THE COMPLETE
AMELIA BUTTERWORTH
MYSTERY SERIES

ALSO BY ANNA KATHARINE GREEN

The Anna Katharine Green Mystery MEGAPACK® (ebook)
The Leavenworth Case
The Mayor's Wife
The Mystery of the Hasty Arrow
A Strange Disappearance
That Affair Next Door

THE COMPLETE
AMELIA BUTTERWORTH
MYSTERY SERIES

ANNA KATHARINE GREEN

WILDSIDE PRESS

CONTENTS

THAT AFFAIR NEXT DOOR

The First Episode in the Life of Amelia Butterworth

BOOK I: MISS BUTTERWORTH'S WINDOW

CHAPTER I

A Discovery

I am not an inquisitive woman, but when, in the middle of a certain warm night in September, I heard a carriage draw up at the adjoining house and stop, I could not resist the temptation of leaving my bed and taking a peep through the curtains of my window.

First: because the house was empty, or supposed to be so, the family still being, as I had every reason to believe, in Europe; and secondly: because, not being inquisitive, I often miss in my lonely and single life much that it would be both interesting and profitable for me to know.

Luckily I made no such mistake this evening. I rose and looked out, and though I was far from realizing it at the time, took, by so doing, my first step in a course of inquiry which has ended—

But it is too soon to speak of the end. Rather let me tell you what I saw when I parted the curtains of my window in Gramercy Park, on the night of September 17, 1895.

Not much at first glance, only a common hack drawn up at the neighboring curb-stone. The lamp which is supposed to light our part of the block is some rods away on the opposite side of the street, so that I obtained but a shadowy glimpse of a young man and woman standing below me on the pavement. I could see, however, that the woman—and not the man—was putting money into the driver's hand. The next moment they were on the stoop of this long-closed house, and the coach rolled off.

It was dark, as I have said, and I did not recognize the young people—at least their figures were not familiar to me; but when, in another instant, I heard the click of a night-key, and saw them, after a rather tedious fumbling at the lock, disappear from the stoop, I took it for granted that the gentleman was Mr. Van Burnam's eldest son Franklin, and the lady some relative of the family; though why this, its most punctilious member, should bring a guest at so late an hour into a house devoid of everything necessary to make the least exacting visitor comfortable, was a mystery that I retired to bed to meditate upon.

I did not succeed in solving it, however, and after some ten minutes had elapsed, I was settling myself again to sleep when I was re-aroused by a fresh sound from the quarter mentioned. The door I had so lately heard shut, opened again, and though I had to rush for it, I succeeded in getting to my window in time to catch a glimpse of the departing figure of the young man hurrying away towards Broadway. The young woman was not with him, and as I realized that he had left her behind him in the great, empty house, without apparent light and certainly without any companion, I began to question if this was like Franklin Van Burnam. Was it not more in keeping with the recklessness of his more easy-natured and less reliable brother, Howard, who, some two or three years back, had married a young wife of no very satisfactory antecedents, and who, as I had heard, had been ostracized by the family in consequence?

Whichever of the two it was, he had certainly shown but little consideration for his companion, and thus thinking, I fell off to sleep just as the clock struck the half hour after midnight.

Next morning as soon as modesty would permit me to approach the window, I surveyed the neighboring house minutely. Not a blind was open, nor a shutter displaced. As I am an early riser, this did not disturb me at the time, but when after breakfast I looked again and still failed to detect any evidences of life in the great barren front beside me, I began to feel uneasy. But I did nothing till noon, when going into my rear garden and observing that the back windows of the Van Burnam house were as closely shuttered as the front, I became so anxious that I stopped the next policeman I saw going by, and telling him my suspicions, urged him to ring the bell.

No answer followed the summons.

"There is no one here," said he.

"Ring again!" I begged.

And he rang again but with no better result.

"Don't you see that the house is shut up?" he grumbled. "We have had orders to watch the place, but none to take the watch off."

"There is a young woman inside," I insisted. "The more I think over last night's occurrence, the more I am convinced that the matter should be looked into."

He shrugged his shoulders and was moving away when we both observed a common-looking woman standing in front looking at us. She had a bundle in her hand, and her face, unnaturally ruddy though it was, had a scared look which was all the more remarkable from the fact that it was one of those wooden-like countenances which under ordinary circumstances are capable of but little expression. She was not a stranger to me; that is, I had seen her before in or about the house in which we were at that moment so interested; and not stopping to put any curb on my excitement, I rushed down to the pavement and accosted her.

"Who are you?" I asked. "Do you work for the Van Burnams, and do you know who the lady was who came here last night?"

The poor woman, either startled by my sudden address or by my manner which may have been a little sharp, gave a quick bound backward, and was only deterred by the near presence of the policeman from attempting flight. As it was, she stood her ground, though the fiery flush, which made her face so noticeable, deepened till her cheeks and brow were scarlet.

"I am the scrub-woman," she protested. "I have come to open the windows and air the house,"—ignoring my last question.

"Is the family coming home?" the policeman asked.

"I don't know; I think so," was her weak reply.

"Have you the keys?" I now demanded, seeing her fumbling in her pocket.

She did not answer; a sly look displaced the anxious one she had hitherto displayed, and she turned away.

"I don't see what business it is of the neighbors," she muttered, throwing me a dissatisfied scowl over her shoulder.

"If you've got the keys, we will go in and see that things are all right," said the policeman, stopping her with a light touch.

She trembled; I saw that she trembled, and naturally became excited. Something was wrong in the Van Burnam mansion, and I was going to be present at its discovery. But her next words cut my hopes short.

"I have no objection to *your* going in," she said to the policeman, "but I will not give up my keys to *her*. What right has she in our house any way." And I thought I heard her murmur something about a meddlesome old maid.

The look which I received from the policeman convinced me that my ears had not played me false.

"The lady's right," he declared; and pushing by me quite disrespectfully, he led the way to the basement door, into which he and the so-called cleaner presently disappeared.

I waited in front. I felt it to be my duty to do so. The various passersby stopped an instant to stare at me before proceeding on their way, but I did not flinch from my post. Not till I had heard that the young woman whom I had seen enter these doors at midnight was well, and that her delay in opening the windows was entirely due to fashionable laziness, would I feel justified in returning to my own home and its affairs. But it took patience and some courage to remain there. Several minutes elapsed before I perceived the shutters in the third story open, and a still longer time before a window on the second floor flew up and the policeman looked out, only to meet my inquiring gaze and rapidly disappear again.

Meantime three or four persons had stopped on the walk near me, the nucleus of a crowd which would not be long in collecting, and I was beginning to feel I was paying dearly for my virtuous resolution, when the front door burst violently open and we caught sight of the trembling form and shocked face of the scrub-woman.

"She's dead!" she cried, "she's dead! Murder!" and would have said more had not the policeman pulled her back, with a growl which sounded very much like a suppressed oath.

He would have shut the door upon me had I not been quicker than lightning. As it was, I got in before it slammed, and happily too; for just at that moment the house-cleaner, who had grown paler every instant, fell in a heap in the entry, and the policeman, who was not the man I would want about me in any trouble, seemed somewhat embarrassed by this new emergency, and let me lift the poor thing up and drag her farther into the hall.

She had fainted, and should have had something done for her, but anxious though I always am to be of help where help is needed, I had no sooner got within range of the parlor door with my burden, than I beheld a sight so terrifying that I involuntarily let the poor woman slip from my arms to the floor.

In the darkness of a dim corner (for the room had no light save that which came through the doorway where I stood) lay the form of a woman under a fallen piece of furniture. Her skirts and distended arms alone were visible; but no one who saw the rigid outlines of her limbs could doubt for a moment that she was dead.

At a sight so dreadful, and, in spite of all my apprehensions, so unexpected, I felt a sensation of sickness which in another moment might have ended in my fainting also, if I had not realized that it would never do for me to lose my wits in the presence of a man who had none too many of his own. So I shook off my momentary weakness, and turning to the policeman, who was hesitating between the unconscious figure of the woman outside the door and the dead form of the one within I cried sharply:

"Come, man, to business! The woman inside there is dead, but this one is living. Fetch me a pitcher of water from below if you can, and then go for whatever assistance you need. I'll wait here and bring this woman to. She is a strong one, and it won't take long."

"You'll stay here alone with that—" he began.

But I stopped him with a look of disdain.

"Of course I will stay here; why not? Is there anything in the dead to be afraid of? Save me from the living, and I undertake to save myself from the dead."

But his face had grown very suspicious.

"You go for the water," he cried. "And see here! Just call out for someone to telephone to Police Headquarters for the Coroner and a detective. I don't quit this room till one or the other of them comes."

Smiling at a caution so very ill-timed, but abiding by my invariable rule of never arguing with a man unless I see some way of getting the better of him, I did what he bade me, though I hated dreadfully to leave the spot and its woful mystery, even for so short a time as was required.

"Run up to the second story," he called out, as I passed by the prostrate figure of the cleaner. "Tell them what you want from the window, or we will have the whole street in here."

So I ran upstairs—I had always wished to visit this house, but had never been encouraged to do so by the Misses Van Burnam—and making my way into the front room, the door of which stood wide open, I rushed to the window and hailed the crowd, which by this time extended far out beyond the curb-stone.

"An officer!" I called out, "a police officer! An accident has occurred and the man in charge here wants the Coroner and a detective from Police Headquarters."

"Who's hurt?" "Is it a man?" "Is it a woman?" shouted up one or two; and "Let us in!" shouted others; but the sight of a boy rushing off to meet an advancing policeman satisfied me that help would soon be forthcoming, so I drew in my head and looked about me for the next necessity—water.

I was in a lady's bed-chamber, probably that of the eldest Miss Van Burnam; but it was a bed-chamber which had not been occupied for some months, and naturally it lacked the very articles which would have been of assistance to me in the present emergency. No *eau de Cologne* on the bureau, no camphor on the mantel-shelf. But there was water in the pipes (something I had hardly hoped for), and a mug on the wash-stand; so I filled the mug and ran with it to the door, stumbling, as I did so, over some small object which I presently perceived to be a little round pincushion. Picking it up, for I hate anything like disorder, I placed it on a table near by, and continued on my way.

The woman was still lying at the foot of the stairs. I dashed the water in her face and she immediately came to.

Sitting up, she was about to open her lips when she checked herself;

a fact which struck me as odd, though I did not allow my surprise to become apparent.

Meantime I stole a glance into the parlor. The officer was standing where I had left him, looking down on the prostrate figure before him.

There was no sign of feeling in his heavy countenance, and he had not opened a shutter, nor, so far as I could see, disarranged an object in the room.

The mysterious character of the whole affair fascinated me in spite of myself, and leaving the now fully aroused woman in the hall, I was half-way across the parlor floor when the latter stopped me with a shrill cry:

"Don't leave me! I have never seen anything before so horrible. The poor dear! The poor dear! Why don't he take those dreadful things off her?"

She alluded not only to the piece of furniture which had fallen upon the prostrate woman, and which can best be described as a cabinet with closets below and shelves above, but to the various articles of *bric-à-brac* which had tumbled from the shelves, and which now lay in broken pieces about her.

"He will do so; they will do so very soon," I replied. "He is waiting for someone with more authority than himself; for the Coroner, if you know what that means."

"But what if she's alive! Those things will crush her. Let us take them off. I'll help. I'm not too weak to help."

"Do you know who this person is?" I asked, for her voice had more feeling in it than I thought natural to the occasion, dreadful as it was.

"I?" she repeated, her weak eyelids quivering for a moment as she tried to sustain my scrutiny. "How should I know? I came in with the policeman and haven't been any nearer than I now be. What makes you think I know anything about her? I'm only the scrub-woman, and don't even know the names of the family."

"I thought you seemed so very anxious," I explained, suspicious of her suspiciousness, which was of so sly and emphatic a character that it changed her whole bearing from one of fear to one of cunning in a moment.

"And who wouldn't feel the like of that for a poor creature lying crushed under a heap of broken crockery!"

Crockery! those Japanese vases worth hundreds of dollars! that ormulu clock and those Dresden figures which must have been more than a couple of centuries old!

"It's a poor sense of duty that keeps a man standing dumb and staring like that, when with a lift of his hand he could show us the like of her pretty face, and if it's dead she be or alive."

As this burst of indignation was natural enough and not altogether uncalled for from the standpoint of humanity, I gave the woman a nod of approval, and wished I were a man myself that I might lift the heavy cabinet or whatever it was that lay upon the poor creature before us. But not being a man, and not judging it wise to irritate the one representative of that sex then present, I made no remark, but only took a few steps farther into the room, followed, as it afterwards appeared, by the scrub-woman.

The Van Burnam parlors are separated by an open arch. It was to the right of this arch and in the corner opposite the doorway that the dead woman lay. Using my eyes, now that I was somewhat accustomed to the semi-darkness enveloping us, I noticed two or three facts which had hitherto escaped me. One was, that she lay on her back with her feet pointing towards the hall door, and another, that nowhere in the room, save in her immediate vicinity, were there to be seen any signs of struggle or disorder. All was as set and proper as in my own parlor when it has been undisturbed for any length of time by guests; and though I could not see far into the rooms beyond, they were to all appearance in an equally orderly condition.

Meanwhile the cleaner was trying to account for the overturned cabinet.

"Poor dear! poor dear! she must have pulled it over on herself! But however did she get into the house? And what was she doing in this great empty place?"

The policeman, to whom these remarks had evidently been addressed, growled out some unintelligible reply, and in her perplexity the woman turned towards me.

But what could I say to her? I had my own private knowledge of the matter, but she was not one to confide in, so I stoically shook my head. Doubly disappointed, the poor thing shrank back, after looking first at the policeman and then at me in an odd, appealing way, difficult to understand. Then her eyes fell again on the dead girl at her feet, and being nearer now than before, she evidently saw something that startled her, for she sank on her knees with a little cry and began examining the girl's skirts.

"What are you looking at there?" growled the policeman. "Get up, can't you! No one but the Coroner has right to lay hand on anything here."

"I'm doing no harm," the woman protested, in an odd, shaking voice. "I only wanted to see what the poor thing had on. Some blue stuff, isn't it?" she asked me.

"Blue serge," I answered; "store-made, but very good; must have come from Altman's or Stern's."

"I—I'm not used to sights like this," stammered the scrub-woman, stumbling awkwardly to her feet, and looking as if her few remaining wits had followed the rest on an endless vacation. "I—I think I shall have to go home." But she did not move.

"The poor dear's young, isn't she?" she presently insinuated, with an odd catch in her voice that gave to the question an air of hesitation and doubt.

"I think she is younger than either you or myself," I deigned to reply. "Her narrow pointed shoes show she has not reached the years of discretion."

"Yes, yes, so they do!" ejaculated the cleaner, eagerly—too eagerly for perfect ingenuousness. "That's why I said 'Poor dear!' and spoke of her pretty face. I am sorry for young folks when they get into trouble, aint you? You and me might lie here and no one be much the worse for it, but a sweet lady like this—"

This was not very flattering to me, but I was prevented from rebuking her by a prolonged shout from the stoop without, as a rush was made against the front door, followed by a shrill peal of the bell.

"Man from Headquarters," stolidly announced the policeman. "Open the door, ma'am; or step back into the further hall if you want me to do it."

Such rudeness was uncalled for; but considering myself too important a witness to show feeling, I swallowed my indignation and proceeded with all my native dignity to the front door.

CHAPTER II

Questions

As I did so, I could catch the murmur of the crowd outside as it seethed forward at the first intimation of the door being opened; but my attention was not so distracted by it, loud as it sounded after the quiet of the shut-up house, that I failed to notice that the door had not been locked by the gentleman leaving the night before, and that, consequently, only the night latch was on. With a turn of the knob it opened, showing me the mob of shouting boys and the forms of two gentlemen awaiting admittance on the door-step. I frowned at the mob and smiled on the gentlemen, one of whom was portly and easy-going in appearance, and the other spare, with a touch of severity in his aspect. But for some reason these gentlemen did not seem to appreciate the honor I had done them, for they both gave me a displeased glance, which was so odd and unsympathetic in its character that I bridled a little, though I soon returned to my natural manner. Did they realize at the first glance that I was destined to prove a thorn in the sides of every one connected with this matter, for days to come?

"Are you the woman who called from the window?" asked the larger of the two, whose business here I found it difficult at first to determine.

"I am," was my perfectly self-possessed reply. "I live next door and my presence here is due to the anxious interest I always take in my neighbors. I had reason to think that all was not as it should be in this house, and I was right. Look in the parlor, sirs."

They were already as far as the threshold of that room and needed no further encouragement to enter. The heavier man went first and the other followed, and you may be sure I was not far behind. The sight meeting our eyes was ghastly enough, as you know; but these men were evidently accustomed to ghastly sights, for they showed but little emotion.

"I thought this house was empty," observed the second gentleman, who was evidently a doctor.

"So it was till last night," I put in; and was about to tell my story, when I felt my skirts jerked.

Turning, I found that this warning had come from the cleaner who stood close beside me.

"What do you want?" I asked, not understanding her and having nothing to conceal.

"I?" she faltered, with a frightened air. "Nothing, ma'am, nothing."

"Then don't interrupt me," I harshly admonished her, annoyed at an interference that tended to throw suspicion upon my candor. "This woman came here to scrub and clean," I now explained; "it was by means of the key she carried that we were enabled to get into the house. I never spoke to her till a half hour ago."

At which, with a display of subtlety I was far from expecting in one of her appearance, she let her emotions take a fresh direction, and pointing towards the dead woman, she impetuously cried:

"But the poor child there! Aint you going to take those things off of her? It's wicked to leave her under all that stuff. Suppose there was life in her!"

"Oh! there's no hope of that," muttered the doctor, lifting one of the hands, and letting it fall again.

"Still—" he cast a side look at his companion, who gave him a meaning nod—"it might be well enough to lift this cabinet sufficiently for me to lay my hand on her heart."

They accordingly did this; and the doctor, leaning down, placed his hand over the poor bruised breast.

"No life," he murmured. "She has been dead some hours. Do you think we had better release the head?" he went on, glancing up at the portly man at his side.

But the latter, who was rapidly growing serious, made a slight protest with his finger, and turning to me, inquired, with sudden authority:

"What did you mean when you said that the house had been empty till last night?"

"Just what I said, sir. It was empty till about midnight, when two persons—" Again I felt my dress twitched, this time very cautiously. What did the woman want? Not daring to give her a look, for these men were only too ready to detect harm in everything I did, I gently drew my skirt away and took a step aside, going on as if no interruption had occurred. "Did I say persons? I should have said a man and a woman drove up to the house and entered. I saw them from my window."

"You did?" murmured my interlocutor, whom I had by this time decided to be a detective. "And this is the woman, I suppose?" he proceeded, pointing to the poor creature lying before us.

"Why, yes, of course. Who else can she be? I did not see the lady's face last night, but she was young and light on her feet, and ran up the stoop gaily."

"And the man? Where is the man? I don't see him here."

"I am not surprised at that. He went very soon after he came, not ten minutes after, I should say. That is what alarmed me and caused me to have the house investigated. It did not seem natural or like any of the Van Burnams to leave a woman to spend the night in so large a house alone."

"You know the Van Burnams?"

"Not well. But that don't signify. I know what report says of them; they are gentlemen."

"But Mr. Van Burnam is in Europe."

"He has two sons."

"Living here?"

"No; the unmarried one spends his nights at Long Branch, and the other is with his wife somewhere in Connecticut."

"How did the young couple you saw get in last night? Was there any one here to admit them?"

"No; the gentleman had a key."

"Ah, he had a key."

The tone in which this was said recurred to me afterwards, but at the moment I was much more impressed by a peculiar sound I heard behind me, something between a gasp and a click in the throat, which came I knew from the scrub-woman, and which, odd and contradictory as it may appear, struck me as an expression of satisfaction, though what there was in my admission to give satisfaction to this poor creature I could not conjecture. Moving so as to get a glimpse of her face, I went on with the grim self-possession natural to my character:

"And when he came out he walked briskly away. The carriage had not waited for him."

"Ah!" again muttered the gentleman, picking up one of the broken pieces of china which lay haphazard about the floor, while I studied the cleaner's face, which, to my amazement, gave evidences of a confusion of emotions most unaccountable to me.

Mr. Gryce may have noticed this too, for he immediately addressed her, though he continued to look at the broken piece of china in his hand.

"And how come you to be cleaning the house?" he asked. "Is the family coming home?"

"They are, sir," she answered, hiding her emotion with great skill the moment she perceived attention directed to herself, and speaking with a sudden volubility that made us all stare. "They are expected any day. I didn't know it till yesterday—was it yesterday? No, the day before—when young Mr. Franklin—he is the oldest son, sir, and a very nice man, a *very* nice man—sent me word by letter that I was to get the house ready. It isn't the first time I have done it for them, sir, and as soon as I could get the basement key from the agent, I came here, and worked all day yesterday, washing up the floors and dusting. I should have been at them again this morning if my husband hadn't been sick. But I had to go to the infirmary for medicine, and it was noon when I got here, and then I found this lady standing outside with a policeman, a very nice lady, a very *nice* lady indeed, sir, I pay my respects to her"—and she actually dropped me a curtsey like a peasant woman in a play—"and they took my key from me, and the policeman opens the door, and he and me go upstairs and into all the rooms, and when we come to this one—"

She was getting so excited as to be hardly intelligible. Stopping herself with a jerk, she fumbled nervously with her apron, while I asked myself how she could have been at work in this house the day before without my knowing it. Suddenly I remembered that I was ill in the morning and busy in the afternoon at the Orphan Asylum, and somewhat relieved at finding so excellent an excuse for my ignorance, I looked up to see if the detective had noticed anything odd in this woman's behavior. Presumably he had, but having more experience than myself with the susceptibility of ignorant persons in the presence of danger and distress, he attached less importance to it than I did, for which I was secretly glad, without exactly knowing my reasons for being so.

"You will be wanted as a witness by the Coroner's jury," he now remarked to her, looking as if he were addressing the piece of china he was turning over in his hand. "Now, no nonsense!" he protested, as she commenced to tremble and plead. "You were the first one to see this dead woman, and you must be on hand to say so. As I cannot tell you when the inquest will be held, you had better stay around till the Coroner comes. He'll be here soon. You, and this other woman too."

By other woman he meant *me*, Miss Butterworth, of Colonial ancestry and no inconsiderable importance in the social world. But though I did not relish this careless association of myself with this poor scrub-woman, I was careful to show no displeasure, for I reasoned that as witnesses we were equal before the law, and that it was solely in this light he regarded us.

There was something in the manner of both these gentlemen which convinced me that while my presence was considered desirable in the house, it was not especially wanted in the room. I was therefore moving reluctantly away, when I felt a slight but peremptory touch on the arm, and turning, saw the detective at my side, still studying his piece of china.

He was, as I have said, of portly build and benevolent aspect; a fatherly-looking man, and not at all the person one would be likely to associate with the police. Yet he could take the lead very naturally, and when he spoke, I felt bound to answer him.

"Will you be so good, madam, as to relate over again, what you saw from your window last night? I am likely to have charge of this matter, and would be pleased to hear all you may have to say concerning it."

"My name is Butterworth," I politely intimated.

"And my name is Gryce."

"A detective?"

"The same."

"You must think this matter very serious," I ventured.

"Death by violence is always serious."

"You must regard this death as something more than an accident, I mean."

His smile seemed to say: "You will not know today how I regard it."

"And you will not know today what I think of it either," was my inward rejoinder, but I said nothing aloud, for the man was seventy-five if he was a day, and I have been taught respect for age, and have practised the same for fifty years and more.

I must have shown what was passing in my mind, and he must have seen it reflected on the polished surface of the porcelain he was contemplating, for his lips showed the shadow of a smile sufficiently sarcastic for me to see that he was far from being as easy-natured as his countenance indicated.

"Come, come," said he, "there is the Coroner now. Say what you have to say, like the straightforward, honest woman you appear."

"I don't like compliments," I snapped out. Indeed, they have always been obnoxious to me. As if there was any merit in being honest and straightforward, or any distinction in being told so!

"I am Miss Butterworth, and not in the habit of being spoken to as if I were a simple countrywoman," I objected. "But I will repeat what I saw last night, as it is no secret, and the telling of it won't hurt me and may help you."

Accordingly I went over the whole story, and was much more loquacious than I had intended to be, his manner was so insinuating and his inquiries so pertinent. But one topic we both failed to broach, and that was the peculiar manner of the scrub-woman. Perhaps it had not struck him as peculiar and perhaps it should not have struck me so, but in the silence which was preserved on the subject I felt I had acquired an advantage over him, which might lead to consequences of no small importance. Would I have felt thus or congratulated myself quite so much upon my fancied superiority, if I had known he was the man who managed the Leavenworth case, and who in his early years had experienced that very wonderful adventure on the staircase of the Heart's Delight? Perhaps I would; for though I have had no adventures, I feel capable of them, and as for any peculiar acumen he may have shown in his long and eventful career, why that is a quality which others may share with him, as I hope to be able to prove before finishing these pages.

CHAPTER III

Amelia Discovers Herself

There is a small room at the extremity of the Van Burnam mansion. In this I took refuge after my interview with Mr. Gryce. As I picked out the chair which best suited me and settled myself for a comfortable communion with my own thoughts, I was astonished to find how much I was enjoying myself, notwithstanding the thousand and one duties awaiting me on the other side of the party-wall.

Even this very solitude was welcome, for it gave me an opportunity to consider matters. I had not known up to this very hour that I had any special gifts. My father, who was a shrewd man of the old New England type, said more times than I am years old (which was not saying it as often as some may think) that Araminta (the name I was christened by, and the name you will find in the Bible record, though I sign myself Amelia, and insist upon being addressed as Amelia, being, as I hope, a sensible woman and not the piece of antiquated sentimentality suggested by the former cognomen)—that Araminta would live to make her mark; though in what capacity he never informed me, being, as I have observed, a shrewd man, and thus not likely to thoughtlessly commit himself.

I now know he was right; my pretensions dating from the moment I found that this affair, at first glance so simple, and at the next so complicated, had aroused in me a fever of investigation which no reasoning could allay. Though I had other and more personal matters on my mind, my thoughts would rest nowhere but on the details of this tragedy; and having, as I thought, noticed some few facts in connection with it, from which conclusions might be drawn, I amused myself with jotting them down on the back of a disputed grocer's bill I happened to find in my pocket.

Valueless as explaining this tragedy, being founded upon insufficient evidence, they may be interesting as showing the workings of my mind even at this early stage of the matter. They were drawn up under three heads.

First, was the death of this young woman an accident?

Second, was it a suicide?

Third, was it a murder?

Under the first head I wrote:

My reasons for not thinking it an accident.

1. If it had been an accident and she had pulled the cabinet over upon herself, she would have been found with her feet pointing towards the wall where the cabinet had stood.

(But her feet were towards the door and her head under the cabinet.)

2. The decent, even precise, arrangement of the clothing about her feet, which precludes any theory involving accident.

Under the second:

Reason for not thinking it suicide.

She could not have been found in the position observed without having lain down on the floor while living and then pulled the shelves down upon herself.

(A theory obviously too improbable to be considered.)

Under the third:

Reason for not thinking it murder.

She would need to have been held down on the floor while the cabinet was being pulled over on her; something which the quiet aspect of the hands and feet made appear impossible.

To this I added:

Reasons for accepting the theory of murder.

1. The fact that she did not go into the house alone; that a man entered with her, remained ten minutes, and then came out again and disappeared up the street with every appearance of haste and an anxious desire to leave the spot.

2. The front door, which he had unlocked on entering, was not locked by him on his departure, the catch doing the locking. Yet, though he could have re-entered so easily, he had shown no disposition to return.

3. The arrangement of the skirts, which show the touch of a careful hand after death.

Nothing clear, you see. I was doubtful of all; and yet my suspicions tended most toward murder.

I had eaten my luncheon before interfering in this matter, which was fortunate for me, as it was three o'clock before I was summoned to meet the Coroner, of whose arrival I had been conscious some time before.

He was in the front parlor where the dead girl lay, and as I took my way thither I felt the same sensations of faintness which had so nearly overcome me on the previous occasion. But I mastered them, and was quite myself before I crossed the threshold.

There were several gentlemen present, but of them all I only noticed two, one of whom I took to be the Coroner, while the other was my late interlocutor, Mr. Gryce. From the animation observable in the latter, I gathered that the case was growing in interest from the detective stand-point.

"Ah, and is this the witness?" asked the Coroner, as I stepped into the room.

"I am Miss Butterworth," was my calm reply. "*Amelia* Butterworth. Living next door and present at the discovery of this poor murdered body."

"Murdered," he repeated. "Why do you say murdered?"

For reply I drew from my pocket the bill on which I had scribbled my conclusions in regard to this matter.

"Read this," said I.

Evidently astonished, he took the paper from my hand, and, after some curious glances in my direction, condescended to do as I requested. The result was an odd but grudging look of admiration directed towards myself and a quick passing over of the paper to the detective.

The latter, who had exchanged his bit of broken china for a very much used and tooth-marked lead-pencil, frowned with a whimsical air at the latter before he put it in his pocket. Then he read my hurried scrawl.

"Two Richmonds in the field!" commented the Coroner, with a sly chuckle. "I am afraid I shall have to yield to their allied forces. Miss Butterworth, the cabinet is about to be raised; do you feel as if you could endure the sight?"

"I can stand anything where the cause of justice is involved," I replied.

"Very well, then, sit down, if you please. When the whole body is visible I will call you."

And stepping forward he gave orders to have the clock and broken china removed from about the body.

As the former was laid away on one end of the mantel someone observed:

"What a valuable witness that clock might have been had it been running when the shelves fell!"

But the fact was so patent that it had not been in motion for months that no one even answered; and Mr. Gryce did not so much as look towards it. But then we had all seen that the hands stood at three minutes to five.

I had been asked to sit down, but I found this impossible. Side by side with the detective, I viewed the replacing of that heavy piece of furniture against the wall, and the slow disclosure of the upper part of the body which had so long lain hidden.

That I did not give way is a proof that my father's prophecy was not without some reasonable foundation; for the sight was one to try the stoutest nerves, as well as to awaken the compassion of the hardest heart.

The Coroner, meeting my eye, pointed at the poor creature inquiringly.

"Is this the woman you saw enter here last night?"

I glanced down at her dress, noted the short summer cape tied to the neck with an elaborate bow of ribbon, and nodded my head.

"I remember the cape," said I. "But where is her hat? She wore one. Let me see if I can describe it." Closing my eyes I endeavored to recall the dim silhouette of her figure as she stood passing up the change to the driver; and was so far successful that I was ready to announce at the next moment that her hat presented the effect of a soft felt with one feather or one bow of ribbon standing upright from the side of the crown.

"Then the identity of this woman with the one you saw enter here last night is established," remarked the detective, stooping down and drawing from under the poor girl's body a hat, sufficiently like the one I had just described, to satisfy everybody that it was the same.

"As if there could be any doubt," I began.

But the Coroner, explaining that it was a mere formality, motioned me to stand aside in favor of the doctor, who seemed anxious to approach nearer the spot where the dead woman lay. This I was about to do when a sudden thought struck me, and I reached out my hand for the hat.

"Let me look at it for a moment," said I.

Mr. Gryce at once handed it over, and I took a good look at it inside and out.

"It is pretty badly crushed," I observed, "and does not present a very fresh appearance, but for all that it has been worn but once."

"How do you know?" questioned the Coroner.

"Let the other Richmond inform you," was my grimly uttered reply, as I gave it again into the detective's hand.

There was a murmur about me, whether of amusement or displeasure, I made no effort to decide. I was finding out something for myself, and I did not care what they thought of me.

"Neither has she worn this dress long," I continued; "but that is not true of the shoes. They are not old, but they have been acquainted with the pavement, and that is more than can be said of the hem of this gown. There are no gloves on her hands; a few minutes elapsed then before the assault; long enough for her to take them off."

"Smart woman!" whispered a voice in my ear; a half-admiring, half-sarcastic voice that I had no difficulty in ascribing to Mr. Gryce. "But are you sure she wore any? Did you notice that her hand was gloved when she came into the house?"

"No," I answered, frankly; "but so well-dressed a woman would not enter a house like this, without gloves."

"It was a warm night," someone suggested.

"I don't care. You will find her gloves as you have her hat; and you will find them with the fingers turned inside out, just as she drew them from her hand. So much I will concede to the warmth of the weather."

"Like these, for instance," broke in a quiet voice.

Startled, for a hand had appeared over my shoulder dangling a pair of gloves before my eyes, I cried out, somewhat too triumphantly I own:

"Yes, yes, just like those! Did you pick them up here? Are they hers?"

"You say that this is the way hers should look."

"And I repeat it."

"Then allow me to pay you my compliments. These were picked up here."

"But where?" I cried. "I thought I had looked this carpet well over."

He smiled, not at me but at the gloves, and the thought crossed me that he felt as if something more than the gloves was being turned inside out. I therefore pursed my mouth, and determined to stand more on my guard.

"It is of no consequence," I assured him; "all such matters will come out at the inquest."

Mr. Gryce nodded, and put the gloves back in his pocket. With them he seemed to pocket some of his geniality and patience.

"All these facts have been gone over before you came in," said he, which statement I beg to consider as open to doubt.

The doctor, who had hardly moved a muscle during all this colloquy, now rose from his kneeling position beside the girl's head.

"I shall have to ask the presence of another physician," said he. "Will you send for one from your office, Coroner Dahl?"

At which I stepped back and the Coroner stepped forward, saying, however, as he passed me:

"The inquest will be held day after tomorrow in my office. Hold yourself in readiness to be present. I regard you as one of my chief witnesses."

I assured him I would be on hand, and, obeying a gesture of his finger, retreated from the room; but I did not yet leave the house. A straight, slim man, with a very small head but a very bright eye, was leaning on the newel-post in the front hall, and when he saw me, started up so alertly I perceived that he had business with me, and so waited for him to speak.

"You are Miss Butterworth?" he inquired.

"I am, sir."

"And I am a reporter from the New York *World*. Will you allow me—"

Why did he stop? I had merely looked at him. But he did stop, and that is saying considerable for a reporter from the New York *World*.

"I certainly am willing to tell you what I have told every one else," I interposed, considering it better not to make an enemy of so judicious a young man; and seeing him brighten up at this, I thereupon related all I considered desirable for the general public to know.

I was about passing on, when, reflecting that one good turn deserves another, I paused and asked him if he thought they would leave the dead girl in that house all night.

He answered that he did not think they would. That a telegram had been sent some time before to young Mr. Van Burnam, and that they were only awaiting his arrival to remove her.

"Do you mean Howard?" I asked.

"Is he the elder one?"

"No."

"It is the elder one they have summoned; the one who has been staying at Long Branch."

"How can they expect him then so soon?"

"Because he is in the city. It seems the old gentleman is going to return on the *New York*, and as she is due here today, Franklin Van Burnam has come to New York to meet him."

"Humph!" thought I, "lively times are in prospect," and for the first time I remembered my dinner and the orders which had not been given about some curtains which were to have been hung that day, and all the other reasons I had for being at home.

I must have shown my feelings, much as I pride myself upon my impassibility upon all occasions, for he immediately held out his arm, with an offer to pilot me through the crowd to my own house; and I was about to accept it when the door-bell rang so sharply that we involuntarily stopped.

"A fresh witness or a telegram for the Coroner," whispered the reporter in my ear.

I tried to look indifferent, and doubtless made out pretty well, for he added, after a sly look in my face:

"You do not care to stay any longer?"

I made no reply, but I think he was impressed by my dignity. Could he not see that it would be the height of ill-manners for me to rush out in the face of any one coming in?

An officer opened the door, and when we saw who stood there, I am sure that the reporter, as well as myself, was grateful that we listened to the dictates of politeness. It was young Mr. Van Burnam—Franklin; I mean the older and more respectable of the two sons.

He was flushed and agitated, and looked as if he would like to annihilate the crowd pushing him about on his own stoop. He gave an angry glance backward as he stepped in, and then I saw that a carriage covered with baggage stood on the other side of the street, and gathered that he had not returned to his father's house alone.

"What has happened? What does all this mean?" were the words he hurled at us as the door closed behind him and he found himself face to face with a half dozen strangers, among whom the reporter and myself stood conspicuous.

Mr. Gryce, coming suddenly from somewhere, was the one to answer him.

"A painful occurrence, sir. A young girl has been found here, dead, crushed under one of your parlor cabinets."

"A young girl!" he repeated. (Oh, how glad I was that I had been brought up never to transgress the principles of politeness.) "Here! in this shut-up house? What young girl? You mean old woman, do you not? the house-cleaner or someone—"

"No, Mr. Van Burnam, we mean what we say, though possibly I should call her a young lady. She is dressed quite fashionably."

"The ——" Really I cannot repeat in this public manner the word which Mr. Van Burnam used. I excused him at the time, but I will not perpetuate his forgetfulness in these pages.

"She is still lying as we found her," Mr. Gryce now proceeded in his quiet, almost fatherly way. "Will you not take a look at her? Perhaps you can tell us who she is?"

"I?" Mr. Van Burnam seemed quite shocked. "How should I know her! Some thief probably, killed while meddling with other people's property."

"Perhaps," quoth Mr. Gryce, laconically; at which I felt so angry, as tending to mislead my handsome young neighbor, that I irresistibly did what I had fully made up my mind not to do, that is, stepped into view and took a part in this conversation.

"How can you say that," I cried, "when her admittance here was due to a young man who let her in at midnight with a key, and then left her to eat out her heart in this great house all alone."

I have made sensations in my life, but never quite so marked a one as this. In an instant every eye was on me, with the exception of the detective's. His was on the figure crowning the newel-post, and bitterly severe his gaze was too, though it immediately grew wary as the young man started towards me and impetuously demanded:

"Who talks like that? Why, it's Miss Butterworth. Madam, I fear I did not fully understand what you said."

Whereupon I repeated my words, this time very quietly but clearly, while Mr. Gryce continued to frown at the bronze figure he had taken into his confidence. When I had finished, Mr. Van Burnam's countenance had changed, so had his manner. He held himself as erect as before, but not with as much bravado. He showed haste and impatience also, but not the same kind of haste and not quite the same kind of impatience. The corners of Mr. Gryce's mouth betrayed that he noted this change, but he did not turn away from the newel-post.

"This is a remarkable circumstance which you have just told me," observed Mr. Van Burnam, with the first bow I had ever received from him. "I don't know what to think of it. But I still hold that it's some thief. Killed, did you say? Really dead? Well, I'd have given five hundred dollars not to have had it happen in this house."

He had been moving towards the parlor door, and he now entered it. Instantly Mr. Gryce was by his side.

"Are they going to close the door?" I whispered to the reporter, who was taking this all in equally with myself.

"I'm afraid so," he muttered.

And they did. Mr. Gryce had evidently had enough of my interference, and was resolved to shut me out, but I heard one word and caught one glimpse of Mr. Van Burnam's face before the heavy door fell to. The word was: "Oh, so bad as that! How can any one recognize her—" And the glimpse—well, the glimpse proved to me that he was much more profoundly agitated than he wished to appear, and any extraordinary agitation on his part was certainly in direct contradiction to the very sentence he was at that moment uttering.

CHAPTER IV

Silas Van Burnam

"However much I may be needed at home, I I cannot reconcile it with my sense of duty to leave just yet," I confided to the reporter, with what I meant to be a proper show of reason and self-restraint; "Mr. Van Burnam may wish to ask me some questions."

"Of course, of course," acquiesced the other. "You are very right; always are very right, I should judge."

As I did not know what he meant by this, I frowned, always a wise thing to do in an uncertainty; that is—if one wishes to maintain an air of independence and aversion to flattery.

"Will you not sit down?" he suggested. "There is a chair at the end of the hall."

But I had no need to sit. The front door-bell again rang, and simultaneously with its opening, the parlor door unclosed and Mr. Franklin Van Burnam appeared in the hall, just as Mr. Silas Van Burnam, his father, stepped into the vestibule.

"Father!" he remonstrated, with a troubled air; "could you not wait?"

The elder gentleman, who had evidently just been driven up from the steamer, wiped his forehead with an irascible air, that I will say I had noticed in him before and on much less provocation.

"Wait, with a yelling crowd screaming murder in my ear, and Isabella on one side of me calling for salts, and Caroline on the opposite seat getting that blue look about the mouth we have learned to dread so in a hot day like this? No, sir, when there is anything wrong going on I want to know it, and evidently there is something wrong going on here. What is it? Some of Howard's—"

But the son, seizing me by the hand and drawing me forward, put a quick stop to the old gentleman's sentence. "Miss Butterworth, father! Our next-door neighbor, you know."

"Ah! hum! ha! Miss Butterworth. How do you do, ma'am? What the hell is she doing here?" he grumbled, not so low but that I heard both the profanity and the none too complimentary allusion to myself.

"If you will come into the parlor, I will tell you," urged the son. "But what have you done with Isabella and Caroline? Left them in the carriage with that hooting mob about them?"

"I told the coachman to drive on. They are probably half-way around the block by this time."

"Then come in here. But don't allow yourself to be too much affected by what you will see. A sad accident has occurred here, and you must expect the sight of blood."

"Blood! Oh, I can stand that, if Howard—"

The rest was lost in the sound of the closing door.

And now, you will say, I ought to have gone. And you are right, but would you have gone yourself, especially as the hall was full of people who did not belong there?

If you would, then condemn me for lingering just a few minutes longer.

The voices in the parlor were loud, but they presently subsided; and when the owner of the house came out again, he had a subdued look which was as great a contrast to his angry aspect on entering, as was the change I had observed in his son. He was so absorbed indeed that he did not notice me, though I stood directly in his way.

"Don't let Howard come," he was saying in a thick, low voice to his son. "Keep Howard away till we are sure—"

I am confident that his son pressed his arm at this point, for he stopped short and looked about him in a blind and dazed way.

"Oh!" he ejaculated, in a tone of great displeasure. "This is the woman who saw—"

"Miss Butterworth, father," the anxious voice of his son broke in. "Don't try to talk; such a sight is enough to unnerve any man."

"Yes, yes," blustered the old gentleman, evidently taking some hint from the other's tone or manner. "But where are the girls? They will be dead with terror, if we don't relieve their minds. They got the idea it was their brother Howard who was hurt; and so did I, but it's only some wandering waif—some—"

It seemed as if he was not to be allowed to finish any of his sentences, for Franklin interrupted him at this point to ask him what he was going to do with the girls. Certainly he could not bring them in here.

"No," answered the father, but in the dreamy, inconsequential way of one whose thoughts were elsewhere. "I suppose I shall have to take them to some hotel."

Ah, an idea! I flushed as I realized the opportunity which had come to me and had to wait a moment not to speak with too much eagerness.

"Let me play the part of a neighbor," I prayed, "and accommodate the young ladies for the night. My house is near and quiet."

"But the trouble it will involve," protested Mr. Franklin.

"Is just what I need to allay my excitement," I responded. "I shall be glad to offer them rooms for the night. If they are equally glad to accept them—"

"They must be!" the old gentleman declared. "I can't go running round with them hunting up rooms tonight. Miss Butterworth is very good; go find the girls, Franklin; let me have them off my mind, at least."

The young man bowed. I bowed, and was slipping at last from my place by the stairs when, for the third time, I felt my dress twitched.

"Are you going to keep to that story?" a voice whispered in my ear. "About the young man and woman coming in the night, you know."

"Keep to it!" I whispered back, recognizing the scrub-woman, who had sidled up to me from some unknown quarter in the semi-darkness. "Why, it's true. Why shouldn't I keep to it."

A chuckle, difficult to describe but full of meaning, shook the arm of the woman as she pressed close to my side.

"Oh, you are a good one," she said. "I didn't know they made 'em so good!" And with another chuckle full of satisfaction and an odd sort of admiration I had certainly not earned, she slid away again into the darkness.

Certainly there was something in this woman's attitude towards this affair which merited attention.

CHAPTER V

"This Is No One I Know"

I welcomed the Misses Van Burnam with just enough good-will to show that I had not been influenced by any unworthy motives in asking them to my house.

I gave them my guest-chamber, but I invited them to sit in my front room as long as there was anything interesting going on in the street. I knew they would like to look out, and as this chamber boasts of a bay with two windows, we could all be accommodated. From where I sat I could now and then hear what they said, and I considered this but just, for if the young woman who had suffered so untimely an end was in any way connected with them, it was certainly best that the fact should not lie concealed; and one of them, that is Isabella, is such a chatterbox.

Mr. Van Burnam and his son had returned next door, and so far as we could observe from our vantage-point, preparations were being made for the body's removal. As the crowd below, driven away by the policemen one minute, only to collect again in another, swayed and grumbled in a continual expectation that was as continually disappointed, I heard Caroline's voice rise in two or three short sentences.

"They can't find Howard, or he would have been here before now. Did you see her that time when we were coming out of Clark's? Fanny Preston did, and said she was pretty."

"No, I didn't get a glimpse—" A shout from the street below.

"I can't believe it," were the next words I heard, "but Franklin is awfully afraid—"

"Hush! or the ogress—" I am sure I heard her say ogress; but what followed was drowned in another loud murmur, and I caught nothing further till these sentences were uttered by the trembling and over-excited Caroline: "If it is she, pa will never be the same man again. To have her die in our house! O, there's Howard now!"

The interruption came quick and sharp, and it was followed by a double cry and an anxious rustle, as the two girls sprang to their feet in their anxiety to attract their brother's attention or possibly to convey him some warning.

But I did not give much heed to them. My eyes were on the carriage in which Howard had arrived, and which, owing to the ambulance in front, had stopped on the other side of the way. I was anxious to see him descend that I might judge if his figure recalled that of the man I had seen cross the pavement the night before. But he did not descend. Just as his hand was on the carriage door, a half dozen men appeared on the adjoining stoop carrying a burden which they hastened to deposit in the ambulance. He sank back when he saw it, and when his face became visible again, it was so white it seemed to be the only face in the street, though fifty people stood about staring at the house, at the ambulance, and at him.

Franklin Van Burnam had evidently come to the door with the rest; for Howard no sooner showed his face the second time than we saw the former dash down the steps and try to part the crowd in a vain attempt to reach his brother's side. Mr. Gryce was more successful. He had no difficulty in winning his way across the street, and presently I perceived him standing near the carriage exchanging a few words with its occupant. A moment later he drew back, and addressing the driver, jumped into the carriage with Howard, and was speedily driven off. The ambulance followed and some of the crowd, and as soon as a hack could be obtained, Mr. Van Burnam and his son took the same road, leaving us three women in a state of suspense, which as far as one of us was concerned, ended in a nervous attack that was not unlike heart failure. I allude, of course, to Caroline, and it took Isabella and myself a good half hour to bring her back to a normal condition, and when this was done, Isabella thought it incumbent upon her to go off into hysterics, which, being but a weak simulation of the other's state, I met with severity and cured with a frown. When both were in trim again I allowed myself one remark.

"One would think," said I, "that you knew the young woman who has fallen victim to her folly next door."

At which Isabella violently shook her head and Caroline observed:

"It is the excitement which has been too much for me. I am never strong, and this is such a dreadful home-welcoming. When will father and Franklin come back? It was very unkind of them to go off without one word of encouragement."

"They probably did not consider the fate of this unknown woman a matter of any importance to you."

The Van Burnam girls were unlike in appearance and character, but they showed an equal embarrassment at this, casting down their eyes and behaving so strangely that I was driven to wonder, without any show of hysterics I am happy to say, what would be the upshot of this matter, and how far I would become involved in it before the truth came to light.

At dinner they displayed what I should call their best society manner. Seeing this, I assumed my society manner also. It is formed on a different pattern from theirs, but is fully as impressive, I judge.

A most formal meal was the result. My best china was in use, but I had added nothing to my usual course of viands. Indeed, I had abstracted something. An *entrée*, upon which my cook prides herself, was omitted. Was I going to allow these proud young misses to think I had exerted myself to please them? No; rather would I have them consider me niggardly and an enemy to good living; so the *entrée* was, as the French say, suppressed.

In the evening their father came in. He was looking very dejected, and half his bluster was gone. He held a telegram crushed in his hand, and he talked very rapidly. But he confided none of his secrets to me, and I was obliged to say good-night to these young ladies without knowing much more about the matter engrossing us than when I left their house in the afternoon.

But others were not as ignorant as myself. A dramatic and highly exciting scene had taken place that evening at the undertaker's to which the unknown's body had been removed, and as I have more than once heard it minutely described, I will endeavor to transcribe it here with all the impartiality of an outsider.

When Mr. Gryce entered the carriage in which Howard sat, he noted first, that the young man was frightened; and secondly, that he made no effort to hide it. He had heard almost nothing from the detective. He knew that there had been a hue and cry for him ever since noon, and that he was wanted to identify a young woman who had been found dead in his father's house, but beyond these facts he had been told little, and yet he seemed to have no curiosity nor did he venture to express any surprise. He merely accepted the situation and was troubled by it, showing no inclination to talk till very near the end of his destination, when he suddenly pulled himself together and ventured this question:

"How did she—the young woman as you call her—kill herself?"

The detective, who in his long career among criminals and suspected persons, had seen many men and encountered many conditions, roused at this query with much of his old spirit. Turning from the man rather than toward him, he allowed himself a slight shrug of the shoulders as he calmly replied:

"She was found under a heavy piece of furniture; the cabinet with the vases on it, which you must remember stood at the left of the mantelpiece. It had crushed her head and breast. Quite a remarkable means of death, don't you think? There has been but one occurrence like it in my long experience."

"I don't believe what you tell me," was the young man's astonishing reply. "You are trying to frighten me or to make game of me. No lady would make use of any such means of death as that."

"I did not say she was a lady," returned Mr. Gryce, scoring one in his mind against his unwary companion.

A quiver passed down the young man's side where he came in contact with the detective.

"No," he muttered; "but I gathered from what you said, she was no common person; or why," he flashed out in sudden heat, "do you require me to go with you to see her? Have I the name of associating with any persons of the sex who are not ladies?"

"Pardon me," said Mr. Gryce, in grim delight at the prospect he saw slowly unfolding before him of one of those complicated affairs in which minds like his unconsciously revel; "I meant no insinuations. We have requested you, as we have requested your father and brother, to accompany us to the undertaker's, because the identification of the corpse is a most important point, and every formality likely to insure it must be observed."

"And did not they—my father and brother, I mean—recognize her?"

"It would be difficult for any one to recognize her who was not well acquainted with her."

A horrified look crossed the features of Howard Van Burnam, which, if a part of his acting, showed him to have genius for his *rôle*. His head sank back on the cushions of the carriage, and for a moment he closed his eyes. When he opened them again, the carriage had stopped, and Mr. Gryce, who had not noticed his emotion, of course, was looking out of the window with his hand on the handle of the door.

"Are we there already?" asked the young man, with a shudder. "I wish you had not considered it necessary for me to see her. I shall detect nothing familiar in her, I know."

Mr. Gryce bowed, repeated that it was a mere formality, and followed the young gentleman into the building and afterwards into the room where the dead body lay. A couple of doctors and one or two officials stood about, in whose faces the young man sought for something like encouragement before casting his eyes in the direction indicated by the detective. But there was little in any of these faces to calm him, and turning shortly away, he walked manfully across the room and took his stand by the detective.

"I am positive," he began, "that it is not my wife—" At this moment the cloth that covered the body was removed, and he gave a great start of relief. "I said so," he remarked, coldly. "This is no one I know."

His sigh was echoed in double chorus from the doorway. Glancing that way he encountered the faces of his father and elder brother, and moved towards them with a relieved air that made quite another man of him in appearance.

"I have had my say," he remarked. "Shall I wait outside till you have had yours?"

"We have already said all that we had to," Franklin returned. "We declared that we did not recognize this person."

"Of course, of course," assented the other. "I don't see why they should have expected us to know her. Some common suicide who thought the house empty—But how did she get in?"

"Don't you know?" said Mr. Gryce. "Can it be that I forgot to tell you? Why, she was let in at night by a young man of medium height"—his eye ran up and down the graceful figure of the young *élégant* before him as he spoke—"who left her inside and then went away. A young man who had a key—"

"A *key*? Franklin, I—"

Was it a look from Franklin which made him stop? It is possible, for he turned on his heel as he reached this point, and tossing his head with quite a gay air, exclaimed: "But it is of no consequence! The girl is a stranger, and we have satisfied, I believe, all the requirements of the law in saying so, and may now drop the matter. Are you going to the club, Franklin?"

"Yes, but—" Here the elder brother drew nearer and whispered something into the other's ear, who at that whisper turned again towards the place where the dead woman lay. Seeing this movement, his anxious father wiped the moisture from his forehead. Silas Van Burnam had been silent up to this moment and seemed inclined to continue so, but he watched his younger son with painful intentness.

"Nonsense!" broke from Howard's lips as his brother ceased his communication; but he took a step nearer the body, notwithstanding, and then another and another till he was at its side again.

The hands had not been injured, as we have said, and upon these his eyes now fell.

"They are like hers! O God! they are like hers!" he muttered, growing gloomy at once. "But where are the rings? There are no rings to be seen on these fingers, and she wore five, including her wedding-ring."

"Is it of your wife you are speaking?" inquired Mr. Gryce, who had edged up close to his side.

The young man was caught unawares.

He flushed deeply, but answered up boldly and with great appearance of candor:

"Yes; my wife left Haddam yesterday to come to New York, and I have not seen her since. Naturally I have felt some doubts lest this unhappy victim should be she. But I do not recognize her clothing; I do not recognize her form; only the hands look familiar."

"And the hair?"

"Is of the same color as hers, but it's a very ordinary color. I do not dare to say from anything I see that this is my wife."

"We will call you again after the doctor has finished his autopsy," said Mr. Gryce. "Perhaps you will hear from Mrs. Van Burnam before then."

But this intimation did not seem to bring comfort with it. Mr. Van Burnam walked away, white and sick, for which display of emotion there was certainly some cause, and rejoining his father tried to carry off the moment with the *aplomb* of a man of the world.

But that father's eye was fixed too steadily upon him; he faltered as he sat down, and finally spoke up, with feverish energy:

"If it is she, so help me, God, her death is a mystery to me! We have quarrelled more than once lately, and I have sometimes lost my patience with her, but she had no reason to wish for death, and I am ready to swear in defiance of those hands, which are certainly like hers, and the nameless something which Franklin calls a likeness, that it is a stranger who lies there, and that her death in our house is a coincidence."

"Well, well, we will wait," was the detective's soothing reply. "Sit down in the room opposite there, and give me your orders for supper, and I will see that a good meal is served you."

The three gentlemen, seeing no way of refusing, followed the discreet official who preceded them, and the door of the doctor's room closed upon him and the inquiries he was about to make.

CHAPTER VI

New Facts

Mr. Van Burnam and his sons had gone through the formality of a supper and were conversing in the haphazard way natural to men filled with a subject they dare not discuss, when the door opened and Mr. Gryce came in.

Advancing very calmly, he addressed himself to the father:

"I am sorry," said he, "to be obliged to inform you that this affair is much more serious than we anticipated. This young woman was dead before the shelves laden with *bric-à-brac* fell upon her. It is a case of murder; obviously so, or I should not presume to forestall the Coroner's jury in their verdict."

Murder! it is a word to shake the stoutest heart!

The older gentleman reeled as he half rose, and Franklin, his son, betrayed in his own way an almost equal amount of emotion. But Howard, shrugging his shoulders as if relieved of an immense weight, looked about with a cheerful air, and briskly cried:

"Then it is not the body of my wife you have there. No one would murder Louise. I shall go away and prove the truth of my words by hunting her up at once."

The detective opened the door, beckoned in the doctor, who whispered two or three words into Howard's ear.

They failed to awake the emotion he evidently expected. Howard looked surprised, but answered without any change of voice:

"Yes, Louise had such a scar; and if it is true that this woman is similarly marked, then it is a mere coincidence. Nothing will convince me that my wife has been the victim of murder."

"Had you not better take a look at the scar just mentioned?"

"No. I am so sure of what I say that I will not even consider the possibility of my being mistaken. I have examined the clothing on this body you have shown me, and not one article of it came from my wife's wardrobe; nor would my wife go, as you have informed me this woman did, into a dark house at night with any other man than her husband."

"And so you absolutely refuse to acknowledge her."

"Most certainly."

The detective paused, glanced at the troubled faces of the other two gentlemen, faces that had not perceptibly altered during these declarations, and suggestively remarked:

"You have not asked by what means she was killed."

"And I don't care," shouted Howard.

"It was by very peculiar means, also new in my experience."

"It does not interest me," the other retorted.

Mr. Gryce turned to his father and brother.

"Does it interest *you*?" he asked.

The old gentleman, ordinarily so testy and so peremptory, silently nodded his head, while Franklin cried:

"Speak up quick. You detectives hesitate so over the disagreeables. Was she throttled or stabbed with a knife?"

"I have said the means were peculiar. She was stabbed, but not— with a knife."

I know Mr. Gryce well enough now to be sure that he did not glance towards Howard while saying this, and yet at the same time that he did not miss the quiver of a muscle on his part or the motion of an eyelash. But Howard's assumed *sang froid* remained undisturbed and his countenance imperturbable.

"The wound was so small," the detective went on, "that it is a miracle it did not escape notice. It was made by the thrust of some very slender instrument through—"

"The heart?" put in Franklin.

"Of course, of course," assented the detective; "what other spot is vulnerable enough to cause death?"

"Is there any reason why we should not go?" demanded Howard, ignoring the extreme interest manifested by the other two, with a determination that showed great doggedness of character.

The detective ignored *him*.

"A quick stroke, a sure stroke, a fatal stroke. The girl never breathed after."

"But what of those things under which she lay crushed?"

"Ah, in them lies the mystery! Her assailant must have been as subtle as he was sure."

And still Howard showed no interest.

"I wish to telegraph to Haddam," he declared, as no one answered the last remark. Haddam was the place where he and his wife had been spending the summer.

"We have already telegraphed there," observed Mr. Gryce. "Your wife has not yet returned."

"There are other places," defiantly insisted the other. "I can find her if you give me the opportunity."

Mr. Gryce bowed.

"I am to give orders, then, for this body to be removed to the Morgue."

It was an unexpected suggestion, and for an instant Howard showed that he had feelings with the best. But he quickly recovered himself, and avoiding the anxious glances of his father and brother, answered with offensive lightness:

"I have nothing to do with that. You must do as you think proper."

And Mr. Gryce felt that he had received a check, and did not know whether to admire the young man for his nerve or to execrate him for his brutality. That the woman whom he had thus carelessly dismissed to the ignominy of the public gaze was his wife, the detective did not doubt.

CHAPTER VII

Mr. Gryce Discovers Miss Amelia

To return to my own observations. I was almost as ignorant of what I wanted to know at ten o'clock on that memorable night as I was at five, but I was determined not to remain so. When the two Misses Van Burnam had retired to their room, I slipped away to the neighboring house and boldly rang the bell. I had observed Mr. Gryce enter it a few minutes before, and I was resolved to have some talk with him.

The hall-lamp was lit, and we could discern each other's faces as he opened the door. Mine may have been a study, but I am sure his was. He had not expected to be confronted by an elderly lady at that hour of night.

"Well!" he dryly ejaculated, "I am sensible of the honor, Miss Butterworth." But he did not ask me in.

"I expected no less," said I. "I saw you come in, and I followed as soon after as I could. I have something to say to you."

He admitted me then and carefully closed the door. Feeling free to be myself, I threw off the veil I had tied under my chin and confronted him with what I call the true spirit.

"Mr. Gryce," I began, "let us make an exchange of civilities. Tell me what you have done with Howard Van Burnam, and I will tell you what I have observed in the course of this afternoon's investigation."

This aged detective is used to women, I have no doubt, but he is not used to *me*. I saw it by the way he turned over and over the spectacles he held in his hand. I made an effort to help him out.

"I have noted something today which I think has escaped *you*. It is so slight a clue that most women would not speak of it. But being interested in the case, I will mention it, if in return you will acquaint me with what will appear in the papers tomorrow."

He seemed to like it. He peered through his glasses and at them with the smile of a discoverer. "I am your very humble servant," he declared; and I felt as if my father's daughter had received her first recognition.

But he did not overwhelm me with confidences. O, no, he is very sly, this old and well-seasoned detective; and while appearing to be very communicative, really parted with but little information. He said enough, however, for me to gather that matters looked grim for Howard, and if this was so, it must have become apparent that the death they were investigating was neither an accident nor a suicide.

I hinted as much, and he, for his own ends no doubt, admitted at last that a wound had been found on the young woman which could not have been inflicted by herself; at which I felt such increased interest in this remarkable murder that I must have made some foolish display of it, for the wary old gentleman chuckled and ogled his spectacles quite lovingly before shutting them up and putting them into his pocket.

"And now what have you to tell me?" he inquired, sliding softly between me and the parlor door.

"Nothing but this. Question that queer-acting house-cleaner closely. She has something to tell which it is your business to know."

I think he was disappointed. He looked as if he regretted the spectacles he had pocketed, and when he spoke there was an edge to his tone I had not noticed in it before.

"Do you know what that something is?" he asked.

"No, or I should tell you myself."

"And what makes you think she is hiding anything from us?"

"Her manner. Did you not notice her manner?"

He shrugged his shoulders.

"It conveyed much to me," I insisted. "If I were a detective I would have the secret out of that woman or die in the attempt."

He laughed; this sly, old, almost decrepit man laughed outright. Then he looked severely at his old friend on the newel-post, and drawing himself up with some show of dignity, made this remark:

"It is my very good fortune to have made your acquaintance, Miss Butterworth. You and I ought to be able to work out this case in a way that will be satisfactory to all parties."

He meant it for sarcasm, but I took it quite seriously, that is to all appearance. I am as sly as he, and though not quite as old—now *I* am sarcastic—have some of his wits, if but little of his experience.

"Then let us to work," said I. "You have your theories about this murder, and I have mine; let us see how they compare."

If the image he had under his eye had not been made of bronze, I am sure it would have become petrified by the look he now gave it. What to me seemed but the natural proposition of an energetic woman with a special genius for his particular calling, evidently struck him as audacity of the grossest kind. But he confined his display of astonishment to the figure he was eying, and returned me nothing but this most gentlemanly retort:

"I am sure I am obliged to you, madam, and possibly I may be willing to consider your very thoughtful proposition later, but now I am busy, very busy, and if you will await my presence in your house for a half hour—"

"Why not let me wait here," I interposed. "The atmosphere of the place may sharpen my faculties. I already feel that another sharp look into that parlor would lead to the forming of some valuable theory."

"You—" Well, he did not say what I was, or rather, what the image he was apostrophizing, was. But he must have meant to utter a compliment of no common order.

The prim courtesy I made in acknowledgment of his good intention satisfied him that I had understood him fully; and changing his whole manner to one more in accordance with business, he observed after a moment's reflection:

"You came to a conclusion this afternoon, Miss Butterworth, for which I should like some explanation. In investigating the hat which had been drawn from under the murdered girl's remains, you made the remark that it had been worn but once. I had already come to the same conclusion, but by other means, doubtless. Will you tell me what it was that gave point to your assertion?"

"There was but one prick of a hat-pin in it," I observed. "If you have been in the habit of looking into young women's hats, you will appreciate the force of my remark."

"The deuce!" was his certainly uncalled for exclamation. "Women's eyes for women's matters! I am greatly indebted to you, ma'am. You have solved a very important problem for us. A hat-pin! humph!" he muttered to himself. "The devil in a man is not easily balked; even such an innocent article as that can be made to serve, when all other means are lacking."

It is perhaps a proof that Mr. Gryce is getting old, that he allowed these words to escape him. But having once given vent to them, he made no effort to retract them, but proceeded to take me into his confidence so far as to explain:

"The woman who was killed in that room owed her death to the stab of a thin, long pin. We had not thought of a hat-pin, but upon your mentioning it, I am ready to accept it as the instrument of death. There was no pin to be seen in the hat when you looked at it?"

"None. I examined it most carefully."

He shook his head and seemed to be meditating. As I had plenty of time I waited, expecting him to speak again. My patience seemed to impress him. Alternately raising and lowering his hands like one in the act of weighing something, he soon addressed me again, this time in a tone of banter:

"This pin—if pin it was—was found broken in the wound. We have been searching for the end that was left in the murderer's hand, and we have not found it. It is not on the floors of the parlors nor in this hallway. What do you think the ingenious user of such an instrument would do with it?"

This was said, I am now sure, out of a spirit of sarcasm. He was amusing himself with me, but I did not realize it then. I was too full of my subject.

"He would not have carried it away," I reasoned shortly, "at least not far. He did not throw it aside on reaching the street, for I watched his movements so closely that I would have observed him had he done this. It is in the house then, and presumably in the parlor, even if you do not find it on the floor."

"Would you like to look for it?" he impressively asked. I had no means of knowing at that time that when he was impressive he was his least candid and trustworthy self.

"Would I," I repeated; and being spare in figure and much more active in my movements that one would suppose from my age and dignified deportment, I ducked under his arms and was in Mr. Van Burnam's parlor before he had recovered from his surprise.

That a man like him could look foolish I would not have you for a moment suppose. But he did not look very well satisfied, and I had a chance to throw more than one glance around me before he found his tongue again.

"An unfair advantage, ma'am; an unfair advantage! I am old and I am rheumatic; you are young and sound as a nut. I acknowledge my folly in endeavoring to compete with you and must make the best of the situation. And now, madam, where is that pin?"

It was lightly said, but for all that I saw that my opportunity had come. If I could find this instrument of murder, what might I not expect from his gratitude. Nerving myself for the task thus set me, I peered hither and thither, taking in every article in the room before I made a step forward. There had been some attempt to rectify its disorder. The broken pieces of china had been lifted and laid carefully away on newspapers upon the shelves from which they had fallen. The cabinet stood upright in its place, and the clock which had tumbled face upward, had been placed upon the mantel shelf in the same position. The carpet was therefore free, save for the stains which told such a woful story of past tragedy and crime.

"You have moved the tables and searched behind the sofas," I suggested.

"Not an inch of the floor has escaped our attention, madam."

My eyes fell on the register, which my skirts half covered. It was closed; I stooped and opened it. A square box of tin was visible below, at the bottom of which I perceived the round head of a broken hat-pin.

Never in my life had I felt as I did at that minute. Rising up, I pointed at the register and let some of my triumph become apparent; but not all, for I was by no means sure at that moment, nor am I by any means sure now, that he had not made the discovery before I did and was simply testing my pretensions.

However that may be, he came forward quickly and after some little effort drew out the broken pin and examined it curiously.

"I should say that this is what we want," he declared, and from that moment on showed me a suitable deference.

"I account for its being there in this way," I argued. "The room was dark; for whether he lighted it or not to commit his crime, he certainly did not leave it lighted long. Coming out, his foot came in contact with the iron of the register and he was struck by a sudden thought. He had not dared to leave the head of the pin lying on the floor, for he hoped that he had covered up his crime by pulling the heavy cabinet over upon his victim; nor did he wish to carry away such a memento of his cruel deed. So he dropped it down the register, where he doubtless expected it would fall into the furnace pipes out of sight. But the tin box retained it. Is not that plausible, sir?"

"I could not have reasoned better myself, madam. We shall have you on the force, yet."

But at the familiarity shown by this suggestion, I bridled angrily. "I am Miss Butterworth," was my sharp retort, "and any interest I may take in this matter is due to my sense of justice."

Seeing that he had offended me, the astute detective turned the conversation back to business.

"By the way," said he, "your woman's knowledge can help me out at another point. If you are not afraid to remain in this room alone for a moment, I will bring an article in regard to which I should like your opinion."

I assured him I was not in the least bit afraid, at which he made me another of his anomalous bows and passed into the adjoining parlor. He did not stop there. Opening the sliding-doors communicating with the dining-room beyond, he disappeared in the latter room, shutting the doors behind him. Being now alone for a moment on the scene of crime, I crossed over to the mantel-shelf, and lifted the clock that lay there.

Why I did this I scarcely know. I am naturally very orderly (some people call me precise) and it probably fretted me to see so valuable an object out of its natural position. However that was, I lifted it up and set it upright, when to my amazement it began to tick. Had the hands not stood as they did when my eyes first fell on the clock lying face up on the floor at the dead girl's side, I should have thought the works had been started since that time by Mr. Gryce or some other officious person. But they pointed now as then to a few minutes before five and the only conclusion I could arrive at was, that the clock had been in running order when it fell, startling as this fact appeared in a house which had not been inhabited for months.

But if it had been in running order and was only stopped by its fall upon the floor, why did the hands point at five instead of twelve which was the hour at which the accident was supposed to have happened? Here was matter for thought, and that I might be undisturbed in my use of it, I hastened to lay the clock down again, even taking the precaution to restore the hands to the exact position they had occupied before I had started up the works. If Mr. Gryce did not know their secret, why so much the worse for Mr. Gryce.

I was back in my old place by the register before the folding-doors unclosed again. I was conscious of a slight flush on my cheek, so I took from my pocket that perplexing grocer-bill and was laboriously going down its long line of figures, when Mr. Gryce reappeared.

He had to my surprise a woman's hat in his hand.

"Well!" thought I, "what does this mean!"

It was an elegant specimen of millinery, and was in the latest style. It had ribbons and flowers and bird wings upon it, and presented, as it was turned about by Mr. Gryce's deft hand, an appearance which some might have called charming, but to me was simply grotesque and absurd.

"Is that a last spring's hat?" he inquired.

"I don't know, but I should say it had come fresh from the milliner's."

"I found it lying with a pair of gloves tucked inside it on an otherwise empty shelf in the dining-room closet. It struck me as looking too new for a discarded hat of either of the Misses Van Burnam. What do you think?"

"Let me take it," said I.

"O, it's been worn," he smiled, "several times. And the hat-pin is in it, too."

"There is something else I wish to see."

He handed it over.

"I think it belongs to one of them," I declared. "It was made by La Mole of Fifth Avenue, whose prices are simply—wicked."

"But the young ladies have been gone—let me see—five months. Could this have been bought before then?"

"Possibly, for this is an imported hat. But why should it have been left lying about in that careless way? It cost twenty dollars, if not thirty, and if for any reason its owner decided not to take it with her, why didn't she pack it away properly? I have no patience with the modern girl; she is made up of recklessness and extravagance."

"I hear that the young ladies are staying with you," was his suggestive remark.

"They are."

"Then you can make some inquiries about this hat; also about the gloves, which are an ordinary street pair."

"Of what color?"

"Grey; they are quite fresh, size six."

"Very well; I will ask the young ladies about them."

"This third room is used as a dining-room, and the closet where I found them is one in which glass is kept. The presence of this hat there is a mystery, but I presume the Misses Van Burnam can solve it. At all events, it is very improbable that it has anything to do with the crime which has been committed here."

"Very," I coincided.

"So improbable," he went on, "that on second thoughts I advise you not to disturb the young ladies with questions concerning it unless further reasons for doing so become apparent."

"Very well," I returned. But I was not deceived by his second thoughts.

As he was holding open the parlor door before me in a very significant way, I tied my veil under my chin, and was about to leave when he stopped me.

"I have another favor to ask," said he, and this time with his most benignant smile. "Miss Butterworth, do you object to sitting up for a few nights till twelve o'clock?"

"Not at all," I returned, "if there is any good reason for it."

"At twelve o'clock tonight a gentleman will enter this house. If you will note him from your window I will be obliged."

"To see whether he is the same one I saw last night? Certainly I will take a look, but—"

"Tomorrow night," he went on, imperturbably, "the test will be repeated, and I should like to have you take another look; without prejudice, madam; remember, without prejudice."

"I have no prejudices—" I began.

"The test may not be concluded in two nights," he proceeded, without any notice of my words. "So do not be in haste to spot your man, as the vulgar expression is. And now good-night—we shall meet again tomorrow."

"Wait!" I called peremptorily, for he was on the point of closing the door. "I saw the man but faintly; it is an impression only that I received. I would not wish a man to hang through any identification I could make."

"No man hangs on simple identification. We shall have to prove the crime, madam, but identification is important; even such as you can make."

There was no more to be said; I uttered a calm good-night and hastened away. By a judicious use of my opportunities I had become much less ignorant on the all-important topic than when I entered the house.

It was half past eleven when I returned home, a late hour for me to enter my respectable front door alone. But circumstances had warranted my escapade, and it was with quite an easy conscience and a cheerful sense of accomplishment that I went up to my room and prepared to sit out the half hour before midnight.

I am a comfortable sort of person when alone, and found no difficulty in passing this time profitably. Being very orderly, as you must have remarked, I have everything at hand for making myself a cup of tea at any time of day or night; so feeling some need of refreshment, I set out the little table I reserve for such purposes and made the tea and sat down to sip it.

While doing so, I turned over the subject occupying my mind, and endeavored to reconcile the story told by the clock with my preconceived theory of this murder; but no reconcilement was possible. The woman had been killed at twelve, and the clock had fallen at five. How could the two be made to agree, and which, since agreement was impossible, should be made to give way, the theory or the testimony of the clock? Both seemed incontrovertible, and yet one must be false. Which?

I was inclined to think that the trouble lay with the clock; that I had been deceived in my conclusions, and that it was not running at the time of the crime. Mr. Gryce may have ordered it wound, and then have had it laid on its back to prevent the hands from shifting past the point where they had stood at the time of the crime's discovery. It was an unexplainable act, but a possible one; while to suppose that it was going when the shelves fell, stretched improbability to the utmost, there having been, so far as we could learn, no one in the house for months sufficiently dexterous to set so valuable a timepiece; for who could imagine the scrubwoman engaging in a task requiring such delicate manipulation.

No! some meddlesome official had amused himself by starting up the works, and the clue I had thought so important would probably prove valueless.

There was humiliation in the thought, and it was a relief to me to hear an approaching carriage just as the clock on my mantel struck twelve. Springing from my chair, I put out my light and flew to the window.

The coach drew up and stopped next door. I saw a gentleman descend and step briskly across the pavement to the neighboring stoop. The figure he presented was not that of the man I had seen enter the night before.

CHAPTER VIII.

The Misses Van Burnam

Late as it was when I retired, I was up betimes in the morning—as soon, in fact, as the papers were distributed. The *Tribune* lay on the stoop. Eagerly I seized it; eagerly I read it. From its headlines you may judge what it had to say about this murder:

A STARTLING DISCOVERY IN THE VAN BURNAM MANSION IN GRAMERCY PARK.

A Young Girl Found there, Lying Dead
under an Overturned Cabinet.

Evidences that she was Murdered before
it was Pulled down upon her.

Thought by Some to be Mrs. Howard Van Burnam.

A Fearful Crime Involved in an Impenetrable Mystery.

What Mr. Van Burnam Says about it: He does
not Recognize the Woman as his Wife.

So, so, it was his wife they were talking about. I had not expected that. Well! well! no wonder the girls looked startled and concerned. And I paused to recall what I had heard about Howard Van Burnam's marriage.

It had not been a fortunate one. His chosen bride was pretty enough, but she had not been bred in the ways of fashionable society, and the other members of the family had never recognized her. The father, especially, had cut his son dead since his marriage, and had even gone so far as to threaten to dissolve the partnership in which they were all involved. Worse than this, there had been rumors of a disagreement between Howard and his wife. They were not always on good terms, and opinions differed as to which was most in fault. So much for what I knew of these two mentioned parties.

Reading the article at length, I learned that Mrs. Van Burnam was missing; that she had left Haddam for New York the day before her husband, and had not since been heard from. Howard was confident, however, that the publicity given to her disappearance by the papers would bring immediate news of her.

The effect of the whole article was to raise grave doubts as to the candor of Mr. Van Burnam's assertions, and I am told that in some of the less scrupulous papers these doubts were not only expressed, but actual surmises ventured upon as to the identity between the person whom I had seen enter the house with the young girl. As for my own name, it was blazoned forth in anything but a gratifying manner. I was spoken of in one paper—a kind friend told me this—as the prying Miss Amelia. As if my prying had not given the police their only clue to the identification of the criminal.

The New York *World* was the only paper that treated me with any consideration. That young man with the small head and beady eyes was not awed by me for nothing. He mentioned me as the clever Miss Butterworth whose testimony is likely to be of so much value in this very interesting case.

It was the *World* I handed the Misses Van Burnam when they came downstairs to breakfast. It did justice to me and not too much injustice to him. They read it together, their two heads plunged deeply into the paper so that I could not watch their faces. But I could see the sheet shake, and I noticed that their social veneer was not as yet laid on so thickly that they could hide their real terror and heart-ache when they finally confronted me again.

"Did you read—have you seen this horrible account?" quavered Caroline, as she met my eye.

"Yes, and I now understand why you felt such anxiety yesterday. Did you know your sister-in-law, and do you think she could have been beguiled into your father's house in that way?"

It was Isabella who answered.

"We never have seen her and know little of her, but there is no telling what such an uncultivated person as she might do. But that our good brother Howard ever went in there with her is a lie, isn't it, Caroline?—a base and malicious lie?"

"Of course it is, of course, of course. You don't think the man you saw was Howard, do you, dear Miss Butterworth?"

Dear? O dear!

"I am not acquainted with your brother," I returned. "I have never seen him but a few times in my life. You know he has not been a very frequent visitor at your father's house lately."

They looked at me wistfully, *so* wistfully.

"Say it was not Howard," whispered Caroline, stealing up a little nearer to my side.

"And we will never forget it," murmured Isabella, in what I am obliged to say was not her society manner.

"I hope to be able to say it," was my short rejoinder, made difficult by the prejudices I had formed. "When I see your brother, I may be able to decide at a glance that the person I saw entering your house was not he."

"Yes, oh, yes. Do you hear that, Isabella? Miss Butterworth will save Howard yet. O you dear old soul. I could almost love you!"

This was not agreeable to me. I a dear old soul! A term to be applied to a butter-woman not to a Butterworth. I drew back and their sentimentalities came to an end. I hope their brother Howard is not the guilty man the papers make him out to be, but if he is, the Misses Van Burnam's fine phrase, *We could almost love you*, will not deter me from being honest in the matter.

Mr. Gryce called early, and I was glad to be able to tell him that the gentleman who visited him the night before did not recall the impression made upon me by the other. He received the communication quietly, and from his manner I judged that it was more or less expected. But who can be a correct judge of a detective's manner, especially one so foxy and imperturbable as this one? I longed to ask who his visitor was, but I did not dare, or rather—to be candid in little things that you may believe me in great—I was confident he would not tell me, so I would not compromise my dignity by a useless question.

He went after a five minutes' stay, and I was about to turn my attention to household affairs, when Franklin came in.

His sisters jumped like puppets to meet him.

"O," they cried, for once thinking and speaking alike, "have you found her?"

His silence was so eloquent that he did not need to shake his head.

"But you will before the day is out?" protested Caroline.

"It is too early yet," added Isabella.

"I never thought I would be glad to see that woman under any circumstances," continued the former, "but I believe now that if I saw her coming up the street on Howard's arm, I should be happy enough to rush out and—and—"

"Give her a hug," finished the more impetuous Isabella.

It was not what Caroline meant to say, but she accepted the emendation, with just the slightest air of deprecation. They were both evidently much attached to Howard, and ready in his trouble to forget and forgive everything. I began to like them again.

"Have you read the horrid papers?" and "How is papa this morning?" and "What shall we do to save Howard?" now flew in rapid questions from their lips; and feeling that it was but natural they should have their little say, I sat down in my most uncomfortable chair and waited for these first ebullitions to exhaust themselves.

Instantly Mr. Van Burnam took them by the arm, and led them away to a distant sofa.

"Are you happy here?" he asked, in what he meant for a very confidential tone. But I can hear as readily as a deaf person anything which is not meant for my ears.

"O she's kind enough," whispered Caroline, "but so stingy. Do take us where we can get something to eat."

"She puts all her money into china! Such plates!—*and so little on them!*"

At these expressions, uttered with all the emphasis a whisper will allow, I just hugged myself in my quiet corner. The dear, giddy things! But they should see, they should see.

"I fear"—it was Mr. Van Burnam who now spoke—"I shall have to take my sisters from under your kind care today. Their father needs them, and has, I believe, already engaged rooms for them at the Plaza."

"I am sorry," I replied, "but surely they will not leave till they have had another meal with me. Postpone your departure, young ladies, till after luncheon, and you will greatly oblige me. We may never meet so agreeably again."

They fidgeted (which I had expected), and cast secret looks of almost comic appeal at their brother, but he pretended not to see them, being disposed for some reason to grant my request. Taking advantage of the momentary hesitation that ensued, I made them all three my most concil-iatory bow, and said as I retreated behind the portière:

"I shall give my orders for luncheon now. Meanwhile, I hope the young ladies will feel perfectly free in my house. All that I have is at their command." And was gone before they could protest.

When I next saw them, they were upstairs in my front room. They were seated together in the window and looked miserable enough to have a little diversion. Going to my closet, I brought out a band-box. It contained my best bonnet.

"Young ladies, what do you think of this?" I inquired, taking the bonnet out and carefully placing it on my head.

I myself consider it a very becoming article of headgear, but their eyebrows went up in a scarcely complimentary fashion.

"You don't like it?" I remarked. "Well, I think a great deal of young girls' taste; I shall send it back to Madame More's tomorrow."

"I don't think much of Madame More," observed Isabella, "and after Paris—"

"Do you like La Mole better?" I inquired, bobbing my head to and fro before the mirror, the better to conceal my interest in the venture I was making.

"I don't like any of them but D'Aubigny," returned Isabella. "She charges twice what La Mole does—"

Twice! What are these girls' purses made of, or rather their father's!

"But she has the *chic* we are accustomed to see in French millinery. I shall *never* go anywhere else."

"We were recommended to her in Paris," put in Caroline, more lan-guidly. Her interest was only half engaged by this frivolous topic.

"But did you never have one of La Mole's hats?" I pursued, taking down a hand-mirror, ostensibly to get the effect of my bonnet in the back, but really to hide my interest in their unconscious faces.

"Never!" retorted Isabella. "I would not patronize the thing."

"Nor you?" I urged, carelessly, turning towards Caroline.

"No; I have never been inside her shop."

"Then whose is—" I began and stopped. A detective doing the work I was, would not give away the object of his questions so recklessly.

"Then who is," I corrected, "the best person after D'Aubigny? I never can pay *her* prices. I should think it wicked."

"O don't ask us," protested Isabella. "We have never made a study of the best bonnet-maker. At present we wear hats."

And having thus thrown their youth in my face, they turned away to the window again, not realizing that the middle-aged lady they regarded with such disdain had just succeeded in making them dance to her music most successfully.

The luncheon I ordered was elaborate, for I was determined that the Misses Van Burnam should see that I knew how to serve a fine meal, and that my plates were not always better than my viands.

I had invited in a couple of other guests so that I should not seem to have put myself out for two young girls, and as they were quiet people like myself, the meal passed most decorously. When it was finished, the Misses Caroline and Isabella had lost some of their consequential airs, and I really think the deference they have since showed me is due more to the surprise they felt at the perfection of this dainty luncheon, than to any considerate appreciation of my character and abilities.

They left at three o'clock, still without news of Mrs. Van Burnam; and being positive by this time that the shadows were thickening about this family, I saw them depart with some regret and a positive feeling of commiseration. Had they been reared to a proper reverence for their elders, how much more easy it would have been to see earnestness in Caroline and affectionate impulses in Isabella.

The evening papers added but little to my knowledge. Great disclosures were promised, but no hint given of their nature. The body at the Morgue had not been identified by any of the hundreds who had viewed it, and Howard still refused to acknowledge it as that of his wife. The morrow was awaited with anxiety.

So much for the public press!

At twelve o'clock at night, I was again seated in my window. The house next door had been lighted since ten, and I was in momentary expectation of its nocturnal visitor. He came promptly at the hour set, alighted from the carriage with a bound, shut the carriage-door with a slam, and crossed the pavement with cheerful celerity. His figure was not so positively like, nor yet so positively unlike, that of the supposed murderer that I could definitely say, "This is he," or, "This is not he," and I went to bed puzzled, and not a little burdened by a sense of the responsibility imposed upon me in this matter.

And so passed the day between the murder and the inquest.

CHAPTER IX

DEVELOPMENTS

Mr. Gryce called about nine o'clock next morning.

"Well," said he, "what about the visitor who came to see me last night?"

"Like and unlike," I answered. "Nothing could induce me to say he is the man we want, and yet I would not dare to swear he was not."

"You are in doubt, then, concerning him?"

"I am."

Mr. Gryce bowed, reminded me of the inquest, and left. Nothing was said about the hat.

At ten o'clock I prepared to go to the place designated by him. I had never attended an inquest in my life, and felt a little flurried in consequence, but by the time I had tied the strings of my bonnet (the despised bonnet, which, by the way, I did not return to More's), I had conquered this weakness, and acquired a demeanor more in keeping with my very important position as chief witness in a serious police investigation.

I had sent for a carriage to take me, and I rode away from my house amid the shouts of some half dozen boys collected on the curb-stone. But I did not allow myself to feel dashed by this publicity. On the contrary, I held my head as erect as nature intended, and my back kept the line my good health warrants. The path of duty has its thorny passages, but it is for strong minds like mine to ignore them.

Promptly at ten o'clock I entered the room reserved for the inquest, and was ushered to the seat appointed me. Though never a self-conscious woman, I could not but be aware of the many eyes that followed me, and endeavored so to demean myself that there should be no question as to my respectable standing in the community. This I considered due to the memory of my father, who was very much in my thoughts that day.

The Coroner was already in his seat when I entered, and though I did not perceive the good face of Mr. Gryce anywhere in his vicinity, I had no doubt he was within ear-shot. Of the other people I took small note, save of the honest scrub-woman, of whose red face and anxious eyes under a preposterous bonnet (which did *not come* from La Mole's), I caught vague glimpses as the crowd between us surged to and fro.

None of the Van Burnams were visible, but this did not necessarily mean that they were absent. Indeed, I was very sure, from certain indications, that more than one member of the family could be seen in the small room connecting with the large one in which we witnesses sat with the jury.

The policeman, Carroll, was the first man to talk. He told of my stopping him on his beat and of his entrance into Mr. Van Burnam's house with the scrub-woman. He gave the details of his discovery of the dead woman's body on the parlor floor, and insisted that no one—here he looked very hard at me—had been allowed to touch the body till relief had come to him from Headquarters.

Mrs. Boppert, the scrub-woman, followed him; and if she was watched by no one else in that room, she was watched by me. Her manner before the Coroner was no more satisfactory, according to my notion, than it had been in Mr. Van Burnam's parlor. She gave a very perceptible start when they spoke her name, and looked quite scared when the Bible was held out towards her. But she took the oath notwithstanding, and with her testimony the inquiry began in earnest.

"What is your name?" asked the Coroner.

As this was something she could not help knowing, she uttered the necessary words glibly, though in a way that showed she resented his impertinence in asking her what he already knew.

"Where do you live? And what do you do for a living?" rapidly followed.

She replied that she was a scrub-woman and cleaned people's houses, and having said this, she assumed a very dogged air, which I thought strange enough to raise a question in the minds of those who watched her. But no one else seemed to regard it as anything but the embarrassment of ignorance.

"How long have you known the Van Burnam family?" the Coroner went on.

"Two years, sir, come next Christmas."

"Have you often done work for them?"

"I clean the house twice a year, fall and spring."

"Why were you at this house two days ago?"

"To scrub the kitchen floors, sir, and put the pantries in order."

"Had you received notice to do so?"

"Yes, sir, through Mr. Franklin Van Burnam."

"And was that the first day of your work there?"

"No, sir; I had been there all the day before."

"You don't speak loud enough," objected the Coroner; "remember that every one in this room wants to hear you."

She looked up, and with a frightened air surveyed the crowd about her. Publicity evidently made her most uncomfortable, and her voice sank rather than rose.

"Where did you get the key of the house, and by what door did you enter?"

"I went in at the basement, sir, and I got the key at Mr. Van Burnam's agent in Dey Street. I had to go for it; sometimes they send it to me; but not this time."

"And now relate your meeting with the policeman on Wednesday morning, in front of Mr. Van Burnam's house."

She tried to tell her story, but she made awkward work of it, and they had to ply her with questions to get at the smallest fact. But finally she managed to repeat what we already knew, how she went with the policeman into the house, and how they stumbled upon the dead woman in the parlor.

Further than this they did not question her, and I, Amelia Butterworth, had to sit in silence and see her go back to her seat, redder than before, but with a strangely satisfied air that told me she had escaped more easily than she had expected. And yet Mr. Gryce had been warned that she knew more than appeared, and by one in whom he seemed to have placed some confidence!

The doctor was called next. His testimony was most important, and contained a surprise for me and more than one surprise for the others. After a short preliminary examination, he was requested to state how long the woman had been dead when he was called in to examine her.

"More than twelve and less than eighteen hours," was his quiet reply.

"Had the rigor mortis set in?"

"No; but it began very soon after."

"Did you examine the wounds made by the falling shelves and the vases that tumbled with them?"

"I did."

"Will you describe them?"

He did so.

"And now"—there was a pause in the Coroner's question which roused us all to its importance, "which of these many serious wounds was in your opinion the cause of her death?"

The witness was accustomed to such scenes, and was perfectly at home in them. Surveying the Coroner with a respectful air, he turned slowly towards the jury and answered in a slow and impressive manner:

"I feel ready to declare, sirs, that none of them did. She was not killed by the falling of the cabinet upon her."

"Not killed by the falling shelves! Why not? Were they not sufficiently heavy, or did they not strike her in a vital place?"

"They were heavy enough, and they struck her in a way to kill her if she had not been already dead when they fell upon her. As it was, they simply bruised a body from which life had already departed."

As this was putting it very plainly, many of the crowd who had not been acquainted with these facts previously, showed their interest in a very unmistakable manner; but the Coroner, ignoring these symptoms of growing excitement, hastened to say:

"This is a very serious statement you are making, doctor. If she did not die from the wounds inflicted by the objects which fell upon her, from what cause did she die? Can you say that her death was a natural one, and that the falling of the shelves was merely an unhappy accident following it?"

"No, sir; her death was not natural. She was killed, but not by the falling cabinet."

"Killed, and not by the cabinet? How then? Was there any other wound upon her which you regard as mortal?"

"Yes, sir. Suspecting that she had perished from other means than appeared, I made a most rigid examination of her body, when I discovered under the hair in the nape of the neck, a minute spot, which, upon probing, I found to be the end of a small, thin point of steel. It had been thrust by a careful hand into the most vulnerable part of the body, and death must have ensued at once."

This was too much for certain excitable persons present, and a momentary disturbance arose, which, however, was nothing to that in my own breast.

So! so! it was her neck that had been pierced, and not her heart. Mr. Gryce had allowed us to think it was the latter, but it was not this fact which stupefied me, but the skill and diabolical coolness of the man who had inflicted this death-thrust.

After order had been restored, which I will say was very soon, the Coroner, with an added gravity of tone, went on with his questions:

"Did you recognize this bit of steel as belonging to any instrument in the medical profession?"

"No; it was of too untempered steel to have been manufactured for any thrusting or cutting purposes. It was of the commonest kind, and had broken short off in the wound. It was the end only that I found."

"Have you this end with you—the point, I mean, which you found imbedded at the base of the dead woman's brain?"

"I have, sir"; and he handed it over to the jury. As they passed it along, the Coroner remarked:

"Later we will show you the remaining portion of this instrument of death," which did not tend to allay the general excitement. Seeing this, the Coroner humored the growing interest by pushing on his inquiries.

"Doctor," he asked, "are you prepared to say how long a time elapsed between the infliction of this fatal wound and those which disfigured her?"

"No, sir, not exactly; but some little time."

Some little time, when the murderer was in the house only ten minutes! All looked their surprise, and, as if the Coroner had divined this feeling of general curiosity, he leaned forward and emphatically repeated:

"More than ten minutes?"

The doctor, who had every appearance of realizing the importance of his reply, did not hesitate. Evidently his mind was quite made up.

"*Yes; more than ten minutes.*"

This was the shock *I* received from his testimony.

I remembered what the clock had revealed to me, but I did not move a muscle of my face. I was learning self-control under these repeated surprises.

"This is an unexpected statement," remarked the Coroner. "What reasons have you to urge in explanation of it?"

"Very simple and very well known ones; at least, among the profession. There was too little blood seen, for the wounds to have been inflicted before death or within a few minutes after it. Had the woman been living when they were made, or even had she been but a short time dead, the floor would have been deluged with the blood gushing from so many and such serious injuries. But the effusion was slight, so slight that I noticed it at once, and came to the conclusions mentioned before I found the mark of the stab that occasioned death."

"I see, I see! And was that the reason you called in two neighboring physicians to view the body before it was removed from the house?"

"Yes, sir; in so important a matter, I wished to have my judgment confirmed."

"And these physicians were—"

"Dr. Campbell, of 110 East —— Street, and Dr. Jacobs, of —— Lexington Avenue."

"Are these gentlemen here?" inquired the Coroner of an officer who stood near.

"They are, sir."

"Very good; we will now proceed to ask one or two more questions of this witness. You told us that even had the woman been but a few minutes dead when she received these contusions, the floor would have been more or less deluged by her blood. What reason have you for this statement?"

"This; that in a few minutes, let us say ten, since that number has been used, the body has not had time to cool, nor have the blood-vessels had sufficient opportunity to stiffen so as to prevent the free effusion of blood."

"Is a body still warm at ten minutes after death?"

"It is."

"So that your conclusions are logical deductions from well-known facts?"

"Certainly, sir."

A pause of some duration followed.

When the Coroner again proceeded, it was to remark:

"The case is complicated by these discoveries; but we must not allow ourselves to be daunted by them. Let me ask you, if you found any marks upon this body which might aid in its identification?"

"One; a slight scar on the left ankle."

"What kind of a scar? Describe it."

"It was such as a burn might leave. In shape it was long and narrow, and it ran up the limb from the ankle-bone."

"Was it on the right foot?"

"No; on the left."

"Did you call the attention of any one to this mark during or after your examination?"

"Yes; I showed it to Mr. Gryce the detective, and to my two coadjutors; and I spoke of it to Mr. Howard Van Burnam, son of the gentleman in whose house the body was found."

It was the first time this young gentleman's name had been mentioned, and it made my blood run cold to see how many side-long looks and expressive shrugs it caused in the motley assemblage. But I had no time for sentiment; the inquiry was growing too interesting.

"And why," asked the Coroner, "did you mention it to this young man in preference to others?"

"Because Mr. Gryce requested me to. Because the family as well as the young man himself had evinced some apprehension lest the deceased might prove to be his missing wife, and this seemed a likely way to settle the question."

"And did it? Did he acknowledge it to be a mark he remembered to have seen on his wife?"

"He said she had such a scar, but he would not acknowledge the deceased to be his wife."

"Did he see the scar?"

"No; he would not look at it."

"Did you invite him to?"

"I did; but he showed no curiosity."

Doubtless thinking that silence would best emphasize this fact, which certainly was an astonishing one, the Coroner waited a minute. But there was no silence. An indescribable murmur from a great many lips filled up the gap. I felt a movement of pity for the proud family whose good name was thus threatened in the person of this young gentleman.

"Doctor," continued the Coroner, as soon as the murmur had subsided, "did you notice the color of the woman's hair?"

"It was a light brown."

"Did you sever a lock? Have you a sample of this hair here to show us?"

"I have, sir. At Mr. Gryce's suggestion I cut off two small locks. One I gave him and the other I brought here."

"Let me see it."

The doctor passed it up, and in sight of every one present the Coroner tied a string around it and attached a ticket to it.

"That is to prevent all mistake," explained this very methodical functionary, laying the lock aside on the table in front of him. Then he turned again to the witness.

"Doctor, we are indebted to you for your valuable testimony, and as you are a busy man, we will now excuse you. Let Dr. Jacobs be called."

As this gentleman, as well as the witness who followed him, merely corroborated the statements of the other, and made it an accepted fact that the shelves had fallen upon the body of the girl some time after the first wound had been inflicted, I will not attempt to repeat their testimony. The question now agitating me was whether they would endeavor to fix the time at which the shelves fell by the evidence furnished by the clock.

CHAPTER X

Important Evidence

Evidently not; for the next words I heard were: "Miss Amelia Butterworth!"

I had not expected to be called so soon, and was somewhat flustered by the suddenness of the summons, for I am only human. But I rose with suitable composure, and passed to the place indicated by the Coroner, in my usual straightforward manner, heightened only by a sense of the importance of my position, both as a witness and a woman whom the once famous Mr. Gryce had taken more or less into his confidence.

My appearance seemed to awaken an interest for which I was not prepared. I was just thinking how well my name had sounded uttered in the sonorous tones of the Coroner, and how grateful I ought to be for the courage I had displayed in substituting the genteel name of Amelia for the weak and sentimental one of Araminta, when I became conscious that the eyes directed towards me were filled with an expression not easy to understand. I should not like to call it admiration and will not call it amusement, and yet it seemed to be made up of both. While I was puzzling myself over it, the first question came.

As my examination before the Coroner only brought out the facts already related, I will not burden you with a detailed account of it. One portion alone may be of interest. I was being questioned in regard to the appearance of the couple I had seen entering the Van Burnam mansion, when the Coroner asked if the young woman's step was light, or if it betrayed hesitation.

I replied: "No hesitation; she moved quickly, almost gaily."

"And he?"

"Was more moderate; but there is no signification in that; he may have been older."

"No theories, Miss Butterworth; it is facts we are after. Now, do you know that he was older?"

"No, sir."

"Did you get any idea as to his age?"

"The impression he made was that of being a young man."

"And his height?"

"Was medium, and his figure slight and elegant. He moved as a gentleman moves; of this I can speak with great positiveness."

"Do you think you could identify him, Miss Butterworth, if you should see him?"

I hesitated, as I perceived that the whole swaying mass eagerly awaited my reply. I even turned my head because I saw others doing so; but I regretted this when I found that I, as well as others, was glancing towards the door beyond which the Van Burnams were supposed to sit. To cover up the false move I had made—for I had no wish as yet to centre suspicion upon anybody—I turned my face quickly back to the crowd and declared in as emphatic a tone as I could command:

"I have thought I could do so if I saw him under the same circumstances as those in which my first impression was made. But lately I have begun to doubt even that. I should never dare trust to my memory in this regard."

The Coroner looked disappointed, and so did the people around me.

"It is a pity," remarked the Coroner, "that you did not see more plainly. And, now, how did these persons gain an entrance into the house?"

I answered in the most succinct way possible.

I told them how he had used a door-key in entering, of the length of time the man stayed inside, and of his appearance on going away. I also related how I came to call a policeman to investigate the matter next day, and corroborated the statements of this official as to the appearance of the deceased at time of discovery.

And there my examination stopped. I was not asked any questions tending to bring out the cause of the suspicion I entertained against the scrub-woman, nor were the discoveries I had made in conjunction with Mr. Gryce inquired into. It was just as well, perhaps, but I would never approve of a piece of work done for me in this slipshod fashion.

A recess now followed. Why it was thought necessary, I cannot imagine, unless the gentlemen wished to smoke. Had they felt as much interest in this murder as I did, they would not have wanted bite or sup till the dreadful question was settled. There being a recess, I improved the opportunity by going into a restaurant near by where one can get very good buns and coffee at a reasonable price. But I could have done without them.

The next witness, to my astonishment, was Mr. Gryce. As he stepped forward, heads were craned and many women rose in their seats to get a glimpse of the noted detective. I showed no curiosity myself, for by this time I knew his features well, but I did feel a great satisfaction in seeing him before the Coroner, for now, thought I, we shall hear something worth our attention.

But his examination, though interesting, was not complete. The Coroner, remembering his promise to show us the other end of the steel point which had been broken off in the dead girl's brain, limited himself to such inquiries as brought out the discovery of the broken hat-pin in Mr. Van Burnam's parlor register. No mention was made by the witness of any assistance which he may have received in making this discovery; a fact which caused me to smile: men are so jealous of any interference in their affairs.

The end found in the register and the end which the Coroner's physician had drawn from the poor woman's head were both handed to the jury, and it was interesting to note how each man made his little effort to fit the two ends together, and the looks they interchanged as they found themselves successful. Without doubt, and in the eyes of all, the instrument of death had been found. But what an instrument!

The felt hat which had been discovered under the body was now produced and the one hole made by a similar pin examined. Then Mr. Gryce was asked if any other pin had been picked up from the floor of the room, and he replied, no; and the fact was established in the minds of all present that the young woman had been killed by a pin taken from her own hat.

"A subtle and cruel crime; the work of a calculating intellect," was the Coroner's comment as he allowed the detective to sit down. Which expression of opinion I thought reprehensible, as tending to prejudice the jury against the only person at present suspected.

The inquiry now took a turn. The name of Miss Ferguson was called. Who was Miss Ferguson? It was a new name to most of us, and her face when she rose only added to the general curiosity. It was the plainest face imaginable, yet it was neither a bad nor unintelligent one. As I studied it and noted the nervous contraction that disfigured her lip, I could not but be sensible of my blessings. I am not handsome myself, though there have been persons who have called me so, but neither am I ugly, and in contrast to this woman—well, I will say nothing. I only know that, after seeing her, I felt profoundly grateful to a kind Providence.

As for the poor woman herself, she knew she was no beauty, but she had become so accustomed to seeing the eyes of other people turn away from her face, that beyond the nervous twitching of which I have spoken, she showed no feeling.

"What is your full name, and where do you live?" asked the Coroner.

"My name is Susan Ferguson, and I live in Haddam, Connecticut," was her reply, uttered in such soft and beautiful tones that every one was astonished. It was like a stream of limpid water flowing from a most unsightly-looking rock. Excuse the metaphor; I do not often indulge.

"Do you keep boarders?"

"I do; a few, sir; such as my house will accommodate."

"Whom have you had with you this summer?"

I knew what her answer would be before she uttered it; so did a hundred others, but they showed their knowledge in different ways. I did not show mine at all.

"I have had with me," said she, "a Mr. and Mrs. Van Burnam from New York. Mr. Howard Van Burnam is his full name, if you wish me to be explicit."

"Any one else?"

"A Mr. Hull, also from New York, and a young couple from Hartford. My house accommodates no more."

"How long have the first mentioned couple been with you?"

"Three months. They came in June."

"Are they with you still?"

"Virtually, sir. They have not moved their trunks; but neither of them is in Haddam at present. Mrs. Van Burnam came to New York last Monday morning, and in the afternoon her husband also left, presumably for New York. I have seen nothing of either of them since."

(It was on Tuesday night the murder occurred.)

"Did either of them take a trunk?"

"No, sir."

"A hand-bag?"

"Yes; Mrs. Van Burnam carried a bag, but it was a very small one."

"Large enough to hold a dress?"

"O no, sir."

"And Mr. Van Burnam?"

"He carried an umbrella; I saw nothing else."

"Why did they not leave together? Did you hear any one say?"

"Yes; I heard them say Mrs. Van Burnam came against her husband's wishes. He did not want her to leave Haddam, but she would, and he was none too pleased at it. Indeed they had words about it, and as both our rooms overlook the same veranda, I could not help hearing some of their talk."

"Will you tell us what you heard?"

"It does not seem right" (thus this honest woman spoke), "but if it's the law, I must not go against it. I heard him say these words: 'I have changed my mind, Louise. The more I think of it, the more disinclined I am to have you meddle in the matter. Besides, it will do no good. You will only add to the prejudice against you, and our life will become more unbearable than it is now.'"

"Of what were they speaking?"

"I do not know."

"And what did she reply?"

"O, she uttered a torrent of words that had less sense in them than feeling. She wanted to go, she would go, *she* had not changed *her* mind, and considered that her impulses were as well worth following as his cool judgment. She was not happy, had never been happy, and meant there should be a change, even if it were for the worse. But she did not believe it would be for the worse. Was she not pretty? Was she not very pretty when in distress and looking up thus? And I heard her fall on her knees, a movement which called out a grunt from her husband, but whether this was an expression of approval or disapproval I cannot say. A silence followed, during which I caught the sound of his steady tramping up and down the room. Then she spoke again in a petulant way. 'It may seem foolish to *you*' she cried, 'knowing me as you do, and being used to seeing me in all my moods. But to him it will be a surprise, and I will so manage it that it will effect all we want, and more, too, perhaps. I—I have a genius for some things, Howard; and my better angel tells me I shall succeed.'"

"And what did he reply to that?"

"That the name of her better angel was Vanity; that his father would see through her blandishments; that he forbade her to prosecute her schemes; and much more to the same effect. To all of which she answered by a vigorous stamp of her foot, and the declaration that she was going to do what she thought best in spite of all opposition; that it was a lover, and not a tyrant that she had married, and that if he did not know what was good for himself, she did, and that when he received an intimation from his father that the breach in the family was closed, then he would acknowledge that if she had no fortune and no connections, she had at least a plentiful supply of wit. Upon which he remarked: 'A poor qualification when it verges upon folly!' which seemed to close the conversation, for I heard no more till the sound of her skirts rustling past my door assured me she had carried her point and was leaving the house. But this was not done without great discomfiture to her husband, if one may judge from the few brief but emphatic words that escaped him before he closed his own door and followed her down the hall."

"Do you remember those words?"

"They were swear words, sir; I am sorry to say it, but he certainly cursed her and his own folly. Yet I always thought he loved her."

"Did you see her after she passed your door?"

"Yes, sir, on the walk outside."

"Was she then on the way to the train?"

"Yes, sir."

"Carrying the bag of which you have spoken?"

"Yes, sir; another proof of the state of feeling between them, for he was very considerate in his treatment of ladies, and I never saw him do anything ungallant before."

"You say you watched her as she went down the walk?"

"Yes, sir; it is human nature, sir; I have no other excuse to offer."

It was an apology I myself might have made. I conceived a liking for this homely matter-of-fact woman.

"Did you note her dress?"

"Yes, sir; that is human nature also, or, rather, woman's nature."

"Particularly, madam; so that you can describe it to the jury before you?"

"I think so."

"Will you, then, be good enough to tell us what sort of a dress Mrs. Van Burnam wore when she left your house for the city?"

"It was a black and white plaid silk, very rich—"

Why, what did this mean? We had all expected a very different description.

"It was made fashionably, and the sleeves—well, it is impossible to describe the sleeves. She wore no wrap, which seemed foolish to me, for we have very sudden changes sometimes in September."

"A plaid dress! And did you notice her hat?"

"O, I have seen the hat often. It was of every conceivable color. It would have been called bad taste at one time, but now-a-days—"

The pause was significant. More than one man in the room chuckled, but the women kept a discreet silence.

"Would you know that hat if you saw it?"

"I should think I would!"

The emphasis was that of a countrywoman, and amused some people notwithstanding the melodious tone in which it was uttered. But it did not amuse me; my thoughts had flown to the hat which Mr. Gryce had found in the third room of Mr. Van Burnam's house, and which was of every color of the rainbow.

The Coroner asked two other questions, one in regard to the gloves worn by Mrs. Van Burnam, and the other in regard to her shoes. To the first, Miss Ferguson replied that she did not notice her gloves, and to the other, that Mrs. Van Burnam was very fashionable, and as pointed shoes were the fashion, in cities at least, she probably wore pointed shoes.

The discovery that Mrs. Van Burnam had been differently dressed on that day from the young woman found dead in the Van Burnam parlors, had acted as a shock upon most of the spectators. They were just beginning to recover from it when Miss Ferguson sat down. The Coroner was the only one who had not seemed at a loss. Why, we were soon destined to know.

CHAPTER XI

The Order Clerk

A lady well known in New York society was the next person summoned. She was a friend of the Van Burnam family, and had known Howard from childhood. She had not liked his marriage; indeed, she rather participated in the family feeling against it, but when young Mrs. Van Burnam came to her house on the preceding Monday, and begged the privilege of remaining with her for one night, she had not had the heart to refuse her. Mrs. Van Burnam had therefore slept in her house on Monday night.

Questioned in regard to that lady's appearance and manner, she answered that her guest was unnaturally cheerful, laughing much and showing a great vivacity; that she gave no reason for her good spirits, nor did she mention her own affairs in any way—rather took pains not to do so.

"How long did she stay?"

"Till the next morning."

"And how was she dressed?"

"Just as Miss Ferguson has described."

"Did she bring her hand-bag to your house?"

"Yes, and left it there. We found it in her room after she was gone."

"Indeed! And how do you account for that?"

"She was preoccupied. I saw it in her cheerfulness, which was forced and not always well timed."

"And where is that bag now?"

"Mr. Van Burnam has it. We kept it for a day and as she did not call for it, sent it down to the office on Wednesday morning."

"Before you had heard of the murder?"

"O yes, before I had heard anything about the murder."

"As she was your guest, you probably accompanied her to the door?"

"I did, sir."

"Did you notice her hands? Can you say what was the color of her gloves?"

"I do not think she wore any gloves on leaving; it was very warm, and she held them in her hand. I remembered this, for I noticed the sparkle of her rings as she turned to say good-bye."

"Ah, you saw her rings!"

"Distinctly."

"So that when she left you she was dressed in a black and white plaid silk, had a large hat covered with flowers on her head, and wore rings?"

"Yes, sir."

And with these words ringing in the ears of the jury, the witness sat down.

What was coming? Something important, or the Coroner would not look so satisfied, or the faces of the officials about him so expectant. I waited with great but subdued eagerness for the testimony of the next witness, who was a young man by the name of Callahan.

I don't like young men in general. They are either over-suave and polite, as if they condescended to remember that you are elderly and that it is their duty to make you forget it, or else they are pert and shallow and disgust you with their egotism. But this young man looked sensible and business-like, and I took to him at once, though what connection he could have with this affair I could not imagine.

His first words, however, settled all questions as to his personality: He was the order clerk at Altman's.

As he acknowledged this, I seemed to have some faint premonition of what was coming. Perhaps I had not been without some vague idea of the truth ever since I had put my mind to work on this matter; perhaps my wits only received their real spur then; but certainly I knew what he was going to say as soon as he opened his lips, which gave me quite a good opinion of myself, whether rightfully or not, I leave you to judge.

His evidence was short, but very much to the point. On the seventeenth of September, as could be verified by the books, the firm had received an order for a woman's complete outfit, to be sent, C.O.D., to Mrs. James Pope at the Hotel D——, on Broadway. Sizes and measures and some particulars were stated, and as the order bore the words *In haste* underlined upon it, several clerks had assisted him in filling this order, which when filled had been sent by special messenger to the place designated.

Had he this order with him?

He had.

And could he identify the articles sent to fill it?

He could.

At which the Coroner motioned to an officer and a pile of clothing was brought forward from some mysterious corner and laid before the witness.

Immediately expectation rose to a high pitch, for every one recognized, or thought he did, the apparel which had been taken from the victim.

The young man, who was of the alert, nervous type, took up the articles one by one and examined them closely.

As he did so, the whole assembled crowd surged forward and lightning-like glances from a hundred eyes followed his every movement and expression.

"Are they the same?" inquired the Coroner.

The witness did not hesitate. With one quick glance at the blue serge dress, black cape, and battered hat, he answered in a firm tone:

"They are."

And a clue was given at last to the dreadful mystery absorbing us.

The deep-drawn sigh which swept through the room testified to the universal satisfaction; then our attention became fixed again, for the Coroner, pointing to the undergarments accompanying the articles already mentioned, demanded if they had been included in the order.

There was as little hesitation in the reply given to this question as to the former. He recognized each piece as having come from his establishment. "You will note," said he, "that they have never been washed, and that the pencil marks are still on them."

"Very good," observed the Coroner, "and you will note that one article there is torn down the back. Was it in that condition when sent?"

"It was not, sir."

"All were in perfect order?"

"Most assuredly, sir."

"Very good, again. The jury will take cognizance of this fact, which may be useful to them in their future conclusions. And now, Mr. Callahan, do you notice anything lacking here from the list of articles forwarded by you?"

"No, sir."

"Yet there is one very necessary adjunct to a woman's outfit which is not to be found here."

"Yes, sir, the shoes; but I am not surprised at that. We sent shoes, but they were not satisfactory, and they were returned."

"Ah, I see. Officer, show the witness the shoes that were taken from the deceased."

This was done, and when Mr. Callahan had examined them, the Coroner inquired if they came from his store. He replied no.

Whereupon they were held up to the jury, and attention called to the fact that, while rather new than old, they gave signs of having been worn more than once; which was not true of anything else taken from the victim.

This matter settled, the Coroner proceeded with his questions.

"Who carried the articles ordered, to the address given?"

"A man in our employ, named Clapp."

"Did he bring back the amount of the bill?"

"Yes, sir; less the five dollars charged for the shoes."

"What was the amount, may I ask?"

"Here is our cash-book, sir. The amount received from Mrs. James Pope, Hotel D——, on the seventeenth of September, is, as you see, seventy-five dollars and fifty-eight cents."

"Let the jury see the book; also the order."

They were both handed to the jury, and if ever I wished myself in any one's shoes, save my own very substantial ones, it was at that moment. I did so want a peep at that order.

It seemed to interest the jury also, for their heads drew together very eagerly over it, and some whispers and a few knowing looks passed between them. Finally one of them spoke:

"It is written in a very odd hand. Do you call this a woman's writing or a man's?"

"I have no opinion to give on the subject," rejoined the witness. "It is intelligible writing, and that is all that comes within my province."

The twelve men shifted on their seats and surveyed the Coroner eagerly. Why did he not proceed? Evidently he was not quick enough to suit them.

"Have you any further questions for this witness?" asked that gentleman after a short delay.

Their nervousness increased, but no one ventured to follow the Coroner's suggestion. A poor lot, I call them, a very poor lot! I would have found plenty of questions to put to him.

I expected to see the man Clapp called next, but I was disappointed in this. The name uttered was Henshaw, and the person who rose in answer to it was a tall, burly man with a shock of curly black hair. He was the clerk of the Hotel D——, and we all forgot Clapp in our eagerness to hear what this man had to say.

His testimony amounted to this:

That a person by the name of Pope was registered on his books. That she came to his house on the seventeenth of September, some time near noon. That she was not alone; that a person she called her husband accompanied her, and that they had been given a room, at her request, on the second floor overlooking Broadway.

"Did you see the husband? Was it his handwriting we see in your register?"

"No, sir. He came into the office, but he did not approach the desk. It was she who registered for them both, and who did all the business in fact. I thought it queer, but took it for granted he was ill, for he held his head very much down, and acted as if he felt disturbed or anxious."

"Did you notice him closely? Would you be able to identify him on sight?"

"No, sir, I should not. He looked like a hundred other men I see every day: medium in height and build, with brown hair and brown moustache. Not noticeable in any way, sir, except for his hang-dog air and evident desire not to be noticed."

"But you saw him later?"

"No, sir. After he went to his room he stayed there, and no one saw him. I did not even see him when he left the house. His wife paid the bill and he did not come into the office."

"But you saw her well; you would know her again?"

"Perhaps, sir; but I doubt it. She wore a thick veil when she came in, and though I might remember her voice, I have no recollection of her features for I did not see them."

"You can give a description of her dress, though; surely you must have looked long enough at a woman who wrote her own and her husband's name in your register, for you to remember her clothes."

"Yes, for they were very simple. She had on what is called a gossamer, which covered her from neck to toe, and on her head a hat wrapped all about with a blue veil."

"So that she might have worn any dress under that gossamer?"

"Yes, sir."

"And any hat under that veil?"

"Any one that was large enough, sir."

"*Very* good. Now, did you see her hands?"

"Not to remember them."

"Did she have gloves on?"

"I cannot say. I did not stand and watch her, sir."

"That is a pity. But you say you heard her voice."

"Yes, sir."

"Was it a lady's voice? Was her tone refined and her language good?"

"They were, sir."

"When did they leave? How long did they remain in your house?"

"They left in the evening; after tea, I should say."

"How? On foot or in a carriage?"

"In a carriage; one of the hacks that stand in front of the door."

"Did they bring any baggage with them?"

"No, sir."

"Did they take any away?"

"The lady carried a parcel."

"What kind of a parcel?"

"A brown-paper parcel, like clothing done up."

"And the gentleman?"

"I did not see him."

"Was she dressed the same in going as in coming?"

"To all appearance, except her hat. That was smaller."

"She had the gossamer on still, then?"

"Yes, sir."

"And a veil?"

"Yes, sir."

"Only that the hat it covered was smaller?"

"Yes, sir."

"And now, how did you account to yourself for the parcel and the change of hat?"

"I didn't account for them. I didn't think anything about them at the time; but, since I have had the subject brought to my mind, I find it easy enough. She had a package delivered to her while she was in our house, or rather packages; they were quite numerous, I believe."

"Can you recall the circumstances of their delivery?"

"Yes, sir; the man who brought the packages said that they had not been paid for, so I allowed him to carry them to Mrs. James Pope's room. When he went away, he had but one small parcel with him; the rest he had left."

"And this is all you can tell us about this singular couple? Had they no meals in your house?"

"No, sir; the gentleman—or I suppose I should say the lady, sir, for the order was given in her voice—sent for two dozen oysters and a bottle of ale, which were furnished to them in their rooms; but they didn't come to the dining-room."

"Is the boy here who carried up those articles?"

"He is, sir."

"And the chambermaid who attended to their rooms?"

"Yes, sir."

"Then you may answer this question, and we will excuse you. How was the gentleman dressed when you saw him?"

"In a linen duster and a felt hat."

"Let the jury remember that. And now let us hear from Richard Clapp. Is Richard Clapp in the room?"

"I am, sir," answered a cheery voice; and a lively young man with a shrewd eye and a wide-awake manner popped up from behind a portly woman on a side seat and rapidly came forward.

He was asked several questions before the leading one which we all expected; but I will not record them here. The question which brought the reply most eagerly anticipated was this:

"Do you remember being sent to the Hotel D—— with several packages for a Mrs. James Pope?"

"I do, sir."

"Did you deliver them in person? Did you see the lady?"

A peculiar look crossed his face and we all leaned forward. But his answer brought a shock of disappointment with it.

"No, I didn't, sir. She wouldn't let me in. She bade me lay the things down by the door and wait in the rear hall till she called me."

"And you did this?"

"Yes, sir."

"But you kept your eye on the door, of course?"

"Naturally, sir."

"And saw—"

"A hand steal out and take in the things."

"A woman's hand?"

"No; a man's. I saw the white cuff."

"And how long was it before they called you?"

"Fifteen minutes, I should say. I heard a voice cry 'Here!' and seeing their door open, I went toward it. But by the time I reached it, it was shut again, and I only heard the lady say that all the articles but the shoes were satisfactory, and would I thrust the bill in under the door. I did so, and they were some minutes counting out the change, but presently the door opened slightly, and I saw a man's hand holding out the money, which was correct to the cent. 'You need not receipt the bill,' cried the lady from somewhere in the room. 'Give him the shoes and let him go.' So I received the shoes in the same mysterious way I had the money, and seeing no reason for waiting longer, pocketed the bills and returned to the store."

"Has the jury any further questions to ask the witness?"

Of course not. They were ninnies, all of them, and— But, contrary to my expectation, one of them did perk up courage, and, wriggling very much on his seat, ventured to ask if the cuff he had seen on the man's hand when it was thrust through the doorway had a button in it.

The answer was disappointing. The witness had not noticed any.

The juror, somewhat abashed, sank into silence, at which another of the precious twelve, inspired no doubt by the other's example, blurted out:

"Then what was the color of the coat sleeve? You surely can remember that."

But another disappointment awaited us.

"He did not wear any coat. It was a shirt sleeve I saw."

A shirt sleeve! There was no clue in that. A visible look of dejection spread through the room, which was not dissipated till another witness stood up.

This time it was the bell-boy of the hotel who had been on duty that day. His testimony was brief, and added but little to the general knowledge. He had been summoned more than once by these mysterious parties, but only to receive his orders through a closed door. He had not entered the room at all.

He was followed by the chambermaid, who testified that she was in the room once while they were there; that she saw them both then, but did not catch a glimpse of their faces; Mr. Pope was standing in the window almost entirely shielded by the curtains, and Mrs. Pope was busy hanging up something in the wardrobe. The gentleman had on his duster and the lady her gossamer; it was but a few minutes after their arrival.

Questioned in regard to the state of the room after they left it, she said that there was a lot of brown paper lying about, marked B. Altman, but nothing else that did not belong there.

"Not a tag, nor a hat-pin, nor a bit of memorandum, lying on bureau or table?"

"Nothing, sir, so far as I mind. I wasn't on the look-out for anything, sir. They were a queer couple, but we have lots of queer couples at our house, and the most I notices, sir, is those what remember the chambermaid and those what don't. This couple was of the kind what don't."

"Did you sweep the room after their departure?"

"I always does. They went late, so I swept the room the next morning."

"And threw the sweepings away, of course?"

"Of course; would you have me keep them for treasures?"

"It might have been well if you had," muttered the Coroner. "The combings from the lady's hair might have been very useful in establishing her identity."

The porter who has charge of the lady's entrance was the last witness from this house. He had been on duty on the evening in question and had noticed this couple leaving. They both carried packages, and had attracted his attention first, by the long, old-fashioned duster which the gentleman wore, and secondly, by the pains they both took not to be observed by any one. The woman was veiled, as had already been said, and the man held his package in such a way as to shield his face entirely from observation.

"So that you would not know him if you saw him again?" asked the Coroner.

"Exactly, sir," was the uncomprising answer.

As he sat down, the Coroner observed: "You will note from this testimony, gentlemen, that this couple, signing themselves Mr. and Mrs. James Pope of Philadelphia, left this house dressed each in a long garment eminently fitted for purposes of concealment—he in a linen duster, and she in a gossamer. Let us now follow this couple a little farther and see what became of these disguising articles of apparel. Is Seth Brown here?"

A man, who was so evidently a hackman that it seemed superfluous to ask him what his occupation was, shuffled forward at this.

It was in his hack that this couple had left the D———. He remembered them very well as he had good reason to. First, because the man paid him before entering the carriage, saying that he was to let them out at the northwest corner of Madison Square, and secondly— But here the Coroner interrupted him to ask if he had seen the gentleman's face when he paid him. The answer was, as might have been expected, No. It was dark, and he had not turned his head.

"Didn't you think it queer to be paid before you reached your destination?"

"Yes, but the rest was queerer. After I had taken the money—I never refuses money, sir—and was expecting him to get into the hack, he steps up to me again and says in a lower tone than before: 'My wife is very nervous. Drive slow, if you please, and when you reach the place I have named, watch your horses carefully, for if they should move while she is getting out, the shock would throw her into a spasm.' As she had looked very pert and lively, I thought this mighty queer, and I tried to get a peep at his face, but he was too smart for me, and was in the carriage before I could clap my eye on him."

"But you were more fortunate when they got out? You surely saw one or both of them then?"

"No, sir, I didn't. I had to watch the horses' heads, you know. I shouldn't like to be the cause of a young lady having a spasm."

"Do you know in what direction they went?"

"East, I should say. I heard them laughing long after I had whipped up my horses. A queer couple, sir, that puzzled me some, though I should not have thought of them twice if I had not found next day—"

"Well?"

"The gentleman's linen duster and the neat brown gossamer which the lady had worn, lying folded under the two back cushions of my hack; a present for which I was very much obliged to them, but which I was not long allowed to enjoy, for yesterday the police—"

"Well, well, no matter about that. Here is a duster and here is a brown gossamer. Are these the articles you found under your cushions?"

"If you will examine the neck of the lady's gossamer, you can soon tell, sir. There was a small hole in the one I found, as if something had been snipped out of it; the owner's name, most likely."

"Or the name of the place where it was bought," suggested the Coroner, holding the garment up to view so as to reveal a square hole under the collar.

"That's it!" cried the hackman. "That's the very one. Shame, I say, to spoil a new garment that way."

"Why do you call it new?" asked the Coroner.

"Because it hasn't a mud spot or even a mark of dust upon it. We looked it all over, my wife and I, and decided it had not been long off the shelf. A pretty good haul for a poor man like me, and if the police—"

But here he was cut short again by an important question:

"There is a clock but a short distance from the place where you stopped. Did you notice what time it was when you drove away?"

"Yes, sir. I don't know why I remember it, but I do. As I turned to go back to the hotel, I looked up at this clock. It was half-past eleven."

CHAPTER XII

The Keys

We were all by this time greatly interested in the proceedings; and when another hackman was called we recognized at once that an effort was about to be made to connect this couple with the one who had alighted at Mr. Van Burnam's door.

The witness, who was a melancholy chap, kept his stand on the east side of the Square. At about twenty minutes to twelve, he was awakened from a nap he had been taking on the top of his coach, by a sharp rap on his whip arm, and looking down, he saw a lady and gentleman standing at the door of his vehicle.

"We want to go to Gramercy Park," said the lady. "Drive us there at once."

"I nodded, for what is the use of wasting words when it can be avoided; and they stepped at once into the coach."

"Can you describe them—tell us how they looked?"

"I never notice people; besides, it was dark; but he had a swell air, and she was pert and merry, for she laughed as she closed the door."

"Can't you remember how they were dressed?"

"No, sir; she had on something that flapped about her shoulders, and he had a dark hat on his head, but that was all I saw."

"Didn't you see his face?"

"Not a bit of it; he kept it turned away. He didn't want nobody looking at *him*. She did all the business."

"Then you saw *her* face?"

"Yes, for a minute. But I wouldn't know it again. She was young and purty, and her hand which dropped the money into mine was small, but I couldn't say no more, not if you was to give me the town."

"Did you know that the house you stopped at was Mr. Van Burnam's, and that it was supposed to be empty?"

"No, sir, I'm not one of the swell ones. My acquaintances live in another part of the town."

"But you noticed that the house was dark?"

"I may have. I don't know."

"And that is all you have to tell us about them?"

"No, sir; the next morning, which was yesterday, sir, as I was a-dusting out the coach I found under the cushions a large blue veil, folded and lying very flat. But it had been slit with a knife and could not be worn."

This was strange too, and while more than one person about me ventured an opinion, I muttered to myself, "James Pope, his mark!" astonished at a coincidence which so completely connected the occupants of the two coaches.

But the Coroner was able to produce a witness whose evidence carried the matter on still farther. A policeman in full uniform testified next, and after explaining that his beat led him from Madison Avenue to Third on Twenty-seventh Street, went on to say that as he was coming up this street on Tuesday evening some few minutes before midnight, he encountered, somewhere between Lexington Avenue and Third, a man and woman walking rapidly towards the latter avenue, each carrying a parcel of some dimensions; that he noted them because they seemed so merry, but would have thought nothing of it, if he had not presently perceived them coming back without the parcels. They were chatting more gaily than ever. The lady wore a short cape, and the gentleman a dark coat, but he could give no other description of their appearance, for they went by rapidly, and he was more interested in wondering what they had done with such large parcels in such a short time at that hour of night, than in noting how they looked or whither they were going. He did observe, however, that they proceeded towards Madison Square, and remembers now that he heard a carriage suddenly drive away from that direction.

The Coroner asked him but one question:

"Had the lady no parcel when you saw her last?"

"I saw none."

"Could she not have carried one under her cape?"

"Perhaps, if it was small enough."

"As small as a lady's hat, say?"

"Well, it would have to be smaller than some of them are now, sir."

And so terminated this portion of the inquiry.

A short delay followed the withdrawal of this witness. The Coroner, who was a somewhat portly man, and who had felt the heat of the day very much, leaned back and looked anxious, while the jury, always restless, moved in their seats like a set of school-boys, and seemed to long for the hour of adjournment, notwithstanding the interest which everybody but themselves seemed to take in this exciting investigation.

Finally an officer, who had been sent into the adjoining room, came back with a gentleman, who was no sooner recognized as Mr. Franklin Van Burnam than a great change took place in the countenances of all present. The Coroner sat forward and dropped the large palm-leaf fan he had been industriously using for the last few minutes, the jury settled down, and the whispering of the many curious ones about me grew less audible and finally ceased altogether. A gentleman of the family was about to be interrogated, and such a gentleman!

I have purposely refrained from describing this best known and best reputed member of the Van Burnam family, foreseeing this hour when he would attract the attention of a hundred eyes and when his appearance would require our special notice. I will therefore endeavor to picture him to you as he looked on this memorable morning, with just the simple warning that you must not expect me to see with the eyes of a young girl or even with those of a fashionable society woman. I know a man when I see him, and I had always regarded Mr. Franklin as an exceptionally fine-looking and prepossessing gentleman, but I shall not go into raptures, as I heard a girl behind me doing, nor do I feel like acknowledging him as a paragon of all the virtues—as Mrs. Cunningham did that evening in my parlor.

He is a medium-sized man, with a shape not unlike his brother's. His hair is dark and so are his eyes, but his moustache is brown and his complexion quite fair. He carries himself with distinction, and though his countenance in repose has a precise air that is not perfectly agreeable, it has, when he speaks or smiles, an expression at once keen and amiable.

On this occasion he failed to smile, and though his elegance was sufficiently apparent, his worth was not so much so. Yet the impression generally made was favorable, as one could perceive from the air of respect with which his testimony was received.

He was asked many questions. Some were germane to the matter in hand and some seemed to strike wide of all mark. He answered them all courteously, showing a manly composure in doing so, that served to calm the fever-heat into which many had been thrown by the stories of the two hackmen. But as his evidence up to this point related merely to minor concerns, this was neither strange nor conclusive. The real test began when the Coroner, with a certain bluster, which may have been meant to attract the attention of the jury, now visibly waning, or, as was more likely, may have been the unconscious expression of a secret if hitherto well concealed embarrassment, asked the witness whether the keys to his father's front door had any duplicates.

The answer came in a decidedly changed tone. "No. The key used by our agent opens the basement door only."

The Coroner showed his satisfaction. "No duplicates," he repeated; "then you will have no difficulty in telling us where the keys to your father's front door were kept during the family's absence."

Did the young man hesitate, or was it but imagination on my part— "They were usually in my possession."

"Usually!" There was irony in the tone; evidently the Coroner was getting the better of his embarrassment, if he had felt any. "And where were they on the seventeenth of this month? Were they in your possession then?"

"No, sir." The young man tried to look calm and at his ease, but the difficulty he felt in doing so was apparent. "On the morning of that day," he continued, "I passed them over to my brother."

Ah! here was something tangible as well as important. I began to fear the police understood themselves only too well; and so did the whole crowd of persons there assembled. A groan in one direction was answered by a sigh in another, and it needed all the Coroner's authority to prevent an outbreak.

Meanwhile Mr. Van Burnam stood erect and unwavering, though his eye showed the suffering which these demonstrations awakened. He did not turn in the direction of the room where we felt sure his family was gathered, but it was evident that his thoughts did, and that most painfully. The Coroner, on the contrary, showed little or no feeling; he had brought the investigation up to this critical point and felt fully competent to carry it farther.

"May I ask," said he, "where the transference of these keys took place?"

"I gave them to him in our office last Tuesday morning. He said he might want to go into the house before his father came home."

"Did he say why he wanted to go into the house?"

"No."

"Was he in the habit of going into it alone and during the family's absence?"

"No."

"Had he any clothes there? or any articles belonging to himself or his wife which he would be likely to wish to carry away?"

"No."

"Yet he wanted to go in?"

"He said so."

"And you gave him the keys without question?"

"Certainly, sir."

"Was that not opposed to your usual principles—to your way of doing things, I should say?"

"Perhaps; but principles, by which I suppose you mean my usual business methods, do not govern me in my relations with my brother. He asked me a favor, and I granted it. It would have to have been a much larger one for me to have asked an explanation from him before doing so."

"Yet you are not on good terms with your brother; at least you have not had the name of being, for some time?"

"We have had no quarrel."

"Did he return the keys you lent him?"

"No."

"Have you seen them since?"

"No."

"Would you know them if they were shown you?"

"I would know them if they unlocked our front door."

"But you would not know them on sight?"

"I don't think so."

"Mr. Van Burnam, it is disagreeable for me to go into family matters, but if you have had no quarrel with your brother, how comes it that you and he have had so little intercourse of late?"

"He has been in Connecticut and I at Long Branch. Is not that a good answer, sir?"

"Good, but not good enough. You have a common office in New York, have you not?"

"Certainly, the firm's office."

"And you sometimes meet there, even while residing in different localities?"

"Yes, our business calls us in at times and then we meet, of course."

"Do you talk when you meet?"

"Talk?"

"Of other matters besides business, I mean. Are your relations friendly? Do you show the same spirit towards each other as you did three years ago, say?"

"We are older; perhaps we are not quite so voluble."

"But do you feel the same?"

"No. I see you will have it, and so I will no longer hold back the truth. We are not as brotherly in our intercourse as we used to be; but there is no animosity between us. I have a decided regard for my brother."

This was said quite nobly, and I liked him for it, but I began to feel that perhaps it had been for the best after all that I had never been intimate with the family. But I must not forestall either events or my opinions.

"Is there any reason"—it is the Coroner, of course, who is speaking—"why there should be any falling off in your mutual confidence? Has your brother done anything to displease you?"

"We did not like his marriage."

"Was it an unhappy one?"

"It was not a suitable one."

"Did you know Mrs. Van Burnam well, that you say this?"

"Yes, I knew her, but the rest of the family did not."

"Yet they shared in your disapprobation?"

"They felt the marriage more than I did. The lady—excuse me, I never like to speak ill of the sex—was not lacking in good sense or virtue, but she was not the person we had a right to expect Howard to marry."

"And you let him see that you thought so?"

"How could we do otherwise?"

"Even after she had been his wife for some months?"

"We could not like her."

"Did your brother—I am sorry to press this matter—ever show that he felt your change of conduct towards him?"

"I find it equally hard to answer," was the quick reply. "My brother is of an affectionate nature, and he has some, if not all, of the family's pride. I think he did feel it, though he never said so. He is not without loyalty to his wife."

"Mr. Van Burnam, of whom does the firm doing business under the name of Van Burnam & Sons consist?"

"Of the three persons mentioned."

"No others?"

"No."

"Has there ever been in your hearing any threat made by the senior partner of dissolving this firm as it stands?"

"I have heard"—I felt sorry for this strong but far from heartless man, but I would not have stopped the inquiry at this point if I could; I was far too curious—"I have heard my father say that he would withdraw if Howard did not. Whether he would have done so, I consider open to doubt. My father is a just man and never fails to do the right thing, though he sometimes speaks with unnecessary harshness."

"He made the threat, however?"

"Yes."

"And Howard heard it?"

"Or of it; I cannot say which."

"Mr. Van Burnam, have you noticed any change in your brother since this threat was uttered?"

"How, sir; what change?"

"In his treatment of his wife, or in his attitude towards yourself?"

"I have not seen him in the company of his wife since they went to Haddam. As for his conduct towards myself, I can say no more than I have already. We have never forgotten that we are children of one mother."

"Mr. Van Burnam, how many times have you seen Mrs. Howard Van Burnam?"

"Several. More frequently before they were married than since."

"You were in your brother's confidence, then, at that time; knew he was contemplating marriage?"

"It was in my endeavors to prevent the match that I saw so much of Miss Louise Stapleton."

"Ah! I am glad of the explanation! I was just going to inquire why you, of all members of the family, were the only one to know your brother's wife by sight."

The witness, considering this question answered, made no reply. But the next suggestion could not be passed over.

"If you saw Mrs. Van Burnam so often, you are acquainted with her personal appearance?"

"Sufficiently so; as well as I know that of my ordinary calling-acquaintance."

"Was she light or dark?"

"She had brown hair."

"Similar to this?"

The lock held up was the one which had been cut from the head of the dead girl.

"Yes, somewhat similar to that." The tone was cold; but he could not hide his distress.

"Mr. Van Burnam, have you looked well at the woman who was found murdered in your father's house?"

"I have, sir."

"Is there anything in her general outline or in such features as have escaped disfigurement to remind you of Mrs. Howard Van Burnam?"

"I may have thought so—at first glance," he replied, with decided effort.

"And did you change your mind at the second?"

He looked troubled, but answered firmly: "No, I cannot say that I did. But you must not regard my opinion as conclusive," he hastily added. "My knowledge of the lady was comparatively slight."

"The jury will take that into account. All we want to know now is whether you can assert from any knowledge you have or from anything to be noted in the body itself, that it is not Mrs. Howard Van Burnam?"

"I cannot."

And with this solemn assertion his examination closed.

The remainder of the day was taken up in trying to prove a similarity between Mrs. Van Burnam's handwriting and that of Mrs. James Pope as seen in the register of the Hotel D—— and on the order sent to Altman's. But the only conclusion reached was that the latter might be the former disguised, and even on this point the experts differed.

CHAPTER XIII

Howard Van Burnam

The gentleman who stepped from the carriage and entered Mr. Van Burnam's house at twelve o'clock that night produced so little impression upon me that I went to bed satisfied that no result would follow these efforts at identification.

And so I told Mr. Gryce when he arrived next morning. But he seemed by no means disconcerted, and merely requested that I would submit to one more trial. To which I gave my consent, and he departed.

I could have asked him a string of questions, but his manner did not invite them, and for some reason I was too wary to show an interest in this tragedy superior to that felt by every right-thinking person connected with it.

At ten o'clock I was in my old seat in the court-room. The same crowd with different faces confronted me, amid which the twelve stolid countenances of the jury looked like old friends. Howard Van Burnam was the witness called, and as he came forward and stood in full view of us all, the interest of the occasion reached its climax.

His countenance wore a reckless look that did not serve to prepossess him with the people at whose mercy he stood. But he did not seem to care, and waited for the Coroner's questions with an air of ease which was in direct contrast to the drawn and troubled faces of his father and brother just visible in the background.

Coroner Dahl surveyed him a few minutes before speaking, then he quietly asked if he had seen the dead body of the woman who had been found lying under a fallen piece of furniture in his father's house.

He replied that he had.

"Before she was removed from the house or after it?"

"After."

"Did you recognize it? Was it the body of any one you know?"

"I do not think so."

"Has your wife, who was missing yesterday, been heard from yet, Mr. Van Burnam?"

"Not to my knowledge, sir."

"Had she not—that is, your wife—a complexion similar to that of the dead woman just alluded to?"

"She had a fair skin and brown hair, if that is what you mean. But these attributes are common to too many women for me to give them any weight in an attempted identification of this importance."

"Had they no other similar points of a less general character? Was not your wife of a slight and graceful build, such as is attributed to the subject of this inquiry?"

"My wife was slight and she was graceful, common attributes also."

"And your wife had a scar?"

"Yes."

"On the left ankle?"

"Yes."

"Which the deceased also has?"

"That I do not know. They say so, but I had no interest in looking."

"Why, may I ask? Did you not think it a remarkable coincidence?"

The young man frowned. It was the first token of feeling he had given.

"I was not on the look-out for coincidences," was his cold reply. "I had no reason to think this unhappy victim of an unknown man's brutality my wife, and so did not allow myself to be moved by even such a fact as this."

"You had no reason," repeated the Coroner, "to think this woman your wife. Had you any reason to think she was not?"

"Yes."

"Will you give us that reason?"

"I had more than one. First, my wife would never wear the clothes I saw on the girl whose dead body was shown to me. Secondly, she would never go to any house alone with a man at the hour testified to by one of your witnesses."[1]

"Not with any man?"

"I did not mean to include her husband in my remark, of course. But as I did not take her to Gramercy Park, the fact that the deceased woman entered an empty house accompanied by a man, is proof enough to me that she was not Louise Van Burnam."

"When did you part with your wife?"

"On Monday morning at the depot in Haddam."

"Did you know where she was going?"

"I knew where she said she was going."

"And where was that, may I ask?"

---

1   Why could he not have said Miss Butterworth? These Van Burnams are proud, most vilely proud as the poet has it.—A. B.

"To New York, to interview my father."

"But your father was not in New York?"

"He was daily expected here. The steamer on which he had sailed from Southampton was due on Tuesday."

"Had she an interest in seeing your father? Was there any special reason why she should leave you for doing so?"

"She thought so; she thought he would become reconciled to her entrance into our family if he should see her suddenly and without prejudiced persons standing by."

"And did you fear to mar the effect of this meeting if you accompanied her?"

"No, for I doubted if the meeting would ever take place. I had no sympathy with her schemes, and did not wish to give her the sanction of my presence."

"Was that the reason you let her go to New York alone?"

"Yes."

"Had you no other?"

"No."

"Why did you follow her, then, in less than five hours?"

"Because I was uneasy; because I also wanted to see my father; because I am a man accustomed to carry out every impulse; and impulse led me that day in the direction of my somewhat headstrong wife."

"Did you know where your wife intended to spend the night?"

"I did not. She has many friends, or at least I have, in the city, and I concluded she would go to one of them—as she did."

"When did you arrive in the city? before ten o'clock?"

"Yes, a few minutes before."

"Did you try to find your wife?"

"No. I went directly to the club."

"Did you try to find her the next morning?"

"No; I had heard that the steamer had not yet been sighted off Fire Island, so considered the effort unnecessary."

"Why? What connection is there between this fact and an endeavor on your part to find your wife?"

"A very close one. She had come to New York to throw herself at my father's feet. Now she could only do this at the steamer or in—"

"Why do you not proceed, Mr. Van Burnam?"

"I will. I do not know why I stopped—or in his own house."

"In his own house? In the house in Gramercy Park, do you mean?"

"Yes, he has no other."

"The house in which this dead girl was found?"

"Yes,"—impatiently.

"Did you think she might throw herself at his feet there?"

"She said she might; and as she is romantic, foolishly romantic, I thought her fully capable of doing so."

"And so you did not seek her in the morning?"

"No, sir."

"How about the afternoon?"

This was a close question; we saw that he was affected by it though he tried to carry it off bravely.

"I did not see her in the afternoon. I was in a restless frame of mind, and did not remain in the city."

"Ah! indeed! and where did you go?"

"Unless necessary, I prefer not to say."

"It is necessary."

"I went to Coney Island."

"Alone?"

"Yes."

"Did you see anybody there you know?"

"No."

"And when did you return?"

"At midnight."

"When did you reach your rooms?"

"Later."

"How much later?"

"Two or three hours."

"And where were you during those hours?"

"I was walking the streets."

The ease, the quietness with which he made these acknowledgments were remarkable. The jury to a man honored him with a prolonged stare, and the awe-struck crowd scarcely breathed during their utterance. At the last sentence a murmur broke out, at which he raised his head and with an air of surprise surveyed the people before him. Though he must have known what their astonishment meant, he neither quailed nor blanched, and while not in reality a handsome man, he certainly looked handsome at this moment.

I did not know what to think; so forbore to think anything. Meanwhile the examination went on.

"Mr. Van Burnam, I have been told that the locket I see there dangling from your watch-chain contains a lock of your wife's hair. Is it so?"

"I have a lock of her hair in this; yes."

"Here is a lock clipped from the head of the unknown woman whose identity we seek. Have you any objection to comparing the two?"

"It is not an agreeable task you have set me," was the imperturbable response; "but I have no objection to doing what you ask." And calmly lifting the chain, he took off the locket, opened it, and held it out courteously toward the Coroner. "May I ask you to make the first comparison," he said.

The Coroner, taking the locket, laid the two locks of brown hair together, and after a moment's contemplation of them both, surveyed the young man seriously, and remarked:

"They are of the same shade. Shall I pass them down to the jury?"

Howard bowed. You would have thought he was in a drawing-room, and in the act of bestowing a favor. But his brother Franklin showed a very different countenance, and as for their father, one could not even see his face, he so persistently held up his hand before it.

The jury, wide-awake now, passed the locket along, with many sly nods and a few whispered words. When it came back to the Coroner, he took it and handed it to Mr. Van Burnam, saying:

"I wish you would observe the similarity for yourself. I can hardly detect any difference between them."

"Thank you! I am willing to take your word for it," replied the young man, with most astonishing *aplomb*. And Coroner and jury for a moment looked baffled, and even Mr. Gryce, of whose face I caught a passing glimpse at this instant, stared at the head of his cane, as if it were of thicker wood than he expected and had more knotty points on it than even his accustomed hand liked to encounter.

Another effort was not out of place, however; and the Coroner, summoning up some of the pompous severity he found useful at times, asked the witness if his attention had been drawn to the dead woman's hands.

He acknowledged that it had. "The physician who made the autopsy urged me to look at them, and I did; they were certainly very like my wife's."

"Only like."

"I cannot say that they were my wife's. Do you wish me to perjure myself?"

"A man should know his wife's hands as well as he knows her face."

"Very likely."

"And you are ready to swear these were not the hands of your wife?"

"I am ready to swear I did not so consider them."

"And that is all?"

"That is all."

The Coroner frowned and cast a glance at the jury. They needed prodding now and then, and this is the way he prodded them. As soon as they gave signs of recognizing the hint he gave them, he turned back, and renewed his examination in these words:

"Mr. Van Burnam, did your brother at your request hand you the keys of your father's house on the morning of the day on which this tragedy occurred?"

"He did."

"Have you those keys now?"

"I have not."

"What have you done with them? Did you return them to your brother?"

"No; I see where your inquiries are tending, and I do not suppose you will believe my simple word; but I lost the keys on the day I received them; that is why—"

"Well, you may continue, Mr. Van Burnam."

"I have no more to say; my sentence was not worth completing."

The murmur which rose about him seemed to show dissatisfaction; but he remained imperturbable, or rather like a man who did not hear. I began to feel a most painful interest in the inquiry, and dreaded, while I anxiously anticipated, his further examination.

"You lost the keys; may I ask when and where?"

"That I do not know; they were missing when I searched for them; missing from my pocket, I mean."

"Ah! and when did you search for them?"

"The next day—after I had heard—of—of what had taken place in my father's house."

The hesitations were those of a man weighing his reply. They told on the jury, as all such hesitations do; and made the Coroner lose an atom of the respect he had hitherto shown this easy-going witness.

"And you do not know what became of them?"

"No."

"Or into whose hands they fell?"

"No, but probably into the hands of the wretch—"

To the astonishment of everybody he was on the verge of vehemence; but becoming sensible of it, he controlled himself with a suddenness that was almost shocking.

"Find the murderer of this poor girl," said he, with a quiet air that was more thrilling than any display of passion, "and ask *him* where he got the keys with which he opened the door of my father's house at midnight."

Was this a challenge, or just the natural outburst of an innocent man. Neither the jury nor the Coroner seemed to know, the former looking startled and the latter nonplussed. But Mr. Gryce, who had moved now into view, smoothed the head of his cane with quite a loving touch, and did not seem at this moment to feel its inequalities objectionable.

"We will certainly try to follow your advice," the Coroner assured him. "Meanwhile we must ask how many rings your wife is in the habit of wearing?"

"Five. Two on the left hand and three on the right."

"Do you know these rings?"

"I do."

"Better than you know her hands?"

"As well, sir."

"Were they on her hands when you parted from her in Haddam?"

"They were."

"Did she always wear them?"

"Almost always. Indeed I do not ever remember seeing her take off more than one of them."

"Which one?"

"The ruby with the diamond setting."

"Had the dead girl any rings on when you saw her?"

"No, sir."

"Did you look to see?"

"I think I did in the first shock of the discovery."

"And you saw none?"

"No, sir."

"And from this you concluded she was not your wife?"

"From this and other things."

"Yet you must have seen that the woman was in the habit of wearing rings, even if they were not on her hands at that moment?"

"Why, sir? What should I know about her habits?"

"Is not that a ring I see now on your little finger?"

"It is; my seal ring which I always wear."

"Will you pull it off?"

"Pull it off!"

"If you please; it is a simple test I am requiring of you, sir."

The witness looked astonished, but pulled off the ring at once.

"Here it is," said he.

"Thank you, but I do not want it. I merely want you to look at your finger."

The witness complied, evidently more nonplussed than disturbed by this command.

"Do you see any difference between that finger and the one next it?"

"Yes; there is a mark about my little finger showing where the ring has pressed."

"Very good; there were such marks on the fingers of the dead girl, who, as you say, had no rings on. I saw them, and perhaps you did yourself?"

"I did not; I did not look closely enough."

"They were on the little finger of the right hand, on the marriage finger of the left, and on the forefinger of the same. On which fingers did your wife wear rings?"

"On those same fingers, sir, but I will not accept this fact as proving her identity with the deceased. Most women do wear rings, and on those very fingers."

The Coroner was nettled, but he was not discouraged. He exchanged looks with Mr. Gryce, but nothing further passed between them and we were left to conjecture what this interchange of glances meant.

The witness, who did not seem to be affected either by the character of this examination or by the conjectures to which it gave rise, preserved his *sang-froid*, and eyed the Coroner as he might any other questioner, with suitable respect, but with no fear and but little impatience. And yet he must have known the horrible suspicion darkening the minds of many people present, and suspected, even if against his will, that this examination, significant as it was, was but the forerunner of another and yet more serious one.

"You are very determined," remarked the Coroner in beginning again, "not to accept the very substantial proofs presented you of the identity between the object of this inquiry and your missing wife. But we are not yet ready to give up the struggle, and so I must ask if you heard the description given by Miss Ferguson of the manner in which your wife was dressed on leaving Haddam?

"I have."

"Was it a correct account? Did she wear a black and white plaid silk and a hat trimmed with various colored ribbons and flowers?"

"She did."

"Do you remember the hat? Were you with her when she bought it, or did you ever have your attention drawn to it in any particular way?"

"I remember the hat."

"Is this it, Mr. Van Burnam?"

I was watching Howard, and the start he gave was so pronounced and the emotion he displayed was in such violent contrast to the self-possession he had maintained up to this point, that I was held spell-bound by the shock I received, and forebore to look at the object which the Coroner had suddenly held up for inspection. But when I did turn my head towards it, I recognized at once the multi-colored hat which Mr. Gryce had brought in from the third room of Mr. Van Burnam's house on the evening I was there, and realized almost in the same breath that great as this mystery had hitherto seemed it was likely to prove yet greater before its proper elucidation was arrived at.

"Was that found in my father's house? Where—where was that hat found?" stammered the witness, so far forgetting himself as to point towards the object in question.

"It was found by Mr. Gryce in a closet off your father's dining-room, a short time after the dead girl was carried out."

"I don't believe it," vociferated the young man, paling with something more than anger, and shaking from head to foot.

"Shall I put Mr. Gryce on his oath again?" asked the Coroner, mildly.

The young man stared; evidently these words failed to reach his understanding.

"*Is* it your wife's hat?" persisted the Coroner with very little mercy. "Do you recognize it for the one in which she left Haddam?"

"Would to God I did not!" burst in vehement distress from the witness, who at the next moment broke down altogether and looked about for the support of his brother's arm.

Franklin came forward, and the two brothers stood for a moment in the face of the whole surging mass of curiosity-mongers before them, arm in arm, but with very different expressions on their two proud faces. Howard was the first to speak.

"If that was found in the parlors of my father's house," he cried, "then the woman who was killed there was my wife." And he started away with a wild air towards the door.

"Where are you going?" asked the Coroner, quietly, while an officer stepped softly before him, and his brother compassionately drew him back by the arm.

"I am going to take her from that horrible place; she is my wife. Father, you would not wish her to remain in that spot for another moment, would you, while we have a house we call our own?"

Mr. Van Burnam the senior, who had shrunk as far from sight as possible through these painful demonstrations, rose up at these words from his agonized son, and making him an encouraging gesture, walked hastily out of the room; seeing which, the young man became calmer, and though he did not cease to shudder, tried to restrain his first grief, which to those who looked closely at him was evidently very sincere.

"I would not believe it was she," he cried, in total disregard of the presence he was in, "I *would not* believe it; but now—" A certain pitiful gesture finished the sentence, and neither Coroner nor jury seemed to know just how to proceed, the conduct of the young man being so markedly different from what they had expected. After a short pause, painful enough to all concerned, the Coroner, perceiving that very little could be done with the witness under the circumstances, adjourned the sitting till afternoon.

CHAPTER XIV

A Serious Admission

I went at once to a restaurant. I ate because it was time to eat, and because any occupation was welcome that would pass away the hours of waiting. I was troubled; and I did not know what to make of myself. I was no friend to the Van Burnams; I did not like them, and certainly had never approved of any of them but Mr. Franklin, and yet I found myself altogether disturbed over the morning's developments, Howard's emotion having appealed to me in spite of my prejudices. I could not but think ill of him, his conduct not being such as I could honestly commend. But I found myself more ready to listen to the involuntary pleadings of my own heart in his behalf than I had been prior to his testimony and its somewhat startling termination.

But they were not through with him yet, and after the longest three hours I ever passed, we were again convened before the Coroner.

I saw Howard as soon as anybody did. He came in, arm in arm as before, with his faithful brother, and sat down in a retired corner behind the Coroner. But he was soon called forward.

His face when the light fell on it was startling to most of us. It was as much changed as if years, instead of hours, had elapsed since last we saw it. No longer reckless in its expression, nor easy, nor politely patient, it showed in its every lineament that he had not only passed through a hurricane of passion, but that the bitterness, which had been its worst feature, had not passed with the storm, but had settled into the core of his nature, disturbing its equilibrium forever. My emotions were not allayed by the sight; but I kept all expression of them out of view. I must be sure of his integrity before giving rein to my sympathies.

The jury moved and sat up quite alert when they saw him. I think that if these especial twelve men could have a murder case to investigate every day, they would grow quite wide-awake in time. Mr. Van Burnam made no demonstration. Evidently there was not likely to be a repetition of the morning's display of passion. He had been iron in his impassibility at that time, but he was steel now, and steel which had been through the fiercest of fires.

The opening question of the Coroner showed by what experience these fires had been kindled.

"Mr. Van Burnam, I have been told that you have visited the Morgue in the interim which has elapsed since I last questioned you. Is that true?"

"It is."

"Did you, in the opportunity thus afforded, examine the remains of the woman whose death we are investigating, attentively enough to enable you to say now whether they are those of your missing wife?"

"I have. The body is that of Louise Van Burnam; I crave your pardon and that of the jury for my former obstinacy in refusing to recognize it. I thought myself fully justified in the stand I took. I see now that I was not."

The Coroner made no answer. There was no sympathy between him and this young man. Yet he did not fail in a decent show of respect; perhaps because he did feel some sympathy for the witness's unhappy father and brother.

"You then acknowledge the victim to have been your wife?"

"I do."

"It is a point gained, and I compliment the jury upon it. We can now proceed to settle, if possible, the identity of the person who accompanied Mrs. Van Burnam into your father's house."

"Wait," cried Mr. Van Burnam, with a strange air, "*I acknowledge I was that person.*"

It was coolly, almost fiercely said, but it was an admission that well-nigh created a hubbub. Even the Coroner seemed moved, and cast a glance at Mr. Gryce which showed his surprise to be greater than his discretion.

"You acknowledge," he began—but the witness did not let him finish.

"I acknowledge that I was the person who accompanied her into that empty house; but I do not acknowledge that I killed her. She was alive and well when I left her, difficult as it is for me to prove it. It was the realization of this difficulty which made me perjure myself this morning."

"So," murmured the Coroner, with another glance at Mr. Gryce, "you acknowledge that you perjured yourself. Will the room be quiet!"

But the lull came slowly. The contrast between the appearance of this elegant young man and the significant admissions he had just made (admissions which to three quarters of the persons there meant more, much more, than he acknowledged), was certainly such as to provoke interest of the deepest kind. I felt like giving rein to my own feelings, and was not surprised at the patience shown by the Coroner. But order was restored at last, and the inquiry proceeded.

"We are then to consider the testimony given by you this morning as null and void?"

"Yes, so far as it contradicts what I have just stated."

"Ah, then you will no doubt be willing to give us your evidence again?"

"Certainly, if you will be so kind as to question me."

"Very well; where did your wife and yourself first meet after your arrival in New York?"

"In the street near my office. She was coming to see me, but I prevailed upon her to go uptown."

"What time was this?"

"After ten and before noon. I cannot give the exact hour."

"And where did you go?"

"To a hotel on Broadway; you have already heard of our visit there."

"You are, then, the Mr. James Pope, whose wife registered in the books of the Hotel D—— on the seventeenth of this month?"

"I have said so."

"And may I ask for what purpose you used this disguise, and allowed your wife to sign a wrong name?"

"To satisfy a freak. She considered it the best way of covering up a scheme she had formed; which was to awaken the interest of my father under the name and appearance of a stranger, and not to inform him who she was till he had given some evidence of partiality for her."

"Ah, but for such an end was it necessary for her to assume a strange name before she saw your father, and for you both to conduct yourselves in the mysterious way you did all that day and evening?"

"I do not know. She thought so, and I humored her. I was tired of working against her, and was willing she should have her own way for a time."

"And for this reason you let her fit herself out with clothes down to her very undergarments?"

"Yes; strange as it may seem, I was just such a fool. I had entered into her scheme, and the means she took to change her personality only amused me. She wished to present herself to my father as a girl obliged to work for her living, and was too shrewd to excite suspicion in the minds of any of the family by any undue luxury in her apparel. At least that was the excuse she gave me for the precautions she took, though I think the delight she experienced in anything romantic and unusual had as much to do with it as anything else. She enjoyed the game she was playing, and wished to make as much of it as possible."

"Were her own garments much richer than those she ordered from Altman's?"

"Undoubtedly. Mrs. Van Burnam wore nothing made by American seamstresses. Fine clothes were her weakness."

"I see, I see; but why such an attempt on your part to keep yourself in the background? Why let your wife write your assumed names in the hotel register, for instance, instead of doing it yourself?"

"It was easier for her; I know no other reason. She did not mind putting down the name Pope. I did."

It was an ungracious reflection upon his wife, and he seemed to feel it so; for he almost immediately added: "A man will sometimes lend himself to a scheme of which the details are obnoxious. It was so in this case; but she was too interested in her plans to be affected by so small a matter as this."

This explained more than one mysterious action on the part of this pair while they were at the Hotel D——. The Coroner evidently considered it in this light, for he dwelt but little longer on this phase of the case, passing at once to a fact concerning which curiosity had hitherto been roused without receiving any satisfaction.

"In leaving the hotel," said he, "you and your wife were seen carrying certain packages, which were missing from your arms when you alighted at Mr. Van Burnam's house. What was in those packages, and where did you dispose of them before you entered the second carriage?"

Howard made no demur in answering.

"My wife's clothes were in them," said he, "and we dropped them somewhere on Twenty-seventh Street near Third Avenue, just as we saw an old woman coming along the sidewalk. We knew that she would stop and pick them up, and she did, for we slid into a dark shadow made by a projecting stoop and watched her. Is that too simple a method for disposing of certain encumbering bundles, to be believed, sir?"

"That is for the jury to decide," answered the Coroner, stiffly. "But why were you so anxious to dispose of these articles? Were they not worth some money, and would it not have been simpler and much more natural to have left them at the hotel till you chose to send for them? That is, if you were simply engaged in playing, as you say, a game upon your father, and not upon the whole community?"

"Yes," Mr. Van Burnam acknowledged, "that would have been the natural thing, no doubt; but we were not following natural instincts at the time, but a woman's *bizarre* caprices. We did as I said; and laughed long, I assure you, over its unqualified success; for the old woman not only grabbed the packages with avidity, but turned and fled away with them, just as if she had expected this opportunity and had prepared herself to make the most of it."

"It was very laughable, certainly," observed the Coroner, in a hard voice. "*You* must have found it very ridiculous"; and after giving the witness a look full of something deeper than sarcasm, he turned towards the jury as if to ask them what they thought of these very forced and suspicious explanations.

But they evidently did not know what to think, and the Coroner's looks flew back to the witness who of all the persons present seemed the least impressed by the position in which he stood.

"Mr. Van Burnam," said he, "you showed a great deal of feeling this morning at being confronted with your wife's hat. Why was this, and why did you wait till you saw this evidence of her presence on the scene of death to acknowledge the facts you have been good enough to give us this afternoon?"

"If I had a lawyer by my side, you would not ask me that question, or if you did, I would not be allowed to answer it. But I have no lawyer here, and so I will say that I was greatly shocked by the catastrophe which had happened to my wife, and under the stress of my first over-powering emotions had the impulse to hide the fact that the victim of so dreadful a mischance was my wife. I thought that if no connection was found between myself and this dead woman, I would stand in no danger of the suspicion which must cling to the man who came into the house with her. But like most first impulses, it was a foolish one and gave way under the strain of investigation. I, however, persisted in it as long as possible, partially because my disposition is an obstinate one, and partially because I hated to acknowledge myself a fool; but when I saw the hat, and recognized it as an indisputable proof of her presence in the Van Burnam house that night, my confidence in the attempt I was making broke down all at once. I could deny her shape, her hands, and even the scar, which she might have had in common with other women, but I could not deny her hat. Too many persons had seen her wear it."

But the Coroner was not to be so readily imposed upon.

"I see, I see," he repeated with great dryness, "and I hope the jury will be satisfied. And they probably will, unless they remember the anxiety which, according to your story, was displayed by your wife to have her whole outfit in keeping with her appearance as a working girl. If she was so particular as to think it necessary to dress herself in store-made undergarments, why make all these precautions void by carrying into the house a hat with the name of an expensive milliner inside it?"

"Women are inconsistent, sir. She liked the hat and hated to part with it. She thought she could hide it somewhere in the great house, at least that was what she said to me when she tucked it under her cape."

The Coroner, who evidently did not believe one word of this, stared at the witness as if curiosity was fast taking the place of indignation. And I did not wonder. Howard Van Burnam, as thus presented to our notice by his own testimony, was an anomaly, whether we were to believe what he was saying at the present time or what he had said during the morning session. But I wished I had had the questioning of him.

His next answer, however, opened up one dark place into which I had been peering for some time without any enlightenment. It was in reply to the following query:

"All this," said the Coroner, "is very interesting; but what explanation have you to give for taking your wife into your father's empty house at an hour so late, and then leaving her to spend the best part of the dark night alone?"

"None," said he, "that will strike you as sensible and judicious. But we were not sensible that night, neither were we judicious, or I would not be standing here trying to explain what is not explainable by any of the ordinary rules of conduct. She was set upon being the first to greet my father on his entrance into his own home, and her first plan had been to do so in her own proper character as my wife, but afterwards the freak took her, as I have said, to personify the housekeeper whom my father had cabled us to have in waiting at his house—a cablegram which had reached us too late for any practical use, and which we had therefore ignored—and fearing he might come early in the morning, before she could be on hand to make the favorable impression she intended, she wished to be left in the house that night; and I humored her. I did not foresee the suffering that my departure might cause her, or the fears that were likely to spring from her lonely position in so large and empty a dwelling. Or rather, I should say, *she* did not foresee them; for she begged me not to stay with her, when I hinted at the darkness and dreariness of the place, saying that she was too jolly to feel fear or think of anything but the surprise my father and sisters would experience in discovering that their very agreeable young housekeeper was the woman they had so long despised."

"And why," persisted the Coroner, edging forward in his interest and so allowing me to catch a glimpse of Mr. Gryce's face as he too leaned forward in his anxiety to hear every word that fell from this remarkable witness—"why do you speak of her fear? What reason have you to think she suffered apprehension after your departure?"

"Why?" echoed the witness, as if astounded by the other's lack of perspicacity. "Did she not kill herself in a moment of terror and discouragement? Leaving her, as I did, in a condition of health and good spirits, can you expect me to attribute her death to any other cause than a sudden attack of frenzy caused by terror?"

"Ah!" exclaimed the Coroner in a suspicious tone, which no doubt voiced the feelings of most people present; "then you think your wife committed suicide?"

"Most certainly," replied the witness, avoiding but two pairs of eyes in the whole crowd, those of his father and brother.

"*With* a hat-pin," continued the Coroner, letting his hitherto scarcely suppressed irony become fully visible in voice and manner, "thrust into the back of her neck at a spot young ladies surely would have but little reason to know is peculiarly fatal! Suicide! when she was found crushed under a pile of *bric-à-brac*, which was thrown down or fell upon her hours after she received the fatal thrust!"

"I do not know how else she could have died," persisted the witness, calmly, "unless she opened the door to some burglar. And what burglar would kill a woman in that way, when he could pound her with his fists? No; she was frenzied and stabbed herself in desperation; or the thing was done by accident, God knows how! And as for the testimony of the experts—we all know how easily the wisest of them can be mistaken even in matters of as serious import as these. *If all the experts in the world"*—here his voice rose and his nostrils dilated till his aspect was actually commanding and impressed us all like a sudden transformation—*"If all the experts in the world were to swear that those shelves were thrown upon her after she had lain therefor four hours dead, I would not believe them. Appearances or no appearances, blood or no blood, I here declare that she pulled that cabinet over in her death-struggle; and upon the truth of this fact I am ready to rest my honor as a man and my integrity as her husband."*

An uproar immediately followed, amid which could be heard cries of "He lies!" "He's a fool!" The attitude taken by the witness was so unexpected that the most callous person present could not fail to be affected by it. But curiosity is as potent a passion as surprise, and in a few minutes all was still again and everybody intent to hear how the Coroner would answer these asseverations.

"I have heard of a blind man denying the existence of light," said that gentleman, "but never before of a sensible being like yourself urging the most untenable theories in face of such evidence as has been brought before us during this inquiry. If your wife committed suicide, or if the entrance of the point of a hat-pin into her spine was effected by accident, how comes the head of the pin to have been found so many feet away from her and in such a place as the parlor register?"

"It may have flown there when it broke, or, what is much more probable, been kicked there by some of the many people who passed in and out of the room between the time of her death and that of its discovery."

"But the register was found closed," urged the Coroner. "Was it not, Mr. Gryce?"

That person thus appealed to, rose for an instant.

"It was," said he, and deliberately sat down again.

The face of the witness, which had been singularly free from expression since his last vehement outbreak, clouded over for an instant and his eye fell as if he felt himself engaged in an unequal struggle. But he recovered his courage speedily, and quietly observed:

"The register may have been closed by a passing foot. I have known of stranger coincidences than that."

"Mr. Van Burnam," asked the Coroner, as if weary of subterfuges and argument, "have you considered the effect which this highly contradictory evidence of yours is likely to have on your reputation?"

"I have."

"And are you ready to accept the consequences?"

"If any especial consequences follow, I must accept them, sir."

"When did you lose the keys which you say you have not now in your possession? This morning you asserted that you did not know; but perhaps this afternoon you may like to modify that statement."

"I lost them after I left my wife shut up in my father's house."

"Soon?"

"Very soon."

"How soon?"

"Within an hour, I should judge."

"How do you know it was so soon?"

"I missed them at once."

"Where were you when you missed them?"

"I don't know; somewhere. I was walking the streets, as I have said. I don't remember just where I was when I thrust my hands into my pocket and found the keys gone."

"You do not?"

"No."

"But it was within an hour after leaving the house?"

"Yes."

"Very good; the keys have been found."

The witness started, started so violently that his teeth came together with a click loud enough to be heard over the whole room.

"Have they?" said he, with an effort at nonchalance which, however, failed to deceive any one who noticed his change of color. "*You* can tell me, then, where I lost them."

"They were found," said the Coroner, "in their usual place above your brother's desk in Duane Street."

"Oh!" murmured the witness, utterly taken aback or appearing so. "I cannot account for their being found in the office. I was so sure I dropped them in the street."

"I did not think you could account for it," quietly observed the Coroner. And without another word he dismissed the witness, who staggered to a seat as remote as possible from the one where he had previously been sitting between his father and brother.

CHAPTER XV

A Reluctant Witness

A pause of decided duration now followed; an exasperating pause which tried even me, much as I pride myself upon my patience. There seemed to be some hitch in regard to the next witness. The Coroner sent

Mr. Gryce into the neighboring room more than once, and finally, when the general uneasiness seemed on the point of expressing itself by a loud murmur, a gentleman stepped forth, whose appearance, instead of allaying the excitement, renewed it in quite an unprecedented and remarkable way.

I did not know the person thus introduced.

He was a handsome man, a very handsome man, if the truth must be told, but it did not seem to be this fact which made half the people there crane their heads to catch a glimpse of him. Something else, something entirely disconnected with his appearance there as a witness, appeared to hold the people enthralled and waken a subdued enthusiasm which showed itself not only in smiles, but in whispers and significant nudges, chiefly among the women, though I noticed that the jurymen stared when somebody obliged them with the name of this new witness. At last it reached my ears, and though it awakened in me also a decided curiosity, I restrained all expression of it, being unwilling to add one jot to this ridiculous display of human weakness.

Randolph Stone, as the intended husband of the rich Miss Althorpe, was a figure of some importance in the city, and while I was very glad of this opportunity of seeing him, I did not propose to lose my head or forget, in the marked interest his person invoked, the very serious cause which had brought him before us. And yet I suppose no one in the room observed his figure more minutely.

He was elegantly made and possessed, as I have said, a face of peculiar beauty. But these were not his only claims to admiration. He was a man of undoubted intelligence and great distinction of manner. The intelligence did not surprise me, knowing, as I did, how he had raised himself to his present enviable position in society in the short space of five years. But the perfection of his manner astonished me, though how I could have expected anything less in a man honored by Miss Althorpe's regard, I cannot say. He had that clear pallor of complexion which in a smooth-shaven face is so impressive, and his voice when he spoke had that music in it which only comes from great cultivation and a deliberate intent to please.

He was a friend of Howard's, that I saw by the short look that passed between them when he first entered the room; but that it was not as a friend he stood there was apparent from the state of amazement with which the former recognized him, as well as from the regret to be seen underlying the polished manner of the witness himself. Though perfectly self-possessed and perfectly respectful, he showed by every means possible the pain he felt in adding one feather-weight to the evidence against a man with whom he was on terms of more or less intimacy.

But let me give his testimony. Having acknowledged that he knew the Van Burnam family well, and Howard in particular, he went on to state that on the night of the seventeenth he had been detained at his office by business of a more than usual pressing nature, and finding that he could expect no rest for that night, humored himself by getting off the cars at Twenty-first Street instead of proceeding on to Thirty-third Street, where his apartments were.

The smile which these words caused (Miss Althorpe lives in Twenty-first Street) woke no corresponding light on his face. Indeed, he frowned at it, as if he felt that the gravity of the situation admitted of nothing frivolous or humorsome. And this feeling was shared by Howard, for he started when the witness mentioned Twenty-first Street, and cast him a haggard look of dismay which happily no one saw but myself, for every one else was concerned with the witness. Or should I except Mr. Gryce?

"I had of course no intentions beyond a short stroll through this street previous to returning to my home," continued the witness, gravely; "and am sorry to be obliged to mention this freak of mine, but find it necessary in order to account for my presence there at so unusual an hour."

"You need make no apologies," returned the Coroner. "Will you state on what line of cars you came from your office?"

"I came up Third Avenue."

"Ah! and walked towards Broadway?"

"Yes."

"So that you necessarily passed very near the Van Burnam mansion?"

"Yes."

"At what time was this, can you say?"

"At four, or nearly four. It was half-past three when I left my office."

"Was it light at that hour? Could you distinguish objects readily?"

"I had no difficulty in seeing."

"And what did you see? Anything amiss at the Van Burnam mansion?"

"No, sir, nothing amiss. I merely saw Howard Van Burnam coming down the stoop as I went by the corner."

"You made no mistake. It was the gentleman you name, and no other whom you saw on this stoop at this hour?"

"I am very sure that it was he. I am sorry——"

But the Coroner gave him no opportunity to finish.

"You and Mr. Van Burnam are friends, you say, and it was light enough for you to recognize each other; then you probably spoke?"

"No, we did not. I was thinking—well of other, things," and here he allowed the ghost of a smile to flit suggestively across his firm-set lips. "And Mr. Van Burnam seemed preoccupied also, for, as far as I know, he did not even look my way."

"And you did not stop?"

"No, he did not look like a man to be disturbed."

"And this was at four on the morning of the eighteenth?"

"At four."

"You are certain of the hour and of the day?"

"I am certain. I should not be standing here if I were not very sure of my memory. I am sorry," he began again, but he was stopped as peremptorily as before by the Coroner.

"Feeling has no place in an inquiry like this." And the witness was dismissed.

Mr. Stone, who had manifestly given his evidence under compulsion, looked relieved at its termination. As he passed back to the room from which he had come, many only noticed the extreme elegance of his form and the proud cast of his head, but I saw more than these. I saw the look of regret he cast at his friend Howard.

A painful silence followed his withdrawal, then the Coroner spoke to the jury:

"Gentlemen, I leave you to judge of the importance of this testimony. Mr. Stone is a well-known man of unquestionable integrity, but perhaps Mr. Van Burnam can explain how he came to visit his father's house at four o'clock in the morning on that memorable night, when according to his latest testimony he left his wife there at twelve. We will give him the opportunity."

"There is no use," began the young man from the place where he sat. But gathering courage even while speaking, he came rapidly forward, and facing Coroner and jury once more, said with a false kind of energy that imposed upon no one:

"I can explain this fact, but I doubt if you will accept my explanation. I was at my father's house at that hour, but not in it. My restlessness drove me back to my wife, but not finding the keys in my pocket, I came down the stoop again and went away."

"Ah, I see now why you prevaricated this morning in regard to the time when you missed those keys."

"I know that my testimony is full of contradictions."

"You feared to have it known that you were on the stoop of your father's house for the second time that night?"

"Naturally, in face of the suspicion I perceived everywhere about me."

"And this time you did not go in?"

"No."

"Nor ring the bell?"

"No."

"Why not, if you left your wife within, alive and well?"

"I did not wish to disturb her. My purpose was not strong enough to surmount the least difficulty. I was easily deterred from going where I had little wish to be."

"So that you merely went up the stoop and down again at the time Mr. Stone saw you?"

"Yes, and if he had passed a minute sooner he would have seen this: seen me go up, I mean, as well as seen me come down. I did not linger long in the doorway."

"But you did linger there a moment?"

"Yes; long enough to hunt for the keys and get over my astonishment at not finding them."

"Did you notice Mr. Stone going by on Twenty-first Street?"

"No."

"Was it as light as Mr. Stone has said?"

"Yes, it was light."

"And you did not notice him?"

"No."

"Yet you must have followed very closely behind him?"

"Not necessarily. I went by the way of Twentieth Street, sir. Why, I do not know, for my rooms are uptown. I do not know why I did half the things I did that night."

"I can readily believe it," remarked the Coroner.

Mr. Van Burnam's indignation rose.

"You are trying," said he, "to connect me with the fearful death of my wife in my father's lonely house. You cannot do it, for I am as innocent of that death as you are, or any other person in this assemblage. Nor did I pull those shelves down upon her as you would have this jury think, in my last thoughtless visit to my father's door. She died according to God's will by her own hand or by means of some strange and unaccountable accident known only to Him. And so you will find, if justice has any place in these investigations and a manly intelligence be allowed to take the place of prejudice in the breasts of the twelve men now sitting before me."

And bowing to the Coroner, he waited for his dismissal, and receiving it, walked back not to his lonely corner, but to his former place between his father and brother, who received him with a wistful air and strange looks of mingled hope and disbelief.

"The jury will render their verdict on Monday morning," announced the Coroner, and adjourned the inquiry.

BOOK II: THE WINDINGS OF A LABYRINTH

CHAPTER XVI

COGITATIONS

My cook had prepared for me a most excellent dinner, thinking that I needed all the comfort possible after a day of such trying experiences. But I ate little of it; my thoughts were too busy, my mind too much exercised. What would be the verdict of the jury, and could this especial jury be relied upon to give a just verdict?

At seven I had left the table and was shut up in my own room. I could not rest till I had fathomed my own mind in regard to the events of the day.

The question—the great question, of course, now—was how much of Howard's testimony was to be believed, and whether he was, notwithstanding his asseverations to the contrary, the murderer of his wife. To most persons the answer seemed easy. From the expression of such people as I had jostled in leaving the court-room, I judged that his sentence had already been passed in the minds of most there present. But these hasty judgments did not influence me. I hope I look deeper than the surface, and my mind would not subscribe to his guilt, notwithstanding the bad impression made upon me by his falsehoods and contradictions.

Now why would not my mind subscribe to it? Had sentiment got the better of me, Amelia Butterworth, and was I no longer capable of looking a thing squarely in the face? Had the Van Burnams, of all people in the world, awakened my sympathies at the cost of my good sense, and was I disposed to see virtue in a man in whom every circumstance as it came to light revealed little but folly and weakness? The lies he had told—for there is no other word to describe his contradictions—would have been sufficient under most circumstances to condemn a man in my estimation. Why, then, did I secretly look for excuses to his conduct?

Probing the matter to the bottom, I reasoned in this way: The latter half of his evidence was a complete contradiction of the first, purposely so. In the first, he made himself out a cold-hearted egotist with not enough interest in his wife to make an effort to determine whether she and the murdered woman were identical; in the latter, he showed himself in the light of a man influenced to the point of folly by a woman to whom he had been utterly unyielding a few hours before.

Now, knowing human nature to be full of contradictions, I could not satisfy myself that I should be justified in accepting either half of his testimony as absolutely true. The man who is all firmness one minute may be all weakness the next, and in face of the calm assertions made by this one when driven to bay by the unexpected discoveries of the police, I dared not decide that his final assurances were altogether false, and that he was not the man I had seen enter the adjoining house with his wife.

Why, then, not carry the conclusion farther and admit, as reason and probability suggested, that he was also her murderer; that he had killed her during his first visit and drawn the shelves down upon her in the second? Would not this account for all the phenomena to be observed in connection with this otherwise unexplainable affair? Certainly, all but one—one that was perhaps known to nobody but myself, and that was the testimony given by the clock. *It* said that the shelves fell at five, whereas, according to Mr. Stone's evidence, it was four, or thereabouts, when Mr. Van Burnam left his father's house. But the clock might not have been a reliable witness. It might have been set wrong, or it might not have been running at all at the time of the accident. No, it would not do for me to rely too much upon anything so doubtful, nor did I; yet I could not rid myself of the conviction that Howard spoke the truth when he declared in face of Coroner and jury that they could not connect him with this crime; and whether this conclusion sprang from sentimentality or intuition, I was resolved to stick to it for the present night at least. The morrow might show its futility, but the morrow had not come.

Meanwhile, with this theory accepted, what explanation could be given of the very peculiar facts surrounding this woman's death? Could the supposition of suicide advanced by Howard before the Coroner be entertained for a moment, or that equally improbable suggestion of accident?

Going to my bureau drawer, I drew out the old grocer-bill which has already figured in these pages, and re-read the notes I had scribbled on its back early in the history of this affair. They related, if you will remember, to this very question, and seemed even now to answer it in a more or less convincing way. Will you pardon me if I transcribe these notes again, as I cannot imagine my first deliberations on this subject to have made a deep enough impression for you to recall them without help from me.

The question raised in these notes was threefold, and the answers, as you will recollect, were transcribed before the cause of death had been determined by the discovery of the broken pin in the dead woman's brain.

These are the queries:

First: was her death due to accident?

Second: was it effected by her own hand?

Third: was it a murder?

The replies given are in the form of reasons, as witness:

My reasons for not thinking it an accident.

1. If it had been an accident, and she had pulled the cabinet over

upon herself,[2] she would have been found with her feet pointing towards the wall where the cabinet had stood. But her feet were towards the door and her head under the cabinet.

2. The precise arrangement of the clothing about her feet, which precluded any theory involving accident.

My reason for not thinking it a suicide.

She could not have been found in the position observed without having lain down on the floor while living, and then pulled the shelves down upon herself. (A theory obviously too improbable to be considered.)

My reason for not thinking it murder.

She would need to have been held down on the floor while the cabinet was being pulled over on her, a thing which the quiet aspect of the hands and feet make appear impossible. (Very good, but we know now that she was dead when the shelves fell over, so that my one excuse for not thinking it a murder is rendered null.)

My reasons for thinking it a murder.

———But I will not repeat these. My reasons for not thinking it an accident or a suicide remained as good as when they were written, and if her death had not been due to either of these causes, then it must have been due to some murderous hand. Was that hand the hand of her husband? I have already given it as my opinion that it was not.

Now, how to make that opinion good, and reconcile me again to myself; for I am not accustomed to have my instincts at war with my judgment. Is there any reason for my thinking as I do? Yes, the manliness of man. He only looked well when he was repelling the suspicion he saw in the surrounding faces. But that might have been assumed, just as his careless manner was assumed during the early part of the inquiry. I must have some stronger reason than this for my belief. The two hats? Well, he had explained how there came to be two hats on the scene of crime, but his explanation had not been very satisfactory. *I* had seen no hat in her hand when she crossed the pavement to her father's house. But then she might have carried it under her cape without my seeing it—perhaps. The discovery of two hats and of two pairs of gloves in Mr. Van Burnam's parlors was a fact worth further investigation, and mentally I made a note of it, though at the moment I saw no prospect of engaging in this matter further than my duties as a witness required.

And now what other clue was offered me, save the one I have already mentioned as being given by the clock? None that I could seize upon; and feeling the weakness of the cause I had so obstinately embraced, I rose from my seat at the tea-table and began making such alterations in my toilet as would prepare me for the evening and my inevitable callers.

"Amelia," said I to myself, as I encountered my anything but satis-

2   As was asserted by her husband in his sworn examination.

fied reflection in the glass, "can it be that you ought, after all, to have been called Araminta? Is a momentary display of spirit on the part of a young man of doubtful principles, enough to make you forget the dictates of good sense which have always governed you up to this time?"

The stern image which confronted me from the mirror made me no reply, and smitten with sudden disgust, I left the glass and went below to greet some friends who had just ridden up in their carriage.

They remained one hour, and they discussed one subject: Howard Van Burnam and his probable connection with the crime which had taken place next door. But though I talked some and listened more, as is proper for a woman in her own house, I said nothing and heard nothing which had not been already said and heard in numberless homes that night. Whatever thoughts I had which in any way differed from those generally expressed, I kept to myself—whether guided by discretion or pride, I cannot say; probably by both, for I am not deficient in either quality.

Arrangements had already been made for the burial of Mrs. Van Burnam that night, and as the funeral ceremony was to take place next door, many of my guests came just to sit in my windows and watch the coming and going of the few people invited to the ceremony.

But I discouraged this. I have no patience with idle curiosity. Consequently by nine I was left alone to give the affair such real attention as it demanded; something which, of course, I could not have done with a half dozen gossiping friends leaning over my shoulder.

CHAPTER XVII

Butterworth Versus Gryce

The result of this attention can be best learned from the conversation I held with Mr. Gryce the next morning.

He came earlier than usual, but he found me up and stirring.

"Well," he cried, accosting me with a smile as I entered the parlor where he was seated, "it is all right this time, is it not? No trouble in identifying the gentleman who entered your neighbor's house last night at a quarter to twelve?"

Resolved to probe this man's mind to the bottom, I put on my sternest air.

"I had not expected any one to enter there so late last night," said I. "Mr. Van Burnam declared so positively at the inquest that he was the person we have been endeavoring to identify, that I did not suppose you would consider it necessary to bring him to the house for me to see."

"And so you were not in the window?"

"I did not say that; I am always where I have promised to be, Mr.

Gryce."

"Well, then?" he inquired sharply.

I was purposely slow in answering him—I had all the longer time to search his face. But its calmness was impenetrable, and finally I declared:

"The man you brought with you last night—you were the person who accompanied him, were you not—was *not* the man I saw alight there four nights ago."

He may have expected it; it may have been the very assertion he desired from me, but his manner showed displeasure, and the quick "How?" he uttered was sharp and peremptory.

"I do not ask who it was," I went on, with a quiet wave of my hand that immediately restored him to himself, "for I know you will not tell me. But what I do hope to know is the name of the man who entered that same house at just ten minutes after nine. He was one of the funeral guests, and he arrived in a carriage that was immediately preceded by a coach from which four persons alighted, two ladies and two gentlemen."

"I do not know the gentleman, ma'am," was the detective's half-surprised and half-amused retort. "I did not keep track of every guest that attended the funeral."

"Then you didn't do your work as well as I did mine," was my rather dry reply. "For I noted every one who went in; and that gentleman, whoever he was, was more like the person I have been trying to identify than any one I have seen enter there during my four midnight vigils."

Mr. Gryce smiled, uttered a short "*Indeed!*" and looked more than ever like a sphinx. I began quietly to hate him, under my calm exterior.

"Was Howard at his wife's funeral?" I asked.

"He was, ma'am."

"And did he come in a carriage?"

"He did, ma'am."

"Alone?"

"He thought he was alone; yes, ma'am."

"Then may it not have been he?"

"I can't say, ma'am."

Mr. Gryce was so obviously out of his element under this cross-examination that I could not suppress a smile even while I experienced a very lively indignation at his reticence. He may have seen me smile and he may not, for his eyes, as I have intimated, were always busy with some object entirely removed from the person he addressed; but at all events he rose, leaving me no alternative but to do the same.

"And so you didn't recognize the gentleman I brought to the neighboring house just before twelve o'clock," he quietly remarked, with a calm ignoring of my last question which was a trifle exasperating.

"No."

"Then, ma'am," he declared, with a quick change of manner, meant, I should judge, to put me in my proper place, "I do not think we can depend upon the accuracy of your memory;" and he made a motion as if to leave.

As I did not know whether his apparent disappointment was real or not, I let him move to the door without a reply. But once there I stopped him.

"Mr. Gryce," said I, "I don't know what you think about this matter, nor whether you even wish my opinion upon it. But I am going to express it, for all that. *I* do not believe that Howard killed his wife with a hat-pin."

"No?" retorted the old gentleman, peering into his hat, with an ironical smile which that inoffensive article of attire had certainly not merited. "And why, Miss Butterworth, why? You must have substantial reasons for any opinion you would form."

"I have an intuition," I responded, "backed by certain reasons. The intuition won't impress you very deeply, but the reasons may not be without some weight, and I am going to confide them to you."

"Do," he entreated in a jocose manner which struck me as inappropriate, but which I was willing to overlook on account of his age and very fatherly manner.

"Well, then," said I, "this is one. If the crime was a premeditated one, if he hated his wife and felt it for his interest to have her out of the way, a man of Mr. Van Burnam's good sense would have chosen any other spot than his father's house to kill her in, knowing that her identity could not be hidden if once she was associated with the Van Burnam name. If, on the contrary, he took her there in good faith, and her death was the unexpected result of a quarrel between them, then the means employed would have been simpler. An angry man does not stop to perform a delicate surgical operation when moved to the point of murder, but uses his hands or his fists, just as Mr. Van Burnam himself suggested."

"Humph!" grunted the detective, staring very hard indeed into his hat.

"You must not think me this young man's friend," I went on, with a well meant desire to impress him with the impartiality of my attitude. "I never have spoken to him nor he to me, but I am the friend of justice, and I must declare that there was a note of surprise in the emotion he showed at sight of his wife's hat, that was far too natural to be assumed."

The detective failed to be impressed. I might have expected this, knowing his sex and the reliance such a man is apt to place upon his own powers.

"Acting, ma'am, acting!" was his laconic comment. "A very uncommon character, that of Mr. Howard Van Burnam. I do not think you do it full justice."

"Perhaps not, but see that you don't slight mine. I do not expect you to heed these suggestions any more than you did those I offered you in connection with Mrs. Boppert, the scrub-woman; but my conscience is eased by my communication, and that is much to a solitary woman like myself who is obliged to spend many a long hour alone with no other companion."

"Something has been accomplished, then, by this delay," he observed. Then, as if ashamed of this momentary display of irritation, he added in the genial tones more natural to him: "I don't blame you for your good opinion of this interesting, but by no means reliable, young man, Miss Butterworth. A woman's kind heart stands in the way of her proper judgment of criminals."

"You will not find its instincts fail even if you do its judgment."

His bow was as full of politeness as it was lacking in conviction.

"I hope you won't let your instincts lead you into any unnecessary detective work," he quietly suggested.

"That I cannot promise. If you arrest Howard Van Burnam for murder, I may be tempted to meddle with matters which don't concern me."

An amused smile broke through his simulated seriousness.

"Pray accept my congratulations, then, in advance, ma'am. My health has been such that I have long anticipated giving up my profession; but if I am to have such assistants as you in my work, I shall be inclined to remain in it some time longer."

"When a man as busy as you stops to indulge in sarcasm, he is in more or less good spirits. Such a condition, I am told, only prevails with detectives when they have come to a positive conclusion concerning the case they are engaged upon."

"I see you already understand the members of your future profession."

"As much as is necessary at this juncture," I retorted. Then seeing him about to repeat his bow, I added sharply: "You need not trouble yourself to show me too much politeness. If I meddle in this matter at all it will not be as your coadjutor, but as your rival."

"My rival?"

"Yes, your rival; and rivals are never good friends until one of them is hopelessly defeated."

"Miss Butterworth, I see myself already at your feet."

And with this sally and a short chuckle which did more than anything he had said towards settling me in my half-formed determination to do as I had threatened, he opened the door and quietly disappeared.

CHAPTER XVIII

The Little Pincushion

The verdict rendered by the Coroner's jury showed it to be a more discriminating set of men than I had calculated upon. It was murder inflicted by a hand unknown.

I was so gratified by this that I left the court-room in quite an agitated frame of mind, so agitated, indeed, that I walked through one door instead of another, and thus came unexpectedly upon a group formed almost exclusively of the Van Burnam family.

Starting back, for I dislike anything that looks like intrusion, especially when no great end is to be gained by it, I was about to retrace my steps when I felt two soft arms about my neck.

"Oh, Miss Butterworth, isn't it a mercy that this dreadful thing is over! I don't know when I have ever felt anything so keenly."

It was Isabella Van Burnam.

Startled, for the embraces bestowed on me are few, I gave a subdued sort of grunt, which nevertheless did not displease this young lady, for her arms tightened, and she murmured in my ear: "You dear old soul! I like you *so* much."

"We are going to be very good neighbors," cooed a still sweeter voice in my other ear. "Papa says we must call on you soon." And Caroline's demure face looked around into mine in a manner some would have thought exceedingly bewitching.

"Thank you, pretty poppets!" I returned, freeing myself as speedily as possible from embraces the sincerity of which I felt open to question. "My house is always open to you." And with little ceremony, I walked steadily out and betook myself to the carriage awaiting me.

I looked upon this display of feeling as the mere gush of two over-excited young women, and was therefore somewhat astonished when I was interrupted in my afternoon nap by an announcement that the two Misses Van Burnam awaited me in the parlor.

Going down, I saw them standing there hand in hand and both as white as a sheet.

"O Miss Butterworth!" they cried, springing towards me, "Howard has been arrested, and we have no one to say a word of comfort to us."

"Arrested!" I repeated, greatly surprised, for I had not expected it to happen so soon, if it happened at all.

"Yes, and father is just about prostrated. Franklin, too, but he keeps up, while father has shut himself into his room and won't see anybody, not even us. O, I don't know how we are to bear it! Such a disgrace, and such a wicked, wicked shame! For Howard never had anything to do with his wife's death, had he, Miss Butterworth?"

"No," I returned, taking my ground at once, and vigorously, for I really believed what I said. "He is innocent of her death, and I would like the chance of proving it."

They evidently had not expected such an unqualified assertion from me, for they almost smothered me with kisses, and called me *their only friend*! and indeed showed so much real feeling this time that I neither pushed them away nor tried to withdraw myself from their embraces.

When their emotions were a little exhausted I led them to a sofa and sat down before them. They were motherless girls, and my heart, if hard, is not made of adamant or entirely unsusceptible to the calls of pity and friendship.

"Girls," said I, "if you will be calm, I should like to ask you a few questions."

"Ask us anything," returned Isabella; "nobody has more right to our confidence than you."

This was another of their exaggerated expressions, but I was so anxious to hear what they had to tell, I let it pass. So instead of rebuking them, I asked where their brother had been arrested, and found it had been at his rooms and in presence of themselves and Franklin. So I inquired further and learned that, so far as they knew, nothing had been discovered beyond what had come out at the inquest except that Howard's trunks had been found packed, as if he had been making preparations for a journey when interrupted by the dreadful event which had put him into the hands of the police. As there was a certain significance in this, the girls seemed almost as much impressed by it as I was, but we did not discuss it long, for I suddenly changed my manner, and taking them both by the hand, asked if they could keep a secret.

"Secret?" they gasped.

"Yes, a secret. You are not the girls I should confide in ordinarily; but this trouble has sobered you."

"O, we can do anything," began Isabella; and "Only try us," murmured Caroline.

But knowing the volubility of the one and the weakness of the other, I shook my head at their promises, and merely tried to impress them with the fact that their brother's safety depended upon their discretion. At which they looked very determined for poppets, and squeezed my hands so tightly that I wished I had left off some of my rings before engaging in this interview.

When they were quiet again and ready to listen I told them my plans. They were surprised, of course, and wondered how I could do anything towards finding out the real murderer of their sister-in-law; but seeing how resolved I looked, changed their tone and avowed with much feeling their perfect confidence in me and in the success of anything I might undertake.

This was encouraging, and ignoring their momentary distrust, I proceeded to say:

"But for me to be successful in this matter, no one must know my interest in it. You must pay me no visits, give me no confidences, nor, if you can help it, mention my name before *any one*, not even before your father and brother. So much for precautionary measures, my dears; and now for the active ones. I have no curiosity, as I think you must see, but I shall have to ask you a few questions which under other circumstances would savor more or less of impertinence. Had your sister-in-law any special admirers among the other sex?"

"Oh," protested Caroline, shrinking back, while Isabella's eyes grew round as a frightened child's. "None that we ever heard of. She wasn't that kind of a woman, was she, Belle? It wasn't for any such reason papa didn't like her."

"No, no, *that* would have been too dreadful. It was her family we objected to, that's all."

"Well, well," I apologized, tapping their hands reassuringly, "I only asked—let me now say—from curiosity, though I have not a particle of that quality, I assure you."

"Did you think—did you have any idea—" faltered Caroline, "that—"

"Never mind," I interrupted. "You must let my words go in one car and out of the other after you have answered them. I wish"—here I assumed a brisk air—"that I could go through your parlors again before every trace of the crime perpetrated there has been removed."

"Why, you can," replied Isabella.

"There is no one in them now," added Caroline, "Franklin went out just before we left."

At which I blandly rose, and following their leadership, soon found myself once again in the Van Burnam mansion.

My first glance upon re-entering the parlors was naturally directed towards the spot where the tragedy had taken place. The cabinet had been replaced and the shelves set back upon it; but the latter were empty, and neither on them nor on the adjacent mantel-piece did I see the clock. This set me thinking, and I made up my mind to have another look at that clock. By dint of judicious questions I found that it had been carried into the third room, where we soon found it lying on a shelf of the same closet where the hat had been discovered by Mr. Gryce. Franklin had put it there, fearing that the sight of it might affect Howard, and from the fact that the hands stood as I had left them, I gathered that neither he nor any of the family had discovered that it was in running condition.

Assured of this, I astonished them by requesting to have it taken down and set up on the table, which they had no sooner done than it started to tick just as it had done under my hand a few nights before.

The girls, greatly startled, surveyed each other wonderingly.

"Why, it's going!" cried Caroline.

"Who could have wound it!" marvelled Isabella.

"Hark!" I cried. The clock had begun to strike.

It gave forth five clear notes.

"Well, it's a mystery!" Isabella exclaimed. Then seeing no astonishment in my face, she added: "Did you know about this, Miss Butterworth?"

"My dear girls," I hastened to say, with all the impressiveness characteristic of me in my more serious moments. "I do not expect you to ask me for any information I do not volunteer. This is hard, I know; but some day I will be perfectly frank with you. Are you willing to accept my aid on these terms?"

"O yes," they gasped, but they looked not a little disappointed.

"And now," said I, "leave the clock where it is, and when your brother comes home, show it to him, and say that having the curiosity to examine it you were surprised to find it going, and that you had left it there for him to see. He will be surprised also, and as a consequence will question first you and then the police to find out who wound it. If they acknowledge having done it, you must notify me at once, for that's what I want to know. Do you understand, Caroline? And, Isabella, do you feel that you can go through all this without dropping a word concerning me and my interest in this matter?"

Of course they answered yes, and of course it was with so much effusiveness that I was obliged to remind them that they must keep a check on their enthusiasm, and also to suggest that they should not come to my house or send me any notes, but simply a blank card, signifying: "No one knows who wound the clock."

"How delightfully mysterious!" cried Isabella. And with this girlish exclamation our talk in regard to the clock closed.

The next object that attracted our attention was a paper-covered novel I discovered on a side-table in the same room.

"Whose is this?" I asked.

"Not mine."

"Not mine."

"Yet it was published this summer," I remarked.

They stared at me astonished, and Isabella caught up the book. It was one of those summer publications intended mainly for railroad distribution, and while neither ragged nor soiled, bore evidence of having been read.

"Let me take it," said I.

Isabella at once passed it into my hands.

"Does your brother smoke?" I asked.

"Which brother?"

"Either of them."

"Franklin sometimes, but Howard, never. It disagrees with him, I believe."

"There is a faint odor of tobacco about these pages. Can it have been brought here by Franklin?"

"O no, he never reads novels, not such novels as this, at all events. He loses a lot of pleasure, we think."

I turned the pages over. The latter ones were so fresh I could almost put my finger on the spot where the reader had left off. Feeling like a bloodhound who has just run upon a trail, I returned the book to Caroline, with the injunction to put it away; adding, as I saw her air of hesitation: "If your brother Franklin misses it, it will show that he brought it here, and then I shall have no further interest in it." Which seemed to satisfy her, for she put it away at once on a high shelf.

Perceiving nothing else in these rooms of a suggestive character, I led the way into the hall. There I had a new idea.

"Which of you was the first to go through the rooms upstairs?" I inquired.

"Both of us," answered Isabella. "We came together. Why do you ask, Miss Butterworth?"

"I was wondering if you found everything in order there?"

"We did not notice anything wrong, did we, Caroline? Do you think that the—the person who committed that awful crime went *upstairs*? I couldn't sleep a wink if I thought so."

"Nor I," Caroline put in. "O, don't say that he went upstairs, Miss Butterworth!"

"I do not know it," I rejoined.

"But you asked—"

"And I ask again. Wasn't there some little thing out of its usual place? I was up in your front chamber after water for a minute, but I didn't touch anything but the mug."

"We missed the mug, but—O Caroline, the pin-cushion! Do you suppose Miss Butterworth means the pin-cushion?"

I started. Did she refer to the one I had picked up from the floor and placed on a side-table?

"What about the pin-cushion?" I asked.

"O nothing, but we did not know what to make of its being on the table. You see, we had a little pin-cushion shaped like a tomato which always hung at the side of our bureau. It was tied to one of the brackets and was never taken off; Caroline having a fancy for it because it kept her favorite black pins out of the reach of the neighbor's children when they came here. Well, this cushion, this sacred cushion which none of us dared touch, was found by us on a little table by the door, with the ribbon hanging from it by which it had been tied to the bureau. Some one had pulled it off, and very roughly too, for the ribbon was all ragged and torn. But there is nothing in a little thing like that to interest you, is there, Miss Butterworth?"

"No," said I, not relating my part in the affair; "not if our neighbor's children were the marauders."

"But none of them came in for days before we left."

"Are there pins in the cushion?"

"When we found it, do you mean? No."

I did not remember seeing any, but one cannot always trust to one's memory.

"But you had left pins in it?"

"Possibly, I don't remember. Why should I remember such a thing as that?"

I thought to myself, "I would know whether I left pins on my pincushion or not," but every one is not as methodical as I am, more's the pity.

"Have you anywhere about you a pin like those you keep on that cushion?" I inquired of Caroline.

She felt at her belt and neck and shook her head.

"I may have upstairs," she replied.

"Then get me one." But before she could start, I pulled her back. "Did either of you sleep in that room last night?"

"No, we were going to," answered Isabella, "but afterwards Caroline took a freak to sleep in one of the rooms on the third floor. She said she wanted to get away from the parlors as far as possible."

"Then I should like a peep at the one overhead."

The wrenching of the pin-cushion from its place had given me an idea.

They looked at me wistfully as they turned to mount the stairs, but I did not enlighten them further. What would an idea be worth shared by them!

Their father undoubtedly lay in the back room, for they moved very softly around the head of the stairs, but once in front they let their tongues run loose again. I, who cared nothing for their babble when it contained no information, walked slowly about the room and finally stopped before the bed.

It had a fresh look, and I at once asked them if it had been lately made up. They assured me that it had not, saying that they always kept their beds spread during their absence, as they did so hate to enter a room disfigured by bare mattresses.

I could have read them a lecture on the niceties of housekeeping, but I refrained; instead of that I pointed to a little dent in the smooth surface of the bed nearest the door.

"Did either of you two make that?" I asked.

They shook their heads in amazement.

"What is there in that?" began Caroline; but I motioned her to bring me the little cushion, which she no sooner did than I laid it in the little dent, which it fitted to a nicety.

"You wonderful old thing!" exclaimed Caroline. "How ever did you think—"

But I stopped her enthusiasm with a look. I may be wonderful, but I am not old, and it is time they knew it.

"Mr. *Gryce* is *old*," said I; and lifting the cushion, I placed it on a perfectly smooth portion of the bed. "Now take it up," said I, when, lo! a second dent similar to the first.

"You see where that cushion has lain before being placed on the table," I remarked, and reminding Caroline of the pin I wanted, I took my leave and returned to my own house, leaving behind me two girls as much filled with astonishment as the giddiness of their pates would allow.

CHAPTER XIX

A Decided Step Forward

I felt that I had made an advance. It was a small one, no doubt, but it was an advance. It would not do to rest there, however, or to draw definite conclusions from what I had seen without further facts to guide me. Mrs. Boppert could supply these facts, or so I believed. Accordingly I decided to visit Mrs. Boppert.

Not knowing whether Mr. Gryce had thought it best to put a watch over my movements, but taking it for granted that it would be like him to do so, I made a couple of formal calls on the avenue before I started eastward. I had learned Mrs. Boppert's address before leaving home, but I did not ride directly to the tenement where she lived. I chose, instead, to get out at a little fancy store I saw in the neighborhood.

It was a curious place. I never saw so many or such variety of things in one small spot in my life, but I did not waste any time upon this quaint interior, but stepped immediately up to the good woman I saw leaning over the counter.

"Do you know a Mrs. Boppert who lives at 803?" I asked.

The woman's look was too quick and suspicious for denial; but she was about to attempt it, when I cut her short by saying:

"I wish to see Mrs. Boppert very much, but not in her own rooms. I will pay any one well who will assist me to five minutes' conversation with her in such a place, say, as that I see behind the glass door at the end of this very shop."

The woman, startled by so unexpected a proposition, drew back a step, and was about to shake her head, when I laid on the counter before her (shall I say how much? Yes, for it was not thrown away) a five-dollar bill, which she no sooner saw than she gave a gasp of delight.

"Will you give me *that*?" she cried.

For answer I pushed it towards her, but before her fingers could clutch it, I resolutely said:

"Mrs. Boppert must not know there is anybody waiting here to see her, or she will not come. I have no ill-will towards her, and mean her only good, but she's a timid sort of person, and—"

"I know she's timid," broke in the good woman, eagerly. "And she's had enough to make her so! What with policemen drumming her up at night, and innocent-looking girls and boys luring her into corners to tell them what she saw in that grand house where the murder took place, she's grown that feared of her shadow you can hardly get her out after sundown. But I think I can get her here; and if you mean her no harm, why, ma'am—" Her fingers were on the bill, and charmed with the feel of it, she forgot to finish her sentence.

"Is there any one in the room back there?" I asked, anxious to recall her to herself.

"No, ma'am, no one at all. I am a poor widder, and not used to such company as you; but if you will sit down, I will make myself look more fit and have Mrs. Boppert over here in a minute." And calling to someone of the name of Susie to look after the shop, she led the way towards the glass door I have mentioned.

Relieved to find everything working so smoothly and determined to get the worth of my money out of Mrs. Boppert when I saw her, I followed the woman into the most crowded room I ever entered. The shop was nothing to it; there you could move without hitting anything; here you could not. There were tables against every wall, and chairs where there were no tables. Opposite me was a window-ledge filled with flowering plants, and at my right a grate and mantel-piece covered, that is the latter, with innumerable small articles which had evidently passed a long and forlorn probation on the shop shelves before being brought in here. While I was looking at them and marvelling at the small quantity of dust I found, the woman herself disappeared behind a stack of boxes, for which there was undoubtedly no room in the shop. Could she have gone for Mrs. Boppert already, or had she slipped into another room to hide the money which had come so unexpectedly into her hands?

I was not long left in doubt, for in another moment she returned with a flower-bedecked cap on her smooth gray head, that transformed her into a figure at once so complacent and so ridiculous that, had my nerves not been made of iron, I should certainly have betrayed my amusement. With it she had also put on her company manner, and what with the smiles she bestowed upon me and her perfect satisfaction with her own appearance, I had all I could do to hold my own and keep her to the matter in hand. Finally she managed to take in my anxiety and her own duty, and saying that Mrs. Boppert could never refuse a cup of tea, offered to send her an invitation to supper. As this struck me favorably, I nodded, at which she cocked her head on one side and insinuatingly whispered:

"And would you pay for the tea, ma'am?"

I uttered an indignant "No!" which seemed to surprise her. Immediately becoming humble again, she replied it was no matter, that she had tea enough and that the shop would supply cakes and crackers; to all of which I responded with a look which awed her so completely that she almost dropped the dishes with which she was endeavoring to set one of the tables.

"She does so hate to talk about the murder that it will be a perfect godsend to her to drop into good company like this with no prying neighbors about. Shall I set a chair for you, ma'am?"

I declined the honor, saying that I would remain seated where I was, adding, as I saw her about to go:

"Let her walk straight in, and she will be in the middle of the room before she sees me. That will suit her and me too; for after she has once seen me, she won't be frightened. *But you are not to listen at the door.*"

This I said with great severity, for I saw the woman was becoming very curious, and having said it, I waved her peremptorily away.

She didn't like it, but a thought of the five dollars comforted her. Casting one final look at the table, which was far from uninvitingly set, she slipped out and I was left to contemplate the dozen or so photographs that covered the walls. I found them so atrocious and their arrangement so distracting to my bump of order, which is of a pronounced character, that I finally shut my eyes on the whole scene, and in this attitude began to piece my thoughts together. But before I had proceeded far, steps were heard in the shop, and the next moment the door flew open and in popped Mrs. Boppert, with a face like a peony in full blossom. She stopped when she saw me and stared.

"Why, if it isn't the lady—"

"Hush! Shut the door. I have something very particular to say to you."

"O," she began, looking as if she wanted to back out. But I was too quick for her. I shut the door myself and, taking her by the arm, seated her in the corner.

"You don't show much gratitude," I remarked.

I did not know what she had to be grateful to me for, but she had so plainly intimated at our first interview that she regarded me as having done her some favor, that I was disposed to make what use of it I could, to gain her confidence.

"I know, ma'am, but if you could see how I've been harried, ma'am. It's the murder, and nothing but the murder all the time; and it was to get away from the talk about it that I came here, ma'am, and now it's you I see, and you'll be talking about it too, or why be in such a place as this, ma'am?"

"And what if I do talk about it? You know I'm your friend, or I never would have done you that good turn the morning we came upon the poor girl's body."

"I know, ma'am, and grateful I am for it, too; but I've never understood it, ma'am. Was it to save me from being blamed by the wicked police, or was it a dream you had, and the gentleman had, for I've heard what he said at the inquest, and it's muddled my head till I don't know where I'm standing."

What I had said and what the gentleman had said! What did the poor thing mean? As I did not dare to show my ignorance, I merely shook my head.

"Never mind what caused us to speak as we did, as long as we helped *you*. And we did help you? The police never found out what you had to do with this woman's death, did they?"

"No, ma'am, O no, ma'am. When such a respectable lady as you said that you saw the young lady come into the house in the middle of the night, how was they to disbelieve it. They never asked me if I knew any different."

"No," said I, almost struck dumb by my success, but letting no hint of my complacency escape me. "And I did not mean they should. You are a decent woman, Mrs. Boppert, and should not be troubled."

"Thank you, ma'am. But how did you know she had come to the house before I left. Did you see her?"

I hate a lie as I do poison, but I had to exercise all my Christian principles not to tell one then.

"No," said I, "I didn't see her, but I don't always have to use my eyes to know what is going on in my neighbor's houses." Which is true enough, if it is somewhat humiliating to confess it.

"O ma'am, how smart you are, ma'am! I wish I had some smartness in me. But my husband had all that. He was a man—O what's that?"

"Nothing but the tea-caddy; I knocked it over with my elbow."

"How I do jump at everything! I'm afraid of my own shadow ever since I saw that poor thing lying under that heap of crockery."

"I don't wonder."

"She must have pulled those things over herself, don't you think so, ma'am? No one went in there to murder her. But how came she to have those clothes on. She was dressed quite different when I let her in. I say it's all a muddle, ma'am, and it will be a smart man as can explain it."

"Or a smart woman," I thought.

"Did I do wrong, ma'am? That's what plagues me. She begged so hard to come in, I didn't know how to shut the door on her. Besides her name was Van Burnam, or so she told me."

Here was a coil. Subduing my surprise, I remarked:

"If she asked you to let her in, I do not see how you could refuse her. Was it in the morning or late in the afternoon she came?"

"Don't you know, ma'am? I thought you knew all about it from the way you talked."

Had I been indiscreet? Could she not bear questioning? Eying her with some severity, I declared in a less familiar tone than any I had yet used:

"Nobody knows more about it than I do, but I do not know just the hour at which this lady came to the house. But I do not ask you to tell me if you do not want to."

"O ma'am," she humbly remonstrated, "I am sure I am willing to tell you everything. It was in the afternoon while I was doing the front basement floor."

"And she came to the basement door?"

"Yes, ma'am."

"And asked to be let in?"

"Yes, ma'am."

"Young Mrs. Van Burnam?"

"Yes, ma'am."

"Dressed in a black and white plaid silk, and wearing a hat covered with flowers?"

"Yes, ma'am, or something like that. I know it was very bright and becoming."

"And why did she come to the basement door—a lady dressed like that?"

"Because she knew I couldn't open the front door; that I hadn't the key. O she talked beautiful, ma'am, and wasn't proud with me a bit. She made me let her stay in the house, and when I said it would be dark after a while and that I hadn't done nothing to the rooms upstairs, she laughed and said she didn't care, that she wasn't afraid of the dark and had just as lieve as not stay in the big house alone all night, for she had a book—Did you say anything, ma'am?"

"No, no, go on, she had a book."

"Which she could read till she got sleepy. I never thought anything would happen to her."

"Of course not, why should you? And so you let her into the house and left her there when you went out of it? Well, I don't wonder you were shocked to see her lying dead on the floor next morning."

"Awful, ma'am. I was afraid they would blame me for what had happened. But I didn't do nothing to make her die. I only let her stay in the house. Do you think they will do anything to me if they know it?"

"No," said I, trying to understand this woman's ignorant fears, "they don't punish such things. More's the pity!"—this in confidence to myself. "How could you know that a piece of furniture would fall on her before morning. Did you lock her in when you left the house?"

"Yes, ma'am. She told me to."

Then she was a prisoner.

Confounded by the mystery of the whole affair, I sat so still the woman looked up in wonder, and I saw I had better continue my questions.

"What reason did she give for wanting to stay in the house all night?"

"What reason, ma'am? I don't know. Something about her having to be there when Mr. Van Burnam came home. I didn't make it out, and I didn't try to. I was too busy wondering what she would have to eat."

"And what did she have?"

"I don't know, ma'am. She said she had something, but I didn't see it."

"Perhaps you were blinded by the money she gave you. She gave you some, of course?"

"O, not much, ma'am, not much. And I wouldn't have taken a cent if it had not seemed to make her so happy to give it. The pretty, pretty thing! A real lady, whatever they say about her!"

"And happy? You said she was happy, cheerful-looking, and pretty."

"O yes, ma'am; *she* didn't know what was going to happen. I even heard her sing after she went upstairs."

I wished that my ears had been attending to their duty that day, and I might have heard her sing too. But the walls between my house and that of the Van Burnams are very thick, as I have had occasion to observe more than once.

"Then she went upstairs before you left?"

"To be sure, ma'am; what would she do in the kitchen?"

"And you didn't see her again?"

"No, ma'am; but I heard her walking around."

"In the parlors, you mean?"

"Yes, ma'am, in the parlors."

"You did not go up yourself?"

"No, ma'am, I had enough to do below."

"Didn't you go up when you went away?"

"No, ma'am; I didn't like to."

"When did you go?"

"At five, ma'am; I always go at five."

"How did you know it was five?"

"The kitchen clock told me; I wound it, ma'am and set it when the whistles blew at twelve."

"Was that the only clock you wound?"

"Only clock? Do you think I'd be going around the house winding any others?"

Her face showed such surprise, and her eyes met mine so frankly, that I was convinced she spoke the truth. Gratified—I don't know why— I bestowed upon her my first smile, which seemed to affect her, for her face softened, and she looked at me quite eagerly for a minute before she said:

"You don't think so very bad of me, do you, ma'am?"

But I had been struck by a thought which made me for the moment oblivious to her question. *She* had wound the clock in the kitchen for her own uses, and why may not the lady above have wound the one in the parlor for hers? Filled with this startling idea, I remarked:

"The young lady wore a watch, of course?"

But the suggestion passed unheeded. Mrs. Boppert was as much absorbed in her own thoughts as I was.

"Did young Mrs. Van Burnam wear a watch?" I persisted.

Mrs. Boppert's face remained a blank.

Provoked at her impassibility, I shook her with an angry hand, imperatively demanding:

"What are you thinking of? Why don't you answer my questions?"

She was herself again in an instant.

"O ma'am, I beg your pardon. I was wondering if you meant the parlor clock."

I calmed myself, looked severe to hide my more than eager interest, and sharply cried:

"Of course I mean the parlor clock. Did you wind it?"

"O no, no, no, I would as soon think of touching gold or silver. But the young lady did, I'm sure, ma'am, for I heard it strike when she was setting of it."

Ah! If my nature had not been an undemonstrative one, and if I had not been bred to a strong sense of social distinctions, I might have betrayed my satisfaction at this announcement in a way that would have made this homely German woman start. As it was I sat stock-still, and even made her think I had not heard her. Venturing to rouse *me* a bit, she spoke again after a minute's silence.

"She might have been lonely, you know, ma'am; and the ticking of a clock is such company."

"Yes," I answered with more than my accustomed vivacity, for she jumped as if I had struck her. "You have hit the nail on the head, Mrs. Boppert, and are a much smarter woman than I thought. But when did she wind the clock?"

"At five o'clock, ma'am; just before I left the house."

"O, and did she know you were going?"

"I think so, ma'am, for I called up, just before I put on my bonnet, that it was five o'clock and that I was going."

"O, you did. And did she answer back?"

"Yes, ma'am. I heard her step in the hall and then her voice. She asked if I was sure it was five, and I told her yes, because I had set the kitchen clock at twelve. She didn't say any more, but just after that I heard the parlor clock begin to strike."

O, thought I, what cannot be got out of the most stupid and unwilling witness by patience and a judicious use of questions. To know that this clock was started after five o'clock, that is, after the hour at which the hands pointed when it fell, and that it was set correctly in starting, and so would give indisputable testimony of the hour when the shelves fell, were points of the greatest importance. I was so pleased I gave the woman another smile.

Instantly she cried:

"But you won't say anything about it, will you, ma'am? They might make me pay for all the things that were broke."

My smile this time was not one of encouragement simply. But it might have been anything for all effect it had on her. The intricacies of the affair had disturbed her poor brain again, and all her powers of mind were given up to lament.

"O," she bemoaned, "I wish I had never seen her! My head wouldn't ache so with the muddle of it. Why, ma'am, her husband said he came to the house at midnight with his wife! How could he when she was inside of it all the time. But then perhaps he said that, just as you did, to save me blame. But why should a gentleman like him do that?"

"It isn't worth while for you to bother your head about it," I expostulated. "It is enough that *my* head aches over it."

I don't suppose she understood me or tried to. Her wits had been sorely tried and my rather severe questioning had not tended to clear them. At all events she went on in another moment as if I had not spoken:

"But what became of her pretty dress? I was never so astonished in my life as when I saw that dark skirt on her."

"She might have left her fine gown upstairs," I ventured, not wishing to go into the niceties of evidence with this woman.

"So she might, so she might, and that may have been her petticoat we saw." But in another moment she saw the impossibility of this, for she added: "But I saw her petticoat, and it was a brown silk one. She showed it when she lifted her skirt to get at her purse. I don't understand it, ma'am."

As her face by this time was almost purple, I thought it a mercy to close the interview; so I uttered some few words of a soothing and encouraging nature, and then seeing that something more tangible was necessary to restore her to any proper condition of spirits, I took out my pocket-book and bestowed on her some of my loose silver.

This was something she *could* understand. She brightened immediately, and before she was well through her expressions of delight, I had quitted the room and in a few minutes later the shop.

I hope the two women had their cup of tea after that.

CHAPTER XX

Miss Butterworth's Theory

I was so excited when I entered my carriage that I rode all the way home with my bonnet askew and never knew it. When I reached my room and saw myself in the glass, I was shocked, and stole a glance at Lena, who was setting out my little tea-table, to see if she noticed what a ridiculous figure I cut. But she is discretion itself, and for a girl with two undeniable dimples in her cheeks, smiles seldom—at least when I am looking at her. She was not smiling now, and though, for the reason given above, this was not as comforting as it may appear, I chose not to worry myself any longer about such a trifle when I had matters of so much importance on my mind.

Taking off my bonnet, whose rakish appearance had given me such a shock, I sat down, and for half an hour neither moved nor spoke. I was thinking. A theory which had faintly suggested itself to me at the inquest was taking on body with these later developments. Two hats had been found on the scene of the tragedy, and two pairs of gloves, and now I had learned that there had been two women there, the one whom Mrs. Boppert had locked into the house on leaving it, and the one whom I had seen enter at midnight with Mr. Van Burnam. Which of the two had perished? We had been led to think, and Mr. Van Burnam had himself acknowledged, that it was his wife; but his wife had been dressed quite differently from the murdered woman, and was, as I soon began to see, much more likely to have been the assassin than the victim. Would you like to know my reasons for this extraordinary statement? If so, they are these:

I had always seen a woman's hand in this work, but having no reason to believe in the presence of any other woman on the scene of crime than the victim, I had put this suspicion aside as untenable. But now that I had found the second woman, I returned to it.

But how connect her with the murder? It seemed easy enough to do so if this other woman was her rival. We have heard of no rival, but she may have known of one, and this knowledge may have been at the bottom of her disagreement with her husband and the half-crazy determination she evinced to win his family over to her side. Let us say, then, that the second woman was Mrs. Van Burnam's rival. That he brought her there not knowing that his wife had effected an entrance into the house; brought her there after an afternoon spent at the Hotel D——, during which he had furnished her with a new outfit of less pronounced type, perhaps, than that she had previously worn. The use of the two carriages and the care they took to throw suspicion off their track, may have been part of a scheme of future elopement, for I had no idea they meant to remain in Mr. Van Burnam's house. For what purpose, then, did they go there? To meet Mrs. Van Burnam and kill her, that their way might be clearer for flight? No; I had rather think that they went to the house without a thought of whom they would encounter, and that only after they had entered the parlors did he realize that the two women he least wished to see together had been brought by his folly face to face.

The presence in the third room of Mrs. Van Burnam's hat, gloves, and novel seemed to argue that she had spent the evening in reading by the dining-room table, but whether this was so or not, the stopping of a carriage in front and the opening of the door by an accustomed hand undoubtedly assured her that either the old gentleman or some other member of the family had unexpectedly arrived. She was, therefore, in or near the parlor-door when they entered, and the shock of meeting her hated rival in company with her husband, under the very roof where she had hoped to lay the foundations of her future happiness, must have been great, if not maddening. Accusations, recriminations even, did not satisfy her. She wanted to kill; but she had no weapon. Suddenly her eyes fell on the hat-pin which her more self-possessed rival had drawn from her hat, possibly before their encounter, and she conceived a plan which seemed to promise her the very revenge she sought. How she carried it out; by what means she was enabled to approach her victim and inflict with such certainty the fatal stab which laid her enemy at her feet, can be left to the imagination. But that she, a woman, and not Howard, a man, drove this woman's weapon into the stranger's spine, I will yet prove, or lose all faith in my own intuitions.

But if this theory is true, how about the shelves that fell at daybreak, and how about her escape from the house without detection? A little thought will explain all that. The man, horrified, no doubt, at the result of his imprudence, and execrating the crime to which it had led, left the house almost immediately. But the woman remained there, possibly because she had fainted, possibly because he would have nothing to do with her; and coming to herself, saw her victim's face staring up at her with an accusing beauty she found it impossible to meet. What should she do to escape it? Where should she go? She hated it so she could have trampled on it, but she restrained her passions till daybreak, when in one wild burst of fury and hatred she drew down the cabinet upon it, and then fled the scene of horror she had herself caused. This was at five, or, to be exact, three minutes before that hour, as shown by the clock she had carelessly set in her lighter moments.

She escaped by the front door, which her husband had mercifully forborne to lock; and she had not been discovered by the police, because her appearance did not tally with the description which had been given them. How did I know this? Remember the discoveries I had made in Miss Van Burnam's room, and allow them to assist you in understanding my conclusions.

Some one had gone into that room; someone who wanted pins; and keeping this fact before my eyes, I saw through the motive and actions of the escaping woman. She had on a dress separated at the waist, and finding, perhaps, a spot of blood on the skirt, she conceived the plan of covering it with her petticoat, which was also of silk and undoubtedly as well made as many women's dresses. But the skirt of the gown was longer than the petticoat and she was obliged to pin it up. Having no pins herself, and finding none on the parlor floor, she went upstairs to get some. The door at the head of the stairs was locked, but the front room was open, so she entered there. Groping her way to the bureau, for the place was very dark, she found a pin-cushion hanging from a bracket. Feeling it to be full of pins, and knowing that she could see nothing where she was, she tore it away and carried it towards the door. Here there was some light from the skylight over the stairs, so setting the cushion down on the bed, she pinned up the skirt of her gown.

When this was done she started away, brushing the cushion off the bed in her excitement, and fearing to be traced by her many-colored hat, or having no courage remaining for facing again the horror in the parlor, she slid out without one and went, God knows whither, in her terror and remorse.

So much for my theory; now for the facts standing in the way of its complete acceptance. They were two: the scar on the ankle of the dead girl, which was a peculiarity of Louise Van Burnam, and the mark of the rings on her fingers. But who had identified the scar? Her husband. No one else. And if the other woman had, by some strange freak of chance, a scar also on her left foot, then the otherwise unaccountable apathy he had shown at being told of this distinctive mark, as well as his temerity in afterwards taking it as a basis for his false identification, becomes equally consistent and natural; and as for the marks of the rings, it would be strange if such a woman did not wear rings and plenty of them.

Howard's conduct under examination and the contradiction between his first assertions and those that followed, all become clear in the light of this new theory. He had seen his wife kill a defenceless woman before his eyes, and whether influenced by his old affection for her or by his pride in her good name, he could not but be anxious to conceal her guilt even at the cost of his own truthfulness. As long then as circumstances permitted, he preserved his indifferent attitude, and denied that the dead woman was his wife. But when driven to the wall by the indisputable proof which was brought forth of his wife having been in the place of murder, he saw, or thought he did, that a continued denial on his part of Louise Van Burnam being the victim might lead sooner or later to the suspicion of her being the murderer, and influenced by this fear, took the sudden resolution of profiting by all the points which the two women had in common by acknowledging, what everybody had expected him to acknowledge from the first, that the woman at the Morgue was his wife. This would exonerate her, rid him of any apprehension he may have entertained of her ever returning to be a disgrace to him, and would (and perhaps this thought influenced him most, for who can understand such men or the passions that sway them) insure the object of his late devotion a decent burial in a Christian cemetery. To be sure, the risk he ran was great, but the emergency was great, and he may not have stopped to count the cost. At all events, the fact is certain that he perjured himself when he said that it was his wife he brought to the house from the Hotel D——, and if he perjured himself in this regard, he probably perjured himself in others, and his testimony is not at all to be relied upon.

Convinced though I was in my own mind that I had struck a truth which would bear the closest investigation, I was not satisfied to act upon it till I had put it to the test. The means I took to do this were daring, and quite in keeping with the whole desperate affair. They promised, however, a result important enough to make Mr. Gryce blush for the disdain with which he had met my threats of interference.

CHAPTER XXI

A Shrewd Conjecture

The test of which I speak was as follows:

I would advertise for a person dressed as I believed Mrs. Van Burnam to have been when she left the scene of crime. If I received news of such a person, I might safely consider my theory established.

I accordingly wrote the following advertisement:

"Information wanted of a woman who applied for lodgings on the morning of the eighteenth inst., dressed in a brown silk skirt and a black and white plaid blouse of fashionable cut. She was without a hat, or if a person so dressed wore a hat, then it was bought early in the morning at some store, in which case let shopkeepers take notice. The person answering this description is eagerly sought for by her relatives, and to any one giving positive information of the same, a liberal reward will be paid. Please address, T. W. Alvord, —— Liberty Street."

I purposely did not mention her personal appearance, for fear of attracting the attention of the police.

This done, I wrote the following letter:

"Dear Miss Ferguson:

"One clever woman recognizes another. I am clever and am not ashamed to own it. You are clever and should not be ashamed to be told so. I was a witness at the inquest in which you so notably distinguished yourself, and I said then, 'There is a woman after my own heart!' But a truce to compliments! What I want and ask of you to procure for me is a photograph of Mrs. Van Burnam. I am a friend of the family, and consider them to be in more trouble than they deserve. If I had her picture I would show it to the Misses Van Burnam, who feel great remorse at their treatment of her, and who want to see how she looked. Cannot you find one in their rooms? The one in Mr. Howard's room here has been confiscated by the police.[3]

"Hoping that you will feel disposed to oblige me in this—and I assure you that my motives in making this request are most excellent—I remain,

"Cordially yours,
"Amelia Butterworth.

"P. S.—Address me, if you please, at 564 —— Avenue. Care of J. H. Denham."

This was my grocer, with whom I left word the next morning to deliver this package in the next bushel of potatoes he sent me.

3   This was *so* probable, it cannot be considered an untruth.—A. B.

My smart little maid, Lena, carried these two communications to the east side, where she posted the letter herself and entrusted the advertisement to a lover of hers who carried it to the *Herald* office. While she was gone I tried to rest by exercising my mind in other directions. But I could not. I kept going over Howard's testimony in the light of my own theory, and remarking how the difficulty he experienced in maintaining the position he had taken, forced him into inconsistencies and far-fetched explanations. With his wife for a companion at the Hotel D——, his conduct both there and on the road to his father's house was that of a much weaker man than his words and appearance led one to believe; but if, on the contrary, he had with him a woman with whom he was about to elope (and what did the packing up of all his effects mean, if not that?), all the precautions they took seemed reasonable.

Later, my mind fixed itself on one point. If it was his wife who was with him, as he said, then the bundle they dropped at the old woman's feet contained the much-talked of plaid silk. If it was not, then it was a gown of some different material. Now, could this bundle be found? If it could, then why had not Mr. Gryce produced it? The sight of Mrs. Van Burnam's plaid silk spread out on the Coroner's table would have had a great effect in clinching the suspicion against her husband. But no plaid silk had been found (because it was not dropped in the bundle, but worn away on the murderess's back), and no old woman. I thought I knew the reason of this too. There was no old woman to be found, and the bundle they carried had been got rid of some other way. What way? I would take a walk down that same block and see, and I would take it at the midnight hour too, for only so could I judge of the possibilities there offered for concealing or destroying such an article.

Having made this decision, I cast about to see how I could carry it into effect. I am not a coward, but I have a respectability to maintain, and what errand could Miss Butterworth be supposed to have in the streets at twelve o'clock at night! Fortunately, I remembered that my cook had complained of toothache when I gave her my orders for breakfast, and going down at once into the kitchen, where she sat with her cheek propped up in her hand waiting for Lena, I said with an asperity which admitted of no reply:

"You have a dreadful tooth, Sarah, and you must have something done for it at once. When Lena comes home, send her to me. I am going to the drug-store for some drops, and I want Lena to accompany me."

She looked astounded, of course, but I would not let her answer me. "Don't speak a word," I cried, "it will only make your toothache worse; and don't look as if some hobgoblin had jumped up on the kitchen table. I guess I know my duty, and just what kind of a breakfast I will have in the morning, if you sit up all night groaning with the toothache." And I was out of the room before she had more than begun to say that it was not so bad, and that I needn't trouble, and all that, which was true enough, no doubt, but not what I wanted to hear at that moment.

When Lena came in, I saw by the brightness of her face that she had accomplished her double errand. I therefore signified to her that I was satisfied, and asked if she was too tired to go out again, saying quite peremptorily that Sarah was ill, and that I was going to the drug-store for some medicine, and did not wish to go alone.

Lena's round-eyed wonder was amusing; but she is very discreet, as I have said before, and she ventured nothing save a meek, "It's very late, Miss Butterworth," which was an unnecessary remark, as she soon saw.

I do not like to obtrude my aristocratic tendencies too much into this narrative, but when I found myself in the streets alone with Lena, I could not help feeling some secret qualms lest my conduct savored of impropriety. But the thought that I was working in the cause of truth and justice came to sustain me, and before I had gone two blocks, I felt as much at home under the midnight skies as if I were walking home from church on a Sunday afternoon.

There is a certain drug-store on Third Avenue where I like to deal, and towards this I ostensibly directed my steps. But I took pains to go by the way of Lexington Avenue and Twenty-seventh Street, and upon reaching the block where this mysterious couple were seen, gave all my attention to the possible hiding-places it offered.

Lena, who had followed me like my shadow, and who was evidently too dumfounded at my freak to speak, drew up to my side as we were half-way down it and seized me tremblingly by the arm.

"Two men are coming," said she.

"I am not afraid of men," was my sharp rejoinder. But I told a most abominable lie; for I am afraid of them in such places and under such circumstances, though not under ordinary conditions, and never where the tongue is likely to be the only weapon employed.

The couple who were approaching us now seemed to be in a merry mood. But when they saw us keep to our own side of the way, they stopped their chaffing and allowed us to go by, with just a mocking word or two.

"Sarah ought to be very much obliged to you," whispered Lena.

At the corner of Third Avenue I paused. I had seen nothing so far but bare stoops and dark area-ways. Nothing to suggest a place for the disposal of such cumbersome articles as these persons had made way with. Had the avenue anything better to offer? I stopped under the gas-lamp at the corner to consider, notwithstanding Lena's gentle pull towards the drug-store. Looking to left and right and over the muddy crossings, I sought for inspiration. An almost obstinate belief in my own theory led me to insist in my own mind that they had encountered no old woman, and consequently had not dropped their bundles in the open street. I even entered into an argument about it, standing there with the cable cars whistling by me and Lena tugging away at my arm. "If," said I to myself, "the woman with him had been his wife and the whole thing nothing more than a foolish escapade, they might have done this; but she was not his wife, and the game they were playing was serious, if they did laugh over it, and so their disposal of these tell-tale articles would be serious and such as would protect their secret. Where, then, could they have thrust them?"

My eyes, as I muttered this, were on the one shop in my line of vision that was still open and lighted. It was the den of a Chinese laundryman, and through the windows in front I could see him still at work, ironing.

"Ah!" thought I, and made such a start across the street that Lena gasped in dismay and almost fell to the ground in her frightened attempt to follow me.

"Not that way!" she called. "Miss Butterworth, you are going wrong."

But I kept right on, and only stopped when I reached the laundry.

"I have an errand here," I explained. "Wait in the doorway, Lena, and don't act as if you thought me crazy, for I was never saner in my life."

I don't think this reassured her much, lunatics not being supposed to be very good judges of their own mental condition, but she was so accustomed to obey, that she drew back as I opened the door before me and entered. The surprise on the face of the poor Chinaman when he turned and saw before him a lady of years and no ordinary appearance, daunted me for an instant. But another look only showed me that his very surprise was inoffensive, and gathering courage from the unexpectedness of my own position, I inquired with all the politeness I could show one of his abominable nationality:

"Didn't a gentleman and a heavily veiled lady leave a package with you a few days ago at about the same hour of night as this?"

"Some lalee clo' washee? Yes, ma'am. No done. She tellee me no callee for one week."

"Then that's all right; the lady has died very suddenly, and the gentleman gone away; you will have to keep the clothes a long time."

"Me wantee money, no wantee clo'!"

"I'll pay you for them; I don't care about them being ironed."

"Givee tickee, givee clo'! No givee tickee, no givee clo'!"

This was a poser! But as I did not want the clothes so much as a look at them, I soon got the better of this difficulty.

"I don't want them tonight," said I. "I only wanted to make sure you had them. What night were these people here?"

"Tuesday night, velly late; nicee man, nicee lalee. She wantee talk. Nicee man he pullee she; I no hear if muchee stasch. All washee, see!" he went on, dragging a basket out of the corner, "him no ilon."

I was in such a quiver; so struck with amazement at my own perspicacity in surmising that here was a place where a bundle of underclothing could be lost indefinitely, that I just stared while he turned over the clothes in the basket. For by means of the quality of the articles he was preparing to show me, the question which had been agitating me for hours could be definitely decided. If they proved to be fine and of foreign manufacture, then Howard's story was true and all my fine-spun theories must fall to the ground. But if, on the contrary, they were such as are usually worn by American women, then my own idea as to the identity of the woman who left them here was established, and I could safely consider her as the victim and Louise Van Burnam as the murderess, unless further facts came to prove that he was the guilty one, after all.

The sight of Lena's eyes staring at me with great anxiety through the panes of the door distracted my attention for a moment, and when I looked again, he was holding up two or three garments before me. The articles thus revealed told their story in a moment. They were far from fine, and had even less embroidery on them than I expected.

"Are there any marks on them?" I asked.

He showed me two letters stamped in indelible ink on the band of a skirt. I did not have my glasses with me, but the ink was black, and I read O. R. "The minx's initials," thought I.

When I left the place my complacency was such that Lena did not know what to make of me. She has since informed me that I looked as if I wanted to shout Hurrah! but I cannot believe I so far forgot myself as that. But pleased as I was, I had only discovered how one bundle had been disposed of. The dress and outside fixings still had to be accounted for, and I was the woman to do it.

We had mechanically moved in the direction of the drug-store and were near the curb-stone when I reached this point in my meditations. It had rained a little while before, and a small stream was running down the gutter and emptying itself into the sewer opening. The sight of it sharpened my wits.

If I wanted to get rid of anything of a damaging character, I would drop it at the mouth of one of these holes and gently thrust it into the sewer with my foot, thought I. And never doubting that I had found an explanation of the disappearance of the second bundle, I walked on, deciding that if I had the police at my command I would have the sewer searched at those four corners.

We rode home after visiting the drug-store. I was not going to subject Lena or myself to another midnight walk through Twenty-seventh Street.

CHAPTER XXII

A Blank Card

The next day at noon Lena brought me up a card on her tray. It was a perfectly blank one.

"Miss Van Burnam's maid said you sent for this," was her demure announcement.

"Miss Van Burnam's maid is right," said I, taking the card and with it a fresh installment of courage.

Nothing happened for two days, then there came word from the kitchen that a bushel of potatoes had arrived. Going down to see them, I drew from their midst a large square envelope, which I immediately carried to my room. It failed to contain a photograph; but there was a letter in it couched in these terms:

> "Dear Miss Butterworth:
> "The esteem which you are good enough to express for me is returned. I regret that I cannot oblige you. There are no photographs to be found in Mrs. Van Burnam's rooms. Perhaps this fact may be accounted for by the curiosity shown in those apartments by a very spruce new boarder we have had from New York. His taste for that particular quarter of the house was such that I could not keep him away from it except by lock and key. If there was a picture there of Mrs. Van Burnam, he took it, for he departed very suddenly one night. I am glad he took nothing more with him. The talks he had with my servant-girl have almost led to my dismissing her.
> "Praying your pardon for the disappointment I am forced to give you, I remain,
> "Yours sincerely,
> "Susan Ferguson."

So! so! balked by an emissary of Mr. Gryce. Well, well, we would do without the photograph! Mr. Gryce might need it, but not Amelia Butterworth.

This was on a Thursday, and on the evening of Saturday the long-desired clue was given me. It came in the shape of a letter brought me by Mr. Alvord.

Our interview was not an agreeable one. Mr. Alvord is a clever man and an adroit one, or I should not persist in employing him as my lawyer; but he never understood *me*. At this time, and with this letter in his hand, he understood me less than ever, which naturally called out my powers of self-assertion and led to some lively conversation between us. But that is neither here nor there. He had brought me an answer to my advertisement and I was presently engrossed by it. It was an uneducated woman's epistle and its chirography and spelling were dreadful; so I will just mention its contents, which were highly interesting in themselves, as I think you will acknowledge.

She, that is, the writer, whose name, as nearly as I could make out, was Bertha Desberger, knew such a person as I described, and could give me news of her if I would come to her house in West Ninth Street at four o'clock Sunday afternoon.

If I would! I think my face must have shown my satisfaction, for Mr. Alvord, who was watching me, sarcastically remarked:

"You don't seem to find any difficulties in that communication. Now, what do you think of this one?"

He held out another letter which had been directed to him, and which he had opened. Its contents called up a shade of color to my cheek, for I did not want to go through the annoyance of explaining myself again:

"Dear Sir:

"From a strange advertisement which has lately appeared in the *Herald*, I gather that information is wanted of a young woman who on the morning of the eighteenth inst. entered my store without any bonnet on her head, and saying she had met with an accident, bought a hat which she immediately put on. She was pale as a girl could be and looked so ill that I asked her if she was well enough to be out alone; but she gave me no reply and left the store as soon as possible. That is all I can tell you about her."

With this was enclosed his card:

PHINEAS COX,

Millinery,
Trimmed and Untrimmed Hats,
—— Sixth Avenue.

"Now, what does this mean?" asked Mr. Alvord. "The morning of the eighteenth was the morning when the murder was discovered in which you have shown such interest."

"It means," I retorted with some spirit, for simple dignity was thrown away on this man, "that I made a mistake in choosing your office as a medium for my business communications."

This was to the point and he said no more, though he eyed the letter in my hand very curiously, and seemed more than tempted to renew the hostilities with which we had opened our interview.

Had it not been Saturday, and late in the day at that, I would have visited Mr. Cox's store before I slept, but as it was I felt obliged to wait till Monday. Meanwhile I had before me the still more important interview with Mrs. Desberger.

As I had no reason to think that my visiting any number in Ninth Street would arouse suspicion in the police, I rode there quite boldly the next day, and with Lena at my side, entered the house of Mrs. Bertha Desberger.

For this trip I had dressed myself plainly, and drawn over my eyes—and the puffs which I still think it becoming in a woman of my age to wear—a dotted veil, thick enough to conceal my features, without robbing me of that aspect of benignity necessary to the success of my mission. Lena wore her usual neat gray dress, and looked the picture of all the virtues.

A large brass door-plate, well rubbed, was the first sign vouchsafed us of the respectability of the house we were about to enter; and the parlor, when we were ushered into it, fully carried out the promise thus held forth on the door-step. It was respectable, but in wretched taste as regards colors. I, who have the nicest taste in such matters, looked about me in dismay as I encountered the greens and blues, the crimsons and the purples which everywhere surrounded me.

But I was not on a visit to a temple of art, and resolutely shutting my eyes to the offending splendor about me—worsted splendor, you understand—I waited with subdued expectation for the lady of the house.

She came in presently, bedecked in a flowered gown that was an epitome of the blaze of colors everywhere surrounding us; but her face was a good one, and I saw that I had neither guile nor over-much shrewdness to contend with.

She had seen the coach at the door, and she was all smiles and flutter.

"You have come for the poor girl who stopped here a few days ago," she began, glancing from my face to Lena's with an equally inquiring air, which in itself would have shown her utter ignorance of social distinctions if I had not bidden Lena to keep at my side and hold her head up as if she had business there as well as myself.

"Yes," returned I, "we have. Lena here, has lost a relative (which was true), and knowing no other way of finding her, I suggested the insertion of an advertisement in the paper. You read the description given, of course. Has the person answering it been in this house?"

"Yes; she came on the morning of the eighteenth. I remember it because that was the very day my cook left, and I have not got another one yet." She sighed and went on. "I took a great interest in that unhappy young woman—Was she your sister?" This, somewhat doubtfully, to Lena, who perhaps had too few colors on to suit her.

"No," answered Lena, "she wasn't my sister, but—"

I immediately took the words out of her mouth.

"At what time did she come here, and how long did she stay? We want to find her very much. Did she give you any name, or tell where she was going?"

"She said her name was Oliver." (I thought of the O. R. on the clothes at the laundry.) "But I knew this wasn't so; and if she had not looked so very modest, I might have hesitated to take her in. But, lor! I can't resist a girl in trouble, and she was in trouble, if ever a girl was. And then she had money—Do you know what her trouble was?" This again to Lena, and with an air at once suspicious and curious. But Lena has a good face, too, and her frank eyes at once disarmed the weak and good-natured woman before us.

"I thought"—she went on before Lena could answer—"that whatever it was, *you* had nothing to do with it, nor this lady either."

"No," answered Lena, seeing that I wished her to do the talking. "And we don't know" (which was true enough so far as Lena went) "just what her trouble was. Didn't she tell you?"

"She told nothing. When she came she said she wanted to stay with me a little while. I sometimes take boarders—" She had twenty in the house at that minute, if she had one. Did she think I couldn't see the length of her dining-room table through the crack of the parlor door? "'I can pay,' she said, which I had not doubted, for her blouse was a very expensive one; though I thought her skirt looked queer, and her hat—Did I say she had a hat on? You seemed to doubt that fact in your advertisement. Goodness me! if she had had no hat on, she wouldn't have got as far as my parlor mat. But her blouse showed her to be a lady—and then her face—it was as white as your handkerchief there, madam, but so sweet—I thought of the Madonna faces I had seen in Catholic churches."

I started; inwardly commenting: "Madonna-like, *that* woman!" But a glance at the room about me reassured me. The owner of such hideous sofas and chairs and of the many pictures effacing or rather defacing the paper on the walls, could not be a judge of Madonna faces.

"You admire everything that is good and lovely," I suggested, for Mrs. Desberger had paused at the movement I made.

"Yes, it is my nature to do so, ma'am. I love the beautiful," and she cast a half-apologetic, half-proud look about her. "So I listened to the girl and let her sit down in my parlor. She had had nothing to eat that morning, and though she didn't ask for it, I went to order her a cup of tea, for I knew she couldn't get upstairs without it. Her eyes followed me when I went out of the room in a way that haunted me, and when I came back—I shall never forget it, ma'am—there she lay stretched out on the floor with her face on the ground and her hands thrown out. Wasn't it horrible, ma'am? I don't wonder you shudder."

Did I shudder? If I did, it was because I was thinking of that other woman, the victim of this one, whom I had seen, with her face turned upward and her arms outstretched, in the gloom of Mr. Van Burnam's half-closed parlor.

"She looked as if she was dead," the good woman continued, "but just as I was about to call for help, her fingers moved and I rushed to lift her. She was neither dead nor had she fainted; she was simply dumb with misery. What could have happened to her? I have asked myself a hundred times."

My mouth was shut very tight, but I shut it still tighter, for the temptation was great to cry: "She had just committed murder!" As it was, no sound whatever left my lips, and the good woman doubtless thought me no better than a stone, for she turned with a shrug to Lena, repeating still more wistfully than before:

"*Don't* you know what her trouble was?"

But, of course, poor Lena had nothing to say, and the woman went on with a sigh:

"Well, I suppose I shall never know what had used that poor creature up so completely. But whatever it was, it gave me enough trouble, though I do not want to complain of it, for why are we here, if not to help and comfort the miserable. It was an hour, ma'am; it was an hour, miss, before I could get that poor girl to speak; but when I did succeed, and had got her to drink the tea and eat a bit of toast, then I felt quite repaid by the look of gratitude she gave me and the way she clung to my sleeve when I tried to leave her for a minute. It was this sleeve, ma'am," she explained, lifting a cluster of rainbow flounces and ribbons which but a minute before had looked little short of ridiculous in my eyes, but which in the light of the wearer's kind-heartedness had lost some of their offensive appearance.

"Poor Mary!" murmured Lena, with what I considered most admirable presence of mind.

"What name did you say?" cried Mrs. Desberger, eager enough to learn all she could of her late mysterious lodger.

"I had rather not tell her name," protested Lena, with a timid air that admirably fitted her rather doll-like prettiness. "*She* didn't tell you what it was, and *I* don't think I ought to."

Good for little Lena! And she did not even know for whom or what she was playing the *rôle* I had set her.

"I thought you said Mary. But I won't be inquisitive with you. I wasn't so with her. But where was I in my story? Oh, I got her so she could speak, and afterwards I helped her upstairs; but she didn't stay there long. When I came back at lunch time—I have to do my marketing no matter what happens—I found her sitting before a table with her head on her hands. She had been weeping, but her face was quite composed now and almost hard.

"'O you good woman!' she cried as I came in. 'I want to thank you.' But I wouldn't let her go on wasting words like that, and presently she was saying quite wildly: 'I want to begin a new life. I want to act as if I had never had a yesterday. I have had trouble, overwhelming trouble, but I will get something out of existence yet. I *will* live, and in order to do so, I will work. Have you a paper, Mrs. Desberger, I want to look at the advertisements?' I brought her a *Herald* and went to preside at my lunch table. When I saw her again she looked almost cheerful. 'I have found just what I want,' she cried, 'a companion's place. But I cannot apply in this dress,' and she looked at the great puffs of her silk blouse as if they gave her the horrors, though why, I cannot imagine, for they were in the latest style and rich enough for a millionaire's daughter, though as to colors I like brighter ones myself. 'Would you'—she was very timid about it—'buy me some things if I gave you the money?'

"If there is one thing more than another that I like, it is to shop, so I expressed my willingness to oblige her, and that afternoon I set out with a nice little sum of money to buy her some clothes. I should have enjoyed it more if she had let me do my own choosing—I saw the loveliest pink and green blouse—but she was very set about what she wanted, and so I just got her some plain things which I think even you, ma'am, would have approved of. I brought them home myself, for she wanted to apply immediately for the place she had seen advertised, but, O dear, when I went up to her room—"

"Was she gone?" burst in Lena.

"O no, but there was such a smudge in it, and—and I could cry when I think of it—there in the grate were the remains of her beautiful silk blouse, all smoking and ruined. She had tried to burn it, and she had succeeded too. I could not get a piece out as big as my hand."

"But you got some of it!" blurted out Lena, guided by a look which I gave her.

"Yes, scraps, it was so handsome. I think I have a bit in my work-basket now."

"O get it for me," urged Lena. "I want it to remember her by."

"My work-basket is here." And going to a sort of *etagère* covered with a thousand knick-knacks picked up at bargain counters, she opened a little cupboard and brought out a basket, from which she presently pulled a small square of silk. It was, as she said, of the richest weaving, and was, as I had not the least doubt, a portion of the dress worn by Mrs. Van Burnam from Haddam.

"Yes, it was hers," said Lena, reading the expression of my face, and putting the scrap away very carefully in her pocket.

"Well, I would have given her five dollars for that blouse," murmured Mrs. Desberger, regretfully. "But girls like her are so improvident."

"And did she leave that day?" I asked, seeing that it was hard for this woman to tear her thoughts away from this coveted article.

"Yes, ma'am. It was late, and I had but little hopes of her getting the situation she was after. But she promised to come back if she didn't; and as she did not come back I decided that she was more successful than I had anticipated."

"And don't you know where she went? Didn't she confide in you at all?"

"No; but as there were but three advertisements for a lady-companion in the *Herald* that day, it will be easy to find her. Would you like to see those advertisements? I saved them out of curiosity."

I assented, as you may believe, and she brought us the clippings at once. Two of them I read without emotion, but the third almost took my breath away. It was an advertisement for a lady-companion accustomed to the typewriter and of some taste in dressmaking, and the address given was that of Miss Althorpe.

If this woman, steeped in misery and darkened by crime, should be there!

As I shall not mention Mrs. Desberger again for some time, I will here say that at the first opportunity which presented itself I sent Lena to the shops with orders to buy and have sent to Mrs. Desberger the ugliest and most flaunting of silk blouses that could be found on Sixth Avenue; and as Lena's dimples were more than usually pronounced on her return, I have no doubt she chose one to suit the taste and warm the body of the estimable woman, whose kindly nature had made such a favorable impression upon me.

CHAPTER XXIII

Ruth Oliver

From Mrs. Desberger's I rode immediately to Miss Althorpe's, for the purpose of satisfying myself at once as to the presence there of the unhappy fugitive I was tracing.

Six o'clock Sunday night is not a favorable hour for calling at a young lady's house, especially when that lady has a lover who is in the habit of taking tea with the family. But I was in a mood to transgress all rules and even to forget the rights of lovers. Besides, much is forgiven a woman of my stamp, especially by a person of the good sense and amiability of Miss Althorpe.

That I was not mistaken in my calculations was evident from the greeting I received. Miss Althorpe came forward as graciously and with as little surprise in her manner as any one could expect under the circumstances, and for a moment I was so touched by her beauty and the unaffected charm of her manners that I forgot my errand and only thought of the pleasure of meeting a lady who fairly comes up to the standard one has secretly set for one's self. Of course she is much younger than I— some say she is only twenty-three; but a lady is a lady at any age, and Ella Althorpe might be a model for a much older woman than myself.

The room in which we were seated was a large one, and though I could hear Mr. Stone's voice in the adjoining apartment, I did not fear to broach the subject I had come to discuss.

"You may think this intrusion an odd one," I began, "but I believe you advertised a few days ago for a young lady-companion. Have you been suited, Miss Althorpe?"

"O yes; I have a young person with me whom I like very much."

"Ah, you are supplied! Is she any one you know?"

"No, she is a stranger, and what is more, she brought no recommendations with her. But her appearance is so attractive and her desire for the place was so great, that I consented to try her. And she is very satisfactory, poor girl! very satisfactory indeed!"

Ah, here was an opportunity for questions. Without showing too much eagerness and yet with a proper show of interest, I smilingly remarked:

"No one can be called poor long who remains under your roof, Miss Althorpe. But perhaps she has lost friends; so many nice girls are thrown upon their own resources by the death of relatives?"

"She does not wear mourning; but she is in some great trouble for all that. But this cannot interest you, Miss Butterworth; have you some *protégé* whom you wished to recommend for the position?"

I heard her, but did not answer at once. In fact, I was thinking how to proceed. Should I take her into my confidence, or should I continue in the ambiguous manner in which I had begun. Seeing her smile, I became conscious of the awkward silence.

"Pardon me," said I, resuming my best manner, "but there is something I want to say which may strike you as peculiar."

"O no," said she.

"I *am* interested in the girl you have befriended, and for very different reasons from those you suppose. I fear—I have great reason to fear— that she is not just the person you would like to harbor under your roof."

"Indeed! Why, what do you know about her? Anything bad, Miss Butterworth?"

I shook my head, and prayed her first to tell me how the girl looked and under what circumstances she came to her; for I was desirous of making no mistake concerning her identity with the person of whom I was in search.

"She is a sweet-looking girl," was the answer I received; "not beautiful, but interesting in expression and manner. She has brown hair,"—I shuddered—"brown eyes, and a mouth that would be lovely if it ever smiled. In fact, she is very attractive and so lady-like that I have desired to make a companion of her. But while attentive to all her duties, and manifestly grateful to me for the home I have given her, she shows so little desire for company or conversation that I have desisted for the last day or so from urging her to speak at all. But you asked me under what circumstances she came to me?"

"Yes, on what day, and at what time of day? Was she dressed well, or did her clothes look shabby?"

"She came on the very day I advertised; the eighteenth—yes, it was the eighteenth of this month; and she was dressed, so far as I noticed, very neatly. Indeed, her clothes appeared to be new. They needed to have been, for she brought nothing with her save what was contained in a small hand-bag."

"Also new?" I suggested.

"Very likely; I did not observe."

"O Miss Althorpe!" I exclaimed, this time with considerable vehemence, "I fear, or rather I hope, she is the woman I want."

"*You* want!"

"Yes, *I*; but I cannot tell you for what just yet. I must be sure, for I would not subject an innocent person to suspicion any more than you would."

"Suspicion! She is not honest, then? That would worry me, Miss Butterworth, for the house is full now, as you know, of wedding presents, and—But I cannot believe such a thing of *her*. It is some other fault she has, less despicable and degrading."

"I do not say she has any faults; I only said I feared. What name does she go by?"

"Oliver; Ruth Oliver."

Again I thought of the O. R. on the clothes at the laundry.

"I wish I could see her," I ventured. "I would give anything for a peep at her face unobserved."

"I don't know how I can manage *that*; she is very shy, and never shows herself in the front of the house. She even dines in her own room, having begged for that privilege till after I was married and the household settled on a new basis. But you can go to her room with me. If she is all right, she can have no objection to a visitor; and if she is *not*, it would be well for me to know it at once."

"Certainly," said I, and rose to follow her, turning over in my mind how I should account to this young woman for my intrusion. I had just arrived at what I considered a sensible conclusion, when Miss Althorpe, leaning towards me, said with a whole-souled impetuosity for which I could not but admire her:

"The girl is very nervous, she looks and acts like a person who has had some frightful shock. Don't alarm her, Miss Butterworth, and don't accuse her of anything wrong too suddenly. Perhaps she is innocent, and perhaps if she is not innocent, she has been driven into evil by very great temptations. I am sorry for her, whether she is simply unhappy or deeply remorseful. For I never saw a sweeter face, or eyes with such boundless depths of misery in them."

Just what Mrs. Desberger had said! Strange, but I began to feel a certain sort of sympathy for the wretched being I was hunting down.

"I will be careful," said I. "I merely want to satisfy myself that she is the same girl I heard of last from a Mrs. Desberger."

Miss Althorpe, who was now half-way up the rich staircase which makes her house one of the most remarkable in the city, turned and gave me a quick look over her shoulder.

"I don't know Mrs. Desberger," she remarked.

At which I smiled. Did she think Mrs. Desberger in society?

At the end of an upper passage-way we paused.

"This is the door," whispered Miss Althorpe. "Perhaps I had better go in first and see if she is at all prepared for company."

I was glad to have her do so, for I felt as if I needed to prepare myself for encountering this young girl, over whom, in my mind, hung the dreadful suspicion of murder.

But the time between Miss Althorpe's knock and her entrance, short as it was, was longer than that which elapsed between her going in and her hasty reappearance.

"You can have your wish," said she. "She is lying on her bed asleep, and you can see her without being observed. But," she entreated, with a passionate grip of my arm, which proclaimed her warm nature, "doesn't it seem a little like taking advantage of her?"

"Circumstances justify it in this case," I replied, admiring the consideration of my hostess, but not thinking it worth while to emulate it. And with very little ceremony I pushed open the door and entered the room of the so-called Ruth Oliver.

The hush and quiet which met me, though nothing more than I had reason to expect, gave me my first shock, and the young figure outstretched on a bed of dainty whiteness, my second. Everything about me was so peaceful, and the delicate blue and white of the room so expressive of innocence and repose, that my feet instinctively moved more softly over the polished floor and paused, when they did pause, before that dimly shrouded bed, with something like hesitation in their usually emphatic tread.

The face of that bed's occupant, which I could now plainly see, may have had an influence in producing this effect. It was so rounded with health, and yet so haggard with trouble. Not knowing whether Miss Althorpe was behind me or not, but too intent upon the sleeping girl to care, I bent over the half-averted features and studied them carefully.

They were indeed Madonna-like, something which I had not expected, notwithstanding the assurances I had received to that effect, and while distorted with suffering, amply accounted for the interest shown in her by the good-hearted Mrs. Desberger and the cultured Miss Althorpe.

Resenting this beauty, which so poorly accommodated itself to the character of the woman who possessed it, I leaned nearer, searching for some defect in her loveliness, when I saw that the struggle and anguish visible in her expression were due to some dream she was having.

Moved, even against my will, by the touching sight of her trembling eyelids and working mouth, I was about to wake her when I was stopped by the gentle touch of Miss Althorpe on my shoulder.

"Is she the girl you are looking for?"

I gave one quick glance around the room, and my eyes lighted on the little blue pin-cushion on the satin-wood bureau.

"Did you put those pins there?" I asked, pointing to a dozen or more black pins grouped in one corner.

"*I* did not, no; and I doubt if Crescenze did. Why?"

I drew a small black pin from my belt where I had securely fastened it, and carrying it over to the cushion, compared it with those I saw. They were identical.

"A small matter," I inwardly decided, "but it points in the right direction"; then, in answer to Miss Althorpe, added aloud: "I fear she is. At least I have seen no reason yet for doubting it. But I must make sure. Will you allow me to wake her?"

"O it seems cruel! She is suffering enough already. See how she twists and turns!"

"It will be a mercy, it seems to me, to rouse her from dreams so full of pain and trouble."

"Perhaps, but I will leave you alone to do it. What will you say to her? How account for your intrusion?"

"O I will find means, and they won't be too cruel either. You had better stand back by the bureau and listen. I think I had rather not have the responsibility of doing this thing alone."

Miss Althorpe, not understanding my hesitation, and only half comprehending my errand, gave me a doubtful look but retreated to the spot I had mentioned, and whether it was the rustle of her silk dress or whether the dream of the girl we were watching had reached its climax, a momentary stir took place in the outstretched form before me, and next moment she was flinging up her hands with a cry.

"O how can I touch her! She is dead, and I have never touched a dead body."

I fell back breathing hard, and Miss Althorpe's eyes, meeting mine, grew dark with horror. Indeed she was about to utter a cry herself, but I made an imperative motion, and she merely shrank farther away towards the door.

Meantime I had bent forward and laid my hand on the trembling figure before me.

"Miss Oliver," I said, "rouse yourself, I pray. I have a message for you from Mrs. Desberger."

She turned her head, looked at me like a person in a daze, then slowly moved and sat up.

"Who are you?" she asked, surveying me and the space about her with eyes which seemed to take in nothing till they lit upon Miss Althorpe's figure standing in an attitude of mingled shame and sympathy by the half-open door.

"Oh, Miss Althorpe!" she entreated, "I pray you to excuse me. I did not know you wanted me. I have been asleep."

"It is this lady who wants you," answered Miss Althorpe. "She is a friend of mine and one in whom you can confide."

"Confide!" This was a word to rouse her. She turned livid, and in her eyes as she looked my way both terror and surprise were visible. "Why should you think I had anything to confide? If I had, I should not pass by you, Miss Althorpe, for another."

There were tears in her voice, and I had to remember the victim just laid away in Woodlawn, not to bestow much more compassion on this woman than she rightfully deserved. She had a magnetic voice and a magnetic presence, but that was no reason why I should forget what she had done.

"No one asks for your confidence," I protested, "though it might not hurt you to accept a friend whenever you can get one. I merely wish, as I said before, to give you a message from Mrs. Desberger, under whose roof you stayed before coming here."

"I am obliged to you," she responded, rising to her feet, and trembling very much. "Mrs. Desberger is a kind woman; what does she want of me?"

So I was on the right track; she acknowledged Mrs. Desberger.

"Nothing but to return you this. It fell out of your pocket while you were dressing." And I handed her the little red pin-cushion I had taken from the Van Burnams' front room.

She looked at it, shrunk violently back, and with difficulty prevented herself from showing the full depth of her feelings.

"I don't know anything about it. It is not mine, I don't know it!" And her hair stirred on her forehead as she gazed at the small object lying in the palm of my hand, proving to me that she saw again before her all the horrors of the house from which it had been taken.

"Who are *you*?" she suddenly demanded, tearing her eyes from this simple little cushion and fixing them wildly on my face. "Mrs. Desberger never sent me this. I—"

"You are right to stop there," I interposed, and then paused, feeling that I had forced a situation which I hardly knew how to handle.

The instant's pause she had given herself seemed to restore her self-possession. Leaving me, she moved towards Miss Althorpe.

"I don't know who this lady is," said she, "or what her errand here with me may mean. But I hope that it is nothing that will force me to leave this house which is my only refuge."

Miss Althorpe, too greatly prejudiced in favor of this girl to hear this appeal unmoved, notwithstanding the show of guilt with which she had met my attack, smiled faintly as she answered:

"Nothing short of the best reasons would make me part from you now. If there are such reasons, you will spare me the pain of making use of them. I think I can so far trust you, Miss Oliver."

No answer; the young girl looked as if she could not speak.

"Are there any reasons why I should not retain you in my house, Miss Oliver?" the gentle mistress of many millions went on. "If there are, you will not wish to stay, I know, when you consider how near my marriage day is, and how undisturbed my mind should be by any cares unattending my wedding."

And still the girl was silent, though her lips moved slightly as if she would have spoken if she could.

"But perhaps you are only unfortunate," suggested Miss Althorpe, with an almost angelic look of pity—I don't often see angels in women. "If that is so, God forbid that you should leave my protection or my house. What do you say, Miss Oliver?"

"That you are God's messenger to me," burst from the other, as if her tongue had been suddenly loosed. "That misfortune, and not wickedness, has driven me to your doors; and that there is no reason why I should leave you unless my secret sufferings make my presence unwelcome to you."

Was this the talk of a frivolous woman caught unawares in the meshes of a fearful crime? If so, she was a more accomplished actress than we had been led to expect even from her own words to her disgusted husband.

"You look like one accustomed to tell the truth," proceeded Miss Althorpe. "Do you not think you have made some mistake, Miss Butterworth?" she asked, approaching me with an ingenuous smile.

I had forgotten to caution her not to make use of my name, and when it fell from her lips I looked to see her unhappy companion recoil from me with a scream.

But strange to say she evinced no emotion, and seeing this, I became more distrustful of her than ever; for, for her to hear without apparent interest the name of the chief witness in the inquest which had been held over the remains of the woman with whose death she had been more or less intimately concerned, argued powers of duplicity such as are only associated with guilt or an extreme simplicity of character. And she was not simple, as the least glance from her deep eyes amply showed.

Recognizing, therefore, that open measures would not do with this woman, I changed my manner at once, and responding to Miss Althorpe, with a gracious smile, remarked with an air of sudden conviction:

"Perhaps I have made some mistake. Miss Oliver's words sound very ingenuous, and I am disposed, if you are, to take her at her word. It is so easy to draw false conclusions in this world." And I put back the pin-cushion into my pocket with an air of being through with the matter, which seemed to impose upon the young woman, for she smiled faintly, showing a row of splendid teeth as she did so.

"Let me apologize," I went on, "if I have intruded upon Miss Oliver against her wishes." And with one comprehensive look about the room which took in all that was visible of her simple wardrobe and humble belongings, I led the way out. Miss Althorpe immediately followed.

"This is a much more serious affair than I have led you to suppose," I confided to her as soon as we were at a suitable distance from Miss Oliver's door. "If she is the person I think her, she is amenable to law, and the police will have to be notified of her whereabouts."

"She *has* stolen, then?"

"Her fault is a very grave one," I returned.

Miss Althorpe, deeply troubled, looked about her as if for guidance. I, who could have given it to her, made no movement to attract her attention to myself, but waited calmly for her own decision in this matter.

"I wish you would let me consult Mr. Stone," she ventured at last. "I think his judgment might help us."

"I had rather take no one into our confidence—especially no man. He would consider your welfare only and not hers."

I did not consider myself obliged to acknowledge that the work upon which I was engaged could not be shared by one of the male sex without lessening my triumph over Mr. Gryce.

"Mr. Stone is very just," she remarked, "but he might be biased in a matter of this kind. What way do you see out of the difficulty?"

"Only this. To settle at once and unmistakably, whether she is the person who carried certain articles from the house of a friend of mine. If she is, there will be some evidence of the fact visible in her room or on her person. She has not been out, I believe?"

"Not since she came into the house."

"And has remained for the most part in her own apartment?"

"Always, except when I have summoned her to my assistance."

"Then what I want to know I can learn there. But how can I make my investigations without offence?"

"What do you want to know, Miss Butterworth?"

"Whether she has in her keeping some half dozen rings of considerable value."

"Oh! she could conceal rings so easily."

"She does conceal them; I have no more doubt of it than I have of my standing here; but I must know it before I shall feel ready to call the attention of the police to her."

"Yes, we should both know it. Poor girl! poor girl! to be suspected of a crime! How great must have been her temptation!"

"*I* can manage this matter, Miss Althorpe, if you will entrust it to me."

"How, Miss Butterworth?"

"The girl is ill; let me take care of her."

"Really ill?"

"Yes, or will be so before morning. There is fever in her veins; she has worried herself ill. Oh, I will be good to her."

This in answer to a doubtful look from Miss Althorpe.

"This is a difficult problem you have set me," that lady remarked after a moment's thought. "But anything seems better than sending her away, or sending for the police. But do you suppose she will allow you in her room?"

"I think so; if her fever increases she will not notice much that goes on about her, and I think it will increase; I have seen enough of sickness to be something of a judge."

"And you will search her while she is unconscious?"

"Don't look so horrified, Miss Althorpe. I have promised you I will not worry her. She may need assistance in getting to bed. While I am giving it to her I can judge if there is anything concealed upon her person."

"Yes, perhaps."

"At all events, we shall know more than we do now. Shall I venture, Miss Althorpe?"

"I cannot say no," was the hesitating answer; "you seem so very much in earnest."

"And I am in earnest. I have reasons for being; consideration for you is one of them."

"I do not doubt it. And now will you come down to supper, Miss Butterworth?"

"No," I replied. "My duty is here. Only send word to Lena that she is to drive home and take care of my house in my absence. I shall want nothing, so do not worry about me. Join your lover now, dear; and do not bestow another thought upon this self-styled Miss Oliver or what I am about to do in her room."

CHAPTER XXIV

A House of Cards

I did not return immediately to my patient. I waited till her supper came up. Then I took the tray, and assured by the face of the girl who brought it that Miss Althorpe had explained my presence in her house sufficiently for me to feel at my ease before her servants, I carried in the dainty repast she had provided and set it down on the table.

The poor woman was standing where we had left her; but her whole figure showed languor, and she more than leaned against the bedpost behind her. As I looked up from the tray and met her eyes, she shuddered and seemed to be endeavoring to understand who I was and what I was doing in her room. My premonitions in regard to her were well based. She was in a raging fever, and was already more than half oblivious to her surroundings.

Approaching her, I spoke as gently as I could, for her hapless condition appealed to me in spite of my well founded prejudices against her; and seeing she was growing incapable of response, I drew her up on the bed and began to undress her.

I half expected her to recoil at this, or at least to make some show of alarm, but she submitted to my ministrations almost gratefully, and neither shrank nor questioned me till I laid my hands upon her shoes. Then indeed she quivered, and drew her feet away with such an appearance of terror that I was forced to desist from my efforts or drive her into violent delirium.

This satisfied me that Louise Van Burnam lay before me. The scar concerning which so much had been said in the papers would be ever present in the thoughts of this woman as the tell-tale mark by which she might be known, and though at this moment she was on the borders of unconsciousness, the instinct of self-preservation still remained in sufficient force to prompt her to make this effort to protect herself from discovery.

I had told Miss Althorpe that my chief reason for intruding upon Miss Oliver, was to determine if she had in her possession certain rings supposed to have been taken from a friend of mine; and while this was in a measure true—the rings being an important factor in the proof I was accumulating against her—I was not so anxious to search for them at this time as to find the scar which would settle at once the question of her identity.

When she drew her foot away from me then, so violently, I saw that I needed to search no farther for the evidence required, and could give myself up to making her comfortable. So I bathed her temples, now throbbing with heat, and soon had the satisfaction of seeing her fall into a deep and uneasy slumber. Then I tried again to draw off her shoes, but the start she gave and the smothered cry which escaped her warned me that I must wait yet longer before satisfying my curiosity; so I desisted at once, and out of pure compassion left her to get what good she might from the lethargy into which she had fallen.

Being hungry, or at least feeling the necessity of some slight aliment to help me sustain the fatigues of the night, I sat down now at the table and partook of some of the dainties with which Miss Althorpe had kindly provided me. After which I made out a list of such articles as were necessary to my proper care of the patient who had so strangely fallen into my hands, and then, feeling that I had a right at last to indulge in pure curiosity, I turned my attention to the clothing I had taken from the self-styled Miss Oliver.

The dress was a simple gray one, and the skirts and underclothing all white. But the latter was of the finest texture, and convinced me, before I had given them more than a glance, that they were the property of Howard Van Burnam's wife. For, besides the exquisite quality of the material, there were to be seen, on the edges of the bands and sleeves, the marks of stitches and clinging threads of lace, where the trimming had been torn off, and in one article especially, there were tucks such as you see come from the hands of French needlewomen only.

This, taken with what had gone before, was proof enough to satisfy me that I was on the right track, and after Crescenze had come and gone with the tray and all was quiet in this remote part of the house, I ventured to open a closet door at the foot of the bed. A brown silk skirt was hanging within, and in the pocket of that skirt I found a purse so gay and costly that all doubt vanished as to its being the property of Howard's luxurious wife.

There were several bills in this purse, amounting to about fifteen dollars in money, but no change and no memoranda, which latter seemed a pity. Restoring the purse to its place and the skirt to its peg, I came softly back to the bedside and examined my patient still more carefully than I had done before. She was asleep and breathing heavily, but even with this disadvantage her face had its own attraction, an attraction which evidently had more or less influenced men, and which, for the reason perhaps that I have something masculine in my nature, I discovered to be more or less influencing me, notwithstanding my hatred of an intriguing character.

However, it was not her beauty I came to study, but her hair, her complexion, and her hands. The former was brown, the brown of that same lock I remembered to have seen in the jury's hands at the inquest; and her skin, where fever had not flushed it, was white and smooth. So were her hands, and yet they were not a lady's hands. That I noticed when I first saw her. The marks of the rings she no longer wore, were not enough to blind me to the fact that her fingers lacked the distinctive shape and nicety of Miss Althorpe's, say, or even of the Misses Van Burnam; and though I do not object to this, for I like strong-looking, capable hands myself, they served to help me understand the face, which otherwise would have looked too spiritual for a woman of the peevish and self-satisfied character of Louise Van Burnam. On this innocent and appealing expression she had traded in her short and none too happy career. And as I noted it, I recalled a sentence in Miss Ferguson's testimony, in which she alluded to Mrs. Van Burnam's confidential remark to her husband upon the power she exercised over people when she raised her eyes in entreaty towards them. "Am I not pretty," she had said, "when I am in distress and looking up in this way?" It was the suggestion of a scheming woman, but from what I had seen and was seeing of the woman before me, I could imagine the picture she would thus make, and I do not think she overrated its effects.

Withdrawing from her side once more, I made a tour of the room. Nothing escaped my eyes; nothing was too small to engage my attention. But while I failed to see anything calculated to shake my confidence in the conclusions I had come to, I saw but little to confirm them. This was not strange; for, apart from a few toilet articles and some knitting-work on a shelf, she appeared to have no belongings; everything else in sight being manifestly the property of Miss Althorpe. Even the bureau drawers were empty, and her bag, found under a small table, had not so much in it as a hair-pin, though I searched it inside and out for her rings, which I was positive she had with her, even if she dared not wear them.

When every spot was exhausted I sat down and began to brood over what lay before this poor being, whose flight and the great efforts she made at concealment proved only too conclusively the fatal part she had played in the crime for which her husband had been arrested. I had reached her arraignment before a magistrate, and was already imagining her face with the appeal in it which such an occasion would call forth, when there came a low knock at the door, and Miss Althorpe re-entered.

She had just said good-night to her lover, and her face recalled to me a time when my own cheek was round and my eye was bright and—Well! what is the use of dwelling on matters so long buried in oblivion! A maiden-woman, as independent as myself, need not envy any girl the doubtful blessing of a husband. I chose to be independent, and I am, and what more is there to be said about it? Pardon the digression.

"Is Miss Oliver any better?" asked Miss Althorpe; "and have you found—"

I put up my finger in warning. Of all things, it was most necessary that the sick woman should not know my real reason for being there.

"She is asleep," I answered quietly, "and I *think* I have found out what is the matter with her."

Miss Althorpe seemed to understand. She cast a look of solicitude towards the bed and then turned towards me.

"I cannot rest," said she, "and will sit with you for a little while, if you don't mind."

I felt the implied compliment keenly.

"You can do me no greater favor," I returned.

She drew up an easy-chair. "That is for you," she smiled, and sat down in a little low rocker at my side.

But she did not talk. Her thoughts seemed to have recurred to some very near and sweet memory, for she smiled softly to herself and looked so deeply happy that I could not resist saying:

"These are delightful days for you, Miss Althorpe."

She sighed softly—how much a sigh can reveal!—and looked up at me brightly. I think she was glad I spoke. Even such reserved natures as hers have their moments of weakness, and she had no mother or sister to appeal to.

"Yes," she replied, "I am very happy; happier than most girls are, I think, just before marriage. It is such a revelation to me—this devotion and admiration from one I love. I have had so little of it in my life. My father—"

She stopped; I knew why she stopped. I gave her a look of encouragement.

"People have always been anxious for my happiness, and have warned me against matrimony since I was old enough to know the difference between poverty and wealth. Before I was out of short dresses I was warned against fortune-seekers. It was not good advice; it has stood in the way of my happiness all my life, made me distrustful and unnaturally reserved. But now—ah, Miss Butterworth, Mr. Stone is so estimable a man, so brilliant and so universally admired, that all my doubts of manly worth and disinterestedness have disappeared as if by magic. I trust him implicitly, and—Do I talk too freely? Do you object to such confidences as these?"

"On the contrary," I answered. I liked Miss Althorpe so much and agreed with her so thoroughly in her opinion of this man, that it was a real pleasure to me to hear her speak so unreservedly.

"We are not a foolish couple," she went on, warming with the charm of her topic till she looked beautiful in the half light thrown upon her by the shaded lamp. "We are interested in people and things, and get half our delight from the perfect congeniality of our natures. Mr. Stone has given up his club and all his bachelor pursuits since he knew me, and—"

O love, if at any time in my life I have despised thee, I did not despise thee then! The look with which she finished this sentence would have moved a cynic.

"Forgive me," she prayed. "It is the first time I have poured out my heart to any one of my own sex. It must sound strange to you, but it seemed natural while I was doing it, for you looked as if you could understand."

This to me, to *me*, Amelia Butterworth, of whom men have said I had no more sentiment than a wooden image. I looked my appreciation, and she, blushing slightly, whispered in a delicious tone of mingled shyness and pride:

"Only two weeks now, and I shall have someone to stand between me and the world. *You* have never needed any one, Miss Butterworth, for you do not fear the world, but it awes and troubles me, and my whole heart glows with the thought that I shall be no longer alone in my sorrows or my joys, my perplexities or my doubts. Am I to blame for anticipating this with so much happiness?"

I sighed. It was a less eloquent sigh than hers, but it was a distinct one and it had a distinct echo. Lifting my eyes, for I sat so as to face the bed, I was startled to observe my patient leaning towards us from her pillows, and staring upon us with eyes too hollow for tears but filled with unfathomable grief and yearning.

She had heard this talk of love, she, the forsaken and crime-stained one. I shuddered and laid my hand on Miss Althorpe's.

But I did not seek to stop the conversation, for as our looks met, the sick woman fell back and lapsed, or seemed to lapse, into immediate insensibility again.

"Is Miss Oliver worse?" inquired Miss Althorpe.

I rose and went to the bedside, renewed the bandages on my patient's head, and forced a drop or two of medicine between her half-shut lips.

"No," I returned, "I think her fever is abating." And it was, though the suffering on her face was yet heart-rendingly apparent.

"Is she asleep?"

"She seems to be."

Miss Althorpe made an effort.

"I am not going to talk any more about myself." Then as I came back and sat down by her side, she quietly asked:

"What do you think of the Van Burnam murder?"

Dismayed at the introduction of this topic, I was about to put my hand over her mouth, when I noticed that her words had made no evident impression upon my patient, who lay quietly and with a more composed expression than when I left her bedside. This assured me, as nothing else could have done, that she was really asleep, or in that lethargic state which closes the eyes and ears to what is going on.

"I think," said I, "that the young man Howard stands in a very unfortunate position. Circumstances certainly do look very black against him."

"It is dreadful, unprecedently dreadful. I do not know what to think of it all. The Van Burnams have borne so good a name, and Franklin especially is held in such high esteem. I don't think anything more shocking has ever happened in this city, do you, Miss Butterworth? You saw it all, and should know. Poor, poor Mrs. Van Burnam!"

"She is to be pitied!" I remarked, my eyes fixed on the immovable face of my patient.

"When I heard that a young woman had been found dead in the Van Burnam mansion," Miss Althorpe pursued with such evident interest in this new theme that I did not care to interrupt her unless driven to it by some token of consciousness on the part of my patient, "my thoughts flew instinctively to Howard's wife. Though why, I cannot say, for I never had any reason to expect so tragic a termination to their marriage relations. And I cannot believe now that he killed her, can you, Miss Butterworth? Howard has too much of the gentleman in him to do a brutal thing, and there was brutality as well as adroitness in the perpetration of this crime. Have you thought of that, Miss Butterworth?"

"Yes," I nodded, "I have looked at the crime on all sides."

"Mr. Stone," said she, "feels dreadfully over the part he was forced to play at the inquest. But he had no choice, the police would have his testimony."

"That was right," I declared.

"It has made us doubly anxious to have Howard free himself. But he does not seem able to do so. If his wife had only known—"

Was there a quiver in the lids I was watching? I half raised my hand and then I let it drop again, convinced that I had been mistaken. Miss Althorpe at once continued:

"She was not a bad-hearted woman, only vain and frivolous. She had set her heart on ruling in the great leather-merchant's house, and she did not know how to bear her disappointment. I have sympathy for her myself. When I saw her—"

Saw her! I started, upsetting a small work-basket at my side which for once I did not stop to pick up.

"You have seen her!" I repeated, dropping my eyes from the patient to fix them in my unbounded astonishment on Miss Althorpe's face.

"Yes, more than once. She was—if she were living I would not repeat this—a nursery governess in a family where I once visited. That was before her marriage; before she had met either Howard or Franklin Van Burnam."

I was so overwhelmed, that for once I found difficulty in speaking. I glanced from her to the white form in the shrouded bed, and back again in ever-growing astonishment and dismay.

"You have seen her!" I at last reiterated in what I meant to be a whisper, but which fell little short of being a cry, "and you took in this girl?"

Her surprise at this burst was almost equal to mine.

"Yes, why not; what have they in common?"

I sank back, my house of cards was trembling to its foundations.

"Do they—do they not look alike?" I gasped. "I thought—I imagined—"

"Louise Van Burnam look like that girl! O no, they were very different sort of women. What made you think there was any resemblance between them?"

I did not answer her; the structure I had reared with such care and circumspection had fallen about my ears and I lay gasping under the ruins.

CHAPTER XXV

"The Rings! Where Are the Rings?"

Had Mr. Gryce been present, I would have instantly triumphed over my disappointment, bottled up my chagrin, and been the inscrutable Amelia Butterworth before he could say, "Something has gone wrong with this woman!" But Mr. Gryce was not present, and though I did not betray the half I felt. I yet showed enough emotion for Miss Althorpe to remark:

"You seemed surprised by what I have told you. Has any one said that these two women were alike?"

Having to speak, I became myself again in a trice, and nodded vigorously.

"Some one was so foolish," I remarked.

Miss Althorpe looked thoughtful. While she was interested she was not so interested as to take the subject in fully. Her own concerns made her abstracted, and I was very glad of it.

"Louise Van Burnam had a sharp chin and a very cold blue eye. Yet her face was a fascinating one to some."

"Well, it was a dreadful tragedy!" I observed, and tried to turn the subject aside, which fortunately I was able to do after a short effort.

Then I picked the basket up, and perceiving the sick woman's lips faintly moving, I went over to her and found her murmuring to herself.

As Miss Althorpe had risen when I did, I did not dare to listen to these murmurs, but when my charming hostess had bidden me good-night, with many injunctions not to tire myself, and to be sure and re-member that a decanter and a plate of biscuits stood on a table outside, I hastened back to the bedside, and leaning over my patient, endeavored to catch the words as they fell from her lips.

As they were simple and but the echo of those running at that very moment through my own brain, I had no difficulty in distinguishing them.

"Van Burnam!" she was saying, "Van Burnam!" varied by a short "Howard!" and once by a doubtful "Franklin!"

"Ah," thought I, with a sudden reaction, "she is the woman I seek, if she is not Louise Van Burnam." And unheeding the start she gave, I pulled off the blanket I had spread over her, and willy-nilly drew off her left shoe and stocking.

Her bare ankle showed no scar, and covering it quickly up I took up her shoe. Immediately the trepidation she had shown at the approach of a stranger's hand towards that article of clothing was explained. In the lining around the top were sewn bills of no ordinary amount, and as the other shoe was probably used as a like depository, she naturally felt con-cern at any approach which might lead to a discovery of her little fortune.

Amazed at a mystery possessing so many points of interest, I tucked the shoe in under the bedclothes and sat down to review the situation.

The mistake I had made was in concluding that because the fugitive whose traces I had followed had worn the clothes of Louise Van Burnam, she must necessarily be that unfortunate lady. Now I saw that the mur-dered woman was Howard's wife after all, and this patient of mine her probable rival.

But this necessitated an entire change in my whole line of reason-ing. If the rival and not the wife lay before me, then which of the two accompanied him to the scene of tragedy? He had said it was his wife; I had proven to myself that it was the rival; was he right, or was I right, or were neither of us right?

Not being able to decide, I fixed my mind upon another query. When did the two women exchange clothes, or rather, when did this woman procure the silk habiliments and elaborate adornments of her more opu-lent rival? Was it before either of them entered Mr. Van Burnam's house? Or was it after their encounter there?

Running over in my mind certain little facts of which I had hitherto attempted no explanation, I grouped them together and sought amongst them for inspiration.

These are the facts:

1. One of the garments found on the murdered woman had been torn down the back. As it was a new one, it had evidently been subjected to some quick strain, not explainable by any appearance of struggle.

2. The shoes and stockings found on the victim were the only articles she wore which could not be traced back to Altman's. In the re-dressing of the so-called Mrs. James Pope, these articles had not been changed. Could not that fact be explained by the presence of a considerable sum of money in her shoes?

3. The going out bareheaded of a fugitive, anxious to avoid observation, leaving hat and gloves behind her in a dining-room closet.

I had endeavored to explain this last anomalous action by her fear of being traced by so conspicuous an article as this hat; but it was not a satisfactory explanation to me then and much less so now.

4. And last, and most vital of all, the words which I had heard fall from this half-conscious girl: "*O how can I touch her! She is dead, and I have never touched a dead body!*"

Could inspiration fail me before such a list? Was it not evident that the change had been made after death, and by this seemingly sensitive girl's own hands?

It was a horrible thought and led to others more horrible. For the very commission of such a revolting act argued a desire for concealment only to be explained by great guilt. She had been the offender and the wife the victim; and Howard—Well, his actions continued to be a mystery, but I would not admit his guilt even now. On the contrary, I saw his innocence in a still stronger light. For if he had openly or even covertly connived at his wife's death, would he have so immediately forsaken the accomplice of his guilt, to say nothing of leaving to her the dreadful task of concealing the crime? No, I would rather think that the tragedy took place after his departure, and that his action in denying his wife's identity, as long as it was possible to do so, was to be explained by the fact of his ignorance in regard to his wife's presence in the house where he had supposed himself to have simply left her rival. As the exchange made in the clothing worn by the two women could only have taken place later, and as he naturally judged the victim by her clothing, perhaps he was really deceived himself as to her identity. It was certainly not an improbable supposition, and accounted for much that was otherwise inexplicable in Mr. Van Burnam's conduct.

But the rings? Why could I not find the rings? If my present reasoning were correct, this woman should have those evidences of guilt about her. But had I not searched for them in every available place without success? Annoyed at my failure to fix this one irrefutable proof of guilt upon her, I took up the knitting-work I saw in Miss Oliver's basket, and began to ply the needles by way of relief to my thoughts. But I had no sooner got well under way than some movement on the part of my patient drew my attention again to the bed, and I was startled by beholding her sitting up again, but this time with a look of fear rather than of suffering on her features.

"Don't!" she gasped, pointing with an unsteady hand at the work in my hand. "The click, click of the needles is more than I can stand. Put them down, pray; put them down!"

Her agitation was so great and her nervousness so apparent that I complied at once. However much I might be affected by her guilt, I was not willing to do the slightest thing to worry her nerves even at the expense of my own. As the needles fell from my hand, she sank back and a quick, short sigh escaped her lips. Then she was again quiet, and I allowed my thoughts to return to the old theme. The rings! the rings! Where were the rings, and was it impossible for me to find them?

CHAPTER XXVI

A Tilt With Mr. Gryce

At seven o'clock the next morning my patient was resting so quietly that I considered it safe to leave her for a short time. So I informed Miss Althorpe that I was obliged to go down-town on an important errand, and requested Crescenze to watch over the sick girl in my absence. As she agreed to this, I left the house as soon as breakfast was over and went immediately in search of Mr. Gryce. I wished to make sure that he knew nothing about the rings.

It was eleven o'clock before I succeeded in finding him. As I was certain that a direct question would bring no answer, I dissembled my real intention as much as my principles would allow, and accosted him with the eager look of one who has great news to impart.

"O, Mr. Gryce!" I impetuously cried, just as if I were really the weak woman he thought me, "I have found something; something in connection with the Van Burnam murder. You know I promised to busy myself about it if you arrested Howard Van Burnam."

His smile was tantalizing in the extreme. "Found something?" he repeated. "And may I ask if you have been so good as to bring it with you?"

He was playing with me, this aged and reputable detective. I subdued my anger, subdued my indignation even, and smiling much in his own way, answered briefly:

"I never carry valuables on my person. A half-dozen expensive rings stand for too much money for me to run any undue risk with them."

He was caressing his watch-chain as I spoke, and I noticed that he paused in this action for just an infinitesimal length of time as I said the word rings. Then he went on as before, but I knew I had caught his attention.

"Of what rings do you speak, madam? Of those missing from Mrs. Van Burnam's hands?"

I took a leaf from his book, and allowed myself to indulge in a little banter.

"O, no," I remonstrated, "not those rings, of course. The Queen of Siam's rings, any rings but those in which we are specially interested."

This meeting him on his own ground evidently puzzled him.

"You are facetious, madam. What am I to gather from such levity? That success has crowned your efforts, and that you have found a guiltier party than the one now in custody?"

"Possibly," I returned, limiting my advance by his. "But it would be going too fast to mention that yet. What I want to know is whether *you* have found the rings belonging to Mrs. Van Burnam?"

My triumphant tone, the almost mocking accent I purposely gave to the word *you*, accomplished its purpose. He never dreamed I was playing with him; he thought I was bursting with pride; and casting me a sharp glance (the first, by the way, I had received from him), he inquired with perceptible interest:

"Have *you?*"

Instantly convinced that the whereabouts of these jewels was as little known to him as to me, I rose and prepared to leave. But seeing that he was not satisfied, and that he expected an answer, I assumed a mysterious air and quietly remarked:

"If you will come to my house tomorrow I will explain myself. I am not prepared to more than intimate my discoveries today."

But he was not the man to let one off so easily.

"Excuse me," said he, "but matters of this kind do not admit of delay. The grand jury sits within the week, and any evidence worth presenting them must be collected at once. I must ask you to be frank with me, Miss Butterworth."

"And I will be, tomorrow."

"Today," he insisted, "today."

Seeing that I should gain nothing by my present course, I reseated myself, bestowing upon him a decidedly ambiguous smile as I did so.

"You acknowledge then," said I, "that the old maid can tell you something after all. I thought you regarded all my efforts in the light of a jest. What has made you change your mind?"

"Madam, I decline to bandy words. Have you found those rings, or have you not?"

"I have *not*," said I, "but neither have you, and as that is what I wanted to make sure of, I will now take my leave without further ceremony."

Mr. Gryce is not a profane man, but he allowed a word to slip from him which was not entirely one of blessing. He made amends for it next moment, however, by remarking:

"Madam, I once said, as you will doubtless remember, that the day would come when I should find myself at your feet. That day has arrived. And now is there any other little cherished fact known to the police which you would like to have imparted to you?"

I took his humiliation seriously.

"You are very good," I rejoined, "but I will not trouble you for any *facts—those* I am enabled to glean for myself; but what I should like you to tell me is this: Whether if you came upon those rings in the possession of a person known to have been on the scene of crime at the time of its perpetration, you would not consider them as an incontrovertible proof of guilt?"

"Undoubtedly," said he, with a sudden alteration in his manner which warned me that I must muster up all my strength if I would keep my secret till I was quite ready to part with it.

"Then," said I, with a resolute movement towards the door, "that's the whole of my business for today. Good-morning, Mr. Gryce; tomorrow I shall expect you."

He made me stop though my foot had crossed the threshold; not by word or look but simply by his fatherly manner.

"Miss Butterworth," he observed, "the suspicions which you have entertained from the first have within the last few days assumed a definite form. In what direction do they point?—tell me."

Some men and most women would have yielded to that imperative *tell me*! But there was no yielding in Amelia Butterworth. Instead of that I treated him to a touch of irony.

"Is it possible," I asked, "that you think it worth while to consult *me*? I thought your eyes were too keen to seek assistance from mine. You are as confident as I am that Howard Van Burnam is innocent of the crime for which you have arrested him."

A look that was dangerously insinuating crossed his face at this. He came forward rapidly and, joining me where I stood, said smilingly:

"Let us join forces, Miss Butterworth. You have from the first refused to consider the younger son of Silas Van Burnam as guilty. Your reasons then were slight and hardly worth communicating. Have you any better ones to advance now? It is not too late to mention them, if you have."

"It will not be too late tomorrow," I retorted.

Convinced that I was not to be moved from my position, he gave me one of his low bows.

"I forgot," said he, "that it was as a rival and not as a coadjutor you meddled in this matter." And he bowed again, this time with a sarcastic air I felt too self-satisfied to resent.

"Tomorrow, then?" said I.

"Tomorrow."

At that I left him.

I did not return immediately to Miss Althorpe. I visited Cox's millinery store, Mrs. Desberger's house, and the offices of the various city railways. But I got no clue to the rings; and finally satisfied that Miss Oliver, as I must now call her, had not lost or disposed of them on her way from Gramercy Park to her present place of refuge, I returned to Miss Althorpe's with even a greater determination than before to search that luxurious home till I found them.

But a decided surprise awaited me. As the door opened I caught a glimpse of the butler's face, and noticing its embarrassed expression, I at once asked what had happened.

His answer showed a strange mixture of hesitation and bravado.

"Not much, ma'am; only Miss Althorpe is afraid you may not be pleased. Miss Oliver is gone, ma'am; she ran away while Crescenze was out of the room."

CHAPTER XXVII

Found

I gave a low cry and rushed down the steps.

"Don't go!" I called out to the driver. "I shall want you in ten minutes." And hurrying back, I ran upstairs in a condition of mind such as I have no reason to be proud of. Happily Mr. Gryce was not there to see me.

"Gone? Miss Oliver gone?" I cried to the maid whom I found trembling in a corner of the hall.

"Yes, ma'am; it was my fault, ma'am. She was in bed so quiet, I thought I might step out for a minute, but when I came back her clothes were missing and she was gone. She must have slipped out at the front door while Dan was in the back hall. I don't see how ever she had the strength to do it."

Nor did I. But I did not stop to reason about it; there was too much to be done. Rushing on, I entered the room I had left in such high hopes a few hours before. Emptiness was before me, and I realized what it was to be baffled at the moment of success. But I did not waste an instant in inactivity. I searched the closets and pulled open the drawers; found her coat and hat gone, but not Mrs. Van Burnam's brown skirt, though the purse had been taken out of the pocket.

"Is her bag here?" I asked.

Yes, it was in its old place under the table; and on the wash-stand and bureau were the simple toilet articles I had been told she had brought there. In what haste she must have fled to leave these necessities behind her!

But the greatest shock I received was the sight of the knitting-work, with which I had so inconsiderately meddled the evening before, lying in ravelled heaps on the table, as if torn to bits in a frenzy. This was a proof that the fever was yet on her; and as I contemplated this fact I took courage, thinking that one in her condition would not be allowed to run the streets long, but would be picked up and put in some hospital.

In this hope I began my search. Miss Althorpe, who came in just as I was about to leave the house, consented to telephone to Police Head-quarters a description of the girl, with a request to be notified if such a person should be found in the streets or on the docks or at any of the station-houses that night. "Not," I assured her, as we left the telephone and I prepared to say good-bye for the day, "that you need expect her to be brought back to this house, for I do not mean that she shall ever darken your doors again. So let me know if they find her, and I will relieve you of all further responsibility in the matter."

Then I started out.

To name the streets I traversed or the places I visited that day, would take more space than I would like to devote to the subject. Dusk came, and I had failed in obtaining the least clue to her whereabouts; evening followed, and still no trace of the fugitive. What was I to do? Take Mr. Gryce into my confidence after all? That would be galling to my pride, but I began to fear I should have to submit to this humiliation when I happened to think of the Chinaman. To think of him once was to think of him twice, and to think of him twice was to be conscious of an irresist-ible desire to visit his place and find out if any one but myself had been there to inquire after the lost one's clothes.

Accompanied by Lena, I hurried away to Third Avenue. The laundry was near Twenty-seventh Street. As we approached I grew troubled and unaccountably expectant. When we reached it I understood my excite-ment and instantly became calm. For there stood Miss Oliver, gazing like one under a spell through the lighted window-panes into the narrow shop where the owner bent over his ironing. She had evidently stood there some time, for a small group of half-grown lads were watching her with every symptom of being about to break into a mischievous display of curiosity. Her hands, which were without gloves, were pressed against the glass, and her whole attitude showed an intensity of fatigue which would have laid her on the ground had she not been sustained by an equal intensity of purpose.

Sending Lena for a carriage, I approached the poor creature and drew her forcibly from the window.

"Do you want anything here?" I asked. "I will go in with you if you do."

She surveyed me with strange apathy, and yet with a certain sort of relief too. Then she slowly shook her head.

"I don't know anything about it. My head swims and everything looks queer, but someone or something sent me to this place."

"Come in," I urged, "come in for a minute." And half supporting her, half dragging her, I managed to get her across the threshold and into the Chinaman's shop.

Immediately a dozen faces were pressed where hers had been.

The Chinaman, a stolid being, turned as he heard the little bell tinkle which announced a customer.

"Is this the lady who left the clothes here a few nights ago?" I asked.

He stopped and stared, recognizing me slowly, and remembering by degrees what had passed between us at our last interview.

"You tellee me lalee die; how him lalee when lalee die?"

"The lady is not dead; I made a mistake. Is this the lady?"

"Lalee talk; I no see face, I hear speak."

"Have you seen this man before?" I inquired of my nearly insensible companion.

"I think so in a dream," she murmured, trying to recall her poor wandering wits back from some region into which they had strayed.

"Him lalee!" cried the Chinaman, overjoyed at the prospect of getting his money. "Pletty speak, I knowee him. Lalee want clo?"

"Not tonight. The lady is sick; see, she can hardly stand." And overjoyed at this seeming evidence that the police had failed to get wind of my interest in this place, I slipped a coin into the Chinaman's hand, and drew Miss Oliver away towards the carriage I now saw drawing up before the shop.

Lena's eyes when she came up to help me were a sight to see. They seemed to ask who this girl was and what I was going to do with her. I answered the look by a very brief and evidently wholly unexpected explanation.

"This is your cousin who ran away," I remarked. "Don't you recognize her?"

Lena gave me up then and there; but she accepted my explanation, and even lied in her desire to carry out my whim.

"Yes, ma'am," said she, "and glad I am to see her again." And with a deft push here and a gentle pull there, she succeeded in getting the sick woman into the carriage.

The crowd, which had considerably increased by this time, was beginning to flock about us with shouts of no little derision. Escaping it as best I could, I took my seat by the poor girl's side, and bade Lena give the order for home. When we left the curb-stone behind, I felt that the last page in my adventures as an amateur detective had closed.

But I counted without my cost. Miss Oliver, who was in an advanced stage of fever, lay like a dead weight on my shoulder during the drive down the avenue, but when we entered the Park and drew near my house, she began to show such signs of violent agitation that it was with difficulty that the united efforts of Lena and myself could prevent her from throwing herself out of the carriage door which she had somehow managed to open.

As the carriage stopped she grew worse, and though she made no further efforts to leave it, I found her present impulses even harder to contend with than the former. For now she would not be pushed out or dragged out, but crouched back moaning and struggling, her eyes fixed on the stoop, which is not unlike that of the adjoining house; till with a sudden realization that the cause of her terror lay in her fear of re-entering the scene of her late terrifying experiences, I bade the coachman drive on, and reluctantly, I own, carried her back to the house she had left in the morning.

And this is how I came to spend a second night in Miss Althorpe's hospitable mansion.

CHAPTER XXVIII

Taken Aback

One incident more and this portion of my story is at an end. My poor patient, sicker than she had been the night before, left me but little leisure for thought or action disconnected with my care for her. But towards morning she grew quieter, and finding in an open drawer those tangled threads of yarn of which I have spoken, I began to rewind them, out of a natural desire to see everything neat and orderly about me. I had nearly finished my task when I heard a strange noise from the bed. It was a sort of gurgling cry which I found hard to interpret, but which only stopped when I laid my work down again. Manifestly this sick girl had very nervous fancies.

When I went down to breakfast the next morning, I was in that complacent state of mind natural to a woman who feels that her abilities have asserted themselves and that she would soon receive a recognition of the same at the hands of the one person for whose commendation she had chiefly been working. The identification of Miss Oliver by the Chinaman was the last link in the chain connecting her with the Mrs. James Pope who had accompanied Mr. Van Burnam to his father's house in Gramercy Park, and though I would fain have had the murdered woman's rings to show, I was contented enough with the discoveries I had made to wish for the hour which would bring me face to face with the detective.

But a surprise awaited me at the breakfast table in the shape of a communication from that gentleman. It had just been brought from my house by Lena, and it ran thus:

"Dear Miss Butterworth:

"Pardon our interference. *We* have found the rings which you think so conclusive an evidence of guilt against the person secreting them; and, *with your permission* [this was basely underlined], Mr. Franklin Van Burnam will be in custody today.

"I will wait upon you at ten.

"Respectfully yours,

"Ebenezar Gryce."

Franklin Van Burnam! Was I dreaming? *Franklin* Van Burnam accused of this crime and in custody! What did it mean? I had found no evidence against Franklin Van Burnam.

BOOK III: THE GIRL IN GRAY

CHAPTER XXIX

Amelia Becomes Peremptory

"Madam, I hope I see you satisfied?"

This was Mr. Gryce's greeting as he entered my parlor on that memorable morning.

"Satisfied?" I repeated, rising and facing him with what he afterwards described as a stony glare.

"Pardon me! I suppose you would have been still more satisfied if we had waited for *you* to point out the guilty man to *us*. But you must make some allowances for professional egotism, Miss Butterworth. We really could not allow you to take the initiatory step in a matter of such importance."

"Oh!" was my sole response; but he has since told me that there was a great deal in that *oh*; so much, that even he was startled by it.

"You set today for a talk with me," he went on; "probably relying upon what you intended to assure yourself of yesterday. But our discovery at the same time as yourself of the rings in Mr. Van Burnam's office, need not interfere with your giving us your full confidence. The work you have done has been excellent, and we are disposed to give you considerable credit for it."

"Indeed!"

I had no choice but to thus indulge in ejaculations. The communication he had just made was so startling, and his assumption of my complete understanding of and participation in the discovery he professed to have made, so puzzling, that I dared not venture beyond these simple exclamations, lest he should see the state of mind into which he had thrown me, and shut up like an oyster.

"We have kept counsel over what we have found," the wary old detective continued, with a smile, which I wish I could imitate, but which unhappily belongs to him alone. "I hope that you, or your maid, I should say, have been equally discreet."

My maid!

"I see you are touched; but women find it so hard to keep a secret. But it does not matter. Tonight the whole town will know that the older and not the younger brother has had these rings in his keeping."

"It will be nuts for the papers," I commented; then making an effort, I remarked: "You are a most judicious man, Mr. Gryce, and must have other reasons than the discovery of these rings for your threatened arrest of a man of such excellent repute as Silas Van Burnam's eldest son. I should like to hear them, Mr. Gryce. I should like to hear them very much."

My attempt to seem at ease under these embarrassing conditions must have given a certain sharpness to my tone; for, instead of replying, he remarked, with well simulated concern and a fatherly humoring of my folly peculiarly exasperating to one of my temperament: "You are displeased, Miss Butterworth, because we did not let *you* find the rings."

"Perhaps; but we were engaged in an open field. I could not expect the police to stand aside for me."

"Exactly! Especially when you have the secret satisfaction of having put the police on the track of these jewels."

"How?"

"We were simply fortunate in laying our hands on them first. You, or your maid rather, showed us where to look for them."

Lena again.

I was so dumfounded by this last assertion, I did not attempt to reply. Fortunately, he misinterpreted my silence and the "stony glare" with which it was accompanied.

"I know that it must seem to you altogether too bad, to be tripped up at the moment of your anticipated triumph. But if apologies will suffice to express our sense of presumption, then I pray you to accept them, Miss Butterworth, both on my own part and on that of the Superintendent of Police."

I did not understand in the least what he was talking about, but I recognized the sarcasm of his final expression, and had spirit enough to reply:

"The subject is too important for any more nonsense. Whereabouts in Franklin Van Burnam's desk were these rings found, and how do you know that his brother did not put them there?"

"Your ignorance is refreshing, Miss Butterworth. If you will ask a certain young girl dressed in gray, upon what object connected with Mr. Van Burnam's desk she laid her hands yesterday morning, you will have an answer to your first question. The second one is still more easily answered. Mr. Howard Van Burnam did not conceal the rings in the Duane Street office for the reason that he has not been in that office since his wife was killed. Regarding this fact we are as well advised as yourself. Now you change color, Miss Butterworth. But there is no necessity. For an amateur you have made less trouble and fewer mistakes than were to be expected."

Worse and worse! He was patronizing me now, and for results I had done nothing to bring about. I surveyed him in absolute amazement. Was he amusing himself with me, or was he himself deceived as to the nature and trend of my late investigations. This was a question to settle, and at once; and as duplicity had hitherto proved my best weapon in dealing with Mr. Gryce, I concluded to resort to it in this emergency. Clearing my brow, I regarded with a more amenable air the little Hungarian vase he had taken up on entering the room, and into which he had been talking ever since he thought it worth while to compliment its owner.

"I do not wish," said I, "to be published to the world as the discoverer of Franklin Van Burnam's guilt. But I do want credit with the police, if only because one of their number has chosen to look upon my efforts with disdain. I mean you, Mr. Gryce; so, if you are in earnest"—he smiled at the vase most genially—"I will accept your apologies just so far as you honor me with your confidence. I know you are anxious to hear what evidence I have collected, or you would not be wasting time on me this busy morning."

"Shrewd!" was the short ejaculation he shot into the mouth of the vase he was handling.

"If that term of admiration is intended for me," I remarked, "I am sure I am only too sensible of the honor. But flattery has never succeeded in making me talk against my better judgment. I may be shrewd, but a fool could see what you are after this morning. Compliment me when I have deserved it. I can wait."

"I begin to think that what you withhold so resolutely has more than common value, Miss Butterworth. If this is so, I must not be the only one to listen to your explanations. Is not that a carriage I hear stopping? I am expecting Inspector Z——. If that is he you have been wise to delay your communications till he came."

A carriage *was* stopping, and it was the Inspector who alighted from it. I began to feel my importance in a way that was truly gratifying, and cast my eyes up at the portrait of my father with a secret longing that its original stood by to witness the verification of his prophecy.

But I was not so distracted by these thoughts as not to make one attempt to get something from Mr. Gryce before the Inspector joined us.

"Why do you speak to me of my maid in one breath and of a girl in gray in another? Did you think Lena—"

"Hush!" he enjoined, "we will have ample opportunities to discuss this subject later."

"Will we?" thought I. "We will discuss nothing till I know more positively what you are aiming at."

But I showed nothing of this determination in my face. On the contrary, I became all affability as the Inspector entered, and I did the honors of the house in a way I hope my father would have approved of, had he been alive and present.

Mr. Gryce continued to stare into the vase.

"Miss Butterworth,"—it was the Inspector who was speaking—"I have been told that you take great interest in the Van Burnam murder, and that you have even gone so far as to collect some facts in connection with it which you have not as yet given to the police."

"You have heard correctly," I returned. "I have taken a deep interest in this tragedy, and have come into possession of some facts in reference to it which as yet I have imparted to no living soul."

Mr. Gryce's interest in my poor little vase increased marvellously. Seeing this, I complacently continued:

"I could not have accomplished so much had I indulged in a confidant. Such work as I have attempted depends for its success upon the secrecy with which it is carried on. That is why amateur work is sometimes more effective than professional. No one suspected me of making inquiries, unless it was this gentleman, and he was forewarned of my possible interference. I told him that in case Howard Van Burnam was put under arrest, I should take it upon myself to stir up matters; and I have."

"Then you do not believe in Mr. Van Burnam's guilt? Not even in his complicity, I suppose?" ventured the Inspector.

"I do not know anything about his complicity; but I do not believe the stroke given to his wife came from his hand."

"I see, I see. You believe it the work of his brother."

I stole a look at Mr. Gryce before replying. He had turned the vase upside down, and was intently studying its label; but he could not conceal his expectation of an affirmative answer. Greatly relieved, I immediately took the position I had resolved upon, and calmly but vigorously observed:

"What I believe, and what I have learned in support of my belief, will sound as well in your ears ten minutes hence as now. Before I give you the result of such inquiries as I have been enabled to make, I require to know what evidence you have yourself collected against the gentleman you have just named, and in what respect it is as criminating as that against his brother?"

"Is not that peremptory, Miss Butterworth? And do you think us called upon to part with all or any of the secrets of our office? We have informed you that we have new and startling evidence against the older brother; should not that be sufficient for you?"

"Perhaps so if I were an assistant of yours, or even in your employ. But I am neither; I stand alone, and although I am a woman and unused to this business, I have earned, as I think you will acknowledge later, the right to some consideration on your part. I cannot present the facts I have to relate in a proper manner till I know just how the case stands."

"It is not curiosity that troubles Miss Butterworth—Madam, I said it was not curiosity—but a laudable desire to have the whole matter arranged with precision," dropped now in his dryest tones from the detective's lips.

"Mr. Gryce has a most excellent understanding of my character," I gravely observed.

The Inspector looked nonplussed. He glanced at Mr. Gryce and he glanced at me, but the smile of the former was inscrutable, and my expression, if I showed any, must have betrayed but little relenting.

"If called as a witness, Miss Butterworth,"—this was how he sought to manage me—"you will have no choice in the matter. You will be compelled to speak or show contempt of court."

"That is true," I acknowledged. "But it is not what I might feel myself called upon to say then, but what I can say now, that is of interest to you at this present moment. So be generous, gentlemen, and satisfy my curiosity, for such Mr. Gryce considers it, in spite of his assertions to the contrary. Will it not all come out in the papers a few hours hence, and have I not earned as much at your hands as the reporters?"

"The reporters are our bane. Do not liken yourself to the reporters."

"Yet they sometimes give you a valuable clue."

Mr. Gryce looked as if he would like to disclaim this, but he was a judicious soul, and merely gave a twist to the vase which I thought would cost me that small article of vertu.

"Shall we humor Miss Butterworth?" asked the Inspector.

"We will do better," answered Mr. Gryce, setting the vase down with a precision that made me jump; for I am a worshipper of *bric-à-brac*, and prize the few articles I own, possibly beyond their real value. "We will treat her as a coadjutor, which, by the way, she says she is not, and by the trust we place in her, secure that discretionary use of our confidence which she shows with so much spirit in regard to her own."

"Begin then," said I.

"I will," said he, "but first allow me to acknowledge that you are the person who first put us on the track of Franklin Van Burnam."

CHAPTER XXX

The Matter as Stated by Mr. Gryce

I had exhausted my wonder, so I accepted this statement with no more display of surprise than a grim smile.

"When you failed to identify Howard Van Burnam as the man who accompanied his wife into the adjacent house, I realized that I must look elsewhere for the murderer of Louise Van Burnam. You see I had more confidence in the excellence of your memory than you had yourself, so much indeed that I gave you more than one chance to exercise it, having, by certain little methods I sometimes employ, induced different moods in Mr. Van Burnam at the time of his several visits, so that his bearing might vary, and you have every opportunity to recognize him for the man you had seen on that fatal night."

"Then it was he you brought here each time?" I broke in.

"It was he."

"Well!" I ejaculated.

"The Superintendent and some others whom I need not mention,"— here Mr. Gryce took up another small object from the table—"believed implicitly in his guilt; conjugal murder is so common and the causes which lead to it so frequently puerile. Therefore I had to work alone. But this did not cause me any concern. *Your* doubts emphasized mine, and when you confided to me that you had seen a figure similar to the one we were trying to identify, enter the adjoining house on the evening of the funeral, I made immediate inquiries and discovered that the gentleman who had entered the house right after the four persons described by you was *Franklin Van Burnam*. This gave me a definite clue, and this is why I say that it was you who gave me my first start in this matter."

"Humph!" thought I to myself, as with a sudden shock I remembered that one of the words which had fallen from Miss Oliver's lips during her delirium had been this very name of Franklin.

"I had had my doubts of this gentleman before," continued the detective, warming gradually with his subject. "A man of my experience doubts every one in a case of this kind, and I had formed at odd times a sort of side theory, so to speak, into which some little matters which came up during the inquest seemed to fit with more or less nicety; but I had no real justification for suspicion till the event of which I speak. That you had evidently formed the same theory as myself and were bound to enter into the lists with me, put me on my mettle, madam, and with your knowledge or without it, the struggle between us began."

"So your disdain of me," I here put in with a triumphant air I could not subdue, "was only simulated? I shall know what to think of you hereafter. But don't stop, go on, this is all deeply interesting to me."

"I can understand that. To proceed then; my first duty, of course, was to watch *you*. You had reasons of your own for suspecting this man, so by watching you I hoped to surprise them."

"Good!" I cried, unable to entirely conceal the astonishment and grim amusement into which his continued misconception of the trend of my suspicions threw me.

"But you led us a chase, madam; I must acknowledge that you led us a chase. Your being an amateur led me to anticipate your using an amateur's methods, but you showed skill, madam, and the man I sent to keep watch over Mrs. Boppert against your looked-for visit there, was foiled by the very simple strategy you used in meeting her at a neighboring shop."

"Good!" I again cried, in my relief that the discovery made at that meeting had not been shared by him.

"We had sounded Mrs. Boppert ourselves, but she had seemed a very hopeless job, and I do not yet see how you got any water out of that stone—if you did."

"No?" I retorted ambiguously, enjoying the Inspector's manifest delight in this scene as much as I did my own secret thoughts and the prospect of the surprise I was holding in store for them.

"But your interference with the clock and the discovery you made that it had been going at the time the shelves fell, was not unknown to us, and we have made use of it, good use as you will hereafter see."

"So! those girls could not keep a secret after all," I muttered; and waited with some anxiety to hear him mention the pin-cushion; but he did not, greatly to my relief.

"Don't blame the girls!" he put in (his ears evidently are as sharp as mine); "the inquiries having proceeded from Franklin, it was only natural for me to suspect that he was trying to mislead us by some hocus-pocus story. So *I* visited the girls. That I had difficulty in getting to the root of the matter is to their credit, Miss Butterworth, seeing that you had made them promise secrecy."

"You are right," I nodded, and forgave them on the spot. If I could not withstand Mr. Gryce's eloquence—and it affected me at times—how could I expect these girls to. Besides, they had not revealed the more important secret I had confided to them, and in consideration of this I was ready to pardon them most anything.

"That the clock was going at the time the shelves fell, and that he should be the one to draw our attention to it would seem to the superficial mind proof positive that he was innocent of the deed with which it was so closely associated," the detective proceeded. "But to one skilled in the subterfuges of criminals, this seemingly conclusive fact in his favor was capable of an explanation so in keeping with the subtlety shown in every other feature of this remarkable crime, that I began to regard it as a point against him rather than in his favor. Of which more hereafter.

"Not allowing myself to be deterred, then, by this momentary setback, and rejoicing in an affair considered as settled by my superiors, I proceeded to establish Franklin Van Burnam's connection with the crime which had been laid with so much apparent reason at his brother's door.

"The first fact to be settled was, of course, whether your identification of him as the gentleman who accompanied his victim into Mr. Van Burnam's house could be corroborated by any of the many persons who had seen the so-called Mr. James Pope at the Hotel D———.

"As none of the witnesses who attended the inquest had presumed to recognize in either of these sleek and haughty gentlemen the shrinking person just mentioned, I knew that any open attempt on my part to bring about an identification would result disastrously. So I employed strategy—like my betters, Miss Butterworth" (here his bow was overpowering in its mock humility); "and rightly considering that for a person to be satisfactorily identified with another, he must be seen under the same circumstances and in nearly the same place, I sought out Franklin Van Burnam, and with specious promises of some great benefit to be done his brother, induced him to accompany me to the Hotel D———.

"Whether he saw through my plans and thought that a brave front and an assumption of candor would best serve him in this unexpected dilemma, or whether he felt so entrenched behind the precautions he had taken as not to fear discovery under any circumstances, he made but one demur before preparing to accompany me. This demur was significant, however, for it was occasioned by my advice to change his dress for one less conspicuously fashionable, or to hide it under an ulster or mackintosh. And as a proof of his hardihood—remember, madam, that his connection with this crime has been established—he actually did put on the ulster, though he must have known what a difference it would make in his appearance.

"The result was all I could desire. As we entered the hotel, I saw a certain hackman start and lean forward to look after him. It was the one who had driven Mr. and Mrs. Pope away from the hotel. And when we passed the porter, the wink which I gave him was met by a lift of his eyelids which he afterwards interpreted into 'Like! very like!'

"But it was from the clerk I received the most unequivocal proof of his identity. On entering the office I had left Mr. Van Burnam as near as possible to the spot where Mr. Pope had stood while his so-called wife was inscribing their names in the register, and bidding him to remain in the background while I had a few words at the desk, all in his brother's interests of course, I succeeded in secretly directing Mr. Henshaw's attention towards him. The start which he gave and the exclamation he uttered were unequivocal. 'Why, there's the man now!' he cried, happily in a whisper. 'Anxious look, drooping head, brown moustache, everything but the duster.' 'Bah!' said I; 'that's Mr. *Franklin* Van Burnam you are looking at! What are you thinking of?' 'Can't help it,' said he; 'I saw both of the brothers at the inquest, and saw nothing in them then to remind me of our late mysterious guest. But as he stands there, he's a —— sight more like James Pope than the other one is, and don't you forget it.' I shrugged my shoulders, told him he was a fool, and that fools had better keep their follies to themselves, and came away with my man, outwardly disgusted but inwardly in most excellent trim for pursuing an investigation which had opened so auspiciously.

"Whether this man possessed any motive for a crime so seemingly out of accordance with his life and disposition was, of course, the next point to settle. His conduct at the inquest certainly showed no decided animosity toward his brother's wife, nor was there on the surface of affairs any token of the mortal hatred which alone could account for a crime at once so deliberate and so brutal. But we detectives plunge below the surface, and after settling the question of Franklin's identity with the so-called Mr. Pope of the Hotel D——, I left New York and its interests—among which I reckoned your efforts at detective work, Miss Butterworth—to a young man in my office, who, I am afraid, did not quite understand the persistence of your character; for he had nothing to tell me concerning you on my return, save that you had been cultivating Miss Althorpe, which, of course, was such a natural thing for you to do, I wonder he thought it necessary to mention it.

"My destination was Four Corners, the place where Howard first met his future wife. In relating what I learned there, I shall doubtless repeat facts with which you are acquainted, Miss Butterworth."

"That is of no consequence," I returned, with almost brazen duplicity; for I not only was ignorant of what he was going to say, but had every reason to believe that it would bear as remote a connection as possible to the secret then laboring in my breast. "A statement of the case from your lips," I pursued, "will emphasize what I know. Do not stint any of your disclosures, then, I beg. I have an ear for all." This was truer than my rather sarcastic tone would convey, for might not his story after all prove to have some unexpected relation with the facts I had myself gathered together.

"It is a pleasure," said he, "to think I am capable of giving any information to Miss Butterworth, and as I did not run across you or your very nimble and pert little maid during my stay at Four Corners, I shall take it for granted that you confined your inquiries to the city and the society of which you are such a shining light."

This in reference to my double visit at Miss Althorpe's, no doubt.

"Four Corners is a charming town in Southern Vermont, and here, three years ago, Howard Van Burnam first met Miss Stapleton. She was living in a gentleman's family at that time as travelling companion to his invalid daughter."

Ah, now I could see what explanation this wary old detective gave himself of my visits to Miss Althorpe, and began to hug myself in anticipation of my coming triumph over him.

"The place did not fit her, for Miss Stapleton only shone in the society of men; but Mr. Harrison had not yet discovered this special idiosyncrasy of hers, and as his daughter was able to see a few friends, and in fact needed some diversion, the way was open to her companion for that acquaintance with Mr. Van Burnam which has led to such disastrous results.

"The house at which their meeting took place was a private one, and I soon found out many facts not widely known in this city. First, that she was not so much in love with Howard as he was with her. *He* succumbed to her fascinations at once, and proposed, I believe, within two weeks after seeing her; but though she accepted him, few of those who saw them together thought her affections very much engaged till Franklin suddenly appeared in town, when her whole manner underwent a change, and she became so sparklingly and irresistibly beautiful that her avowed lover became doubly enslaved, and Franklin—Well, there is evidence to prove that he was not insensible to her charms either; that, in spite of her engagement to his brother and the attitude which honor bade him hold towards his prospective sister-in-law, he lost his head for a short time at least, and under her seductions I do not doubt, for she was a double-faced woman according to general repute, went so far as to express his passion in a letter of which I heard much before I was so fortunate as to obtain a sight of it. This was three years ago, and I think Miss Stapleton would have been willing to have broken with Howard and married Franklin if the latter had had the courage to meet his brother's reproaches. But he evidently was deficient in this quality. His very letter, which is a warm one, but which holds out no hope to her of any closer bond between them than that offered by her prospective union with his brother, shows that he still retained some sense of honor, and as he presently left Four Corners and did not appear again where they were till just before their marriage, it is probable that all would have gone well if the woman had shared this sentiment with him. But she was made up of mean materials, and while willing to marry Howard for what he could give her or what she thought he could give her, she yet cherished an implacable grudge against Franklin for his weakness, as she called it, in not following the dictates of his heart. Being sly as well as passionate, she hid her feelings from every one but a venial, though apparently devoted confidante, a young girl named—"

"Oliver," I finished in my own mind.

But the name he mentioned was quite different.

"Pigot," he said, looking at the filigree basket he held in his hand as if he picked this word out from one of its many interstices. "She was French, and after once finding her, I had but little difficulty in learning all she had to tell. She had been Miss Harrison's maid, but she was not above serving Miss Stapleton in many secret and dishonorable ways. As a consequence, she could give me the details of an interview which that lady had held with Franklin Van Burnam on the evening of her wedding. It took place in Mr. Harrison's garden, and was supposed to be a secret one, but the woman who arranged the meeting was not the person to keep away from it when it occurred, and consequently I have been enabled to learn with more or less accuracy what took place between them. It was not to Miss Stapleton's credit. Mr. Van Burnam merely wanted his letter back, but she refused to return it unless he would promise her a complete recognition by his family of her marriage and ensure her a reception in his father's house as Howard's wife. This was more than he could engage himself to perform. He had already, according to his own story, made every effort possible to influence the old gentleman in her favor, but had only succeeded in irritating him against himself. It was an acknowledgment which would have satisfied most women, but it did not satisfy her. She declared her intention of keeping the letter for fear he would cease his exertions; and heedless of the effect produced upon him by the barefaced threat, proceeded to inveigh against his brother for the very love which made her union with him possible; and as if this was not bad enough, showed at the same time such a disposition to profit by whatever worldly good the match promised, that Franklin lost all regard for her, and began to hate her.

"As he made no effort to conceal his feelings, she must have become immediately aware of the change which had taken place in them. But however affected by this, she gave no sign of relenting in her purpose. On the contrary, she persisted in her determination to retain his letter, and when he remonstrated with her and threatened to leave town before her marriage, she retorted by saying that, if he did so, she would show his letter to his brother as soon as the minister had made them one. This threat seemed to affect Franklin deeply, and while it intensified his feeling of animosity towards her, subjected him for the moment to her whim. He stayed in Four Corners till the ceremony was performed, but was such a gloomy guest that all united in saying that he did the occasion no credit.

"So much for my work in Four Corners."

I had by this time become aware that Mr. Gryce was addressing himself chiefly to the Inspector, being gratified no doubt at this opportunity of presenting his case at length before that gentleman. But true to his special habits, he looked at neither of us, but rather at the fretted basket, upon the handle of which he tapped out his arguments as he quickly proceeded:

"The young couple spent the first months of their married life in Yonkers; so to Yonkers I went next. There I learned that Franklin had visited the place twice; both times, as I judge, upon a peremptory summons from her. The result was mutual fret and heartburning, for she had made no progress in her endeavors to win recognition from the Van Burnams; and even had had occasion to perceive that her husband's love, based as it was upon her physical attributes, had begun to feel the stress of her uneasiness and dissatisfaction. She became more anxious than ever for social recognition and distinction, and when the family went to Europe, consented to accompany her husband into the quiet retreat he thought best calculated to win the approbation of his father, only upon the assurance of better times in the fall and a possible visit to Washington in the winter. But the quiet to which she was subjected had a bad effect upon her. Under it she grew more and more restless, and as the time approached for the family's return, conceived so many plans for conciliating them that her husband could not restrain his disgust. But the worst plan of all and the one which undoubtedly led to her death, he never knew. This was to surprise Franklin at his office and, by renewed threats of showing this old love-letter to his brother, win an absolute promise from him to support her in a fresh endeavor to win his father's favor. You see she did not understand Silas Van Burnam's real character, and persisted in holding the most extravagant views concerning Franklin's ascendancy over him as well as over the rest of the family. She even went so far as to insist in the interview, which Jane Pigot overheard, that it was

Franklin himself who stood in the way of her desires, and that if he chose he could obtain for her an invitation to take up her abode with the rest of them in Gramercy Park. To Duane Street she therefore went before making her appearance at Mrs. Parker's; a fact which was not brought out at the inquest; Franklin not disclosing it of course, and the clerk not recognizing her under the false name she chose to give. Of the details of this interview I am ignorant, but as she was closeted with him some time, it is only natural to suppose that conversation of some importance took place between them. The clerk who works in the outer office did not, as I have said, know who she was at the time, but he noticed her face when she came out, and he declares that it was insolent with triumph, while Mr. Franklin, who was polite enough or calculating enough to bow her out of the room, was pale with rage, and acted so unlike himself that everybody observed it. She held his letter in her hand, a letter easily distinguishable by the violet-colored seal on the back, and she filliped with it in a most aggravating way as she crossed the floor, pretending to lay it down on Howard's desk as she went by and then taking it up again with an arch look at Franklin, pretty enough to see but hateful in its effect on him. As he went back to his own room his face was full of anger, and such was the effect of this visit on him that he declined to see any one else that day. She had probably shown such determination to reveal his past perfidy to her husband, that his fears were fully aroused at last, and he saw he was not only likely to lose his good name but the esteem with which he was accustomed to be regarded by this younger and evidently much-loved brother.

"And now, considering his intense pride, as well as his affection for Howard, do you not see the motive which this seemingly good man had for putting his troublesome sister-in-law out of existence? He wanted that letter back, and to obtain it had to resort to crime. Or such is my present theory of this murder, Miss Butterworth. Does it correspond with yours?"

CHAPTER XXXI

Some Fine Work

"O perfectly!" I assented, with just the shade of irony necessary to rob the assertion of its mendacity. "But go on, go on. You have not begun to satisfy me yet. You did not stop with finding a motive for the crime I am sure."

"Madam, you are a female Shylock; you will have the whole of the bond or none."

"We are not here to draw comparisons," I retorted. "Keep to the subject, Mr. Gryce; keep to the subject."

He laughed; laid down the little basket he held, took it up again, and finally resumed:

"Madam, you are right; we did not stop at finding a motive. Our next step was to collect evidence directly connecting him with the crime."

"And you succeeded in this?"

My tone was unnecessarily eager, this was all so unaccountable to me; but he did not appear to notice it.

"We did. Indeed the evidence against him is stronger than that against his brother. For if we ignore the latter part of Howard's testimony, which was evidently a tissue of lies, what remains against him? Three things: his dogged persistency in not recognizing his wife in the murdered woman; the receiving of the house keys from his brother; and the fact that he was seen on the stoop of his father's house at an unusual hour in the morning following this murder. Now what have we against Franklin? Many things.

"First:

"That he can no more account for the hours between half-past eleven on Tuesday morning and five o'clock on the following Wednesday morning than his brother can. In one breath he declares that he was shut up in his rooms at the hotel, for which no corroborative evidence is forthcoming; and in another that he was on a tramp after his brother, which seems equally improbable and incapable of proof.

"Second:

"That he and not Howard was the man in a linen duster, and that he and not Howard was in possession of the keys that night. As these are serious statements to make, I will give you my reasons for them. They are distinct from the recognition of his person by the inmates of the Hotel D——, and added to that recognition, form a strong case against him. The janitor who has charge of the offices in Duane Street, happening to have a leisure moment on the morning of the day on which Mrs. Van Burnam was murdered, was making the most of it by watching the unloading of a huge boiler some four doors below the Van Burnam warehouse. He was consequently looking intently in that direction when Howard passed him, coming from the interview with his brother in which he had been given the keys. Mr. Van Burnam was walking briskly, but finding the sidewalk blocked by the boiler to which I have alluded, paused for a moment to let it pass, and being greatly heated, took out his handkerchief to wipe his forehead. This done, he moved on, just as a man dressed in a long duster came up behind him, stopping where he stopped and picking up from the ground something which the first gentleman had evidently dropped. This last man's figure looked more or less familiar to the janitor, so did the duster, and later he discovered that the latter was the one which he had seen hanging for so long a time in the little disused closet under the warehouse stairs. Its wearer was Franklin Van Burnam, who, as I took pains to learn, had left the office immediately in the wake of his brother, and the object he picked up was the bunch of keys which the latter had inadvertently dropped. He may have thought he lost them later, but it was then and there they slipped from his pocket. I will here add that the duster found by the hackman in his coach has been identified as the one missing from the closet just mentioned.

"Third:

"The keys with which Mr. Van Burnam's house was unlocked were found hanging in their usual place by noon of the next day. They could not have been taken there by Howard, for he was not seen at the office after the murder. By whom then were they returned, if not by Franklin?

"Fourth:

"The letter, for the possession of which I believe this crime to have been perpetrated, was found by us in a supposedly secret drawer of this gentleman's desk. It was much crumpled, and bore evidences of having been rather rudely dealt with since it was last seen in Mrs. Van Burnam's hand in that very office.

"But the fact which is most convincing, and which will tell most heavily against him, is the unexpected discovery of the murdered lady's rings, also in this same desk. How *you* became aware that anything of such importance could be found there, knowing even the exact place in which they were secreted, I will not stop to ask at this moment. Enough that when your maid entered the Van Burnam offices and insisted with so much ingenuousness that she was expected by Mr. Van Burnam and would wait for his return, the clerk most devoted to my interests became distrustful of her intentions, having been told to be on the look-out for a girl in gray or a lady in black with puffs on each side of two very sharp eyes. You will pardon me, Miss Butterworth. He therefore kept his eyes on the girl and presently espied her stretching out her hand towards a hook at the side of Mr. Franklin Van Burnam's desk. As it is upon this hook this gentleman strings his unanswered letters, the clerk rose from his place as quickly as possible, and coming forward with every appearance of polite solicitude—did she not say he was polite, Miss Butterworth?—inquired what she wished, thinking she was after some letter, or possibly anxious for a specimen of someone's handwriting. But she gave him no other reply than a blush and a confused look, for which you must rebuke her, Miss Butterworth, if you are going to continue to employ her as your agent in these very delicate affairs. And she made another mistake. She should not have left so abruptly upon detection, for that gave the clerk an opportunity to telephone for me, which he immediately did. I was at liberty, and I came at once, and, after hearing his story, decided that what was of interest to you must be of interest to me, and so took a look at the letters she had handled, and discovered, what she also must have discovered before she let them slip from her hand, that the five missing rings we were all in search of were hanging on this same hook amid the sheets of Franklin's correspondence. You can imagine, madam, my satisfaction, and the gratitude which I felt towards my agent, who by his quickness had retained to me the honors of a discovery which it would have been injurious to my pride to have had confined entirely to yourself."

"I can understand," I repeated, and trusted myself to say no more, hot as my secret felt upon my lips.

"You have read Poe's story of the filigree basket?" he now suggested, running his finger up and down the filigree work he himself held.

I nodded. I saw what he meant at once.

"Well, the principle involved in that story explains the presence of the rings in the midst of this stack of letters. Franklin Van Burnam, if he is the murderer of his sister-in-law, is one of the subtlest villains this city has ever produced, and knowing that, if once suspected, every secret drawer and professed hiding-place within his reach would be searched, he put these dangerous evidences of his guilt in a place so conspicuous, and yet so little likely to attract attention, that even so old a hand as myself did not think of looking for them there."

He had finished, and the look he gave me was for myself alone.

"And now, madam," said he, "that I have stated the facts of the case against Franklin Van Burnam, has not the moment come for you to show your appreciation of my good nature by a corresponding show of confidence on your part?"

I answered with a distinct negative. "There is too much that is unexplained as yet in your case against Franklin," I objected. "You have shown that he had motive for the murder and that he was connected more or less intimately with the crime we are considering, but you have by no means explained all the phenomena accompanying this tragedy. How, for instance, do you account for Mrs. Van Burnam's whim in changing her clothing, if her brother-in-law, instead of her husband, was her companion at the Hotel D———?"

You see I was determined to know the whole story before introducing Miss Oliver's name into this complication.

He who had seen through the devices of so many women in his day did not see through mine, perhaps because he took a certain professional pleasure in making his views on this subject clear to the attentive Inspector. At all events, this is the way he responded to my half-curious, half-ironical question:

"A crime planned and perpetrated for the purpose I have just mentioned, Miss Butterworth, could not have been a simple one under any circumstances. But conceived as this one was by a man of more than ordinary intelligence, and carried out with a skill and precaution little short of marvellous, the features which it presents are of such a varying and subtle character that only by the exercise of a certain amount of imagination can they be understood at all. Such an imagination I possess, but how can I be sure that you do?"

"By testing it," I suggested.

"Very good, madam, I will. Not from actual knowledge, then, but from a certain insight I have acquired in my long dealing with such matters, I have come to the conclusion that Franklin Van Burnam did not in the beginning plan to kill this woman in his father's house.

"On the contrary, he had fixed upon a hotel room as the scene of the conflict he foresaw between them, and that he might carry it on without endangering their good names, had urged her to meet him the next morning in the semi-disguise of a gossamer over her fine dress and a heavy veil over her striking features; making the pretence, no doubt, of this being the more appropriate costume for her to appear in before the old gentleman should he so far concede to her demands as to take her to the steamer. For himself he had planned the adoption of a disfiguring duster which had been hanging for a long time in a closet on the ground-floor of the building in Duane Street. All this promised well, but when the time came and he was about to leave his office, his brother unexpectedly appeared and asked for the key to their father's house. Disconcerted no doubt by the appearance of the very person he least wished to see, and astonished by a request so out of keeping with all that had hitherto passed between them, he nevertheless was in too much haste to question him, so gave him what he wanted and Howard went away. As soon after as he could lock his desk and don his hat, Franklin followed, and merely stopping to cover his coat with the old duster, he went out and hastened towards the place of meeting. Under most circumstances all this might have happened without the brothers encountering each other again, but a temporary obstruction on the sidewalk having, as we know, detained Howard, Franklin was enabled to approach him sufficiently close to see him draw his pocket-handkerchief out of his pocket, and with it the keys which he had just given him. The latter fell, and as there was a great pounding of iron going on in the building just over their heads, Howard did not perceive his loss but went quickly on. Franklin coming up behind him picked up the keys, and with a thought, or perhaps as yet with no thought, of the use to which they might be applied, put them in his own pocket before proceeding on his way.

"New York is a large place, and much can take place in it without comment. Franklin Van Burnam and his sister-in-law met and went together to the Hotel D—— without being either recognized or suspected till later developments drew attention to them. That *she* should consent to accompany him to this place, and that after she was there should submit, as she did, to taking all the business of the scheme upon herself, would be inconceivable in a woman of a self-respecting character; but Louise Van Burnam cared for little save her own aggrandisement, and rather enjoyed, so far as we can see, this very doubtful escapade, whose real meaning and murderous purpose she was so far from understanding.

"As the steamer, contrary to all expectation, had not yet been sighted off Fire Island, they took a room and prepared to wait for it. That is, *she* prepared to wait. He had no intention of waiting for its arrival or of going to it when it came; he only wanted his letter. But Louise Van Burnam was not the woman to relinquish it till she had obtained the price she had put on it, and he becoming very soon aware of this fact, began to ask himself if he should not be obliged to resort to extreme measures in order to regain it. One chance only remained for avoiding these. He would seem to embrace her later and probably much-talked-of scheme of presenting herself before his father in his own house rather than at the steamer; and by urging her to make its success more certain by a different style of dress from that she wore, induce a change of clothing, during which he might come upon the letter he was more than confident she carried about her person. Had this plan worked; had he been able to seize upon this compromising bit of paper, even at the cost of a scratch or two from her vigorous fingers, we should not be sitting here at this moment trying to account for the most complicated crime on record. But Louise Van Burnam, while weak and volatile enough to enjoy the romantic features of this transformation scene, even going so far as to write out the order herself with the same effort at disguise she had used in registering their assumed names at the desk, was not entirely his dupe, and having hidden the letter in her shoe—"

"What!" I cried.

"*Having hidden the letter in her shoe*," repeated Mr. Gryce, with his finest smile, "she had but to signify that the boots sent by Altman were a size too small, for her to retain her secret and keep the one article she traded upon from his envious clutch. You seem struck dumb by this, Miss Butterworth. Have I enlightened you on a point that has hitherto troubled you?"

"Don't ask me; don't look at me." As if he ever looked at any one! "Your perspicacity is amazing, but I will try and not show my sense of it, if it is going to make you stop."

He smiled; the Inspector smiled: neither understood me.

"Very well then, I will go on; but the non-change of shoes had to be accounted for, Miss Butterworth."

"You are right; and it *has* been, of course."

"Have you any better explanation to give?"

I had, or thought I had, and the words trembled on my tongue. But I restrained myself under an air of great impatience. "Time is flying!" I urged, with as near a simulation of his own manner in saying the words as I could affect. "Go on, Mr. Gryce."

And he did, though my manner evidently puzzled him.

"Being foiled in this his last attempt, this smooth and diabolical villain hesitated no longer in carrying out the scheme which had doubtless been maturing in his mind ever since he dropped the key of his father's house into his own pocket. His brother's wife must die, but not in a hotel room with him for a companion. Though scorned, detested, and a stumbling-block in the way of the whole family's future happiness and prosperity, she still was a Van Burnam, and no shadow must fall upon her reputation. Further than this, for he loved life and his own reputation also, and did not mean to endanger either by this act of self-preservation, she must perish as if from accident, or by some blow so undiscoverable that it would be laid to natural causes. He thought he knew how this might be brought about. He had seen her put on her hat with a very thin and sharp pin, and he had heard how one thrust into a certain spot in the spine would effect death without a struggle. A wound like that would be small; almost indiscernible. True it would take skill to inflict it, and it would require dissimulation to bring her into the proper position for the contemplated thrust; but he was not lacking in either of these characteristics; and so he set himself to the task he had promised himself, and with such success that ere long the two left the hotel and proceeded to the house in Gramercy Park with all the caution necessary for preserving a secret which meant reputation to the one, and liberty, if not life, to the other. That he and not she felt the greater need of secrecy, witness their whole conduct, and when, their goal reached, she and not he put the money into the driver's hand, the last act of this curious drama of opposing motives was reached, and only the final catastrophe was wanting.

"With what arts he procured her hat-pin, and by what show of simulated passion he was able to approach near enough to her to inflict that cool and calculating thrust which resulted in her immediate death, I leave to *your* imagination. Enough that he compassed his ends, killing her and regaining the letter for the possession of which he had been willing to take a life. Afterwards—"

"Well, afterwards?"

"The deed he had thought so complete began to assume a different aspect. The pin had broken in the wound, and, knowing the scrutiny which the body would receive at the hands of a Coroner's jury, he began to see what consequences might follow its discovery. So to hide that wound and give to her death the wished-for appearance of accident, he went back and drew down the cabinet under which she was found. Had he done this at once his hand in the tragedy might have escaped detection, but he waited, and by waiting allowed the blood-vessels to stiffen and all that phenomena to become apparent by means of which the eyes of the physicians were opened to the fact that they must search deeper for the cause of death than the bruises she had received. Thus it is that Justice opens loop-holes in the finest web a criminal can weave."

"A just remark, Mr. Gryce, but in this fine-spun web of *your* weaving, you have not explained how the clock came to be running and to stop at five."

"Cannot you see? A man capable of such a crime would not forget to provide himself with an alibi. He expected to be in his rooms at five, so before pulling down the shelves at three or four, he wound the clock and set it at an hour when he could bring forward testimony to his being in another place. Is not such a theory consistent with his character and with the skill he has displayed from the beginning to the end of this woful affair?"

Aghast at the deftness with which this able detective explained every detail of this crime by means of a theory necessarily hypothetical if the discoveries I had made in the matter were true, and for the moment subjected to the overwhelming influence of his enthusiasm, I sat in a maze, asking myself if all the seemingly irrefutable evidence upon which men had been convicted in times gone by was as false as this. To relieve myself and to gain renewed confidence in my own views and the discoveries I had made in this matter, I repeated the name of Howard, and asked how, in case the whole crime was conceived and perpetrated by his brother, he came to utter such equivocations and to assume that position of guilt which had led to his own arrest.

"Do you think," I inquired, "that he was aware of his brother's part in this affair, and that out of compassion for him he endeavored to take the crime upon his own shoulders?"

"No, madam. Men of the world do not carry their disinterestedness so far. He not only did not know the part his brother took in this crime, but did not even suspect it, or why acknowledge that he lost the key by which the house was entered?"

"I do not understand Howard's actions, even under these circumstances. They seem totally inconsistent to me."

"Madam, they are easily explainable to one who knows the character of his mind. He prizes his honor above every consideration, and regarded it as threatened by the suggestion that his wife had entered his father's empty house at midnight with another man. To save himself that shame, he was willing not only to perjure himself, but to take upon himself the consequences of his perjury. Quixotic, certainly, but some men are constituted that way, and he, for all his amiable characteristics, is the most dogged man I ever encountered. That he ran against snags in his attempted explanations, seemed to make no difference to him. He was bound that no one should accuse him of marrying a false woman, even if he must bear the opprobrium of her death. It is hard to understand such a nature, but re-read his testimony, and see if this explanation of his conduct is not correct."

And still I mechanically repeated: "I do not understand."

Mr. Gryce may not have been a patient man under all circumstances, but he was patient with me that day.

"It was his ignorance, Miss Butterworth, his total ignorance of the whole affair that led him into the inconsistencies he manifested. Let me present his case as I already have his brother's. He knew that his wife had come to New York to appeal to his father, and he gathered from what she said that she intended to do this either in his house or on the dock. To cut short any opportunity she might have for committing the first folly, he begged the key of the house from his brother, and, supposing that he had it all right, went to his rooms, not to Coney Island as he said, and began to pack up his trunks. For he meant to flee the country if his wife disgraced him. He was tired of her caprices and meant to cut them short as far as he was himself concerned. But the striking of the midnight hour brought better counsel. He began to wonder what she had been doing in his absence. Going out, he haunted the region of Gramercy Park for the better part of the night, and at daybreak actually mounted the steps of his father's house and prepared to enter it by means of the key he had obtained from his brother. But the key was not in his pocket, so he came down again and walked away, attracting the attention of Mr. Stone as he did so. The next day he heard of the tragedy which had taken place within those very walls; and though his first fears led him to believe that the victim was his wife, a sight of her clothes naturally dispelled this apprehension, for he knew nothing of her visit to the Hotel D—— or of the change in her habiliments which had taken place there. His father's persistent fears and the quiet pressure brought to bear upon him by the police only irritated him, and not until confronted by the hat found on the scene of death, an article only too well known as his wife's, did he yield to the accumulated evidence in support of her identity. Immediately he felt the full force of his unkindness towards her, and rushing to the Morgue had her poor body taken to that father's house and afterwards given a decent burial. But he could not accept the shame which this acknowledgment naturally brought with it, and, blind to all consequences, insisted, when brought up again for examination, that he was the man with whom she came to that lonely house. The difficulties into which this plunged him were partly foreseen and partly prepared for, and he showed some skill in surmounting them. But falsehoods never fit like truths, and we all felt the strain on our credulity as he met and attempted to parry the Coroner's questions.

"And now, Miss Butterworth, let me again ask if your turn has not come at last for adding the sum of your evidence to ours against Franklin Van Burnam?"

It had; I could not deny it, and as I realized that with it had also come the opportunity for justifying the pretensions I had made, I raised my head with suitable spirit and, after a momentary pause for the purpose of making my words the more impressive, I asked:

"And what has made you think that *I* was interested in fixing the guilt on Franklin Van Burnam?"

CHAPTER XXXII

Iconoclasm

The surprise which this very simple question occasioned, showed itself differently in the two men who heard it. The Inspector, who had never seen me before, simply stared, while Mr. Gryce, with that admirable command over himself which has helped to make him the most successful man on the force, retained his impassibility, though I noticed a small corner drop from my filigree basket as if crushed off by an inadvertent pressure of his hand.

"I judged," was his calm reply, as he laid down the injured toy with an apologetic grunt, "that the clearing of Howard from suspicion meant the establishment of another man's guilt; and so far as we can see there has been no other party in the case besides these two brothers."

"No? Then I fear a great surprise awaits you, Mr. Gryce. This crime, which you have fixed with such care and seeming probability upon Franklin Van Burnam, was not, in my judgment, perpetrated either by him or any other man. It was the act of a woman."

"A woman?"

Both men spoke: the Inspector, as if he thought me demented; Mr. Gryce, as if he would like to have considered me a fool but dared not.

"Yes, a *woman*," I repeated, dropping a quiet curtsey. It was a proper expression of respect when I was young, and I see no reason why it should not be a proper expression of respect now, except that we have lost our manners in gaining our independence, something which is to be regretted perhaps. "A woman whom I know; a woman whom I can lay my hands on at a half-hour's notice; a young woman, sirs; a pretty woman, the owner of one of the two hats found in the Van Burnam parlors."

Had I exploded a bomb-shell the Inspector could not have looked more astounded. The detective, who was a man of greater self-command, did not betray his feelings so plainly, though he was not entirely without them, for, as I made this statement, he turned and looked at me; *Mr. Gryce* looked at me.

"Both of those hats belonged to Mrs. Van Burnam," he protested; "the one she wore from Haddam; the other was in the order from Altman's."

"She never ordered anything from Altman's," was my uncompromising reply. "The woman whom I saw enter next door, and who was the same who left the Hotel D—— with the man in the linen duster, was not Louise Van Burnam. She was that lady's rival, and let me say it, for I dare to think it, not only her rival but the prospective taker of her life. O you need not shake your heads at each other so significantly, gentlemen. I have been collecting evidence as well as yourselves, and what I have learned is very much to the point; very much, indeed."

"The deuce you have!" muttered the Inspector, turning away from me; but Mr. Gryce continued to eye me like a man fascinated.

"Upon what," said he, "do you base these extraordinary assertions? I should like to hear what that evidence is."

"But first," said I, "I must take a few exceptions to certain points you consider yourself to have made against Franklin Van Burnam. You believe him to have committed this crime because you found in a secret drawer of his desk a letter known to have been in Mrs. Van Burnam's hands the day she was murdered, and which you, naturally enough, I acknowledge, conceive he could only have regained by murdering her. But have you not thought of another way in which he could have obtained it, a perfectly harmless way, involving no one either in deceit or crime? May it not have been in the little hand-bag returned by Mrs. Parker on the morning of the discovery, and may not its crumpled condition be accounted for by the haste with which Franklin might have thrust it into his secret drawer at the untoward entrance of someone into his office?"

"I acknowledge that I have not thought of such a possibility," growled the detective, below his breath, but I saw that his self-satisfaction had been shaken.

"As for any proof of complicity being given by the presence of the rings on the hook attached to his desk, I grieve for your sake to be obliged to dispel that illusion also. Those rings, Mr. Gryce and Mr. Inspector, were not discovered there by the girl in gray, but taken there; and hung there at the very moment your spy saw her hand fumbling with the papers."

"Taken there, and hung there by your maid! By the girl Lena, who has so evidently been working in *your* interests! What sort of a confession are you making, Miss Butterworth?"

"Ah, Mr. Gryce," I gently remonstrated, for I actually pitied the old man in his hour of humiliation, "other girls wear gray besides Lena. It was the woman of the Hotel D—— who played this trick in Mr. Van Burnam's office. Lena was not out of my house that day."

I had never thought Mr. Gryce feeble, though I knew he was over seventy if not very near the octogenarian age. But he drew up a chair at this and hastily sat down.

"Tell me about this other girl," said he.

But before I repeat what I said to him, I must explain by what reasoning I had arrived at the conclusion I have just mentioned. That Ruth Oliver was the visitor in Mr. Van Burnam's office there was but little reason to doubt; that her errand was one in connection with the rings was equally plain. What else would have driven her from her bed when she was hardly able to stand, and sent her in a state of fever, if not delirium, down town to this office?

She feared having these rings found in her possession, and she also cherished a desire to throw whatever suspicion was attached to them upon the man who was already compromised. She may have thought it was Howard's desk she approached, and she may have known it to be Franklin's. On that point I was in doubt, but the rest was clear to me from the moment Mr. Gryce mentioned the girl in gray; and even the spot where she had kept them in the interim since the murder was no longer an unsolved mystery to me. Her emotion when I touched her knitting-work and the shreds of unravelled wool I had found lying about after her departure, had set my wits working, and I comprehended now *that they had been wound up in the ball of yarn I had so carelessly handled.*

But what had I to say to Mr. Gryce in answer to his question. Much; and seeing that further delay was injudicious, I began my story then and there. Prefacing my tale with the suspicions I had always had of Mrs. Boppert, I told them of my interview with that woman and of the valuable clue she had given me by confessing that she had let Mrs. Van Burnam into the house prior to the visit of the couple who entered there at midnight. Knowing what an effect this must produce upon Mr. Gryce, utterly unprepared for it as he was, I looked for some burst of anger on his part, or at least some expression of self-reproach. But he only broke a second piece off my little filigree basket, and, totally unconscious of the demolition he was causing, cried out with true professional delight:

"Well! well! I've always said this was a remarkable case, a very remarkable case; but if we don't look out it will go ahead of that one at Sibley. *Two* women in the affair, and one of them in the house before the arrival of the so-called victim and her murderer! What do you think of that, Inspector? Rather late for us to find out so important a detail, eh?"

"Rather," was the dry reply. At which Mr. Gryce's face grew long and he exclaimed, half shamefacedly, half jocularly:

"Outwitted by a woman! Well, it's a new experience for me, Inspector, and you must not be surprised if it takes me a minute or so to get accustomed to it. A scrub-woman too! It cuts, Inspector, it cuts."

But as I went on, and he learned how I had obtained definite proof of the clock having been not only wound by the lady thus admitted to the house, but set also and that correctly, his face grew even longer, and he gazed quite dolefully at the small figure in the carpet to which he had transferred his attention.

"So! so!" came in almost indistinguishable murmur from his lips. "All my pretty theory in regard to its being set by the criminal for the purpose of confirming his attempt at a false alibi was but a figment of my imagination, eh? Sad! sad! But it was neat enough to have been true, was it not, Inspector?"

"Quite," that gentleman good-humoredly admitted, yet with a shade of irony in his tone that made me suspect that, for all his confidence in and evident admiration for this brilliant old detective, he felt a certain amount of pleasure at seeing him for once at fault. Perhaps it gave him more confidence in his own judgment, seeing that their ideas on this case had been opposed from the start.

"Well! well! I'm getting old; that's what they'll say at Headquarters tomorrow. But go on, Miss Butterworth; let us hear what followed; for I am sure your investigations did not stop there."

I complied with his request with as much modesty as possible. But it was hard to suppress all triumph in face of the unrestrained enthusiasm with which he received my communication. When I told him of the doubts I had formed in regard to the disposal of the packages brought from the Hotel D——, and how to settle those doubts I had taken that midnight walk down Twenty-seventh Street, he looked astonished, his lips worked, and I really expected to see him try to pluck that flower up from the carpet, he ogled it so lovingly. But when I mentioned the lighted laundry and my discoveries there, his admiration burst all bounds, and he cried out, seemingly to the rose in the carpet, really to the Inspector:

"Didn't I tell you she was a woman in a thousand? See now! we ought to have thought of that laundry ourselves; but we didn't, none of us did; we were too credulous and too easily satisfied with the evidence given at the inquest. Well, I'm seventy-seven, but I'm not too old to learn. Proceed, Miss Butterworth."

I admired him and I was sorry for him, but I never enjoyed myself so much in my whole life. How could I help it, or how could I prevent myself from throwing a glance now and then at the picture of my father smiling upon me from the opposite wall?

It was my task now to mention the advertisement I had inserted in the newspapers, and the reflections which had led to my rather daring description of the wandering woman as one dressed thus and so, and *without a hat*. This seemed to strike him—as I had expected it would—and he interrupted me with a quick slap of his leg, for which only that leg was prepared.

"Good!" he ejaculated; "a fine stroke! The work of a woman of genius! I could not have done better myself, Miss Butterworth. And what came of it? Something, I hope; talent like yours should not go unrewarded."

"Two letters came of it," said I. "One from Cox, the milliner, saying that a bareheaded girl had bought a hat in his shop early on the morning designated; and another from a Mrs. Desberger appointing a meeting at which I obtained a definite clue to this girl, who, notwithstanding she wore Mrs. Van Burnam's clothes from the scene of tragedy, is not Mrs. Van Burnam herself, but a person by the name of Oliver, now to be found at Miss Althorpe's house in Twenty-first Street."

As this was in a measure putting the matter into their hands, I saw them both grow impatient in their anxiety to see this girl for themselves. But I kept them for a few minutes longer while I related my discovery of the money in her shoes, and hinted at the explanation it afforded for her not changing those articles under the influence of the man who accompanied her.

This was the last blow I dealt to the pride of Mr. Gryce. He quivered under it, but soon recovered, and was able to enjoy what he called another fine point in this remarkable case.

But the acme of his delight was reached when I informed him of my ineffectual search for the rings, and my final conclusion that they had been wound up in the ball of yarn attached to her knitting-work.

Whether his pleasure lay chiefly in the talent shown by Miss Oliver in her choice of a hiding-place for these jewels, or in the acumen displayed by myself in discovering it, I do not know; but he evinced an unbounded satisfaction in my words, crying aloud:

"Beautiful! I don't know of anything more interesting! We have not seen the like in years! I can almost congratulate myself upon my mistakes, the features of the case they have brought out are so fine!"

But his satisfaction, great as it was, soon gave way to his anxiety to see this girl who, if not the criminal herself, was so important a factor in this great crime.

I was anxious myself to have him see her, though I feared her condition was not such as to promise him any immediate enlightenment on the doubtful portions of this far from thoroughly mastered problem. And I bade him interview the Chinaman also, and Mrs. Desberger, and even

Mrs. Boppert, for I did not wish him to take for granted anything I had said, though I saw he had lost his attitude of disdain and was inclined to accept my opinions quite seriously.

He answered in quite an off-hand manner while the Inspector stood by, but when that gentleman had withdrawn towards the door, Mr. Gryce remarked with more earnestness than he had yet used:

"You have saved me from committing a folly, Miss Butterworth. If I had arrested Franklin Van Burnam today, and tomorrow all these facts had come to light, I should never have held up my head again. As it is, there will be numerous insinuations uttered by men on the force, and many a whisper will go about that Gryce is getting old, that Gryce has seen his best days."

"Nonsense!" was my vigorous rejoinder. "You didn't have the clue, that is all. Nor did I get it through any keenness on my part, but from the force of circumstances. Mrs. Boppert thought herself indebted to me, and so gave me her confidence. Your laurels are very safe yet. Besides, there is enough work left on this case to keep more than one great detective like you busy. While the Van Burnams have not been proved guilty, they are not so freed from suspicion that you can regard your task as completed. If Ruth Oliver committed this crime, which of these two brothers was involved in it with her? The facts seem to point towards Franklin, but not so unerringly that no doubt is possible on the subject."

"True, true. The mystery has deepened rather than cleared. Miss Butterworth, you will accompany me to Miss Althorpe's."

CHAPTER XXXIII

"Known, Known, All Known"

Mr. Gryce possesses one faculty for which I envy him, and that is his skill in the management of people. He had not been in Miss Althorpe's house five minutes before he had won her confidence and had everything he wished at his command. *I* had to talk some time before getting so far, but *he*—a word and a look did it.

Miss Oliver, for whom I hesitated to inquire, lest I should again find her gone or in a worse condition than when I left, was in reality better, and as we went upstairs I allowed myself to hope that the questions which had so troubled us would soon be answered and the mystery ended.

But Mr. Gryce evidently knew better, for when we reached her door he turned and said:

"Our task will not be an easy one. Go in first and attract her attention so that I can enter unobserved. I wish to study her before addressing her; but, mind, no words about the murder; leave that to me."

I nodded, feeling that I was falling back into my own place; and knocking softly entered the room.

A maid was sitting with her. Seeing me, she rose and advanced, saying:

"Miss Oliver is sleeping."

"Then I will relieve you," I returned, beckoning Mr. Gryce to come in.

The girl left us and we two contemplated the sick woman silently. Presently I saw Mr. Gryce shake his head. But he did not tell me what he meant by it.

Following the direction of his finger, I sat down in a chair at the head of the bed; he took his station at the side of it in a large arm-chair he saw there. As he did so I saw how fatherly and kind he really looked, and wondered if he was in the habit of so preparing himself to meet the eye of all the suspected criminals he encountered. The thought made me glance again her way. She lay like a statue, and her face, naturally round but now thinned out and hollow, looked up from the pillow in pitiful quiet, the long lashes accentuating the dark places under her eyes.

A sad face, the saddest I ever saw and one of the most haunting.

He seemed to find it so also, for his expression of benevolent interest deepened with every passing moment, till suddenly she stirred; then he gave me a warning glance, and stooping, took her by the wrist and pulled out his watch.

She was deceived by the action. Opening her eyes, she surveyed him languidly for a moment, then heaving a great sigh, turned aside her head.

"Don't tell me I am better, doctor. I do not want to live."

The plaintive tone, the refined accent, seemed to astonish him. Laying down her hand, he answered gently:

"I do not like to hear that from such young lips, but it assures me that I was correct in my first surmise, that it is not medicine you need but a friend. And I can be that friend if you will but allow me."

Moved, encouraged for the instant, she turned her head from side to side, probably to see if they were alone, and not observing me, answered softly:

"You are very good, very thoughtful, doctor, but"—and here her despair returned again—"it is useless; you can do nothing for me."

"You think so," remonstrated the old detective, "but you do not know me, child. Let me show you that I can be of benefit to you." And he drew from his pocket a little package which he opened before her astonished eyes. "Yesterday, in your delirium, you left these rings in an office downtown. As they are valuable, I have brought them back to you. Wasn't I right, my child?"

"No! no!" She started up, and her accents betrayed terror and anguish, "I do not want them; I cannot bear to see them; they do not belong to *me*; they belong to *them*."

"To *them*? Whom do you mean by them?" queried Mr. Gryce, insinuatingly.

"The—the Van Burnams. Is not that the name? Oh, do not make me talk; I am so weak! Only take the rings back."

"I will, child, I will." Mr. Gryce's voice was more than fatherly now, it was tender, really and sincerely tender. "I will take them back; but to which of the brothers shall I return them? To"—he hesitated softly—"to Franklin or to Howard?"

I expected to hear her respond, his manner was so gentle and apparently sincere. But though feverish and on the verge of wildness, she had still some command over herself, and after giving him a look, the intensity of which called out a corresponding expression on his face, she faltered out:

"I—I don't care; I don't know either of the gentlemen; but to the one you call Howard, I think."

The pause which followed was filled by the tap-tap of Mr. Gryce's fingers on his knee.

"That is the one who is in custody," he observed at last. "The other, that is Franklin, has gone scot-free thus far, I hear."

No answer from her close-shut lips.

He waited.

Still no answer.

"If you do not know either of these gentlemen," he insinuated at last, "how did you come to leave the rings at their office?"

"I knew their names—I inquired my way—It is all a dream now. Please, please do not ask me questions. O doctor! do you not see I cannot bear it?"

He smiled—I never could smile like that under any circumstances— and softly patted her hand.

"I see it makes you suffer," he acknowledged, "but I must make you suffer in order to do you any good. If you would tell me all you know about these rings—"

She passionately turned away her head.

"I might hope to restore you to health and happiness. You know with what they are associated?"

She made a slight motion.

"And that they are an invaluable clue to the murderer of Mrs. Van Burnam?"

Another motion.

"How then, my child, did *you* come to have them?"

Her head, which was rolling to and fro on the pillow, stopped and she gasped, rather than uttered:

"I was *there*."

He knew this, yet it was terrible to hear it from her lips; she was so young and had such an air of purity and innocence. But more heartrending yet was the groan with which she burst forth in another moment, as if impelled by conscience to unburden herself from some overwhelming load:

"I took them; I could not help it; but I did not keep them; you know that I did not keep them. I am no thief, doctor; whatever I am, I am no thief."

"Yes, yes, I see that. But why take them, child? What were you doing in that house, and whom were you with?"

She threw up her arms, but made no reply.

"Will you not tell?" he urged.

A short silence, then a low "No," evidently wrung from her by the deepest anguish.

Mr. Gryce heaved a sigh; the struggle was likely to be a more serious one than he had anticipated.

"Miss Oliver," said he, "more facts are known in relation to this affair than you imagine. Though unsuspected at first, it has secretly been proven that the man who accompanied the woman into the house where the crime took place, was *Franklin* Van Burnam."

A low gasp from the bed, and that was all.

"You know this to be correct, don't you, Miss Oliver?"

"O must you ask?" She was writhing now, and I thought he must desist out of pure compassion. But detectives are made out of very stern stuff, and though he looked sorry he went inexorably on.

"Justice and a sincere desire to help you, force me, my child. Were you not the woman who entered Mr. Van Burnam's house at midnight with this man?"

"I entered the house."

"At midnight?"

"Yes."

"And with this man?"

Silence.

"You do not speak, Miss Oliver."

Again silence.

"It was Franklin who was with you at the Hotel D——?"

She uttered a cry.

"And it was Franklin who connived at your change of clothing there, and advised or allowed you to dress yourself in a new suit from Altman's?"

"Oh!" she cried again.

"Then why should it not have been he who accompanied you to the Chinaman's, and afterwards took you in a second hack to the house in Gramercy Park?"

"Known, known, all known!" was her moan.

"Sin and crime cannot long remain hidden in this world, Miss Oliver. The police are acquainted with all your movements from the moment you left the Hotel D——. That is why I have compassion on you. I wish to save you from the consequences of a crime you saw committed, but in which you took no hand."

"O," she exclaimed in one involuntary burst, as she half rose to her knees, "if you could save me from appearing in the matter at all! If you would let me run away—"

But Mr. Gryce was not the man to give her hope on any such score.

"Impossible, Miss Oliver. You are the only person who can witness for the guilty. If *I* should let you go, the police would not. Then why not tell at once whose hand drew the hat-pin from your hat and—"

"Stop!" she shrieked; "stop! you kill me! I cannot bear it! If you bring that moment back to my mind I shall go mad! I feel the horror of it rising in me now! Be still! I pray you, for God's sake, to be still!"

This was mortal anguish; there was no acting in this. Even he was startled by the emotion he had raised, and sat for a moment without speaking. Then the necessity of providing against all further mistakes by fixing the guilt where it belonged, drove him on again, and he said:

"Like many another woman before you, you are trying to shield a guilty man at your own expense. But it is useless, Miss Oliver; the truth always comes to light. Be advised, then, and make a confidant of one who understands you better than you think."

But she would not listen to this.

"No one understands me. I do not understand myself. I only know that I shall make a confidant of no one; that I shall never speak." And turning from him, she buried her head in the bedclothes.

To most men her tone and the action which accompanied it would have been final. But Mr. Gryce possessed great patience. Waiting for just a moment till she seemed more composed, he murmured gently:

"Not if you must suffer more from your silence than from speaking? Not if men—I do not mean myself, child, for I am your friend—will think that *you* are to blame for the death of the woman whom you saw fall under a cruel stab, and whose rings you have?"

"*I!*" Her horror was unmistakable; so were her surprise, her terror, and her shame, but she added nothing to the word she had uttered, and he was forced to say again:

"The world, and by that I mean both good people and bad, will believe all this. *He* will let them believe all this. Men have not the devotion of women."

"Alas! alas!" It was a murmur rather than a cry, and she trembled so the bed shook visibly under her. But she made no response to the entreaty in his look and gesture, and he was compelled to draw back unsatisfied.

When a few heavy minutes had passed, he spoke again, this time in a tone of sadness.

"Few men are worth such sacrifices, Miss Oliver, and a criminal never. But a woman is not moved by that thought. She should be moved by this, however. If either of these brothers is to blame in this matter, consideration for the guiltless one should lead you to mention the name of the guilty."

But even this did not visibly affect her.

"I shall mention no names," said she.

"A sign will answer."

"I shall make no sign."

"Then Howard must go to his trial?"

A gasp, but no words.

"And Franklin proceed on his way undisturbed?"

She tried not to answer, but the words would come. Pray God! I may never see such a struggle again.

"That is as God wills. I can do nothing in the matter." And she sank back crushed and wellnigh insensible.

Mr. Gryce made no further effort to influence her.

CHAPTER XXXIV

Exactly Half-Past Three

"She is more unfortunate than wicked," was Mr. Gryce's comment as we stepped into the hall. "Nevertheless, watch her closely, for she is in just the mood to do herself a mischief. In an hour, or at the most two, I shall have a woman here to help you. You can stay till then?"

"All night, if you say so."

"That you must settle with Miss Althorpe. As soon as Miss Oliver is up I shall have a little scheme to propose, by means of which I hope to arrive at the truth of this affair. I must know which of these two men she is shielding."

"Then you think she did not kill Mrs. Van Burnam herself?"

"I think the whole matter one of the most puzzling mysteries that has ever come to the notice of the New York police. We are sure that the murdered woman was Mrs. Van Burnam, that this girl was present at her death, and that she availed herself of the opportunity afforded by that death to make the exchange of clothing which has given such a complicated twist to the whole affair. But beyond these facts, we know little more than that it was Franklin Van Burnam who took her to the Gramercy Park house, and Howard who was seen in that same vicinity some two or four hours later. But on which of these two to fix the responsibility of Mrs. Van Burnam's death, is the question."

"She had a hand in it herself," I persisted; "though it may have been without evil intent. No man ever carried that thing through without feminine help. To this opinion I shall stick, much as this girl draws upon my sympathies."

"I shall not try to persuade you to the contrary. But the point is to find out how much help, and to whom it was given."

"And your scheme for doing this?"

"Cannot be carried out till she is on her feet again. So cure her, Miss Butterworth, cure her. When she can go downstairs, Ebenezer Gryce will be on the scene to test his little scheme."

I promised to do what I could, and when he was gone, I set diligently to work to soothe the child, as he had called her, and get her in trim for the delicate meal which had been sent up. And whether it was owing to a change in my own feelings, or whether the talk with Mr. Gryce had so unnerved her that any womanly ministration was welcome, she responded much more readily to my efforts than ever before, and in a little while lay in so calm and grateful a mood that I was actually sorry to see the nurse when she came. Hoping that something might spring from an interview with Miss Althorpe whereby my departure from the house might be delayed, I descended to the library, and was fortunate enough to find the mistress of the house there. She was sorting invitations, and looked anxious and worried.

"You see me in a difficulty, Miss Butterworth. I had relied on Miss Oliver to oversee this work, as well as to assist me in a great many other details, and I don't know of any one whom I can get on short notice to take her place. My own engagements are many and—"

"Let me help you," I put in, with that cheerfulness her presence invariably inspires. "I have nothing pressing calling me home, and for once in my life I should like to take an active part in wedding festivities. It would make me feel quite young again."

"But—" she began.

"Oh," I hastened to say, "you think I would be more of a hindrance to you than a help; that I would do the work, perhaps, but in my own way rather than in yours. Well, that would doubtless have been true of me a month since, but I have learned a great deal in the last few weeks—you will not ask me how—and now I stand ready to do your work in your way, and to take a great deal of pleasure in it too."

"Ah, Miss Butterworth," she exclaimed, with a burst of genuine feeling which I would not have lost for the world, "I always knew that you had a kind heart; and I am going to accept your offer in the same spirit in which it is made."

So that was settled, and with it the possibility of my spending another night in this house.

At ten o'clock I stole away from the library and the delightful company of Mr. Stone, who had insisted upon sharing my labors, and went up to Miss Oliver's room. I met the nurse at the door.

"You want to see her," said she. "She's asleep, but does not rest very easily. I don't think I ever saw so pitiful a case. She moans continually, but not with physical pain. Yet she seems to have courage too; for now and then she starts up with a loud cry. Listen."

I did so, and this is what I heard:

"I do not want to live; doctor, I do not want to live; why do you try to make me better?"

"That is what she is saying all the time. Sad, isn't it?"

I acknowledged it to be so, but at the same time wondered if the girl were not right in wishing for death as a relief from her troubles.

Early the next morning I inquired at her door again. Miss Oliver was better. Her fever had left her, and she wore a more natural look than at any time since I had seen her. But it was not an untroubled one, and it was with difficulty I met her eyes when she asked if they were coming for her that day, and if she could see Miss Althorpe before she left. As she was not yet able to leave her bed I could easily answer her first question, but I knew too little of Mr. Gryce's intentions to be able to reply to the second. But I was easy with this suffering woman, very easy, more easy than I ever supposed I could be with any one so intimately associated with crime.

She seemed to accept my explanations as readily as she already had my presence, and I was struck again with surprise as I considered that my name had never aroused in her the least emotion.

"Miss Althorpe has been so good to me I should like to thank her; from my despairing heart, I should like to thank her," she said to me as I stood by her side before leaving. "Do you know"—she went on, catching me by the dress as I was turning away—"what kind of a man she is going to marry? She has such a loving heart, and marriage is such a fearful risk."

"Fearful?" I repeated.

"Is it not fearful? To give one's whole soul to a man and be met by—I must not talk of it; I must not think of it—But is he a good man? Does he love Miss Althorpe? Will she be happy? I have no right to ask, perhaps, but my gratitude towards her is such that I wish her every joy and pleasure."

"Miss Althorpe has chosen well," I rejoined. "Mr. Stone is a man in ten thousand."

The sigh that answered me went to my heart.

"I will pray for her," she murmured; "that will be something to live for."

I did not know what reply to make to this. Everything which this girl said and did was so unexpected and so convincing in its sincerity, I felt moved by her even against my better judgment. I pitied her and yet I dared not urge her on to speak, lest I should fail in my task of making her well. I therefore confined myself to a few haphazard expressions of sympathy and encouragement, and left her in the hands of the nurse.

Next day Mr. Gryce called.

"Your patient is better," said he.

"Much better," was my cheerful reply. "This afternoon she will be able to leave the house."

"Very good; have her down at half-past three and I will be in front with a carriage."

"I dread it," I cried; "but I will have her there."

"You are beginning to like her, Miss Butterworth. Take care! You will lose your head if your sympathies become engaged."

"It sits pretty firmly on my shoulders yet," I retorted; "and as for sympathies, you are full of them yourself. I saw how you looked at her yesterday."

"Bah, *my* looks!"

"You cannot deceive me, Mr. Gryce; you are as sorry for the girl as you can be; and so am I too. By the way, I do not think I should speak of her as a girl. From something she said yesterday I am convinced she is a married woman; and that her husband—"

"Well, madam?"

"I will not give him a name, at least not before your scheme has been carried out. Are you ready for the undertaking?"

"I will be this afternoon. At half-past three she is to leave the house. Not a minute before and not a minute later. Remember."

CHAPTER XXXV

A Ruse

It was a new thing for me to enter into any scheme blindfold. But the past few weeks had taught me many lessons and among them to trust a little in the judgment of others.

Accordingly I was on hand with my patient at the hour designated, and, as I supported her trembling steps down the stairs, I endeavored not to betray the intense interest agitating me, or to awaken by my curiosity any further dread in her mind than that involved by her departure from this home of bounty and good feeling, and her entrance upon an unknown and possibly much to be apprehended future.

Mr. Gryce was awaiting us in the lower hall, and as he caught sight of her slender figure and anxious face his whole attitude became at once so protecting and so sympathetic, I did not wonder at her failure to associate him with the police.

As she stepped down to his side he gave her a genial nod.

"I am glad to see you so far on the road to recovery," he remarked. "It shows me that my prophecy is correct and that in a few days you will be quite yourself again."

She looked at him wistfully.

"You seem to know so much about me, doctor, perhaps you can tell me where they are going to take me."

He lifted a tassel from a curtain near by, looked at it, shook his head at it, and inquired quite irrelevantly:

"Have you bidden good-bye to Miss Althorpe?"

Her eyes stole towards the parlors and she whispered as if half in awe of the splendor everywhere surrounding her:

"I have not had the opportunity. But I should be sorry to go without a word of thanks for her goodness. Is she at home?"

The tassel slipped from his hand.

"You will find her in a carriage at the door. She has an engagement out this afternoon, but wishes to say good-bye to you before leaving."

"Oh, how kind she is!" burst from the girl's white lips; and with a hurried gesture she was making for the door when Mr. Gryce stepped before her and opened it.

Two carriages were drawn up in front, neither of which seemed to possess the elegance of so rich a woman's equipage. But Mr. Gryce appeared satisfied, and pointing to the nearest one, observed quietly:

"You are expected. If she does not open the carriage door for you, do not hesitate to do it yourself. She has something of importance to say to you."

Miss Oliver looked surprised, but prepared to obey him. Steadying herself by the stone balustrade, she slowly descended the steps and advanced towards the carriage. I watched her from the doorway and Mr. Gryce from the vestibule. It seemed an ordinary situation, but something in the latter's face convinced me that interests of no small moment depended upon the interview about to take place.

But before I could decide upon their nature or satisfy myself as to the full meaning of Mr. Gryce's manner, she had started back from the carriage door and was saying to him in a tone of modest embarrassment:

"There is a gentleman in the carriage; you must have made some mistake."

Mr. Gryce, who had evidently expected a different result from his stratagem, hesitated for a moment, during which I felt that he read her through and through; then he responded lightly:

"I made a mistake, eh? Oh, possibly. Look in the other carriage, my child."

With an unaffected air of confidence she turned to do so, and I turned to watch her, for I began to understand the "scheme" at which I was assisting, and foresaw that the emotion she had failed to betray at the door of the first carriage might not necessarily be lacking on the opening of the second.

I was all the more assured of this from the fact that Miss Althorpe's stately figure was very plainly to be seen at that moment, not in the coach Miss Oliver was approaching, but in an elegant victoria just turning the corner.

My expectations were realized; for no sooner had the poor girl swung open the door of the second hack, than her whole body succumbed to a shock so great that I expected to see her fall in a heap on the pavement. But she steadied herself up with a determined effort, and with a sudden movement full of subdued fury, jumped into the carriage and violently shut the door just as the first carriage drove off to give place to Miss Althorpe's turn-out.

"Humph!" sprang from Mr. Gryce's lips in a tone so full of varied emotions that it was with difficulty I refrained from rushing down the stoop to see for myself who was the occupant of the coach into which my late patient had so passionately precipitated herself. But the sight of Miss Althorpe being helped to the ground by her attendant lover, recalled me so suddenly to my own anomalous position on her stoop, that I let my first impulse pass and concerned myself instead with the formation of those apologies I thought necessary to the occasion. But those apologies were never uttered. Mr. Gryce, with the infinite tact he displays in all serious emergencies, came to my rescue, and so distracted Miss Althorpe's attention that she failed to observe that she had interrupted a situation of no small moment.

Meanwhile the coach containing Miss Oliver had, at a signal from the wary detective, drawn off in the wake of the first one, and I had the doubtful satisfaction of seeing them both roll down the street without my having penetrated the secret of either.

A glance from Mr. Stone, who had followed Miss Althorpe up the stoop, interrupted Mr. Gryce's flow of eloquence, and a few minutes later I found myself making those adieux which I had hoped to avoid by departing in Miss Althorpe's absence. Another instant and I was hastening down the street in the direction taken by the two carriages, one of which had paused at the corner a few rods off.

But, spry as I am for one of my settled habits and sedate character, I found myself passed by Mr. Gryce; and when I would have accelerated my steps, he darted forward quite like a boy and, without a word of explanation or any acknowledgment of the mutual understanding which certainly existed between us, leaped into the carriage I was endeavoring to reach, and was driven away. But not before I caught a glimpse of Miss Oliver's gray dress inside.

Determined not to be baffled by this man, I turned about and followed the other carriage. It was approaching a crowded part of the avenue, and in a few minutes I had the gratification of seeing it come to a standstill only a few feet from the curb-stone. The opportunity thus afforded me of satisfying my curiosity was not to be slighted. Without pausing to consider consequences or to question the propriety of my conduct, I stepped boldly up in front of its half-lowered window and looked in. There was but one person inside, and that person was Franklin Van Burnam.

What was I to conclude from this? That the occupant of the other carriage was Howard, and that Mr. Gryce now knew with which of the two brothers Miss Oliver's memories were associated.

LOST MAN'S LANE

THE SECOND EPISODE IN THE LIFE OF AMELIA BUTTERWORTH

DEDICATION

To Elizabeth D. Shepard, cousin and friend, this book is affectionately inscribed.

PREFACE

A word to my readers before they begin these pages.

As a woman of inborn principle and strict Presbyterian training, I hate deception and cannot abide subterfuge. This is why, after a year or more of hesitation, I have felt myself constrained to put into words the true history of the events surrounding the solution of that great mystery which made Lost Man's Lane the dread of the neighboring country. Feminine delicacy, and a natural shrinking from revealing to the world certain weaknesses on my part, inseparable from a true relation of this tale, led me to consent to the publication of that meagre and decidedly falsified account of the matter which has appeared in some of our leading papers.

But conscience has regained its sway in my breast, and with all due confidence in your forbearance, I herein take my rightful place in these annals, of whose interest and importance I now leave you to judge.

Amelia Butterworth.

Gramercy Park, New York.

BOOK I: THE KNOLLYS FAMILY

CHAPTER I

A Visit from Mr. Gryce

Ever since my fortunate—or shall I say unfortunate?—connection with that famous case of murder in Gramercy Park, I have had it intimated to me by many of my friends—and by some who were not my friends—that no woman who had met with such success as myself in detective work would ever be satisfied with a single display of her powers, and that sooner or later I would find myself again at work upon some other case of striking peculiarities.

As vanity has never been my foible, and as, moreover, I never have forsaken and never am likely to forsake the plain path marked out for my sex, at any other call than that of duty, I invariably responded to these insinuations by an affable but incredulous smile, striving to excuse the presumption of my friends by remembering their ignorance of my nature and the very excellent reasons I had for my one notable interference in the police affairs of New York City.

Besides, though I appeared to be resting quietly, if not in entire contentment, on my laurels, I was not so utterly removed from the old atmosphere of crime and its detection as the world in general considered me to be. Mr. Gryce still visited me; not on business, of course, but as a friend, for whom I had some regard; and naturally our conversation was not always confined to the weather or even to city politics, provocative as the latter subject is of wholesome controversy.

Not that he ever betrayed any of the secrets of his office—oh no; that would have been too much to expect—but he did sometimes mention the outward aspects of some celebrated case, and though I never ventured upon advice—I know too much for that, I hope—I found my wits more or less exercised by a conversation in which he gained much without acknowledging it, and I gave much without appearing conscious of the fact.

I was therefore finding life pleasant and full of interest, when suddenly (I had no right to expect it, and I do not blame myself for not expecting it or for holding my head so high at the prognostications of my friends) an opportunity came for a direct exercise of my detective powers in a line seemingly so laid out for me by Providence that I felt I would be slighting the Powers above if I refused to enter upon it, though now I see that the line was laid out for me by Mr. Gryce, and that I was obeying anything but the call of duty in following it.

But this is not explicit. One night Mr. Gryce came to my house looking older and more feeble than usual. He was engaged in a perplexing case, he said, and missed his early vigor and persistency. Would I like to hear about it? It was not in the line of his usual work, yet it had points—and well!—it would do him good to talk about it to a non-professional who was capable of sympathizing with its baffling and worrisome features and yet would never have to be told to hold her peace.

I ought to have been on my guard. I ought to have known the old fox well enough to feel certain that when he went so manifestly out of his way to take me into his confidence he did it for a purpose. But Jove nods now and then—or so I have been assured on unimpeachable authority—and if Jove has ever been caught napping, surely Amelia Butterworth may be pardoned a like inconsistency.

"It is not a city crime," Mr. Gryce went on to explain, and here he was base enough to sigh. "At my time of life this is an important consideration. It is no longer a simple matter for me to pack up a valise and go off to some distant village, way up in the mountains perhaps, where comforts are few and secrecy an impossibility. Comforts have become indispensable to my threescore years and ten, and secrecy—well, if ever there was an affair where one needs to go softly, it is this one; as you will see if you will allow me to give you the facts of the case as known at Headquarters today."

I bowed, trying not to show my surprise or my extreme satisfaction. Mr. Gryce assumed his most benignant aspect (always a dangerous one with him), and began his story.

CHAPTER II

I Am Tempted

"Some ninety miles from here, in a more or less inaccessible region, there is a small but interesting village, which has been the scene of so many unaccountable disappearances that the attention of the New York police has at last been directed to it. The village, which is at least two miles from any railroad, is one of those quiet, placid little spots found now and then among the mountains, where life is simple, and crime, to all appearance, an element so out of accord with every other characteristic of the place as to seem a complete anomaly. Yet crime, or some other hideous mystery almost equally revolting, has during the last five years been accountable for the disappearance in or about this village of four persons of various ages and occupations. Of these, three were strangers and one a well-known vagabond accustomed to tramp the hills and live on the bounty of farmers' wives. All were of the male sex, and in no case has any clue ever come to light as to their fate. That is the matter as it stands before the police today."

"A serious affair," I remarked. "Seems to me I have read of such things in novels. Is there a tumbled-down old inn in the vicinity where beds are made up over trap-doors?"

His smile was a mild protest against my flippancy.

"I have visited the town myself. There is no inn there, but a comfortable hotel of the most matter-of-fact sort, kept by the frankest and most open-minded of landlords. Besides, these disappearances, as a rule, did not take place at night, but in broad daylight. Imagine this street at noon. It is a short one, and you know every house on it, and you think you know every lurking-place. You see a man enter it at one end and you expect him to issue from it at the other. But suppose he never does. More than that, suppose he is never heard of again, and that this thing should happen in this one street four times during five years."

"I should move," I dryly responded.

"Would you? Many good people have moved from the place I speak of, but that has not helped matters. The disappearances go on just the same and the mystery continues."

"You interest me," I said. "Come to think of it, if this street were the scene of such an unexplained series of horrors as you have described, I do not think I should move."

"I thought not," he curtly rejoined. "But since you are interested in this matter, let me be more explicit in my statements. The first person whose disappearance was noted—"

"Wait," I interrupted. "Have you a map of the place?"

He smiled, nodded quite affectionately to a little statuette on the mantel-piece, which had had the honor of sharing his confidences in days gone by, but did not produce the map.

"That detail will keep," said he. "Let me go on with my story. As I was saying, madam, the first person whose disappearance was noted in this place was a peddler of small wares, accustomed to tramp the mountains. On this occasion he had been in town longer than usual, and was known to have sold fully half of his goods. Consequently he must have had quite a sum of money upon him. One day his pack was found lying under a cluster of bushes in a wood, but of him nothing was ever again heard. It made an excitement for a few days while the woods were being searched for his body, but, nothing having been discovered, he was forgotten, and everything went on as before, till suddenly public attention was again aroused by the pouring in of letters containing inquiries in regard to a young man who had been sent there from Duluth to collect facts in a law case, and who after a certain date had failed to communicate with his firm or show up at any of the places where he was known. Instantly the village was in arms. Many remembered the young man, and some two or three of the villagers could recall the fact of having seen him go up the street with his hand-bag in his hand as if on his way to the Mountain-station. The landlord of the hotel could fix the very day at which he left his house, but inquiries at the station failed to establish the fact that he took train from there, nor were the most minute inquiries into his fate ever attended by the least result. He was not known to have carried much money, but he carried a very handsome watch and wore a ring of more than ordinary value, neither of which has ever shown up at any pawnbroker's known to the police. This was three years ago.

"The next occurrence of a like character did not take place till a year after. This time it was a poor old man from Hartford, who vanished almost as it were before the eyes of these astounded villagers. He had come to town to get subscriptions for a valuable book issued by a well-known publisher. He had been more or less successful, and was looking very cheerful and contented, when one morning, after making a sale at a certain farmhouse, he sat down to dine with the family, it being close on to noon. He had eaten several mouthfuls and was chatting quite freely, when suddenly they saw him pause, clap his hand to his pocket, and rise up very much disturbed. 'I have left my pocket-book behind me at Deacon Spear's,' he cried. 'I cannot eat with it out of my possession. Excuse me if I go for it.' And without any further apologies, he ran out of the house and down the road in the direction of Deacon Spear's. He never reached Deacon Spear's, nor was he ever seen in that village again or in his home in Hartford. This was the most astonishing mystery of all. Within a half-mile's radius, in a populous country town, this man disappeared as if the road had swallowed him and closed again. It was marvellous, it was incredible, and remained so even after the best efforts of the country police to solve the mystery had exhausted themselves. After this, the town began to acquire a bad name, and one or two families moved away. Yet no one was found who was willing to admit that these various persons had been the victims of foul play till a month later another case came to light of a young man who had left the village for the hillside station, and had never arrived at that or any other destination so far as could be learned. As he was a distant relative of a wealthy cattle owner in Iowa, who came on post-haste to inquire into his nephew's fate, the excitement ran high, and through his efforts and that of one of the town's leading citizens, the services of our office were called into play. But the result has been nil. We have found neither the bodies of these men nor any clue to their fate."

"Yet *you* have been there?" I suggested.

He nodded.

"Wonderful! And you came upon no suspicious house, no suspicious person?"

The finger with which he was rubbing his eyeglasses went round and round the rims with a slower and slower and still more thoughtful motion.

"Every town has its suspicious-looking houses," he slowly remarked, "and, as for persons, the most honest often wear a lowering look in which an unbridled imagination can see guilt. I never trust to appearances of that kind."

"What else can you trust in, when a case is as impenetrable as this one?" I asked.

His finger, going slower and slower, suddenly stopped.

"In my knowledge of persons," he replied. "In my knowledge of their fears, their hopes, and their individual concerns. If I were twenty years younger"—here he stole a glance at me in the mirror which made me bridle; did he think I was only twenty years younger than himself?—"I would," he went on, "make myself so acquainted with every man, woman, and child there, that—" Here he drew himself up with a jerk. "But the day for that is passed," said he. "I am too old and too crippled to succeed in such an undertaking. Having been there once, I am a marked man. My very walk betrays me. He whose good fortune it will be to get at the bottom of these people's hearts must awaken no suspicions as to his connection with the police. Indeed, I do not think that any man can succeed in doing this now."

I started. This was a frank showing of his hand at least. No man! It was then a woman's aid he was after. I laughed as I thought of it. I had not thought him either so presumptuous or so appreciative of talents of a character so directly in line with his own.

"Don't you agree with me, madam?"

I did agree with him; but I had a character of great dignity to maintain, so I simply surveyed him with an air of well-tempered severity.

"I do not know of any woman who would undertake such a task," I calmly observed.

"No?" he smiled with that air of forbearance which is so exasperating to me. "Well, perhaps there isn't any such woman to be found. It would take one of very uncommon characteristics, I own."

"Pish!" I cried. "Not so very!"

"Indeed, I think you have not fully taken in the case," he urged in quiet superiority. "The people there are of the higher order of country folk. Many of them are of extreme refinement. One family"—here his tone changed a trifle—"is poor enough and cultivated enough to interest even such a woman as yourself."

"Indeed!" I ejaculated, with just a touch of my father's hauteur to hide the stir of curiosity his words naturally evoked.

"It is in some such home," he continued with an ease that should have warned me he had started on this pursuit with a quiet determination to win, "that the clue will be found to the mystery we are considering. Yes, you may well look startled, but that conclusion is the one thing I brought away with me from—X., let us say. I regard it as one of some moment. What do you think of it?"

"Well," I admitted, "it makes me feel like recalling that *pish* I uttered a few minutes ago. It would take a woman of uncommon characteristics to assist you in this matter."

"I am glad we have got that far," said he.

"A lady," I went on.

"Most assuredly a lady."

I paused. Sometimes discreet silence is more sarcastic than speech.

"Well, what lady would lend herself to this scheme?" I demanded at last.

The tap, tap of his fingers on the rim of his glasses was my only answer.

"I do not know of any," said I.

His eyebrows rose perhaps a hair's-breadth, but I noted the implied sarcasm, and for an instant forgot my dignity.

"Now," said I, "this will not do. You mean me, Amelia Butterworth; a woman who—but I do not think it is necessary to tell you either who or what I am. You have presumed, sir—Now do not put on that look of innocence, and above all do not attempt to deny what is so manifestly in your thoughts, for that would make me feel like showing you the door."

"Then," he smiled, "I shall be sure to deny nothing. I am not anxious to leave—yet. Besides, whom could I mean but you? A lady visiting friends in this remote and beautiful region—what opportunities might she not have to probe this important mystery if, like yourself, she had tact, discretion, excellent understanding, and an experience which if not broad or deep is certainly such as to give her a certain confidence in herself, and an undoubted influence with the man fortunate enough to receive her advice."

"Bah!" I exclaimed. It was one of his favorite expressions. That was perhaps why I used it. "One would think I was a member of your police."

"You flatter us too deeply," was his deferential answer. "Such an honor as that would be beyond our deserts."

To this I gave but the faintest sniff. That he should think that I, Amelia Butterworth, could be amenable to such barefaced flattery! Then I faced him with some asperity, and said bluntly: "You waste your time. I have no more intention of meddling in another affair than—"

"You had in meddling in the first," he politely, too politely, interpolated. "I understand, madam."

I was angry, but made no show of being so. I was not willing he should see that I could be affected by anything he could say.

"The Van Burnams are my next-door neighbors," I remarked sweetly. "I had the best of excuses for the interest I took in their affairs."

"So you had," he acquiesced. "I am glad to be reminded of the fact. I wonder I was able to forget it."

Angry now to the point of not being able to hide it, I turned upon him with firm determination.

"Let us talk of something else," I said.

But he was equal to the occasion. Drawing a folded paper from his pocket, he opened it out before my eyes, observing quite naturally: "That is a happy thought. Let us look over this sketch you were sharp enough to ask for a few moments ago. It shows the streets of the village and the places where each of the persons I have mentioned was last seen. Is not that what you wanted?"

I know that I should have drawn back with a frown, that I never should have allowed myself the satisfaction of casting so much as a glance toward the paper, but the human nature which links me to my kind was too much for me, and with an involuntary "Exactly!" I leaned over it with an eagerness I strove hard, even at that exciting moment, to keep within the bounds I thought proper to my position as a non-professional, interested in the matter from curiosity alone.

This is what I saw:

"Mr. Gryce," said I, after a few minutes' close contemplation of this diagram, "I do not suppose you want any opinion from me."

"Madam," he retorted, "it is all you have left me free to ask for."

Receiving this as a permission to speak, I put my finger on the road marked with a cross.

"Then," said I, "so far as I can gather from this drawing, all the disappearances seem to have taken place in or about this especial road."

"You are as correct as usual," he returned. "What you have said is so true, that the people of the vicinity have already given to this winding way a special cognomen of its own. For two years now it has been called Lost Man's Lane."

"Indeed!" I cried. "They have got the matter down as close as that, and yet have not solved its mystery? How long is this road?"

"A half mile or so."

I must have looked my disgust, for his hands opened deprecatingly.

"The ground has undergone a thorough search," said he. "Not a square foot in those woods you see on either side of the road, but has been carefully examined."

"And the houses? I see there are three houses on this road."

"Oh, they are owned by most respectable people—*most* respectable people," he repeated, with a lingering emphasis that gave me an inward shudder. "I think I had the honor of intimating as much to you a few minutes ago."

I looked at him earnestly, and irresistibly drew a little nearer to him over the diagram.

"Have none of these houses been visited by you?" I asked. "Do you mean to say you have not seen the inside of them all?"

"Oh," he replied, "I have been in them all, of course; but a mystery such as we are investigating is not written upon the walls of parlors or halls."

"You freeze my blood," was my uncharacteristic rejoinder. Somehow the sight of the homes indicated on this diagram seemed to bring me into more intimate sympathy with the affair.

His shrug was significant.

"I told you that this was no vulgar mystery," he declared; "or why should I be considering it with *you*? It is quite worthy of your interest. Do you see that house marked A?"

"I do," I nodded.

"Well, that is a decayed mansion of imposing proportions, set in a forest of overgrown shrubbery. The ladies who inhabit it—"

"Ladies!" I put in, with a small shock of horror.

"Young ladies," he explained, "of a refined if not over-prosperous appearance. They are the interesting residue of a family of some repute. Their father was a judge, I believe."

"And do they live there alone," I asked—"two young ladies in a house so large and in a neighborhood so full of mystery?"

"Oh, they have a brother with them, a lout of no great attractions," he responded carelessly—too carelessly, I thought.

I made a note of the house A in my mind.

"And who lives in the house marked B?" I now queried.

"A Mr. Trohm. You will remember that it was through his exertions the services of the New York police were secured. His place there is one of the most interesting in town, and he does not wish to be forced to leave it, but he will be obliged to do so if the road is not soon relieved of its bad name; and so will Deacon Spear. The very children shun the road now. I do not know of a lonelier place."

"I see a little mark made here on the verge of the woods. What does that mean?"

"That stands for a hut—it can hardly be called a cottage—where a poor old woman lives called Mother Jane. She is a harmless imbecile, against whom no one has ever directed a suspicion. You may take your finger off that mark, Miss Butterworth."

I did so, but I did not forget that it stood very near the footpath branching off to the station.

"You entered this hut as well as the big houses?" I intimated.

"And found," was his answer, "four walls; nothing more."

I let my finger travel along the footpath I have just mentioned.

"Steep," was his comment. "Up, up, all the way, but no precipices. Nothing but pine woods on either side, thickly carpeted with needles."

My finger came back and stopped at the house marked M.

"Why is a letter affixed to this spot?" I asked.

"Because it stands at the head of the lane. Any one sitting at the window L can see whoever enters or leaves the lane at this end. And some-one is always sitting there. The house contains two crippled children, a boy and a girl. One of them is always in that window."

"I see," said I. Then abruptly: "What do you think of Deacon Spear?"

"Oh, he's a well-meaning man, none too fine in his feelings. He does not mind the neighborhood; likes quiet, he says. I hope you will know him for yourself some day," the detective slyly added.

At this return to the forbidden subject, I held myself very much aloof.

"Your diagram is interesting," I remarked, "but it has not in the least changed my determination. It is you who will return to X., and that, very soon."

"Very soon?" he repeated. "Whoever goes there on this errand must go at once; tonight, if possible; if not, tomorrow at the latest."

"Tonight! tomorrow!" I expostulated. "And you thought—"

"No matter what I thought," he sighed. "It seems I had no reason for my hopes." And folding up the map, he slowly rose. "The young man we have left there is doing more harm than good. That is why I say that someone of real ability must replace him immediately. The detective from New York must seem to have left the place."

I made him my most ladylike bow of dismissal.

"I shall watch the papers," I said. "I have no doubt that I shall soon be gratified by seeing in them some token of your success."

He cast a rueful look at his hands, took a painful step toward the door, and dolefully shook his head.

I kept my silence undisturbed.

He took another painful step, then turned.

"By the way," he remarked, as I stood watching him with an uncompromising air, "I have forgotten to mention the name of the town in which these disappearances have occurred. It is called X., and it is to be found on one of the spurs of the Berkshire Hills." And, being by this time at the door, he bowed himself out with all the insinuating suavity which distinguishes him at certain critical moments. The old fox was so sure of his triumph that he did not wait to witness it. He knew—how, it is easy enough for me to understand now—that X. was a place I had often threatened to visit. The family of one of my dearest friends lived there, the children of Althea Knollys. She had been my chum at school, and when she died I had promised myself not to let many months go by without making the acquaintance of her children. Alas! I had allowed years to elapse.

CHAPTER III

I Succumb

That night the tempter had his own way with me. Without much difficulty he persuaded me that my neglect of Althea Burroughs' children was without any excuse; that what had been my duty toward them when I knew them to be left motherless and alone, had become an imperative demand upon me now that the town in which they lived had become overshadowed by a mystery which could not but affect the comfort and happiness of all its inhabitants. I could not wait a day. I recalled all that I had heard of poor Althea's short and none too happy marriage, and immediately felt such a burning desire to see if her dainty but spirited beauty—how well I remembered it—had been repeated in her daughters, that I found myself packing my trunk before I knew it.

I had not been from home for a long time—all the more reason why I should have a change now—and when I notified Mrs. Randolph and the servants of my intention of leaving on the early morning train, it created quite a sensation in the house.

But I had the best of explanations to offer. I had been thinking of my dead friend, and my conscience would not let me neglect her dear and possibly unhappy progeny any longer. I had purposed many times to visit X., and now I was going to do it. When I come to a decision, it is usually suddenly, and I never rest after having once made up my mind.

My sentiment went so far that I got down an old album and began hunting up the pictures I had brought away with me from boarding-school. Hers was among them, and I really did experience more or less compunction when I saw again the delicate yet daring features which had once had a very great influence over my mind. What a teasing sprite she was, yet what a will she had, and how strange it was that, having been so intimate as girls, we never knew anything of each other as women! Had it been her fault or mine? Was her marriage to blame for it or my spinsterhood? Difficult to tell then, impossible to tell now. I would not even think of it again, save as a warning. Nothing must stand between me and her children now that my attention has been called to them again.

I did not mean to take them by surprise—that is, not entirely. The invitation which they had sent me years ago was still in force, making it simply necessary for me to telegraph them that I had decided to make them a visit, and that they might expect me by the noon train. If in times gone by they had been properly instructed by their mother in regard to the character of her old friend, this need not put them out. I am not a woman of unbounded expectations. I do not look for the comforts abroad I am accustomed to find at home, and if, as I have reason to believe, their means are not of the greatest, they would only provoke me by any show of effort to make me feel at home in the humble cottage suited to their fortunes.

So the telegram was sent, and my preparations completed for an early departure.

But, resolved as I was to make this visit, my determination came near receiving a check. Just as I was leaving the house—at the very moment, in fact, when the hackman was carrying out my trunk, I perceived a man approaching me with every evidence of haste. He had a letter in his hand, which he held out to me as soon as he came within reach.

"For Miss Butterworth," he announced. "Private and immediate."

"Ah," thought I, "a communication from Mr. Gryce," and hesitated for a moment whether to open it on the spot or to wait and read it at my leisure on the cars. The latter course promised me less inconvenience than the first, for my hands were cumbered with the various small articles I consider indispensable to the comfortable enjoyment of the shortest journey, and the glasses without which I cannot read a word, were in the very bottom of my pocket under many other equally necessary articles.

But something in the man's expectant look warned me that he would never leave me till I had read the note, so with a sigh I called Lena to my aid, and after several vain attempts to reach my glasses, succeeded at last in pulling them out, and by their help reading the following hurried lines:

"Dear Madam:

"I send you this by a swifter messenger than myself. Do not let anything that I may have said last night influence you to leave your comfortable home. The adventure offers too many dangers for a woman. Read the inclosed. G."

The inclosed was a telegram from X., sent during the night, and evidently just received at Headquarters. Its contents were certainly not reassuring:

"Another person missing. Last seen in Lost Man's Lane. A harmless lad known as Silly Rufus. What's to be done? Wire orders. Trohm."

"Mr. Gryce bade me say that he would be up here some time before noon," said the man, seeing me look with some blankness at these words.

Nothing more was needed to restore my self-possession. Folding up the letter, I put it in my bag.

"Say to Mr. Gryce from me that my intended visit cannot be postponed," I replied. "I have telegraphed to my friends to expect me, and only a great emergency would lead me to disappoint them. I will be glad to receive Mr. Gryce on my return." And without further parley, I took my bundles back from Lena, and proceeded at once to the carriage. Why should I show any failure of courage at an event that was but a repetition of the very ones which made my visit necessary? Was I a likely person to fall victim to a mystery to which my eyes had been opened? Had I not been sufficiently warned of the dangers of Lost Man's Lane to keep myself at a respectable distance from the place of peril? I was going to visit the children of my once devoted friend. If there were perils of no ordinary nature to be encountered in so doing, was I not all the more called upon to lend them the support of my presence?

Yes, Mr. Gryce, and nothing now should hold me back. I even felt an increased desire to reach the scene of these mysteries, and chafed some at the length of the journey, which was of a more tedious character than I expected. A poor beginning for events requiring patience as well as great moral courage; but I little knew what was before me, and only considered that every moment spent on this hot and dusty train kept me thus much longer from the embraces of Althea's children.

I recovered my equanimity, however, as we approached X. The scenery was really beautiful, and the consciousness that I should soon alight at the mountain station which had played a more or less serious part in Mr. Gryce's narrative, awakened in me a pleasurable excitement which should have been a sufficient warning to me that the spirit of investigation which had led me so triumphantly through that affair next door had seized me again in a way that meant equal absorption if not equal success.

The number of small packages I carried gave me enough to think of at the moment of alighting, but as soon as I was safely again on terra firma I threw a hasty glance around to see if any of Althea's children were on hand to meet me.

I felt that I ought to know them at first glance. Their mother had been so characteristically pretty, she could not have failed to transmit some of her most charming traits to her offspring. But while there were two or three country maidens to be seen standing in and around the little pavilion known here as the Mountain-station, I saw no one who by any stretch of imagination could be regarded as of Althea Burroughs' blood or breeding.

Somewhat disappointed, for I had expected different results from my telegram, I stepped up to the station-master, and asked him whether I would have any difficulty in procuring a carriage to take me to Miss Knollys' house. He stared, it seemed to me, unnecessarily long, before replying.

"Waal," said he, "Simmons is usually here, but I don't see him around today. Perhaps some of these farmer lads will drive you in."

But they all drew back with a scared look, and I was beginning to tuck up my skirts preparatory to walking, when a little old man of exceedingly meek appearance drove up in a very old-fashioned coach, and with a hesitating air, springing entirely from bashfulness, managed to ask if I was Miss Butterworth. I hastened to assure him that I was that lady, whereupon he stammered out some words about Miss Knollys, and how sorry she was that she could not come for me herself. Then he pointed to his coach, and made me understand that I was to step into it and go with him.

This I had not counted upon doing, for I desired to both see and hear as much as possible before reaching my destination. There was but one way out of it. To his astonishment, I insisted that my belongings be put inside the coach, while I rode on the box.

It was an inauspicious beginning to a very doubtful adventure. I understood this when I saw the heads of the various onlookers draw together and many curious looks directed at both us and the conveyance that was to carry us. But I was in no mood to be daunted now, and mounting to the box with what grace I could, prepared myself for a ride into town.

But it seems I was not to be allowed to leave the spot without another warning. While the old man was engaged in fetching my trunk, the station-master approached me with great civility, and asked if it was my intention to spend a few days with the Misses Knollys. I told him that it was, and thinking it best to establish my position at once in the eyes of the whole town, added with a politeness equal to his own, that I was an old friend of the family, and had been coming to visit them for years, but had never found it convenient till now, and that I hoped they were all well and would be glad to see me.

His reply showed considerable embarrassment.

"Perhaps you have not heard that this village is under a cloud just now?"

"I have heard that one or two men have disappeared from here somewhat mysteriously," I returned. "Is that what you mean?"

"Yes, ma'am. One person, a boy, disappeared only two days ago."

"That's bad," I said. "But what has it to do with me?" I smilingly added, for I saw that he was not at the end of his talk.

"Oh, nothing," he eagerly replied, "only I didn't know but you might be timid—"

"Oh, I'm not at all timid," I hastened to interject. "If I were, I should not have come here at all. Such matters don't affect me." And I spread out my skirts and arranged myself for my ride with as much care and precision as if the horrors he had mentioned had made no more impression upon me than if his chat had been of the weather.

Perhaps I overdid it, for he looked at me for another moment in a curious, lingering way; then he walked off, and I saw him enter the circle of gossips on the platform, where he stood shaking his head as long as we were within sight.

My companion, who was the shyest man I ever saw, did not speak a word while we were descending the hill. I talked, and endeavored to make him follow my example, but his replies were mere grunts or half-syllables which conveyed no information whatever. As we cleared the thicket, however, he allowed himself an ejaculation or two as he pointed out the beauties of the landscape. And indeed it was well worth his admiration and mine had my mind been free to enjoy it. But the houses, which now began to appear on either side of the way, drew my attention from the mountains. Though still somewhat remote from the town, we were rapidly approaching the head of that lane of evil fame with whose awe-inspiring history my thoughts were at this time full. I was so anxious not to pass it without one look into its grewsome recesses that I kept my head persistently turned that way till I felt I was attracting the attention of my companion. As this was not desirable, I put on a nonchalant look and began chatting about what I saw. But he had lapsed into his early silence, and seemed wholly engrossed in his attempt to remove with the butt-end of his whip a bit of rag which had somehow become entangled in the spokes of one of the front wheels. The furtive look he cast me as he succeeded in doing this struck me oddly at the moment, but it was too small a matter to hold my attention long or to cause any cessation in the flow of small talk with which I was endeavoring to enliven the situation.

My desire for conversation lagged, however, as I saw rising up before us the dark boughs of a pine thicket. We were nearing Lost Man's Lane; we were abreast of it; we were—yes, we were turning into it!

I could not repress an exclamation of dismay.

"Where are we going?" I asked.

"To Miss Knollys' house," he found words to say, with a sidelong glance at me full of uneasy inquiry.

"Do they live on this road?" I cried, remembering with a certain shock Mr. Gryce's suspicious description of the two young ladies who with their brother inhabited the dilapidated mansion marked A in the map he had shown me.

"Where else?" was his laconic answer; and, obliged to be satisfied with this curtest of curt replies, I drew myself up with just one longing look behind me at the cheerful highway we were so rapidly leaving. A cottage, with an open window, in which a child's head could be seen nodding eagerly toward me, met my eyes and filled me with quite an odd sense of discomfort as I realized that I had caught the attention of one of the little cripples who, according to Mr. Gryce, always kept watch over this entrance into Lost Man's Lane. Another moment and the pine branches had shut the vision out, but I did not soon forget that eager, childish face and pointing hand, marking me out as a possible victim to the horrors of this ill-reputed lane. But I was aware of no secret flinching from the adventure into which I was plunging. On the contrary, I felt a strange and fierce delight in thus being thrust into the very heart of the mystery I had only expected to approach by degrees. The warning message sent me by Mr. Gryce had acquired a deeper and more significant meaning, as did the looks which had been cast me by the station-master and his gossips on the hillside, but in my present mood these very tokens of the serious nature of my undertaking only gave an added spur to my courage. I felt my brain clear and my heart expand, as if at this moment, before I had so much as set eyes on the faces of these young people, I recognized the fact that they were the victims of a web of circumstances so tragic and incomprehensible that only a woman like myself would be able to dissipate them and restore these girls to the confidence of the people around them.

I forgot that these girls had a brother and that—But not a word to forestall the truth. I wish this story to grow upon you just as it did upon me, and with just as little preparation.

The farmer who drove me, and who I afterwards learned was called Simsbury, showed a certain dogged interest in my behavior that would have amused me, or, at least, have awakened my disdain under circumstances of a less thrilling nature. I saw his eye roll in a sort of wonder over my person, which may have been held a little more stiffly than was necessary, and settle finally on my face, with a look I might have thought complimentary had I had any thought to bestow on such matters. Not till we had passed the path branching up through the woods toward the mountain did he see fit to withdraw it, nor did I fail to find it fixed again upon me as we rode by the little hut occupied by the old woman considered so harmless by Mr. Gryce.

Perhaps he had a reason for this, as I was very much interested in this hut and its occupant, about whom I felt free to cherish my own secret doubts—so interested that I cast it a very sharp glance, and was glad when I caught a glimpse through the doorway of the old crone mumbling over a piece of bread she was engaged in eating as we passed her.

"That's Mother Jane," explained my companion, breaking the silence of many minutes. "And yonder is Miss Knollys' house," he added, lifting his whip and pointing toward the half-concealed façade of a large and pretentious dwelling a few rods farther on down the road. "She will be powerful glad to see you, Miss. Company is scarce in these parts."

Astonished at this sudden launch into conversation by one whose reserve I had hitherto found it impossible to penetrate, I gave him the affable answer he evidently expected, and then looked eagerly toward the house. It was as Mr. Gryce had intimated, exceedingly forbidding even at that distance, and as we approached nearer and I was given a full view of its worn and discolored front, I felt myself forced to acknowledge that never in my life had my eyes fallen upon a habitation more given over to neglect or less promising in its hospitality.

Had it not been for the thin circle of smoke eddying up from one of its broken chimneys, I would have looked upon the place as one which had not known the care or presence of man for years. There was a riot of shrubbery in the yard, a lack of the commonest attention to order in the way the vines drooped in tangled masses over the face of the desolate porch, that gave to the broken pilasters and decayed window-frames of this dreariest of façades that look of abandonment which only becomes picturesque when nature has usurped the prerogative of man and taken entirely to herself the empty walls and falling casements of what was once a human dwelling. That any one should be living in it now and that I, who have never been able to see a chair standing crooked or a curtain awry, without a sensation of the keenest discomfort, should be on the point of deliberately entering its doors as an inmate, filled me at the moment with such a sense of unreality, that I descended from the carriage in a sort of a dream and was making my way through one of the gaps in the high antique fence that separated the yard from the gateway, when Mr. Simsbury stopped me and pointed out the gate.

I did not think it worth while to apologize for my mistake, for the broken palings certainly offered as good an entrance as the gate, which had slipped from its hinges and hung but a few inches open. But I took the course he indicated, holding up my skirts, and treading gingerly for fear of the snails and toads that incumbered such portions of the path as the weeds had left visible. As I proceeded on my way, something in the silence of the spot struck me. Was I becoming over-sensitive to impressions or was there something really uncanny in the absolute lack of sound or movement in a dwelling of such dimensions? But I should not have said movement, for at that instant I saw a flash in one of the upper windows as of a curtain being stealthily drawn and as stealthily let fall again, and though it gave me the promise of some sort of greeting, there was a furtiveness in the action, so in keeping with the suspicions of Mr. Gryce that I felt my nerves braced at once to mount the half-dozen uninviting-looking steps that led to the front door.

But no sooner had I done this, with what I am fain to consider my best air, than I suddenly collapsed with what I am bound to regard as a comprehensible and quite excusable fear; for, while I do not quail before men, and have a reasonable fortitude in the presence of most dangers, corporeal and moral, I am not quite myself in face of a rampant and barking dog. It is my one weakness, and while I usually can, and under most circumstances do, succeed in hiding my inner trepidation under the emergency just mentioned, I always feel that it would be a happy relief for me if the day should ever come when these so-called domestic animals would be banished from the affections and homes of men. Then I think I would begin to live in good earnest and perhaps enjoy trips into the country, which now, for all my apparent bravery, I regard more in the light of a penance than a pleasure.

Imagine, then, how hard I found it to retain my self-possession or even any appearance of dignity, when at the moment I was stretching forth my hand toward the knocker of this inhospitable mansion I heard rising from some unknown quarter a howl so keen, piercing, and prolonged that it frightened the very birds over my head and sent them flying from the vines in clouds.

It was the unhappiest kind of welcome for me. I did not know whether it came from within or without, and when after a moment of indecision I saw the door open, I am not sure whether the smile I called up to grace the occasion had any of the real Amelia Butterworth in it, so much was my mind divided between a desire to produce a favorable impression and a very decided and not-to-be-hidden fear of the dog who had greeted my arrival with such an ominous howl.

"Call off the dog!" I cried almost before I saw what sort of person I was addressing.

Mr. Gryce, when I saw him later, declared this to be the most significant introduction I could have made of myself upon entering the Knollys mansion.

CHAPTER IV

A Ghostly Interior

The hall into which I had stepped was so dark that for a few minutes I could see nothing but the indistinct outline of a young woman with a very white face. She had uttered some sort of murmur at my words, but for some reason was strangely silent, and, if I could trust my eyes, seemed rather to be looking back over her shoulder than into the face of her advancing guest. This was odd, but before I could quite satisfy myself as to the cause of her abstraction, she suddenly bethought herself, and throwing open the door of an adjoining room, let in a stream of light by which we were enabled to see each other and exchange the greetings suitable to the occasion.

"Miss Butterworth, my mother's old friend," she murmured, with an almost pitiful effort to be cordial, "we are so glad to have you visit us. Won't you—won't you sit down?"

What did it mean? She had pointed to a chair in the sitting-room, but her face was turned away again as if drawn irresistibly toward some secret object of dread. Was there anyone or anything at the top of the dim staircase I could faintly see in the distance? It would not do for me to ask, nor was it wise for me to show that I thought this reception a strange one. Stepping into the room she pointed out, I waited for her to follow me, which she did with manifest reluctance. But when she was once out of the atmosphere of the hall, or out of reach of the sight or sound of whatever it was that frightened her, her face took on a smile that ingratiated her with me at once and gave to her very delicate aspect, which up to that moment had not suggested the remotest likeness to her mother, a piquant charm and subtle fascination that were not unworthy of the daughter of Althea Burroughs.

"You must not mind the poverty of your welcome," she said, with a half-proud, half-apologetic look around her, which I must say the bareness and shabby character of the room we were in fully justified. "We have not been very well off since father died and mother left us. Had you given us a chance we should have written you that our home would not offer many inducements to you after your own, but you have come unexpectedly and—"

"There, there," I put in, for I saw that her embarrassment would soon get the better of her, "do not speak of it. I did not come to enjoy your home, but to see you. Are you the eldest, my dear, and where are your sister and brother?"

"I am not the eldest," she said. "I am Lucetta. My sister"—here her head stole irresistibly back to its old position of listening—"will—will come soon. My brother is not in the house."

"Well," said I, astonished that she did not ask me to take off my things, "you are a pretty girl, but you do not look very strong. Are you quite well, my dear?"

She started, looked at me eagerly, almost anxiously, for a moment, then straightened herself and began to lose some of her abstraction.

"I am not a strong person," she smiled, "but neither am I so very weak either. I was always small. So was my mother, you know."

I was glad to have her talk of her mother. I therefore answered her in a way to prolong the conversation.

"Yes, your mother was small," I admitted, "but never thin or pallid. She was like a fairy among us schoolgirls. Does it seem odd to hear so old a woman as I speak of herself as a schoolgirl?"

"Oh, no!" she said, but there was no heart in her voice.

"I had almost forgotten those days till I happened to hear the name of Althea mentioned the other day," I proceeded, seeing I must keep up the conversation if we were not to sit in total silence. "Then my early friendship with your mother recurred to me, and I started up—as I always do when I come to any decision, my dear—and sent that telegram, which I hope I have not followed by an unwelcome presence."

"Oh, no," she repeated, but this time with some feeling; "we need friends, and if you will overlook our shortcomings—But you have not taken off your hat. What will Loreen say to me?"

And with a sudden nervous action as marked as her late listlessness, she jumped up and began busying herself over me, untying my bonnet and laying aside my bundles, which up to this moment I had held in my hands.

"I—I am so absent-minded," she murmured. "I—I did not think—I hope you will excuse me. Loreen would have given you a much better welcome."

"Then Loreen should have been here," I said, with a smile. I could not restrain this slight rebuke, yet I liked the girl; notwithstanding everything I had heard and her own odd and unaccountable behavior, there was a sweetness in her face, when she chose to smile, that proved an irresistible attraction. And then, for all her absent-mindedness and abstracted ways, she was such a lady! Her plain dress, her restrained manner, could not hide this fact. It was apparent in every line of her thin but graceful form and in every inflection of her musical but constrained voice. Had I seen her in my own parlor instead of between these bare and moldering walls, I should have said the same thing: "She is such a lady!" But this only passed through my mind at the time. I was not studying her personality, but trying to understand why my presence in the house had so visibly disturbed her. Was it the embarrassment of poverty, not knowing how to meet the call made so suddenly upon it? I hardly thought so. Fear would not enter into a sensation of this kind, and fear was what I had seen in her face before the front door had closed upon me. But that fear? Was it connected with me or with something threatening her from another portion of the house?

The latter supposition seemed the probable one. The way her ear was turned, the slight start she gave at every sound, convinced me that her cause of dread lay elsewhere than with myself, and therefore was worthy of my closest attention. Though I chatted and tried in every way to arouse her confidence, I could not help asking myself between the sentences, if the cause of her apprehension lay with her sister, her brother, or in something entirely apart from either, and connected with the dreadful matter which had drawn me to X. Or another supposition still, was it merely the sign of an habitual distemper which, misunderstood by Mr. Gryce, had given rise to the suspicions which it was my possible mission here to dispel?

Anxious to force things a little, I remarked, with a glance at the dismal branches that almost forced their way into the open casements: "What a scene for young eyes like yours! Do you never get tired of these pine-boughs and clustering shadows? Would not a little cottage in the sunnier part of the town be preferable to all this dreary grandeur?"

She looked up with sudden wistfulness that made her smile piteous.

"Some of my happiest days have been passed here and some of my saddest. I do not think I should like to leave it for any sunny cottage. We were not made for bonny homes," she continued. "The sombreness of this old house suits us."

"And of this road," I ventured. "It is the darkest and most picturesque I ever rode through. I thought I was threading a wilderness."

For a moment she forgot her cause of anxiety and looked at me quite intently, while a subtle shade of doubt passed slowly over her features.

"It is a solitary one," she acquiesced. "I do not wonder it struck you as dismal. Have you heard—has any one ever told you that—that it was not considered quite safe?"

"Safe?" I repeated, with—God forgive me!—an expression of mild wonder in my eyes.

"Yes, it has not the best of reputations. Strange things have happened in it. I thought that someone might have been kind enough to tell you this at the station."

There was a gentle sort of sarcasm in the tone; only that, or so it seemed to me at the time. I began to feel myself in a maze.

"Somebody—I suppose it was the station-master—did say something to me about a boy lost somewhere in this portion of the woods. Do you mean that, my dear?"

She nodded, glancing again over her shoulder and partly rising as if moved by some instinct of flight.

"They are dark enough, for more than one person to have been lost in their recesses," I observed with another look toward the heavily curtained windows.

"They certainly are," she assented, reseating herself and eying me nervously while she spoke. "We are used to the terrors they inspire in strangers, but if you"—she leaped to her feet in manifest eagerness and her whole face changed in a way she little realized herself—"if you have any fear of sleeping amid such gloomy surroundings, we can procure you a room in the village where you will be more comfortable, and where we can visit you almost as well as we can here. Shall I do it? Shall I call—"

My face must have assumed a very grim look, for her words tripped at that point, and a flush, the first I had seen on her cheek, suffused her face, giving her an appearance of great distress.

"Oh, I wish Loreen would come! I am not at all happy in my suggestions," she said, with a deprecatory twitch of her lip that was one of her subtle charms. "Oh, there she is! Now I may go," she cried; and without the least appearance of realizing that she had said anything out of place, she rushed from the room almost before her sister had entered it.

But not before their eyes had met in a look of unusual significance.

CHAPTER V

A Strange Household

Had I not surprised this look of mutual understanding, I might have received an impression of Miss Knollys which would in a measure have counteracted that made by the more nervous and less restrained Lucetta. The dignified reserve of her bearing, the quiet way in which she approached, and, above all, the even tones in which she uttered her welcome, were such as to win my confidence and put me at my ease in the house of which she was the nominal mistress. But that look! With that in my memory, I was enabled to pierce below the surface of this placid nature, and in the very constraint she put upon herself, detect the presence of the same secret uneasiness which had been so openly, if unconsciously, manifested by her sister.

She was more beautiful than Lucetta in form and feature, and even more markedly elegant in her plain black gown and fine lawn ruffles, but she lacked her sister's evanescent charm, and though admirable to all appearance, was less lovable on a short acquaintance.

But this delays my tale, which is one of action rather than reflection. I had naturally expected that with the appearance of the elder Miss

Knollys I should be taken to my room; but, on the contrary, she sat down and with an apologetic air informed me that she was sorry she could not show me the customary attentions. Circumstances over which she had no control had made it impossible, she said, for her to offer me the guest-chamber, but if I would be so good as to accept another for this one night, she would endeavor to provide me with better accommodations on the morrow.

Satisfied of the almost painful nature of their poverty and determined to submit to privations rather than leave a house so imbued with mystery, I hastened to assure her that any room would be acceptable to me; and with a display of good feeling not wholly insincere, began to gather up my wraps in anticipation of being taken at once upstairs.

But Miss Knollys again surprised me by saying that my room was not yet ready; that they had not been able to complete all their arrangements, and begged me to make myself at home in the room where I was till evening.

As this was asking a good deal of a woman of my years, fresh from a railroad journey and with natural habits of great neatness and order, I felt somewhat disconcerted, but hiding my feelings in consideration of reasons before given, replaced my bundles on the table and endeavored to make the best of a somewhat trying situation.

Launching at once into conversation, I began, as with Lucetta, to talk about her mother. I had never known, save in the vaguest way, why Mrs. Knollys had taken the journey which had ended in her death and burial in a foreign land. Rumor had it that she had gone abroad for her health which had begun to fail after the birth of Lucetta; but as Rumor had not added why she had gone unaccompanied by her husband or children, there remained much which these girls might willingly tell me, which would be of the greatest interest to me. But Miss Knollys, intentionally or unintentionally, assumed an air so cold at my well meant questions, that I desisted from pressing them, and began to talk about myself in a way which I hoped would establish really friendly relations between us and make it possible for her to tell me later, if not at the present moment, what it was that weighed so heavily upon the household, that no one could enter this home without feeling the shadow of the secret terror enveloping it.

But Miss Knollys, while more attentive to my remarks than her sister had been, showed, by certain unmistakable signs, that her heart and interest were anywhere but in that room; and while I could not regard this as throwing any discredit upon my powers of pleasing—which have rarely failed when I have exerted them to their utmost—I still could not but experience the dampening effect of her manner. I went on chatting, but in a desultory way, noting all that was odd in her unaccountable reception of me, but giving, as I firmly believe, no evidence of my concern and rapidly increasing curiosity.

The peculiarities observable in this my first interview with these interesting but by no means easily-to-be-understood sisters continued all day. When one sister came in, the other stepped out, and when dinner was announced and I was ushered down the bare and dismal hall into an equally bare and unattractive dining-room, it was to find the chairs set for four, and Lucetta only seated at the table.

"Where is Loreen?" I asked wonderingly, as I took the seat she pointed out to me with one of her faint and quickly vanishing smiles.

"She cannot come at present," my young hostess stammered with an unmistakable glance of distress at the large, hearty-looking woman who had summoned me to the dining-room.

"Ah," I ejaculated, thinking that possibly Loreen had found it necessary to assist in the preparation of the meal, "and your brother?"

It was the first time he had been mentioned since my first inquiries. I had shrunk from the venture out of a motive of pure compassion, and they had not seen fit to introduce his name into any of our conversations. Consequently I awaited her response, with some anxiety, having a secret premonition that in some way he was at the bottom of my strange reception.

Her hasty answer, given, however, without any increase of embarrassment, somewhat dispelled this supposition.

"Oh, he will be in presently," said she. "William is never very punctual."

But when he did come in, I could not help seeing that her manner instantly changed and became almost painfully anxious. Though it was my first meeting with the real head of the house, she waited for an interchange of looks with him before giving me the necessary introduction, and when, this duty performed, he took his seat at the table, her thoughts and attention remained so fixed upon him that she well-nigh forgot the ordinary civilities of a hostess. Had it not been for the woman I have spoken of, who in her good-natured attention to my wants amply made up for the abstraction of her mistress, I should have fared ill at this meal, good and ample as it was, considering the resources of those who provided it.

She seemed to dread to have him speak, almost to have him move. She watched him with her lips half open, ready, as it appeared, to stop any inadvertent expression he might utter in his efforts to be agreeable. She even kept her left hand disengaged, with the evident intention of stretching it out in his direction if in his lumbering stupidity he should utter a sentence calculated to open my eyes to what she so passionately desired to have kept secret. I saw it all as plainly as I saw his heavy indifference to her anxiety; and knowing from experience that it is in just such stolid louts as these that the worst passions are often hidden, I took advantage of my years and forced a conversation in which I hoped some flash of his real self would appear, despite her wary watch upon him.

Not liking to renew the topic of the lane itself, I asked with a very natural show of interest, who was their nearest neighbor. It was William who looked up and William who answered.

"Old Mother Jane is the nearest," said he; "but she's no good. We never think of her. Mr. Trohm is the only neighbor I care for. Such peaches as the old fellow raises! Such grapes! Such melons! He gave me two of the nicest you ever saw this morning. By Jupiter, I taste them yet!"

Lucetta's face, which should have crimsoned with mortification, turned most unaccountably pale. Yet not so pale as it had previously done when, a few minutes before, he began to say, "Loreen wants some of this soup saved for"—and stopped awkwardly, conscious perhaps that Loreen's wants should not be mentioned before me.

"I thought you promised me that you would never again ask Mr. Trohm for any of his fruit," remonstrated Lucetta.

"Oh, I didn't ask! I just stood at the fence and looked over. Mr. Trohm and I are good friends. Why shouldn't I eat his fruit?"

The look she gave him might have moved a stone, but he seemed perfectly impervious to it. Seeing him so stolid, her head drooped, and she did not answer a word. Yet somehow I felt that even while she was so manifestly a prey to the deepest mortification, her attention was not wholly given over to this one emotion. There was something else she feared. Hoping to relieve her and lighten the situation, I forced myself to smile on the young man as I said:

"Why don't you raise melons yourself? I think if I possessed your land I should be anxious to raise everything I could on it."

"Oh, you're a woman!" he retorted, almost roughly. "It's good business for women; and for men, too, perhaps, who love to see fruit hang, but I only care to eat it."

"Don't," Lucetta put in, but not with the vigor I had expected.

"I like to hunt, train dogs, and enjoy other people's fruit," he laughed, with a nod at the blushing Lucetta. "I don't see any use in a man's putting himself out for things he can get for the asking. Life's too short for such folly. I mean to have a good time while I'm on this blessed sphere."

"William!"

The cry was irresistible, yet it was not the cry I had been looking for. Painful as was this exhibition of his stupidity and utter want of feeling, it was not the one thing she stood in dread of, or why was her protest so much weaker than her appearance had given token of?

"Oh!" he shouted in great amusement, while she shrunk back with a horrified look. "Lucetta don't like to hear me say that. She thinks a man ought to work, plow, harrow, dig, make a slave of himself, to keep up a place that's no good anyway. But I tell her that work is something she'll never get out of me. I was born a gentleman, and a gentleman I will live if the place tumbles down over our heads. Perhaps it would be the best way to get rid of it. Then I could go live with Mr. Trohm, and have melons from early morn till late at night." And again his coarse laugh rang out.

This, or was it his words, seemed to rouse her as nothing had done before. Thrusting out her hand, she laid it on his mouth, with a look of almost frenzied appeal at the woman who was standing at his back.

"Mr. William, how can you!" that woman protested; and when he would have turned upon her angrily, she leaned over and whispered in his ear a few words that seemed to cow him, for he gave a short grunt through his sister's trembling fingers and, with a shrug of his heavy shoulders, subsided into silence.

To all this I was a simple spectator, but I did not soon forget a single feature of the scene.

The remainder of the dinner passed quietly, William and myself eating with more or less heartiness, Lucetta tasting nothing at all. In mercy to her I declined coffee, and as soon as William gave token of being satisfied, we hurriedly rose. It was the most uncomfortable meal I ever ate in my life.

CHAPTER VI

A Sombre Evening

The evening, like the afternoon, was spent in the sitting-room with one of the sisters. One event alone is worth recording. I had become excessively tired of a conversation that always languished, no matter on what topic it started, and, observing an old piano in one corner—I once played very well—I sat down before it and impulsively struck a few chords from the yellow keys. Instantly Lucetta—it was Lucetta who was with me then—bounded to my side with a look of horror.

"Don't do that!" she cried, laying her hand on mine to stop me. Then, seeing my look of dignified astonishment, she added with an appealing smile, "I beg pardon, but every sound goes through me tonight."

"Are you not well?" I asked.

"I am never very well," she returned, and we went back to the sofa and renewed our forced and pitiful attempts at conversation.

Promptly at nine o'clock Miss Knollys came in. She was very pale and cast, as usual, a sad and uneasy look at her sister before she spoke to me. Immediately Lucetta rose, and, becoming very pale herself, was hurrying toward the door when her sister stopped her.

"You have forgotten," she said, "to say good-night to our guest."

Instantly Lucetta turned, and, with a sudden, uncontrollable impulse, seized my hand and pressed it convulsively.

"Good-night," she cried. "I hope you will sleep well," and was gone before I could say a word in response.

"Why does Lucetta go out of the room when you come in?" I asked, determined to know the reason for this peculiar conduct. "Have you any other guests in the house?"

The reply came with unexpected vehemence. "No," she cried, "why should you think so? There is no one here but the family." And she turned away with a dignity she must have inherited from her father, for Althea Burroughs had every interesting quality but that. "You must be very tired," she remarked. "If you please we will go now to your room."

I rose at once, glad of the prospect of seeing the upper portion of the house. She took my wraps on her arm, and we passed immediately into the hall. As we did so, I heard voices, one of them shrill and full of distress; but the sound was so quickly smothered by a closing door that I failed to discover whether this tone of suffering proceeded from a man or a woman.

Miss Knollys, who was preceding me, glanced back in some alarm, but as I gave no token of having noticed anything out of the ordinary, she speedily resumed her way upstairs. As the sounds I had heard proceeded from above, I followed her with alacrity, but felt my enthusiasm diminish somewhat when I found myself passing door after door down a long hall to a room as remote as possible from what seemed to be the living portion of the house.

"Is it necessary to put me off quite so far?" I asked, as my young hostess paused and waited for me to join her on the threshold of the most forbidding room it had ever been my fortune to enter.

The blush which mounted to her brow showed that she felt the situation keenly.

"I am sure," she said, "that it is a matter of great regret to me to be obliged to offer you so mean a lodging, but all our other rooms are out of order, and I cannot accommodate you with anything better tonight."

"But isn't there some spot nearer you?" I urged. "A couch in the same room with you would be more acceptable to me than this distant room."

"I—I hope you are not timid," she began, but I hastened to disabuse her mind on this score.

"I am not afraid of any earthly thing but dogs," I protested warmly. "But I do not like solitude. I came here for companionship, my dear. I really would like to sleep with one of you."

This, to see how she would meet such urgency. She met it, as I might have known she would, by a rebuff.

"I am very sorry," she again repeated, "but it is quite impossible. If I could give you the comforts you are accustomed to, I should be glad, but we are unfortunate, we girls, and—" She said no more, but began to busy herself about the room, which held but one object that had the least look of comfort in it. That was my trunk, which had been neatly placed in one corner.

"I suppose you are not used to candles," she remarked, lighting what struck me as a very short end, from the one she held in her hand.

"My dear," said I, "I can accommodate myself to much that I am not used to. I have very few old maid's ways or notions. You shall see that I am far from being a difficult guest."

She heaved a sigh, and then, seeing my eye travelling slowly over the gray discolored walls which were not relieved by so much as a solitary print, she pointed to a bell-rope near the head of the bed, and considerately remarked:

"If you wish anything in the night, or are disturbed in any way, pull that. It communicates with my room, and I will be only too glad to come to you."

I glanced up at the rope, ran my eye along the wire communicating with it, and saw that it was broken sheer off before it even entered into the wall.

"I am afraid you will not hear me," I answered, pointing to the break.

She flushed a deep scarlet, and for a moment looked as embarrassed as ever her sister had done.

"I did not know," she murmured. "The house is so old, everything is more or less out of repair." And she made haste to quit the room.

I stepped after her in grim determination.

"But there is no key to the door," I objected.

She came back with a look that was as nearly desperate as her placid features were capable of.

"I know," she said, "I know. We have nothing. But if you are not afraid—and of what could you be afraid in this house, under our protection, and with a good dog outside?—you will bear with things tonight, and—Good God!" she murmured, but not so low but that my excited sense caught every syllable, "can she have heard? Has the reputation of this place gone abroad? Miss Butterworth," she repeated earnestly, "the house contains no cause of terror for you. Nothing threatens our guest, nor need you have the least concern for yourself or us, whether the night passes in quiet or whether it is broken by unaccountable sounds. They will have no reference to anything in which you are interested."

"Ah, ha," thought I, "won't they! You give me credit for much indifference, my dear." But I said nothing beyond a few soothing phrases, which I made purposely short, seeing that every moment I detained her was just so much unnecessary torture to her. Then I went back to my room and carefully closed the door. My first night in this dismal and strangely ordered house had opened anything but propitiously.

CHAPTER VII

The First Night

I spoke with a due regard to truth when I assured Miss Knollys that I entertained no fears at the prospect of sleeping apart from the rest of the family. I am a woman of courage—or so I have always believed—and at home occupy my second floor alone without the least apprehension. But there is a difference in these two abiding-places, as I think you are ready by this time to acknowledge, and, though I felt little of what is called fear, I certainly did not experience my usual satisfaction in the minute preparations with which I am accustomed to make myself comfortable for the night. There was a gloom both within and without the four bare walls between which I now found myself shut, which I would have been something less than human not to feel, and though I had no dread of being overcome by it, I was glad to add something to the cheer of the spot by opening my trunk and taking out a few of those little matters of personal equipment without which the brightest room looks barren and a den like this too desolate for habitation.

Then I took a good look about me to see how I could obtain for myself some sense of security. The bed was light and could be pulled in front of the door. This was something. There was but one window, and that was closely draped with some thick, dark stuff, very funereal in its appearance. Going to it, I pulled aside the thick folds and looked out. A mass of heavy foliage at once met my eye, obstructing the view of the sky and adding much to the lonesomeness of the situation. I let the curtain fall again and sat down in a chair to think.

The shortness of the candle-end with which I had been provided had struck me as significant, so significant that I had not allowed it to burn long after Miss Knollys had left me. If these girls, charming, no doubt, but sly, had thought to shorten my watch by shortening my candle, I would give them no cause to think but that their ruse had been successful. The foresight which causes me to add a winter wrap to my stock of clothing even when the weather is at the hottest, leads me to place a half dozen or so of candles in my travelling trunk, and so I had only to open a little oblong box in the upper tray to have the means at my disposal of keeping a light all night.

So far, so good. I had a light, but had I anything else in case William Knollys—but with this thought Miss Knollys's look and reassuring words recurred to me. "Whatever you may hear—if you hear anything—will have no reference to yourself and need not disturb you."

This was comforting certainly, from a selfish standpoint; but did it relieve my mind concerning others?

Not knowing what to think of it all, and fully conscious that sleep would not visit me under existing circumstances, I finally made up my mind not to lie down till better assured that sleep on my part would be desirable. So after making the various little arrangements already alluded to, I drew over my shoulders a comfortable shawl and set myself to listen for what I feared would be more than one dreary hour of this not to be envied night.

And here just let me stop to mention that, carefully considered as all my precautions were, I had forgotten one thing upon leaving home which at this minute made me very nearly miserable. I had not included among my effects the alcohol lamp and all the other private and particular conveniences which I possess for making tea in my own apartment. Had I but had them with me, and had I been able to make and sip a cup of my own delicious tea through the ordeal of listening for whatever sounds might come to disturb the midnight stillness of this house, what relief it would have been to my spirits and in what a different light I might have regarded Mr. Gryce and the mission with which I had been intrusted. But I not only lacked this element of comfort, but the satisfaction of thinking that it was any one's fault but my own. Lena had laid her hand on that teapot, but I had shaken my head, fearing that the sight of it might offend the eyes of my young hostesses. But I had not calculated upon being put in a remote corner like this of a house large enough to accommodate a dozen families, and if ever I travel again—

But this is a matter personal to Amelia Butterworth, and of no interest to you. I will not inflict my little foibles upon you again.

Eleven o'clock came and went. I had heard no sound. Twelve, and I began to think that all was not quite so still as before; that I certainly could hear now and then faint noises as of a door creaking on its hinges, or the smothered sound of stealthily moving feet. Yet all was so far from being distinct, that for some time I hesitated to acknowledge to myself that anything could be going on in the house, which was not to be looked for in a home professing to be simply the abode of a decent young man and two very quiet-appearing young ladies; and even after the noises and whispering had increased to such an extent that I could even distinguish the sullen tones of the brother from the softer and more carefully modulated accents of Lucetta and her sister, I found myself ready to explain the matter by any conjecture short of that which involved these delicate young ladies in any scheme of secret wickedness.

But when I found there was likely to be no diminution in the various noises and movements that were taking place in the front of the house, and that only something much out of the ordinary could account for so much disturbance in a country home so long after midnight, I decided that only a person insensible to all sight and sound could be expected to remain asleep under such circumstances, and that I would be perfectly justified in their eyes in opening my door and taking a peep down the corridor. So without further ado, I drew my bed aside and glanced out.

All was perfectly dark and silent in the great house. The only light visible came from the candle burning in the room behind me, and as for sound, it was almost too still—it was the stillness of intent rather than that of natural repose.

This was so unexpected that for an instant I stood baffled and wondering. Then my nose went up, and I laughed quietly to myself. I could see nothing and I could hear nothing; but Amelia Butterworth, like most of her kind, boasts of more than two senses, and happily there was something to smell. A quickly blown-out candle leaves a witness behind it to sensitive nostrils like mine, and this witness assured me that the darkness was deceptive. Some one had just passed the head of my corridor with a light, and because the light was extinguished it did not follow that the person who held it was far away. Indeed, I thought that now I heard a palpitating breath.

"Humph," I cried aloud, but as if in unconscious communion with myself, "it is not often I have so vivid a dream! I was sure that I heard steps in the hall. I fear I'm growing nervous."

Nothing moved. No one answered me.

"Miss Knollys!" I called firmly.

No reply.

"Lucetta, dear!"

I thought this appeal would go unanswered also, but when I raised my voice for the third time, a sudden rushing sound took place down the corridor, and Lucetta's excited figure, fully dressed, appeared in the faint circle of light caused by my now rapidly waning candle.

"Miss Butterworth, what is the matter?" she asked, making as if she would draw me into my room—a proceeding which I took good care she should not succeed in.

Giving a glance at her dress, which was the same she had worn at the supper table, I laughingly retorted:

"Isn't that a question I might better ask you? It is two o'clock by my watch, and you, for all your apparent delicacy, are still up. What does it mean, my dear? Have I put you out so completely by my coming that none of you can sleep?"

Her eyes, which had fallen before mine, quickly looked up.

"I am sorry," she began, flushing and trying to take a peep into my room, possibly to see if I had been to bed. "We did not mean to disturb you, but—but—oh, Miss Butterworth, pray excuse our makeshifts and our poverty. We wished to fix up another room for you, and were ashamed to have you see how little we had to do it with, so we were moving some things out of our own room tonight, and—"

Here her voice broke, and she burst into an almost uncontrollable flood of tears.

"Don't," she entreated, "don't," as, quite thoroughly ashamed, I began to utter some excuses. "I shall be all right in a moment. I am used to humiliations. Only"—and her whole body seemed to join in the plea, it trembled so—"do not, I pray, speak quite so loud. My brother is more sensitive than even Loreen and myself about these things, and if he should hear—"

Here a suppressed oath from way down the hall assured me that he did hear, but I gave no sign of my recognition of this fact, and Lucetta added quickly: "He would not forgive us for our carelessness in waking you. He is rough sometimes, but so good at heart, so good."

This, with the other small matter I have just mentioned, caused a revulsion in my feelings. He good? I did not believe it. Yet her eyes showed no wavering when I interrogated them with mine, and feeling that I had perhaps been doing them all an injustice, and that what I had seen was, as she evidently meant to intimate, due to their efforts to make a sudden guest comfortable amid their poverty, I put the best face I could on the matter and gave the poor, pitiful, pleading face a kiss. I was startled to feel how cold her forehead was, and, more and more concerned, loaded her down with such assurances of appreciation as came to my lips, and sent her back to her own room with an injunction not to trouble herself any more about fixing up any other room for me. "Only," I added, as her whole face showed relief, "we will go to the locksmith tomorrow and get a key; and after tonight you will be kind enough to see that I have a cup of tea brought to my room just before I retire. I am no good without my cup of tea, my dear. What keeps other people awake makes me sleep."

"Oh, you shall have your tea!" she cried, with an eagerness that was almost unnatural, and then, slipping from my grasp, she uttered another hasty apology for having roused me from my sleep and ran hastily back.

I stretched out my arm for the candle guttering in my room and held it up to light her. She seemed to shrink at sight of its rays, and the last vision I had of her speeding figure showed me that same look of dread on her pallid features which had aroused my interest in our first interview.

"She may have explained why the three of them are up at this time of night," I muttered, "but she has not explained why her every conversation is seasoned by an expression of fear."

And thus brooding, I went back to my room and, pushing the bed again against the door, lay down upon it and out of sheer chagrin fell fast asleep.

CHAPTER VIII

On the Stairs

I did not wake up till morning. The room was so dark that in all probability I should not have wakened then, if my habits of exact punctuality had not been aided by a gentle knock at my door.

"Who's there?" I called, for I could not say "Come in" till I had moved my bed and made way for the door to open.

"Hannah with warm water," replied a voice, at which I made haste to rise. Hannah was the woman who had waited on us at dinner.

The sight of her pleasant countenance, which nevertheless looked a trifle haggard, was a welcome relief after the sombre features of the night. Addressing her with my usual brusqueness, but with quite my usual kindness, I asked how the young ladies were feeling this morning.

Her answer made a great show of frankness.

"Oh, they are much as usual," said she. "Miss Loreen is in the kitchen and Miss Lucetta will soon be here to inquire how you are. I hope you passed a good night yourself, ma'am."

I had slept more than I ought to, perhaps, and made haste to reassure her as to my own condition. Then seeing that a little talk would not be unwelcome to this hearty woman, tired to death possibly with life in this dreary house, I made some excuse for keeping her a few minutes, saying as I did so:

"What an immense dwelling this is for four persons to live in, or have you another inmate whom I have not seen?"

I thought her buxom color showed a momentary sign of failing, but it all came back with her answer, which was given in a round, hearty voice.

"Oh, I'm the only maid, ma'am. I cook and sweep and all. I couldn't abide another near me. Even Mr. Simsbury, who tends the cow and horse and who only comes in for his dinner, worries me by spells. I like to have my own way in the kitchen, except when the young ladies choose to come in. Is there anything more you want, ma'am, and do you prefer tea or coffee for breakfast?"

I told her that I always drank coffee in the morning, and would have liked to have added a question or two, but she gave me no chance. As she went out I saw her glance at my candlestick. There was only a half-burned end in it. She is calculating, too, how long I sat up, thought I.

Lucetta stood at the head of the stairs as I went down.

"Will you excuse me for a few moments?" said she. "I am not quite ready to follow you, but will be soon."

"I will take a look at the grounds."

I thought she hesitated for a moment; then her face lighted up. "Be sure you don't encounter the dog," she cried, and slipped hastily down a side hall I had not noticed the night before.

"Ah, a good way to keep me in," I reasoned. "But I shall see the grounds yet if I have to poison that dog." Notwithstanding, I made no haste to leave the house. I don't believe in tempting Providence, especially where a dog is concerned.

Instead of that, I stood still and looked up and down the halls, endeavoring to get some idea of their plan and of the location of my own room in reference to the rest.

I found that the main hall ran at right angles to the long corridor down which I had just come, and noting that the doors opening into it were of a size and finish vastly superior to those I had passed in the corridor just mentioned, I judged that the best bedrooms all lay front, and that I had been quartered at the end of what had once been considered as the servants' hall. At my right, as I looked down the stairs, ran a wall with a break, which looked like an opening into another corridor, and indeed I afterward learned that the long series of rooms of which mine was the last, had its counterpart on the other side of this enormous dwelling, giving to the house the shape of a long, square U.

I was looking in some wonderment at this opening and marvelling over the extravagant hospitality of those old days which necessitated such a number of rooms in a private gentleman's home, when I heard a door open and two voices speaking. One was rough and careless, unmistakably that of William Knollys. The other was slow and timid, and was just as unmistakably that of the man who had driven me to this house the day before. They were talking of some elderly person, and I had good sense enough not to allow my indignation to blind me to the fact that by that elderly person they meant me. This is important, for their words were not without significance.

"How shall we keep the old girl out of the house till it is all over?" was what I heard from William's surly lips.

"Lucetta has a plan," was the hardly distinguishable answer. "I am to take—"

That was all I could hear; a closing door shut off the remainder. Something, then, was going on in this house, of a dark if not mysterious character, and the attempts made by these two interesting and devoted girls to cover up the fact, by explanations founded on their poverty, had been but subterfuges after all. Grieved on their account, but inwardly grateful to the imprudence of their more than reckless brother, for this not-to-be-mistaken glimpse into the truth, I slowly descended the stairs, in that state of complete self-possession which is given by a secret knowledge of the intentions formed against us by those whose actions we have reason to suspect.

Henceforth I had but one duty—to penetrate the mystery of this household. Whether it was the one suspected by Mr. Gryce or another of a less evil and dangerous character hardly mattered in my eyes. While the blight of it rested upon this family, eyes would be lowered and heads shaken at their name. This, if I could help it, must no longer be. If guilt lay at the bottom of all this fear, then this guilt must be known; if innocence—I thought of the brother's lowering brow and felt it incompatible with innocence, but remembering Mr. Gryce's remarks on this subject, read an instant lecture to myself and, putting all conclusions aside, devoted the few minutes in which I found myself alone in the dining-room to a careful preparation of my mind for its duty, which was not likely to be of the simplest character if Lucetta's keen wits were to be pitted against mine.

CHAPTER IX

A New Acquaintance

When my mind is set free from doubt and fully settled upon any course, I am capable of much good nature and seeming simplicity. I was therefore able to maintain my own at the breakfast-table with some success, so that the meal passed off without any of the disagreeable experiences of the night before. Perhaps the fact that Loreen presided at the coffee-urn instead of Lucetta had something to do with this. Her calm, even looks seemed to put some restraint upon the boisterous outbursts to which William was only too liable, while her less excitable nature suffered less if by any chance he did break out and startle the decorous silence by one of his rude guffaws.

I am a slow eater, but I felt forced to hurry through the meal or be left eating alone at the end. This did not put me in the best of humor, for I hated to risk an indigestion just when my faculties needed to be unusually alert. I compromised by leaving the board hungry, but I did it with such a smile that I do not think Miss Knollys knew I had not risen from any table so ill satisfied in years.

"I will leave you to my brother for a few minutes," said she, hastily tripping from the room. "I pray that you will not think of going to your room till we have had an opportunity of arranging it."

I instantly made up my mind to disobey this injunction. But first, it was necessary to see what I could make of William.

He was not a very promising subject as he turned and led the way toward the front of the house.

"I thought you might like to see the grounds," he growled, evidently not enjoying the rôle assigned him. "They are so attractive," he sneered. "Children hereabout call them the jungle."

"Who's to blame for that?" I asked, with only a partial humoring of his ill nature. "You have a sturdy pair of arms of your own, and a little trimming here and a little trimming there would have given quite a different appearance to this undergrowth. A gentleman usually takes pride in his place."

"Yes, when it's all his. This belongs to my sisters as much as to me. What's the use of my bothering myself about it?"

The man was so selfish he did not realize the extent of the exhibition he made of it. Indeed he seemed to take pride in what he probably called his independence. I began to feel the most intense aversion for him, and only with the greatest difficulty could prolong this conversation unmoved.

"I should think it would be a pleasure to give that much assistance to your sisters. They do not seem to be sparing in their attempts to please you."

He snapped his fingers, and I was afraid a dog or two would come leaping around the corner of the house. But it was only his way of expressing disdain.

"Oh, the girls are well enough," he grumbled; "but they will stick to the place. Lucetta might have married a half-dozen times, and once I thought she was going to, but suddenly she turned straight about and sent her lover packing, and that made me mad beyond everything. Why should she hang on to me like a burr when there are other folks willing to take on the burden?"

It was the most palpable display of egotism I had ever seen and one of the most revolting. I was so disgusted by it that I spoke up without any too much caution.

"Perhaps she thinks she can be useful to you," I said. "I have known sisters give up their own happiness on no better grounds."

"Useful?" he sneered. "It's a usefulness a man like me can dispense with. Do you know what I would like?"

We were standing in one of the tangled pathways, with our faces turned toward the house. As he spoke, he looked up and made a rude sort of gesture toward the blank expanse of empty and curtainless windows.

"I would like that great house all to myself, to make into one huge, bachelor's hall. I should like to feel that I could tramp from one end of it to the other without awakening an echo I did not choose to hear there. I should not find it too big. I should not find it too lonesome. I and my dogs would know how to fill it, wouldn't we, Saracen? Oh, I forgot, Saracen is locked up."

The way he mumbled the last sentence showed displeasure, but I gave little heed to that. The gloating way in which he said he and his dogs would fill it had given me a sort of turn. I began to have more than an aversion for the man. He inspired me with something like terror.

"Your wishes," said I, with as little expression as possible, "seem to leave your sisters entirely out of your calculations. How would your mother regard that if she could see you from the place where she is gone?"

He turned upon me with a look of anger that made his features positively ugly.

"What do you mean by speaking to me of my mother? Have I spoken of her to you? Is there any reason why you should lug my mother into this conversation? If so, say so, and be—"

He did not swear at me; he did not dare to, but he came precious near to it, and that was enough to make me recoil.

"She was my friend," said I. "I knew and loved her before you were born. That was why I spoke of her, and I think it very natural myself."

He seemed to feel ashamed. He grumbled out some sort of apology and looked about quite helplessly, possibly for the dog he manifestly was in the habit of seeing forever at his heels. I took advantage of this momentary abstraction on his part to smooth my own disturbed features.

"She was a beautiful girl," I remarked, on the principle that, the ice once broken, one should not hesitate about jumping in. "Was your father equally handsome for a man?"

"My father—yes, let's talk of father. He was a judge of horses, he was. When he died, there were three mares in the stable not to be beat this side of Albany, but those devils of executors sold them, and I—well, you had a chance to test the speed of old Bess yesterday. You weren't afraid of being thrown out, I take it. Great Scott, to think of a man of my tastes owning no other horse than that!"

"You have not answered my question," I suggested, turning him about and moving toward the gate.

"Oh, about the way my father looked! What does that matter? He was handsome, though. Folks say that I get whatever good looks I have from him. He was big—bigger than I am, and while he lived—What did you make a fellow talk for?"

I don't know why I did, but I was certainly astonished at the result. This great, huge lump of selfish clay had actually shown feeling and was ashamed of it, like the lout he was.

"Yesterday," said I, anxious to change the subject, "I had difficulty in getting in through that gate we are pointing for. Couldn't you set it straight, with just a little effort?"

He paused, looked at me to see if I were in earnest, then took a dogged step toward the gate I was still indicating with my resolute right hand, but before he could touch it he perceived something on that deserted and ominous highway which made him start in sudden surprise.

"Why, Trohm," he cried, "is that you? Well, it's an age since I have seen you turn that corner on a visit to us."

"Sometime, certainly," answered a hearty and pleasant voice, and before I could quite drop the look of severity with which I was endeavoring to shame this young man into some decent show of interest in this place, and assume the more becoming aspect of a lady caught unawares at an early morning hour plucking flowers from a stunted syringa, a gentleman stepped into sight on the other side of the fence with a look and a bow so genial and devoid of mystery that I experienced for the first time since entering the gloomy precincts of this town a decided sensation of pleasure.

"Miss Butterworth," explained Mr. Knollys with a somewhat forced gesture in my direction. "A guest of my sisters," he went on, and looked as if he hoped I would retire, though he made no motion to welcome Mr. Trohm in, but rather leaned a little conspicuously on the gate as if anxious to show that he had no idea that the other's intention went any further than the passing of a few neighborly comments at the gate.

I like to please the young even when they are no more agreeable than my surly host, and if the gentleman who had just shown himself had been equally immature, I would certainly have left them to have their talk out undisturbed. But he was not. He was older; he was even of sufficient years for his judgment to have become thoroughly matured and his every faculty developed. I therefore could not see why my society should be considered an intrusion by him, so I waited. His next sentence was addressed to me.

"I am happy," said he, "to have the pleasure of a personal introduction to Miss Butterworth. I did not expect it. The surprise is all the more agreeable. I only anticipated being allowed to leave this package and letter with the maid. They are addressed to you, madam, and were left at my house by mistake."

I could not hide my astonishment.

"I live in the next house below," said he. "The boy who brought these from the post office was a stupid lad, and I could not induce him to come any farther up the road. I hope you will excuse the present messenger and believe there has been no delay."

I bowed with what must have seemed an abstracted politeness. The letter was from New York, and, as I strongly suspected, from Mr. Gryce. Somehow this fact created in me an unmistakable embarrassment. I put both letter and package into my pocket and endeavored to meet the gentleman's eye with my accustomed ease in the presence of strangers. But, strange to say, I had no sooner done so than I saw that he was no more at his ease than myself. He smiled, glanced at William, made an offhand remark or so about the weather, but he could not deceive eyes sharpened by such experience as mine. Something disturbed him, something connected with me. It made my cheek a little hot to acknowledge this even to myself, but it was so very evident that I began to cast about for the means of ridding ourselves of William when that blundering youth suddenly spoke:

"I suppose he was afraid to come up the lane. Do you know, I think you're brave to attempt it, Trohm. We haven't a very good name here." And with a sudden, perfectly unnatural burst, he broke out into one of his huge guffaws that so shook the old gate on which he was leaning that I thought it would tumble down with him before our eyes.

I saw Mr. Trohm start and cast him a look in which I seemed to detect both surprise and horror, before he turned to me and with an air of polite deprecation anxiously said:

"I am afraid Miss Butterworth will not understand your allusions, Mr. Knollys. I hear this is her first visit in town."

As his manner showed even more feeling than the occasion seemed to warrant, I made haste to answer that I was well acquainted with the tradition of the lane; that its name alone showed what had happened here.

His bearing betrayed an instant relief.

"I am glad to find you so well informed," said he. "I was afraid"— here he cast another very strange glance at William—"that your young friends might have shrunk, from some sense of delicacy, from telling you what might frighten most guests from a lonely road like this. I compliment you upon their thoughtfulness."

William bowed as if the words of the other contained no other suggestion than that which was openly apparent. Was he so dull, or was he—I had not time to finish my conjectures even in my own mind, for at this moment a quick cry rose behind us, and Lucetta's light figure appeared running toward us with every indication of excitement.

"Ah," murmured Mr. Trohm, with an appearance of great respect, "your sister, Mr. Knollys. I had better be moving on. Good-morning, Miss Butterworth. I am sorry that circumstances make it impossible for me to offer you those civilities which you might reasonably expect from so near a neighbor. Miss Lucetta and I are at swords' points over a matter upon which I still insist she is to blame. See how shocked she is to see me even standing at her gate."

Shocked! I would have said terrified. Nothing but fear—her old fear aggravated to a point that made all attempt at concealment impossible—could account for her white, drawn features and trembling form. She looked as if her whole thought was, "Have I come in time?"

"What—what has procured us the honor of this visit?" she asked, moving up beside William as if she would add her slight frame to his bulky one to keep this intruder out.

"Nothing that need alarm you," said the other with a suggestive note in his kind and mellow voice. "I was rather unexpectedly intrusted this morning with a letter for your agreeable guest here, and I have merely come to deliver it."

Her look of astonishment passing from him to me, I thrust my hand into my pocket and drew out the letter which I had just received.

"From home," said I, without properly considering that this was in some measure an untruth.

"Oh!" she murmured as if but half convinced. "William could have gone for it," she added, still eying Mr. Trohm with a pitiful anxiety.

"I was only too happy," said the other, with a low and reassuring bow. Then, as if he saw that her distress would only be relieved by his departure, he raised his hat and stepped back into the open highway. "I will not intrude again, Miss Knollys," were his parting words. "If you want anything of Obadiah Trohm, you know where to find him. His doors will always be open to you."

Lucetta, with a start, laid her hand on her brother's arm as if to restrain the words she saw slowly laboring to his lips, and leaning breathlessly forward, watched the fine figure of this perfect country gentleman till it had withdrawn quite out of sight. Then she turned, and with a quick abandonment of all self-control, cried out with a pitiful gesture toward her brother, "I thought all was over; I feared he meant to come into the house," and fell stark and seemingly lifeless at our feet.

CHAPTER X

Secret Instructions

For a moment William and myself stood looking at each other over this frail and prostrate figure. Then he stooped, and with an unexpected show of kindness raised her up and began carrying her toward the house.

"Lucetta is a fool," he cried suddenly, stopping and giving me a quick glance over his shoulder. "Because folks are terrified of this road and come to see us but seldom, she has got to feel a most unreasonable dread of visitors. She was even set against your coming till we showed her what folly it was for her to think we could always live here like hermits. Then she doesn't like Mr. Trohm; thinks he is altogether too friendly to me—as if that was any of her business. Am I an idiot? Have I no sense? Cannot I be trusted to take care of my own affairs and keep my own secrets? She's a weak, silly chit, to go and flop over like this when, d—n it, we have enough to look after without nursing her up and—I mean," he said, tripping himself up with an air of polite consideration so out of keeping with his usual churlishness as to be more than noticeable, "that it cannot add much to the pleasure of your visit to have such things happen as this."

"Oh, don't worry about me!" I curtly responded. "Get the poor girl in. I'll look after her."

But as if she heard these words and was startled by them, Lucetta roused in her brother's arms and struggled passionately to her feet. "Oh! what has happened to me?" she cried. "Have I said anything? William, have I said anything?" she asked wildly, clinging to her brother in terror.

He gave her a look and pushed her off.

"What are you talking about?" he cried. "One would think you had something to conceal."

She steadied herself up in an instant.

"I am the weakest of the family," said she, walking straight up to me and taking me affectionately by the arm. "All my life I have been delicate and these turns are nothing new to me. Sometimes I think I will die in one of them; but I am quite restored now," she hastily added, as I could not help showing my concern. "See! I can walk quite alone." And she ran, rather than walked, up the few short steps of the porch, at which we had now arrived. "Don't tell Loreen," she begged, as I followed her into the house. "She worries so about me, and it will do no good."

William had stalked off toward the stables. We were therefore alone. I turned and laid a finger on her arm.

"My dear," said I, "I never make foolish promises, but I can be trusted never to heedlessly slight any one's wishes. If I see no good reason why I should tell your sister of this fainting fit, I shall certainly hold my peace."

She seemed moved by my manner, if not by my words.

"Oh," she cried, seizing my hand and pressing it. "If I dared to tell you of my troubles! But it is impossible, quite impossible." And before I could urge a plea for her confidence she was gone, leaving me in the company of Hannah, who at this moment was busying herself with something at the other end of the hall.

I had no wish to interfere with Hannah just then. I had my letter to read, and did not wish to be disturbed. So I slipped into the sitting-room and carefully closed the door. Then I opened my letter.

It was, as I supposed, from Mr. Gryce, and ran thus:

"Dear Miss Butterworth:

"I am astonished at your determination, but since your desire to visit your friends is such as to lead you to brave the dangers of Lost Man's Lane, allow me to suggest certain precautions.

"First.—Do not trust anybody.

"Second.—Do not proceed anywhere alone or on foot.

"Third.—If danger comes to you, and you find yourself in a condition of real peril, blow once shrilly on the whistle I inclose with this. If, however, the danger is slight, or you wish merely to call the attention of those who will be set to watch over you, let the blast be short, sharp, and repeated—twice to summon assistance, three times to call attention.

"I advise you to fasten this whistle about your neck in a way to make it easily obtainable.

"I have advised you to trust nobody. I should have excepted Mr. Trohm, but I do not think you will be given an opportunity to speak to him. Remember that all depends upon your not awakening suspicion. If, however, you wish advice or desire to make any communication to me or the man secretly holding charge over this affair in X., seek the first opportunity of riding into town and go at once to the hotel where you will ask for Room 3. It has been retained in your service, and once shown into it, you, may expect a visitor who will be the man you seek.

"As you will see, every confidence is put in your judgment."

There was no signature to this—it needed none—and in the packet which came with it was the whistle. I was glad to see it, and glad to hear that I was not left entirely without protection in my somewhat hazardous enterprise.

The events of the morning had been so unexpected that till this moment I had forgotten my early determination to go to my room before any change there could be made. Recalling it now, I started for the staircase, and did not stop though I heard Hannah calling me back. The consequence was that I ran full tilt against Miss Knollys coming down the hall with a tray in her hand.

"Ah," I cried; "someone sick in the house?"

The attack was too sudden. I saw her recoil and for one instant hesitate before replying. Then her natural self-possession came to her aid, and she placidly remarked:

"We were all up to a late hour last night, as you know. It was necessary for us to have some food."

I accepted the explanation and made no further remark, but as in passing her I had detected on this tray of food supposed to have been sent up the night before, the half-eaten portion of a certain dish we had had for breakfast, I reserved to myself the privilege of doubting her exact truthfulness. To me the sight of this partially consumed breakfast was proof positive of there being in the house some person of whose presence I was supposed to be ignorant—not a pleasant thought under the circumstances, but quite an important fact to have established. I felt that in this one discovery I had clutched the thread that would yet lead me out of the labyrinth of this mystery.

Miss Knollys, who was on her way downstairs, called Hannah to take the tray, and, coming back, beckoned me toward a door opening into one of the front rooms.

"This is to be your room," she announced, "but I do not know that I can move you today."

She was so calm, so perfectly mistress of herself, that I could not but admire her. Lucetta would have flushed and fidgeted, but Loreen stood as erect and placid as if no trouble weighed upon her heart and the words were as unimportant in their character as they seemed.

"Do not distress yourself," said I. "I told Lucetta last night that I was perfectly comfortable and had no wish to change my quarters. I am sorry you should have thought it necessary to disturb yourself on my account last night. Don't do it again, I pray. A woman like myself had rather put herself to some slight inconvenience than move.

"I am much obliged to you," said she, and came at once from the door. I don't know but after all I like Lucetta's fidgety ways better than Loreen's unmovable self-possession.

"Shall I order the coach for you?" she suddenly asked, as I turned toward the corridor leading to my room.

"The coach?" I repeated.

"I thought that perhaps you might like to ride into town. Mr. Simsbury is at leisure this morning. I regret that neither Lucetta nor myself will be able to accompany you."

I thought what this same Mr. Simsbury had said about Lucetta's plan, and hesitated. It was evidently their wish to have me spend my morning elsewhere than with them. Should I humor them, or find excuses for remaining home? Either course had its difficulties. If I went, what might not take place in my absence! If I remained, what suspicions might I not rouse! I decided to compromise matters, and start for town even if I did not go there.

"I am hesitating," said I, "because of the two or three rather threatening-looking clouds toward the east. But if you are sure Mr. Simsbury can be spared, I think I will risk it. I really would like to get a key for my door; and then riding in the country is so pleasant."

Miss Knollys, with a bow, passed immediately downstairs. I went in a state of some doubt toward my own room. "Am I surveying these occurrences through highly magnifying glasses?" thought I. It was very possible, yet not so possible but that I cast very curious glances at the various closed doors I had to pass before reaching my own. Such a little thing would make me feel like trying them. Such a little thing—that is, added to the other things which had struck me as unexplainable.

I found my bed made and everything in apple-pie order. I had therefore nothing to do but to prepare for going out. This I did quickly, and was downstairs sooner perhaps than I was expected. At all events Lucetta and William parted very suddenly when they saw me, she in tears and he with a dogged shrug and some such word as this:

"You're a fool to take on so. Since it's got to be, the sooner the better, I say. Don't you see that every minute makes less our chances of concealment?"

It made me feel like changing my mind and staying home. But the habit of a lifetime is not easily broken into. I kept to my first decision.

CHAPTER XI

Men, Women, And Ghosts

Mr. Simsbury gave me quite an amiable bow as I entered the buggy. This made it easy for me to say:

"You are on hand early this morning. Do you sleep in the Knollys house?"

The stare he gave me had the least bit of suspicion in it.

"I live over yonder," he said, pointing with his whip across the intervening woods to the main road. "I come through the marshes to my breakfast; my old woman says they owes me three meals, and three meals I must have."

It was the longest sentence with which he had honored me. Finding him in a talkative mood, I prepared to make myself agreeable, a proceeding which he seemed to appreciate, for he began to sniff and pay great attention to his horse, which he was elaborately turning about.

"Why do you go that way?" I protested. "Isn't it the longest way to the village?"

"It's the way I'm most accustomed to," said he. "But we can go the other way if you like. Perhaps we will get a glimpse of Deacon Spear. He's a widower, you know."

The leer with which he said this was intolerable. I bridled up—but no, I will not admit that I so much as manifested by my manner that I understood him. I merely expressed my wish to go the old way.

He whipped up the horse at once, almost laughing outright. I began to think this man capable of most any wicked deed. He was forced, however, to pull up suddenly. Directly in our path was the stooping figure of a woman. She did not move as we advanced, and so we had no alternative but to stop. Not till the horse's head touched her shoulder did she move. Then she rose up and looked at us somewhat indignantly.

"Didn't you hear us?" I asked, willing to open conversation with the old crone, whom I had no difficulty in recognizing as Mother Jane.

"She's deaf—deaf, as a post," muttered Mr. Simsbury. "No use shouting at her." His tone was brusque, yet I noticed he waited with great patience for her to hobble out of the way.

Meanwhile I was watching the old creature with much interest. She had not a common face or a common manner. She was gray, she was toothless, she was haggard, and she was bent, but she was not ordinary or just one of the crowd of old women to be seen on country doorsteps. There was force in her aged movements and a strong individuality in the glances she shot at us as she backed slowly out of the roadway.

"Do they say she is imbecile?" I asked. "She looks far from foolish to me."

"Hearken a bit," said he. "Don't you see she is muttering? She talks to herself all the time." And in fact her lips were moving.

"I cannot hear her," I said. "Make her come nearer. Somehow the old creature interests me."

He at once beckoned to the crone; but he might as well have beckoned to the tree against which she had pushed herself. She neither answered him nor gave any indication that she understood the gesture he had made. Yet her eyes never moved from our faces.

"Well, well," said I, "she seems dull as well as deaf. You had better drive on." But before he could give the necessary jerk of the reins, I caught sight of some pennyroyal growing about the front of the cottage a few steps beyond, and, pointing to it with some eagerness, I cried: "If there isn't some of the very herb I want to take home with me! Do you think she would give me a handful of it if I paid her?"

With an obliging grunt he again pulled up. "If you can make her understand," said he.

I thought it worth the effort. Though Mr. Gryce had been at pains to tell me there was no harm in this woman and that I need not even consider her in any inquiries I might be called upon to make, I remembered that Mr. Gryce had sometimes made mistakes in just such matters as these, and that Amelia Butterworth had then felt herself called upon to set him right. If that could happen once, why not twice? At all events, I was not going to lose the least chance of making the acquaintance of the people living in this lane. Had he not himself said that only in this way could we hope to come upon the clue that had eluded all open efforts to find it?

Knowing that the sight of money is the strongest appeal that can be made to one living in such abject poverty as this woman, making the blind to see and the deaf to hear, I drew out my purse and held up before her a piece of silver. She bounded as if she had been shot, and when I held it toward her came greedily forward and stood close beside the wheels looking up.

"For you," I indicated, after making a motion toward the plant which had attracted my attention.

She glanced from me to the herb and nodded with quick appreciation. As in a flash she seemed to take in the fact that I was a stranger, a city lady with memories of the country and this humble plant, and hurrying to it with the same swiftness she had displayed in advancing to the carriage, she tore off several of the sprays and brought them back to me, holding out her hand for the money.

I had never seen greater eagerness, and I think even Mr. Simsbury was astonished at this proof of her poverty or her greed. I was inclined to think it the latter, for her portly figure was far from looking either ill-fed or poorly cared for. Her dress was of decent calico, and her pipe had evidently been lately filled, for I could smell the odor of tobacco about her. Indeed, as I afterward heard, the good people of X. had never allowed her to suffer. Yet her fingers closed upon that coin as if in it she grasped the salvation of her life, and into her eyes leaped a light that made her look almost young, though she must have been fully eighty.

"What do you suppose she will do with that?" I asked Mr. Simsbury, as she turned away in an evident fear I might repent of my bargain.

"Hark!" was his brief response. "She is talking now."

I did hearken, and heard these words fall from her quickly moving lips:

"Seventy; twenty-eight; and now ten."

Jargon; for I had given her twenty-five cents, an amount quite different from any she had mentioned.

"Seventy!" She was repeating the figures again, this time in a tone of almost frenzied elation. "Seventy; twenty-eight; and now ten! Won't Lizzie be surprised! Seventy; twenty—" I heard no more—she had bounded into her cottage and shut the door.

"Waal, what do you think of her now?" chuckled Mr. Simsbury, touching up his horse. "She's always like that, saying over numbers, and muttering about Lizzie. Lizzie was her daughter. Forty years ago she ran off with a man from Boston, and for thirty-eight years she's been lying in a Massachusetts grave. But her mother still thinks she is alive and is coming back. Nothing will ever make her think different. But she's harmless, perfectly harmless. You needn't be afeard of her."

This, because I cast a look behind me of more than ordinary curiosity, I suppose. Why were they all so sure she was harmless? I had thought her expression a little alarming at times, especially when she took the money from my hand. If I had refused it or even held it back a little, I think she would have fallen upon me tooth and nail. I wished I could take a peep into her cottage. Mr. Gryce had described it as four walls and nothing more, and indeed it was small and of the humblest proportions; but the fluttering of some half-dozen pigeons about its eaves proved it to be a home and, as such, of interest to me, who am often able to read character from a person's habitual surroundings.

There was no yard attached to this simple building, only a small open place in front in which a few of the commonest vegetables grew, such as turnips, carrots, and onions. Elsewhere towered the forest—the great pine forest through which this portion of the road ran.

Mr. Simsbury had been so talkative up to now that I was in hope he would enter into some details about the persons and things we encountered, which might assist me in the acquaintanceship I was anxious to make. But his loquaciousness ended with this small adventure I have just described. Not till we were well quit of the pines and had entered into the main thoroughfare did he deign to respond to any of my suggestions, and then it was in a manner totally unsatisfactory and quite uncommunicative. The only time he deigned to offer a remark was when we emerged from the forest and came upon the little crippled child, looking from its window. Then he cried:

"Why, how's this? That's Sue you see there, and her time isn't till arternoon. Rob allers sits there of a mornin'. I wonder if the little chap's sick. S'pose I ask."

As this was just what I would have suggested if he had given me time, I nodded complacently, and we drove up and stopped.

The piping voice of the child at once spoke up:

"How d' ye do, Mr. Simsbury? Ma's in the kitchen. Rob isn't feelin' good today."

I thought her tone had a touch of mysteriousness in it. I greeted the pale little thing, and asked if Rob was often sick.

"Never," she answered, "except, like me, he can't walk. But I'm not to talk about it, ma says. I'd like to, but—"

Ma's face appearing at this moment over her shoulder put an end to her innocent garrulity.

"How d' ye do, Mr. Simsbury?" came a second time from the window, but this time in very different tones. "What's the child been saying? She's so sot up at being allowed to take her brother's place in the winder that she don't know how to keep her tongue still. Rob's a little languid, that's all. You'll see him in his old place tomorrow." And she drew back as if in polite intimation that we might drive on.

Mr. Simsbury responded to the suggestion, and in another moment we were trotting down the road. Had we stayed a minute longer, I think the child would have said something more or less interesting to hear.

The horse, which had brought us thus far at a pretty sharp trot, now began to lag, which so attracted Mr. Simsbury's attention, that he forgot to answer even by a grunt more than half of my questions. He spent most of his time looking at the nag's hind feet, and finally, just as we came in sight of the stores, he found his tongue sufficiently to announce that the horse was casting a shoe and that he would be obliged to go to the blacksmith's with her.

"Humph, and how long will that take?" I asked.

He hesitated so long, rubbing his nose with his finger, that I grew suspicious and cast a glance at the horse's foot myself. The shoe was loose. I began to hear it clang.

"Waal, it may be a matter of a couple of hours," he finally drawled. "We have no blacksmith in town, and the ride up there is two miles. Sorry it happened, ma'am, but there's all sorts of shops here, you see, and I've allers heard that a woman can easily spend two hours haggling away in shops."

I glanced at the two ill-furnished windows he pointed out, thought of Arnold & Constable's, Tiffany's, and the other New York establishments I had been in the habit of visiting, and suppressed my disdain. Either the man was a fool or he was acting a part in the interests of Lucetta and her family. I rather inclined to the latter supposition. If the plan was to keep me out most of the morning why could that shoe not have been loosened before the mare left the stable?

"I made all necessary purchases while in New York," said I, "but if you must get the horse shod, why, take her off and do it. I suppose there is a hotel parlor near here where I can sit."

"Oh, yes," and he made haste to point out to me where the hotel stood. "And it's a very nice place, ma'am. Mrs. Carter, the landlady, is the nicest sort of person. Only you won't try to go home, ma'am, on foot? You'll wait till I come back for you?"

"It isn't likely I'll go streaking through Lost Man's Lane alone," I exclaimed indignantly. "I'd rather sit in Mrs. Carter's parlor till night."

"And I would advise you to," he said. "No use making gossip for the village folks. They have enough to talk about as it is."

Not exactly seeing the force of this reasoning, but quite willing to be left to my own devices for a little while, I pointed to a locksmith's shop I saw near by, and bade him put me down there.

With a sniff I declined to interpret into a token of disapproval, he drove me up to the shop and awkwardly assisted me to alight.

"Trunk key missing?" he ventured to inquire before getting back into his seat.

I did not think it necessary to reply, but walked immediately into the shop. He looked dissatisfied at this, but whatever his feelings were he refrained from any expression of them, and presently mounted to his place and drove off. I was left confronting the decent man who represented the lock-fitting interests in X.

I found some difficulty in broaching my errand. Finally I said:

"Miss Knollys, who lives up the road, wishes a key fitted to one of her doors. Will you come or send a man to her house today? She is too occupied to see about it herself."

The man must have been struck by my appearance, for he stared at me quite curiously for a minute. Then he gave a hem and a haw and said:

"Certainly. What kind of a door is it?" When I had answered, he gave me another curious glance and seemed uneasy to step back to where his assistant was working with a file.

"You will be sure to come in time to have the lock fitted before night?" I said in that peremptory manner of mine which means simply, "I keep my promises and expect you to keep yours."

His "Certainly" struck me as a little weaker this time, possibly because his curiosity was excited. "Are you the lady from New York who is staying with them?" he asked, stepping back, seemingly quite unawed by my positive demeanor.

"Yes," said I, thawing a trifle; "I am Miss Butterworth."

He looked at me almost as if I were a curiosity.

"And did you sleep there last night?" he urged.

I thought it best to thaw still more.

"Of course," I said. "Where do you think I would sleep? The young ladies are friends of mine."

He rapped abstractedly on the counter with a small key he was holding.

"Excuse me," said he, with some remembrance of my position toward him as a stranger, "but weren't you afraid?"

"Afraid?" I echoed. "Afraid in Miss Knollys' house?"

"Why, then, do you want a key to your door?" he asked, with a slight appearance of excitement. "We don't lock doors here in the village; at least we didn't."

"I did not say it was my door," I began, but, feeling that this was a prevarication not only unworthy of me, but one that he was entirely too sharp to accept, I added stiffly: "It is for my door. I am not accustomed even at home to sleep with my room unlocked."

"Oh," he murmured, totally unconvinced, "I thought you might have got a scare. Folks somehow are afraid of that old place, it's so big and ghost-like. I don't think you would find any one in this village who would sleep there all night."

"A pleasing preparation for my rest tonight," I grimly laughed. "Dangers on the road and ghosts in the house. Happily I don't believe in the latter."

The gesture he made showed incredulity. He had ceased rapping with the key or even to show any wish to join his assistant. All his thoughts for the moment seemed to be concentrated on me.

"You don't know little Rob," he inquired, "the crippled lad who lives at the head of the lane?"

"No," I said; "I haven't been in town a day yet, but I mean to know Rob and his sister too. Two cripples in one family rouse my interest."

He did not say why he had spoken of the child, but began tapping with his key again.

"And you are sure you saw nothing?" he whispered. "Lots of things can happen in a lonely road like that."

"Not if everybody is as afraid to enter it as you say your villagers are," I retorted.

But he didn't yield a jot.

"Some folks don't mind present dangers," said he. "Spirits—"

But he received no encouragement in his return to this topic. "You don't believe in spirits?" said he. "Well, they are doubtful sort of folks, but when honest and respectable people such as live in this town, when children even, see what answers to nothing but phantoms, then I remember what a wiser man than any of us once said— But perhaps you don't read Shakespeare, madam?"

Nonplussed for the moment, but interested in the man's talk more than was consistent with my need of haste, I said with some spirit, for it struck me as very ridiculous that this country mechanic should question my knowledge of the greatest dramatist of all time, "Shakespeare and the Bible form the staple of my reading." At which he gave me a little nod of apology and hastened to say:

"Then you know what I mean—Hamlet's remark to Horatio, madam, 'There are more things,' etc. Your memory will readily supply you with the words."

I signified my satisfaction and perfect comprehension of his meaning, and, feeling that something important lay behind his words, I endeavored to make him speak more explicitly.

"The Misses Knollys show no terror of their home," I observed. "They cannot believe in spirits either."

"Miss Knollys is a woman of a great deal of character," said he. "But look at Lucetta. There is a face for you, for a girl not yet out of her twenties; and such a round-cheeked lass as she was once! Now what has made the change? The sights and sounds of that old house, I say. Nothing else would give her that scared look—nothing merely mortal, I mean."

This was going a step too far. I could not discuss Lucetta with this stranger, anxious as I was to hear what he had to say about her.

"I don't know," I remonstrated, taking up my black satin bag, without which I never stir. "One would think the terrors of the lane she lives in might account for some appearance of fear on her part."

"So it might," he assented, but with no great heartiness. "But Lucetta has never spoken of those dangers. The people in the lane do not seem to fear them. Even Deacon Spear says that, set aside the wickedness of the thing, he rather enjoys the quiet which the ill repute of the lane gives him. I don't understand this indifference myself. I have no relish for horrible mysteries or for ghosts either."

"You won't forget the key?" I suggested shortly, preparing to walk out, in my dread lest he should again introduce the subject of Lucetta.

"No," said he, "I won't forget it." His tone should have warned me that I need not expect to have a locked door that night.

CHAPTER XII

The Phantom Coach

Ghosts! What could the fellow have meant? If I had pressed him he would have told me, but it did not seem quite a lady's business to pick up information in this way, especially when it involved a young lady like Lucetta. Yet did I think I would ever come to the end of this matter without involving Lucetta? No. Why, then, did I allow my instincts to triumph over my judgment? Let those answer who understand the workings of the human heart. I am simply stating facts.

Ghosts! Somehow the word startled me as if in some way it gave a rather unwelcome confirmation to my doubts. Apparitions seen in the Knollys mansion or in any of the houses bordering on this lane! That was a serious charge; how serious seemed to be but half comprehended by this man. But I comprehended it to the full, and wondered if it was on account of such gossip as this that Mr. Gryce had persuaded me to enter Miss Knollys' house as a guest.

I was crossing the street to the hotel as I indulged in these conjectures, and intent as my mind was upon them, I could not but note the curiosity and interest which my presence excited in the simple country folk invariably to be found lounging about a country tavern. Indeed, the whole neighborhood seemed agog, and though I would have thought it derogatory to my dignity to notice the fact, I could not but see how many faces were peering at me from store doors and the half-closed blinds of adjoining cottages. No young girl in the pride of her beauty could have awakened more interest, and this I attributed, as was no doubt right, not to my appearance, which would not perhaps be apt to strike these simple villagers as remarkable, or to my dress, which is rather rich than fashionable, but to the fact that I was a stranger in town, and, what was more extraordinary, a guest of the Misses Knollys.

My intention in approaching the hotel was not to spend a couple of dreary hours in the parlor with Mrs. Carter, as Mr. Simsbury had suggested, but to obtain if possible a conveyance to carry me immediately back to the Knollys mansion. But this, which would have been a simple matter in most towns, seemed well-nigh an impossibility in X. The landlord was away, and Mrs. Carter, who was very frank with me, told me it would be perfectly useless to ask one of the men to drive me through the lane. "It's an unwholesome spot," said she, "and only Mr. Carter and the police have the courage to brave it."

I suggested that I was willing to pay well, but it seemed to make very little difference to her. "Money won't hire them," said she, and I had the satisfaction of knowing that Lucetta had triumphed in her plan, and that, after all, I must sit out the morning in the precincts of the hotel parlor with Mrs. Carter.

It was my first signal defeat, but I was determined to make the best of it, and if possible glean such knowledge from the talk of this woman as would make me feel that I had lost nothing by my disappointment. She was only too ready to talk, and the first topic was little Rob.

I saw the moment I mentioned his name that I was introducing a subject which had already been well talked over by every eager gossip in the village.

Her attitude of importance, the air of mystery she assumed, were preparations I had long been accustomed to in women of this kind, and I was not at all surprised when she announced in a way that admitted of no dispute:

"Oh, there's no wonder the child is sick. We would be sick under the circumstances. *He has seen the phantom coach.*"

The phantom coach! So that was what the locksmith meant. A phantom coach! I had heard of every kind of phantom but that. Somehow the idea was a thrilling one, or would have been to a nature less practical than mine.

"I don't know what you mean," said I. "Some superstition of the place? I never heard of a ghostly appearance of that nature before."

"No, I expect not. It belongs to X. I never heard of it beyond these mountains. Indeed, I have never known it to have been seen but upon one road. I need not mention what road, madam. You can guess."

Yes, I could guess, and the guessing made me set my lips a little grimly.

"Tell me more about this thing," I urged, half laughing. "It ought to be of some interest to me."

She nodded, drew her chair a trifle nearer, and impetuously began:

"You see this is a very old town. It has more than one ancient country house similar to the one you are now living in, and it has its early traditions. One is, that an old-fashioned coach, perfectly noiseless, drawn by horses through which you can see the moonlight, haunts the highroad at intervals and flies through the gloomy forest road we have christened of late years Lost Man's Lane. It is a superstition, possibly, but you cannot find many families in town but believe in it as a fact, for there is not an old man or woman in the place but has either seen it in the past or has had some relative who has seen it. It passes only at night, and it is thought to presage some disaster to those who see it. My husband's uncle died the next morning after it flew by him on the highway. Fortunately years elapse between its going and coming. It is ten years, I think they say, since it was last seen. Poor little Rob! It has frightened him almost out of his wits."

"I should think so," I cried with becoming credulity. "But how came he to see it? I thought you said it only passed at night."

"At midnight," she repeated. "But Rob, you see, is a nervous lad, and night before last he was so restless he could not sleep, so he begged to be put in the window to cool off. This his mother did, and he sat there for a good half-hour alone, looking out at the moonlight. As his mother is an economical woman there was no candle lit in the room, so he got his pleasure out of the shadows which the great trees made on the highroad, when suddenly—you ought to hear the little fellow tell it—he felt the hair rise on his forehead and all his body grow stiff with a terror that made his tongue feel like lead in his mouth. A something he would have called a horse and a carriage in the daytime, but which, in this light and under the influence of the mortal terror he was in, took on a distorted shape which made it unlike any team he was accustomed to, was going by, not as if being driven over the earth and stones of the road—though there was a driver in front, a driver with an odd three-cornered hat on his head and a cloak about his shoulders, such as the little fellow remembered to have seen hanging in his grandmother's closet—but as if it floated along without sound or stir; in fact, a spectre team which seemed to find its proper destination when it turned into Lost Man's Lane and was lost among the shadows of that ill-reputed road."

"Pshaw!" was my spirited comment as she paused to take her breath and see how I was affected by this grewsome tale. "A dream of the poor little lad! He had heard stories of this apparition and his imagination supplied the rest."

"No; excuse me, madam, he had been carefully kept from hearing all such tales. You could see this by the way he told his story. He hardly believed what he had himself seen. It was not till some foolish neighbor blurted out, 'Why, that was the phantom coach,' that he had any idea he was not relating a dream."

My second *Pshaw!* was no less marked than the first.

"He did know about it, notwithstanding," I insisted. "Only he had forgotten the fact. Sleep often supplies us with these lost memories."

"Very true, and your supposition is very plausible, Miss Butterworth, and might be regarded as correct, if he had been the only person to see this apparition. But Mrs. Jenkins saw it too, and she is a woman to be believed."

This was becoming serious.

"Saw it before he did or afterwards?" I asked. "Does she live on the highway or somewhere in Lost Man's Lane?"

"She lives on the highway about a half-mile from the station. She was sitting up with her sick husband and saw it just as it was going down the hill. She said it made no more noise than a cloud slipping by. She expects to lose old Rause. No one could behold such a thing as that and not have some misfortune follow."

I laid all this up in my mind. My hour of waiting was not likely to prove wholly unprofitable.

"You see," the good woman went on, with a relish for the marvellous that stood me in good stead, "there is an old tradition of that road connected with a coach. Years ago, before any of us were born, and the house where you are now staying was a gathering-place for all the gay young bloods of the county, a young man came up from New York to visit Mr. Knollys. I do not mean the father or even the grandfather of the folks you are visiting, ma'am. He was great-grandfather to Lucetta, and a very fine gentleman, if you can trust the pictures that are left of him. But my story has not to do with him. He had a daughter at that time, a widow of great and sparkling attractions, and though she was older than the young man I have mentioned, every one thought he would marry her, she was so handsome and such an heiress.

"But he failed to pay his court to her, and though he was handsome himself and made a fool of more than one girl in the town, every one thought he would return as he had come, a free-hearted bachelor, when suddenly one night the coach was missed from the stables and he from the company, which led to the discovery that the young widow's daughter was gone too, a chit who was barely fifteen, and without a hundredth part of the beauty of her mother. Love only could account for this, for in those days young ladies did not ride with gentlemen in the evening for pleasure, and when it came to the old gentleman's ears, and, what was worse, came to the mother's, there was a commotion in the great house, the echoes of which, some say, have never died out. Though the pipers were playing and the fiddles were squeaking in the great room where they used to dance the night away, Mrs. Knollys, with her white brocade tucked up about her waist, stood with her hand on the great front door, waiting for the horse upon which she was determined to follow the flying lovers. The father, who was a man of eighty years, stood by her side. He was too old to ride himself, but he made no effort to hold her back, though the jewels were tumbling from her hair and the moon had vanished from the highway.

"'I will bring her back or die!' the passionate beauty exclaimed, and not a lip said her nay, for they saw, what neither man nor woman had been able to see up to that moment, that her very life and soul were wrapped up in the man who had stolen away her daughter.

"Shrilly piped the pipes, squeak and hum went the fiddles, but the sound that was sweetest to her was the pound of the horses' hoofs on the road in front. That was music indeed, and as soon as she heard it she bestowed one wild kiss on her father and bounded from the house. An instant later and she was gone. One flash of her white robe at the gate, then all was dark on the highway, and only the old father stood in the wide-open door, waiting, as he vowed he would wait, till his daughter returned.

"She did not go alone. A faithful groom was behind her, and from him was learned the conclusion of that quest. For an hour and a half they rode; then they came upon a chapel in the mountains, in which were burning unwonted lights. At the sight the lady drew rein and almost fell from her horse into the arms of her lackey. 'A marriage!' she murmured; 'a marriage!' and pointed to an empty coach standing in the shadow of a wide-spreading tree. It was their family coach. How well she knew it! Rousing herself, she made for the chapel door. 'I will stop these unhallowed rites!' she cried! 'I am her mother, and she is not of age.' But the lackey drew her back by her rich white dress. 'Look!' he cried, pointing in at one of the windows, and she looked. The man she loved stood before the altar with her daughter. He was smiling in that daughter's face with a look of passionate devotion. It went like a dagger to her heart. Crushing her hands against her face, she wailed out some fearful protest; then she dashed toward the door with 'Stop! stop!' on her lips. But the faithful lackey at her side drew her back once more. 'Listen!' was his word, and she listened. The minister, whose form she had failed to note in her first hurried look, was uttering his benediction. She had come too late. The young couple were married.

"Her servant said, or so the tradition runs, that when she realized this she grew calm as walking death. Making her way into the chapel, she stood ready at the door to greet them as they issued forth, and when they saw her there, with her rich bedraggled robe and the gleam of jewels on a neck she had not even stopped to envelop in more than the veil from her hair, the bridegroom seemed to realize what he had done and stopped the bride, who in her confusion would have fled back to the altar where she had just been made a wife. 'Kneel!' he cried. 'Kneel, Amarynth! Only thus can we ask pardon of our mother.' But at that word, a word which seemed to push her a million miles away from these two beings who but two hours before had been the delight of her life, the unhappy woman gave a cry and fled from their presence. 'Go! go!' were her parting words. 'As you have chosen, you must abide. But let no tongue ever again call me mother.'

"They found her lying on the grass outside. As she could no longer sustain herself on a horse, they put her into the coach, gave the reins to her devoted lackey, and themselves rode off on horseback. One man, the fellow who had driven them to that place, said that the clock struck twelve from the chapel tower as the coach turned away and began its rapid journey home. This may and may not be so. We only know that its apparition always enters Lost Man's Lane a few minutes before one, which is the very hour at which the real coach came back and stopped before Mr. Knollys' gate. And now for the worst, Miss Butterworth. When the old gentleman went down to greet the runaways, he found the lackey on the box and his daughter sitting all alone in the coach. But the soil on the brocaded folds of her white dress was no longer that of mud only. She had stabbed herself to the heart with a bodkin she wore in her hair, and it was a corpse which the faithful negro had been driving down the highway that night."

I am not a sentimental woman, but this story as thus told gave me a thrill I do not know as I really regret experiencing.

"What was this unhappy mother's name?" I asked.

"Lucetta," was the unexpected and none too reassuring answer.

CHAPTER XIII

GOSSIP

This name once mentioned called for more gossip, but of a somewhat different nature.

"The Lucetta of today is not like her ancient namesake," observed Mrs. Carter. "She may have the heart to love, but she is not capable of showing that love by any act of daring."

"I don't know about that," I replied, astonished that I felt willing to enter into a discussion with this woman on the very subject I had just shrunk from talking over with the locksmith. "Girls as frail and nervous as she is, sometimes astonish one at a pinch. I do not think Lucetta lacks daring."

"You don't know her. Why, I have seen her jump at the sight of a spider, and heaven knows that they are common enough among the decaying walls in which she lives. A puny chit, Miss Butterworth; pretty enough, but weak. The very kind to draw lovers, but not to hold them. Yet every one pities her, her smile is so heart-broken."

"With ghosts to trouble her and a lover to bemoan, she has surely some excuse for that," said I.

"Yes, I don't deny it. But why has she a lover to bemoan? He seemed a proper man and much beyond the ordinary. Why let him go as she did? Even her sister admits that she loved him."

"I am not acquainted with the circumstances," I suggested.

"Well, there isn't much of a story to it. He is a young man from over the mountains, well educated, and with something of a fortune of his own. He came here to visit the Spears, I believe, and seeing Lucetta leaning one day on the gate in front of her house, he fell in love with her and began to pay her his attentions. That was before the lane got its present bad name, but not before one or two men had vanished from among us. William—that is her brother, you know—has always been anxious to have his sisters marry, so he did not stand in the way, and no more did Miss Knollys, but after two or three weeks of doubtful courtship, the young man went away, and that was the end of it. And a great pity, too, say I, for once clear of that house, Lucetta would grow into another person. Sunshine and love are necessities to most women, Miss Butterworth, especially to such as are weakly and timid."

I thought the qualification excellent.

"You are right," I assented, "and I should like to see the result of them upon Lucetta." Then, with an attempt to still further sound this woman's mind and with it the united mind of the whole village, I remarked: "The young do not usually throw aside such prospects without excellent reasons. Have you never thought that Lucetta was governed by principle in discarding this very excellent young man?"

"Principle? What principle could she have had in letting a desirable husband go?"

"She may have thought the match an undesirable one for him."

"For him? Well, I never thought of that. True, she may. They are known to be poor, but poverty don't count in such old families as theirs. I hardly think she would be influenced by any such consideration. Now, if this had happened since the lane got its bad name and all this stir had been made about the disappearance of certain folks within its precincts, I might have given some weight to your suggestion—women are so queer. But this happened long ago and at a time when the family was highly thought of, leastwise the girls, for William does not go for much, you know—too stupid and too brutal."

William! Would the utterance of that name heighten my suggestion?

I surveyed her closely, but could detect no change in her somewhat puzzled countenance.

"My allusions were not in reference to the disappearances," said I. "I was thinking of something else. Lucetta is not well."

"Ah, I know! They say she has some kind of heart complaint, but that was not true then. Why, her cheeks were like roses in those days, and her figure as plump and pretty as any you could see among our village beauties. No, Miss Butterworth, it was through her weakness she lost him. She probably palled upon his taste. It was noticed that he held his head very high in going out of town."

"Has he married since?" I asked.

"Not to my knowledge, ma'am."

"Then he loved her," I declared.

She looked at me quite curiously. Doubtless that word sounds a little queer on my lips, but that shall not deter me from using it when the circumstances seem to require. Besides, there was once a time—But there, I promised to fall into no digressions.

"You should have been married yourself, Miss Butterworth," said she.

I was amazed, first at her daring, and secondly that I was so little angry at this sudden turning of the tables upon myself. But then the woman meant no offence, rather intended a compliment.

"I am very well contented as I am," I returned. "*I* am neither sickly nor timid."

She smiled, looked as if she thought it only common politeness to agree with me, and tried to say so, but finding the situation too much for her, coughed and discreetly held her peace. I came to her rescue with a new question:

"Have the women of the Knollys family ever been successful in love? The mother of these girls, say—she who was Miss Althea Burroughs—was her life with her husband happy? I have always been curious to know. She and I were schoolmates."

"You were? You knew Althea Knollys when she was a girl? Wasn't she charming, ma'am? Did you ever see a livelier girl or one with more knack at winning affection? Why, she couldn't sit down with you a half-hour before you felt like sharing everything you had with her. It made no difference whether you were man or woman, it was all the same. She had but to turn those mischievous, pleading eyes upon you for you to become a fool at once. Yet her end was sad, ma'am; too sad, when you remember that she died at the very height of her beauty alone and in a foreign land. But I have not answered your question. Were she and the judge happy together? I have never heard to the contrary, ma'am. I'm sure he mourned her faithfully enough. Some think that her loss killed him. He did not survive her more than three years."

"The children do not favor her much," said I, "but I see an expression now and then in Lucetta which reminds me of her mother."

"They are all Knollys," said she. "Even William has traits which, with a few more brains back of them, would remind you of his grandfather, who was the plainest of his race."

I was glad that the talk had reverted to William.

"He seems to lack heart, as well as brains," I said. "I marvel that his sisters put up with him as well as they do."

"They cannot help it. He is not a fellow to be fooled with. Besides, he holds third share in the house. If they could sell it! But, deary me, who would buy an old tumble-down place like that, on a road you cannot get folks who have any consideration for their lives to enter for love or money? But excuse me, ma'am; I forgot that you are living just now on that very road. I'm sure I beg a thousand pardons."

"I am living there as a guest," I returned. "I have nothing to do with its reputation—except to brave it."

"A courageous thing to do, ma'am, and one that may do the road some good. If you can spend a month with the Knollys girls and come out of their house at the end as hale and hearty as you entered it, it will be the best proof possible that there is less to be feared there than some people think. I shall be glad if you can do it, ma'am, for I like the girls and would be glad to have the reputation of the place restored."

"Pshaw!" was my final comment. "The credulity of the town has had as much to do with its loss as they themselves. That educated people such as I see here should believe in ghosts!"

I say final, for at this moment the good lady, springing up, put an end to our conversation. She had just seen a buggy pass the window.

"It's Mr. Trohm," she exclaimed. "Ma'am, if you wish to return home before Mr. Simsbury comes back you may be able to do so with this gentleman. He's a most obliging man, and lives less than a quarter of a mile from the Misses Knollys."

I did not say I had already met the gentleman. Why, I do not know. I only drew myself up and waited with some small inner perturbation for the result of the inquiry I saw she had gone to make.

CHAPTER XIV

I Forget My Age, or, Rather, Remember It

Mr. Trohm did not disappoint my expectations. In another moment I perceived him standing in the open doorway with the most genial smile on his lips.

"Miss Butterworth," said he, "I feel too honored. If you will deign to accept a seat in my buggy, I shall only be too happy to drive you home."

I have always liked the manners of country gentlemen. There is just a touch of formality in their bearing which has been quite eliminated from that of their city brothers. I therefore became gracious at once and accepted the seat he offered me without any hesitation.

The heads that showed themselves at the neighboring windows warned us to hasten on our route. Mr. Trohm, with a snap of his whip, touched up his horse, and we rode in dignified calm away from the hotel steps into the wide village street known as the main road. The fact that Mr. Gryce had told me that this was the one man I could trust, joined to my own excellent knowledge of human nature and the persons in whom explicit confidence can be put, made the moment one of great satisfaction to me. I was about to make my appearance at the Knollys mansion two hours before I was expected, and thus outwit Lucetta by means of the one man whose assistance I could conscientiously accept.

We were not slow in beginning conversation. The fine air, the prosperous condition of the town offered themes upon which we found it quite easy to dilate, and so naturally and easily did our acquaintanceship progress that we had turned the corner into Lost Man's Lane before I quite realized it. The entrance from the village offered a sharp contrast to the one I had already traversed. There it was but a narrow opening between sombre and unduly crowding trees. Here it was the gradual melting of a village street into a narrow and less frequented road, which only after passing Deacon Spear's house assumed that aspect of wildness which a quarter of a mile farther on deepened into something positively sombre and repellent.

I speak of Deacon Spear because he was sitting on his front doorstep when we rode by. As he was a resident in the lane, I did not fail to take notice of him, though guardedly and with such restraint as a knowledge of his widowed condition rendered both wise and proper.

He was not an agreeable-looking person, at least to me. His hair was sleek, his beard well cared for, his whole person in good if not prosperous condition, but he had the self-satisfied expression I detest, and looked after us with an aspect of surprise I chose to consider a trifle impertinent. Perhaps he envied Mr. Trohm. If so, he may have had good reason for it—it is not for me to judge.

Up to now I had seen only a few scrub bushes at the side of the road, with here and there a solitary poplar to enliven the dead level on either side of us; but after we had ridden by the fence which sets the boundary to the good deacon's land, I noticed such a change in the appearance of the lane that I could not but exclaim over the natural as well as cultivated beauties which every passing moment was bringing before me.

Mr. Trohm could not conceal his pleasure.

"These are my lands," said he. "I have bestowed unremitting attention upon them for years. It is my hobby, madam. There is not a tree you see that has not received my careful attention. Yonder orchard was set out by me, and the fruit it yields—Madam, I hope you will remain long enough with us to taste a certain rare and luscious peach that I brought from France a few years ago. It gives promise of reaching its full perfection this year, and I shall be gratified indeed if you can give it your approval."

This was politeness indeed, especially as I knew what value men like him set upon each individual fruit they watch ripen under their care. Testifying my appreciation of his kindness, I endeavored to introduce another and less harmless and perhaps less personally interesting topic of conversation. The chimneys of his house were beginning to show over the trees, and I had heard nothing from this man on the subject which should have been the most interesting of all to me at this moment. And he was the only person in town I was at liberty to really confide in, and possibly the only man in town who could give me a reliable statement of the reasons why the family I was visiting was regarded in a doubtful light not only by the credulous villagers, but by the New York police. I began by an allusion to the phantom coach.

"I hear," said I, "that this lane has other claims to attention beyond those afforded by the mysteries connected with it. I hear that it has at times a ghostly visitant in the shape of a spectral horse and carriage."

"Yes," he replied, with a seeming understanding that was very flattering; "do not spare the lane one of its honors. It has its nightly horror as well as its daily fear. I wish the one were as unreal as the other."

"You act as if both were unreal to you," said I. "The contrast between your appearance and that of some other members of the lane is quite marked."

"You refer"—he seemed to hate to speak—"to the Misses Knollys, I presume."

I endeavored to treat the subject lightly.

"To your young enemy, Lucetta," I smilingly replied.

He had been looking at me in a perfectly modest and respectful manner, but he dropped his eyes at this and busied himself abstractedly, and yet I thought with some intention, in removing a fly from the horse's flank with the tip of his whip.

"I will not acknowledge her as an enemy," he quietly returned in strictly modulated tones. "I like the girl too well."

The fly had been by this time dislodged, but he did not look up.

"And William?" I suggested. "What do you think of William?"

Slowly he straightened himself. Slowly he dropped the whip back into its socket. I thought he was going to answer, when suddenly his whole attitude changed and he turned upon me a beaming face full of nothing but pleasure.

"The road takes a turn here. In another moment you will see my house." And even while he spoke it burst upon us, and I instantly forgot that I had just ventured on a somewhat hazardous question.

It was such a pretty place, and it was so beautifully and exquisitely kept. There was a charm about its rose-encircled porch that is only to be found in very old places that have been appreciatively cared for. A high fence painted white inclosed a lawn like velvet, and the house itself, shining with a fresh coat of yellow paint, bore signs of comfort in its white-curtained windows not usually to be found in the solitary dwelling of a bachelor. I found my eyes roving over each detail with delight, and almost blushed, or, rather, had I been twenty years younger might have been thought to blush, as I met his eyes and saw how much my pleasure gratified him.

"You must excuse me if I express too much admiration for what I see before me," I said, with what I have every reason to believe was a highly successful effort to hide my confusion. "I have always had a great leaning towards well-ordered walks and trimly kept flower-beds—a leaning, alas! which I have found myself unable to gratify."

"Do not apologize," he hastened to say. "You but redouble my own pleasure in thus honoring my poor efforts with your regard. I have spared no pains, madam, I have spared no pains to render this place beautiful, and most of what you see, I am proud to say, has been accomplished by my own hands."

"Indeed!" I cried in some surprise, letting my eye rest with satisfaction on the top of a long well-sweep that was one of the picturesque features of the place.

"It may have been folly," he remarked, with a gloating sweep of his eye over the velvet lawn and flowering shrubs—a peculiar look that seemed to express something more than the mere delight of possession, "but I seemed to begrudge any hired assistance in the tending of plants every one of which seems to me like a personal friend."

"I understand," was my somewhat un-Butterworthian reply. I really did not quite know myself. "What a contrast to the dismal grounds at the other end of the lane!"

This was more in my usual vein. He seemed to feel the difference, for his expression changed at my remark.

"Oh, that den!" he exclaimed, bitterly; then, seeing me look a little shocked, he added, with an admirable return to his old manner, "I call any place a den where flowers do not grow." And jumping from the buggy, he gathered an exquisite bunch of heliotrope, which he pressed upon me. "I love sunshine, beds of roses, fountains, and a sweep of lawn like this we see before us. But do not let me bore you. You have probably lingered long enough at the old bachelor's place and now would like to drive on. I will be with you in a moment. Doubtful as it is whether I shall soon again be so fortunate as to be able to offer you any hospitality, I would like to bring you a glass of wine—or, for I see your eyes roaming longingly toward my old-fashioned well, would you like a draft of water fresh from the bucket?"

I assured him I did not drink wine, at which I thought his eyes brightened, but that neither did I indulge in water when in a heat, as at present, at which he looked disappointed and came somewhat reluctantly back to the buggy.

He brightened up, however, the moment he was again at my side.

"Now for the woods," he exclaimed, with what was undoubtedly a forced laugh.

I thought the opportunity one I ought not to slight.

"Do you think," said I, "that it is in those woods the disappearances occur of which Miss Knollys has told me?"

He showed the same hesitancy as before to enter upon this subject.

"I think the less you allow your mind to dwell on this matter the better," said he—"that is, if you are going to remain long in this lane. I do not expend any more thought upon it than is barely necessary, or I should not retain sufficient courage to remain among my roses and my fruits. I wonder—pardon me the indiscretion—that you could bring yourself to enter so ill-reputed a neighborhood. You must be a very brave woman."

"I thought it my duty—" I began. "Althea Knollys was my friend, and I felt I owed a duty toward her children. Besides—" Should I tell Mr. Trohm my real errand in this place? Mr. Gryce had intimated that he was in the confidence of the police, and if so, his assistance in case of necessity might be of inestimable value to me. Yet if no such necessity should arise would I want this man to know that Amelia Butterworth—No, I would not take him into my confidence—not yet. I would only try to get at his idea of where the blame lay—that is, if he had any.

"Besides," he suggested in polite reminder, after waiting a minute or two for me to continue.

"Did I say besides?" was my innocent rejoinder. "I think I meant that after seeing them my sense of the importance of that duty had increased. William especially seems to be a young man of very doubtful amiability."

Immediately the non-commital look returned to Mr. Trohm's face.

"I have no fault to find with William," said he. "He's not the most agreeable companion in the world perhaps, but he has a pretty fancy for fruit—a very pretty fancy."

"One can hardly wonder at that in a neighbor of Mr. Trohm," said I, watching his look, which was fixed somewhat gloomily upon the forest of trees now rapidly closing in around us.

"Perhaps not, perhaps not, madam. The sight of a blossoming honeysuckle hanging from an arbor such as runs along my south walls is a great stimulant to one's taste, madam, I'll not deny that."

"But William?" I repeated, determined not to let the subject go; "have you never thought he was a little indifferent to his sisters?"

"A little, madam."

"And a trifle rough to everything but his dogs?"

"A trifle, madam."

Such reticence seemed unnecessary. I was almost angry, but restrained myself and pursued quietly, "The girls, on the contrary, seem devoted to him?"

"Women have that weakness."

"And act as if they would do—what would they not do for him?"

"Miss Butterworth, I have never seen a more amiable woman than yourself. Will you promise me one thing?"

His manner was respect itself, his smile genial and highly contagious. I could not help responding to it in the way he expected.

"Do not talk to me about this family. It is a painful subject to me. Lucetta—you know the girl, and I shall not be able to prejudice you against her—has conceived the idea that I encourage William in an intimacy of which she does not approve. She does not want him to talk to me. William has a loose tongue in his head and sometimes drops unguarded words about their doings, which if any but William spoke—But there, I am forgetting one of the most important rules of my own life, which is to keep my mouth from babbling and my tongue from guile. Influence of a congenial companion, madam; it is irresistible sometimes, especially to a man living so much alone as myself."

I considered his fault very pardonable, but did not say so lest I should frighten his confidences away.

"I thought there was something wrong between you," I said. "Lucetta acted almost afraid of you this morning. I should think she would be glad of the friendship of so good a neighbor."

His face took on a very sombre look.

"She is afraid of me," he admitted, "afraid of what I have seen or may see of—their poverty," he added, with an odd emphasis. I scarcely think he expected to deceive me.

I did not push the subject an inch farther. I saw it had gone as far as discretion permitted at this time.

We had reached the heart of the forest and were rapidly approaching the Knollys house. As the tops of its great chimneys rose above the foliage, I saw his aspect suddenly change.

"I don't know why I should so hate to leave you here," he remarked.

I myself thought the prospect of re-entering the Knollys mansion somewhat uninviting after the pleasant ride I had had and the glimpse which had been given me of a really cheery home and pleasant surroundings.

"This morning I looked upon you as a somewhat daring woman, the progress of whose stay here would be watched by me with interest, but after the companionship of the last half-hour I am conscious of an anxiety in your regard which makes me doubly wish that Miss Knollys had not shut me out from her home. Are you sure you wish to enter this house again, madam?"

I was surprised—really surprised—at the feeling he showed. If my well-disciplined heart had known how to flutter it would probably have fluttered then, but happily the restraint of years did not fail me in this emergency. Taking advantage of the emotion which had betrayed him into an acknowledgment of his real feelings regarding the dangers lurking in this home, despite the check he had endeavored to put upon his lips, I said, with an attempt at *naïveté* only to be excused by the exigencies of the occasion:

"Why, I thought you considered this domicile perfectly harmless. You like the girls and have no fault to find with William. Can it be that this great building has another occupant? I do not allude to ghosts. Neither of us are likely to believe in the supernatural."

"Miss Butterworth, you have me at a disadvantage. I do not know of any other occupant which the house can hold save the three young people you have mentioned. If I seem to feel any doubt of them—but I don't feel any doubt. I only dread any place for you which is not watched over by someone interested in your defence. The danger threatening the inhabitants of this lane is such a veiled one. If we knew where it lurked, we would no longer call it danger. Sometimes I think the ghosts you allude to are not as innocent as mere spectres usually are. But don't let me frighten you. Don't—" How quick his voice changed! "Ah, William, I have brought back your guest, you see! I couldn't let her sit out the noon hour in old Carter's parlor. That would be too much for even so amiable a person as Miss Butterworth to endure."

I had hardly realized we were so near the gate and certainly was surprised to find William anywhere within hearing. That his appearance at this moment was anything but welcome, must be evident to every one. The sentence which it interrupted might have contained the most important advice, or at the least a warning I could ill afford to lose. But destiny was against me, and being one who accepts the inevitable with good grace, I prepared to alight, with Mr. Trohm's assistance.

The bunch of heliotrope I held was a little in my way or I should have managed the jump with confidence and dignified agility. As it was, I tripped slightly, which brought out a chuckle from William that at the moment seemed more wicked to me than any crime. Meanwhile he had not let matters proceed thus far without putting more than one question.

"And where's Simsbury? And why did Miss Butterworth think she had got to sit in Carter's parlor?"

"Mr. Simsbury," said I as soon as I could recover from the mingled exertion and embarrassment of my descent to terra firma, "felt it necessary to take the horse to the shoer's. That is a half-day's work, as you know, and I felt confident that he and especially you would be glad to have me accept any means for escaping so dreary a waiting."

The grunt he uttered was eloquent of anything but satisfaction.

"I'll go tell the girls," he said. But he didn't go till he had seen Mr. Trohm enter his buggy and drive slowly off.

That all this did not add to my liking for William goes without saying.

BOOK II: THE FLOWER PARLOR

CHAPTER XV

Lucetta Fulfils My Expectation Of Her

It was not till Mr. Trohm had driven away that I noticed, in the shadow of the trees on the opposite side of the road, a horse tied up, whose empty saddle bespoke a visitor within. At any other gate and on any other road this would not have struck me as worthy of notice, much less of comment. But here, and after all that I had heard during the morning, the circumstance was so unexpected I could not help showing my astonishment.

"A visitor?" I asked.

"Some one to see Lucetta."

William had no sooner said this than I saw he was in a state of high excitement. He had probably been in this condition when we drove up, but my attention being directed elsewhere I had not noticed it. Now, however, it was perfectly plain to me, and it did not seem quite the excitement of displeasure, though hardly that of joy.

"She doesn't expect you yet," he pursued, as I turned sharply toward the house, "and if you interrupt her—D—n it, if I thought you would interrupt her—"

I thought it time to teach him a lesson in manners.

"Mr. Knollys," I interposed somewhat severely, "I am a lady. Why should I interrupt your sister or give her or you a moment of pain?"

"I don't know," he muttered. "You are so very quick I was afraid you might think it necessary to join her in the parlor. She is perfectly able to take care of herself, Miss Butterworth, and if she don't do it—" The rest was lost in indistinct guttural sounds.

I made no effort to answer this tirade. I took my usual course in quite my usual way to the front steps and proceeded to mount them without so much as looking behind me to see whether or not this uncouth representative of the Knollys name had kept at my heels or not.

Entering the door, which was open, I came without any effort on my part upon Lucetta and her visitor, who proved to be a young gentleman. They were standing together in the middle of the hall and were so absorbed in what they were saying that they neither saw nor heard me. I was therefore enabled to catch the following sentences, which struck me as of some moment. The first was uttered by her, and in very pleading tones:

"A week—I only ask a week. Then perhaps I can give you an answer which will satisfy you."

His reply, in manner if not in matter, proclaimed him the lover of whom I had so lately heard.

"I cannot, dear girl; indeed, I cannot. My whole future depends upon my immediately making the move in which I have asked you to join me. If I wait a week, my opportunity will be gone, Lucetta. You know me and you know how I love you. Then come—"

A rude hand on my shoulder distracted my attention. William stood lowering behind me and, as I turned, whispered in my ear:

"You must come round the other way. Lucetta is so touchy, the sight of you will drive every sensible idea out of her head."

His blundering whisper did what my presence and by no means light footsteps had failed to do. With a start Lucetta turned and, meeting my eye, drew back in visible confusion. The young man followed her hastily.

"Is it good-by, Lucetta?" he pleaded, with a fine, manly ignoring of our presence that roused my admiration.

She did not answer. Her look was enough. William, seeing it, turned furious at once, and, bounding by me, faced the young man with an oath.

"You're a fool to take no from a silly chit like that," he vociferated. "If I loved a girl as you say you love Lucetta, I'd have her if I had to carry her away by force. She'd stop screaming before she was well out of the lane. I know women. While you listen to them they'll talk and talk; but once let a man take matters into his own hands and—" A snap of his fingers finished the sentence. I thought the fellow brutal, but scarcely so stupid as I had heretofore considered him.

His words, however, might just as well have been uttered into empty air. The young man he so violently addressed appeared hardly to have heard him, and as for Lucetta, she was so nearly insensible from misery that she had sufficient ado to keep herself from falling at her lover's feet.

"Lucetta, Lucetta, is it then good-by? You will not go with me?"

"I cannot. William, here, knows that I cannot. I must wait till—"

But here her brother seized her so violently by the wrist that she stopped from sheer pain, I fear. However that was, she turned pale as death under his clutch, and, when he tried to utter some hot, passionate words into her ear, shook her head, but did not speak, though her lover was gazing with a last, final appeal into her eyes. The delicate girl was bearing out my estimate of her.

Seeing her thus unresponsive, William flung her hand from him and turned upon me.

"It's your fault," he cried. "You *would* come in—"

But, at this, Lucetta, recovering her poise in a moment, cried out shrilly:

"For shame, William! What has Miss Butterworth to do with this? You are not helping me with your roughness. God knows I find this hour hard enough, without this show of anxiety on your part to be rid of me."

"There's woman's gratitude for you," was his snarling reply. "I offer to take all the responsibilities on my own shoulders and make it right with—with her sister, and all that, and she calls it desire to get rid of her. Well, have your own way," he growled, storming down the hall; "I'm done with it for one."

The young man, whose attitude of reserve, mixed with a strange and lingering tenderness for this girl, whom he evidently loved without fully understanding her, was every minute winning more and more of my admiration, had meanwhile raised her trembling hand to his lips in what was, as we all could see, a last farewell.

In another moment he was walking by us, giving me as he passed a low bow that for all its grace did not succeed in hiding from me the deep and heartfelt disappointment with which he quitted this house. As his figure passed through the door, hiding for one moment the sunshine, I felt an oppression such as has not often visited my healthy nature, and when it passed and disappeared, something like the good spirit of the place seemed to go with it, leaving in its place doubt, gloom, and a morbid apprehension of that unknown something which in Lucetta's eyes had rendered his dismissal necessary.

"Where's Saracen? I declare I'm nothing but a fool without that dog," shouted William. "If he has to be tied up another day—" But shame was not entirely eliminated from his breast, for at Lucetta's reproachful "William!" he sheepishly dropped his head and strode out, muttering some words I was fain to accept as an apology.

I had expected to encounter a wreck in Lucetta, as, this episode in her life closed, she turned toward me. But I did not yet know this girl, whose frailty seemed to lie mostly in her physique. Though she was suffering far more than her defence of me to her brother would seem to denote, there was a spirit in her approach and a steady look in her dark eye which assured me that I could not calculate upon any loss in Lucetta's keenness, in case we came to an issue over the mystery that was eating into the happiness as well as the honor of this household.

"I am glad to see you," were her unexpected words. "The gentleman who has just gone out was a lover of mine; at least he once professed to care for me very much, and I should have been glad to have married him, but there were reasons which I once thought most excellent why this seemed anything but expedient, and so I sent him away. Today he came without warning to ask me to go away with him, after the hastiest of ceremonies, to South America, where a splendid prospect has suddenly opened for him. You see, don't you, that I could not do that; that it would be the height of selfishness in me to leave Loreen—to leave William—"

"Who seems only too anxious to be left," I put in, as her voice trailed off in the first evidence of embarrassment she had shown since she faced me.

"William is a difficult man to understand," was her firm but quiet retort. "From his talk you would judge him to be morose, if not positively unkind, but in action—" She did not tell me how he was in action. Perhaps her truthfulness got the better of her, or perhaps she saw it would be hard work to prejudice me now in his favor.

CHAPTER XVI

LOREEN

Lucetta had said to her departing lover, that in a week she might be able (were he willing or in a position to wait) to give him a more satisfactory answer. Why in a week?

That her hesitation sprang from the mere dislike of leaving her sister so suddenly, or that she had sacrificed her life's happiness to any childish idea of decorum, I did not think probable. The spirit she had shown, her immovable attitude under a temptation which had not only romance to recommend it, but everything else which could affect a young and sensitive woman, argued in my mind the existence of some uncompleted duty of so exacting and imperative a nature that she could not even consider the greatest interests of her own life until this one thing was out of her way. William's rude question of the morning, "What shall we do with the old girl till it is all over?" recurred to me in support of this theory, making me feel that I needed no further confirmation, to be quite certain that a crisis was approaching in this house which would tax my powers to the utmost and call perhaps for the use of the whistle which I had received from Mr. Gryce, and which, following his instructions, I had tied carefully about my neck. Yet how could I associate Lucetta with crime, or dream of the police in connection with the serene Loreen, whose every look was a rebuke to all that was false, vile, or even common? Easily, my readers, easily, with that great, hulking William in my remembrance. To shield *him*, to hide perhaps his deformity of soul from the world, even such gentle and gracious women as these have been known to enter into acts which to an unprejudiced eye and an unbiased conscience would seem little short of fiendish. Love for an unworthy relative, or rather the sense of duty toward those of one's own blood, has driven many a clearminded woman to her ruin, as may be seen any day in the police annals.

I am quite aware that I have not as yet put into definite words the suspicion upon which I was now prepared to work. Up to this time it had been too vague, or rather of too monstrous a character for me not to consider other theories, such as, for instance, the possible connection of old Mother Jane with the unaccountable disappearances which had taken place in this lane. But after this scene, the increased assurance I was hourly receiving that something extraordinary and out of keeping with the customary appearances of the household was secretly going on in one of the various chambers of that long corridor I had been prevented from entering, forced me to accept and act upon the belief that these young women held in charge a prisoner of some kind, of whose presence in the house they dreaded the discovery.

Now, who could this prisoner be?

Common sense supplied me with but one answer; Silly Rufus, the boy who within a few days had vanished from among the good people of this seemingly guileless community.

This theory once established in my mind, I applied myself to a consideration of the means at my disposal for determining its validity. The simplest, surest, but least satisfactory to one of my nature was to summon the police and have the house thoroughly searched, but this involved, in case I had been deceived by appearances—as was possible even to a woman of my experience and discrimination—a scandal and an opprobrium which I would be the last to inflict upon Althea's children, unless justice to the rest of the world demanded it.

It was in consideration of this very fact, perhaps, that I had been chosen for this duty instead of some regular police spy. Mr. Gryce, as I very well knew, has made it his rule of life never to risk the reputation of any man or woman without reasons so excellent as to carry their own exoneration with them, and should I, a woman, with full as much heart as himself, if not quite as much brain (at least in the estimation of people in general), by any premature exposure of my suspicions, subject these young friends of mine to humiliations they are far too weak and too poor to rise above?

No, rather would I trust a little longer to my own perspicacity and make sure by the use of my own eyes that the situation called for the interference I had, as you may say, at the end of the cord I wore about my neck.

Lucetta had not asked me how I came to be back so much sooner than she had reason to expect me. The unlooked-for arrival of her lover had probably put all idea of her former plans out of her head. I therefore gave her the shortest of explanations when we met at the dinner table. Nothing further seemed to be necessary, for the girls were even more abstracted than before, and William positively boorish till a warning glance from Loreen recalled him to his better self, which meant silence.

The afternoon was spent in very much the same way as the evening before. Neither sister remained an instant with me after the other entered my company, and though the alternations were less frequent than at that time, their peculiarities were more marked and less naturally accounted for. It was while Loreen was with me that I made the suggestion which had been hovering on my lips ever since the noon.

"I consider this," I observed, in one of the pauses of our more than fitful conversation, "one of the most interesting houses it has ever been my good fortune to enter. Would you mind my roaming about a bit just to enjoy the old-time flavor of its great empty rooms? I know they are mostly closed and possibly unfurnished, but to a connoisseur like myself in colonial architecture, this rather adds to, than detracts from, their interest."

"Impossible," she was going to say, but caught herself back in time and changed the imperative word to one more conciliatory if equally unyielding.

"I am sorry, Miss Butterworth, to deny you this gratification, but the condition of the rooms and the unhappy excitement into which we have been thrown by the unfortunate visit paid to Lucetta by a gentleman to whom she is only too much attached, make it quite impossible for me to consider any such undertaking today. Tomorrow I may find it easier; but, if not, be assured you shall see every nook and corner of this house before you finally leave it."

"Thank you. I will remember that. To one of my tastes an ancient room in a time-honored mansion like this, affords a delight not to be understood by one who knows less of the last century's life. The legends connected with your great drawing-room below [we were sitting in my room, I having refused to be cooped up in their dreary side parlor, and she not having offered me any other spot more cheerful] are sufficient in themselves to hold me entranced for an hour. I heard one of them today."

"Which?"

She spoke more quickly than usual, and for her quite sharply.

"That of Lucetta's namesake," I explained. "She who rode through the night after a daughter who had won her lover's heart away from her.

"Ah, it is a well-known tale, but I think Mrs. Carter might have left its relation to us. Did she tell you anything else?"

"No other tradition of this place," I assured her.

"I am glad she was so considerate. But why—if you will pardon me—did she happen to light upon that story? We have not heard those incidents spoken of for years."

"Not since the phantom coach flew through this road the last time," I ventured, with a smile that should have disarmed her from suspecting any ulterior motive on my part in thus introducing a subject which could not be altogether pleasing to her.

"The phantom coach! Have you heard of that?"

I wish it had been Lucetta who had said this and to whom my reply was due. The opportunities would have been much greater for an injudicious display of feeling on her part and for a suitable conclusion on mine.

But it was Loreen, and she never forgot herself. So I had to content myself with the persuasion that her voice was just a whit less clear than usual and her serenity enough impaired for her to look out of my one high and dismal window instead of into my face.

"My dear,"—I had not called her this before, though the term had frequently risen to my lips in answer to Lucetta—"you should have gone with me into the village today. Then you would not need to ask if I had heard of the phantom coach."

The probe had reached the quick at last. She looked quite startled.

"You amaze me," she said. "What do you mean, Miss Butterworth? Why should I not have needed to ask?"

"Because you would have heard it whispered about in every lane and corner. It is common talk in town today. You must know why, Miss Knollys."

She was not looking out of the window now. She was looking at me.

"I assure you," she murmured, "I do not know at all. Nothing could be more incomprehensible to me. Explain yourself, I entreat you. The phantom coach is but a myth to me, interesting only as involving certain long-vanished ancestors of mine."

"Of course," I assented. "No one of real sense could regard it in any other light. But villagers will talk, and they say—you will soon know what, if I do not tell you myself—that it passed through the lane on

Tuesday night."

"Tuesday night!" Her composure had been regained, but not so entirely but that her voice slightly trembled. "That was before you came. I hope it was not an omen."

I was in no mood for pleasantry.

"They say that the passing of this apparition denotes misfortune to those who see it. I am therefore obviously exempt. But you—did you see it? I am just curious to know if it is visible to those who live in the lane. It ought to have turned in here. Were you fortunate enough to have been awake at that moment and to have seen this spectral appearance?"

She shuddered. I was not mistaken in believing I saw this sign of emotion, for I was watching her very closely, and the movement was unmistakable.

"I have never seen anything ghostly in my life," said she. "I am not at all superstitious."

If I had been ill-natured or if I had thought it wise to press her too closely, I might have inquired why she looked so pale and trembled so visibly.

But my natural kindness, together with an instinct of caution, restrained me, and I only remarked:

"There you are sensible, Miss Knollys—doubly so as a denizen of this house, which, Mrs. Carter was obliging enough to suggest to me, is considered by many as haunted."

The straightening of Miss Knollys' lips augured no good to Mrs. Carter.

"Now I only wish it was," I laughed dryly. "I should really like to meet a ghost, say, in your great drawing-room, which I am forbidden to enter."

"You are not forbidden," she hastily returned. "You may explore it now if you will excuse me from accompanying you; but you will meet no ghosts. The hour is not propitious."

Taken aback by her sudden amenity, I hesitated for a moment. Would it be worth while for me to search a room she was willing to have me enter? No, and yet any knowledge which could be obtained in regard to this house might be of use to me or to Mr. Gryce. I decided to embrace her offer, after first testing her with one other question.

"Would you prefer to have me steal down these corridors at night and dare their dusky recesses at a time when spectres are supposed to walk the halls they once flitted through in happy consciousness?"

"Hardly." She made the greatest effort to sustain the jest, but her concern and dread were manifest. "I think I had better give you the keys now, than subject you to the drafts and chilling discomforts of this old place at midnight."

I rose with a semblance of eager anticipation.

"I will take you at your word," said I. "The keys, my dear. I am going to visit a haunted room for the first time in my life."

I do not think she was deceived by this feigned ebullition. Perhaps it was too much out of keeping with my ordinary manner, but she gave no sign of surprise and rose in her turn with an air suggestive of relief.

"Excuse me, if I precede you," she begged. "I will meet you at the head of the corridor with the keys."

I was in hopes she would be long enough in obtaining them to allow me to stroll along the front hall to the opening into the corridor I was so anxious to enter. But the spryness I showed, seemed to have a corresponding effect upon her, for she almost flew down the passageway before me and was back at my side before I could take a step in the coveted direction.

"These will take you into any room on the first floor," said she. "You will meet with dust and Lucetta's abhorrence, spiders, but for these I shall make no apologies. Girls who cannot provide comforts for the few rooms they utilize, cannot be expected to keep in order the large and disused apartments of a former generation."

"I hate dirt and despise spiders," was my dry retort, "but I am willing to brave both for the pleasure of satisfying my love for the antique." At which she handed me the keys, with a calm smile which was not without its element of sadness.

"I will be here on your return," she said, leaning over the banisters to speak to me as I took my first steps down. "I shall want to hear whether you are repaid for your trouble."

I thanked her and proceeded on my way, somewhat doubtful whether by so doing I was making the best possible use of my opportunities.

CHAPTER XVII

The Flower Parlor

The lower hall did not correspond exactly with the one above. It was larger, and through its connection with the front door, presented the shape of a letter T—that is, to the superficial observer who was not acquainted with the size of the house and had not had the opportunity of remarking that at the extremities of the upper hall making this T, were two imposing doors usually found shut except at meal-times, when the left-hand one was thrown open, disclosing a long and dismal corridor similar to the ones above. Half-way down this corridor was the dining-room, into which I had now been taken three times.

The right-hand one, I had no doubt, led the way into the great drawing-room or dancing-hall which I had started out to see.

Proceeding first to the front of the house, where some glimmer of light penetrated from the open sitting-room door, I looked the keys over and read what was written on the several tags attached to them. They were seven in number, and bore some such names as these: "Blue Chamber," "Library," "Flower Parlor," "Shell Cabinet," "Dark Parlor"—all of which was very suggestive, and, to an antiquarian like myself, most alluring.

But it was upon a key marked "A" I first fixed my attention. This, I had been told, would open the large door at the extremity of the upper hall, and when I made a trial with it I found it to move easily, though somewhat gratingly, in the lock, releasing the great doors, which in another moment swung inward with a growling sound which might have been startling to a nervous person filled with the legends of the place.

But in me the only emotion awakened was one of disgust at the nauseous character of the air which instantly enveloped me. Had I wished for any further proof than was afforded by the warning given me by the condition of the hinges, that the foot of man had not lately invaded these precincts, I would have had it in the mouldy atmosphere and smell of dust that greeted me on the threshold. Neither human breath nor a ray of outdoor sunshine seemed to have disturbed its gloomy quiet for years, and when I moved, as I presently did, to open one of the windows I dimly discerned at my right, I felt such a movement of something foul and noisome amid the decaying rags of the carpet through which I was stumbling that I had to call into use the stronger elements of my character not to back out of a place so given over to rot and the creatures that infest it.

"What a spot," thought I, "for Amelia Butterworth to find herself in!" and wondered if I could ever wear again the three-dollar-a-yard silk dress in which I was then enveloped. Of my shoes I took no account. They were ruined, of course.

I reached the window in safety, but could not open it; neither could I move the adjoining one. There were sixteen in all, or so I afterwards found, and not till I reached the last (you see, I am very persistent) did I succeed in loosening the bar that held its inner shutter in place. This done, I was able to lift the window, and for the first time in years, perhaps, let in a ray of light into this desolated apartment.

The result was disappointing. Mouldy walls, worm-eaten hangings, two very ancient and quaint fireplaces, met my eyes, and nothing more. The room was absolutely empty. For a few minutes I allowed my eyes to roam over the great rectangular space in which so much that was curious and interesting had once taken place, and then, with a vague sense of defeat, turned my eyes outward, anxious to see what view could be obtained from the window I had opened. To my astonishment, I saw before me a high wall with here and there a window in it, all tightly barred and closed, till by a careful inspection about me I realized that I was looking upon the other wing of the building, and that between these wings extended a court so narrow and long that it gave to the building the shape, as I have before said, of the letter U. A dreary prospect, reminding one of the view from a prison, but it had its point of interest, for in the court below me, the brick pavement of which was half obliterated by grass, I caught sight of William in an attitude so different from any I had hitherto seen him assume that I found it difficult to account for it till I caught sight of the jaws of a dog protruding from under his arms, and then I realized he was hugging Saracen.

The dog was tied, but the comfort which William seemed to take in just this physical contact with his rough skin was something worth seeing. It made me quite thoughtful for a moment.

I detest dogs, and it gives me a creepy sensation to see them fondled, but sincerity of feeling appeals to me, and no one could watch William Knollys with his dogs without seeing that he really loved the brutes. Thus in one day I had witnessed the best and worst side of this man. But wait! Had I seen the worst? I was not so sure that I had.

He had not noticed my peering, for which I was duly thankful, and after another fruitless survey of the windows in the wall before me, I drew back and prepared to leave the place. This was by no means a pleasant undertaking. I could now see what I had only felt before, and to traverse the space before me amid beetles and spiders required a determination of no ordinary nature. I was glad when I reached the great doors and more than glad when they closed behind me.

"So much for Room A," thought I.

The next most promising apartment was in the same corridor as the dining-room. It was called the Dark Parlor. Entering it, I found it dark indeed, but not because of lack of light, but because its hangings were all of a dismal red and its furniture of the blackest ebony. As this mainly consisted of shelves and cabinets placed against three of its four walls, the effect was gloomy indeed, and fully accounted for the name which the room had received. I lingered in it, however, longer than I had in the big drawing-room, chiefly because the shelves contained books.

Had anything better offered I might not have continued my explorations, but not seeing exactly how I could pass away the time more profitably, I chose out another key and began to search for the Flower Parlor. I found it beyond the dining-room in the same hall as the Dark Parlor.

It was, as I might have expected from the name, the brightest and most cheerful spot I had yet found in the whole house. The air in it was even good, as if sunshine and breeze had not been altogether shut out of it, yet I had no sooner taken one look at its flower-painted walls and pretty furniture than I felt an oppression difficult to account for. Something was wrong about this room. I am not superstitious and have no faith in premonitions, but once seized by a conviction, I have never known myself to be mistaken as to its import. Something was wrong about this room—what, it was my business to discover.

Letting in more light, I took a closer survey of the objects I had hitherto seen but dimly. They were many and somewhat contradictory in character. The floor was bare—the first bare floor I had come upon—but the shades in the windows, the chintz-covered lounges drawn up beside tables bestrewn with books and other objects of comfort and luxury, bespoke a place in common if not every-day use.

A faint smell of tobacco assured me in whose use, and from the minute I recognized that this was William's sanctum, my curiosity grew unbounded and I neglected nothing which would be likely to attract the keenest-eyed detective in Mr. Gryce's force. There were several things to be noted there: First, that this lumbering lout of a man read, but only on one topic—vivisection; secondly, that he was not a reader merely, for there were instruments in the cases heaped up on the tables about me, and in one corner—it made me a little sick, but I persevered in searching out the corners—a glass case with certain horrors in it which I took care to note, but which it is not necessary for me to describe. Another corner was blocked up by a closet which stood out in the room in a way to convince me it had been built in after the room was otherwise finished. As I crossed over to examine the door, which did not appear to me to be quite closed, I noticed on the floor at my feet a huge discoloration. This was the worst thing I had yet encountered, and while I did not feel quite justified in giving it a name, I could not but feel some regret for the worm-eaten rags of the drawing-room, which, after all, are more comfortable underfoot than bare boards with such suggestive marks upon them as these.

The door to the closet was, as I had expected, slightly ajar, a fact for which I was profoundly grateful, for, set it down to breeding or a natural recognition of other people's rights, I would have found it most difficult to turn the knob of a closet door, inspection of which had not been offered me.

But finding it open, I gave it just a little pull and found—well, it was a surprise, much more so than the sight of a skeleton would have been—that the whole interior was taken up by a small circular staircase such as you find in public libraries where the books are piled up in tiers. It stretched from the floor to the ceiling, and dark as it was I thought I detected the outlines of a trap-door by means of which communication was established with the room above. Anxious to be convinced of this, I consulted with myself as to what a detective would do in my place.

The answer came readily enough: "Mount the stairs and feel for yourself whether there is a lock there." But my delicacy or—shall I acknowledge it for once?—an instinct of timidity seemed to restrain me, till a remembrance of Mr. Gryce's sarcastic look which I had seen honoring lesser occasions than these, came to nerve me, and I put foot on the stairs which had last been trod—by whom, shall I say? William? Let us hope by William, and William only.

Being tall, I had to mount but a few steps before reaching the ceiling. Pausing for breath, the air being close and the stairs steep, I reached up and felt for the hinge or clasp I had every reason to expect to encounter. I found it almost immediately, and, satisfied now that nothing but a board separated me from the room above, I tried that board with my finger and was astonished to feel it yield. As this was a wholly unexpected discovery I drew back and asked myself if it would be wise to pursue it to the point of raising this door, and had hardly settled the question in my own mind, when the sound of a voice raised in a soothing murmur, revealed the fact that the room above was not empty, and that I would be committing a grave indiscretion in thus tampering with a means of entrance possibly under the very eye of the person speaking.

If the voice I had heard had been all that had come to my ears, I might have ventured after a moment of hesitation to brave the displeasure of Miss Knollys by an attempt which would have at once satisfied me as to the correctness of the suspicions which were congealing my blood as I stood there, but another voice—the heavy and threatening voice of William—had broken into this murmur, and I knew that if I so much as awakened in him the least suspicion of my whereabouts, I would have to dread an anger that might not know where to stop.

I therefore rested from further efforts in this direction, and fearing he might bethink him of some errand which would bring him to the trapdoor himself, I began a retreat which I made slow only from my desire not to make any noise. I succeeded as well as if my feet had been shod in velvet and my dress had been made of wool instead of a rustling silk, and when once again I found myself planted in the centre of the Flower Parlor, the closet door closed, and no evidence remaining of my late attempt to probe this family secret, I drew a deep breath of relief that was but a symbol of my devout thankfulness.

I did not mean to remain much longer in this spot of evil suggestions, but spying the corner of a book protruding from under a cushion of one of the lounges, I had a curiosity to see if it were similar to the others I had handled. Drawing it out, I took one look at it.

I need not tell what it was, but after a hasty glance here and there through its pages, I put it back, shuddering. If any doubt remained in my breast that William was one of those monsters who feed their morbid cravings by experiments upon the weak and defenceless, it had been dispelled by what I had just seen in this book.

However, I did not leave the room immediately. As it was of the greatest importance that I should be able to locate in which of the many apartments on the floor above, the supposed prisoner was lodged, I cast about me for the means of doing this through the location of the room in which I then was. As this could only be done by affixing some token to the window, which could be recognized from without, I thought, first, of thrusting the end of my handkerchief through one of the slats of the outside blinds; secondly, of simply leaving one of these blinds ajar; and finally, of chipping off a piece with the penknife I always carry with innumerable other small things in the bag I invariably wear at my side. (Fashion, I hold, counts for nothing against convenience.)

This last seemed by much the best device. A handkerchief could be discovered and pulled out, an open blind could be shut, but a sliver once separated from the wood of the casement, nothing could replace it or even cover it up without itself attracting attention.

Taking out my knife, I glanced at the door leading into the hall, found it still shut and everything quiet behind it. Then I took a look into the shrubs and bushes of the yard outside, and, observing nothing to disturb me, snipped off a bit from one of the outer edges of the slats and then carefully reclosed the blinds and the window.

I was crossing the threshold when I heard a rapid footstep in the hall. Miss Knollys was hastening down the hall to my side.

"Oh, Miss Butterworth," she exclaimed, with one quick look into the room I was leaving, "this is William's den, the one spot he never allows any of us to enter. I don't know how the key came to be upon the string. It never was before, and I am afraid he never will forgive me."

"He need never know that I have been the victim of such a mistake," said I. "My feet leave no trail, and as I use no perfumes he will never suspect that I have enjoyed a glimpse of these old-fashioned walls and ancient cabinets."

"The slats of the blinds are a little open," she remarked, her eyes searching my face for some sign that I am sure she did not find there. "Were they so when you came in?"

"I hardly think so; it was very dark. Shall I put them as I found them?"

"No. He will not notice." And she hurried me out, still eying me breathlessly as if she half distrusted my composure.

"Come, Amelia," I now whispered in self-admonition, "the time for exertion has come. Show this young woman, who is not much behind you in self-control, some of the lighter phases of your character. Charm her, Amelia, charm her, or you may live to rue this invasion into family secrets more than you may like to acknowledge at the present moment."

A task of some difficulty, but I rejoice in difficult tasks, and before another half-hour had passed, I had the satisfaction of seeing Miss Knollys entirely restored to that state of placid melancholy which was the natural expression of her calm but unhappy nature.

We visited the Shell Cabinet, the Blue Parlor, and another room, the peculiarities of which I have forgotten. Frightened by the result of leaving me to my own devices, she did not quit me for an instant, and when, my curiosity quite satisfied, I hinted that a short nap in my own room would rest me for the evening, she proceeded with me to the door of my apartment.

"The locksmith whom I saw this morning has not kept his word," I remarked as she was turning away.

"None of the tradesmen here do that," was her cold answer. "I have given up expecting having any attention paid to my wants."

"Humph," thought I. "Another pleasant admission. Amelia Butterworth, this has not been a cheerful day."

CHAPTER XVIII

The Second Night

I cannot say that I looked forward to the night with any very cheerful anticipations. The locksmith having failed to keep his appointment, I was likely to have no more protection against intrusion than I had had the night before, and while I cannot say that I especially feared any unwelcome entrance into my apartment, I should have gone to my rest with a greater sense of satisfaction if a key had been in the lock and that key had been turned by my own hand on my own side of the door.

The atmosphere of gloom which settled down over the household after the evening meal, seemed like the warning note of something strange and evil awaiting us. So marked was this, that many in my situation would have further disturbed these girls by some allusion to the fact. But that was not the rôle I had set myself to play at this crisis. I remembered what Mr. Gryce had said about winning their confidence, and though the turmoil evident in Lucetta's mind and the distraction visible even in the careful Miss Knollys led me to expect a culmination of some kind before the night was over, I not only hid my recognition of this fact, but succeeded in sufficiently impressing them with the contentment which my own petty employments afforded me (I am never idle even in other persons' houses) for them to spare me the harassment of their alternate visits, which, in their present mood and mine promised little in the way of increased knowledge of their purposes and much in the way of distraction and the loss of that nerve upon which I calculated for a successful issue out of the possible difficulties of this night.

Had I been a woman of ordinary courage, I would have sounded three premonitory notes upon my whistle before blowing out my candle, but while I am not lacking, I hope, in many of the finer feminine qualities which link me to my sex, I have but few of that sex's weaknesses and none of its instinctive reliance upon others which leads it so often to neglect its own resources. Till I saw good reasons for summoning the police, I proposed to preserve a discreet silence, a premature alarm being in their eyes, as I knew from many talks with Mr. Gryce, the one thing suggestive of a timid and inexperienced mind.

Hannah had brought me a delicious cup of tea at ten, the influence of which was to make me very drowsy at eleven, but I shook this weakness off and began my night's watch in a state of stern composure which I verily believe would have awakened Mr. Gryce's admiration had it been consonant with the proprieties for him to have seen it. Indeed the very seriousness of the occasion was such that I could not have trembled if I would, every nerve and faculty being strained to their utmost to make the most of every sound which might arise in the now silent and discreetly darkened house.

I had purposely omitted the precaution of pushing my bed against the door of my room, as I had done the night before, being anxious to find myself in a position to cross its threshold at the least alarm. That this would come, I felt positive, for Hannah in leaving my room had taken pains to say, in unconscious imitation of what Miss Knollys had remarked the night before:

"Don't let any queer sounds you may hear disturb you, Miss Butterworth. There's nothing to hurt you in this house; nothing at all." An admonition which I am sure her young mistresses would not have allowed her to utter if they had been made acquainted with her intention.

But though in a state of high expectation, and listening, as I supposed, with every faculty alert, the sounds I apprehended delayed so long that I began after an hour or two unaccountably to nod in my chair, and before I knew it I was asleep, with the whistle in my hand and my feet pressed against the panels of the door I had set myself to guard. How deep that sleep was or how long I indulged in it, I can only judge from the state of emotion in which I found myself when I suddenly woke. I was sitting there still, but my usually calm frame was in a violent tremble, and I found it difficult to stir, much more to speak. Some one or something was at my door.

An instant and my powerful nature would have asserted itself, but before this could happen the stealthy step drew nearer, and I heard the quiet, almost noiseless, insertion of a key into the lock, and the quick turn which made me a prisoner.

This, with the indignation it caused, brought me quickly to myself. So the door had a key after all, and this was the use it was reserved for. Rising quickly to my feet, I shouted out the names of Loreen, Lucetta, and William, but received no other response than the rapid withdrawal of feet down the corridor. Then I felt for the whistle, which had somehow slipped from my hand, but failed to find it in the darkness, nor when I went to search for the matches to relight the candle I had left standing on a table near by, could I by any means succeed in igniting one, so that I presently had the pleasure of finding myself shut up in my room, with no means of communicating with the world outside and with no light to render the situation tolerable. This was having the tables turned upon me with a vengeance and in a way for which I could not account. I could understand why they had locked me in the room and why they had not heeded my cry of indignant appeal, but I could not comprehend how my whistle came to be gone, nor why the matches, which were sufficiently plentiful in the safe, refused one and all to perform their office.

On these points I felt it necessary to come to some sort of conclusion before I proceeded to invent some way out of my difficulties. So, dropping on my knees by the chair in which I had been sitting, I began a quiet search for the petty object upon which, nevertheless, hung not my safety perhaps, but all chances of success in an undertaking which was every moment growing more serious. I did not find it, but I did find where it had gone. In the floor near the door, my hand encountered a hole which had been covered up by a rug early in the evening, but which I now distinctly remembered having pushed aside with my feet when I took my seat there. This aperture was not large, but it was so deep that my hand failed to reach to the bottom of it; and into this hole by some freak of chance had slipped the small whistle I had so indiscreetly taken into my hand. The mystery of the matches was less easy of solution; so I let it go after a moment of indecisive thought and bent my energies once again to listen, when suddenly and without the least warning there rose from somewhere in the house a cry so wild and unearthly that I started up appalled, and for a moment could not tell whether I was laboring under some fearful dream or a still more fearful reality.

A rushing of feet in the distance and an involuntary murmur of voices soon satisfied me, however, on this score, and drawing upon every energy I possessed, I listened for a renewal of the cry which was yet curdling my blood. But none came, and presently all was as still as if no sound had arisen to disturb the midnight, though every fibre in my body told me that the event I had feared—the event of which I hardly dared mention the character even to myself—had taken place, and that I, who was sent there to forestall it, was not only a prisoner in my room, but a prisoner through my own folly and my inordinate love of tea.

The anger with which I contemplated this fact, and the remorse I felt at the consequences which had befallen the innocent victim whose scream I had just heard, made me very wide-awake indeed, and after an ineffectual effort to make my voice heard from the window, I called my usual philosophy to my aid and decided that since the worst had happened and I, a prisoner, had to await events like any other weak and defenceless woman, I might as well do it with calmness and in a way to win my own approval at least. The dupe of William and his sisters, I would not be the dupe of my own fears or even of my own regrets.

The consequence was a renewed equanimity and a gentle brooding over the one event of the day which brought no regret in its train. The ride with Mr. Trohm, and the acquaintanceship to which it had led, were topics upon which I could rest with great soothing effect through the weary hours stretching between me and daylight. Consequently of Mr. Trohm I thought.

Whether the almost deathly quiet into which the house had now fallen, or the comforting nature of my meditations held inexorably to the topic I had chosen, acted as a soporific upon me I cannot tell, but greatly as I dislike to admit it, feeling sure that you will expect to hear I kept myself awake all that night, I insensibly sank from great alertness to an easy indifference to my surroundings, and from that to vague dreams in which beds of lilies and trellises covered with roses mingled strangely with narrow, winding staircases whose tops ended in the swaying branches of great trees; and so, into quiet and a nothingness that were only broken into by a rap at my door and a cheerful:

"Eight o'clock, ma'am. The young ladies are waiting."

I bounded, literally bounded from my chair. Such a summons, after such a night! What did it mean? I was sitting half dressed in my chair before my door in a straightened and uncomfortable attitude, and therefore had not dreamed that I had been upon the watch all night, yet the sunshine in the room, the cheery tones such as I had not heard even from this woman before, seemed to argue that my imagination had played me false and that no horrors had come to disturb my rest or render my waking distressing.

Stretching out my hand toward the door, I was about to open it, when I bethought me.

"Turn the key in the lock," said I. "Somebody was careful enough of my safety to fasten me in last night."

An exclamation of astonishment came from outside the door.

"There is no key here, ma'am. The door is not locked. Shall I open it and come in?"

I was about to say yes in my anxiety to talk to the woman, but remembering that nothing was to be gained by letting it be seen to what an extent I had carried my suspicions, I hastily disrobed and crept into bed. Pulling the coverings about me, I assumed a comfortable attitude and then cried:

"Come in."

The door immediately opened.

"There, ma'am! What did I tell you? Locked?—this door? Why, the key has been lost for months."

"I cannot help it," I protested, but with little if any asperity, for it did not suit me that she should see I was moved by any extraordinary feeling. "A key was put in that lock about midnight, and I was locked in. It was about the time someone screamed in your own part of the house."

"Screamed?" Her brows took a fine pucker of perplexity. "Oh, that must have been Miss Lucetta."

"Lucetta?"

"Yes, ma'am; she had an attack, I believe. Poor Miss Lucetta! She often has attacks like that."

Confounded, for the woman spoke so naturally that only a suspicious nature like mine would fail to have been deceived by it, I raised myself on my elbow and gave her an indignant look.

"Yet you said just now that the young ladies were expecting me to breakfast."

"Yes, and why not?" Her look was absolutely guileless. "Miss Lucetta sometimes keeps us up half the night, but she does not miss breakfast on that account. When the turn is over, she is as well as ever she was. A fine young lady, Miss Lucetta. I'd lose my two hands for her any day."

"She certainly is a remarkable girl," I declared, not, however, as dryly as I felt. "I can hardly believe I dreamed about the key. Let me feel of your pocket," I laughed.

She, without the smallest hesitancy, pulled aside her apron.

"I am sorry you put so little confidence in my word, ma'am, but Lor' me, what you heard is nothing to what some of our guests have complained of—in the days, I mean, when we did have guests. I have known them to scream out themselves in the middle of the night and vow they saw white figures creeping up and down the halls—all nonsense, ma'am, but believed in by some folks. You don't look as if you believed in ghosts."

"And I don't," I said, "not a whit. It would be a poor way to try to frighten me. How is Mr. William this morning?"

"Oh, he's well and feeding the dogs, ma'am. What made you think of him?"

"Politeness, Hannah," I found myself forced to say. "He's the only man in the house. Why shouldn't I think of him?"

She fingered her apron a minute and laughed.

"I didn't know you liked him. He's so rough, it isn't everybody who understands him," she said.

"Must one understand a person to like him?" I queried good-humoredly. I was beginning to think I might have dreamed about that key.

"I don't know," she said, "I don't always understand Miss Lucetta, but I like her through and through, ma'am, as I like this little finger," and holding up this member to my inspection, she crossed the room for my water-pitcher, which she proposed to fill with hot water.

I followed her closely with my eyes. When she came back, I saw her attention caught by the break in the flooring, which she had not noticed on entering.

"Oh," she exclaimed, "what a shame!" her honest face coloring as she drew the rug back over the small black gap. "I am sure, ma'am," she cried, "you must think very poorly of us. But I assure you, ma'am, it's honest poverty, nothing but honest poverty as makes them so neglectful," and with an air as far removed from mystery as her frank, good-natured manner seemed to be from falsehood, she slid from the room with a kind:

"Don't hurry, ma'am. It is Miss Knollys' turn in the kitchen, and she isn't as quick as Miss Lucetta."

"Humph," thought I, "supposing I had called in the police."

But by the time she had returned with the water, my doubts had reawakened. She was not changed in manner, though I have no doubt she had recounted all that I had said, below, but I was, for I remembered the matches and thought I saw a way of tripping her up in her self-complacency.

Just as she was leaving me for the second time I called her back.

"What is the matter with your matches?" I asked. "I couldn't make them light last night."

With a wholly undisturbed countenance she turned toward the bureau and took up the china trinket that held the few remaining matches I had not scraped on the piece of sandpaper I myself had fastened up alongside the door. A sheepish cry of dismay at once escaped her.

"Why, these are old matches!" she declared, showing me the box in which a half-dozen or so burned matches stood with their burned tops all turned down.

"I thought they were all right. I'm afraid we are a little short of matches."

I did not like to tell her what I thought about it, but it made me doubly anxious to join the young ladies at breakfast and judge for myself from their conduct and expression if I had been deceived by my own fears into taking for realities the phantasies of a nightmare, or whether I was correct in ascribing to fact that episode of the key with all the possibilities that lay behind it.

I did not let my anxiety, however, stand in the way of my duty. Mr. Gryce had bid me carry the whistle he had sent me constantly about my person, and I felt that he would have the right to reproach me if I left my room without making some endeavor to recover this lost article. How to do this without aid or appliances of any kind was a problem. I knew where it was, but I could not see it, much less reach it. Besides, they were waiting for me—never a pleasant thought. It occurred to me that I might lower into the hole a lighted candle hung by a string.

Looking over my effects, I chose out a hairpin, a candle, and two corset laces, (Pardon me. I am as modest as most of my sex, but I am not squeamish. Corset laces are strings, and as such only I present them to your notice.) I should like to have added a button-hook to my collection, but not having as yet discarded the neatly laced boot of my ancestor, I could only produce a small article from my toilet-service which shall remain unmentioned, as I presently discarded it and turned my whole attention to the other objects I have named. A poor array, but out of them I hoped to find the means of fishing up my lost whistle.

My intention was to lower first a lighted candle into the hole by means of a string tied about its middle, then to drop a line on the whistle thus discovered and draw it up with the point of a bent hairpin, which I fondly hoped I could make do the service of a hook. To think was to try. The candle was soon down in the hole, and by its light the whistle was easily seen. The string and bent hairpin went down next. I was successful in hooking the prize and proceeded to pull it up with great care. For an instant I realized what a ridiculous figure I was cutting, stooping over a hole in the floor on both knees, a string in each hand, leading apparently to nowhere, and I at work cautiously steadying one and as carefully pulling on the other. Having hooked the string holding the whistle over the first finger of the hand holding the candle, I may have become too self-conscious to notice the slight release of weight on the whistle hand. Whatever the reason, when the end of the string came in sight there was no whistle on it. The charred end showed me that the candle had burned the cord, letting the whistle fall again out of reach. Down went the candle again. It touched bottom, but no whistle was to be seen. After a long and fruitless search, I concluded to abandon my whistle-fishing excursion, and, rising from my cramped and undignified position, I proceeded to pull up the candle. To my surprise and delight, I found the whistle firmly stuck to the lower side of it. Some drops of candle grease had fallen upon the whistle where it lay. The candle coming in contact with it, the two had adhered, and I became indebted to accident rather than to acumen for the restoration of the precious article.

CHAPTER XIX

A Knot of Crape

I was prepared for some change in the appearance of my young hostesses, but not for so great a one as I saw on entering the dining-room that memorable morning. The blinds, which were always half closed, were now wide open, and under the cheerful influence of the light which was thus allowed to enter, the table and all its appointments had a much less dreary look than before. Behind the urn sat Miss Knollys, with a smile on her lips, and in the window William stood whistling a cheerful air, unrebuked. Lucetta was not present, but to my great astonishment she presently walked in with her hands laden with sprays of morning-glory, which she flung down in the centre of the board. It was the first time I had seen any attempt made by any of them to lighten the sombreness of their surroundings, and it was also the first time I had seen the three together.

I was more disconcerted by this simple show of improved spirits than I like to acknowledge. In the first place, they were natural and not forced; and, secondly, they were to all appearance unconscious.

They were not marked enough to show relief, and in Lucetta especially did not serve to hide the underlying melancholy of a disappointed girl, yet it was not what I expected from my supposed experiences of the night, and led me to answer a little warily when, with a frank laugh, Loreen exclaimed:

"So you have lost your character as a practical woman, Miss Butterworth? Hannah tells me you were the victim of a ghostly visit last night."

"Hannah gossips unmercifully," was my cautious and somewhat peevish reply. "If I chose to dream that I was locked into my room by some erratic spectre, I cannot see why she should take the confession of my folly out of my mouth. I was going to relate the fact myself, with all the accompaniments of rushing steps and wild and unearthly cries which are expected by the listeners to a veritable ghost story. But now I have simply to defend myself from a charge of credulity. It's too bad, Miss Knollys, much too bad. I did not come to a haunted house for this."

My manner, rather than my words, seemed to completely deceive them. Perhaps it deceived myself, for I began to feel a loss of the depression which had weighed upon me ever since that scream rang in my ears at midnight. It disappeared still further when Lucetta said:

"If your ramblings through the old rooms on this floor were the occasion of this nightmare, you must be prepared for a recurrence of the same tonight, for I am going to take you through the upper rooms myself this morning. Isn't that the programme, Loreen? Or have you changed your mind and planned a drive for Miss Butterworth?"

"She shall do both," Loreen answered. "When she is tired of tramping through dusty chambers and examining the decayed remnants of old furniture which encumber them, William stands ready to drive her over the hills, where she will find views well worth her attention."

"Thank you," said I. "It is a pleasant prospect." But inwardly I uttered anything but thanks; rather asked myself if I had not played the part of a fool in ascribing so much importance to the events of the past night, and decided almost without an argument that I had.

However, beliefs die hard in a mind like mine, and though I was ready to consider that an inflamed imagination may often carry us beyond the bounds of fact and even into the realm of fancy and misconception, I yet was not ready to give up my suspicions altogether, or to acknowledge that I had no foundation for the fear that something uncanny if not awful had taken place under this roof the night before. The very naturalness I observed in this hitherto restrained trio might be the result of the removal of some great strain, and if that was the case—Ah, well, alertness is the motto of the truly wise. It is when vigilance sleeps that the enemy gains the victory. I would not let myself be deceived even at the cost of a little ridicule. Amelia Butterworth was still awake, even under a semblance of well-laid suspicion.

My footsteps were not dogged after this as they had hitherto been in my movements about the house. I was allowed to go and come and even to stray into the second long corridor, without any other let than my own discretion and good breeding. Lucetta joined me, to be sure, after a while, but only as guide and companion. She took me into rooms I forgot the next minute, and into others I remember to this day as quaint memorials of a past ever and always interesting to me. We ransacked the house, yet after all was over and I sat down to rest in my own room, two formidable questions rose in my mind for which I found no satisfactory answer. Why, with so many more or less attractive bedchambers at their command, had they chosen to put me into a hole, where the very flooring was unsafe, and the outlook the most dismal that could be imagined? and why, in all our peregrinations in and out of rooms, had we always passed one door without entering? She had said that it was William's—a sufficient explanation, if true, and I have no doubt it was—but the change of countenance with which she passed it and the sudden lightening of her tread (so instinctive that she was totally unconscious of it) marked that door as one it would be my duty to enter if fate should yet give me the opportunity. That it was the one in communication with the Flower Parlor I felt satisfied, but in order to make assurance doubly sure I resolved upon a tour through the shrubbery outside, that I might compare the location of the window having the chipped blind with that of this room, which was, as well as I could calculate, the third from the rear on the left-hand side.

When, therefore, William called up to know if I was ready for my drive, I answered back that I found myself very tired and would be glad to exchange the pleasure he offered, for a visit to the stables.

This, as I expected, caused considerable comment and some disturbance. They wanted me to repeat my experience of the day before and spend two if not more hours of the morning out of the house. But I did not mean to gratify them. Indeed I felt that my duty held me to the house, and was so persistent in my wishes, or rather in my declaration of them, that all opposition had to give way, even in the stubborn William.

"I thought you had a dread of dogs," was the final remark with which he endeavored to turn me aside from my purpose. "I have three in the barn and two in the stable, and they make a great fuss when I come around, I assure you."

"Then they will have enough to do without noticing me," said I, with a brazen assumption of courage sufficiently surprising if I had had any real intention of invading a place so guarded. But I had not. I no more meant to enter the stables than to jump off the housetop, but it was necessary that I should start for them and make the start from the left wing of the house.

How I managed the intractable William and led him as I did from bush to bush and shrub to shrub, up and down the length of that interminable façade of the left wing, would make an interesting story in itself. The curiosity I showed in plants, even such plants as had survived the neglect that had made a wilderness of this old-time garden; the indifference which, contrary to all my habits, I persisted in manifesting to every inconvenience I encountered in the way of straightforward walking to any object I set my fancy upon examining; the knowledge I exhibited, and the interest which I took it for granted he felt in all I discovered and all I imparted to him, would form the basis of a farce of no ordinary merit had it not had its birth in interests and intents bordering on the tragic.

A row of bushes of various species ran along the wall and covered in some instances the lower ledges of the first row of windows. As I made for a certain shrub which I had observed growing near what I supposed to be the casement from whose blind I had chipped a small sliver, I allowed my enthusiasm to bubble over, in my evident desire to display my erudition.

"This," said I, "is, without any doubt at all, a stunted but undoubted specimen of that rare tree found seldom north of the thirtieth degree, the *Magnolia grandiflora*. I have never seen it but once before, and that was in the botanical gardens in Washington. Note its leaves. You have noted its flowers, smaller undoubtedly than they should be—but then you must acknowledge it has been in a measure neglected—are they not fine?"

Here I pulled a branch down which interfered with my view of the window. There was no chip visible in the blinds thus discovered. Seeing this, I let the branch go. "But the oddest feature of this tree and one with which you are perhaps not acquainted" (I wonder if anybody is?) "is that it will not grow within twenty feet of any plant which scatters pollen. See for yourself. This next shrub bears no flower" (I was moving along the wall), "nor this." I drew down a branch as I spoke, caught sight of the mark I was looking for, and let the bough spring back. I had found the window I wanted.

His grunts and groans during all this formed a running accompaniment which would have afforded me great secret amusement had my purpose been less serious. As it was, I could pay but little attention to him, especially after I had stepped back far enough to take a glance at the window over the one I had just located as that of the Flower Parlor. It was, as I expected, the third one from the rear corner; but it was not this fact which gave me a thrill of feeling so strong that I have never had harder work to preserve my equanimity. *It was the knot of black crêpe with which the shutters were tied together.*

CHAPTER XX

Questions

I kept the promise I had made to myself and did not go to the stables. Had I intended to go there, I could not have done so after the discovery I have just mentioned. It awakened too many thoughts and contradictory surmises. If this knot was a signal, for whom was this signal meant? If it was a mere acknowledgment of death, how reconcile the sentimentality which prompted such an acknowledgment with the monstrous and diseased passions lying at the base of the whole dreadful occurrence? Lastly, if it was the result of pure carelessness, a bit of crêpe having been caught up and used for a purpose for which any ordinary string would have answered, what a wonderful coincidence between it and my thoughts—a coincidence, indeed, amounting almost to miracle!

Marvelling at the whole affair and deciding nothing, I allowed myself to stroll down alone to the gate, William having left me at my peremptory refusal to drag my skirts any longer through the briers. The day being bright and the sunshine warm, the road looked less gloomy than usual, especially in the direction of the village and Deacon Spear's cottage. The fact is, that anything seemed better than the grim and lowering walls of the house behind me. If my home was there, so was my dread, and I welcomed the sight of Mother Jane's heavy figure bent over her herbs at the door of her hut, a few paces to my left, where the road turned.

Had she not been deaf, I believed I would have called her. As it was, I contented myself with watching the awkward swayings of her body as she pottered to and fro among her turnips and carrots. My eyes were still on her when I suddenly heard the clatter of a horse's hoofs on the highway. Looking up, I encountered the trim figure of Mr. Trohm, bending to me from a fine sorrel.

"Good morning, Miss Butterworth. It's a great relief to me to see you in such good health and spirits this morning," were the pleasant words with which he endeavored, perhaps, to explain his presence in a spot more or less under a ban.

It was certainly a surprise. What right had I to look for such attentions from a man whose acquaintance I had made only the day before? It touched me, little as I am in the habit of allowing myself to be ruled by trivial sentimentalities, and though I was discreet enough to avoid any further recognition of his kindness than was his due from a lady of great self-respect, he was evidently sufficiently gratified by my response to draw rein and pause for a moment's conversation under the pine trees. This for the moment seemed so natural that I forgot that more than one pair of eyes might be watching me from the windows behind us—eyes which might wonder at a meeting which to the foolish understandings of the young might have the look of premeditation. But, pshaw! I am talking as if I were twenty instead of—Well, I will leave you to consult our family record on that point. There are certain secrets which even the wisest among us cannot be blamed for preserving.

"How did you pass the night?" was Mr. Trohm's first question. "I hope in all due peace and quiet."

"Thank you," I returned, not seeing why I should increase his anxiety in my regard. "I have nothing to complain of. I had a dream; but dreams are to be expected where one has to pass a half-dozen empty rooms to one's apartment."

He could not restrain his curiosity.

"A dream!" he repeated. "I do not believe in sleep that is broken by dreams, unless they are of the most cheerful sort possible. And I judge from what you say that yours were not cheerful."

I wanted to confide in him. I felt that in a way he had a right to know what had happened to me, or what I thought had happened to me, under this roof. And yet I did not speak. What I could tell would sound so puerile in the broad sunshine that enveloped us. I merely remarked that cheerfulness was not to be expected in a domicile so given over to the ravages of time, and then with that lightness and versatility which characterize me under certain exigencies, I introduced a topic we could discuss without any embarrassment to himself or me.

"Do you see Mother Jane over there?" I asked. "I had some talk with her yesterday. She seems like a harmless imbecile."

"Very harmless," he acquiesced; "her only fault is greed; that is insatiable. Yet it is not strong enough to take her a quarter of a mile from this place. Nothing could do that, I think. She believes that her daughter Lizzie is still alive and will come back to the hut some day. It's very sad when you think that the girl's dead, and has been dead nearly forty years."

"Why does she harp on numbers?" I asked. "I heard her mutter certain ones over and over."

"That is a mystery none of us have ever been able to solve," said he. "Possibly she has no reason for it. The vagaries of the witless are often quite unaccountable."

He remained looking at me long after he had finished speaking, not, I felt sure, from any connection he found between what he had just said and anything to be observed in me, but from—Well, I was glad that I had been carefully trained in my youth to pay the greatest attention to my morning toilets. Any woman can look well at night and many women in the flush of a bright afternoon, but the woman who looks well in the morning needs not always to be young to attract the appreciative gaze of a man of real penetration. Mr. Trohm was such a man, and I did not begrudge him the pleasure he showed in my neat gray silk and carefully adjusted collar. But he said nothing, and a short silence ensued, which was perhaps more of a compliment than otherwise. Then he uttered a short sigh and lifted the reins.

"If only I were not debarred from entering," he smiled, with a short gesture toward the house.

I did not answer. Even I understand that on occasion the tongue plays but a sorry part in interviews of this nature.

He sighed again and uttered some short encouragement to his horse, which started that animal up and sent him slowly pacing down the road toward the cheerful clearing whither my own eyes were looking with what I was determined should not be construed even by the most sanguine into a glance of anything like wistfulness. As he went he made a bow I have never seen surpassed in my own parlor in Gramercy Park, and upon my bestowing upon him a return nod, glanced up at the house with an intentness which seemed to increase as some object, invisible to me at that moment, caught his eye. As that eye was directed toward the left wing, and lifted as far as the second row of windows, I could not help asking myself if he had seen the knot of crêpe which had produced upon me so lugubrious an impression. Before I could make sure of this he had passed from sight, and the highway fell again into shadow—why, I hardly knew, for the sun certainly had been shining a few minutes before.

CHAPTER XXI

Mother Jane

"Well, well, what did Trohm want here this morning?" cried a harsh voice from amid the tangled walks behind me. "Seems to me he finds this place pretty interesting all of a sudden."

I turned upon the intruder with a look that should have daunted him. I had recognized William's courteous tones and was in no mood to endure a questioning so unbecoming in one of his age to one of mine. But as I met his eye, which had something in it besides anger and suspicion— something that was quizzical if not impertinent—I changed my intention and bestowed upon him a conciliatory smile, which I hope escaped the eye of the good angel who records against man all his small hypocrisies and petty deceits.

"Mr. Trohm rides for his health," said I. "Seeing me looking up the road at Mother Jane, he stopped to tell me some of the idiosyncrasies of that old woman. A very harmless courtesy, Mr. Knollys."

"Very," he echoed, not without a touch of sarcasm. "I only hope that is all," he muttered, with a sidelong look back at the house. "Lucetta hasn't a particle of belief in that man's friendship, or, rather, she believes he never goes anywhere without a particular intention, and I do believe she's right, or why should he come spying around here just at a time when"—he caught himself up with almost a look of terror—"when— when you are here?" he completed lamely.

"I do not think," I retorted, more angrily than the occasion perhaps warranted, "that the word spying applies to Mr. Trohm. But if it does, what has he to gain from a pause at the gate and a word to such a new acquaintance as I am?"

"I don't know," William persisted suspiciously. "Trohm's a sharp fellow. If there was anything to see, he would see it without half looking. But there isn't. You don't know of anything wrong here, do you, which such a man as that, hand in glove with the police as we know him to be, might consider himself interested in?"

Astonished both at this blundering committal of himself and at the certain sort of anxious confidence he showed in me, I hesitated for a moment, but only for a moment, since, if half my suspicions were true, this man must not know that my perspicacity was more to be feared than even Mr. Trohm's was.

"If Mr. Trohm shows an increased interest in this household during the last two days," said I, with a heroic defiance of ridicule which I hope Mr. Gryce has duly appreciated, "I beg leave to call your attention to the fact that on yesterday morning he came to deliver a letter addressed to me which had inadvertently been left at his house, and that this morning he called to inquire how I had spent the night, which, in consideration of the ghosts which are said to haunt this house and the strange and uncanny apparitions which only three nights ago made the entrance to this lane hideous to one pair of eyes at least, should not cause a gentleman's son like yourself any astonishment. It does not seem odd to me, I assure you."

He laughed. I meant he should, and, losing almost instantly his air of doubt and suspicion, turned toward the gate from which I had just moved away, muttering:

"Well, it's a small matter to me anyway. It's only the girls that are afraid of Mr. Trohm. I am not afraid of anything but losing Saracen, who has pined like the deuce at his long confinement in the court. Hear him now; just hear him."

And I could hear the low and unhappy moaning of the hound distinctly. It was not a pleasant sound, and I was almost tempted to bid William unloose the dog, but thought better of it.

"By the way," said he, "speaking of Mother Jane, I have a message to her from the girls. You will excuse me if I speak to the poor woman."

Alarmed by his politeness more than I ever have been by his roughness and inconsiderate sarcasms, I surveyed him inquiringly as he left the gate, and did not know whether to stand my ground or retreat to the house. I decided to stand my ground; a message to this woman seeming to me a matter of some interest.

I was glad I did, for after some five minutes' absence, during which he had followed her into the house, I saw him come back again in a state of sullen displeasure, which, however, partially disappeared when he saw me still standing by the gate.

"Ah, Miss Butterworth, you can do me a favor. The old creature is in one of her stubborn fits today, and won't give me a hearing. She may not be so deaf to you; she isn't apt to be to women. Will you cross the road and speak to her? I will go with you. You needn't be afraid."

The way he said this, the confidence he expected to inspire, had almost a ghastly effect upon me. Did he know or suspect that the only thing I feared in this lane was he? Evidently not, for he met my eye quite confidently.

It would not do to shake his faith at such a moment as this, so calling upon Providence to see me safely through this adventure, I stepped into the highway and went with him into Mother Jane's cottage.

Had I been favored with any other companion than himself, I should have been glad of this opportunity. As it was, I found myself ignoring any possible danger I might be running, in my interest in the remarkable interior to which I was thus introduced.

Having been told that Mother Jane was poor, I had expected to confront squalor and possibly filth, but I never have entered a cleaner place or one in which order made the poorest belongings look more decent. The four walls were unfinished, and so were the rafters which formed the ceiling, but the floor, neatly laid in brick, was spotless, and the fireplace, also of brick, was as deftly swept as one could expect from the little scrub I saw hanging by its side. Crouched within this fireplace sat the old woman we had come to interview. Her back was to us, and she looked helplessly and hopelessly deaf.

"Ask her," said William, pointing towards her with a rude gesture, "if she will come to the house at sunset. My sisters have some work for her to do. They will pay her well."

Advancing at his bidding, I passed a rocking-chair, in the cushion of which a dozen patches met my eye. This drew my eyes toward a bed, over which a counterpane was drawn, made up of a thousand or more pieces of colored calico, and noticing their varied shapes and the intricacy with which they were put together, I wondered whether she ever counted them. The next moment I was at her back.

"Seventy," burst from her lips as I leaned over her shoulder and showed her the coin which I had taken pains to have in my hand.

"Yours," I announced, pointing in the direction of the house, "if you will do some work for Miss Knollys tonight."

Slowly she shook her head before burying it deeper in the shawl she wore wrapped about her shoulders. Listening a minute, I thought I heard her mutter: "Twenty-eight, ten, but no more. I can count no more. Go away!"

But I'm nothing if not persistent. Feeling for her hands, which were hidden away somewhere under her shawl, I touched them with the coin and cried again:

"This and more for a small piece of work tonight. Come, you are strong; earn it."

"What kind of work is it?" I asked innocently, or it must have appeared innocently, of Mr. Knollys, who was standing at my back.

He frowned, all the black devils in his heart coming into his look at once.

"How do I know! Ask Loreen; she's the one who sent me. I don't take account of what goes on in the kitchen."

I begged his pardon, somewhat sarcastically I own, and made another attempt to attract the attention of the old crone, who had remained perfectly callous to my allurements.

"I thought you liked money," I said. "For Lizzie, you know, for Lizzie."

But she only muttered in lower and lower gutturals, "I can count no more"; and, disgusted at my failure, being one who accounts failure as little short of disgrace, I drew back and made my way toward the door, saying: "She's in a different mood from what she was yesterday when she snatched a quarter from me at the first intimation it was hers. I don't think you can get her to do any work tonight. Innocents take these freaks. Isn't there someone else you can call in?"

The scowl that disfigured his none too handsome features was a fitting prelude to his words.

"You talk," said he, "as if we had the whole village at our command. How did you succeed with the locksmith yesterday? Came, didn't he? Well, that's what we have to expect whenever we want any help."

Whirling on his heel, he led the way out of the hut, whither I would have immediately followed him if I had not stopped to take another look at the room, which struck me, even upon a second scrutiny, as one of the best ordered and best kept I had ever entered. Even the strings and strings of dried fruits and vegetables, which hung in festoons from every beam of the roof, were free from dust and cobwebs, and though the dishes were few and the pans scarce, they were bright and speckless, giving to the shelf along which they were ranged a semblance of ornament.

"Wise enough to keep her house in order," thought I, and actually found it hard to leave, so attractive to my eyes are absolute neatness and order.

William was pushing at his own gate when I joined him. He looked as if he wished I had spent the morning with Mother Jane, and was barely civil in our walk up to the house. I was not, therefore, surprised when he burst into a volley of oaths at the doorway and turned upon me almost as if he would forbid me the house, for tap, tap, tap, from some distant quarter came a distinct sound like that of nails being driven into a plank.

CHAPTER XXII

The Third Night

Mother Jane must have changed her mind after we left her. For late in the evening I caught a glimpse of her burly figure in the kitchen as I went to give Hannah some instructions concerning certain little changes in the housekeeping arrangements which the girls and I had agreed were necessary to our mutual comfort.

I wished to address the old crone, but warned, by the ill-concealed defiance with which Hannah met my advances, that any such attempt on my part would be met by anything but her accustomed good-nature, I refrained from showing my interest in her strange visitor, or from even appearing conscious of her own secret anxieties and evident preoccupation.

Loreen and Lucetta exchanged a meaning look as I rejoined them in the sitting-room; but my volubility in regard to the domestic affair which had just taken me to the kitchen seemed to speedily reassure them, and when a few minutes later I said good-night and prepared to leave the room, it was with the conviction that I had relieved their mind at the expense of my own. Mother Jane in the kitchen at this late hour meant business. What that business was, I seemed to know only too well.

I had formed a plan for the night which required some courage. Recalling Lucetta's expression of the morning, that I might expect a repetition of the former night's experiences, I prepared to profit by the warning in a way she little meant. Satisfied that if there was any truth in the suspicions I had formed, there would be an act performed in this house tonight which, if seen by me, would forever settle the question agitating the whole countryside, I made up my mind that no locked door should interfere with my opportunity of doing so. How I effected this result I will presently relate.

Lucetta had accompanied me to my door with a lighted candle.

"I hear you had some trouble with matches last night," said she. "You will find them all right now. Hannah must be blamed for some of this carelessness." Then as I began some reassuring reply, she turned upon me with a look that was almost fond, and, throwing out her arms, cried entreatingly: "Won't you give me a little kiss, Miss Butterworth? We have not given you the best of welcomes, but you are my mother's old friend, and sometimes I feel a little lonely."

I could easily believe that, and yet I found it hard to embrace her. Too many shadows swam between Althea's children and myself. She saw my hesitancy (a hesitancy I could not but have shown even at the risk of losing her confidence), and, paling slightly, dropped her hands with a pitiful smile.

"You don't like me," she said. "I do not wonder, but I was in hopes you would for my mother's sake. I have no claims myself."

"You are an interesting girl, and you have, what your mother had not, a serious side to your nature that is anything but displeasing to me. But my kisses, Lucetta, are as rare as my tears. I had rather give you good advice, and that is a fact. Perhaps it is as strong a proof of affection as any ordinary caress would be."

"Perhaps," she assented, but she did not encourage me to give it to her notwithstanding. Instead of that, she drew back and bade me a gentle good-night, which for some reason made me sadder than I wished to be at a crisis demanding so much nerve. Then she walked quickly away, and I was left to face the night alone.

Knowing that I should be rather weakened than helped by the omission of any of the little acts of preparation with which I am accustomed to calm my spirits for the night, I went through them all, with just as much precision as if I had expected to spend the ensuing hours in rest. When all was done and only my cup of tea remained to be quaffed, I had a little struggle with myself, which ended in my not drinking it at all. Nothing, not even this comfortable solace for an unsatisfactory day, should stand in the way of my being the complete mistress of my wits this night. Had I known that this tea contained a soporific in the shape of a little harmless morphine, I would have found this act of self-denial much easier.

It was now eleven. Confident that nothing would be done while my light was burning, I blew it out, and, taking a candle and some matches in my hand, softly opened my door and, after a moment of intense listening, stepped out and closed it carefully behind me. Nothing could be stiller than the house or darker than the corridor.

"Am I watched or am I not watched?" I queried, and for an instant stood undecided. Then, seeing nothing and hearing nothing, I slipped down the hall to the door beyond mine and, opening it with all the care possible, stepped inside.

I knew the room. I had taken especial note of it in my visit of the morning. I knew that it was nearly empty and that there was a key in the lock which I could turn. I therefore felt more or less safe in it, especially as its window was undarkened by the branches that hung so thickly across my own casement, shutting me in, or seeming to shut me in, from all communication with the outside world and the unknown guardian which I had been assured constantly attended my summons.

That I might strengthen my spirits by one glimpse of this same outside world, before settling down for the watch I had set for myself, I stepped softly to the window and took one lingering look without. A belt of forest illumined by a gibbous moon met my eyes; nothing else. Yet this sight was welcome, and it was only after I had been struck by the possibility of my own figure being seen at the casement by some possible watcher in the shadows below, that I found the hardihood necessary to withdraw into the darker precincts of the room, and begin that lonely watch which my doubts and expectations rendered necessary.

This was the third I had been forced to keep, and it was by far the most dismal; for though the bolted door between me and the hall promised me personal safety, there presently rose in some far-off place a smothered repetition of that same tap, tap, tap which had sent the shudders over me upon my sudden entrance into the house early in the morning. Heard now, it caused me to tremble in a way I had not supposed possible to one of my hardy nature, and while with this recognition of my feminine susceptibility to impressions there came a certain pride in the stanchness of purpose which led me to restrain all acknowledgment of fear, by any recourse to my whistle, I was more than glad when even this sound ceased, and I had only to expect the swishing noise of a skirt down the hall, and that stealthy locking of the door of the room I had taken the precaution of leaving.

It came sooner than I expected, came just in the way it had previously done, only that the person paused a moment to listen before hastening back. The silence within must have satisfied her, for I heard a low sigh like that of relief, before the steps took themselves back. That they would turn my way gave me a momentary concern, but I had too completely lulled my young hostesses' suspicions, or (let me be faithful to all the possibilities of the case) they had put too much confidence in the powder with which they had seasoned my nightly cup of tea, for them to doubt that I was soundly asleep in my own quarters.

Three minutes later I followed those steps as far down the corridor as I dared to go. For, since my last appearance in it, a candle had been lit in the main hall, and faint as was its glimmer, it was still a glimmer into the circle of which I felt it would be foolhardiness for me to step. At some twenty paces, then, from the opening, I paused and gave myself up to listening. Alas, there was plenty now for me to hear.

You have heard the sound; we all have heard the sound, but few of us in such a desolate structure and at the hour and under the influences of midnight! The measured tread of men struggling under a heavy weight, and that weight—how well I knew it! as well as if I had seen it, as I really did in my imagination.

They advanced from the adjoining corridor, from the room I had as yet found no opportunity of entering, and they approached surely and slowly the main hall near which I was standing in such a position as rendered it impossible for me to see anything if they took the direct course to the head of the stairs and so down, as there was every reason to expect they would. I did not dare to draw nearer, however, so concentrated my faculties anew upon listening, when suddenly I perceived on the great white wall in front of me—the wall of the main hall, I mean, toward which the opening looked—the shapeless outline of a drooping head, and realized that the candle had been placed in such a position that the wall must receive the full shadow of the passing cortège.

And thus it was I saw it, huge, distorted, and suggestive beyond any picture I ever beheld—the passing of a body to its long home, carried by six anxious figures, four of which seemed to be those of women.

But that long home! Where was it located—in the house or in the grounds? It was a question so important that for a moment I could think of nothing but how I could follow the small procession, without running the risk of discovery. It had reached the head of the stairs by this time, and I heard Miss Knollys' low, firm voice enjoining silence. Then the six bearers began to descend with their burden.

Ere they reached the foot, a doubt struck me. Would it be better to follow them or to take the opportunity afforded by every member of the household being engaged in this task, to take a peep into the room where the death had occurred? I had not decided, when I heard them take the forward course from the foot of the stairs to what, to my straining ear, seemed to be the entrance to the dining-room corridor. But as in my anxiety to determine this fact I slipped far enough forward to make sure that their destination lay somewhere within reach of the Flower Parlor, I was so struck by the advantages to be gained by a cautious use of the trap-door in William's room, that I hesitated no longer, but sped with what swiftness I could toward the spot from which I had so lately heard this strange procession advance.

A narrow band of light lying across the upper end of the long corridor, proved that the door was not only ajar, but that a second candle was burning in the room I was about to invade; but this was scarcely to be regretted, since there could be no question of the emptiness of the room. The six figures I had seen go by embraced every one who by any possibility could be considered as having part in this transaction—William, Mr. Simsbury, Miss Knollys, Lucetta, Hannah, and Mother Jane. No one else was left to guard this room, so I pushed the door open quite boldly and entered.

What I saw there I will relate later, or, rather, I will but hint at now. A bed with a sheet thrown back, a stand covered with vials, a bureau with a man's shaving paraphernalia upon it, and on the wall such pictures as only sporting gentlemen delight in. The candle was guttering on a small table upon which, to my astonishment, a Bible lay open. Not having my glasses with me, I could not see what portion of the sacred word was thus disclosed, but I took the precaution to indent the upper leaf with my thumb-nail, so that I might find it again in case of future opportunity. My attention was attracted by other small matters that would be food for thought at a more propitious moment, but at that instant the sound of voices coming distinctly to my ear from below, warned me that a halt had been made at the Flower Parlor, and that the duty of the moment was to locate the trap-door and if possible determine the means of raising it.

This was less difficult than I anticipated. Either this room was regarded as so safe from intrusion that a secret like this could be safely left unguarded, or the door which was plainly to be seen in one corner had been so lately lifted, that it had hardly sunk back into its place. I found it, if the expression may be used of a horizontal object, slightly ajar and needing but the slightest pull to make it spring upright.

The hole thus disclosed was filled with the little staircase up which I had partly mounted in my daring explorations of the day before. It was dark now, darker than it was then, but I felt that I must descend by it, for plainly to be heard now through the crack in the closet door, which seemed to have a knack of standing partly open, I could hear the heavy tread of the six bearers as they entered the parlor below, still carrying their burden, concerning the destination of which I was so anxious to be informed.

That it could be in the room itself was too improbable for consideration. Yet if they took up their stand in this room it was for a purpose, and what that purpose was I was determined to know. The noise their feet made on the bare boards of the floor and the few words I now heard uttered in William's stolid tones and Lucetta's musical treble assured me that my own light steps would no more be heard, than my dark gown of quiet wool would be seen through the narrow slit through which I was preparing to peer. Yet it took no small degree of what my father used to call pluck, for me to put foot on this winding staircase and descend almost, as it were, into the midst of what I must regard as the last wicked act of a most cowardly and brutal murder.

I did it, however, and after a short but grim communion with my own heart, which would persist in beating somewhat noisily, I leaned forward with all the precaution possible and let my gaze traverse the chamber in which I had previously seen such horrors as should have prepared me for this last and greatest one.

In a moment I understood the whole. A long square hole in the floor, lately sawed, provided an opening through which the plain plank coffin, of which I now caught sight, was to be lowered into the cellar and so into the grave which had doubtless been dug there. The ropes in the hands of the six persons, in whose identity I had made no mistake, was proof enough of their intention; and, satisfied as I now was of the means and mode of the interment which had been such a boundless mystery to me, I shrank a step upward, fearing lest my indignation and the horror I could not but feel, from this moment on, of Althea's children, would betray me into some exclamation which might lead to my discovery and a similar fate.

One other short glance, in which I saw them all ranged around the dark opening, and I was up out of their reach, Lucetta's face and Lucetta's one sob as the ropes began to creak, being the one memory which followed me the most persistently. She, at least, was overwhelmed with remorse for a deed she was perhaps only answerable for in that she failed to make known to the world her brother's madness and the horrible crimes to which it gave rise.

I took one other look around his room before I fled to my own, or rather, to the one in which I had taken refuge while my own was under lock and key. That I spent the next two hours on my knees no one can wonder. When my own room was unlocked, as it was before the day broke, I hastened to enter it and lay my head with all its unhappy knowledge on my pillow. But I did not sleep; and, what was stranger still, never once thought of sounding a single note on the whistle which would have brought the police into this abode of crime. Perhaps it was a wise omission. I had seen enough that was horrible that night without beholding Althea's children arrested before my eyes.

BOOK III: FORWARD AND BACK

CHAPTER XXIII

Room 3, Hotel Carter

I rose at my usual hour. I dressed myself with my usual care. I was, to a superficial observer at least, in all respects my usual self when Hannah came to my door to ask what she could do for me. As there was nothing I wanted but to get out of this house, which had become unbearable to me, I replied with the utmost cheerfulness that my wants were all supplied and that I would soon be down, at which she answered that in that case she must bestir herself or the breakfast would not be ready, and hurried away.

There was no one in the dining-room when I entered, and judging from appearances that several minutes must elapse before breakfast would be ready, I took occasion to stroll through the grounds and glance up at the window of William's room. The knot of crêpe was gone.

I would have gone farther, but just then I heard a great rushing and scampering, and, looking up, saw an enormous dog approaching at full gallop from the stables. Saracen was loose.

I did not scream or give way to other feminine expressions of fear, but I did return as quickly as possible to the house, where I now saw I must remain till William chose to take me into town.

This I was determined should take place as soon after breakfast as practicable. The knowledge which I now possessed warranted, nay, demanded, instant consultation with the police, and as this could best be effected by following out the orders I had received from Mr. Gryce, I did not consider any other plan than that of meeting the man on duty in Room No. 3 at the hotel.

Loreen, Lucetta, and William were awaiting me in the hall, and made no apology for the flurry into which I had been thrown by my rapid escape from Saracen. Indeed I doubt if they noticed it, for with all the attempt they made to seem gay and at ease, the anxieties and fatigue of the foregoing nights were telling upon them, and from Miss Knollys down, they looked physically exhausted. But they also looked mentally relieved. In the clear depths of Lucetta's eye there was now no wavering, and the head which was always turning in anxious anticipation over her shoulder rested firm, though not as erect as her sister's, who had less cause perhaps for regret and sorrow.

William was joyful to a degree, but it was a forced joviality which only became real when he heard a sudden, quick bark under the window and the sound of scraping paws against the mastic coating of the wall outside. Then he broke out into a loud laugh of unrestrained pleasure, crying out thoughtlessly:

"There's Saracen. How quick he knows—"

A warning look from Lucetta stopped him.

"I mean," he stammered, "it's a dull dog that cannot find his master. Miss Butterworth, you will have to overcome your fear of dogs if you stay with us long. Saracen is unbound this morning, and"—he used a great oath—"he's going to remain so."

By which I came to understand that it was not out of consideration for me he had been tied up in the court till now, but for reasons connected with their own safety and the preservation of the secret which they so evidently believed had been buried with the body, which I did not like to remember lay at that very minute too nearly under our feet for my own individual comfort.

However, this has nothing to do with the reply I made to William.

"I hope he does not run with the buggy," I objected. "I want to take a ride very much this morning and could get small pleasure out of it if that dog must be our companion."

"I cannot go out this morning," William began, but changed his sentence, possibly at the touch of his sister's foot under the table, into: "But if you say I must, why, I must. You women folks are so plagued unreasonable."

Had he been ten years younger I would have boxed his ears; had he been that much older I would have taken cue and packed my trunk before he could have finished the cup of coffee he was drinking. But he was just too old to reprimand in the way just mentioned, and not old enough to appreciate any display of personal dignity or self-respect on the part of the person he had offended. Besides, he was a knave; so I just let his impertinence pass with the remark:

"I have purchases to make in the village": and so that matter ended, manifestly to the two girls' relief, who naturally did not like to see me insulted, even if they did not possess sufficient power over their brother to prevent it.

One other small episode and then I will take you with me to the village. As we were leaving the table, where I ate less than common, notwithstanding all my efforts to seem perfectly unconcerned, Lucetta, who had waited for her brother to go out, took me gently by the arm, and, eying me closely, said:

"Did you have any dreams last night, Miss Butterworth? You know I promised you some."

The question disconcerted me, and for a moment I felt like taking the two girls into my confidence and bidding them fly from the shame and doom so soon to fall upon their brother; but the real principle underlying all such momentary impulses on my part deterred me, and in as light a tone as I could command and not be an absolute hypocrite, I replied that I was sorry to disappoint her, but I had had no dreams, which seemed to please her more than it should, for if I had had no dreams I certainly had suffered from the most frightful realities.

I will not describe our ride into town. Saracen did go with us, and indignation not only rendered me speechless, but gave to my thoughts a turn which made that half-hour of very little value to me. Mother Jane's burly figure crouching in her doorway might otherwise have given me opportunity for remark, and so might the dubious looks of people we met on the highroad—looks to which I am so wholly unaccustomed that I had difficulty in recognizing myself as the butt of so much doubt and possibly dislike. I attributed this, however, all to the ill repute under which William so deservedly labored, and did not allow myself to more than notice it. Indeed, I could only be sorry for people who did not know in what consideration I was held at home, and who, either through ignorance or prejudice, allowed themselves privileges they would be the first to regret did they know the heart and mind of Amelia Butterworth.

Once in the village, I took the direction of affairs.

"Set me down at the hotel," I commanded, "and then go about such business as you may have here in town. I am not going to allow myself to be tracked all over by that dog."

"I have no business," was the surly reply.

"Then make some," was my sharp retort. "I want to see the locksmith—that locksmith who wouldn't come to do an honest piece of work for me in your house; and I want to buy dimities and wools and sewing silks at the dry-goods store over there. Indeed I have a thousand things to do, and expect to spend half the morning before the counters. Why, man, I haven't done any shopping for a week."

He gaped at me perfectly aghast (as I meant he should), and, having but little experience of city ladies, took me at my word and prepared to beat an honorable retreat. As a result, I found myself ten minutes later standing on the top step of the hotel porch, watching William driving away with Saracen perched on the seat beside him. Then I realized that the village held no companions for him, and did not know whether I felt glad or sorry.

To the clerk who came to meet me, I said quietly, "Room No. 3, if you please," at which he gave a nod of intelligence and led me as unostentatiously as possible into a small hall, at the end of which I saw a door with the aforesaid number on it.

"If you will take a seat inside," said he, "I will send you whatever you may desire for your comfort."

"I think you know what that is," I rejoined, at which he nodded again and left me, closing the door carefully behind him as he went.

The few minutes which elapsed before my quiet was disturbed were spent by me in thinking. There were many little questions to settle in my own mind, for which a spell of uninterrupted contemplation was necessary. One of these was whether, in the event of finding the police amenable, I should reveal or hide from these children of my old friend, the fact that it was through my instrumentality that their nefarious secret had been discovered. I wished—nay, I hoped—that the affair might be so concluded, but the possibility of doing so seemed so problematical, especially since Mr. Gryce was not on hand to direct matters, that I spent very little time on the subject, deep and important as it was to all concerned.

What most occupied me was the necessity of telling my story in such a way as to exonerate the girls as much as possible. They were mistaken in their devotion and most unhappy in the exercise of it, but they were not innately wicked and should not be made to appear so. Perhaps the one thing for which I should yet have the best cause to congratulate myself, would be the opportunity I had gained of giving to their connection with this affair its true and proper coloring.

I was still dwelling on this thought when there came a knock at my door which advised me that the visitor I expected had arrived. To open and admit him was the work of a moment, but it took more than a moment for me to overcome my surprise at seeing in my visitor no lesser person than Mr. Gryce himself, who in our parting interview had assured me he was too old and too feeble for further detective work and must therefore delegate it to me.

"Ah!" I ejaculated slowly. "It is you, is it? Well, I am not surprised." (I shouldn't have been.) "When you say you are old, you mean old enough to pull the wool over other people's eyes, and when you say you are lame, you mean that you only halt long enough to let others get far enough ahead for them not to see how fast you hobble up behind them. But do not think I am not happy to see you. I am, Mr. Gryce, for I have discovered the secret of Lost Man's Lane, and find it somewhat too heavy a one for my own handling."

To my surprise he showed this was more than he expected.

"You have?" he asked, with just that shade of incredulity which it is so tantalizing to encounter. "Then I suppose congratulations are in order. But are you sure, Miss Butterworth, that you really have obtained a clue to the many strange and fearful disappearances which have given to this lane its name?"

"Quite sure," I returned, nettled. "Why do you doubt it? Because I have kept so quiet and not sounded one note of alarm from my whistle?"

"No," said he. "Knowing your self-restraint so well, I cannot say that that is my reason."

"What is it, then?" I urged.

"Well," said he, "my real reason for doubting if you have been quite as successful as you think, is that we ourselves have come upon a clue about which there can be no question. Can you say the same of yours?"

You will expect my answer to have been a decided "Yes," uttered with all the positiveness of which you know me capable. But for some reason, perhaps because of the strange influence this man's personality exercises upon all—yes, all—who do not absolutely steel themselves against him, I faltered just long enough for him to cry:

"I thought not. The clue is outside the Knollys house, not in it, Miss Butterworth, for which, of course, you are not to be blamed or your services scorned. I have no doubt they have been invaluable in unearthing *a* secret, if not *the* secret."

"Thank you," was my quiet retort. I thought his presumption beyond all bounds, and would at that moment have felt justified in snapping my fingers at the clue he boasted of, had it not been for one thing. What that thing is I am not ready yet to state.

"You and I have come to issue over such matters before," said he, "and therefore need not take too much account of the feelings it is likely to engender. I will merely state that my clue points to Mother Jane, and ask if you have found in the visit she paid at the house last night anything which would go to strengthen the suspicion against her."

"Perhaps," said I, in a state of disdain that was more or less unpardonable, considering that my own suspicions previous to my discovery of the real tragedy enacted under my eyes at the Knollys mansion had played more or less about this old crone.

"Only perhaps?" He smiled, with a playful forbearance for which I should have been truly grateful to him.

"She was there for no good purpose," said I, "and yet if you had not characterized her as the person most responsible for the crimes we are here to investigate, I should have said from all that I then saw of her conduct that she acted as a supernumerary rather than principal, and that it is to me you should look for the correct clue to the criminal, notwithstanding your confidence in your own theories and my momentary hesitation to assert that there was no possible defect in mine."

"Miss Butterworth,"—I thought he looked a trifle shaken—"what did Mother Jane do in that closely shuttered house last night?"

Mother Jane? Well! Did he think I was going to introduce my tragic story by telling what Mother Jane did? I must have looked irritated, and indeed I think I had cause.

"Mother Jane ate her supper," I snapped out angrily. "Miss Knollys gave it to her. Then she helped a little with a piece of work they had on hand. It will not interest you to know what. It has nothing to do with your clue, I warrant."

He did not get angry. He has an admirable temper, has Mr. Gryce, but he did stop a minute to consider.

"Miss Butterworth," he said at last, "most detectives would have held their peace and let you go on with what you have to tell without a hint that it was either unwelcome or unnecessary, but I have consideration for persons' feelings and for persons' secrets so long as they do not come in collision with the law, and my opinion is, or was when I entered this room, that such discoveries as you have made at your old friend's house" (Why need he emphasize friend—did he think I forgot for a moment that Althea was my friend?) "were connected rather with some family difficulty than with the dreadful affair we are considering. That is why I hastened to tell you that we had found a clue to the disappearances in Mother Jane's cottage. I wished to save the Misses Knollys."

If he had thought to mollify me by this assertion, he did not succeed. He saw it and made haste to say:

"Not that I doubt your consideration for them, only the justness of your conclusions."

"You have doubted those before and with more reason," I replied, "yet they were not altogether false."

"That I am willing to acknowledge, so willing that if you still think after I have told my story that yours is *apropos*, then I will listen to it only too eagerly. My object is to find the real criminal in this matter. I say at the present moment it is Mother Jane."

"God grant you are right," I said, influenced in spite of myself by the calm assurance of his manner. "If she was at the house night before last between eleven and twelve, then perhaps she is all you think her. But I see no reason to believe it—not yet, Mr. Gryce. Supposing you give me one. It would be better than all this controversy. One small reason, Mr. Gryce, as good as"—I did not say what, but the fillip it gave to his intention stood me in good stead, for he launched immediately into the matter with no further play upon my curiosity, which was now, as you can believe, thoroughly aroused, though I could not believe that anything he had to bring up against Mother Jane could for a moment stand against the death and the burial I had witnessed in Miss Knollys' house during the two previous nights.

CHAPTER XXIV

The Enigma of Numbers

"When in our first conversation on this topic I told you that Mother Jane was not to be considered in this matter, I meant she was not to be considered by you. She was a subject to be handled by the police, and we have handled her. Yesterday afternoon I made a search of her cabin." Here Mr. Gryce paused and eyed me quizzically. He sometimes does eye me, which same I cannot regard as a compliment, considering how fond he is of concentrating all his wisdom upon small and insignificant objects.

"I wonder," said he, "what you would have done in such a search as that. It was no common one, I assure you. There are not many hiding-places between Mother Jane's four walls."

I felt myself begin to tremble, with eagerness, of course.

"I wish I had been given the opportunity," said I—"that is, if any-thing was to be found there."

He seemed to be in a sympathetic mood toward me, or perhaps—and this is the likelier supposition—he had a minute of leisure and thought he could afford to give himself a little quiet amusement. However that was, he answered me by saying:

"The opportunity is not lost. You have been in her cabin and have noted, I have no doubt, its extreme simplicity. Yet it contains, or rather did contain up till last night, distinct evidences of more than one of the crimes which have been perpetrated in this lane."

"Good! And you want me to guess where you found them? Well, it's not fair."

"Ah, and why not?"

"Because you probably did not find them on your first attempt. You had time to look about. I am asked to guess at once and without second trial what I warrant it took you several trials to determine."

He could not help but laugh. "And why do you think it took me several trials?"

"Because there is more than one thing in that room made up of parts."

"Parts?" He attempted to look puzzled, but I would not have it.

"You know what I mean," I declared; "seventy parts, twenty-eight, or whatever the numbers are she so constantly mutters."

His admiration was unqualified and sincere.

"Miss Butterworth," said he, "you are a woman after my own heart. How came you to think that her mutterings had anything to do with a hiding-place?'"

"Because it did not have anything to do with the amount of money I gave her. When I handed her twenty-five cents, she cried, 'Seventy, twenty-eight, and now ten!' Ten what? Not ten cents or ten dollars, but ten—"

"Why do you stop?"

"I do not want to risk my reputation on a guess. There is a quilt on the bed made up of innumerable pieces. There is a floor of neatly laid brick—"

"And there is a Bible on the stand whose leaves number many over seventy."

"Ah, it was in the Bible you found—"

His smile put mine quite to shame.

"I must acknowledge," he cried, "that I looked in the Bible, but I found nothing there beyond what we all seek when we open its sacred covers. Shall I tell my story?"

He was evidently bursting with pride. You would think that after a half-century of just such successes, a man would take his honors more quietly. But pshaw! Human nature is just the same in the old as in the young. He was no more tired of compliment or of awakening the astonishment of those he confided in, than when he aroused the admiration of the force by his triumphant handling of the Leavenworth Case. Of course in presence of such weakness I could do nothing less than give him a sympathetic ear. I may be old myself some day. Besides, his story was likely to prove more or less interesting.

"Tell your story?" I repeated. "Don't you see that I am"—I was going to say "on pins and needles till I hear it," but the expression is too vulgar for a woman of my breeding; so I altered the words, happily before they were spoken, into "that I am in a state of the liveliest curiosity concerning the whole matter? Tell your story, of course."

"Well, Miss Butterworth, if I do, it is because I know you will appreciate it. You, like myself, placed weight upon the numbers she is forever running over, and you, like myself, have conceived the possibility of these numbers having reference to something in the one room she inhabits. At first glance the extreme bareness of the spot seemed to promise nothing to my curiosity. I looked at the floor and detected no signs of any disturbance having taken place in its symmetrically laid bricks for years. Yet I counted up to seventy one way and twenty-eight the other, and marking the brick thus selected, began to pry it out. It came with difficulty and showed me nothing underneath but green mold and innumerable frightened insects. Then I counted the bricks the other way, but nothing came of it. The floor does not appear to have been disturbed for years. Turning my attention away from the floor, I began upon the quilt.

This was a worse job than the other, and it took me an hour to rip apart the block I settled upon as the suspicious one, but my labor was entirely wasted. There was no hidden treasure in the quilt. Then I searched the walls, using the measurements seventy by twenty-eight, but no result followed these endeavors, and—well, what do you think I did then?"

"You will tell me," I said, "if I give you one more minute to do it in."

"Very well," said he. "I see you do not know, madam. Having searched below and around me, I next turned my attention overhead. Do you remember the strings and strings of dried vegetables that decorate the beams above?"

"I do," I replied, not stinting any of the astonishment I really felt.

"Well, I began to count them next, and when I reached the seventieth onion from the open doorway, I crushed it between my fingers and—these fell out, madam—worthless trinkets, as you will immediately see, but—"

"Well, well," I urged.

"They have been identified as belonging to the peddler who was one of the victims in whose fate we are interested."

"Ah, ah!" I ejaculated, somewhat amazed, I own. "And number twenty-eight?"

"That was a carrot, and it held a really valuable ring—a ruby surrounded by diamonds. If you remember, I once spoke to you of this ring. It was the property of young Mr. Chittenden and worn by him while he was in this village. He disappeared on his way to the railway station, having taken, as many can vouch, the short detour by Lost Man's Lane, which would lead him directly by Mother Jane's cottage."

"You thrill me," said I, keeping down with admirable self-possession my own thoughts in regard to this matter. "And what of No. ten, beyond which she said she could not count?"

"In ten was your twenty-five-cent piece, and in various other vegetables, small coins, whose value taken collectively would not amount to a dollar. The only numbers which seemed to make any impression on her mind were those connected with these crimes. Very good evidence, Miss Butterworth, that Mother Jane holds the clue to this matter, even if she is not responsible for the death of the individuals represented by this property."

"Certainly," I acquiesced, "and if you examined her after her return from the Knollys mansion last night you would probably have found upon her some similar evidence of her complicity in the last crime of this terrible series. It would needs have been small, as Silly Rufus neither indulged in the brass trinkets sold by the old peddler nor the real jewelry of a well-to-do man like Mr. Chittenden."

"Silly Rufus?"

"He was the last to disappear from these parts, was he not?"

"Yes, madam."

"And as such, should have left some clue to his fate in the hands of this old crone, if her motive in removing him was, as you seem to think, entirely that of gain."

"I did not say it was entirely so. Silly Rufus would be the last person any one, even such a *non compos mentis* as Mother Jane, would destroy for hope of gain."

"But what other motive could she have? And, Mr. Gryce, where could she bestow the bodies of so many unfortunate victims, even if by her great strength she could succeed in killing them?"

"There you have me," said he. "We have not been able as yet to un-earth any bodies. Have you?"

"No," said I, with some little show of triumph showing through my disdain, "but I can show *you* where to unearth one."

He should have been startled, profoundly startled. Why wasn't he? I asked this of myself over and over in the one instant he weighed his words before answering.

"You have made some definite discoveries, then," he declared. "You have come across a grave or a mound which you have taken for a grave."

I shook my head.

"No mound," said I. Why should I not play for an instant or more with his curiosity? He had with mine.

"Ah, then, why do you talk of unearthing? No one has told you where you can lay hand on Silly Rufus' body, I take it."

"No," said I. "The Knollys house is not inclined to give up its se-crets."

He started, glancing almost remorsefully first at the tip, then at the head of the cane he was balancing in his hand.

"It's too bad," he muttered, "but you've been led astray, Miss But-terworth—excusably, I acknowledge, quite excusably, but yet in a way to give you quite wrong conclusions. The secret of the Knollys house—But wait a moment. Then you were not locked up in your room last night?"

"Scarcely," I returned, wavering between the doubts he had awak-ened by his first sentence and the surprise which his last could not fail to give me.

"I might have known they would not be likely to catch you in a trap," he remarked. "So you were up and in the halls?"

"I was up," I acknowledged, "and in the halls. May I ask where you were?"

He paid no heed to the last sentence. "This complicates matters," said he, "and yet perhaps it is as well. I understand you now, and in a few minutes you will understand me. You thought it was Silly Rufus who was buried last night. That was rather an awful thought, Miss Butterworth. I wonder, with that in your mind, you look as well as you do this morning, madam. Truly you are a wonderful woman—a very wonderful woman."

"A truce to compliments," I begged. "If you know as much as your words imply of what went on in that ill-omened house last night, you ought to show some degree of emotion yourself, for if it was not Silly Rufus who was laid away under the Flower Parlor, who, then, was it? No one for whom tears could openly be shed or of whose death public acknowledgment could be made, or we would not be sitting here talking away at cross purposes the morning after his burial."

"Tears are not shed or public acknowledgment made for the subject of a half-crazy man's love for scientific investigation. It was no human being whom you saw buried, madam, but a victim of Mr. Knollys' passion for vivisection."

"You are playing with me," was my indignant answer; "outrageously and inexcusably playing with me. Only a human being would be laid away in such secrecy and with such manifestations of feeling as I was witness to. You must think me in my dotage, or else—"

"We will take the rest of the sentence for granted," he dryly interpolated. "You know that I can have no wish to insult your intelligence, Miss Butterworth, and that if I advance a theory on my own account I must have ample reasons for it. Now can you say the same for yours? Can you adduce irrefutable proof that the body we buried last night was that of a man? If you can, there is no more to be said, or, rather, there is everything to be said, for this would give to the transaction a very dreadful and tragic significance which at present I am not disposed to ascribe to it."

Taken aback by his persistence, but determined not to acknowledge defeat until forced to it, I stolidly replied: "You have made an assertion, and it is for you to adduce proof. It will be time enough for me to talk when your own theory is proved untenable."

He was not angry: fellow-feeling for my disappointment made him unusually gentle. His voice was therefore very kind when he said:

"Madam, if you know it to have been a man, say so. I do not wish to waste my time."

"I do not know it."

"Very well, then, I will tell you why I think my supposition true. Mr. Knollys, as you probably have already discovered, is a man with a secret passion for vivisection."

"Yes, I have discovered that."

"It is known to his family, and it is known to a very few others, but it is not known to the world at large, not even to his fellow-villagers.'

"I can believe it," said I.

"His sisters, who are gentle girls, regard the matter as the gentle-hearted usually do. They have tried in every way to influence him to abandon it, but unsuccessfully so far, for he is not only entirely unamenable to persuasion, but has a nature of such brutality he could not live without some such excitement to help away his life in this dreary house. All they can do, then, is to conceal these cruelties from the eyes of the people who already execrate him for his many roughnesses and the undoubted shadow under which he lives. Time was when I thought this shadow had a substance worth our investigation, but a further knowledge of his real fault and a completer knowledge of his sisters' virtues turned my inquiries in a new direction, where I have found, as I have told you, actual reason for arresting Mother Jane. Have you anything to say against these conclusions? Cannot you see that all your suspicions can be explained by the brother's cruel impulses and the sisters' horror of having those impulses known?"

I thought a moment; then I cried out boldly: "No, I cannot, Mr. Gryce. The anxiety, the fear, which I have seen depicted on these sisters' faces for days might be explained perhaps by this theory; but the knot of crêpe on the window-shutter, the open Bible in the room of death—William's room, Mr. Gryce—proclaim that it was a human being, and nothing less, for whom Lucetta's sobs went up."

"I do not follow you," he said, moved for the first time from his composure. "What do you mean by a knot of crêpe, and when was it you obtained entrance into William's room?"

"Ah," I exclaimed in dry retort; "you are beginning to see that I have something as interesting to report as yourself. Did you think me a superficial egotist, without facts to back my assertions?"

"I should not have done you that injustice."

"I have penetrated, I think, deeper than even yourself, into William's character. I think him capable—But do satisfy my curiosity on one point first, Mr. Gryce. How came you to know as much as you do about last night's proceedings? You could not have been in the house. Did Mother Jane talk after she got back?"

The tip of his cane was up, and he frowned at it. Then the handle took its place, and he gave it a good-natured smile.

"Miss Butterworth," said he, "I have not succeeded in making Mother Jane at any time go beyond her numerical monologue. But you have been more successful." And with a sudden marvellous change of expression, pose, and manner he threw over his head my shawl, which had fallen to the floor in my astonishment, and, rocking himself to and fro before me, muttered grimly:

"Seventy! Twenty-eight! Ten! No more! I can count no more! Go."

"Mr. Gryce, it was you—"

"Whom you interviewed in Mother Jane's cottage with Mr. Knollys," he finished. "And it was *I* who helped to bury what you now declare, to my real terror and astonishment, to have been a human being. Miss Butterworth, what about the knot of crêpe? Tell me."

CHAPTER XXV

Trifles, But Not Trifling

I was so astounded I hardly took in this final question.

He had been the sixth party in the funeral cortège I had seen pause in the Flower Parlor. Well, what might I not expect from this man next!

But I am methodical even under the greatest excitement and at the most critical instants, as those who have read *That Affair Next Door* have had ample opportunity to know. Once having taken in the startling fact he mentioned, I found it impossible to proceed to establish my standpoint till I knew a little more about his.

"Wait," I said; "tell me first if I have ever seen the real Mother Jane; or were you the person I saw stooping in the road, and of whom I bought the pennyroyal?"

"No," he replied; "that was the old woman herself. My appearance in the cottage dates from yesterday noon. I felt the need of being secretly near you, and I also wished for an opportunity to examine this humble interior unsuspected and unobserved. So I prevailed upon the old woman to exchange places with me; she taking up her abode in the woods for the night and I her old stool on the hearthstone. She was the more willing to do this from the promise I gave her to watch out for Lizzie. That I would don her own Sunday suit and personate her in her own home she evidently did not suspect. Had not wit enough, I suppose. At the present moment she is back in her old place."

I nodded my thanks for this explanation, but was not deterred from pressing the point I was anxious to have elucidated.

"If," I went on to urge, "you took advantage of your disguise to act as assistant in the burial which took place last night, you are in a much better situation than myself to decide the question we are at present considering. Was it because of any secret knowledge thus gained you declare so positively that it was not a human being you helped lower in its grave?"

"Partially. Having some skill in these disguises, especially where my own infirmities can have full play, as in the case of this strong but half-bent woman, I had no reason to think my own identity was suspected, much less discovered. Therefore I could trust to what I saw and heard as being just what Mother Jane herself would be allowed to see or hear under the same circumstances. If, therefore, these young people and this old crone had been, as you seem to think they are, in league for murder,

Lucetta would hardly have greeted me as she did when she came down to meet me in the kitchen."

"And how was that? What did she say?"

"She said: 'Ah, Mother Jane, we have a piece of work for you. You are strong, are you not?'"

"Humph!"

"And then she commiserated me a bit and gave me food which, upon my word, I found hard to eat, though I had saved my appetite for the occasion. Before she left me she bade me sit in the inglenook till she wanted me, adding in Hannah's ear as she passed her: 'There is no use trying to explain anything to her. Show her when the time comes what there is to do and trust to her short memory to forget it before she leaves the house. She could not understand my brother's propensity or our shame in pandering to it. So attempt nothing, Hannah. Only keep the money in her view.'"

"So, and that gave you no idea?"

"It gave me the idea I have imparted to you, or, rather, added to the idea which had been instilled in me by others."

"And this idea was not affected by what you saw afterwards?"

"Not in the least—rather strengthened. Of the few words I overheard, one was uttered in reference to yourself by Miss Knollys. She said: 'I have locked Miss Butterworth again into her room. If she accuses me of having done so, I shall tell her our whole story. Better she should know the family's disgrace than imagine us guilty of crimes of which we are utterly incapable.'"

"So! so!" I cried, "you heard that?"

"Yes, madam, I heard that, and I do not think she knew she was dropping that word into the ear of a detective, but on this point you are, of course, at liberty to differ with me."

"I am not yet ready to avail myself of the privilege," I retorted. "What else did these girls let fall in your hearing?"

"Not much. It was Hannah who led me into the upper hall, and Hannah who by signs and signals rather than words showed me what was expected of me. However, when, after the box was lowered into the cellar, Hannah was drawing me away, Lucetta stepped up and whispered in her ear: 'Don't give her the biggest coin. Give her the little one, or she may mistake our reasons for secrecy. I wouldn't like even a fool to do that even for the moment it would remain lodged in Mother Jane's mind.'"

"Well, well," I again cried, certainly puzzled, for these stray expressions of the sisters were in a measure contradictory not only of the suspicions I entertained, but of the facts which had seemingly come to my attention.

Mr. Gryce, who was probably watching my face more closely than he did the cane with whose movements he was apparently engrossed, stopped to give a caressing rub to the knob of that same cane before remarking:

"One such peep behind the scenes is worth any amount of surmise expended on the wrong side of the curtain. I let you share my knowledge because it is your due. Now if you feel willing to explain what you mean by a knot of crêpe on the shutter, I am at your service, madam."

I felt that it would be cruel to delay my story longer, and so I began it. It was evidently more interesting than he expected, and as I dilated upon the special features which had led me to believe that it was a thinking, suffering mortal like ourselves who had been shut up in William's room and afterwards buried in the cellar under the Flower Parlor, I saw his face lengthen and doubt take the place of the quiet assurance with which he had received my various intimations up to this time. The cane was laid aside, and from the action of his right forefinger on the palm of his left hand I judged that I was making no small impression on his mind. When I had finished, he sat for a minute silent; then he said:

"Thanks, Miss Butterworth; you have more than fulfilled my hopes. What we buried was undoubtedly human, and the question now is, Who was it, and of what death did he die?" Then, after a meaning pause: "*You* think it was Silly Rufus."

I will astonish you with my reply. "No," said I, "I do not. That is where you make a mistake, Mr. Gryce."

CHAPTER XXVI

A Point Gained

He was surprised, for all his attempts to conceal it.

"No?" said he. "Who, then? You are becoming interesting, Miss Butterworth."

This I thought I could afford to ignore.

"Yesterday," I proceeded, "I would have declared it to be Silly Rufus, in the face of God and man, but after what I saw in William's room during the hurried survey I gave it, I am inclined to doubt if the explanation we have to give to this affair is so simple as that would make it. Mr. Gryce, in one corner of that room, from which the victim had so lately been carried, was a pair of shoes that could never have been worn by any boy-tramp I have ever seen or known of."

"They were Loreen's, or possibly Lucetta's."

"No, Loreen and Lucetta both have trim feet, but these were the shoes of a child of ten, very dainty at that, and of a cut and make worn by women, or rather, I should say, by girls. Now, what do you make of that?"

He did not seem to know what to make of it. Tap, tap went his finger on his seasoned palm, and as I watched the slowness with which it fell, I said to myself, "I have proposed a problem this time that will tax even Mr. Gryce's powers of deduction."

And I had. It was minutes before he ventured an opinion, and then it was with a shade of doubt in his tone that I acknowledge to have felt some pride in producing.

"They were Lucetta's shoes. The emotions under which you labored—very pardonable emotions, madam, considering the circumstances and the hour—"

"Excuse me," said I. "We do not want to waste a moment. I was excited, suitably and duly excited, or I would have been a stone. But I never lose my head under excitement, nor do I part with my sense of proportion. The shoes were not Lucetta's. She never wore any approaching them in smallness since her tenth year."

"Has Simsbury a daughter? Has there not been a child about the house some time to assist the cook in errands and so on?"

"No, or I should have seen her. Besides, how would the shoes of such a person come into William's room?"

"Easily. Secrecy was required. You were not to be disturbed; so shoes were taken off that quiet might result."

"Was Lucetta shoeless or William or even Mother Jane? You have not told me that you were requested to walk in stocking feet up the hall. No, Mr. Gryce, the shoes were the shoes of a girl. I know it because it was matched by a dress I saw hanging up in a sort of wardrobe."

"Ah! You looked into the wardrobe?"

"I did and felt justified in doing so. It was after I had spied the shoes."

"Very good. And you saw a dress?"

"A little dress; a dress with a short skirt. It was of silk too; another anomaly—and the color, I think, was blue, but I cannot swear to that point. I was in great haste and took the briefest glance. But my brief glances can be trusted, Mr. Gryce. That, I think, you are beginning to know."

"Certainly," said he, "and as proof of it we will now act upon these two premises—that the victim in whose burial I was an innocent partaker was a human being and that this human being was a girl-child who came into the house well dressed. Now where does that lead us? Into a maze, I fear."

"We are accustomed to mazes," I observed.

"Yes," he answered somewhat gloomily, "but they are not exactly desirable in this case. I want to find the Knollys family innocent."

"And I. But William's character, I fear, will make that impossible."

"But this girl? Who is she, and where did she come from? No girl has been reported to us as missing from this neighborhood."

"I supposed not."

"A visitor—But no visitor could enter this house without it being known far and wide. Why, I heard of your arrival here before I left the train on which I followed you. Had we allowed ourselves to be influenced by what the people about here say, we would have turned the Knollys house inside out a week ago. But I don't believe in putting too much confidence in the prejudice of country people. The idea they suggested, and which you suggest without putting it too clearly into words, is much too horrible to be acted upon without the best of reasons. Perhaps we have found those reasons, yet I still feel like asking, Where did this girl come from and how could she have become a prisoner in the Knollys house without the knowledge of—Madam, have you met Mr. Trohm?"

The question was so sudden I had not time to collect myself. But perhaps it was not necessary that I should, for the simple affirmation I used seemed to satisfy Mr. Gryce, who went on to say:

"It is he who first summoned us here, and it is he who has the greatest interest in locating the source of these disappearances, yet he has seen no child come here."

"Mr. Trohm is not a spy," said I, but the remark, happily, fell unheeded.

"No one has," he pursued. "We must give another turn to our suppositions."

Suddenly a silence fell upon us both. His finger ceased to lay down the law, and my gaze, which had been searching his face inquiringly, became fixed. At the same moment and in much the same tone of voice we both spoke, he saying, "Humph!" and I, "Ah!" as a prelude to the simultaneous exclamation:

"The phantom coach!"

We were so pleased with this discovery that we allowed a moment to pass in silent contemplation of each other's satisfaction. Then he quietly added:

"Which on the evening preceding your arrival came from the mountains and passed into Lost Man's Lane, from which no one ever saw it emerge."

"It was no phantom," I put in.

"It was their own old coach bringing to the house a fresh victim."

This sounded so startling we both sat still for a moment, lost in the horror of it, then I spoke:

"People living in remote and isolated quarters like this are naturally superstitious. The Knollys family know this, and, remembering the old legend, forbore to contradict the conclusions of their neighbors. Loreen's emotion when the topic was broached to her is explained by this theory."

"It is not a pleasant one, but we cannot be wrong in contemplating it."

"Not at all. This apparition, as they call it, was seen by two persons; therefore it was no apparition but a real coach. It came from the mountains, that is, from the Mountain Station, and it glided—ah!"

"Well?"

"Mr. Gryce, it was its noiselessness that gave it its spectral appearance. Now I remember a petty circumstance which I dare you to match, in corroboration of our suspicions."

"You do?"

I could not repress a slight toss of my head. "Yes, I do," I repeated.

He smiled and made the slightest of deprecatory gestures.

"You have had advantages—" he began.

"And disadvantages," I finished, determined that he should award me my full meed of praise. "You are probably not afraid of dogs. I am. You could visit the stables."

"And did; but I found nothing there."

"I thought not!" I could not help the exclamation. It is so seldom one can really triumph over this man. "Not having the cue, you would not be apt to see what gives this whole thing away. I would never have thought of it again if we had not had this talk. Is Mr. Simsbury a neat man?"

"A neat man? Madam, what do you mean?"

"Something important, Mr. Gryce. If Mr. Simsbury is a neat man, he will have thrown away the old rags which, I dare promise you, cumbered his stable floor the morning after the phantom coach was seen to enter the lane. If he is not, you may still find them there. One of them, I know, you will not find. He pulled it off of his wheel with his whip the afternoon he drove me down from the station. I can see the sly look he gave me as he did it. It made no impression on me then, but now—"

"Madam, you have supplied the one link necessary to the establishment of this theory. Allow me to felicitate you upon it. But whatever our satisfaction may be from a professional standpoint, we cannot but feel the unhappy nature of the responsibility incurred by these discoveries. If this seemingly respectable family stooped to such subterfuge, going to the length of winding rags around the wheels of their lumbering old coach to make it noiseless, and even tying up their horse's feet for this same purpose, they must have had a motive dark enough to warrant your worst suspicions. And William was not the only one involved. Simsbury, at least, had a hand in it, nor does it look as if the girls were as innocent as we would like to consider them."

"I cannot stop to consider the girls," I declared. "I can no longer consider the girls."

"Nor I," he gloomily assented. "Our duty requires us to sift this matter, and it shall be sifted. We must first find if any child alighted from the cars at the Mountain Station on that especial night, or, what is more probable, from the little station at C., five miles farther back in the mountains."

"And—" I urged, seeing that he had still something to say.

"We must make sure who lies buried under the floor of the room you call the Flower Parlor. You may expect me at the Knollys house some time today. I shall come quietly, but in my own proper person. You are not to know me, and, unless you desire it, need not appear in the matter."

"I do not desire it."

"Then good-morning, Miss Butterworth. My respect for your abilities has risen even higher than before. We part in a similar frame of mind for once."

And this he expected me to regard as a compliment.

CHAPTER XXVII

The Text Witnesseth

I have a grim will when I choose to exert it. After Mr. Gryce left the hotel, I took a cup of tea with the landlady and then made a round of the stores. I bought dimity, sewing silk, and what not, as I said I would, but this did not occupy long (to the regret probably of the country merchants, who expected to make a fool of me and found it a by no means easy task), and was quite ready for William when he finally drove up.

The ride home was a more or less silent one. I had conceived such a horror of the man beside me, that talking for talk's sake was impossible, while he was in a mood which it would be charity to call non-communicative. It may be that my own reticence was at the bottom of this, but I rather think not. The remark he made in passing Deacon Spear's house showed that something more than spite was working in his slow but vindictive brain.

"There's a man of your own sort," he cried. "You won't find him doing anything out of the way; oh, no. Pity your visit wasn't paid there. You'd have got a better impression of the lane."

To this I made no reply.

At Mr. Trohm's he spoke again:

"I suppose that you and Trohm had the devil of a say about Lucetta and the rest of us. I don't know why, but the whole neighborhood seems to feel they've a right to use our name as they choose. But it isn't going to be so, long. We have played poor and pinched and starved all I'm going to. I'm going to have a new horse, and Lucetta shall have a dress, and that mighty quick too. I'm tired of all this shabbiness, and mean to have a change."

I wanted to say, "No change yet; change under the present circumstances would be the worst thing possible for you all," but I felt that this would be treason to Mr. Gryce, and refrained, saying simply, as he looked sideways at me for a word:

"Lucetta needs a new dress. That no one can deny. But you had better let me get it for her, or perhaps that is what you mean."

The grunt which was my only answer might be interpreted in any way. I took it, however, for assent.

As soon as I was relieved of his presence and found myself again with the girls, I altered my whole manner and cried out in querulous tones:

"Mrs. Carter and I have had a difference." (This was true. We did have a difference over our cup of tea. I did not think it necessary to say this difference was a forced one. Some things we are perfectly justified in keeping to ourselves.) "She remembers a certain verse in the New Testament one way and I in another. We had not time to settle it by a consultation with the sacred word, but I cannot rest till it is settled, so will you bring your Bible to me, my dear, that I may look that verse up?"

We were in the upper hall, where I had taken a seat on the old-fashioned sofa there. Lucetta, who was standing before me, started immediately to do my bidding, without stopping to think, poor child, that it was very strange I did not go to my own room and consult my own Bible as any good Presbyterian would be expected to do. As she was turning toward the large front room I stopped her with the quiet injunction:

"Get me one with good print, Lucetta. My eyes won't bear much straining."

At which she turned and to my great relief hurried down the corridor toward William's room, from which she presently returned, bringing the very volume I was anxious to consult.

Meanwhile I had laid aside my hat. I felt flurried and unhappy, and showed it. Lucetta's pitiful face had a strange sweetness in it this morning, and I felt sure as I took the sacred book from her hand that her thoughts were all with the lover she had sent from her side and not at all with me or with what at the moment occupied me. Yet my thoughts at this moment involved, without doubt, the very deepest interests of her life, if not that very lover she was brooding over in her darkened and resigned mind. As I realized this I heaved an involuntary sigh, which seemed to startle her, for she turned and gave me a quick look as she was slipping away to join her sister, who was busy at the other end of the hall.

The Bible I held was an old one, of medium size and most excellent print. I had no difficulty in finding the text and settling the question which had been my ostensible reason for wanting the book, but it took me longer to discover the indentation which I had made in one of its pages; but when I did, you may imagine my awe and the turmoil into which my mind was cast, when I found that it marked those great verses in Corinthians which are so universally read at funerals:

"Behold I shew you a mystery. We shall not all sleep, but we shall all be changed."

"In a moment, in the twinkling of an eye—"

CHAPTER XXVIII

An Intrusion

I was so moved by this discovery that I was not myself for several moments.

The reading of these words over the body which had been laid away under the Flower Parlor was in keeping with the knot of crêpe on the window-shutter and argued something more than remorse on the part of someone of the Knollys family. Who was this one, and why, with such feelings in the breast of any of the three, had the deceit and crime to which I had been witness succeeded to such a point as to demand the attention of the police? An impossible problem of which I dared seek no solution, even in the faces of these seemingly innocent girls.

I was, of course, in no position to determine what plan Mr. Gryce intended to pursue. I only knew what course I myself meant to follow, which was to remain quiet and sustain the part I had already played in this house as visitor and friend. It was therefore as such both in heart and manner that I hastened from my room late in the afternoon to inquire the meaning of the cry I had just heard issue from Lucetta's lips. It had come from the front of the house, and, as I hastened thither, I met the two Misses Knollys, looking more openly anxious and distraught than at any former time of anxiety and trouble.

As they looked up and saw my face, Loreen paused and laid her hand on Lucetta's arm. But Lucetta was not to be restrained.

"He has dared to enter our gates, bringing a police officer with him," was her hoarse and almost unintelligible cry. "We know that the man with him is a police officer because he was here once before, and though he was kind enough then, he cannot have come the second time except to—"

Here the pressure of Loreen's hand was so strong as to make the feeble Lucetta quiver. She stopped, and Miss Knollys took up her words:

"Except to make us talk on subjects much better buried in oblivion. Miss Butterworth, will you go down with us? Your presence may act as a restraint. Mr. Trohm seems to have some respect for you."

"Mr. Trohm?"

"Yes. It is his coming which has so agitated Lucetta. He and a man named Gryce are just coming up the walk. There goes the knocker. Lucetta, you must control yourself or leave me to face these unwelcome visitors alone."

Lucetta, with a sudden fierce effort, subdued her trembling.

"If he must be met," said she, "my anger and disdain may give some weight to your quiet acceptance of the family's disgrace. I shall not accept his denunciations quietly, Loreen. You must expect me to show some of the feelings that I have held in check all these years." And without waiting for reply, without waiting even to see what effect these strange words might have upon me, she dashed down the stairs and pulled open the front door.

We had followed rapidly, too rapidly for speech ourselves, and were therefore in the hall when the door swung back, revealing the two persons I had been led to expect. Mr. Trohm spoke first, evidently in answer to the defiance to be seen in Lucetta's face.

"Miss Knollys, a thousand pardons. I know I am transgressing, but, I assure you, the occasion warrants it. I am certain you will acknowledge this when you hear what my errand is."

"Your errand? What can your errand be but to—"

Why did she pause? Mr. Gryce had not looked at her. Yet that it was under his influence she ceased to commit herself I am as convinced as we can be of anything in a world which is half deceit.

"Let us hear your errand," put in Loreen, with that gentle emphasis which is no sign of weakness.

"I will let this gentleman speak for me," returned Mr. Trohm. "You have seen him before—a New York detective of whose business in this town you cannot be ignorant."

Lucetta turned a cold eye upon Mr. Gryce and quietly remarked:

"When he visited this lane a few days ago, he professed to be seeking a clue to the many disappearances which have unfortunately taken place within its precincts."

Mr. Trohm's nod was one of acquiescence. But Lucetta was still looking at the detective.

"Is that your business now?" she asked, appealing directly to Mr. Gryce.

His fatherly accents when he answered her were a great relief after the alternate iciness and fire with which she had addressed his companion and himself.

"I hardly know how to reply without arousing your just anger. If your brother is in—"

"My brother would face you with less patience than we. Tell us your errand, Mr. Gryce, and do not think of calling in my brother till we have failed to answer your questions or satisfy your demands."

"Very well," said he. "The quickest explanation is the kindest in these cases. I merely wish, as a police officer whose business it is to locate the disappearances which have made this lane notorious, and who believes the surest way to do this is to find out once and for all where they did not and could not have taken place, to make an official search of these premises as I already have those of Mother Jane and of Deacon Spear."

"And my errand here," interposed Mr. Trohm, "is to make everything easier by the assurance that my house will be the next to undergo a complete investigation. As all the houses in the lane will be visited alike, none of us need complain or feel our good name attacked."

This was certainly thoughtful of him, but knowing how much they had to fear, I could not expect Loreen or Lucetta to show any great sense either of his kindness or Mr. Gryce's consideration. They were in no position to have a search made of their premises, and, serene as was Loreen's nature and powerful as was Lucetta's will, the apprehension under which they labored was evident to us all, though neither of them attempted either subterfuge or evasion.

"If the police wish to search this house, it is open to them," said Loreen.

"But not to Mr. Trohm," quoth Lucetta, quickly. "Our poverty should be our protection from the curiosity of neighbors."

"Mr. Trohm has no wish to intrude," was Mr. Gryce's conciliatory remark; but Mr. Trohm said nothing. He probably understood why Lucetta wished to curtail his stay in this house better than Mr. Gryce did.

CHAPTER XXIX

In the Cellar

I had meanwhile stood silent. There was no reason for me to obtrude myself, and I was happy not to do so. This does not mean, however, that my presence was not noticed. Mr. Trohm honored me with more than one glance during these trying moments, in which I read the anxiety he felt lest my peace of mind should be too much disturbed, and when, in response to the undoubted dismissal he had received from Lucetta, he prepared to take his leave, it was upon me he bestowed his final look and most deferential bow. It was a tribute to my position and character which all seemed to feel, and I was not at all surprised when Lucetta, after carefully watching his departure, turned to me with childlike impetuosity, saying:

"This must be very unpleasant for you, Miss Butterworth, yet must we ask you to stand our friend. God knows we need one."

"I shall never forget I occupied that position toward your mother," was my straightforward reply, and I did not forget it, not for a moment.

"I shall begin with the cellar," Mr. Gryce announced.

Both girls quivered. Then Loreen lifted her proud head and said quietly:

"The whole house is at your disposal. Only I pray you to be as expeditious as possible. My sister is not well, and the sooner our humiliation is over, the better it will be for her."

And, indeed, Lucetta was in a state that aroused even Mr. Gryce's anxiety. But when she saw us all hovering over her she roused herself with an extraordinary effort, and, waving us aside, led the way to the kitchen, from which, as I gathered, the only direct access could be had to the cellar. Mr. Gryce immediately followed, and behind him came Loreen and myself, both too much agitated to speak. At the Flower Parlor Mr. Gryce paused as if he had forgotten something, but Lucetta urged him feverishly on, and before long we were all standing in the kitchen. Here a surprise awaited us. Two men were sitting there who appeared to be strangers to Hannah, from the lowering looks she cast them as she pretended to be busy over her stove. This was so out of keeping with her usual good humor as to attract the attention even of her young mistress.

"What is the matter, Hannah?" asked Lucetta. "And who are these men?"

"They are my men," said Mr. Gryce. "The job I have undertaken cannot be carried on alone."

The quick look the two sisters interchanged did not escape me, or the quiet air of resignation which was settling slowly over Loreen.

"Must they go into the cellar too?" she asked.

Mr. Gryce smiled his most fatherly smile as he said:

"My dear young ladies, these men are interested in but one thing; they are searching for a clue to the disappearances that have occurred in this lane. As they will not find this in your cellar, nothing else that they may see there will remain in their minds for a moment."

Lucetta said no more. Even her indomitable spirit was giving way before the inevitable discovery that threatened them.

"Do not let William know," were the low words with which she passed Hannah; but from the short glimpse I caught of William's burly figure standing in the stable door, under the guardianship of two detectives, I felt this injunction to be quite superfluous. William evidently did know.

I was not going to descend the cellar stairs, but the girls made me.

"We want you with us," Loreen declared in no ordinary tones, while

Lucetta paused and would not go on till I followed. This surprised me. I no longer seemed to have any clue to their motives; but I was glad to be one of the party.

Hannah, under Loreen's orders, had furnished one of the men with a lighted lantern, and upon our descent into the dark labyrinth below, it became his duty to lead the way, which he did with due circumspection. What all this underground space into which we were thus introduced had ever been used for, it would be difficult to tell. At present it was mostly empty. After passing a small collection of stores, a wine-cellar, the very door of which was unhinged and lay across the cellar bottom, we struck into a hollow void, in which there was nothing worth an instant's investigation save the earth under our feet.

This the two foremost detectives examined very carefully, detaining us often longer, I thought, than Mr. Gryce desired or Lucetta had patience for. But nothing was said in protest nor did the older detective give an order or manifest any special interest in the investigation till he saw the men in front stoop and throw out of the way a coil of rope, when he immediately hurried forward and called upon the party to stop.

The girls, who were on either side of me, crossed glances at this command, and Lucetta, who had been tottering for the last few minutes, fell upon her knees and hid her face in the hollow of her two hands. Loreen came around and stood by her, and I do not know which of them presented the most striking picture of despair, the shrinking Lucetta or Loreen with her quivering form uplifted to meet the shafts of fate without a droop of her eyelids or a murmur from her lips. The light of the one lantern which, intentionally or unintentionally, was concentrated on this pathetic group, made it stand out from the midst of the surrounding darkness in a way to draw the gaze of Mr. Gryce upon them. He looked, and his own brow became overcast. Evidently we were not far from the cause of their fears.

Ordering the candle lifted, he surveyed the ceiling above, at which Loreen's lips opened slightly in secret dread and amazement. Then he commanded the men to move on slowly, while he himself looked overhead rather than underneath, which seemed to astonish his associates, who evidently had heard nothing of the hole which had been cut in the floor of the Flower Parlor.

Suddenly I heard a slight gasp from Lucetta, who had not moved forward with the rest of us. Then her rushing figure flew by us and took up its stand by Mr. Gryce, who had himself paused and was pointing with an imperious forefinger to the ground under his feet.

"You will dig here," said he, not heeding her, though I am sure he was as well acquainted with her proximity as we.

"Dig?" repeated Loreen, in what we all saw was a final effort to stave off disgrace and misery.

"My duty demands it," said he. "Some one else has been digging here within a very few days, Miss Knollys. That is as evident as is the fact that a communication has been made with this place through an opening into the room above. See!" And taking the lantern from the man at his side, he held it up toward the ceiling.

There was no hole there now, but there were ample evidences of there having been one, and that within a very short time. Loreen made no further attempt to stay him.

"The house is at your disposal," she reiterated, but I do not think she knew what she said. The man with the bundle in his arms was already unrolling it on the cellar bottom. A spade came to light, together with some other tools. Lifting the spade, he thrust it smartly into the ground toward which Mr. Gryce's inexorable finger still pointed. At the sight and the sound it made, a thrill passed through Lucetta which made her another creature. Dashing forward, she flung herself down upon the spot with lifted head and outstretched arms.

"Stop your desecrating hand!" she cried. "This is a grave—the grave, sirs, of our mother!"

CHAPTER XXX

Investigation

The shock of these words—if false, most horrible; if true, still more horrible—threw us all aback and made even Mr. Gryce's features assume an aspect quite uncommon to them.

"Your mother's grave?" said he, looking from her to Loreen with very evident doubt. "I thought your mother died seven or more years ago, and this grave has been dug within three days."

"I know," she whispered. "To the world my mother has been dead many, many years, but not to us. We closed her eyes night before last, and it was to preserve this secret, which involves others affecting our family honor, that we resorted to expedients which have perhaps attracted the notice of the police and drawn this humiliation down upon us. I can conceive no other reason for this visit, ushered in as it was by Mr. Trohm."

"Miss Lucetta"—Mr. Gryce spoke quickly; if he had not I certainly could not have restrained some expression of the emotions awakened in my own breast by this astounding revelation—"Miss Lucetta, it is not necessary to bring Mr. Trohm's name into this matter or that of any other person than myself. I saw the coffin lowered here, which you say contained the body of your mother. Thinking this a strange place of burial and not knowing it was your mother to whom you were paying these last dutiful rites, I took advantage of my position as detective to satisfy myself that nothing wrong lay behind so mysterious a death and burial. Can you blame me, Miss? Would I have been a man to trust if I had let such an event as this go by unchallenged?"

She did not answer. She had heard but one sentence of all this long speech.

"You saw my mother's coffin lowered? Where were you that you should see that? In some of these dark passages, let in by I know not what traitor to our peace of mind." And her eyes, which seemed to have grown almost supernaturally large and bright under her emotions, turned slowly in their sockets till they rested with something like doubtful accusation upon mine. But not to remain there, for Mr. Gryce recalled them almost instantly by this short, sharp negative.

"No, I was nearer than that. I lent my strength to this burial. If you had thought to look under Mother Jane's hood, you would have seen what would have forced these explanations then and there."

"And you—"

"I was Mother Jane for the nonce. Not from choice, Miss, but from necessity. I was impersonating the old woman when your brother came to the cottage. I could not give away my plans by refusing the task your brother offered me."

"It is well." Lucetta had risen and was now standing by the side of Loreen. "Such a secret as ours defies concealment. Even Providence takes part against us. What you want to know we must tell, but I assure you it has nothing to do with the business you profess to be chiefly interested in—nothing at all."

"Then perhaps you and your sister will retire," said he. "Distracted as you are by family griefs, I would not wish to add one iota to your distress. This lady, whom you seem to regard with more or less favor as friend or relative, will stay to see that no dishonor is paid to your mother's remains. But your mother's face we must see, Miss Lucetta, if only to lighten the explanations you will doubtless feel called upon to make."

It was Loreen who answered this.

"If it must be," said she, "remember your own mother and deal reverently with ours." Which entreaty and the way it was uttered, gave me my first distinct conviction that these girls were speaking the truth, and that the diminutive body we had come to unearth was that of Althea Knollys, whose fairy-like form I had so long supposed commingled with foreign soil.

The thought was almost too much for my self-possession, and I advanced upon Loreen with a dozen burning questions on my lips when the voice of Mr. Gryce stopped me.

"Explanations later," said he. "For the present we want you here."

It was no easy task for me to linger there with all my doubts unsolved, waiting for the decisive moment when Mr. Gryce should say: "Come! Look! Is it she?" But the will that had already sustained me through so many trying experiences did not fail me now, and, grievous as was the ordeal, I passed steadily through it, being able to say, though not without some emotion, I own: "It is Althea Knollys! Changed almost beyond conception, but still these girls' mother!" which was a happier end to this adventure than that we had first feared, mysterious as the event was, not only to myself, but, as I could see, to the acute detective as well.

The girls had withdrawn long before this, just as Mr. Gryce had desired, and I now expected to be allowed to join them, but Mr. Gryce detained me till the grave was refilled and made decent again, when he turned and to my intense astonishment—for I had thought the matter was all over and the exoneration of this household complete—said softly and with telling emphasis in my ear:

"Our work is not done yet. They who make graves so readily in cellars must have been more or less accustomed to the work. We have still some digging to do."

CHAPTER XXXI

Strategy

I was overwhelmed.

"What," said I, "you still doubt?"

"I always doubt," he gravely replied. "This cellar bottom offers a wide field for speculation. Too wide, perhaps, but, then, I have a plan."

Here he leaned over and whispered a few concise sentences into my ear in a tone so low I should feel that I was betraying his confidence in repeating them. But their import will soon become apparent from what presently occurred.

"Light Miss Butterworth to the stairway," Mr. Gryce now commanded one of the men, and thus accompanied I found my way back to the kitchen, where Hannah was bemoaning uncomforted the shame which had come upon the house.

I did not stop to soothe her. That was not my cue, nor would it have answered my purpose. On the contrary, I broke into angry ejaculations as I passed her:

"What a shame! Those wretches cannot be got away from the cellar. What do you suppose they expect to find there? I left them poking hither and thither in a way that will be very irritating to Miss Knollys when she finds it out. I wonder William stands it."

What she said in reply I do not know. I was half way down the hall before my own words were finished.

My next move was to go to my room and take from my trunk a tiny hammer and some very small, sharp-pointed tacks. Curious articles, you will think, for a woman to carry on her travels, but I am a woman of experience, and have known only too often what it was to want these petty conveniences and not be able to get them. They were to serve me an odd turn now. Taking a half-dozen tacks in one hand and concealing the hammer in my bag, I started boldly for William's room. I knew that the girls were not there, for I had heard them talking together in the sitting-room as I came up. Besides, if they were, I had a ready answer for any demand they might make.

Searching out his boots, I turned them over, and into the sole of each I drove one of my small tacks. Then I put them back in the same place and position in which I found them. Task number one was accomplished.

When I issued from the room, I went as quickly as I could below. I was now ready for a talk with the girls, whom I found as I had anticipated, talking and weeping together in the sitting-room.

They rose as I came in, awaiting my first words in evident anxiety. They had not heard me go upstairs. I immediately allowed my anxiety and profound interest in this matter to have full play.

"My poor girls! What is the meaning of this? Your mother just dead, and the matter kept from me, her friend! It is astounding—incomprehensible! I do not know what to make of it or of you."

"It has a strange look," Loreen gravely admitted; "but we had reasons for this deception, Miss Butterworth. Our mother, charming and sweet as you remember her, has not always done right, or, what you will better understand, she committed a criminal act against a person in this town, the penalty of which is state's prison."

With difficulty the words came out. With difficulty she kept down the flush of shame which threatened to overwhelm her and did overwhelm her more sensitive sister. But her self-control was great, and she went bravely on, while I, in faint imitation of her courage, restrained my own surprise and intolerable sense of shock and bitter sorrow under a guise of simple sympathy.

"It was forgery," she explained. "This has never before passed our lips. Though a cherished wife and a beloved mother, she longed for many things my father could not give her, and in an evil hour she imitated the name of a rich man here and took the check thus signed to New York. The fraud was not detected, and she received the money, but ultimately the rich man whose money she had spent, discovered the use she had made of his name, and, if she had not escaped, would have had her arrested. But she left the country, and the only revenge he took, was to swear that if she ever set foot again in X., he would call the police down upon her. Yes, if she were dying, and they had to drag her from the brink of the grave. And he would have done it; and knowing this, we have lived under the shadow of this fear for eleven years. My father died under it, and my mother—ah, she spent all the remaining years of her life under foreign skies, but when she felt the hand of death upon her, her affection for her own flesh and blood triumphed over her discretion, and she came, secretly, I own, but still with that horror menacing her, to these doors, and begging our forgiveness, lay down under the roof where we were born, and died with the halo of our love about her."

"Ah," said I, thinking of all that had happened since I had come into this house and finding nothing but confirmation of what she was saying, "I begin to understand."

But Lucetta shook her head.

"No," said she, "you cannot understand yet. We who had worn mourning for her because my father wished to make this very return impossible, knew nothing of what was in store for us till a letter came saying she would be at the C. station on the very night we received it. To acknowledge our deception, to seek and bring her home openly to this house, could not be thought of for a moment. How, then, could we satisfy her dying wishes without compromising her memory and ourselves? Perhaps you have guessed, Miss Butterworth. You have had time since we revealed the unhappy secret of this household."

"Yes," said I. "I have guessed."

Lucetta, with her hand laid on mine, looked wistfully into my face.

"Don't blame us!" she cried. "Our mother's good name is everything to us, and we knew no other way to preserve it than by making use of the one superstition of this place. Alas! our efforts were in vain. The phantom coach brought our mother safely to us, but the circumstances which led to our doors being opened to outsiders, rendered it impossible for us to carry out our plans unsuspected. Her grave has been discovered and desecrated, and we—"

She stopped, choked. Loreen took advantage of her silence to pursue the explanations she seemed to think necessary.

"It was Simsbury who undertook to bring our dying mother from C. station to our door. He has a crafty spirit under his meek ways, and dressed himself in a way to lend color to the superstition he hoped to awaken. William, who did not dare to accompany him for fear of arousing gossip, was at the gate when the coach drove in. It was he who lifted our mother out, and it was while she still clung to him with her face pressed close to his breast that we saw her first. Ah! what a pitiable sight it was! She was so wan, so feeble, and yet so radiantly happy.

"She looked up at Lucetta, and her face grew wonderful in its unearthly beauty. She was not the mother we remembered, but a mother whose life had culminated in the one desire to see and clasp her children again. When she could tear her eyes away from Lucetta, she looked at me, and then the tears came, and we all wept together, even William; and thus weeping and murmuring words of welcome and cheer, we carried her upstairs and laid her in the great front chamber. Alas! we did not foresee what would happen the very next morning—I mean the arrival of your telegram, to be followed so soon by yourself."

"Poor girls! Poor girls!" It was all I could say. I was completely overwhelmed.

"The first night after your arrival we moved her into William's room as being more remote and thus a safer refuge for her. The next night she died. The dream which you had of being locked in your room was no dream. Lucetta did that in foolish precaution against your trying to search us out in the night. It would have been better if we had taken you into our confidence."

"Yes," I assented, "that would have been better." But I did not say how much better. That would have been giving away my secret.

Lucetta had now recovered sufficiently to go on with the story.

"William, who is naturally colder than we and less sensitive in regard to our mother's good name, has shown some little impatience at the restraint imposed upon him by her presence, and this was an extra burden, Miss Butterworth, but that and all the others we have been forced to bear" (the generous girl did not speak of her own special grief and loss) "have all been rendered useless by the unhappy chance which has brought into our midst this agent of the police. Ah, if I only knew whether this was the providence of God rebuking us for years of deception, or just the malice of man seeking to rob us of our one best treasure, a mother's untarnished name!"

"Mr. Gryce acts from no malice—" I began, but I saw they were not listening.

"Have they finished down below?" asked Lucetta.

"Does the man you call Gryce seem satisfied?" asked Loreen.

I drew myself up physically and mentally. My second task was about to begin.

"I do not understand those men," said I. "They seem to want to look farther than the sacred spot where we left them. If they are going through a form, they are doing it very thoroughly."

"That is their duty," observed Loreen, but Lucetta took it less calmly.

"It is an unhappy day for us!" cried she. "Shame after shame, disgrace upon disgrace! I wish we had all died in our childhood. Loreen, I must see William. He will be doing some foolish thing, swearing or—"

"My dear, let me go to William," I urgently put in. "He may not like me overmuch, but I will at least prove a restraint to him. You are too feeble. See, you ought to be lying on the couch instead of trying to drag yourself out to the stables."

And indeed at that moment Lucetta's strength gave suddenly out, and she sank into Loreen's arms insensible.

When she was restored, I hurried away to the stables, still in pursuit of the task which I had not yet completed. I found William sitting doggedly on a stool in the open doorway, grunting out short sentences to the two men who lounged in his vicinity on either side. He was angry, but not as angry as I had seen him many times before. The men were townsfolk and listened eagerly to his broken sentences. One or two of these reached my ears.

"Let 'em go it. It won't be now or today they'll settle this business. It's the devil's work, and devils are sly. My house won't give up that secret, or any other house they'll be likely to visit. The place I would ransack—But Loreen would say I was babbling. Goodness knows a fellow's got to talk about something when his fellow-townsfolk come to see him." And here his laugh broke in, harsh, cruel, and insulting. I felt it did him no good, and made haste to show myself.

Immediately his whole appearance changed. He was so astonished to see me there that for a moment he was absolutely silent; then he broke out again into another loud guffaw, but this time in a different tone.

"Why, it's Miss Butterworth," he laughed. "Here, Saracen! Come, pay your respects to the lady who likes you so well."

And Saracen came, but I did not forsake my ground. I had espied in one corner just what I had hoped to see there, and Saracen's presence afforded me the opportunity of indulging in one or two rather curious antics.

"I am not afraid of the dog," I declared, with marked loftiness, shrinking toward the pail of water I had already marked with my eye. "Not at all afraid," I continued, catching up the pail and putting it before me as the dog made a wild rush in my direction. "These gentlemen will not see me hurt." And though they all laughed—they would have been fools if they had not—and the dog jumped the pail and I jumped—not a pail, but a broom-handle that was lying amid all the rest of the disorder on the floor—they did not see that I had succeeded in doing what I wished, which was to place that pail so near to William's feet that—But wait a moment; everything in its own time. I escaped the dog, and next moment had my eye on him. He did not move after that, which rather put a stop to the laughter, which observing, I drew very near to William, and with a sly gesture to the two men, which for some reason they seemed to understand, whispered in the rude fellow's ear:

"They've found your mother's grave under the Flower Parlor. Your sisters told me to tell you. But that is not all. They're trampling hither and yon through all the secret places in the cellar, turning up the earth with their spades. I know they won't find anything, but we thought you ought to know—"

Here I made a feint of being startled, and ceased. My second task was done. The third only remained. Fortunately at that moment Mr. Gryce and his followers showed themselves in the garden. They had just come from the cellar and played their part in the same spirit I had mine. Though they were too far off for their words to be heard, the air of secrecy they maintained and the dubious looks they cast towards the stable, could not but evince even to William's dull understanding that their investigations had resulted in a doubt which left them far from satisfied; but, once this impression made, they did not linger long together. The man with the lantern moved off, and Mr. Gryce turned towards us, changing his whole appearance as he advanced, till no one could look more cheerful and good-humored.

"Well, that is over," he sighed, with a forced air of infinite relief. "Mere form, Mr. Knollys—mere form. We have to go through these pretended investigations at times, and good people like yourself have to submit; but I assure you it is not pleasant, and under the present circumstances—I am sure you understand me, Mr. Knollys—the task has occasioned me a feeling almost of remorse; but that is inseparable from a detective's life. He is obliged every day of his life to ride over the tenderest emotions. Forgive me! And now, boys, scatter till I call you together again. I hope our next search will be without such sorrowful accompaniments."

It succeeded. William stared at him and stared at the men slowly filing off down the yard, but was not for a moment deceived by these overflowing expressions. On the contrary, he looked more concerned than he had while seated between the two men manifestly set to guard him.

"The deuce!" he cried, with a shrug of his shoulders that expressed anything but satisfaction. "Lucetta always said—" But even he knew enough not to finish that sentence, low as he had mumbled it. Watching him and watching Mr. Gryce, who at that moment turned to follow his men, I thought the time had come for action. Making another spring as if in fresh terror of Saracen, who, by the way, was eying me with the meekness of a lamb, I tipped over that pail with such suddenness and with such dexterity that its whole contents poured in one flood over William's feet. My third task was accomplished.

The oath he uttered and the excuses which I volubly poured forth could not have reached Mr. Gryce's ears, for he did not return. And yet from the way his shoulders shook as he disappeared around the corner of the house, I judge that he was not entirely ignorant of the subterfuge by which I hoped to force this blundering booby of ours to change the boots he wore for one of the pairs into which I had driven those little tacks.

CHAPTER XXXII

Relief

The plan succeeded. Mr. Gryce's plans usually do. William went immediately to his room, and in a little while came down and hastened into the cellar.

"I want to see what mischief they have done," said he.

When he came back, his face was beaming.

"All right," he shouted to his sisters, who had come into the hall to meet him. "Your secret's out, but mine—"

"There, there!" interposed Loreen, "you had better go upstairs and prepare for supper. We must eat, William, or rather, Miss Butterworth must eat, whatever our sorrows or disappointments."

He took the rebuke with a grunt and relieved us of his company. Little did he think as he went whistling up the stairs that he had just shown Mr. Gryce where to search for whatever might be lying under the broad sweep of that cellar-bottom.

That night—it was after supper, which I did not eat for all my natural stoicism—Hannah came rushing in where we all sat silent, for the girls showed no disposition to enlarge their confidences in regard to their mother, and no other topic seemed possible, and, closing the door behind her, said quickly and with evident chagrin:

"Those men are here again. They say they forgot something. What do you think it means, Miss Loreen? They have spades and lanterns and—"

"They are the police, Hannah. If they forgot something, they have the right to return. Don't work yourself up about that. The secret they have already found out was our worst. There is nothing to fear after that." And she dismissed Hannah, merely bidding her let us know when the house was quite clear.

Was she right? Was there nothing worse for them to fear? I longed to leave these trembling sisters, longed to join the party below and follow in the track of the tiny impressions made by the tacks I had driven into William's soles. If there was anything hidden under the cellar-bottom, natural anxiety would carry him to the spot he had most to fear; so they would only have to dig at the places where these impressions took a sharp turn.

But was there anything hidden there? From the sisters' words and actions I judged there was nothing serious, but would they know? William was quite capable of deceiving them. Had he done so? It was a question.

It was solved for us by Mr. Gryce's reappearance in the room an hour or so later. From the moment the light fell upon his kindly features I knew that I might breathe again freely. It was not the face he showed in the house of a criminal, nor did his bow contain any of the false deference with which he sometimes tries to hide his secret doubt or contempt.

"I have come to trouble you for the last time, ladies. We have made a double search through this house and through the stables, and feel perfectly justified in saying that our duty henceforth will lead us elsewhere. The secrets we have surprised are your own, and if possible shall remain so. Your brother's propensity for vivisection and the return and death of your mother bear so little on the real question which interests this community that we may be able to prevent their spread as gossip through the town. That this may be done conscientiously, however, I ought to know something more of the latter circumstance. If Miss Butterworth will then be good enough to grant me a few minutes' conference with these ladies, I may be able to satisfy myself to such an extent as to let this matter rest where it is."

I rose with right good will. A mountain weight had been lifted from me, proof positive that I had really come to love these girls.

What they told him, whether it was less or more than they told me, I cannot say, and for the moment did not know. That it had not shaken his faith in them was evident, for when he came out to where I was waiting in the hall his aspect was even more encouraging than it had been before.

"No guile in those girls," he whispered as he passed me. "The clue given by what seemed mysterious in this house has come to naught. To-morrow we take up another. The trinkets found in Mother Jane's cottage are something real. You may sleep soundly tonight, Miss Butterworth. Your part has been well played, but I know you are glad that it has failed."

And I knew that I was glad, too, which is the best proof that there is something in me besides the detective instinct.

The front door had scarcely closed behind him when William came storming in. He had been gossiping over the fence with Mr. Trohm, and had been beguiled into taking a glass of wine in his house. This was evident without his speaking of it.

"Those sneaks!" cried he. "I hear they've been back again, digging and stirring up our cellar-bottom like mad. That's because you're so dreadful shy, you girls. You're afraid of this, you're afraid of that. You don't want folks to know that mother once—Well, well, there it is now! If you had not tried to keep this wretched secret, it would have been an old matter by this time, and my affairs would have been left untouched. But now every fool will cry out at me in this staid, puritanical old town, and all because a few bones have been found of animals which have died in the cause of science. I say it's all your fault! Not that I have anything to be ashamed of, because I haven't, but because this other thing, this d—d wicked series of disappearances, taking place, for aught we know, a dozen rods from our gates (though I think—but no matter what I think—you all like, or say you like, old Deacon Spear), has made every one so touchy in this pharisaical town that to kill a fly has become a crime even if it is to save oneself from poison. I'm going to see if I cannot make folks blink askance at some other man than me. I'm going to find out who or what causes these disappearances."

This was a declaration to make us all stare and look a little bit fool-ish. William playing the detective! Well, what might I not live to see next! But the next moment an overpowering thought struck me. Might this Deacon Spear by any chance be the rich man whose animosity Althea Knollys had awakened?

BOOK IV: THE BIRDS OF THE AIR

CHAPTER XXXIII

Lucetta

The next morning I rose with the lark. I had slept well, and all my old vigor had returned. A new problem was before me; a problem of surpass-ing interest, now that the Knollys family had been eliminated from the list of persons regarded with suspicion by the police. Mother Jane and the jewels were to be Mr. Gryce's starting-point for future investigation. Should they be mine? My decision on this point halted, and thinking it might be helped by a breath of fresh air, I decided upon an early stroll as a means of settling this momentous question.

There was silence in the house when I passed through it on my way to the front door. But that silence had lost its terrors and the old house its absorbing mystery. Yet it was not robbed of its interest. When I real-ized that Althea Knollys, the Althea of my youth, had just died within its walls as ignorant of my proximity as I of hers, I felt that no old-time romance, nor any terror brought by flitting ghost or stalking apparition, could compare with the wonder of this return and the strange and thrill-ing circumstances which had attended it. And the end was not yet. Peace-ful as everything now looked, I still felt that the end had not come.

The fact that Saracen was loose in the yard gave me some slight concern as I opened the great front door and looked out. But the control under which I had held him the day before encouraged me in my venture, and after a few words with Hannah, who was careful not to let me slip away unnoticed, I boldly stepped forth and took my solitary way down to the gate.

It was not yet eight, and the grass was still heavy with dew. At the gate I paused. I wished to go farther, but Mr. Gryce's injunction had been imperative about venturing into the lane alone. Besides—No, that was not a horse's hoof. There could be no one on the road so early as this. I was alarming myself unnecessarily, yet—Well, I held my place, a little awkwardly, perhaps. Self-consciousness is always awkward, and I could not help being a trifle self-conscious at a meeting so unexpected and—But the more I attempt to explain, the more confused my expressions become, so I will just say that, by this very strange chance, I was leaning over the gate when Mr. Trohm rode up for the second time and found me there.

I did not attempt any excuses. He is gentleman enough to understand that a woman of my temperament rises early and must have the morning air. That he should feel the same necessity is a coincidence, natural perhaps, but still a coincidence. So there was nothing to be said about it.

But had there been, I would not have spoken, for he seemed so gratified at finding me enjoying nature at this early hour that any words from me would have been quite superfluous. He did not dismount—that would have shown intention—but he stopped, and—well, we have both passed the age of romance, and what he said cannot be of interest to the general public, especially as it did not deal with the disappearances or with the discoveries made in the Knollys house the day before, or with any of those questions which have absorbed our attention up to this time.

That we were engaged more than five minutes in this conversation I cannot believe. I have always been extremely accurate in regard to time, yet a good half-hour was lost by me that morning for which I have never been able to account. Perhaps it was spent in the short discussion which terminated our interview; a discussion which may be of interest to you, for it was upon the action of the police.

"Nothing came of the investigations made by Mr. Gryce yesterday, I perceive," Mr. Trohm had remarked, with some reluctance, as he gathered up his reins to depart. "Well, that is not strange. How could he have hoped to find any clue to such a mystery as he is engaged to unearth, in a house presided over by Miss Knollys?"

"How could he, indeed! Yet," I added, determined to allay this man's suspicions, which, notwithstanding the openness of his remark, were still observable in his tones, "you say that with an air I should hardly expect from so good a neighbor and friend. Why is this, Mr. Trohm? Surely you do not associate crime with the Misses Knollys?"

"Crime? Oh, no, certainly not. No one could associate crime with the Misses Knollys. If my tone was at fault, it was due perhaps to my embarrassment—this meeting, your kindness, the beauty of the day, and the feeling these all call forth. Well, I may be pardoned if my tones are not quite true in discussing other topics. My thoughts were with the one I addressed."

"Then that tone of doubt was all the more misplaced," I retorted. "I am so frank, I cannot bear innuendo in others. Besides, Mr. Trohm, the worst folly of this home was laid bare yesterday in a way to set at rest all darker suspicions. You knew that William indulged in vivisection. Well, that is bad, but it cannot be called criminal. Let us do him justice, then, and, for his sisters' sake, see how we can re-establish him in the good graces of the community."

But Mr. Trohm, who for all our short acquaintance was not without a very decided appreciation for certain points in my character, shook his head and with a smiling air returned:

"You are asking the impossible not only of the community, but yourself. William can never re-establish himself. He is of too rude a make. The girls may recover the esteem they seem to have lost, but William— Why, if the cause of those disappearances was found today, and found at the remotest end of this road or even up in the mountains, where no one seems to have looked for it, William would still be known throughout the county as a rough and cruel man. I have tried to stand his friend, but it's been against odds, Miss Butterworth. Even his sisters recognize this, and show their lack of confidence in our friendship. But I would like to oblige you."

I knew he ought to go. I knew that if he had simply lingered the five minutes which common courtesy allowed, that curious eyes would be looking from Loreen's window, and that at any minute I might expect some interference from Lucetta, who had read through this man's forbearance toward William the very natural distrust he could not but feel toward so uncertain a character. Yet with such an opportunity at my command, how could I let him go without another question?

"Mr. Trohm," said I, "you have the kindest heart and the closest lips, but have you ever thought that Deacon Spear—"

He stopped me with a really horrified look. "Deacon Spear's house was thoroughly examined yesterday," said he, "as mine will be today. Don't insinuate anything against him! Leave that for foolish William." Then with the most charming return to his old manner, for I felt myself in a measure rebuked, he lifted his hat and urged his horse forward. But, having withdrawn himself a step or two, he paused and with the slightest gesture toward the little hut he was facing, added in a much lower tone than any he had yet used: "Besides, Deacon Spear is much too far away from Mother Jane's cottage. Don't you remember that I told you she never could be got to go more than forty rods from her own doorstep?" And, breaking into a quick canter, he rode away.

I was left to think over his words and the impossibility of my picking up any other clue than that given me by Mr. Gryce.

I was turning toward the house when I heard a slight noise at my feet. Looking down, I encountered the eyes of Saracen. He was crouching at my side, and as I turned toward him, his tail actually wagged. It was a sight to call the color up to my cheek; not that I blushed at this sign of good-will, astonishing as it was, considering my feeling toward dogs, but at his being there at all without my knowing it. So palpable a proof that no woman—I make no exceptions—can listen more than one minute to the expressions of a man's sincere admiration without losing a little of her watchfulness, was not to be disregarded by one as inexorable to her own mistakes as to those of others. I saw myself the victim of vanity, and while somewhat abashed by the discovery, I could not but realize that this solitary proof of feminine weakness was not really to be deplored in one who has not yet passed the line beyond which any such display is ridiculous.

Lucetta met me at the door just as I had expected her to. Giving me a short look, she spoke eagerly but with a latent anxiety, for which I was more or less prepared.

"I am glad to see you looking so bright this morning," she declared. "We are all feeling better now that the incubus of secrecy is removed. But"—here she hesitated—"I would not like to think you told Mr. Trohm what happened to us yesterday."

"Lucetta," said I, "there may be women of my age who delight in gossiping about family affairs with comparative strangers, but I am not that kind of woman. Mr. Trohm, friendly as he has proved himself and worthy as he undoubtedly is of your confidence and trust, will have to learn from some other person than myself anything which you may wish to have withheld from him."

For reply she gave me an impulsive kiss. "I thought I could trust you," she cried. Then, with a dubious look, half daring, half shrinking, she added:

"When you come to know and like us better, you will not care so much to talk to neighbors. They never can understand us or do us justice, Mr. Trohm, especially."

This was a remark I could not let pass.

"Why?" I demanded. "Why do you think Mr. Trohm cherishes such animosity towards you? Has he ever—"

But Lucetta could exercise a repellent dignity when she chose. I did not finish my sentence, though I must have looked the inquiry I thought better not to put into words.

"Mr. Trohm is a man of blameless reputation," she avowed. "If he has allowed himself to cherish suspicions in our regard, he has doubtless had his reasons for it."

And with these quiet words she left me to my thoughts, and I must say to my doubts, which were all the more painful that I saw no immediate opportunity for clearing them up.

Late in the afternoon William burst in with news from the other end of the lane.

"Such a lark!" he cried. "The investigation at Deacon Spear's house was a mere farce, and I just made them repeat it with a few frills. They had dug up my cellar, and I was determined they should dig up his. Oh, the fun it was! The old fellow kicked, but I had my way. They couldn't refuse me, you know; I hadn't refused them. So that man's cellar-bottom has had a stir up. They didn't find anything, but it did me a lot of good, and that's something. I do hate Deacon Spear—couldn't hate him worse if he'd killed and buried ten men under his hearthstone."

"There is no harm in Deacon Spear," said Lucetta, quickly.

"Did they submit Mr. Trohm's house to a search also?" asked Loreen, ashamed of William's heat and anxious to avert any further display of it.

"Yes, they went through that too. I was with them. Glad I was too. I say, girls, I could have laughed to see all the comforts that old bachelor has about him. Never saw such fixings. Why, that house is as neat and pretty from top to bottom as any old maid's. It's silly, of course, for a man, and I'd rather live in an old rookery like this, where I can walk from room to room in muddy boots if I want to, and train my dogs and live in freedom like the man I am. Yet I couldn't help thinking it mighty comfortable, too, for an old fellow like him who likes such things and don't have chick or child to meddle. Why, he had pincushions on all his bureaus, and they had pins in them."

The laugh with which he delivered this last sentence might have been heard a quarter of a mile away. Lucetta looked at Loreen and Loreen looked at me, but none of us joined in the mirth, which seemed to me very ill-timed.

Suddenly Lucetta asked:

"Did they dig up Mr. Trohm's cellar?"

William stopped laughing long enough to say:

"His cellar? Why, it's cemented as hard as an oak floor. No, they didn't polish their spades in his house, which was another source of satisfaction to me. Deacon Spear hasn't even that to comfort him. Oh, how I did enjoy that old fellow's face when they began to root up his old fungi!"

Lucetta turned away with a certain odd constraint I could not but notice.

"It's a humiliating day for the lane," said she. "And what is worse," she suddenly added, "nothing will ever come of it. It will take more than a band of police to reach the root of this matter."

I thought her manner odd, and, moving towards her, took her by the hand with something of a relative's familiarity.

"What makes you say that? Mr. Gryce seems a very capable man."

"Yes, yes, but capability has nothing to do with it. Chance might and pluck might, but wit and experience not. Otherwise the mystery would have been settled long ago. I wish I—"

"Well?" Her hand was trembling violently.

"Nothing. I don't know why I have allowed myself to talk on this subject. Loreen and I once made a compact never to give any opinion upon it. You see how I have kept it."

She had drawn her hand away and suddenly had become quite composed. I turned my attention toward Loreen, but she was looking out of the window and showed no intention of further pursuing the conversation. William had strolled out.

"Well," said I, "if ever a girl had reason for breaking such a compact you are certainly that girl. I could never have been as silent as you have been—that is, if I had any suspicions on so serious a subject. Why, your own good name is impugned—yours and that of every other person living in this lane."

"Miss Butterworth," she replied, "I have gone too far. Besides, you have misunderstood me. I have no more knowledge than anybody else as to the source of these terrible tragedies. I only know that an almost superhuman cunning lies at the bottom of so many unaccountable disappearances, a cunning so great that only a crazy person—"

"Ah," I murmured eagerly, "Mother Jane!"

She did not answer. Instantly I took a resolution.

"Lucetta," said I, "is Deacon Spear a rich man?"

Starting violently, she looked at me amazed.

"If he is, I should like to hazard the guess that he is the man who has held you in such thraldom for years."

"And if he were?" said she.

"I could understand William's antipathy to him and also his suspicions."

She gave me a strange look, then without answering walked over and took Loreen by the hand. "Hush!" I thought I heard her whisper. At all events the two sisters were silent for more than a moment. Then Lucetta said:

"Deacon Spear is well off, but nothing will ever make me accuse living man of crime so dreadful." And she walked away, drawing Loreen after her. In another moment she was out of the room, leaving me in a state of great excitement.

"This girl holds the secret to the whole situation," I inwardly decided. "The belief that nothing more can be learned from her is a false one. I must see Mr. Gryce. William's rodomontades are so much empty air, but Lucetta's silence has a meaning we cannot afford to ignore."

So impressed was I by this, that I took the first opportunity which presented itself of seeing the detective. This was early the next morning. He and several of the townspeople had made their appearance at Mother Jane's cottage, with spades and picks, and the sight had naturally drawn us all down to the gate, where we stood watching operations in a silence which would have been considered unnatural by any one who did not realize the conflicting nature of the emotions underlying it. William, to whom the death of his mother seemed to be a great deliverance, had been inclined to be more or less jocular, but his sallies meeting with no response, he had sauntered away to have it out with his dogs, leaving me alone with the two girls and Hannah.

The latter seemed to be absorbed entirely by the aspect of Mother Jane, who stood upon her doorstep in an attitude so menacing that it was little short of tragic. Her hood, for the first time in the memory of those present, had fallen away from her head, revealing a wealth of gray hair which flew away from her head like a weird halo. Her features we could not distinguish, but the emotion which inspired her, breathed in every gesture of her uplifted arms and swaying body. It was wrath personified, and yet an unreasoning wrath. One could see she was as much dazed as outraged. Her lares and penates were being attacked, and she had come from the heart of her solitude to defend them.

"I declare!" Hannah protested. "It is pitiful. She has nothing in the world but that garden, and now they are going to root that up."

"Do you think that the sight of a little money would appease her?" I inquired, anxious for an excuse to drop a word into the ear of Mr. Gryce.

"Perhaps," said Hannah. "She dearly loves money, but it will not take away her fright."

"It will if she has nothing to be frightened about," said I; and turning to the girls, I asked them, somewhat mincingly for me, if they thought I would make myself conspicuous if I crossed the road on this errand, and when Loreen answered that that would not deter her if she had the money, and Lucetta added that the sight of such misery was too painful for any mere personal consideration, I took advantage of their complaisance, and hastily made my way over to the group, who were debating as to the point they would attack first.

"Gentlemen," said I, "good-morning. I am here on an errand of mercy. Poor old Mother Jane is half imbecile and does not understand why you invade her premises with these implements. Will you object if I endeavor to distract her mind with a little piece of gold I happen to have in my pocket? She may not deserve it, but it will make your task easier and save us some possible concern."

Half of the men at once took off their hats. The other half nudged each other's elbows, and whispered and grimaced like the fools they were. The first half were gentlemen, though not all of them wore gentlemen's clothes.

It was Mr. Gryce who spoke:

"Certainly, madam. Give the old woman anything you please, but—" And here he stepped up to me and began to whisper; "You have something to say. What is it?"

I answered in the same quick way: "The mine you thought exhausted has possibilities in it yet. Question Lucetta. It may prove a more fruitful task than turning up this soil."

The bow he made was more for the onlookers than for the suggestion I had given him. Yet he was not ungrateful for the latter, as I, who was beginning to understand him, could see.

"Be as generous as you please!" he cried aloud. "We would not disturb the old crone if it were not for one of her well-known follies. Nothing will take her over forty rods away from her home. Now what lies within those forty rods? These men think we ought to see."

The shrug I gave answered both the apparent and the concealed question. Satisfied that he would understand it so, I hurried away from him and approached Mother Jane.

"See!" said I, astonished at the regularity of her features, now that I had a good opportunity of observing them. "I have brought you money. Let them dig up your turnips if they will."

She did not seem to perceive me. Her eyes were wild with dismay and her lips trembling with a passion far beyond my power to comfort.

"Lizzie!" she cried. "Lizzie! She will come back and find no home. Oh, my poor girl! My poor, poor girl!"

It was pitiable. I could not doubt her anguish or her sincerity. The delirium of a broken heart cannot be simulated. And this heart was not controlled by reason; that was equally apparent. Immediately my heart, which goes out slowly, but none the less truly on that account, was touched by something more than the surface sympathy of the moment. She may have stolen, she may have done worse, she may even have been at the bottom of the horrible crimes which have given its name to the lane we were in, but her acts, if acts they were, were the result of a clouded mind fixed forever upon the fancied needs of another, and not the expression of personal turpitude or even of personal longing or avarice. Therefore I could pity her, and I did.

Making another appeal, I pressed the coin hard into one of her hands till the contact effected what my words had been unable to do, and she finally looked down and saw what she was clutching. Then indeed her aspect changed, and in a few minutes of slowly growing comprehension she became so quiet and absorbed that she forgot to look at the men and even forgot me, who was probably nothing more than a flitting shadow to her.

"A silk gown," she murmured. "It will buy Lizzie a silk gown. Oh! where did it come from, the good, good gold, the beautiful gold; such a little piece, yet enough to make her look fine, my Lizzie, my pretty, pretty Lizzie?"

No numbers this time. The gift was too overpowering for her even to remember that it must be hidden away.

I walked away while her delight was still voluble. Somehow it eased my mind to have done her this little act of kindness, and I think it eased the minds of the men too. At all events, every hat was off when I repassed them on my way back to the Knollys gateway.

I had left both the girls there, but I found only one awaiting me. Lucetta had gone in, and so had Hannah. On what errand I was soon to know.

"What do you suppose that detective wants of Lucetta now?" asked Loreen as I took my station again at her side. "While you were talking to Mother Jane he stepped over here, and with a word or two induced Lucetta to walk away with him toward the house. See, there they are in those thick shrubs near the right wing. He seems to be pleading with her. Do you think I ought to join them and find out what he is urging upon her so earnestly? I don't like to seem intrusive, but Lucetta is easily agitated, you know, and his business cannot be of an indifferent nature after all he has discovered concerning our affairs."

"No," I agreed, "and yet I think Lucetta will be strong enough to sustain the conversation, judging from the very erect attitude she is holding now. Perhaps he thinks she can tell him where to dig. They seem a little at sea over there, and living, as you do, a few rods from Mother Jane, he may imagine that Lucetta can direct him where to first plant the spade."

"It's an insult," Loreen protested. "All these talks and visits are insults. To be sure, this detective has some excuse, but—"

"Keep your eye on Lucetta," I interrupted. "She is shaking her head and looking very positive. She will prove to him it is an insult. We need not interfere, I think."

But Loreen had grown pensive and did not heed my suggestion. A look that was almost wistful had supplanted the expression of indignant revolt with which she had addressed me, and when next moment the two we had been watching turned and came slowly toward us, it was with decided energy she bounded forward and joined them.

"What is the matter now?" she asked. "What does Mr. Gryce want, Lucetta?"

Mr. Gryce himself spoke.

"I simply want her," said he, "to assist me with a clue from her inmost thoughts. When I was in your house," he explained with a praiseworthy consideration for me and my relations to these girls for which I cannot be too grateful, "I saw in this young lady something which convinced me that, as a dweller in this lane, she was not without her suspicions as to the secret cause of the fatal mysteries which I have been sent here to clear up. Today I have frankly accused her of this, and asked her to confide in me. But she refuses to do so, Miss Loreen. Yet her face shows even at this moment that my old eyes were not at fault in my reading of her. She does suspect somebody, and it is not Mother Jane."

"How can you say that?" began Lucetta, but the eyes which Loreen that moment turned upon her seemed to trouble her, for she did not attempt to say any more—only looked equally obstinate and distressed.

"If Lucetta suspects any one," Loreen now steadily remarked, "then I think she ought to tell you who it is."

"You do. Then perhaps you—" commenced Mr. Gryce—"can persuade her as to her duty," he finished, as he saw her head rise in protest of what he evidently had intended to demand.

"Lucetta will not yield to persuasion," was her quiet reply. "Nothing short of conviction will move the sweetest-natured but the most determined of all my mother's children. What she thinks is right, she will do. I will not attempt to influence her."

Mr. Gryce, with one comprehensive survey of the two, hesitated no longer. I saw the rising of the blood into his forehead, which always precedes the beginning of one of his great moves, and, filled with a sudden excitement, I awaited his next words as a tyro awaits the first unfolding of the plan he has seen working in the brain of some famous strategist.

"Miss Lucetta,"—his very tone was changed, changed in a way to make us all start notwithstanding the preparation his momentary silence had given us—"I have been thus pressing and perhaps rude in my appeal, because of something which has come to my knowledge which cannot but make you of all persons extremely anxious as to the meaning of this terrible mystery. I am an old man, and you will not mind my bluntness. I have been told—and your agitation convinces me there is truth in the report—that you have a lover, a Mr. Ostrander—"

"Ah!" She had sunk as if crushed by one overwhelming blow to the earth. The eyes, the lips, the whole pitiful face that was upturned to us, remain in my memory today as the most terrible and yet the most moving spectacle that has come into my by no means uneventful life. "What has happened to him? Quick, quick, tell me!"

For answer Mr. Gryce drew out a telegram.

"From the master of the ship on which he was to sail," he explained.

"It asks if Mr. Ostrander left this town on Tuesday last, as no news has been received of him."

"Loreen! Loreen! When he left us he passed down that way!" shrieked the girl, rising like a spirit and pointing east toward Deacon Spear's. "He is gone! He is lost! But his fate shall not remain a mystery. I will dare its solution. I—I—Tonight you will hear from me again."

And without another glance at any of us she turned and fled toward the house.

CHAPTER XXXIV

Conditions

But in another moment she was back, her eyes dilated and her whole person exhaling a terrible purpose.

"Do not look at me, do not notice me!" she cried, but in a voice so hoarse no one but Mr. Gryce could fully understand her. "I am for no one's eyes but God's. Pray that he may have mercy upon me." Then as she saw us all instinctively fall back, she controlled herself, and, pointing toward Mother Jane's cottage, said more distinctly: "As for those men, let them dig. Let them dig the whole day long. Secrecy must be kept, a secrecy so absolute that not even the birds of the air must see that our thoughts range beyond the forty rods surrounding Mother Jane's cottage."

She turned and would have fled away for the second time, but Mr. Gryce stopped her. "You have set yourself a task beyond your strength. Can you perform it?"

"I can perform it," she said. "If Loreen does not talk, and I am allowed to spend the day in solitude."

I had never seen Mr. Gryce so agitated—no, not when he left Olive Randolph's bedside after an hour of vain pleading. "But to wait all day! Is it necessary for you to wait all day?"

"It is necessary." She spoke like an automaton. "Tonight at twilight, when the sun is setting, meet me at the great tree just where the road turns. Not a minute sooner, not an hour later. I will be calmer then." And waiting now for nothing, not for a word from Loreen nor a detaining touch from Mr. Gryce, she flew away for the second time. This time Loreen followed her.

"Well, that is the hardest thing I ever had to do," said Mr. Gryce, wiping his forehead and speaking in a tone of real grief and anxiety. "Do you think her delicate frame can stand it? Will she survive this day and carry through whatever it is she has set herself to accomplish?"

"She has no organic disease," said I, "but she loved that young man very much, and the day will be a terrible one to her."

Mr. Gryce sighed.

"I wish I had not been obliged to resort to such means," said he, "but women like that only work under excitement, and she does know the secret of this affair."

"Do you mean," I demanded, almost aghast, "that you have deceived her with a false telegram; that that slip of paper you hold—"

"Read it," he cried, holding it out toward me.

I did read it. Alas, there was no deception in it. It read as he said.

"However—" I began.

But he had pocketed the telegram and was several steps away before I had finished my sentence.

"I am going to start these men up," said he. "You will breathe no word to Miss Lucetta of my sympathy nor let your own interests slack in the investigations which are going on under our noses."

And with a quick, sharp bow, he made his way to the gate, whither I followed him in time to see him set his foot upon a patch of sage.

"You will begin at this place," he cried, "and work east; and, gentlemen, something tells me that we shall be successful."

With almost a simultaneous sound a dozen spades and picks struck the ground. The digging up of Mother Jane's garden had begun in earnest.

CHAPTER XXXV

The Dove

I remained at the gate. I had been bidden to show my interest in what was going on in Mother Jane's garden, and this was the way I did it. But my thoughts were not with the diggers. I knew, as well then as later, that they would find nothing worth the trouble they were taking; and, having made up my mind to this, I was free to follow the lead of my own thoughts.

They were not happy ones; I was neither satisfied with myself nor with the prospect of the long day of cruel suspense that awaited us. When I undertook to come to X., it was with the latent expectation of making myself useful in ferreting out its mystery. And how had I succeeded? I had been the means through which one of its secrets had been discovered, but not *the* secret; and while Mr. Gryce was good enough, or wise enough, to show no diminution in his respect for me, I knew that I had sunk a peg in his estimation from the consciousness I had of having sunk two, if not three pegs, in my own.

This was a galling thought to me. But it was not the only one which disturbed me. Happily or unhappily, I have as much heart as pride, and Lucetta's despair, and the desperate resolve to which it had led, had made an impression upon me which I could not shake off.

Whether she knew the criminal or only suspected him; whether in the heat of her sudden anguish she had promised more or less than she could perform, the fact remained that we (by whom I mean first and above all, Mr. Gryce, the ablest detective on the New York force, and myself, who, if no detective, am at least a factor of more or less importance in an inquiry like this) were awaiting the action of a weak and suffering girl to discover what our own experience should be able to obtain for us unassisted.

That Mr. Gryce felt that he was playing a great card in thus enlisting her despair in our service, did not comfort me. I am not fond of games in which real hearts take the place of painted ones; and, besides, I was not ready to acknowledge that my own capacity for ferreting out this mystery was quite exhausted, or that I ought to remain idle while Lucetta bent under a task so much beyond her strength. So deeply was I impressed by this latter consideration, that I found myself, even in the midst of my apparent interest in what was going on at Mother Jane's cottage, asking if I was bound to accept the defeat pronounced upon my efforts by Mr. Gryce, and if there was not yet time to retrieve myself and save Lucetta. One happy thought, or clever linking of cause to effect, might lead me yet to the clue which we had hitherto sought in vain. And then who would have more right to triumph than Amelia Butterworth, or who more reason to apologize than Ebenezar Gryce! But where was I to get my happy thought, and by what stroke of fortune could I reasonably hope to light upon a clue which had escaped the penetrating eye of my quondam colleague? Lucetta's gesture and Lucetta's exclamation, "He passed that way!" indicated that her suspicions pointed in the direction of Deacon Spear's cottage; so did William's wandering accusations: but this was little help to me, confined as I was to the Knollys demesnes, both by Mr. Gryce's command and by my own sense of propriety. No, I must light on something more tangible; something practical enough to justify me in my own eyes for any interference I might meditate. In short, I must start from a fact, and not from a suspicion. But what fact? Why, there was but one, and that was the finding of certain indisputable tokens of crime in Mother Jane's keeping. That was a clue, a clue, to be sure, which Mr. Gryce, while ostensibly following it in his present action, really felt to lead nowhere, but which I—Here my thoughts paused. I dare not promise myself too satisfactory results to my efforts, even while conscious of that vague elation which presages success, and which I could only overcome by resorting again to reasoning. This time I started with a question. Had Mother Jane committed these crimes herself? I did not think so; neither did Mr. Gryce, for all the persistence he showed in having the ground about her humble dwelling-place turned over. Then, how had the ring of Mr. Chittenden come to be in her possession, when, as all agreed, she never was known to wander more than forty rods away from home? If the crime by which this young gentleman had perished had taken place up the road, as Lucetta's denouncing finger plainly indicated, then this token of Mother Jane's complicity in it had been carried across the intervening space by other means than Mother Jane herself. In other words, it was brought to her by the perpetrator, or it was placed where she could lay hand on it; neither supposition implying guilt on her part, she being in all probability as innocent of wrong as she was of sense. At all events, such should be my theory for the nonce, old theories having exploded or become of little avail in the present aspect of things. To discover, then, the source of crime, I must discover the means by which this ring reached Mother Jane—an almost hopeless task, but not to be despaired of on that account: had I not wrung the truth in times gone by from that piece of obstinate stolidity the Van Burnam scrub-woman? and if I could do this, might I not hope to win an equal confidence from this half-demented creature, with a heart so passionate it beat to but one tune, her Lizzie? I meant at least to try, and, under the impulse of this resolve, I left my position at the gate and recrossed the road to Mother Jane, whose figure I could dimly discern on the farther side of her little house.

Mr. Gryce barely looked up as I passed him, and the men not at all. They were deep in their work, and probably did not see me. Neither did Mother Jane at first. She had not yet wearied of the shining gold she held, though she had begun again upon that chanting of numbers the secret of which Mr. Gryce had discovered in his investigation of her house.

I therefore found it hard to make her hear me when I attempted to speak. She had fixed upon the new number fifteen and seemed never to tire of repeating it. At last I took cue from her speech, and shouted out the word *ten*. It was the number of the vegetable in which Mr. Chittenden's ring had been hidden, and it made her start violently.

"Ten! ten!" I reiterated, catching her eye. "He who brought it has carried it away; come into the house and look."

It was a desperate attempt. I felt myself quake inwardly as I realized how near Mr. Gryce was standing, and what his anger would be if he surprised me at this move after he had cried "Halt!"

But neither my own perturbation nor the thought of his possible anger could restrain the spirit of investigation which had returned to me with the above words; and when I saw that they had not fallen upon deaf ears, but that Mother Jane heard and in a measure understood them, I led the way into the hut and pointed to the string from which the one precious vegetable had been torn.

She gave a spring toward it that was well-nigh maniacal in its fury, and for an instant I thought she was going to rend the air with one of her wild yells, when there came a swishing of wings at one of the open windows, and a dove flew in and nestled in her breast, diverting her attention so, that she dropped the empty husk of the onion she had just grasped and seized the bird in its stead. It was a violent clutch, so violent that the poor dove panted and struggled under it till its head flopped over and I looked to see it die in her hands.

"Stop!" I cried, horrified at a sight I was so unprepared to expect from one who was supposed to cherish these birds most tenderly.

But she heard me no more than she saw the gesture of indignant appeal I made her. All her attention, as well as all her fury, was fixed upon the dove, over whose neck and under whose wings she ran her trembling fingers with the desperation of one looking for something he failed to find.

"Ten! ten!" it was now her turn to shout, as her eyes passed in angry menace from the bird to the empty husk that dangled over her head. "You brought it, did you, and you've taken it, have you? There, then! You'll never bring or carry any more!" And lifting up her hand, she flung the bird to the other side of the room, and would have turned upon me, in which contingency I would for once have met my match, if, in releasing the bird from her hands, she had not at the same time released the coin which she had hitherto managed to hold through all her passionate gestures.

The sight of this piece of gold, which she had evidently forgotten for the moment, turned her thoughts back to the joys it promised her. Recapturing it once more, she sank again into her old ecstasy, upon which I proceeded to pick up the poor, senseless dove, and leave the hut with a devout feeling of gratitude for my undoubted escape.

That I did this quietly and with the dove hidden under my little cape, no one who knows me well will doubt. I had brought something from the hut besides this victim of the old imbecile's fury, and I was no more willing that Mr. Gryce should see the one than detect the other. I had brought away a clue.

"The birds of the air shall carry it." So the Scripture runs. This bird, this pigeon, who now lay panting out his life in my arms had brought her the ring which in Mr. Gryce's eyes had seemed to connect her with the disappearance of young Mr. Chittenden.

CHAPTER XXXVI

An Hour of Startling Experiences

Not till I was safely back in the Knollys grounds, not, indeed, till I had put one or two large and healthy shrubs between me and a certain pair of very prying eyes, did I bring the dove out from under my cape and examine the poor bird for any sign which might be of help to me in the search to which I was newly committed.

But I found nothing, and was obliged to resort to my old plan of reasoning to make anything out of the situation in which I thus so unexpectedly found myself. The dove had brought the ring into old Mother Jane's hands, but whence and through whose agency? This was as much a secret as before, but the longer I contemplated it, the more I realized that it need not remain a secret long; that we had simply to watch the other doves, note where they lighted, and in whose barn-doors they were welcome, for us to draw inferences that might lead to revelations before the day was out. If Deacon Spear—But Deacon Spear's house had been examined as well as that of every other resident in the lane. This I knew, but it had not been examined by me, and unwilling as I was to challenge the accuracy or thoroughness of a search led on by such a man as Mr. Gryce, I could not but feel that, with such a hint as I had received from the episode in the hut, it would be a great relief to my mind to submit these same premises to my own somewhat penetrating survey, no man in my judgment having the same quickness of eyesight in matters domestic as a woman trained to know every inch of a house and to measure by a hair's-breadth every fall of drapery within it.

But how in the name of goodness was I to obtain an opportunity for this survey. Had we not one and all been bidden to confine our attention to what was going on in Mother Jane's cottage, and would it not be treason to Lucetta to run the least risk of awakening apprehension in any possibly guilty mind at the other end of the road? Yes, but for all that I could not keep still if fate, or my own ingenuity, offered me the least chance of pursuing the clue I had wrung from our imbecile neighbor at the risk of my life. It was not in my nature to do so, any more than it was in my nature to yield up my present advantage to Mr. Gryce without making a personal effort to utilize it. I forgot that I failed in this once before in my career, or rather I recalled this failure, perhaps, and felt the great need of retrieving myself.

When, therefore, in my slow stroll towards the house I encountered William in the shrubbery, I could not forbear accosting him with a question or two.

"William," I remarked, gently rubbing the side of my nose with an irresolute forefinger and looking at him from under my lids, "that was a scurvy trick you played Deacon Spear yesterday."

He stood amazed, then burst into one of his loud laughs.

"You think so?" he cried. "Well, I don't. He only got what he deserved, the hard, sanctimonious sneak!"

"Do you say that," I inquired, with some spirit, "because you dislike the man, or because you really believe him to be worthy of hatred?"

William's amusement at this argued little for my hopes.

"*We* are very much interested in the Deacon," he suggested, with a leer; which insolence I allowed to pass unnoticed, because it best suited my plan.

"You have not answered my question," I remarked, with a forced air of anxiety.

"Oh, no," he cried, "so I haven't"; and he tried to look serious too. "Well, well, to be just, I have nothing really against the man but his mean ways. Still, if I were going to risk my life on a hazard as to who is the evil spirit of this lane, I should say Spear and done with it, he has such cursed small eyes."

"*I* don't think his eyes are too small," I returned loftily. Then with a sudden change of manner, I suggested anxiously: "And my opinion is shared by your sisters. They evidently think very well of him."

"Oh!" he sneered; "girls are no judges. They don't know a good man when they see him, and they don't know a bad. You mustn't go by what they say."

I had it on the tip of my tongue to ask if he did not think Lucetta sufficiently understood herself to be trusted in what she contemplated doing that night. But this was neither in accordance with my plan, nor did it seem quite loyal to Lucetta, who, so far as I knew, had not communicated her intentions to this booby brother. I therefore changed this question into a repetition of my first remark:

"Well, I still think the trick you played Deacon Spear yesterday a poor one; and I advise you, as a gentleman, to go and ask his pardon."

This was such a preposterous proposition, he could not hold his peace.

"*I ask his pardon!*" he snorted. "Well, Saracen, did you ever hear the like of that! *I* ask Deacon Spear's pardon for obliging him to be treated with as great attention as I had been myself."

"If you do not," I went on, unmoved, "I shall go and do it myself. I think that is what my friendship for you warrants. I am determined that while I am a visitor in your house no one shall be able to pick a flaw in your conduct."

He stared (as he might well do), tried to read my face, then my intentions, and failing to do both, which was not strange, broke into noisy mirth.

"Oh, ho!" he laughed. "So that is your game, is it! Well, I never! Saracen, Miss Butterworth wants to reform me; wants to make one of her sleek city chaps out of William Knollys. She'll have hard work of it, won't she? But then we're beginning to like her well enough to let her try. Miss Butterworth, I'll go with you to Deacon Spear. I haven't had so much chance for fun in a twelve-month."

I had not expected such success, and was duly thankful. But I made no reference to it aloud. On the contrary, I took his complaisance as a matter of course, and, hiding all token of triumph, suggested quietly that we should make as little ado as possible over our errand, seeing that Mr. Gryce was something of a meddler and *might* take it into his head to interfere. Which suggestion had all the effect I anticipated, for at the double prospect of amusing himself at the Deacon's expense, and of outwitting the man whose business it was to outwit us, he became not only willing but eager to undertake the adventure offered him. So with the understanding that I was to be ready to drive into town as soon as he could hitch up the horse, we parted on the most amicable terms, he proceeding towards the stable and I towards the house, where I hoped to learn something new about Lucetta.

But Loreen, from whom alone I could hope to glean any information, was shut in her room, and did not come out, though I called her more than once, which, if it left my curiosity unsatisfied, at least allowed me to quit the house without awakening hers.

William was waiting for me at the gate when I descended. He was in the best of humors, and helped me into the buggy he had resurrected from some corner of the old stable, with a grimace of suppressed mirth which argued well for the peace of our proposed drive. The horse's head was turned away from the quarter we were bound for, but as we were ostensibly on our way to the village, this showed but common prudence on William's part, and, as such, met with my entire approbation.

Mr. Gryce and his men were hard at work when we passed them. Knowing the detective so well, and rating at its full value his undoubted talent for reading the motives of those about him, I made no attempt at cajolery in the explanation I proffered of our sudden departure, but merely said, in my old, peremptory way, that I found waiting at the gate so tedious that I had accepted William's invitation to drive into town. Which, while it astonished the old gentleman, did not really arouse his suspicions, as a more conciliatory manner and speech might have done. This disposed of, we drove rapidly away.

William's sense of humor once aroused was not easily allayed. He seemed so pleased with his errand that he could talk of nothing else, and turned the subject over and over in his clumsy way, till I began to wonder if he had seen through the object of our proposed visit and was making *me* the butt of his none too brilliant wit.

But no, he was really amused at the part he was called upon to play, and, once convinced of this, I let his humor run on without check till we had re-entered Lost Man's Lane from the other end and were in sight of the low sloping roof of Deacon Spear's old-fashioned farmhouse.

Then I thought it time to speak.

"William," said I, "Deacon Spear is too good a man, and, as I take it, is in possession of too great worldly advantages for you to be at enmity with him. Remember that he is a neighbor, and that you are a landed proprietor in this lane."

"Good for you!" was the elegant reply with which this young boor honored me. "I didn't think you had such an eye for the main chance."

"Deacon Spear is rich, is he not?" I pursued, with an ulterior motive he was far from suspecting.

"Rich? Why, I don't know; that depends upon what you city ladies call rich; *I* shouldn't call him so, but then, as you say, I am a landed proprietor myself."

His laugh was boisterously loud, and as we were then nearly in front of the Deacon's house, it rang in through the open windows, causing such surprise, that more than one head bobbed up from within to see who dared to laugh like that in Lost Man's Lane. While I noted these heads and various other small matters about the house and place, William tied up the horse and held out his hand for me to descend.

"I begin to suspect," he whispered as he helped me out, "why you are so anxious to have me on good terms with the Deacon." At which insinuation I attempted to smile, but only succeeded in forcing a grim twitch or two to my lips, for at that moment and before I could take one step towards the house, a couple of pigeons rose up from behind the house and flew away in a bee-line for Mother Jane's cottage.

"Ha!" thought I; "my instinct has not failed me. Behold the link between this house and the hut in which those tokens of crime were found," and was for the moment so overwhelmed by this confirmation of my secret suspicions, that I quite forgot to advance, and stood stupidly staring after these birds now rapidly disappearing in the distance.

William's voice aroused me.

"Come!" he cried. "Don't be bashful. I don't think much of Deacon Spear myself, but if *you* do—Why, what's the matter now?" he asked, with a startled look at me. I had clutched him by the arm.

"Nothing," I protested, "only—you see that window over there? The one in the gable of the barn, I mean. I thought I saw a hand thrust out—a white hand that dropped crumbs. Have they a child on this place?"

"No," replied William, in an odd voice and with an odd look toward the window I have mentioned. "Did you really see a hand there?"

"I most certainly did," I answered, with an air of indifference I was far from feeling. "Some one is up in the hay-loft; perhaps it is Deacon Spear himself. If so, he will have to come down, for now that we are here, I am determined you shall do your duty."

"Deacon Spear can't climb that hay-loft," was the perplexed answer I received in a hardly intelligible mutter. "I've been there, and I know; only a boy or a very agile young man could crawl along the beams that lead to that window. It is the one hiding-place in this part of the lane; and when I said yesterday that if I were the police and had the same search to make which they have, I knew where I would look, I meant that same little platform up behind the hay, whose only outlook is yonder window. But I forgot that *you* have no suspicions of our good Deacon; that *you* are here on quite a different errand than to search for Silly Rufus. So come along and—"

But I resisted his impelling hand. He was so much in earnest and so evidently under the excitement of what appeared to him a great discovery, that he seemed quite another man. This made my own suspicions less hazardous, and also added to the situation fresh difficulties which could only be met by an appearance on my part of perfect ingenuousness.

Turning back to the buggy as if I had forgotten something, and thus accounting to any one who might be watching us, for the delay we showed in entering the house, I said to William: "You have reasons for thinking this man a villain, or you wouldn't be so ready to suspect him. Now what if I should tell you that I agree with you, and that this is why I have dragged you here this fine morning?"

"I should say you were a deuced smart woman," was his ready answer. "But what can you do here?"

"What have we already done?" I asked. "Discovered that they have someone in hiding in what you call an inaccessible place in the barn. But didn't the police examine the whole place yesterday? They certainly told me they had searched the premises thoroughly."

"Yes," he repeated, with great disdain, "they said and they said; but they didn't climb up to the one hiding-place in sight. That old fellow Gryce declared it wasn't worth their while; that only birds could reach that loophole."

"Oh," I returned, somewhat taken aback; "you called his attention to it, then?"

To which William answered with a vigorous nod and the grumbling words:

"I don't believe in the police. I think they're often in league with the very rogues they—"

But here the necessity of approaching the house became too apparent for further delay. Deacon Spear had shown himself at the front door, and the sight of his astonished face twisted into a grimace of doubtful welcome drove every other thought away than how we were to acquit ourselves in the coming interview. Seeing that William was more or less nonplussed by the situation, I caught him by the arm, and whispering, "Let us keep to our first programme," led him up the walk with much the air of a triumphant captain bringing in a recalcitrant prisoner.

My introduction under these circumstances can be imagined by those who have followed William's awkward ways. But the Deacon, who was probably the most surprised, if not the most disconcerted member of the group, possessed a natural fund of conceit and self-complacency that prevented any outward manifestation of his feelings, though I could not help detecting a carefully suppressed antagonism in his eye when he allowed it to fall upon William, which warned me to exercise my full arts in the manipulation of the matter before me. I accordingly spoke first and with all the prim courtesy such a man might naturally expect from an intruder of my sex and appearance.

"Deacon Spear," said I, as soon as we were seated in his stiff old-fashioned parlor, "you are astonished to see us here, no doubt, especially after the display of animosity shown towards you yesterday by this graceless young friend of mine. But it is on account of this unfortunate occurrence that we are here. After a little reflection and a few hints, I may add, from one who has seen more of life than himself, William felt that he had cause to be ashamed of himself for his show of sport in yesterday's proceedings, and accordingly he has come in my company to tender his apologies and entreat your forbearance. Am I not right, William?"

The fellow is a clown under all and every circumstance, and serious as our real purpose was, and dreadful as was the suspicion he professed to cherish against the suave and seemingly respectable member of the community we were addressing, he could not help laughing, as he blunderingly replied:

"That you are, Miss Butterworth! She's always right, Deacon. I did act like a fool yesterday." And seeming to think that, with this one sentence he had played his part out to perfection, he jumped up and strolled out of the house, almost pushing down as he did so the two daughters of the house, who had crept into the hall from the sitting-room to listen.

"Well, well!" exclaimed the Deacon, "you have done wonders, Miss Butterworth, to bring him to even so small an acknowledgment as that! He's a vicious one, is William Knollys, and if *I* were not such a lover of peace and concord, he should not long be the only aggressive one. But *I* have no taste for strife, and so you may both regard his apology as accepted. But why do you rise, madam? Sit down, I pray, and let me do the honors. Martha! Jemima!"

But I would not allow him to summon his daughters. The man inspired me with too much dislike, if not fear; besides, I was anxious about William. What was he doing, and of what blunder might he not be guilty without my judicious guidance?

"I am obliged to you," I returned; "but I cannot wait to meet your daughters now. Another time, Deacon. There is important business going on at the other end of the lane, and William's presence there may be required."

"Ah," he observed, following me to the door, "they are digging up Mother Jane's garden."

I nodded, restraining myself with difficulty.

"Fool's work!" he muttered. Then with a curious look which made me instinctively draw back, he added, "These things must inconvenience you, madam. I wish you had made your visit to the lane in happier times."

There was a smirk on his face which made him positively repellent. I could scarcely bow my acknowledgments, his look and attitude made the interview so obnoxious. Looking about for William, I stepped down from the stoop. The Deacon followed me.

"Where is William?" I asked.

The Deacon ran his eye over the place, and suddenly frowned with ill-concealed vexation.

"The scapegrace!" he murmured. "What business has he in my barn?"

I immediately forced a smile which, in days long past (I've almost forgotten them now), used to do some execution.

"Oh, he's a boy!" I exclaimed. "Do not mind his pranks, I pray. What a comfortable place you have here!"

Instantly a change passed over the Deacon, and he turned to me with an air of great interest, broken now and then by an uneasy glance behind him at the barn.

"I am glad you like the place," he insinuated, keeping close at my side as I stepped somewhat briskly down the walk. "It is a nice place, worthy of the commendation of so competent a judge as yourself." (It was a barren, hard-worked farm, without one attractive feature.) "I have lived on it now forty years, thirty-two of them with my beloved wife Caroline, and two—" Here he stopped and wiped a tear from the dryest eye I ever saw. "Miss Butterworth, I am a widower."

I hastened my steps. I here duly and with the strictest regard for the truth aver, that I decidedly hastened my steps at this very unnecessary announcement. But he, with another covert glance behind him towards the barn, from which, to my surprise and increasing anxiety, William had not yet emerged, kept well up to me, and only paused when I paused at the side of the road near the buggy.

"Miss Butterworth," he began, undeterred by the air of dignity I assumed, "I have been thinking that your visit here is a rebuke to my unneighborliness. But the business which has occupied the lane these last few days has put us all into such a state of unpleasantness that it was useless to attempt sociability."

His voice was so smooth, his eyes so small and twinkling, that if I could have thought of anything except William's possible discoveries in the barn, I should have taken delight in measuring my wits against his egotism.

But as it was, I said nothing, possibly because I only half heard what he was saying.

"I am no lady's man,"—these were the next words I heard—"but then I judge you're not anxious for flattery, but prefer the square thing uttered by a square man without delay or circumlocution. Madam, I am fifty-three, and I have been a widower two years. I am not fitted for a solitary life, and I am fitted for the companionship of an affectionate wife who will keep my hearth clean and my affections in good working order. Will you be that wife? You see my home,"—here his eye stole behind him with that uneasy look towards the barn which William's presence in it certainly warranted—"a home which I can offer you unencumbered, if you—"

"Desire to live in Lost Man's Lane," I put in, subduing both my surprise and my disgust at this preposterous proposal, in order to throw all the sarcasm of which I was capable into this single sentence.

"Oh!" he exclaimed, "you don't like the neighborhood. Well, we could go elsewhere. I am not set against the city myself—"

Astounded at his presumption, regarding him as a possible criminal, who was endeavoring to beguile me for purposes of his own, I could no longer repress either my indignation or the wrath with which such impromptu addresses naturally inspired me. Cutting him short with a gesture which made him open his small eyes, I exclaimed in continuation of his remark:

"Nor, as I take it, are you set against the comfortable little income somebody has told you I possessed. I see your disinterestedness, Deacon, but I should be sorry to profit by it. Why, man, I never spoke to you before in my life, and do you think—"

"Oh!" he suavely insinuated, with a suppressed chuckle which even his increasing uneasiness as to William could not altogether repress, "I see you are *not* above the flattery that pleases other women. Well, madam, I know a tremendous fine woman when I see her, and from the moment I saw you riding by the other day, I made up my mind I would have you for the second Mrs. Spear, if persistence and a proper advocacy of my cause could accomplish it. Madam, I was going to visit you with this proposal tonight, but seeing you here, the temptation was too great for my discretion, and so I have addressed you on the spot. But you need not answer me at once. I don't need to know any more about *you* than what I can take in with my two eyes, but if you would like a little more acquaintance with *me*, why I can wait a couple of weeks till we've rubbed the edges off our strangeness, when—"

"When you think I will be so charmed with Deacon Spear that I will be ready to settle down with him in Lost Man's Lane, or if that will not do, carry him off to Gramercy Park, where he will be the admiration of all New York and Brooklyn to boot. Why, man, if I was so easily satisfied as that, I would not be in a position today for you to honor me with this proposal. I am not easy to suit, so I advise you to turn your attention to someone much more anxious to be married than I am. But"—and here I allowed some of my real feelings to appear—"if you value your own reputation or the happiness of the lady you propose to inveigle into an union with you, do not venture too far in the matrimonial way till the mystery is dispelled which shrouds Lost Man's Lane in horror. If you were an honest man you would ask no one to share your fortunes whilst the least doubt rests upon your reputation."

"*My* reputation?" He had started very visibly at these words. "Madam, be careful. I admire you, but—"

"No offence," said I. "For a stranger I have been, perhaps, unduly frank. I only mean that any one who lives in this lane must feel himself more or less enveloped by the shadow which rests upon it. When that is lifted, each and every one of you will feel himself a man again. From indications to be seen in the lane today, that time may not be far distant. Mother Jane is a likely source for the mysteries that agitate us. She knows just enough to have no proper idea of the value of a human life."

The Deacon's retort was instantaneous. "Madam," said he, with a snap of his fingers, "I have not that much interest in what is going on down there. If men have been killed in this lane (which I do not believe), old Mother Jane has had no hand in it. My opinion is—and you may value it or not, just as you please—that what the people hereabout call crimes are so many coincidences, which some day or other will receive their due explanation. Every one who has disappeared in this vicinity has disappeared naturally. No one has been killed. That is my theory, and you will find it correct. On this point I have expended more than a little thought."

I was irate. I was also dumfounded at his audacity. Did he think I was the woman to be deceived by any such balderdash as that? But I shut my lips tightly lest I should say something, and he, not finding this agreeable, being no conversationalist himself, drew himself up with a pompously expressed hope that he would see me again after his reputation was cleared, when his attention as well as my own was diverted by seeing William's slouching figure appear in the barn door and make slowly towards us.

Instantly the Deacon forgot me in his interest in William's approach, which was so slow as to be tantalizing to us both.

When he was within speaking distance, Deacon Spear started towards him.

"Well!" he cried; "one would think you had gone back a dozen or so years and were again robbing your neighbor's hen-roosts. Been in the hay, eh?" he added, leaning forward and plucking a wisp or two from my companion's clothes. "Well, what did you find there?"

In trembling fear for what the lout might answer, I put my hand on the buggy rail and struggled anxiously to my seat. William stepped forward and loosened the horse before speaking. Then with a leer he dived into his pocket, and remarking slowly, "I found *this*," brought to light a small riding-whip which we both recognized as one he often carried. "I flung it up in the hay yesterday in one of my fits of laughing, so just thought I would bring it down today. You know it isn't the first time I've climbed about those rafters, Deacon, as you have been good enough to insinuate."

The Deacon, evidently taken aback, eyed the young fellow with a leer in which I saw something more serious than mere suspicion.

"Was that all?" he began, but evidently thought better than to finish, whilst William, with a nonchalance that surprised me, blunderingly avoided his eye, and, bounding into the buggy beside me, started up the horse and drove slowly off.

"Ta, ta, Deacon," he called back; "if you want to see fun, come up to our end of the lane; there's precious little here." And thus, with a laugh, terminated an interview which, all things considered, was the most exciting as well as the most humiliating I have ever taken part in.

"William," I began, but stopped. The two pigeons whose departure I had watched a little while before were coming back, and, as I spoke, fluttered up to the window before mentioned, where they alighted and began picking up the crumbs which I had seen scattered for them. "See!" I suddenly exclaimed, pointing them out to William. "Was I mistaken when I thought I saw a hand drop crumbs from that window?"

The answer was a very grave one for him.

"No," said he, "for I have seen more than a hand, through the loop-hole I made in the hay. I saw a man's leg stretched out as if he were lying on the floor with his head toward the window. It was but a glimpse I got, but the leg moved as I looked at it, and so I know that someone lies hid in that little nook up under the roof. Now it isn't any one belonging to the lane, for I know where every one of us is or ought to be at this blessed moment; and it isn't a detective, for I heard a sound like heavy sobbing as I crouched there. Then who is it? Silly Rufus, I say; and if that hay was all lifted, we would see sights that would make us ashamed of the apologies we uttered to the old sneak just now."

"I want to get home," said I. "Drive fast! Your sisters ought to know this."

"The girls?" he cried. "Yes, it will be a triumph over them. They never would believe I had an atom of judgment. But we'll show them, if William Knollys is altogether a fool."

We were now near to Mr. Trohm's hospitable gateway. Coming from the excitements of my late interview, it was a relief to perceive the genial owner of this beautiful place wandering among his vines and testing the condition of his fruit by a careful touch here and there. As he heard our wheels he turned, and seeing who we were, threw up his hands in ill-restrained pleasure, and came buoyantly forward. There was nothing to do but to stop, so we stopped.

"Why, William! Why, Miss Butterworth, what a pleasure!" Such was his amiable greeting. "I thought you were all busy at your end of the lane; but I see you have just come from town. Had an errand there, I suppose?"

"Yes," William grumbled, eying the luscious pear Mr. Trohm held in his hand.

The look drew a smile from that gentleman.

"Admiring the first fruits?" he observed. "Well, it is a handsome specimen," he admitted, handing it to me with his own peculiar grace. "I beg you will take it, Miss Butterworth. You look tired; pardon me if I mention it." (He is the only person I know who detects any signs of suffering or fatigue on my part.)

"I am worried by the mysteries of this lane," I ventured to remark. "I hate to see Mother Jane's garden uprooted."

"Ah!" he acquiesced, with much evidence of good feeling, "it is a distressing thing to witness. I wish she might have been spared. William, there are other pears on the tree this came from. Tie up the horse, I pray, and gather a dozen or so of these for your sisters. They will never be in better condition for plucking than they are today."

William, whose mouth and eyes were both watering for a taste of the fine fruit thus offered, moved with alacrity to obey this invitation, while I, more startled than pleased—or, rather, as much startled as pleased—by the prospect of a momentary *tête-à-tête* with our agreeable neighbor, sat uneasily eying the luscious fruit in my hand, and wishing I was ten years younger, that the blush I felt slowly stealing up my cheek might seem more appropriate to the occasion.

But Mr. Trohm appeared not to share my wish. He was evidently so satisfied with me as I was, that he found it difficult to speak at first, and when he did—But tut! tut! you have no desire to hear any such confidences as these, I am sure. A middle-aged gentleman's expressions of admiration for a middle-aged lady may savor of romance to her, but hardly to the rest of the world, so I will pass this conversation by, with the single admission that it ended in a question to which I felt obliged to return a reluctant *No*.

Mr. Trohm was just recovering from the disappointment of this, when William sauntered back with his hands and pockets full.

"Ah!" that graceless scamp chuckled, with a suspicious look at our downcast faces, "been improving the opportunity, eh?"

Mr. Trohm, who had fallen back against his old well-curb, surveyed his young neighbor for the first time with a look of anger. But it vanished almost as quickly as it appeared, and he contented himself with a low bow, in which I read real grief.

This was too much for me, and I was about to open my lips with a kind phrase or two, when a flutter took place over our heads, and the two pigeons whose flight I had watched more than once during the last hour, flew down and settled upon Mr. Trohm's arm and shoulders.

"Oh!" I exclaimed, with a sudden shrinking that I hardly understood myself. And though I covered up the exclamation with as brisk a good-by as my inward perturbation would allow, that sight and the involuntary ejaculation I had uttered, were all I saw or heard during our hasty drive homeward.

CHAPTER XXXVII

I Astonish Mr. Gryce and He Astonishes Me

But as we approached the group of curious people which now filled up the whole highway in front of Mother Jane's cottage, I broke from the nightmare into which this last discovery had thrown me, and, turning to William, said with a resolute air:

"You and your sisters are not of one mind regarding these disappearances. You ascribe them to Deacon Spear, but they—whom do they ascribe them to?"

"I shouldn't think it would take a woman of your wit to answer that question."

The rebuke was deserved. I had wit, but I had refused to exercise it; my blind partiality for a man of pleasing exterior and magnetic address had prevented the cool play of my usual judgment, due to the occasion and the trust which had been imposed in me by Mr. Gryce. Resolved that this should end, no matter at what cost to my feelings, I quietly said:

"You allude to Mr. Trohm."

"That is the name," he carelessly assented. "Girls, you know, let their prejudices run away with them. An old grudge—"

"Yes," I tentatively put in; "he persecuted your mother, and so they think him capable of any wickedness."

The growl which William gave was not one of dissent.

"But I don't care what they think," said he, looking down at the heap of fruit which lay between us. "I'm Trohm's friend, and don't believe one word they choose to insinuate against him. What if he didn't like what my mother did! We didn't like it either, and—"

"William," I calmly remarked, "if your sisters knew that Silly Rufus had been found in Deacon Spear's barn they would no longer do Mr. Trohm this injustice."

"No; that would settle them; that would give me a triumph which would last long after this matter was out of the way."

"Very well, then," said I, "I am going to bring about this triumph. I am going to tell Mr. Gryce at once what we have discovered in Deacon Spear's barn."

And without waiting for his ah, yes, or no, I jumped from the buggy and made my way to the detective's side.

His welcome was somewhat unexpected. "Ah, fresh news!" he exclaimed. "I see it in your eye. What have you chanced upon, madam, in your disinterested drive into town?"

I thought I had eliminated all expression from my face, and that my words would bring a certain surprise with them. But it is useless to try to surprise Mr. Gryce.

"You read me like a book," said I; "I have something to add to the situation. Mr. Gryce, I have just come from the other end of the lane, where I found a clue which may shorten the suspense of this weary day, and possibly save Lucetta from the painful task she has undertaken in our interests. Mr. Chittenden's ring—"

I paused for the exclamation of encouragement he is accustomed to give on such occasions, and while I paused, prepared for my accustomed triumph. He did not fail me in the exclamation, nor did I miss my expected triumph.

"Was not found by Mother Jane, or even brought to her in any ordinary way or by any ordinary messenger. It came to her on a pigeon's neck, the pigeon you will find lying dead among the bushes in the Knollys yard."

He was amazed. He controlled himself, but he was very visibly amazed. His exclamations proved it.

"Madam! Miss Butterworth! This ring—Mr. Chittenden's ring, whose presence in her hut we thought an evidence of guilt, was brought to her by one of her pigeons?"

"So she told me. I aroused her fury by showing her the empty husk in which it had been concealed. In her rage at its loss, she revealed the fact I have just mentioned. It is a curious one, sir, and one I am a little proud to have discovered."

"Curious? It is more than curious; it is bizarre, and will rank, I am safe in prophesying, as one of the most remarkable facts that have ever adorned the annals of the police. Madam, when I say I envy you the honor of its discovery, you will appreciate my estimate of it—and you. But when did you find this out, and what explanation are you able to give of the presence of this ring on a pigeon's neck?"

"Sir, to your first question I need only reply that I was here two hours or so ago, and to the second that everything points to the fact that the ring was attached to the bird by the victim himself, as an appeal for succor to whoever might be fortunate enough to find it. Unhappily it fell into the wrong hands. That is the ill-luck which often befalls prisoners."

"Prisoners?"

"Yes. Cannot you imagine a person shut up in an inaccessible place making some such attempt to communicate with his fellow-creatures?"

"But what inaccessible place have we in—"

"Wait," said I. "You have been in Deacon Spear's barn."

"Certainly, many times." But the answer, glib as it was, showed shock. I began to gather courage.

"Well," said I, "there is a hiding-place in that barn which I dare declare you have not penetrated."

"Do you think so, madam?"

"A little loft way up under the eaves, which can only be reached by clambering over the rafters. Didn't Deacon Spear tell you there was such a place?"

"No, but—"

"William, then?" I inexorably pursued. "He says he pointed such a spot out to you, and that you pooh-poohed at it as inaccessible and not worth the searching."

"William is a—Madam, I beg your pardon, but William has just wit enough to make trouble."

"But there is such a place there," I urged; "and, what is more, there is someone hidden in it now. I saw him myself."

"*You* saw him?"

"Saw a part of him; in short, saw his hand. He was engaged in scattering crumbs for the pigeons."

"That does not look like starvation," smiled Mr. Gryce, with the first hint of sarcasm he had allowed himself to make use of in this interview.

"No," said I; "but the time may not have come to inflict this penalty on Silly Rufus. He has been there but a few days, and—well, what have

I said now?"

"Nothing, ma'am, nothing. But what made you think the hand you saw belonged to Silly Rufus?"

"Because he was the last person to disappear from this lane. The last—what am I saying? He wasn't the last. Lucetta's lover was the last. Mr. Gryce, could that hand have belonged to Mr. Ostrander?"

I was intensely excited; so much so that Mr. Gryce made me a warning gesture.

"Hush!" he whispered; "you are attracting attention. That hand *was* the hand of Mr. Ostrander; and the reason why I did not accept William Knollys' suggestion to search the Deacon's barn-loft was because I knew it had been chosen as a place of refuge by this missing lover of Lucetta."

CHAPTER XXXVIII

A Few Words

Never have keener or more conflicting emotions been awakened in my breast than by these simple words. But alive to the necessity of hiding my feelings from those about me, I gave no token of my surprise, but rather turned a stonier face than common upon the man who had caused it.

"Refuge?" I repeated. "He is there, then, of his own free will—or yours?" I sarcastically added, not being able to quite keep down this reproach as I remembered the deception practised upon Lucetta.

"Mr. Ostrander, madam, has been spending the week with Deacon Spear—they are old friends, you know. That he should spend it quietly and, to a degree, in hiding, was as much his plan as mine. For while he found it impossible to leave Lucetta in the doubtful position in which she and her family at present stand, he did not wish to aggravate her misery by the thought that he was thus jeopardizing the position on which all his hopes of future advancement depended. He preferred to watch and wait in secret, seeing which, I did what I could to further his wishes. His usual lodging was with the family, but when the search was instituted, I suggested that he should remove himself to that eyrie back of the hay where you were sharp enough to detect him today."

"Don't attempt any of your flatteries upon me," I protested. "They will not make me forget that I have not been treated fairly. And Lucetta—oh! may I not tell Lucetta—"

"And spoil our entire prospect of solving this mystery? No, madam, you may not tell Lucetta. When Fate has put such a card into our hands as I played with that telegram today, we would be flying in the face of Providence not to profit by it. Lucetta's despair makes her bold; upon that boldness we depend to discover and bring to justice a great criminal."

I felt myself turn pale; for that very reason, perhaps, I assumed a still sterner air, and composedly said:

"If Mr. Ostrander is in hiding at the Deacon's, and he and his host are both in your confidence, then the only man whom *you* can designate in your thoughts by this dreadful title must be Mr. Trohm."

I had perhaps hoped he would recoil at this or give some other evidence of his amazement at an assumption which to me seemed preposterous. But he did not, and I saw, with what feelings may be imagined, that this conclusion, which was half bravado with me, had been accepted by him long enough for no emotion to follow its utterance.

"Oh!" I exclaimed, "how can you reconcile such a suspicion with the attitude you have always preserved towards Mr. Trohm?"

"Madam," said he, "do not criticise my attitude without taking into account existing appearances. They are undoubtedly in Mr. Trohm's favor."

"I am glad to hear you say so," said I, "I am glad to hear you say so. Why, it was in response to his appeal that you came to X. at all."

Mr. Gryce's smile conveyed a reproach which I could not but acknowledge I amply merited. Had he spent evening after evening at my house, entertaining me with tales of the devices and the many inconsistencies of criminals, to be met now by such a puerile disclaimer as this? But beyond that smile he said nothing; on the contrary, he continued as if I had not spoken at all.

"But appearances," he declared, "will not stand before the insight of a girl like Lucetta. She has marked the man as guilty, and we will give her the opportunity of proving the correctness of her instinct."

"But Mr. Trohm's house has been searched, and you have found nothing—nothing," I argued somewhat feebly.

"That is the reason we find ourselves forced to yield our judgment to Lucetta's intuitions," was his quick reply. And smiling upon me with his blandest air, he obligingly added: "Miss Butterworth is a woman of too much character not to abide the event with all her accustomed composure." And with this final suggestion, I was as yet too crushed to resent, he dismissed me to an afternoon of unparalleled suspense and many contradictory emotions.

CHAPTER XXXIX

Under a Crimson Sky

When, in the course of events, the current of my thoughts receive a decided check and I find myself forced to change former conclusions or habituate myself to new ideas and a fresh standpoint, I do it, as I do everything else, with determination and a total disregard of my own previous predilections. Before the afternoon was well over I was ready for any revelations which might follow Lucetta's contemplated action, merely reserving a vague hope that my judgment would yet be found superior to her instinct.

At five o'clock the diggers began to go home. Nothing had been found under the soil of Mother Jane's garden, and the excitement of search which had animated them early in the day had given place to a dull resentment mainly directed towards the Knollys family, if one could judge of these men's feelings by the heavy scowls and significant gestures with which they passed our broken-down gateway.

By six the last man had filed by, leaving Mr. Gryce free for the work which lay before him.

I had retired long before this to my room, where I awaited the hour set by Lucetta with a feverish impatience quite new to me. As none of us could eat, the supper table had not been laid, and though I had no means of knowing what was in store for us, the sombre silence and oppression under which the whole house lay seemed a portent that was by no means encouraging.

Suddenly I heard a knock at my door. Rising hastily, I opened it. Loreen stood before me, with parted lips and terror in all her looks.

"Come!" she cried. "Come and see what I have found in Lucetta's room."

"Then she's gone?" I cried.

"Yes, she's gone, but come and see what she has left behind her."

Hastening after Loreen, who was by this time half-way down the hall, I soon found myself on the threshold of the room I knew to be Lucetta's.

"She made me promise," cried Loreen, halting to look back at me, "that I would let her go alone, and that I would not enter the highway till an hour after her departure. But with these evidences of the extent of her dread before us, how can we stay in this house?" And dragging me to a table, she showed me lying on its top a folded paper and two letters. The folded paper was Lucetta's Will, and the letters were directed severally to Loreen and to myself with the injunction that they were not to be read till she had been gone six hours.

"She has prepared herself for death!" I exclaimed, shocked to my heart's core, but determinedly hiding it. "But you need not fear any such event. Is she not accompanied by Mr. Gryce?"

"I do not know; I do not think so. How could she accomplish her task if not alone? Miss Butterworth, Miss Butterworth, she has gone to brave Mr. Trohm, our mother's persecutor and our life-long enemy, thinking, hoping, believing that in so doing she will rouse his criminal instincts, if he has them, and so lead to the discovery of his crimes and the means by which he has been enabled to carry them out so long undetected. It is noble, it is heroic, it is martyr-like, but—oh! Miss Butterworth, I have never broken a promise to any one before in all my life, but I am going to break the one I made her. Come, let us fly after her! She has her lover's memory, but I have nothing in all the world but her."

I immediately turned and hastened down the stairs in a state of humiliation which should have made ample amends for any show of arrogance I may have indulged in in my more fortunate moments.

Loreen followed me, and when we were in the lower hall she gave me a look and said:

"My promise was not to enter the highway. Would you be afraid to follow me by another road—a secret road—all overgrown with thistles and blackberry bushes which have not been trimmed up for years?"

I thought of my thin shoes, my neat silk dress, but only to forget them the next moment.

"I will go anywhere," said I.

But Loreen was already too far in advance of me to answer. She was young and lithe, and had reached the kitchen before I had passed the Flower Parlor. But when we had sped clear of the house I found that my progress bade fair to be as rapid as hers, for her agitation was a hindrance to her, while excitement always brings out my powers and heightens both my wits and my judgment.

Our way lay past the stables, from which I expected every minute to see two or three dogs jump. But William, who had been discreetly sent out of the way early in the afternoon, had taken Saracen with him, and possibly the rest, so our passing by disturbed nothing, not even ourselves. The next moment we were in a field of prickers, through which we both struggled till we came into a sort of swamp. Here was bad going, but we floundered on, edging continually toward a distant fence beyond which rose the symmetrical lines of an orchard—Mr. Trohm's orchard, in which those pleasant fruits grew which—Bah! should I ever be able to get the taste of them out of my mouth!

At a tiny gateway covered with vines, Loreen stopped.

"I do not believe this has been opened for years, but it must be opened now." And, throwing her whole weight against it, she burst it through, and bidding me pass, hastened after me over the trailing branches and made, without a word, for the winding path we now saw clearly defined on the edge of the orchard before us.

"Oh!" exclaimed Loreen, stopping one moment to catch her breath, "I do not know what I fear or to what our steps will bring us. I only know that I must hunt for Lucetta till I find her. If there is danger where she is,

I must share it. You can rest here or come farther on."

I went farther on.

Suddenly we both started; a man had sprung up from behind the hedgerow that ran parallel with the fence that surrounded Mr. Trohm's place.

"Silence!" he whispered, putting his finger on his lips. "If you are looking for Miss Knollys," he added, seeing us both pause aghast, "she is on the lawn beyond, talking to Mr. Trohm. If you will step here, you can see her. She is in no kind of danger, but if she were, Mr. Gryce is in the first row of trees to the back there, and a call from me—"

That made me remember my whistle. It was still round my neck, but my hand, which had instinctively gone to it, fell again in extraordinary emotion as I realized the situation and compared it with that of the morning when, blinded by egotism and foolish prejudice in favor of this man, I ate of his fruit and hearkened to his outrageous addresses.

"Come!" beckoned Loreen, happily too absorbed in her own emotions to notice mine. "Let us get nearer. If Mr. Trohm is the wicked man we fear, there is no telling what the means are which he uses to get rid of his victims. There was nothing to be found in his house, but who knows where the danger may lurk, and that it may not be near her now? It was evidently to dare it she came, to offer herself as a martyr, that we might know—"

"Hush!" I whispered, controlling my own fears roused against my will by this display of terror in this usually calmest of natures. "No danger can menace her where they stand, unless he is a common assassin and carries a pistol—"

"No pistol," murmured the man, who had crept again near us. "Pistols make a noise. He will not use a pistol."

"Good God!" I whispered. "*You* do not share her sister's fears that it is in the heart of this man to kill Lucetta?"

"Five strong men have disappeared hereabout," said the fellow, never moving his eye from the couple before us. "Why not one weak girl?"

With a cry Loreen started forward. "Run!" she whispered. "Run!"

But as this word left her lips, a slight movement took place in the belt of trees where we had been told Mr. Gryce lay in hiding, and we could see him issue for a moment into sight with his finger like that of his man laid warningly on his lips. Loreen trembled and drew back, seeing which, the man beside us pointed to the hedge and whispered softly:

"There is just room between it and the fence for a person to pass sideways. If you and this lady want to get nearer to Miss Knollys, you might take that road. But Mr. Gryce will expect you to be very quiet. The young lady expressly said, before she came into this place, that she could do nothing if for any reason Mr. Trohm should suspect they were not alone."

"We will be quiet," I assured him, anxious to hide my face, which I felt twitch at every mention of Mr. Trohm's name. Loreen was already behind the hedge.

The evening was one of those which are made for peace. The sun, which had set in crimson, had left a glow on the branches of the forest which had not yet faded into the gray of twilight. The lawn, around which we were skirting, had not lost the mellow brilliancy which made it sparkle, nor had the cluster of varied-hued hollyhocks which set their gorgeousness against the neat yellow of the peaceful doorposts, shown any dimness in their glory, which was on a par with that of the setting sun. But though I saw all this, it no longer appeared to me desirable. Lucetta and Lucetta's fate, the mystery and the impossibility of its being explained out here in the midst of turf and blossoms, filled all my thoughts, and made me forget my own secret cause for shame and humiliation.

Loreen, who had wormed her way along till she crouched nearly opposite to the place where her sister stood, plucked me by the gown as I approached her, and, pointing to the hedge, which pressed up so close it nearly touched our faces, seemed to bid me look through. Searching for a spot where there was a small opening, I put my eye to this and immediately drew back.

"They are moving nearer the gate," I signalled to Loreen, at which she crept along a few paces, but with a stealth so great that, alert as I was, I could not hear a twig snap. I endeavored to imitate her, but not with as much success as I could wish. The sense of horror which had all at once settled upon me, the supernatural dread of something which I could not see, but which I felt, had seized me for the first time and made the ruddy sky and the broad stretch of velvet turf with the shadows playing over it of swaying tree-tops and clustered oleanders, more thrilling and awesome to me than the dim halls of the haunted house of the Knollys family in that midnight hour when I saw a body carried out for burial amid trouble and hush and a mystery so great it would have daunted most spirits for the remainder of their lives.

The very sweetness of the scene made its horror. Never have I had such sensations, never have I felt so deeply the power of the unseen, yet it seemed so impossible that anything could happen here, anything which would explain the total disappearance of several persons at different times, without a trace of their fate being left to the eye, that I could but liken my state to that of nightmare, where visions take the place of realities and often overwhelm them.

I had pressed too close against the hedge as I struggled with these feelings, and the sound I made struck me as distinct, if not alarming; but the tree-tops were rustling overhead, and, while Lucetta might have heard the hedge-branches crack, her companion gave no evidence of doing so. We could distinguish what they were saying now, and realizing this, we stopped moving and gave our whole attention to listening. Mr. Trohm was speaking. I could hardly believe it was his voice, it had so changed in tone, nor could I perceive in his features, distorted as they now were by every evil passion, the once quiet and dignified countenance which had so lately imposed upon me.

"Lucetta, my little Lucetta," he was saying, "so she has come to see me, come to taunt me with the loss of her lover, whom she says I have robbed her of almost before her eyes! I rob her! How can I rob her or any one of a man with a voice and arm of his own stronger than mine? Am I a wizard to dissipate his body in vapor? Yet can you find it in my house or on my lawn? You are a fool, Lucetta; so are all these men about here fools! It is in your house—"

"Hush!" she cried, her slight figure rising till we forgot it was the feeble Lucetta we were gazing at. "No more accusations directed against us. It is you who must expect them now. Mr. Trohm, your evil practices are discovered. Tomorrow you will have the police here in earnest. They did but play with you when they were here before."

"You child!" he gasped, striving, however, to restrain all evidences of shock and terror. "Why, who was it called in the police and set them working in Lost Man's Lane? Was it not I—"

"Yes, that they might not suspect you, and perhaps that they might suspect us. But it was useless, Obadiah Trohm. Althea Knollys' children have been long-suffering, but the limit of their forbearance has been reached. When you laid your hand upon my lover, you roused a spirit in me that nothing but your own destruction can satisfy. Where is he, Mr. Trohm? and where is Silly Rufus and all the rest who have vanished between Deacon Spear's house and the little home of the cripples on the highroad? They have asked me this question, but if any one in Lost Man's Lane can answer, it is you, persecutor of my mother, and traducer of ourselves, whom I here denounce in face of these skies where God reigns and this earth where man lives to harry and condemn."

And then I saw that the instinct of this girl had accomplished what our united acumen and skill had failed to do. The old man—indeed he seemed an old man now—cringed, and the wrinkles came out in his face till he was demoniacally ugly.

"You viper!" he shrieked. "How dare you accuse me of crime—you whose mother would have died in jail but for my forbearance? Have you ever seen me set my foot upon a worm? Look at my fruit and flowers, look at my home, without a spot or blemish to mar its neatness and propriety. Can a man who loves these things stomach the destruction of a man, much less of a silly, yawping boy? Lucetta, you are mad!"

"Mad or sane, my accusation will have its results, Mr. Trohm. I believe too deeply in your guilt not to make others do so."

"Ah," said he, "then you have not done so yet? You believe this and that, but you have not told any one what your suspicions are?"

"No," she calmly returned, though her face blanched to the colorlessness of wax, "I have not said what I think of you yet."

Oh, the cunning that crept into his face!

"She has not said. Oh, the little Lucetta, the wise, the careful little Lucetta!"

"But I will," she cried, meeting his eye with the courage and constancy of a martyr, "though I bring destruction upon myself. I will denounce you and do it before the night has settled down upon us. I have a lover to avenge, a brother to defend. Besides, the earth should be rid of such a monster as you."

"Such a monster as I? Well, my pretty one,"—his voice grown suddenly wheedling, his face a study of mingled passions—"we will see about that. Come just a step nearer, Lucetta. I want to see if you are really the little girl I used to dandle on my knee."

They were now near the gateway. They had been moving all this time. His hand was on the curb of the old well. His face, so turned that it caught the full glare of the setting sun, leaned toward the girl, exerting a fascinating influence upon her. She took the step he asked, and before we could shriek out "Beware!" we saw him bend forward with a sudden quick motion and then start upright again, while her form, which but an instant before had stood there in all its frail and inspired beauty, tottered as if the ground were bending under it, and in another moment disappeared from our appalled sight, swallowed in some dreadful cavern that for an instant yawned in the smoothly cut lawn before us, and then vanished again from sight as if it had never been.

A shriek from my whistle mingled with a simultaneous cry of agony from Loreen. We heard Mr. Gryce rush from behind us, but we ourselves found it impossible to stir, paralyzed as we were by the sight of the old man's demoniacal delight. He was leaping to and fro over the turf, holding up his fingers in the red sunset glare.

"Six!" he shrieked. "Six! and room for two more! Oh, it's a merry life I lead! Flowers and fruit and love-making" (oh, how I cringed at that!), "and now and then a little spice like this! But where is my pretty Lucetta? Surely she was here a moment ago. How could she have vanished, then, so quickly? I do not see her form amid the trees, there is no trace of her presence upon the lawn, and if they search the house from top to bottom and from bottom to top they will find nothing of her—no, not so much as a print of her footstep or the scent of the violets she so often wears tucked into her hair."

These last words, uttered in a different voice from the rest, gave the clue to the whole situation. We saw, even while we all bounded forward to the rescue of the devoted maiden, that he was one of those maniacs who have perfect control over themselves and pass for very decent sort of men except in the moment of triumph; and, noting his look of sinister delight, perceived that half his pleasure and almost his sole reward for the horrible crimes he had perpetrated, was in the mystery surrounding his victims and the entire immunity from suspicion which up to this time he had enjoyed.

Meantime Mr. Gryce had covered the wretch with his pistol, and his man, who succeeded in reaching the place even sooner than ourselves, hampered as we were by the almost impenetrable hedge behind which we had crouched, tried to lift the grass-covered lid we could faintly discern there. But this was impossible until I, with almost superhuman self-possession, considering the imperative nature of the emergency, found the spring hidden in the well-curb which worked the deadly mechanism. A yell from the writhing creature cowering under the detective's pistol guided me unconsciously in its action, and in another moment we saw the fatal lid tip and disclose what appeared to be the remains of a second well, long ago dried up and abandoned for the other.

The rescue of Lucetta followed. As she had fainted in falling she had not suffered much, and soon we had the supreme delight of seeing her eyes unclose.

"Ah," she murmured, in a voice whose echo pierced to every heart save that of the guilty wretch now lying handcuffed on the sward, "I thought I saw Albert! He was not dead, and I—"

But here Mr. Gryce, with an air at once contrite and yet strangely triumphant, interposed his benevolent face between hers and her weeping sister's and whispered something in her ear which turned her pallid cheek to a glowing scarlet. Rising up, she threw her arms around his neck and let him lift her. As he carried her—where was his rheumatism now?—out of those baleful grounds and away from the reach of the maniac's mingled laughs and cries, her face was peace itself. But his—well, his was a study.

CHAPTER XL

Explanations

The hour we all spent together late that night in the old house was unlike any hour which that place had seen for years. Mr. Ostrander, Lucetta, Loreen, William, Mr. Gryce, and myself, all were there, and as an especial grace, Saracen was allowed to enter, that there might not be a cloud upon a single face there assembled. Though it is a small matter, I will add that this dog persisted in lying down by my side, not yielding even to the wiles of his master, whose amusement over this fact kept him good-natured to the last adieu.

There were too few candles in the house to make it bright, but Lucetta's unearthly beauty, the peace in Loreen's soft eyes, made us forget the sombreness of our surroundings and the meagreness of the entertainment Hannah attempted to offer us. It was the promise of coming joy, and when, our two guests departed, I bade good-night to the girls in their grim upper hall, it was with feelings which found their best expression in the two letters I hastened to write as soon as I gained the refuge of my own apartment. I will admit you sufficiently into my confidence to let you read those letters. The first of them ran thus:

"Dear Olive:

"To make others happy is the best way to forget our own misfortunes. A sudden wedding is to take place in this house. Order at once for me from the shops you know me to be in the habit of patronizing, a wedding gown of dainty white taffeta [I did this not to recall too painfully to herself the wedding dress I helped her buy, and which was, as you may remember, of creamy satin], with chiffon trimmings, and a wedding veil of tulle. Add to this a dress suitable for ocean travel and a half-dozen costumes adapted to a southern climate. Let everything be suitable for a delicate but spirited girl who has seen trouble, but who is going to be happy now if a little attention and money can make her so. Do not spare expense, yet show no extravagance, for she is a shy bird, easily frightened. The measurements you will find enclosed; also those of another young lady, her sister, who must also be supplied with a white dress, the material of which, however, had better be of crêpe.

"All these things must be here by Wednesday evening, my own best dress included. On Saturday evening you may look for my return. I shall bring the latter young lady with me, so your present loneliness will be forgotten in the pleasure of entertaining an agreeable guest. Faithfully yours,

"Amelia Butterworth."

The second letter was a longer and more important one. It was directed to the president of the company which had proposed to send Mr. Ostrander to South America. In it I related enough of the circumstances which had kept Mr. Ostrander in X. to interest him in the young couple personally, and then I told him that if he would forgive Mr. Ostrander this delay and allow him to sail with his young bride by the next steamer, I myself would undertake to advance whatever sums might have been lost by this change of arrangement.

I did not know then that Mr. Gryce had already made this matter good with this same gentleman.

The next morning we all took a walk in the lane. (I say nothing about the night. If I did not choose to sleep, or if I had any cause not to feel quite as elevated in spirit as the young people about me, there is surely no reason why I should dwell upon it with you or even apologize for a weakness which you will regard, I hope, as an exception setting off my customary strength.)

Now a walk in this lane was an event. To feel at liberty to stroll among its shadows without fear, to know that the danger had been so located that we all felt free to inhale the autumn air and to enjoy the beauties of the place without a thought of peril lurking in its sweetest nooks and most attractive coverts, gave to this short half-hour a distinctive delight aptly expressed by Loreen when she said:

"I never knew the place was so beautiful. Why, I think I can be happy here now." At which Lucetta grew pensive, till I roused her by saying:

"So much for a constitutional, girls. Now we must to work. This house, as you see it now, has to be prepared for a wedding. William, your business will be to see that these grounds are put in as good order as possible in the short time allotted to you. I will bear the expense, and Loreen—"

But William had a word to say for himself.

"Miss Butterworth," said he, "you're a right good sort of woman, as Saracen has found out, and we, too, in these last few plaguy days. But I'm not such a bad lot either, and if I do like my own way, which may not be other people's way, and if I am sometimes short with the girls for some of their d—d nonsense, I have a little decency about me, too, and I promise to fix these grounds, and out of my own money, too. Now that nine tenths of our income does not have to go abroad, we'll have chink enough to let us live in a respectable manner once more in a place where one horse, if he's good enough, will give a fellow a standing and make him the envy of those who, for some other pesky reasons, may think themselves called upon to fight shy of him. I don't begrudge the old place a few dollars, especially as I mean to live and die in it; so look out, you three women folks, and work as lively as you can on the inside of the old rookery, or the slickness of the outside will put you to open shame, and that would never please Loreen, nor, as I take it, Miss Butterworth either."

It was a challenge we were glad to accept, especially as from the number of persons we now saw come flocking into the lane, it was very apparent that we should experience no further difficulty in obtaining any help we might need to carry out our undertakings.

Meantime my thoughts were not altogether concentrated upon these pleasing plans for Lucetta's benefit. There were certain points yet to be made clear in the matter just terminated, and there was a confession for me to make, without which I could not face Mr. Gryce with all that unwavering composure which our peculiar relations seemed to demand.

The explanations came first. They were volunteered by Mr. Gryce, whom I met in the course of the morning at Mother Jane's cottage. That old crone had been perfectly happy all night, sleeping with the coin in her hand and waking to again devour it with her greedy but loving eyes. As I was alternately watching her and Mr. Gryce, who was directing with his hand the movements of the men who had come to smooth down her garden and make it presentable again, the detective spoke:

"I suppose you have found it difficult, in the light of these new discoveries, to explain to yourself how Mother Jane happened to have those trinkets from the peddler's pack, and also how the ring, which you very naturally thought must have been entrusted to the dove by Mr. Chittenden himself, came to be about its neck when it flew home that day of Mr. Chittenden's disappearance. Madam, we think old Mother Jane must have helped herself out of the peddler's pack before it was found in the woods there back of her hut, and of the other matter our explanation is this:

"One day a young man, equipped for travelling, paused for a glass of water at the famous well in Mr. Trohm's garden just as Mother Jane's pigeons were picking up the corn scattered for them by the former, whose tastes are not confined to the cultivation of fruits and flowers, but extend to dumb animals, to whom he is uniformly kind. The young man wore a ring, and, being nervous, was fiddling with it as he talked to the pleasant old gentleman who was lowering the bucket for him. As he fiddled with it, the earth fell from under him, and as the daylight vanished above his head, the ring flew from his up-thrown hand, and lay, the only token of his now blotted-out existence, upon the emerald sward he had but a moment before pressed with his unsuspicious feet. It burned—this ruby burned like a drop of blood in the grass, when that demon came again to his senses, and being a tell-tale evidence of crime in the eyes of one who had allowed nothing to ever speak against him in these matters, he stared at it as at a deadly thing directed against himself and to be got rid of at once and by means which by no possibility could recoil back upon himself as its author.

"The pigeons stalking near offered to his abnormally acute understanding the only solution which would leave him absolutely devoid of fear. He might have swung open the lid of the well once more and flung it after its owner, but this meant an aftermath of experience from which he shrank, his delight being in the thought that the victims he saw vanish before his eyes were so many encumbrances wiped off the face of the earth by a sweep of the hand. To see or hear them again would be destructive of this notion. He preferred the subtler way and to take advantage of old Mother Jane's characteristics, so he caught one of the pigeons (he has always been able to lure birds into his hands), and tying the ring around the neck of the bird with a blade of grass plucked up from the highway, he let it fly, and so was rid of the bauble which to Mother Jane's eyes, of course, was a direct gift from the heavens through which the bird had flown before lighting on her doorstep."

"Wonderful!" I exclaimed, almost overwhelmed with humiliation, but preserving a brave front. "What invention and what audacity!—the invention and the audacity of a man totally irresponsible for his deeds, was it not?" I asked. "There is no doubt, is there, about his being an absolute maniac?"

"No, madam." What a relief I felt at that word! "Since we entrapped him yesterday and he found himself fully discovered, he has lost all grip upon himself and fills the room we put him in with the unmistakable ravings of a madman. It was through these I learned the facts I have just mentioned."

I drew a deep breath. We were standing in the sight of several men, and their presence there seemed intolerable. Unconsciously I began to walk away. Unconsciously Mr. Gryce followed me. At the end of several paces we both stopped. We were no longer visible to the crowd, and I felt I could speak the words I had been burning to say ever since I saw the true nature of Mr. Trohm's character exposed.

"Mr. Gryce," said I, flushing scarlet—which I here solemnly declare is something which has not happened to me before in years, and if I can help it shall never happen to me again—"I am interested in what you say, because yesterday, at his own gateway, Mr. Trohm proposed to me, and—"

"You did not accept him?"

"No. What do you think I am made of, Mr. Gryce? I did not accept him, but I made the refusal a gentle one, and—this is not easy work, Mr. Gryce," I interrupted myself to say with suitable grimness—"the same thing took place between me and Deacon Spear, and to him I gave a response such as I thought his presumption warranted. The discrimination does not argue well for my astuteness, Mr. Gryce. You see, I crave no credit that I do not deserve. Perhaps you cannot understand that, but it is a part of my nature."

"Madam," said he, and I must own I thought his conduct perfect, "had I not been as completely deceived as yourself I might find words of criticism for this possibly unprofessional partiality. But when an old hand like myself can listen to the insinuations of a maniac, and repose, as I must say I did repose, more or less confidence in the statements he chose to make me, and which were true enough as to the facts he mentioned, but wickedly false and preposterously wrong in suggestion, I can have no words of blame for a woman who, whatever her understanding and whatever her experience, necessarily has seen less of human nature and its incalculable surprises. As to the more delicate matter you have been good enough to confide to me, madam, I have but one remark to make. With such an example of womanhood suddenly brought to their notice in such a wild as this, how could you expect them, sane or insane, to do otherwise than they did? I know many a worthy man who would like to follow their example." And with a bow that left me speechless, Mr. Gryce laid his hand on his heart and softly withdrew.

EPILOGUE

SOME STRAY LEAFLETS FROM AN OLD DIARY OF ALTHEA KNOLLYS, FOUND BY ME IN THE PACKET LEFT IN MY CHARGE BY HER DAUGHTER LUCETTA.

I never thought I should do so foolish a thing as begin a diary. When in my boarding-school days (which I am very glad to be rid of) I used to see Meeley Butterworth sit down every night of her life over a little book which she called the repository of her daily actions, I thought that if ever I reached that point of imbecility I would deserve to have fewer lovers and more sense, just as she so frequently advised me to. And yet here I am, pencil in hand, jotting down the nothings of the moment, and with every prospect of continuing to do so for two weeks at least. For (why was I born such a chatterbox!) I have seen my fate, and must talk to someone about him, if only to myself, nature never having meant me to keep silence on any living topic that interests me.

Yes, with lovers in Boston, lovers in New York, and a most determined suitor on the other side of our own home-walls in Peekskill, I have fallen victim to the grave face and methodical ways of a person I need not name, since he is the only gentleman in this whole town, except—But I won't except anybody. Charles Knollys has no peer here or anywhere, and this I am ready to declare, after only one sight of his face and one look from his eye, though to no one but you, my secret, non-committal confidant—for to acknowledge to any human being that my admiration could be caught, or my heart touched, by a person who had not sued two years at my feet, would be to abdicate an ascendency I am so accustomed to I could not see it vanish without pain. Besides, who knows how I shall feel tomorrow? Meeley Butterworth never shows any hesitation in uttering her opinion either of men or things, but then her opinion never changes, whilst mine is a very thistle-down, blowing hither and thither till I cannot follow its wanderings myself. It is one of my charms, certain fools say, but that is nonsense. If my cheeks lacked color and my eyes were without sparkle, or even if I were two inches taller instead of being the tiniest bit of mortal flesh to be found amongst all the young ladies of my age in our so-called society, I doubt if the lightness of my mind would meet with the approbation of even the warmest woman-lovers of this time. As it is, it just passes, and sometimes, as tonight, for instance, when I can hardly see to inscribe these lines on this page for the vision of two grave, if not quietly reproving eyes which float between it and me, I almost wish I had some of Meeley's responsible characteristics, instead of being the airiest, merriest, and most volatile being that ever tried to laugh down the grandeur of this dreary old house with its century of memories.

Ah! that allusion has given me something to say. This house. What is there about it except its size to make a stranger like me look back continually over her shoulder in going down the long halls, or even when nestling comfortably by the great wood-fire in the immense drawing-room? *I* am not one of your fanciful ones; but I can no more help doing this, than I can help wishing Judge Knollys lived in a less roomy mansion with fewer echoing corners in its innumerable passages. *I* like brightness and cheer, at least in my surroundings. If I must have gloom, or a seriousness which some would call gloom, let me have it in individuals where there is some prospect of a blithe, careless-hearted little midget effecting a change, and not in great towering walls and endless floors which no amount of sunshine or laughter could ever render homelike, or even comfortable.

But there! If one has the man, one must have the home, so I had better say no more against the home till I am quite sure I do not want the man. For—Well, well, I am not a fool, but I *did* hear something just then, a something which makes me tremble yet, though I have spent five good minutes trilling the gayest songs I know.

I think it is very inconsiderate of the witches to bother thus a harmless mite like myself, who only asks for love, light, and money enough to buy a ribbon or a jewel when the fancy takes her, which is not as often as my enemies declare. And now a question! Why are my enemies always to be found among the girls, and among the plainest of them too? I never heard a man say anything against me, though I have sometimes surprised a look on their faces (I saw it today) which might signify reproof if it were not accompanied by a smile showing anything but displeasure.

But this is a digression, as Meeley would say. What I want to do, but which I seem to find it very difficult to do, is to tell how I came to be here, and what I have seen since I came. First, then, to be very short about the matter, I am here because the old folks—that is, my father and Mr. Knollys, have decided Charles and I should know each other.

In thought, I courtesy to the decision; I think we ought to too. For while many other men are handsomer or better known, or have more money, alas! than he, he alone has a way of drawing up to one's side with an air that captivates the eye and sets the heart trembling, a heart, moreover, that never knew before it could tremble, except in the presence of great worldly prosperity and beautiful, beautiful things. So, as this experience is new, I am dutifully obliged for the excitement it gives me, and am glad to be here, awesome as the place is, and destitute of any such pleasures as I have been accustomed to in the gay cities where I have hitherto spent most of my time.

But there! I am rambling again. I have come to X., as you now see, for good and sufficient reasons, and while this house is one of consequence and has been the resort of many notable people, it is a little lonesome, our only neighbor being a young man who has a fine enough appearance, but who has already shown his admiration of me so plainly—of course he was in the road when I drove up to the house—that I lost all interest in him at once, such a nonsensical liking at first sight being, as I take it, a tribute only to my audacious little travelling bonnet and the curl or two which will fall out on my cheek when I move my head about too quickly, as I certainly could not be blamed for doing, in driving into a place where I was expected to make myself happy for two weeks.

He, then, is out of these chronicles. When I say his name is Obadiah Trohm, you will probably be duly thankful. But he is not as stiff and biblical as his name would lead you to expect. On the contrary, he is lithe, graceful, and suave to a point which makes Charles Knollys' judicial face a positive relief to the eye and such little understanding as has been accorded me.

I cannot write another word. It is twelve o'clock, and though I have the cosiest room in the house, all chintz and decorated china, I find myself listening and peering just as I did downstairs in their great barn of a drawing-room. I wonder if any very dreadful things ever happened in this house? I will ask old Mr. Knollys tomorrow, or—or Mr. Charles.

* * * *

I am sorry I was so inquisitive; for the stories Charles told me—I thought I had better not trouble the old gentleman—have only served to people the shadows of this rambling old house with figures of whose acquaintance I am likely to be more or less shy. One tale in particular gave me the shivers. It was about a mother and daughter who both loved the same man (it seems incredible, girls so seldom seeing with the eyes of their mothers), and it was the daughter who married him, while the mother, broken-hearted, fled from the wedding and was driven up to the great door, here, in a coach, dead. They say that the coach still travels the road just before some calamity to the family—a phantom coach which floats along in shadow, turning the air about it to mist that chills the marrow in the bones of the unfortunate who sees it. I am going to see it myself some day, the real coach, I mean, in which this tragic event took place. It is still in the stable, Charles tells me. I wonder if I will have the courage to sit where that poor devoted mother breathed out her miserable existence. I shall endeavor to do so if only to defy the fate which seems to be closing in upon me.

Charles is an able lawyer, but his argument in favor of close bonnets *versus* bewitching little pokes with a rose or two in front, was very weak, I thought, today. He seemed to think so himself, after a while; for when, as the only means of convincing him of the weakness of the cause he was advocating, I ran upstairs and put on a poke similar to the aforesaid, he retracted at once and let the case go by default. For which I, and the poke, made suitable acknowledgments, to the great amusement of papa Knollys, who was on my side from the first.

Not much going on today. Yet I have never felt merrier. Oh, ye hideous, bare old walls! Won't I make you ring if—

* * * *

I won't have it! I won't have that smooth, persistent hypocrite pushing his way into my presence, when my whole heart and attention belong to a man who would love me if he only could get his own leave to do so. Obadiah Trohm has been here today, on one pretext or another, three times. Once he came to bring some very choice apples—as if I cared for apples! The second time he had a question of great importance, no doubt, to put to Charles, and as Charles was in my company, the whole interview lasted, let us say, a good half-hour at least. The third time he came, it was to see *me*, which, as it was now evening, meant talk, talk, talk in the great drawing-room, with just a song interpolated now and then, instead of a cosy chat in the window-seat of the pretty Flower Parlor, with only one pair of ears to please and one pair of eyes to watch. Master Trohm was intrusive, and, if no one felt it but myself, it is because Charles Knollys has set himself up an ideal of womanhood to which I am a contradiction. But that will not affect the end. A woman may be such a contradiction and yet win, if her heart is in the struggle and she has, besides, a certain individuality of her own which appeals to the eye and heart if not to the understanding. I do not despair of seeing Charles Knollys' forehead taking a very deep frown at sight of his handsome and most attentive neighbor. Heigho! why don't I answer Meeley Butterworth's last letter? Am I ashamed to tell her that I have to limit my effusion to just four pages because I have commenced a diary?

* * * *

I declare I begin to regard it a misfortune to have dimples. I never have regarded it so before when I have seen man after man succumb to them, but *now* they have become my bane, for they attract two admirers, just at the time they should attract but one, and it is upon the wrong man they flash the oftenest; why, I leave it to all true lovers to explain. As a consequence, Master Trohm is beginning to assume an air of superiority, and Charles, who may not believe in dimples, but who on that very account, perhaps, seems to be always on the lookout for them, shrinks more or less into the background, as is not becoming in a man with so many claims to respect, if not to love. *I* want to feel that each one of these precious fourteen days contains all that it can of delight and satisfaction, and how can I when Obadiah—oh, the charming and romantic name!—holds my crewels, instead of Charles, and whispers words which, coming from other lips, would do more than waken my dimples!

But if I must have a suitor, just when a suitor is not wanted, let me at least make him useful. Charles shall read his own heart in this man's passion.

* * * *

I don't know why, but I have taken a dislike to the Flower Parlor. It now vies with the great drawing-room in my disregard. Yesterday, in crossing it, I felt a chill, so sudden and so penetrating, that I irresistibly thought of the old saying, "Some one is walking over my grave." *My grave!* where lies it, and why should I feel the shudder of it now? Am I destined to an early death? The bounding life in my veins says no. But I never again shall like that room. It has made me think.

* * * *

I have not only sat in the old coach, but I had (let me drop the words slowly, they are so precious) I—I have had—a *kiss*—given me there. Charles gave me this kiss; he could not help it. I was sitting on the seat in front, in a sort of mock mirth he was endeavoring to frown upon, when suddenly I glanced up and our eyes met, and—He says it was the sauciness of my dimples (oh, those old dimples! they seem to have stood me in good stead after all); but I say it was my sincere affection which drew him, for he stooped like a man forgetful of everything in the whole wide world but the little trembling, panting being before him, and gave me one of those caresses which seals a woman's fate forever, and made me, the feather-brained and thoughtless coquette, a slave to this large-minded and true-hearted man for all my life hereafter.

Why I should be so happy over this event is beyond my understanding. That he should be in the seventh heaven of delight is only to be expected, but that I should find myself tripping through this gloomy old house like one treading on air is a mystery, to the elucidation of which I can only give my dimples. My reason can make nothing out of it. I, who thought of nothing short of a grand establishment in Boston, money, servants, and a husband who would love me blindly whatever my faults, have given my troth—you will say my lips, but the one means the other—to a man who will never be known outside of his own county, never be rich, never be blind even, for he frowns upon me as often as he smiles, and, worst of all, who lives in a house so vast and so full of tragic suggestion that it might well awaken doleful anticipations in much more serious-minded persons than myself.

And yet I am happy, so happy that I have even attempted to make the acquaintance of the grim old portraits and weak pastels which line the walls of many of these bedrooms. Old Mr. Knollys caught me courtesying just now before one of these ancestral beauties, whose face seemed to hold a faint prophecy of my own, and perceiving by my blushes that this was something more than a mere childish freak on my part, he chucked me under the chin and laughingly asked, how long it was likely to be before he might have the honor of adding my pretty face to the collection. Which should have made me indignant, only I am not in an indignant mood just now.

* * * *

Why have I been so foolish? Why did I not let my over-fond neighbor know from the beginning that I detested him, instead of—But what have I done anyway? A smile, a nod, a laughing word mean nothing. When one has eyes which persist in dancing in spite of one's every effort to keep them demure, men who become fools are apt to call one a coquette, when a little good sense would teach them that the woman who smiles always has some other way of showing her regard to the man she really favors. I could not help being on merry terms with Mr. Trohm, if only to hide the effect another's presence has on me. But he thinks otherwise, and today I had ample reason for seeing why his good looks and easy manners have invariably awakened distrust in me rather than admiration. Master Trohm is vindictive, and I should be afraid of him, if I had not observed in him the presence of another passion which will soon engross all his attention and make him forget me as soon as ever I become Charles' wife. Money is his idol, and as fortune seems to favor him, he will soon be happy in the mere pleasure of accumulation. But this is not relating what happened today.

We were walking in the shrubbery (by *we* I naturally mean Charles and myself), and he was saying things which made me at the same time happy and a bit serious, when I suddenly felt myself under the spell of some baleful influence that filled me with a dismay I could neither understand nor escape from.

As this could not proceed from Charles, I turned to look about me, when I encountered the eyes of Obadiah Trohm, who was leaning on the fence separating his grounds from those of Mr. Knollys, looking directly at us. If I flinched at this surveillance, it was but the natural expression of my indignation. His face wore a look calculated to frighten any one, and though he did not respond to the gesture I made him, I felt that my only chance of escaping a scene was to induce Charles to leave me before he should see what I saw in the lowering countenance of his intrusive neighbor. As the situation demanded self-possession and the exercise of a ready wit, and as these are qualities in which I am not altogether deficient, I succeeded in carrying out my intention sooner even than I expected. Charles hurried from my presence at the first word, and proceeded towards the house without seeing Trohm, and I, quivering with dread, turned towards the man whom I felt, rather than saw, approaching me.

He met me with a look I shall never forget. I have had lovers—too many of them—and this is not the first man I have been compelled to meet with rebuff and disdain, but never in the whole course of my none too extended existence have I been confronted by such passion or overwhelmed with such bitter recrimination. He seemed like a man beside himself, yet he was quiet, too quiet, and while his voice did not rise above a whisper, and he approached no nearer than the demands of courtesy required, he produced so terrifying an effect upon me that I longed to cry for help, and would have done so, but that my throat closed with fright, and I could only gurgle forth a remonstrance, too faint even for him to hear.

"You have played with a man's best feelings," he said. "You have led me to believe that I had only to speak to have you for my own. Are you simply foolish, or are you wicked? Did you care for me at all, or was it only your wish to increase the number of men in your train? This one" (here his hand pointed quiveringly towards the house) "has enjoyed a happiness denied me. His hand has touched yours, his lips—" Here his words became almost unintelligible till his purpose gave him strength, and he cried: "But notwithstanding this, notwithstanding any vows you may have exchanged, I have claims upon you that I will not yield. I who have loved no woman before you, will have such a hand in your fate that you will never be able to separate yourself from the influence I shall exert over you. I will not intrude between you and your lover; I will not affect dislike or disturb your outer life with any vain display of my hatred or my passion, but I will work upon your secret thoughts, and create a slowly increasing dread in the inner sanctuary of your heart till you wish you had called up the deadliest of serpents in your pathway rather than the latent fury of Obadiah Trohm. You are a girl now; when you are married and become a mother, you will understand me. For the present I leave you. The shadow of this old house which has never seen much happiness within it will soon rest upon your thoughtless head. What that will not do, your own inherent weakness will. The woman who trifles with a strong man's heart has a flaw in her nature which will work out her own destruction in time. I can afford to let you enjoy your prospective honeymoon in peace. Afterwards—" He cast a threatening look towards the decaying structure behind me, and was silent. But that silence did not unloose my tongue. I was absolutely speechless.

"Ten brides have crossed yonder threshold," he presently went on in a low musing tone freighted with horrible fatality. "One—and she was the girl whose mother was driven up to these doors dead—lived to take her grandchildren on her knees. The rest died early, and most of them unhappily. Oh, I have studied the traditions of your future home! *You* will live, but of all the brides who have triumphed in the honorable name of Knollys, you will lead the saddest life and meet the gloomiest end notwithstanding you stand before me now, with loose locks flying in the wind, and a heart so gay that even my despair can barely pale the roses on your cheek."

This was the raving of a madman. I recognized it as such, and took a little heart. How could he see into my future? How could he prophesy evil to one over whom he will have no control? to one watched over and beloved by a man like Charles? He is a dreamer, a fanatic. His talk about the flaw in my nature is nonsense, and as for the fate lowering over my head, in the shadows falling from the toppling old house in which I am likely to take up my abode—that is only frenzy, and I would be unworthy of happiness to heed it. As I realized this, my indignation grew, and, uttering a few contemptuous words, I was hurrying away when he stopped me with a final warning.

"Wait!" he said, "women like you cannot keep either their joys or their miseries to themselves. But I advise you not to take Charles Knollys into your confidence. If you do, a duel will follow, and if I have not the legal acumen of your intended, I have an eye and a hand before which he must fall, if our passions come to an issue. So beware! never while you live betray what has passed between us at this interview, unless the weariness of a misplaced affection should come to you, and with it the desire to be rid of your husband."

A frightful threat which, unfortunately perhaps, has sealed my lips. Oh, why should such monsters live!

I have been all through the house today with old Mr. Knollys. Every room was opened for my inspection, and I was bidden to choose which should be refurnished for my benefit. It was a gruesome trip, from which I have returned to my own little nook of chintz as to a refuge. Great rooms which for years have been the abode of spiders, are not much to my liking, but I chose out two which at least have fireplaces in them, and these are to be made as cheerful as circumstances will permit. I hope when I again see them, it will not be by the light of a waning November afternoon, when the few leaves still left to flutter from the trees blow, soggy and wet, against the panes of the solitary windows, or lie in sodden masses at the foot of the bare trunks, which cluster so thickly on the lawn as to hide all view of the highroad. I was meant for laughter and joy, flashing lights, and the splendors of ballrooms. Why have I chosen, then, to give up the great world and settle down in this grimmest of grim old houses in a none too lively village? I think it is because I love Charles Knollys, and so, no matter how my heart sinks in the dim shadows that haunt every spot I stray into, I will be merry, will think of Charles instead of myself, and so live down the unhappy prophecies uttered by the wretch who, with his venomous words, has robbed the future of whatever charm my love was likely to cast upon it. The fact that this man left the town today for a lengthy trip abroad should raise my spirits more than it has. If we were going now, Charles and I—But why dream of a Paradise whose doors remain closed to you? It is here our honeymoon is destined to be passed; within these walls and in sight of the bare boughs rattling at this moment against the panes.

I made a misstatement when I said that I had gone into all the rooms of the house this afternoon. *I did not enter the Flower Parlor.*

* * * *

I had been married a month and had, as I thought, no further use for this foolish diary. So one evening when Charles was away, I attempted to burn it.

But when I had flung myself down before the blazing logs of my bedroom fire (I was then young enough to love to crouch for hours on the rug in my lonely room, seeking for all I delighted in and longed for in the glowing embers), some instinct, or was it a premonition? made me withhold from destruction a record which coming events might make worthy of preservation. That was five years ago, and today I have reopened the secret drawer in which this simple book has so long lain undisturbed, and am once more penning lines destined perhaps to pass into oblivion together with the others. Why? I do not know. There is no change in my married life. I have no trouble, no anxiety, no reason for dread; yet—Well, well, some women are made for the simple round of domestic duties, and others are as out of place in the nursery and kitchen as butterflies in a granary. I want just the things Charles cannot give me. I have home, love, children, all that some women most crave, and while I idolize my husband and know of nothing sweeter than my babies, I yet have spells of such wretched weariness, that it would be a relief to me to be a little less comfortable if only I might enjoy a more brilliant existence. But Charles is not rich; sometimes I think he is poor, and however much I may desire change, I cannot have it. Heigho! and, what is worse, I haven't had a new dress in a year; I who so love dress, and become it so well! Why, if it is my lot to go shabby, and tie up my dancing ringlets with faded ribbons, was I made with the figure of a fairy and given a temperament which, without any effort on my part, makes me, diminutive as I am, the centre of every group I enter? If I were plain, or shy, or even self-contained, I might be happy here, but now—There! there! I will go kiss little William, and lay Loreen's baby arm about my neck and see if the wicked demons will fly away. Charles is too busy for me to intrude upon him in that horrid Flower Parlor.

* * * *

I was never superstitious till I entered this house; but now I believe in every sort of thing a sane woman should not. Yesterday, after a neglect of five years, I brought out my diary. Today I have to record in it that there was a reason for my doing so. Obadiah Trohm has returned home. I saw him this morning leaning over his fence in the same place and in very much the same attitude as on that day when he frightened me so, a month before my wedding.

But he did not frighten me today. He merely looked at me very sharply and with a less offensive admiration than in the early days of our first acquaintance. At which I made him my best courtesy. I was not going to remind him of the past in our new relations, and he, thankful perhaps for this, took off his hat with a smile I am trying even yet to explain to myself. Then we began to talk. He had travelled everywhere and I had been nowhere; he wore the dress and displayed the manners of the great world, while I had only a hungry desire to do the same. As for fashion, I needed all my beauty and the fading sparkle of my old animation to enable me to hold up my head before him.

But as for liking him, I did not. I could admire his appearance, but he himself attracted me no more than when he had words of angry fury on his tongue. He is a gentleman, and one who has seen the world, but in other ways he is no more to be compared with my Charles than his pert new house, built in his absence, with the grand old structure with whose fatality he once threatened me.

I do not think he wants to threaten me with disaster now. Time closes such wounds as his very effectually. I wish we had some of his money.

* * * *

I have always heard that the wives of the Knollys, whatever their misfortune, have always loved their husbands. I do not think I am any exception to the rule. When Charles has leisure to give me an hour from his musty old books, the place here seems lively enough, and the children's voices do not sound so shrill. But these hours are so infrequent. If it were not for Mr. Trohm's journal (Did I mention that he had lent me a journal of his travels?) I should often eat my heart out with loneliness. I am beginning to like the man better as I follow him from city to city of the old world. If he had ever mentioned me in its pages, I would not read another line in it, but he seems to have expended both his love and spite when he bade me farewell in the garden underlying these bleak old walls.

* * * *

I am becoming as well acquainted with Mr. Trohm's handwriting as with my own. I read and read and read in his journal, and only stop when the dreaded midnight hour comes with its ghostly suggestions and the unaccountable noises which make this old dwelling so uncanny. Charles often finds me curled up over this book, and when he does he sighs. Why?

* * * *

I have been teaching Loreen to dance. Oh, how merry it has made me! I think I will be happier now. We have the large upper hall to take steps in, and when she makes a misstep we laugh, and that is a good sound to hear in this old place. If I could only have a little money to buy her a fresh frock and some ribbons, I would feel perfectly satisfied; but I do believe Charles is getting poorer and poorer every day; the place costs so much to keep up, he says, and when his father died there were debts to be paid which leaves us, his innocent inheritors, very straitened. Master Trohm has no such difficulties. He has money enough. But I don't like the man for all that, polite as he is to us all. He seems to quite adore Loreen, and as to William, he pets him till I feel almost uncomfortable at times.

* * * *

What shall I do? I am invited to New York, *I*, and Charles says I may go, too—only I have nothing to wear. Oh, for some money! a little money! it is my right to have some money; but Charles tells me he can only spare enough to pay my expenses, that my Sunday frock looks very well, and that, even if it did not, I am pretty enough to do without fine clothes, and other nonsense like that—sweet enough, but totally without point, in fact. If I am pretty, all the more I need a little finery to set me off, and, besides, to go to New York without money—why, I should be perfectly miserable. Charles himself ought to realize this, and be willing to sell his old books before he would let me go into this whirl of temptation without a dollar to spend. As he don't, I must devise some plan of my own for obtaining a little money, for I won't give up my trip—the first offered me since I was married—and neither will I go away and come back without a gift for my two girls, who have grown to womanhood without a jewel to adorn them or a silk dress to make them look like gentlemen's children. But how get money without Charles knowing it? Mr. Trohm is such a good friend, he might lend me a little, but I don't know how to ask him without recalling to his mind certain words long since forgotten by him perhaps, but never to be forgotten by me, feather-brained as many people think me. Is there any one else?

* * * *

I wonder if some things are as wicked as people say they are. I—

* * * *

Here the diary breaks off abruptly. But we know what followed. The forgery, the discovery of it by her suave but secret enemy, his unnatural revenge, and the never-dying enmity which led to the tragic events it has been my unhappy fortune to relate at such length. Poor Althea! with thy name I write *finis* to these pages. May the dust lie lightly on thy breast under the shadow of the Flower Parlor, through which thy footsteps passed with such dread in the old days of thy youthful beauty and innocence!

BOOK IV: THE END OF A GREAT MYSTERY

CHAPTER XXXVI

The Result

I was as much surprised at this result of Mr. Gryce's scheme as he was, and possibly I was more chagrined. But I shall not enter into my feelings on the subject, or weary you any further with my conjectures. You will be much more interested, I know, in learning what occurred to

Mr. Gryce upon entering the carriage holding Miss Oliver.

He had expected, from the intense emotion she displayed at the sight of Howard Van Burnam (for I was not mistaken as to the identity of the person occupying the carriage with her), to find her flushed with the passions incident upon this meeting, and her companion in a condition of mind which would make it no longer possible for him to deny his connection with this woman and his consequently guilty complicity in a murder to which both were linked by so many incriminating circumstances.

But for all his experience, the detective was disappointed in this expectation, as he had been in so many others connected with this case. There was nothing in Miss Oliver's attitude to indicate that she had unburdened herself of any of the emotions with which she was so grievously agitated, nor was there on Mr. Van Burnam's part any deeper manifestation of feeling than a slight glow on his cheek, and even that disappeared under the detective's scrutiny, leaving him as composed and imperturbable as he had been in his memorable inquisition before the Coroner.

Disappointed, and yet in a measure exhilarated by this sudden check in plans he had thought too well laid for failure, Mr. Gryce surveyed the young girl more carefully, and saw that he had not been mistaken in regard to the force or extent of the feelings which had driven her into Mr. Van Burnam's presence; and turning back to that gentleman, was about to give utterance to some very pertinent remarks, when he was forestalled by Mr. Van Burnam inquiring, in his old calm way, which nothing seemed able to disturb:

"Who is this crazy girl you have forced upon me? If I had known I was to be subjected to such companionship I should not have regarded my outing so favorably."

Mr. Gryce, who never allowed himself to be surprised by anything a suspected criminal might do or say, surveyed him quietly for a moment, then turned towards Miss Oliver.

"You hear what this gentleman calls you?" said he.

Her face was hidden by her hands, but she dropped them as the detective addressed her, showing a countenance so distorted by passion that it stopped the current of his thoughts, and made him question whether the epithet bestowed upon her by their somewhat callous companion was entirely unjustified. But soon the something else which was in her face restored his confidence in her sanity, and he saw that while her reason might be shaken it was not yet dethroned, and that he had good cause to expect sooner or later some action from a woman whose misery could wear an aspect of such desperate resolution.

That he was not the only one affected by the force and desperate character of her glance became presently apparent, for Mr. Van Burnam, with a more kindly tone than he had previously used, observed quietly:

"I see the lady is suffering. I beg pardon for my inconsiderate words. I have no wish to insult the unhappy."

Never was Mr. Gryce so nonplussed. There was a mingled courtesy and composure in the speaker's manner which was as far removed as possible from that strained effort at self-possession which marks suppressed passion or secret fear; while in the vacant look with which she met these words there was neither anger nor scorn nor indeed any of the passions one would expect to see there. The detective consequently did not force the situation, but only watched her more and more attentively till her eyes fell and she crouched away from them both. Then he said:

"You can name this gentleman, can you not, Miss Oliver, even if he does not choose to recognize *you*?"

But her answer, if she made one, was inaudible, and the sole result which Mr. Gryce obtained from this venture was a quick look from Mr. Van Burnam and the following uncompromising words from his lips:

"If you think this young girl knows me, or that I know her, you are greatly mistaken. She is as much of a stranger to me as I am to her, and I take this opportunity of saying so. I hope my liberty and good name are not to be made dependent upon the word of a miserable waif like this."

"Your liberty and your good name will depend upon your innocence," retorted Mr. Gryce, and said no more, feeling himself at a disadvantage before the imperturbability of this man and the silent, non-accusing attitude of this woman, from the shock of whose passions he had anticipated so much and obtained so little.

Meantime they were moving rapidly towards Police Headquarters, and fearing that the sight of that place might alarm Miss Oliver more than was well for her, he strove again to rouse her by a kindly word or so. But it was useless. She evidently tried to pay attention and follow the words he used, but her thoughts were too busy over the one great subject that engrossed her.

"A bad case!" murmured Mr. Van Burnam, and with the phrase seemed to dismiss all thought of her.

"A bad case!" echoed Mr. Gryce, "but," seeing how fast the look of resolution was replacing her previous aspect of frenzy, "one that will do mischief yet to the man who has deceived her."

The stopping of the carriage roused her. Looking up, she spoke for the first time.

"I want a police officer," she said.

Mr. Gryce, with all his assurance restored, leaped to the ground and held out his hand.

"I will take you into the presence of one," said he; and she, without a glance at Mr. Van Burnam, whose knee she brushed in passing, leaped to the ground, and turned her face towards Police Headquarters.

CHAPTER XXXVII

"Two Weeks!"

But before she was well in, her countenance changed.

"No," said she, "I want to think first. Give me time to think. I dare not say a word without thinking."

"Truth needs no consideration. If you wish to denounce this man—"

Her look said she did.

"Then now is the time."

She gave him a sharp glance; the first she had bestowed upon him since leaving Miss Althorpe's.

"You are no doctor," she declared. "Are you a police-officer?"

"I am a detective."

"Oh!" and she hesitated for a moment, shrinking from him with very natural distrust and aversion. "I have been in the toils then without knowing it; no wonder I am caught. But I am no criminal, sir; and if you are the one most in authority here, I beg the privilege of a few words with you before I am put into confinement."

"I will take you before the Superintendent," said Mr. Gryce. "But do you wish to go alone? Shall not Mr. Van Burnam accompany you?"

"Mr. Van Burnam?"

"Is it not he you wish to denounce?"

"I do not wish to denounce any one today."

"What do you wish?" asked Mr. Gryce.

"Let me see the man who has power to hold me here or let me go, and I will tell him."

"Very well," said Mr. Gryce, and led her into the presence of the Superintendent.

She was at this moment quite a different person from what she had been in the carriage. All that was girlish in her aspect or appealing in her bearing had faded away, evidently forever, and left in its place something at once so desperate and so deadly, that she seemed not only a woman but one of a very determined and dangerous nature. Her manner, however, was quiet, and it was only in her eye that one could see how near she was to frenzy.

She spoke before the Superintendent could address her.

"Sir," said she, "I have been brought here on account of a fearful crime I was unhappy enough to witness. I myself am innocent of that crime, but, so far as I know, there is no other person living save the guilty man who committed it, who can tell you how or why or by whom it was done. One man has been arrested for it and another has not. If you will give me two weeks of complete freedom, I will point out to you which is the veritable man of blood, and may Heaven have mercy on his soul!"

"She is mad," signified the Superintendent in by-play to Mr. Gryce.

But the latter shook his head; she was not mad yet.

"I know," she continued, without a hint of the timidity which seemed natural to her under other circumstances, "that this must seem a presumptuous request from one like me, but it is only by granting it that you will ever be able to lay your hand on the murderer of Mrs. Van Burnam. For I will never speak if I cannot speak in my own way and at my own time. The agonies I have suffered must have some compensation. Otherwise I should die of horror and my grief."

"And how do you hope to gain compensation by this delay?" expostulated the Superintendent. "Would you not meet with more satisfaction in denouncing him here and now before he can pass another night in fancied security?"

But she only repeated: "I have said two weeks, and two weeks I must have. Two weeks in which to come and go as I please. Two weeks!" And no argument they could advance succeeded in eliciting from her any other response or in altering in any way her air of quiet determination with its underlying suggestion of frenzy.

Acknowledging their mutual defeat by a look, the Superintendent and detective drew off to one side, and something like the following conversation took place between them.

"You think she's sane?"

"I do."

"And will remain so two weeks?"

"If humored."

"You are sure she is implicated in this crime?"

"She was a witness to it."

"And that she speaks the truth when she declares that she is the only person who can point out the criminal?"

"Yes; that is, she is the only one who will do it. The attitude taken by the Van Burnams, especially by Howard just now in the presence of this girl, shows how little we have to expect from them."

"Yet you think they know as much as she does about it?"

"I do not know what to think. For once I am baffled, Superintendent. Every passion which this woman possesses was roused by her unexpected meeting with Howard Van Burnam, and yet their indifference when confronted, as well as her present action, seems to argue a lack of connection between them which overthrows at once the theory of his guilt. Was it the sight of Franklin, then, which really affected her? and was her apparent indifference at meeting him only an evidence of her self-control? It seems an impossible conclusion to draw, and indeed there are nothing but hitches and improbable features in this case. Nothing fits; nothing jibes. I get just so far in it and then I run up against a wall. Either there is a superhuman power of duplicity in the persons who contrived this murder or we are on the wrong tack altogether."

"In other words, you have tried every means known to you to get at the truth of this matter, and failed."

"I have, sir; sorry as I may be to acknowledge it."

"Then we must accept her terms. She can be shadowed?"

"Every moment."

"Very well, then. Extreme cases must be met by extreme measures. We will let her have her swing, and see what comes of it. Revenge is a great weapon in the hands of a determined woman, and from her look I think she will make the most of it."

And returning to where the young girl stood, the Superintendent asked her whether she felt sure the murderer would not escape in the time that must elapse before his apprehension.

Instantly her cheek, which had looked as if it could never show color again, flushed a deep and painful scarlet, and she cried vehemently:

"If any hint of what is here passing should reach him I should be powerless to prevent his flight. Swear, then, that my very existence shall be kept a secret between you two, or I will do nothing towards his apprehension—no, not even to save the innocent."

"We will not swear, but we will promise," returned the Superintendent. "And now, when may we expect to hear from you again?"

"Two weeks from tonight as the clock strikes eight. Be wherever I may chance to be at that hour, and see on whose arm I lay my hand. It will be that of the man who killed Mrs. Van Burnam."

CHAPTER XXXVIII

A White Satin Gown

The events just related did not come to my knowledge for some days after they occurred, but I have recorded them at this time that I might in some way prepare you for an interview which shortly after took place between myself and Mr. Gryce.

I had not seen him since our rather unsatisfactory parting in front of Miss Althorpe's house, and the suspense which I had endured in the interim made my greeting unnecessarily warm. But he took it all very naturally.

"You are glad to see me," said he; "been wondering what has become of Miss Oliver. Well, she is in good hands; with Mrs. Desberger, in short; a woman whom I believe you know."

"With Mrs. Desberger?" I *was* surprised. "Why, I have been looking every day in the papers for an account of her arrest."

"No doubt," he answered. "But we police are slow; we are not ready to arrest her yet. Meanwhile you can do us a favor. She wants to see you; are you willing to visit her?"

My answer contained but little of the curiosity and eagerness I really felt.

"I am always at your command. Do you wish me to go now?"

"Miss Oliver is impatient," he admitted. "Her fever is better, but she is in an excited condition of mind which makes her a little unreasonable. To be plain, she is not quite herself, and while we still hope something from her testimony, we are leaving her very much to her own devices, and do not cross her in anything. You will therefore listen to what she says, and, if possible, aid her in anything she may undertake, unless it points directly towards self-destruction. My opinion is that she will surprise you. But you are becoming accustomed to surprises, are you not?"

"Thanks to you, I am."

"Very well, then, I have but one more suggestion to make. You are working for the police now, madam, and nothing that you see or learn in connection with this girl is to be kept back from us. Am I understood?"

"Perfectly; but it is only proper for me to retort that I am not entirely pleased with the part you assign me. Could you not have left thus much to my good sense, and not put it into so many words?"

"Ah, madam, the case at present is too serious for risks of that kind. Mr. Van Burnam's reputation, to say nothing of his life, depends upon our knowledge of this girl's secret; surely you can stretch a point in a matter of so much moment?"

"I have already stretched several, and I can stretch one more, but I hope the girl won't look at me too often with those miserable appealing eyes of hers; they make me feel like a traitor."

"You will not be troubled by any appeal in them. The appeal has vanished; something harder and even more difficult to meet is to be found in them now: wrath, purpose, and a desire for vengeance. She is not the same woman, I assure you."

"Well," I sighed, "I am sorry; there is something about the girl that lays hold of me, and I hate to see such a change in her. Did she ask for me by name?"

"I believe so."

"I cannot understand her wanting me, but I will go; and I won't leave her either till she shows me she is tired of me. I am as anxious to see the end of this matter as you are." Then, with some vague idea that I had

earned a right to some show of confidence on his part, I added insinuatingly: "I supposed you would feel the case settled when she almost
fainted at the sight of the younger Mr. Van Burnam."

The old ambiguous smile I remembered so well came to modify his
brusque rejoinder.

"If she had been a woman like you, I should; but she is a deep one,
Miss Butterworth; too deep for the success of a little ruse like mine. Are
you ready?"

I was not, but it did not take me long to be so, and before an hour
had elapsed I was seated in Mrs. Desberger's parlor in Ninth Street. Miss
Oliver was in, and ere long made her appearance. She was dressed in
street costume.

I was prepared for a change in her, and yet the shock I felt when I first
saw her face must have been apparent, for she immediately remarked:

"You find me quite well, Miss Butterworth. For this I am partially
indebted to you. You were very good to nurse me so carefully. Will you
be still kinder, and help me in a new matter which I feel quite incompe-
tent to undertake alone?"

Her face was flushed, her manner nervous, but her eyes had an extraordinary look in them which affected me most painfully, notwithstanding the additional effect it gave to her beauty.

"Certainly," said I. "What can I do for you?"

"I wish to buy me a dress," was her unexpected reply. "A handsome
dress. Do you object to showing me the best shops? I am a stranger in
New York."

More astonished than I can express, but carefully concealing it in
remembrance of the caution received from Mr. Gryce, I replied that I
would be only too happy to accompany her on such an errand. Upon
which she lost her nervousness and prepared at once to go out with me.

"I would have asked Mrs. Desberger," she observed while fitting on
her gloves, "but her taste"—here she cast a significant look about the
room—"is not quiet enough for me."

"I should think not!" I cried.

"I shall be a trouble to you," the girl went on, with a gleam in her eye
that spoke of the restless spirit within. "I have many things to buy, and
they must all be rich and handsome."

"If you have money enough, there will be no trouble about that."

"Oh, I have money." She spoke like a millionaire's daughter. "Shall
we go to Arnold's?"

As I always traded at Arnold's, I readily acquiesced, and we left the
house. But not before she had tied a very thick veil over her face.

"If we meet any one, do not introduce me," she begged. "I cannot
talk to people."

"You may rest easy," I assured her.

At the corner she stopped. "Is there any way of getting a carriage?" she asked.

"Do you want one?"

"Yes."

I signalled a hack.

"Now for the dress!" she cried.

We rode at once to Arnold's.

"What kind of a dress do you want?" I inquired as we entered the store.

"An evening one; a white satin, I think."

I could not help the exclamation which escaped me; but I covered it up as quickly as possible by a hurried remark in favor of white, and we proceeded at once to the silk counter.

"I will trust it all to you," she whispered in an odd, choked tone as the clerk approached us. "Get what you would for your daughter—no, no! for Mr. Van Burnam's daughter, if he has one, and do not spare expense. I have five hundred dollars in my pocket."

Mr. Van Burnam's daughter! Well, well! A tragedy of some kind was portending! But I bought the dress.

"Now," said she, "lace, and whatever else I need to make it up suitably. And I must have slippers and gloves. You know what a young girl requires to make her look like a lady. I want to look so well that the most critical eye will detect no fault in my appearance. It can be done, can it not, Miss Butterworth? My face and figure will not spoil the effect, will they?"

"No," said I; "you have a good face and a beautiful figure. You ought to look well. Are you going to a ball, my dear?"

"I am going to a ball," she answered; but her tone was so strange the people passing us turned to look at her.

"Let us have everything sent to the carriage," said she, and went with me from counter to counter with her ready purse in her hand, but not once lifting her veil to look at what was offered us, saying over and over as I sought to consult her in regard to some article: "Buy the richest; I leave it all to you."

Had Mr. Gryce not told me she must be humored, I could never have gone through this ordeal. To see a girl thus expend her hoarded savings on such frivolities was absolutely painful to me, and more than once I was tempted to decline any further participation in such extravagance. But a thought of my obligations to Mr. Gryce restrained me, and I went on spending the poor girl's dollars with more pain to myself than if I had taken them out of my own pocket.

Having purchased all the articles we thought necessary, we were turning towards the door when Miss Oliver whispered:

"Wait for me in the carriage for just a few minutes. I have one more thing to buy, and I must do it alone."

"But—" I began.

"I will do it, and I will not be followed," she insisted, in a shrill tone that made me jump.

And seeing no other way of preventing a scene, I let her leave me, though it cost me an anxious fifteen minutes.

When she rejoined me, as she did at the expiration of that time, I eyed the bundle she held with decided curiosity. But I could make no guess at its contents.

"Now," she cried, as she reseated herself and closed the carriage door, "where shall I find a dressmaker able and willing to make up this satin in five days?"

I could not tell her. But after some little search we succeeded in finding a woman who engaged to make an elegant costume in the time given her. The first measurements were taken, and we drove back to Ninth Street with a lasting memory in my mind of the cold and rigid form of Miss Oliver standing up in Madame's triangular parlor, submitting to the mechanical touches of the modiste with an outward composure, but with a brooding horror in her eyes that bespoke an inward torment.

CHAPTER XXXIX

The Watchful Eye

As I parted with Miss Oliver on Mrs. Desberger's stoop and did not visit her again in that house, I will introduce the report of a person better situated than myself to observe the girl during the next few days. That the person thus alluded to was a woman in the service of the police is evident, and as such may not meet with your approval, but her words are of interest, as witness:

* * * *

"Friday P.M.

"Party went out today in company with an elderly female of respectable appearance. Said elderly female wears puffs, and moves with great precision. I say this in case her identification should prove necessary.

"I had been warned that Miss O. would probably go out, and as the man set to watch the front door was on duty, I occupied myself during her absence in making a neat little hole in the partitions between our two rooms, so that I should not be obliged to offend my next-door neighbor by too frequent visits to her apartment. This done, I awaited her return, which was delayed till it was almost dark. When she did come in, her arms were full of bundles. These she thrust into a bureau-drawer, with the exception of one, which she laid with great care under her pillow. I wondered what this one could be, but could get no inkling from its size or shape. Her manner when she took off her hat was fiercer than before, and a strange smile, which I had not previously observed on her lips, added force to her expression. But it paled after supper-time, and she had a restless night. I could hear her walk the floor long after I thought it prudent on my part to retire, and at intervals through the night I was disturbed by her moaning, which was not that of a sick person but of one very much afflicted in mind.

* * * *

"Saturday.

"Party quiet. Sits most of the time with hands clasped on her knee before the fire. Given to quick starts as if suddenly awakened from an absorbing train of thought. A pitiful object, especially when seized by terror as she is at odd times. No walks, no visitors today. Once I heard her speak some words in a strange language, and once she drew herself up before the mirror in an attitude of so much dignity I was surprised at the fine appearance she made. The fire of her eyes at this moment was remarkable. I should not be surprised at any move she might make.

* * * *

"Sunday.

"She has been writing today. But when she had filled several pages of letter paper she suddenly tore them all up and threw them into the fire. Time seems to drag with her, for she goes every few minutes to the window from which a distant church clock is visible, and sighs as she turns away. More writing in the evening and some tears. But the writing was burned as before, and the tears stopped by a laugh that augurs little good to the person who called it up. The package has been taken from under her pillow and put in some place not visible from my spy-hole.

* * * *

"Monday.

"Party out again today, gone some two hours or more. When she returned she sat down before the mirror and began dressing her hair. She has fine hair, and she tried arranging it in several ways. None seemed to satisfy her, and she tore it down again and let it hang till supper-time, when she wound it up in its usual simple knot. Mrs. Desberger spent some minutes with her, but their talk was far from confidential, and therefore uninteresting. I wish people would speak louder when they talk to themselves.

* * * *

"Tuesday.

"Great restlessness on the part of the young person I am watching. No quiet for her, no quiet for me, yet she accomplishes nothing, and as yet has furnished me no clue to her thoughts.

"A huge box was brought into the room tonight. It seemed to cause her dread rather than pleasure, for she shrank at sight of it, and has not yet attempted to open it. But her eyes have never left it since it was set down on the floor. It looks like a dressmaker's box, but why such emotion over a gown?

* * * *

"Wednesday.

"This morning she opened the box but did not display its contents. I caught one glimpse of a mass of tissue paper, and then she put the cover on again, and for a good half hour sat crouching down beside it, shuddering like one in an ague-fit. I began to feel there was something deadly in the box, her eyes wandered towards it so frequently and with such contradictory looks of dread and savage determination. When she got up it was to see how many more minutes of the wretched day had passed.

* * * *

"Thursday.

"Party sick; did not try to leave her bed. Breakfast brought up by Mrs. Desberger, who showed her every attention, but could not prevail upon her to eat. Yet she would not let the tray be taken away, and when she was alone again or thought herself alone, she let her eyes rest so long on the knife lying across her plate, that I grew nervous and could hardly restrain myself from rushing into the room. But I remembered my instructions, and kept still even when I saw her hand steal towards this possible weapon, though I kept my own on the bell-rope which fortunately hung at my side. She looked quite capable of wounding herself with the knife, but after balancing it a moment in her hand, she laid it down again and turned with a low moan to the wall. She will not attempt death till she has accomplished what is in her mind.

* * * *

"Friday.

"All is right in the next room; that is, the young lady is up; but there is another change in her appearance since last night. She has grown contemptuous of herself and indulges less in brooding. But her impatience at the slow passage of time continues, and her interest in the box is even greater than before. She does not open it, however, only looks at it and lays her trembling hand now and then on the cover.

* * * *

"Saturday.

"A blank day. Party dull and very quiet. Her eyes begin to look like ghastly hollows in her pale face. She talks to herself continually, but in a low mechanical way exceedingly wearing to the listener, especially as no word can be distinguished. Tried to see her in her own room today, but she would not admit me.

* * * *

"Sunday.

"I have noticed from the first a Bible lying on one end of her mantel-shelf. Today she noticed it also, and impulsively reached out her hand to take it down. But at the first word she read she gave a low cry and hastily closed the book and put it back. Later, however, she took it again and read several chapters. The result was a softening in her manner, but she went to bed as flushed and determined as ever.

* * * *

"Monday.

"She has walked the floor all day. She has seen no one, and seems scarcely able to contain her impatience. She cannot stand this long.

* * * *

"Tuesday.

"My surprises began in the morning. As soon as her room had been put in order, Miss O. locked the door and began to open her bundles. First she unrolled a pair of white silk stockings, which she carefully, but without any show of interest, laid on the bed; then she opened a package containing gloves. They were white also, and evidently of the finest qual-ity. Then a lace handkerchief was brought to light, slippers, an evening fan, and a pair of fancy pins, and lastly she opened the mysterious box and took out a dress so rich in quality and of such simple elegance, it al-most took my breath away. It was white, and made of the heaviest satin, and it looked as much out of place in that shabby room as its owner did in the moments of exaltation of which I have spoken.

"Though her face was flushed when she lifted out the gown, it be-came pale again when she saw it lying across her bed. Indeed, a look of passionate abhorrence characterized her features as she contemplated it, and her hands went up before her eyes and she reeled back uttering the first words I have been able to distinguish since I have been on duty. They were violent in character, and seemed to tear their way through her lips almost without her volition. 'It is hate I feel, nothing but hate. Ah, if it were only duty that animated me!'

"Later she grew calmer, and covering up the whole paraphernalia with a stray sheet she had evidently laid by for the purpose, she sent for Mrs. Desberger. When that lady came in she met her with a wan but by no means dubious smile, and ignoring with quiet dignity the very evident curiosity with which that good woman surveyed the bed, she said appealingly:

"'You have been so kind to me, Mrs. Desberger, that I am going to tell you a secret. Will it continue to remain a secret, or shall I see it in the faces of all my fellow-boarders tomorrow?' You can imagine Mrs. Desberger's reply, also the manner in which it was delivered, but not Miss Oliver's secret. She uttered it in these words: 'I am going out tonight, Mrs. Desberger. I am going into great society. I am going to attend Miss Althorpe's wedding.' Then, as the good woman stammered out some words of surprise and pleasure, she went on to say: 'I do not want any one to know it, and I would be so glad if I could slip out of the house without any one seeing me. I shall need a carriage, but you will get one for me, will you not, and let me know the moment it comes. I am shy of what folks say, and besides, as you know, I am neither happy nor well, if I do go to weddings, and have new dresses, and—' She nearly broke down but collected herself with wonderful promptitude, and with a coaxing look that made her almost ghastly, so much it seemed out of accord with her strained and unnatural manner, she raised a corner of the sheet, saying, 'I will show you my gown, if you will promise to help me quietly out of the house,' which, of course, produced the desired effect upon Mrs. Desberger, that woman's greatest weakness being her love of dress.

"So from that hour I knew what to expect, and after sending precautionary advices to Police Headquarters, I set myself to watch her prepare for the evening. I saw her arrange her hair and put on her elegant gown, and was as much startled by the result as if I had not had the least premonition that she only needed rich clothes to look both beautiful and distinguished. The square parcel she had once hidden under her pillow was brought out and laid on the bed, and when Mrs. Desberger's low knock announced the arrival of the carriage, she caught it up and hid it under the cloak she hastily threw about her. Mrs. Desberger came in and put out the light, but before the room sank into darkness I caught one glimpse of Miss Oliver's face. Its expression was terrible beyond anything I had ever seen on any human countenance."

CHAPTER XL

As the Clock Struck

I do not attend weddings in general, but great as my suspense was in reference to Miss Oliver, I felt that I could not miss seeing Miss Althorpe married.

I had ordered a new dress for the occasion, and was in the best of spirits as I rode to the church in which the ceremony was to be performed. The excitement of a great social occasion was for once not disagreeable to me, nor did I mind the crowd, though it pushed me about rather uncomfortably till an usher came to my assistance and seated me in a pew, which I was happy to see commanded a fine view of the chancel.

I was early, but then I always am early, and having ample opportunity for observation, I noted every fine detail of ornamentation with approval, Miss Althorpe's taste being of that fine order which always falls short of ostentation. Her friends are in very many instances my friends, and it was no small part of my pleasure to note their well-known faces among the crowd of those that were strange to me. That the scene was brilliant, and that silks, satins, and diamonds abounded, goes without saying.

At last the church was full, and the hush which usually precedes the coming of the bride was settling over the whole assemblage, when I suddenly observed, in the person of a respectable-looking gentleman seated in a side pew, the form and features of Mr. Gryce, the detective. This was a shock to me, yet what was there in his presence there to alarm me? Might not Miss Althorpe have accorded him this pleasure out of the pure goodness of her heart? I did not look at anybody else, however, after once my eyes fell upon him, but continued to watch his expression, which was non-commital, though a little anxious for one engaged in a purely social function.

The entrance of the clergyman and the sudden peal of the organ in the well-known wedding march recalled my attention to the occasion itself, and as at that moment the bridegroom stepped from the vestry to await his bride at the altar, I was absorbed by his fine appearance and the air of mingled pride and happiness with which he watched the stately approach of the bridal procession.

But suddenly there was a stir through the whole glittering assemblage, and the clergyman made a move and the bridegroom gave a start, and the sound, slight as it was, of moving feet grew still, and I saw advancing from the door on the opposite side of the altar a second bride, clad in white and surrounded by a long veil which completely hid her face. A second bride! and the first was half-way up the aisle, and only one bridegroom stood ready!

The clergyman, who seemed to have as little command of his faculties as the rest of us, tried to speak; but the approaching woman, upon whom every regard was fixed, forestalled him by an authoritative gesture.

Advancing towards the chancel, she took her place on the spot reserved for Miss Althorpe.

Silence had filled the church up to this moment; but at this audacious move, a solitary wailing cry of mingled astonishment and despair went up behind us; but before any of us could turn, and while my own heart stood still, for I thought I recognized this veiled figure, the woman at the altar raised her hand and pointed towards the bridegroom.

"Why does he hesitate?" she cried. "Does he not recognize the only woman with whom he dare face God and man at the altar? Because I am already his wedded wife, and have been so for five long years, does that make my wearing of this veil amiss when he a husband, unreleased by the law, dares enter this sacred place with the hope and expectation of a bridegroom?"

It was Ruth Oliver who spoke. I recognized her voice as I had recognized her apparel; but the emotions aroused in me by her presence and the almost incredible claims she advanced were lost in the horror inspired by the man she thus vehemently accused. No lost spirit from the pit could have shown a more hideous commingling of the most terrible passions known to man than he did in the face of this terrible arraignment; and if Ella Althorpe, cowering in her shame and misery half-way up the aisle, saw him in all his depravity at that instant as I did, nothing could have saved her long-cherished love from immediate death.

Yet he tried to speak.

"It is false!" he cried; "all false! The woman I once called wife is dead."

"Dead, Olive Randolph? Murderer!" she exclaimed. "The blow struck in the dark found another victim!" And pulling the veil from her face, Ruth Oliver advanced to his side and laid her trembling hand with a firm and decisive movement on his arm.

Was it her words, her touch, or the sound of the clock striking eight in the great tower over our heads, which so totally overwhelmed him? As the last stroke of the hour which was to have seen him united with Miss Althorpe died out in the awed spaces above him, he gave a cry such as I am sure never resounded between those sacred walls before, and sank in a heap on the spot where but a few minutes previous he had lifted his head in all the glow and pride of a prospective bridegroom.

CHAPTER XLI

Secret History

It was hours before I found myself able to realize that the scene I had just witnessed had a deeper and much more dreadful significance than appeared to the general eye, and that Ruth Oliver, in her desperate interruption of these treacherous nuptials, had not only made good her prior claim to Randolph Stone as her husband, but had pointed him out to all the world as the villainous author of that crime which for so long a time had occupied my own and the public's attention.

Thinking that you may find the same difficulty in grasping this terrible fact, and being anxious to save you from the suspense under which I myself labored for so many hours, I here subjoin a written statement made by this woman some weeks later, in which the whole mystery is explained. It is signed Olive Randolph; the name to which she evidently feels herself best entitled.

* * * *

"The man known in New York City as Randolph Stone was first seen by me in Michigan five years ago. His name then was John Randolph, and how he has since come to add to this the further appellation of Stone, I must leave to himself to explain.

"I was born in Michigan myself, and till my eighteenth year I lived with my father, who was a widower without any other child, in a little low cottage amid the sand mounds that border the eastern side of the lake.

"I was not pretty, but every man who passed me on the beach or in the streets of the little town where we went to market and to church, stopped to look at me, and this I noticed, and from this perhaps my unhappiness arose.

"For before I was old enough to know the difference between poverty and riches, I began to lose all interest in my simple home duties, and to cast longing looks at the great school building where girls like myself learned to speak like ladies and play the piano. Yet these ambitious promptings might have come to nothing if I had never met *him*. I might have settled down in my own sphere and lived a useful if unsatisfied life like my mother and my mother's mother before her.

"But fate had reserved me for wretchedness, and one day just as I was on the verge of my eighteenth year, I saw John Randolph.

"I was coming out of church when our eyes first met, and I noticed after the first shock my simple heart received from his handsome face and elegant appearance, that he was surveying me with that strange look of admiration I had seen before on so many faces; and the joy this gave me, and the certainty which came with it of my seeing him again, made that moment quite unlike any other in my whole life, and was the beginning of that passion which has undone me, ruined him, and brought death and sorrow to many others of more worth than either of us.

"He was not a resident of the town, but a passing visitor; and his intention had been, as he has since told me, to leave the place on the following day. But the dart which had pierced my breast had not glanced entirely aside from his, and he remained, as he declared, to see what there was in this little country-girl's face to make it so unforgettable. We met first on the beach and afterwards under the strip of pines which separate our cottage from the sand mounds, and though I have no reason to believe he came to these interviews with any honest purpose or deep sincerity of feeling, it is certain he exerted all his powers to make them memorable to me, and that, in doing so, he awoke some of the fire in his own breast which he took such wicked pleasure in arousing in mine.

"In fact he soon showed that this was so, for I could take no step from the house without encountering him; and the one indelible impression remaining to me from those days is the expression his face wore as, one sunny afternoon, he laid my hand on his arm and drew me away to have a look at the lake booming on the beach below us. There was no love in it as I understand love now, but the passion which informed it almost amounted to intoxication, and if such a passion can be understood between a man already cultivated and a girl who hardly knew how to read, it may, in a measure, account for what followed.

"My father, who was no fool, and who saw the selfish quality in this attractive lover of mine, was alarmed by our growing intimacy. Taking an opportunity when we were both in a more sensible mood than common, he put the case before Mr. Randolph in a very decided way. He told him that either he must marry me at once or quit seeing me altogether. No delay was to be considered and no compromise allowed.

"As my father was a man with whom no one ever disputed, John Randolph prepared to leave the town, declaring that he could marry no one at that stage of his career. But before he could carry out his intention, the old intoxication returned, and he came back in a fever of love and impatience to marry me.

"Had I been older or more experienced in the ways of the world, I would have known that such passion as this evinced was short-lived; that there is no witchery in a smile lasting enough to make men like him forget the lack of those social graces to which they are accustomed. But I was mad with happiness, and was unconscious of any cloud lowering upon our future till the day of our first separation came, when an event occurred which showed me what I might expect if I could not speedily raise myself to his level.

"We were out walking, and we met a lady who had known Mr. Randolph elsewhere. She was well dressed, which I was not, though I had not realized it till I saw how attractive she looked in quiet colors and with only a simple ribbon on her hat; and she had, besides, a way of speaking which made my tones sound harsh, and robbed me of that feeling of superiority with which I had hitherto regarded all the girls of my acquaintance.

"But it was not her possession of these advantages, keenly as I felt them, which awakened me to the sense of my position. It was the surprise she showed (a surprise the source of which was not to be mistaken) when he introduced me to her as his wife; and though she recovered herself in a moment, and tried to be kind and gracious, I felt the sting of it and saw that he felt it too, and consequently was not at all astonished when, after she had passed us, he turned and looked at me critically for the first time.

"But his way of showing his dissatisfaction gave me a shock it took me years to recover from. 'Take off that hat,' he cried, and when I had obeyed him, he tore out the spray which to my eyes had been its chief adornment, and threw it into some bushes near by; then he gave me back the hat and asked for the silk neckerchief which I had regarded as the glory of my bridal costume. Giving it to him I saw him put it in his pocket, and understanding now that he was trying to make me look more like the lady we had passed, I cried out passionately: 'It is not these things that make the difference, John, but my voice and way of walking and speaking. Give me money and let me be educated, and then we will see if any other woman can draw your eyes away from me.'

"But he had received a shock that made him cruel. 'You cannot make a silk purse out of a sow's ear,' he sneered, and was silent all the rest of the way home. I was silent too, for I never talk when I am angry, but when we arrived in our own little room I confronted him.

"'Are you going to say any more such cruel things to me?' I asked, 'for if you are, I should like you to say them now and be done with it.'

"He looked desperately angry, but there was yet a little love left in his heart for me, for he laughed after he had looked at me for a minute, and took me in his arms and said some of the fine things with which he had previously won my heart, but not with the old fire and not with the old effect upon me. Yet my love had not grown cold, it had only changed from the unthinking stage to the thinking one, and I was quite in earnest when I said: 'I know I am not as pretty or as nice as the ladies you are accustomed to. But I have a heart that has never known any other passion than its love for you, and from such a heart you ought to expect a lady to grow, and there will. Only give me the chance, John; only let me learn to read and write.'

"But he was in an incredulous state of mind, and it ended in his going away without making any arrangements for my education. He was bound for San Francisco, where he had business to transact, and he promised to be back in four weeks, but before the four weeks elapsed, he wrote me that it would be five, and later on that it would be six, and afterwards that it would be when he had finished a big piece of work he was engaged upon, and which would bring him a large amount of money. I believed him and I doubted him at the same time, but I was not altogether sorry he delayed his return for I had begun school on my own account and was fast laying the foundation of a solid education.

"My means came from my father, who, now it was too late, saw the necessity of my improving myself. The amount of studying I did that first year was amazing, but it was nothing to what I went through the second, for my husband's letters had begun to fail me, and I was forced to work in order to drown grief and keep myself from despair. Finally no letters came at all, and when the second year was over, and I could at least express myself correctly, I woke to the realization that, so far as my husband was concerned, I had gone through all this labor for nothing, and that unless by some fortunate chance I could light upon some clue to his whereabouts in the great world beyond our little town, I would be likely to pass the remainder of my days in widowhood and desolation.

"My father dying at this time and leaving me a thousand dollars, I knew no better way of spending it than in the hopeless search I have just mentioned. Accordingly after his burial I started out on my travels, gaining experience with every mile. I had not been away a week before I realized what a folly I had indulged in in ever hoping to see John Randolph back at my side. I saw the homes in which such men as he lived, and met in cars and on steamboats the kind of people with whom he must associate to be happy, and a gulf seemed to open between us which even such love as mine would be powerless to bridge.

"But though hope thus sank in my breast, I did not lose my old ambition of making myself as worthy of him as circumstances would permit. I read only the best books and I allowed myself to become acquainted with only the best people, and as I saw myself liked by such the awkwardness of my manner gradually disappeared, and I began to feel that the day would come when I should be universally recognized as a lady.

"Meantime I did not advance an iota in the object of my journey; and at last, with every expectation gone of ever seeing my husband again, I made my way to Toledo. Here I speedily found employment, and what was better still to one of my ambitious tendencies, an opportunity to add to the sum of my accomplishments a knowledge of French and music. The French I learned from the family I lived with, and the music from a professor in the same house whose love for his pet art was so great that he found it simple happiness to impart it to one so greedy for improvement as myself.

"Here, in course of time, I also learned type-writing, and it was for the purpose of seeking employment in this capacity that I finally came to New York. This was three months ago.

"I was in complete ignorance of the city when I entered it, and for a day or two I wandered to and fro, searching for a suitable lodging-house. It was while I was on my way to Mrs. Desberger's that I saw advancing towards me a gentleman in whose air and manner I detected a resemblance to the husband who some five years since had deserted me. The shock was too much for my self-control. Quaking in every limb, I stood awaiting his approach, and when he came up to me, and I saw by his startled recognition of me that it was indeed he, I gave a loud cry and threw myself upon his arm. The start he gave was nothing to the frightful expression which crossed his face at this encounter, but I thought both due to his surprise, though now I am convinced they had their origin in the deepest and worst emotions of which a man is capable.

"'John! John!' I cried, and could say no more, for the agitations of five solitary, despairing years were choking me; but he was entirely voiceless, stricken, I have no doubt, beyond any power of mine to realize. How could I dream that in consideration, power, and prestige he had advanced even more rapidly than myself, and that at this very moment he was not only the idol of society, but on the verge of uniting himself to a woman—I will not say of marrying her, for marry her he could not while I lived—who would make him the envied possessor of millions. Such fortune, such daring, yes and such depravity, were beyond the reach of my imagination, and while I thought his pleasure less than mine, I did not dream that my existence was a menace to all his hopes, and that during this moment of speechlessness he was sounding his nature for means to rid himself of me even at the cost of my life.

"His first movement was to push me away, but I clung to him all the harder; at which his whole manner changed and he began to make futile efforts to calm me and lead me away from the spot. Seeing that these attempts were unavailing, he turned pale and raised his arm up passionately, but speedily dropped it again, and casting glances this way and that, broke suddenly into a loud laugh and became, as by the touch of a magician's wand, my old lover again.

"'Why, Olive!' he cried; 'why, Olive! is it you? (Did I say my name was Olive?) Happily met, my dear! I did not know what I had been missing all these years, but now I know it was you. Will you come with me, or shall I go home with you?'

"'I have no home,' said I, 'I have just come into town.'

"'Then I see but one alternative.' He smiled, and what a power there was in his smile when he chose to exert it! 'You must come to my apartments; are you willing?'

"'I am your wife,' I answered.

"He had taken me on his arm by this time and the recoil he made at these words was quite perceptible; but his face still smiled, and I was too mad with joy to be critical.

"'And a very pretty and charming wife you have become,' said he, drawing me on for a few steps. Suddenly he paused, and I felt the old shadow fall between us again. 'But your dress is very shabby,' he remarked.

"It was not; it was not near as shabby as the linen duster he himself wore.

"'Is that rain?' he inquired, looking up as a drop or two fell.

"'Yes, it is raining.'

"'Very well, let us go into this store we are coming to and buy a gossamer. That will cover up your gown. I cannot take you to my house dressed as you are now.'

"Surprised, for I had thought my dress very neat and lady-like, but never dreaming of questioning his taste any more than in the old days in Michigan, I went with him into the shop he had pointed out and bought me a gossamer, for which he paid. When he had helped me to put it on and had tied my veil well over my face, he seemed more at his ease and gave me his arm quite cheerfully.

"'Now,' said he, 'you look well, but how about the time when you will have to take the gossamer off? I tell you what it is, my dear, you will have to refit yourself entirely before I shall be satisfied.' And again I saw him cast about him that furtive and inquiring look which would have awakened more surprise in me than it did had I known that we were in a part of the city where he ran but little chance of meeting any one he knew.

"'This old duster I have on,' he suddenly laughed, 'is a very appropriate companion to your gossamer,' and though I did not agree with him, for my clothes were new, and his old and shabby, I laughed also and never dreamed of evil.

"As this garment which so disfigured him that morning has been the occasion of much false speculation on the part of those whose business it was to inquire into the crime with which it is in a most unhappy way connected, I may as well explain here and now why so fastidious a gentleman as Randolph Stone came to wear it. The gentleman called Howard Van Burnam was not the only person who visited the Van Burnam offices on the morning preceding the murder. Randolph Stone was there also, but he did not see the brothers, for finding them closeted together, he decided not to interrupt them. As he was a frequent visitor there, his presence created no remark nor was his departure noted. Descending the stairs separating the offices from the street, he was about to leave the building, when he noticed that the clouds looked ominous. Being dressed for a luncheon with Miss Althorpe, he felt averse to getting wet, so he stepped back into the adjoining hall and began groping for an umbrella in a little closet under the stairs where he had once before found such an article. While doing this he heard the younger Van Burnam descend and go out, and realizing that he could now see Franklin without difficulty, he was about to return upstairs when he heard that gentleman also come down and follow his brother into the street.

"His first impulse was to join him, but finding nothing but an old duster in the closet, he gave up this intention, and putting on this shabby but protecting garment, started for his apartments, little realizing into what a course of duplicity and crime it was destined to lead him. For to the wearing of this old duster on this especial morning, innocent as the occasion was, I attribute John Randolph's temptation to murder. Had he gone out without it, he would have taken his usual course up Broadway and never met *me*; or even if he had taken the same roundabout way to his apartments as that which led to our encounter, he would never have dared, in his ordinary fine dress, conspicuous as it made him, to have entered upon those measures, which, as he is clever enough to know, lead to disgrace, if they do not end in a felon's cell. It was John Randolph, then, or Randolph Stone, as he is pleased to call himself in New York, and not Franklin Van Burnam (who had doubtless proceeded in another direction) who came up to where Howard had stood, saw the keys he had dropped, and put them in his own pocket. It was as innocent an action as the donning of the duster, and yet it was fraught with the worst consequences to himself and others.

"Being of the same height and complexion as Franklin Van Burnam, and both gentlemen wearing at that time a moustache (my husband shaved his off after the murder), the mistakes which arose out of this strange equipment were but natural. Seen from the rear or in the semi-darkness of a hotel-office they might look alike, though to me or to any one studying them well, their faces are really very different.

"But to return. Leading me through streets of which I knew nothing, he presently stopped before the entrance of a large hotel.

"'I tell you what, Olive,' said he, 'we had better go in here, take a room, and send for such things as you require to make you look like a lady.'

"As I had no objection to anything which kept me at his side, I told him that whatever suited him suited me, and followed him quite eagerly into the office. I did not know then that this hotel was a second-rate one, not having had experience with the best, but if I had, I should not have wondered at his choice, for there was nothing in his appearance, as I have already intimated, or in his manners up to this point, to lead me to think he was one of the city's great swells, and that it was only in such an unfashionable house as this he would be likely to pass unrecognized. How with his markedly handsome features and distinguished bearing he managed so to carry himself as to look like a man of inferior breeding, I can no more explain than I can the singular change which took place in him when once he found himself in the midst of the crowd which lounged about this office.

"From a man to attract all eyes he became at once a man to attract none, and slouched and looked so ordinary that I stared at him in astonishment, little thinking that he had assumed this manner as a disguise. Seeing me at a loss, he spoke up quite peremptorily:

"'Let us keep our secret, Olive, till you can appear in the world full-fledged. And look here, darling, won't you go to the desk and ask for a room? I am no hand at any such business.'

"Confounded at a proposition so unexpected, but too much under the spell of my feelings to dispute his wishes, I faltered out:

"'But supposing they ask me to register?'

"At which he gave me a look which recalled the old days in Michigan, and quietly sneered:

"'Give them a fictitious name. You have learned to write by this time, have you not?'

"Stung by his taunt, but more in love with him than ever, for his momentary display of passion had made him look both masterful and handsome, I went up to the desk to do his bidding.

"'A room!' said I; and when asked to write our names in the book that lay before me, I put down the first that suggested itself. I wrote with my gloves on, which was why the writing looked so queer that it was taken for a disguised hand.

"This done, he rejoined me, and we went upstairs, and I was too happy to be in his company again to wonder at his peculiarities or weigh the consequences of the implicit confidence I accorded him. I was desperately in love once more, and entered into every plan he proposed without a thought beyond the joyous present. He was so handsome without his hat; and when after some short delay he threw aside the duster, I felt myself for the first time in my life in the presence of a finished gentleman. Then his manner was so changed. He was so like his oldest and best self, so dangerously like what he was in those long vanished hours under the pines in my sand-swept home on the shores of Lake Michigan. That he faltered at times and sank into strange spells of silence which had something in them that made my breath come fitfully, did not awaken my apprehension or rouse in me more than a passing curiosity. I thought he regretted the past, and when, after one such pause in our conversation, he drew out of his pocket a couple of keys tied together with a string, and surveyed the card attached to them with a strange look, easily enough to be understood by me now, I only laughed at his abstraction, and indulged in a fresh caress to make him more mindful of my presence.

"These keys were the ones which Mrs. Van Burnam's husband had dropped, and which he had picked up before meeting me; and after he had put them back into his pocket he became more talkative than before, and more systematically lover-like. I think he had not seen his way clearly till this moment, the dark and dreadful way which was to end, as he supposed, in my death.

"But I feared nothing, suspected nothing. Such deep and desperate wickedness as he was planning was beyond the wildest flight of my imagination. When he insisted upon sending for a complete set of clothing for me, and when at his dictation I wrote a list of the articles I wanted, I thought he was influenced by his wish as my husband to see me dressed in articles of his own buying. That it was all a plot to rob me of my identity could not strike such a mind as mine, and when the packages came and were received by him in the sly way already known to the public, I saw nothing in his caution but a playful display of mystery that was to end in my romantic establishment in a home of love and luxury.

"Or rather it is thus that I account for my conduct now, and yet the precaution I took not to change the shoes in which my money was hidden, may argue that I was not without some underlying doubt of his complete sincerity. But if so, I hid it from myself, and, as I have every reason to believe, from him also, doubtless excusing my action to myself by considering that I would be none the worse off for a few dollars of my own, even if he was my husband, and had promised me no end of pleasure and comfort.

"That he did intend to make me happy, he had assured me more than once. Indeed, before we had been long in this hotel room, he informed me that great experiences lay before me; that he had prospered much in the last five years and had now a house of his own to offer me and a large circle of friends to make our life in it agreeable.

"'We will go to our house tonight,' said he. 'I have not been living in it lately, and you may find it a little uncomfortable, but we will remedy that tomorrow. Anything is better than staying here under a false name and I cannot take you to my bachelor apartment.'

"I had doubted some of his previous statements, but this one I implicitly believed. Why should not so elegant a man have a house of his own; and if he had told me it was built of marble and hung with Florentine tapestries, I should still have credited it all. I was in fairy-land and he was my knight of romance, even when he again hung his head in leaving the hotel and looked at once so ordinary and uninteresting.

"The ruse he made use of to cut off all connection between ourselves and the Mr. and Mrs. James Pope who had registered at the Hotel D—— was accepted by me with the same lack of suspicion. That he should wish to carry no remembrance of our old life into our new home I thought a delightful piece of folly, and when he proposed that we should bequeath my gossamer and his own disfiguring duster to the coachman in whose hack we were then riding, I laughed gleefully and helped him fold them up and place them under the cushions, though I did wonder why he cut a piece out of the neck of the former, and pouted with the happy freedom of a self-confident woman when he said:

"'It is the first thing I ever bought for you, and I am just foolish enough to wish to preserve this much of it for a keepsake. Do you object, my dear?'

"As I was conscious of cherishing a similar folly in his regard, and could have pressed even that old duster of his to my heart, I offered him a kiss and said 'No,' and he put the scrap away in his pocket. That it was the portion on which was stamped the name of the firm from which it was bought did not occur to me.

"When the coach stopped, he urged me away on foot in a direction entirely strange to me, saying we would take another hack as soon as we had disposed of the bundles we were carrying. How he intended to do this, I did not know. But presently he drew me towards a Chinese laundry, where he bade me leave one of them as washing, and the other he dropped before the opening of a sewer as we stepped up a neighboring curb-stone.

"And still I did not suspect.

"Our ride to Gramercy Park was short, but during it he had time to put a bill in my hand and tell me I was to pay the driver. He had also time to secure the weapon upon which he had probably had his eye fixed from the first. His manner of doing this I can never forgive, for it was a lover's manner, and as such intended to deceive and cajole me. Drawing my head down on his shoulder, he drew off my veil, saying that it was the only article left of my own buying, and that we would leave it behind us in this coach as we had left the gossamer in the other. 'Only I will make sure that no other woman ever wears it,' he laughed, slitting it up and down with his knife. When this was done he kissed me, and then while my heart was tender and the warm tears stood in my eyes, he drew out the pin from my hat, meeting my remonstrances with the assurance that he hated to see my head covered, and that no hat was as pretty as my own brown hair.

"As this was nonsense, and as the coach was beginning to stop, I shook my head at him and put my hat on again, but he had dropped the pin, or so he said, and I had to alight without it.

"When I had paid the driver and the coach had driven off, I had a chance to look up at the house before which we had stopped. Its height and imposing appearance daunted me in spite of the great expectations I had formed, and I ran up the stoop after him in a condition of mingled awe and wild delight that was the poorest preparation possible for what lay before me in the dark interior we were entering.

"He was fumbling nervously in the keyhole with his key, and I heard a whispered oath escape him. But presently the door fell back, and we stepped in to what looked to me like a cavern of darkness.

"'Do not be frightened!' he admonished me. 'I will strike a light in a moment.' And after carefully closing the street door behind us, he stretched out his hand to take mine, or so I judge, for I heard him whisper impatiently, 'Where are you?'

"I was on the threshold of the parlor, to which I had groped my way while he was closing the front door, so I whispered back, 'Here!' but found voice for nothing further, for at that instant I heard a sound proceeding from the depths of darkness in front of me, and was so struck with terror that I fell back against the staircase, just as he passed me and entered the room from which that stealthy noise had issued.

"'Darling!' he whispered, 'darling!' and went stumbling on in the void of darkness before me, till suddenly by some power I cannot explain I seemed to see, faintly but distinctly, and as if with my mind's eye rather than with my bodily one.

"I perceived the shadowy form of a woman standing in the space before him, and beheld him suddenly grasp her with what he meant to be a loving cry, but which to my ears at that moment sounded strangely ferocious, and after holding her a moment suddenly release her, at which she uttered one low, curdling moan and sank at his feet. At the same instant I heard a click, which I did not understand then, but which I now know to have been the head of the hat-pin striking the register.

"Horrified past all power of speech and action, for I saw that he had intended this blow for me, I cowered against the stairs, waiting for him to pass out. This he did not do at once, though the delay must have been short. He stopped long enough by the prostrate form to stir it with his foot, probably to see if life was extinct, but no longer, yet it seemed an eternity before I perceived him groping his way over the threshold; an eternity in which every act of my life passed before me, and every word and every expression with which he had beguiled me came to rack my soul and made the horror of this mad awakening greater.

"No thought of her, or of the guilt with which he had forever damned his soul, came to me in that first moment of misery. *My* loss, *my* escape, and the danger in which I still stood if the least hint reached him of the mistake he had made, filled my mind too entirely for me to dwell on any less impersonal theme. His words, for he muttered several in that short passage out, showed me in what a fools' paradise I had been revelling, and how certainly I had turned his every thought towards murder when I seized him in the street and proclaimed myself his wife. The satisfaction with which he uttered, 'Well struck!' gave little hint of remorse; and the gloating delight with which he added something about the devil having assisted him to make it a safe blow as well as a deadly one, was proof not only of his having used all his cunning in planning this crime, but of his pleasure in its apparent success.

"That he continued in this frame of mind, and that he never lost confidence in the precautions he had taken and in the mystery with which the deed was surrounded, is apparent from the fact that he revisited the Van Burnam office on the following morning, and hung again on its accustomed nail the keys of the Gramercy Park house.

"When the front door had closed, and I knew that he had gone away in the full belief that it was my form he had left lying behind him on that midnight floor, all the accumulated terrors of the situation came to me in full force, and I began to think of her as well as of myself, and longed for courage to approach her or even the daring to call out for help. But the thought that it was my husband who had committed this crime held me tongue-tied, and though I soon began to move inch by inch in her direction, it was some time before I could so far overcome my terror as to enter the room where she lay.

"I had supposed, and still supposed (as was natural after seeing him open the door with the keys he took from his pocket), that the house was his, and the victim a member of his own household. But when, after innumerable hesitations and a bodily shrinking that was little short of torment, I managed to drag myself into the room and light a match which I found on a farther mantel-shelf, I saw enough in the general appearance of the rooms and of the figure at my feet to make me doubt the truth of both these suppositions. Yet no other explanation came to lighten the mystery of the occasion, and dazed as I was by the horror of my position and the mortal dread I felt of the man who in one instant had turned the heaven of my love into a hell of fathomless horrors, I soon had eyes for the one fact only, that the woman lying before me was sufficiently like myself to inspire me with the hope of preserving my secret and keeping from my would-be slayer the knowledge of my having escaped the doom he had prepared for me.

"For ascribe it to what motive you will, that was the one idea now dominating my mind. I wanted him to believe me dead. I wanted to feel that all connection between us was severed forever. He *had* killed me. By killing my love and faith in him he had murdered the better part of myself, and I shrank with inconceivable horror from anything that would bring me again under his eye, or force me to assert claims that it would be the future business of my life to forget.

"When the first match went out I had not courage to light another, so I crept away in the darkness to listen at the foot of the stairs. There was no sound from above, and a terrifying sense began to pervade me that I was in that house alone. Yet there was safety in the thought, and opportunity for what I was planning, and finally, under the stress of the purpose that was every moment developing within me, I went softly upstairs and listened at all the doors till I was certain that the house was unoccupied. Then I came down and walked resolutely back into the parlor, for I knew if I allowed any time to pass I could never again summon up strength to cross its grisly threshold. Yet I did nothing for hours but crouch in one of its dismal corners, waiting for morning. That I did not go mad in that awful interval is a wonder. I must have been near it more than once.

"I have been asked, and Miss Butterworth has been asked, how in the light of what we now know concerning this poor victim's presence there, we account for her being in the darkness and showing so little terror at our entrance and Mr. Stone's approach. *I* account for it in this way: Two half-burned matches were found in the parlor grate. One I flung there; the other had probably been used by her to light the dining-room gas. If this was still lighted when we drove up, as it may have been, then, alarmed by the sound of the stopping coach, she had put it out, with a vague idea of hiding herself till she knew whether it was the old gentleman who was coming or only her suspicious and unreasonable husband. If it was not lighted then, she was probably aroused from a sleep on the parlor sofa, and was for the moment too dazed to cry out or resent an embrace she had not time to understand before she succumbed to the cruel stab that killed her. Miss Butterworth, however, thinks that the poor creature took the intruder for Franklin till she heard my voice, when she probably became so amazed that she was in a measure paralyzed and found it impossible to move or cry out. As Miss Butterworth is a woman of great discretion I should think her explanation the truest, if I did not consider her a little prejudiced against Mrs. Van Burnam.

"But to return to myself.

"With the first glimmer of light that came through the closed shutters I rose and began my dreadful task. Upheld by a purpose as relentless as that which drove the author of this horror into murder, I stripped the body and put upon it my own clothing, with the one exception of the shoes. Then, when I had re-dressed myself in hers, I steadied up my heart and with one wild pull dragged down the cabinet upon her so that her face might lose its traits and her identification become impossible.

"How I had strength to do this, and how I could contemplate the result without shrieking, I cannot now imagine. Perhaps I was hardly human at this crisis; perhaps something of the demon which had informed him in his awful work had entered into my breast, making this thing possible. I only know that I did what I have said and did it calmly. More than that, that I had mind and judgment left to give to my own appearance. Observing that the dress I had put on was of a conspicuous plaid, I exchanged the skirt portion with the brown silk petticoat under it, and when I observed that it hung below the other, as of course it would, I went through the house till I came upon some pins with which I pinned it up out of sight. Thus equipped, I was still a person to attract attention, especially as I had no hat to put on; my own having fallen from my head and been covered by the dead woman's body, which nothing would induce me to move again.

"But I had confidence in my own powers to escape question, toned up as I was in every nerve by the dreadfulness of my situation, and as soon as I was in decent shape for flight, I opened the front door and prepared to slip out.

"But here the intense dread I felt of my husband, a dread which had actuated all my movements and sustained me in as harrowing a task as ever woman performed, seized me with renewed force, and I quailed at the prospect of entering the streets alone. Supposing he should be on the stoop! Supposing he should be in an opposite window even! Could I encounter him again and live? He was not far away, or so I felt. A murderer, it is said, cannot help haunting the scene of his crime, and if he should see me alive and well, what might I not expect from his astonishment and alarm? I did not dare go out. But neither did I dare remain, so after quaking for a good five minutes on the threshold, I made one wild dash through the door.

"There was no one in sight, and I reached Broadway before I ran across man or woman. Even then I got by without any one speaking to me, and, favored by Providence, found a nook at the end of an alley-way, where I remained undiscovered till it was late enough in the morning for me to enter a shop and buy a hat.

"The rest of my movements are known. I found my way to Mrs. Desberger's, this time without interruption; and from that place sought and found a situation with Miss Althorpe.

"That her fate was in any way connected with mine, or that the Randolph Stone she was engaged to marry was the John Randolph from whose clutches I had just escaped, was, of course, unsuspected by me, and, incredible as it may seem, continued to be unsuspected as long as I remained in the house. There was reason for this. My duties were such as I could well attend to in my own room, and feeling a horror of the world and everything in it, I kept my room as much as possible, and never went out of it when I knew that he was in the house. The very thought of love awakened intolerable emotions in me, and much as I admired and revered Miss Althorpe, I could not bring myself to meet or even talk of the man to whom she was in expectation of being so soon united. There was another thing of which I was ignorant, and that was the circumstances which had invested with so much interest the crime of which I had been witness. I did not know that the victim had been recognized, or that an innocent man had been arrested for her murder. In fact I knew nothing concerning the affair save what I had seen with my own eyes, no one having mentioned the murder in my presence, and I having religiously avoided the very sight of a paper for fear that I should see some account of the horrible affair, and so lose what small remnants of courage I still possessed.

"This apathy concerning a matter so important to myself, or rather this almost frenzied determination to cut myself loose from my dreadful past, may seem strange and unnatural; but it will seem stranger yet when I say that for all these efforts I was haunted night and day by one small fact connected with this past, which made forgetfulness impossible. I had taken the rings from the hands of the dead woman as I had taken away her clothes, and the possession of these valuables, probably because they represented so much money, weighed on my conscience and made me feel like a thief. The purse which I found in a pocket of the skirt I had put on was a trouble to me, but the rings were a source of constant terror and disturbance. I hid them finally in a ball of yarn I was using, but even then I experienced but little peace, for they were not mine, and I lacked the courage to avow it or seek out the person to whom they now rightfully belonged.

"When, therefore, in the intervals of fever which attacked me in Miss Althorpe's house, I overheard enough of a conversation between her and Miss Butterworth to learn that the murdered woman had been a Mrs. Van Burnam, and that her husband or relatives had an office somewhere downtown, I was so seized by the instinct of restitution, that I took the first opportunity that offered to leave my bed and hunt up these people.

"That I would injure them in any way by secretly restoring these jewels, I never dreamed. Indeed, I did not exercise my mind at all on the subject, but only followed the instincts of my delirium; and while to all appearance I showed all the cunning of an insane person, in the pursuit of my purpose, I fail to remember now how I found my way to Duane Street, or by what suggestion of my diseased brain I was induced to slip these rings upon the hook attached to Mr. Van Burnam's desk. Probably the mere utterance of this well-known name into the ears of the passers-by was enough to obtain for me such directions as I needed, but however that may be, the result was misapprehension, and the complications which followed, serious.

"Of the emotion caused in me by the unaccountable discovery of my connection with this crime I need not speak. The love which I at one time felt for John Randolph had turned to gall and bitterness, but enough sense of duty remained in my bruised and broken heart to keep me from denouncing him to the police, till by a sudden stroke of fate or Providence, I saw him in the carriage with Miss Althorpe, and realized that he was not only the man with whom she was upon the point of allying herself, but that it was to preserve his place in her regard and to attain the lofty position promised by this union, he had attempted to murder me, and had murdered another woman only less unfortunate and miserable than myself.

"It was the last and bitterest blow that could come from his hand; and though instinct led me to throw myself into the carriage before which I stood, and thus escape a meeting which I felt I could never survive, I was determined from that moment not only to save Miss Althorpe from an alliance with this villain, but to revenge myself upon him in some never-to-be-forgotten manner.

"That this revenge involved her in a public shame from which her angelic goodness to me should have saved her, I regret now as deeply as even she can wish. But the madness that was upon me made me blind to every other consideration than that of the boundless hatred I bore him; and while I can look for no forgiveness from her on that account, I still hope the day will come when she will see that in spite of my momentary disregard of her feelings, I cherish for her an affection that nothing can efface or make other than the ruling passion of my life."

CHAPTER XLII

With Miss Butterworth's Compliments

They tell me that Mr. Gryce has never been quite the same man since the clearing up of this mystery; that his confidence in his own powers is shaken, and that he hints, more often than is agreeable to his superiors, that when a man has passed his seventy-seventh year it is time for him to give up active connection with police matters. *I* do not agree with him. His mistakes, if we may call them such, were not those of failing faculties, but of a man made oversecure in his own conclusions by a series of old successes. Had he listened to *me*—But I will not pursue this suggestion. You will accuse me of egotism, an imputation I cannot bear with equanimity and will not risk; modest depreciation of myself being one of the chief attributes of my character.[4]

Howard Van Burnam bore his release, as he had his arrest, with great outward composure. Mr. Gryce's explanation of his motives in perjuring himself before the Coroner was correct, and while the mass of people wondered at that instinct of pride which led him to risk the imputation of murder sooner than have the world accuse his wife of an unwomanly action, there were others who understood his peculiarities, and thought his conduct quite in keeping with what they knew of his warped and over-sensitive nature.

That he has been greatly moved by the unmerited fate of his weak but unfortunate wife, is evident from the sincerity with which he still mourns her.

I had always understood that Franklin had never been told of the peril in which his good name had stood for a few short hours. But since a certain confidential conversation which took place between us one evening, I have come to the conclusion that the police were not so reticent as they made themselves out to be. In that conversation he professed to thank me for certain good offices I had done him and his, and waxing warm in his gratitude, confessed that without my interference he would have found himself in a strait of no ordinary seriousness; "For," said he, "there has been no over-statement of the feelings I cherished toward my sister-in-law, nor was there any mistake made in thinking that she uttered some very desperate threats against me during the visit she paid me at my office on Monday. But I never thought of ridding myself of her in any way. I only thought of keeping her and my brother apart till I could escape the country. When therefore he came into the office on Tuesday morning for the keys of our father's house, I felt such a dread of the

4   My attention has been called to the fact that I have not confessed whether it was owing to a mistake made by Mr. Gryce or myself, that Franklin Van Burnam was identified as the man who had entered the adjoining house on the night of the murder. Well, the truth is, neither of us was to blame for that. The man I identified (it was while watching the guests who attended Mrs. Van Burnam's funeral, you remember) was really Mr. Stone; but owing to the fact that this latter gentleman had lingered in the vestibule till he was joined by Franklin and that they had finally entered together, some confusion was created in the mind of the man on duty in the hall, so that when Mr. Gryce asked him who it was that came in immediately after the four who arrived together, he answered Mr. Franklin Van Burnam; being anxious to win his superior's applause and considering that person much more likely to merit the detective's attention than a mere friend of the family like Mr. Stone. In punishment for this momentary display of egotism, he has been discharged from the force, I believe.—A. B.

two meeting there, that I left immediately after my brother for the place where she had told me she would await a final message from me. I hoped to move her by one final plea, for I love my brother sincerely, notwithstanding the wrong I once did him. I was therefore with her in another place at the very time I was thought to be with her at the Hotel D——, a fact which greatly hampered me, as you can see, when I was requested by the police to give an account of how I spent that day. When I left her it was to seek my brother. She had told me of her deliberate intention of spending the night in the Gramercy Park house; and as I saw no way of her doing this without my brother's connivance, I started in search of him, meaning to stick to him when I found him, and keep him away from her till that night was over. I was not successful in my undertaking. He was locked in his rooms it seems, packing up his effects for flight—we always had the same instincts even when boys—and receiving no answer to my knock, I hastened away to Gramercy Park to keep a watch over the house against my brother coming there. This was early in the evening, and for hours afterwards I wandered like a restless spirit in and out of those streets, meeting no one I knew, not even my brother, though he was wandering about in very much the same manner, and with very much the same apprehensions.

"The duplicity of the woman became very evident to me the next morning. In my last interview with her she had shown no relenting in her purpose towards me, but when I entered my office after this restless night in the streets, I found lying on my desk her little hand-bag, which had been sent down from Mrs. Parker's. In it was *the letter*, just as you divined, Miss Butterworth. I had hardly got over the shock of this most unexpected good fortune when the news came that a woman had been found dead in my father's house. What was I to think? That it was she, of course, and that my brother had been the man to let her in there. Miss Butterworth," this is how he ended, "I make no demands upon you, as I have made no demands upon the police, to keep the secret contained in that letter from my much-abused brother. Or, rather, it is too late now to keep it, for I have told him all there was to tell, myself, and he has seen fit to overlook my fault, and to regard me with even more affection than he did before this dreadful tragedy came to harrow up our lives."

Do you wonder I like Franklin Van Burnam?

The Misses Van Burnam call upon me regularly, and when they say "*Dear old thing!*" now, they mean it.

Of Miss Althorpe I cannot trust myself to speak. She was, and is, the finest woman I know, and when the great shadow now hanging over her has lost some of its impenetrability, she will be a useful one again, or I do not rightly read the patient smile which makes her face so beautiful in its sadness.

Olive Randolph has, at my request, taken up her abode in my house. The charm which she seems to have exerted over others she has exerted over me, and I doubt if I shall ever wish to part with her again. In return she gives me an affection which I am now getting old enough to appreciate. Her feeling for me and her gratitude to Miss Althorpe are the only treasures left her out of the wreck of her life, and it shall be my business to make them lasting ones.

The fate of Randolph Stone is too well known for me to enlarge upon it. But before I bid farewell to his name, I must say that after that curt confession of his, "Yes, I did it, in the way and for the motive she alleged," I have often tried to imagine the contradictory feelings with which he must have listened to the facts as they came out at the inquest, and convinced, as he had every reason to be, that the victim was his wife, heard his friend Howard not only accept her for his, but insist that he was the man who accompanied her to that house of death. He has never lifted the veil from those hours, and he never will, but I would give much of the peace of mind which has lately come to me, to know what his sensations were, not only at that time, but when, on the evening, after the murder, he opened the papers and read that the woman whom he had left for dead with her brain pierced by a hat-pin, had been found on that same floor crushed under a fallen cabinet; and what explanation he was ever able to make to himself for a fact so inexplicable.

THE CIRCULAR STUDY

THE THIRD EPISODE IN THE LIFE OF AMELIA BUTTERWORTH

BOOK I: A STRANGE CRIME

CHAPTER I

Red Light

Mr. Gryce was melancholy. He had attained that period in life when the spirits flag and enthusiasm needs a constant spur, and of late there had been a lack of special excitement, and he felt dull and superannuated. He was even contemplating resigning his position on the force and retiring to the little farm he had bought for himself in Westchester; and this in itself did not tend to cheerfulness, for he was one to whom action was a necessity and the exercise of his mental faculties more inspiring than any possible advantage which might accrue to him from their use.

But he was not destined to carry out this impulse yet. For just at the height of his secret dissatisfaction there came a telephone message to Headquarters which roused the old man to something like his former vigor and gave to the close of this gray fall day an interest he had not expected to feel again in this or any other kind of day. It was sent from Carter's well-known drug store, and was to the effect that a lady had just sent a boy in from the street to say that a strange crime had been committed in ———'s mansion round the corner. The boy did not know the lady, and was shy about showing the money she had given him, but that he had money was very evident, also, that he was frightened enough for his story to be true. If the police wished to communicate with him, he could be found at Carter's, where he would be detained till an order for his release should be received.

A *strange* crime! That word "strange" struck Mr. Gryce, and made him forget his years in wondering what it meant. Meanwhile the men about him exchanged remarks upon the house brought thus unexpectedly to their notice. As it was one of the few remaining landmarks of the preceding century, and had been made conspicuous moreover by the shops, club-houses, and restaurants pressing against it on either side, it had been a marked spot for years even to those who knew nothing of its history or traditions.

And now a crime had taken place in it! Mr. Gryce, in whose ears that word "strange" rang with quiet insistence, had but to catch the eye of the inspector in charge to receive an order to investigate the affair. He started at once, and proceeded first to the drug store. There he found the boy, whom he took along with him to the house indicated in the message. On the way he made him talk, but there was nothing the poor waif could add to the story already sent over the telephone. He persisted in saying that a lady (he did not say woman) had come up to him while he was looking at some toys in a window, and, giving him a piece of money, had drawn him along the street as far as the drug store. Here she showed him another coin, promising to add it to the one he had already pocketed if he would run in to the telephone clerk with a message for the police. He wanted the money, and when he grabbed at it she said that all he had to do was to tell the clerk that a strange crime had been committed in the old house on —— Street. This scared him, and he was sliding off, when she caught him again and shook him until his wits came back, after which he ran into the store and delivered the message.

There was candor in the boy's tone, and Mr. Gryce was disposed to believe him; but when he was asked to describe the lady, he showed that his powers of observation were no better than those of most of his class. All he could say was that she was a stunner, and wore shiny clothes and jewels, and Mr. Gryce, recognizing the lad's limitations at the very moment he found himself in view of the house he was making for, ceased to question him, and directed all his attention to the building he was approaching.

Nothing in the exterior bespoke crime or even disturbance. A shut door, a clean stoop, heavily curtained windows (some of which were further shielded by closely drawn shades) were eloquent of inner quiet and domestic respectability, while its calm front of brick, with brownstone trimmings, offered a pleasing contrast to the adjoining buildings jutting out on either side, alive with signs and humming with business.

"Some mistake," muttered Gryce to himself, as the perfect calm reigning over the whole establishment struck him anew. But before he had decided that he had been made the victim of a hoax, a movement took place in the area under the stoop, and an officer stepped out, with a countenance expressive of sufficient perplexity for Mr. Gryce to motion him back with the hurried inquiry: "Anything wrong? Any blood shed?

All seems quiet here."

The officer, recognizing the old detective, touched his hat. "Can't get in," said he. "Have rung all the bells. Would think the house empty if I had not seen something like a stir in one of the windows overhead. Shall I try to make my way into the rear yard through one of the lower windows of Knapp & Co.'s store, next door?"

"Yes, and take this boy with you. Lock him up in one of their offices, and then break your way into this house by some means. It ought to be easy enough from the back yard."

The officer nodded, took the boy by the arm, and in a trice had disappeared with him into the adjoining store. Mr. Gryce remained in the area, where he was presently besieged by a crowd of passers-by, eager to add their curiosity to the trouble they had so quickly scented. The opening of the door from the inside speedily put an end to importunities for which he had as yet no reply, and he was enabled to slip within, where he found himself in a place of almost absolute quiet. Before him lay a basement hall leading to a kitchen, which, even at that moment, he noticed to be in trimmer condition than is usual where much housework is done, but he saw nothing that bespoke tragedy, or even a break in the ordinary routine of life as observed in houses of like size and pretension.

Satisfied that what he sought was not to be found here, he followed the officer upstairs. As they emerged upon the parlor floor, the latter dropped the following information:

"Mr. Raffner of the firm next door says that the man who lives here is an odd sort of person whom nobody knows; a bookworm, I think they call him. He has occupied the house six months, yet they have never seen any one about the premise but himself and a strange old servant as peculiar and uncommunicative as his master."

"I know," muttered Mr. Gryce. He did know, everybody knew, that this house, once the seat of one of New York's most aristocratic families, was inhabited at present by a Mr. Adams, noted alike for his more than common personal attractions, his wealth, and the uncongenial nature of his temperament, which precluded all association with his kind. It was this knowledge which had given zest to this investigation. To enter the house of such a man was an event in itself: to enter it on an errand of life and death—Well, it is under the inspiration of such opportunities that life is reawakened in old veins, especially when those veins connect the heart and brain of a sagacious, if octogenarian, detective.

The hall in which they now found themselves was wide, old-fashioned, and sparsely furnished in the ancient manner to be observed in such time-honored structures. Two doors led into this hall, both of which now stood open. Taking advantage of this fact, they entered the nearest, which was nearly opposite the top of the staircase they had just ascended, and found themselves in a room barren as a doctor's outer office. There was nothing here worth their attention, and they would have left the place as unceremoniously as they had entered it if they had not caught glimpses of richness which promised an interior of uncommon elegance, behind the half-drawn folds of a portière at the further end of the room.

Advancing through the doorway thus indicated, they took one look about them and stood appalled. Nothing in their experience (and they had both experienced much) had prepared them for the thrilling, the solemn nature of what they were here called upon to contemplate.

Shall I attempt its description?

A room small and of circular shape, hung with strange tapestries relieved here and there by priceless curios, and lit, although it was still daylight, by a jet of rose-colored light concentrated, not on the rows and rows of books around the lower portion of the room, or on the one great picture which at another time might have drawn the eye and held the attention, but on the upturned face of a man lying on a bearskin rug with a dagger in his heart and on his breast a cross whose golden lines, sharply outlined against his long, dark, swathing garment, gave him the appearance of a saint prepared in some holy place for burial, save that the dagger spoke of violent death, and his face of an anguish for which Mr. Gryce, notwithstanding his lifelong experience, found no name, so little did it answer to a sensation of fear, pain, or surprise, or any of the emotions usually visible on the countenances of such as have fallen under the unexpected stroke of an assassin.

CHAPTER II

Mysteries

A moment of indecision, of awe even, elapsed before Mr. Gryce recovered himself. The dim light, the awesome silence, the unexpected surroundings recalling a romantic age, the motionless figure of him who so lately had been the master of the house, lying outstretched as for the tomb, with the sacred symbol on his breast offering such violent contradiction to the earthly passion which had driven the dagger home, were enough to move even the tried spirit of this old officer of the law and confuse a mind which, in the years of his long connection with the force, had had many serious problems to work upon, but never one just like this.

It was only for a moment, though. Before the man behind him had given utterance to his own bewilderment and surprise, Mr. Gryce had passed in and taken his stand by the prostrate figure.

That it was that of a man who had long since ceased to breathe he could not for a moment doubt; yet his first act was to make sure of the fact by laying his hand on the pulse and examining the eyes, whose expression of reproach was such that he had to call up all his professional sangfroid to meet them.

He found the body still warm, but dead beyond all question, and, once convinced of this, he forbore to draw the dagger from the wound, though he did not fail to give it the most careful attention before turning his eyes elsewhere. It was no ordinary weapon. It was a curio from some oriental shop. This in itself seemed to point to suicide, but the direction in which the blade had entered the body and the position of the wound were not such as would be looked for in a case of self-murder.

The other clews were few. Though the scene had been one of bloodshed and death, the undoubted result of a sudden and fierce attack, there were no signs of struggle to be found in the well-ordered apartment. Beyond a few rose leaves scattered on the floor, the room was a scene of peace and quiet luxury. Even the large table which occupied the centre of the room and near which the master of the house had been standing when struck gave no token of the tragedy which had been enacted at its side. That is, not at first glance; for though its large top was covered with articles of use and ornament, they all stood undisturbed and presumably in place, as if the shock which had laid their owner low had failed to be communicated to his belongings.

The contents of the table were various. Only a man of complex tastes and attainments could have collected and arranged in one small compass pipes, pens, portraits, weights, measures, Roman lamps, Venetian glass, rare porcelains, medals, rough metal work, manuscript, a scroll of music, a pot of growing flowers, and—and—(this seemed oddest of all) a row of electric buttons, which Mr. Gryce no sooner touched than the light which had been burning redly in the cage of fretted ironwork overhead changed in a twinkling to a greenish glare, filling the room with such ghastly tints that Mr. Gryce sought in haste another button, and, pressing it, was glad to see a mild white radiance take the place of the sickly hue which had added its own horror to the already solemn terrors of the spot.

"Childish tricks for a man of his age and position," ruminated Mr. Gryce; but after catching another glimpse of the face lying upturned at his feet he was conscious of a doubt as to whether the owner of that countenance could have possessed an instinct which was in any wise childish, so strong and purposeful were his sharply cut features. Indeed, the face was one to make an impression under any circumstances. In the present instance, and with such an expression stamped upon it, it exerted a fascination which disturbed the current of the detective's thoughts whenever by any chance he allowed it to get between him and his duty. To attribute folly to a man with such a mouth and such a chin was to own one's self a poor judge of human nature. Therefore, the lamp overhead, with its electric connection and changing slides, had a meaning which at present could be sought for only in the evidences of scientific research observable in the books and apparatus everywhere surrounding him.

Letting the white light burn on, Mr. Gryce, by a characteristic effort, shifted his attention to the walls, covered, as I have said, with tapestries and curios. There was nothing on them calculated to aid him in his research into the secret of this crime, unless—yes, there *was* something, a bent-down nail, wrenched from its place, the nail on which the cross had hung which now lay upon the dead man's heart. The cord by which it had been suspended still clung to the cross and mingled its red threads with that other scarlet thread which had gone to meet it from the victim's wounded breast. Who had torn down that cross? Not the victim himself. With such a wound, any such movement would have been impossible. Besides, the nail and the empty place on the wall were as far removed from where he lay as was possible in the somewhat circumscribed area of this circular apartment. Another's hand, then, had pulled down this symbol of peace and pardon, and placed it where the dying man's fleeting breath would play across it, a peculiar exhibition of religious hope or mad remorse, to the significance of which Mr. Gryce could not devote more than a passing thought, so golden were the moments in which he found himself alone upon this scene of crime.

Behind the table and half-way up the wall was a picture, the only large picture in the room. It was the portrait of a young girl of an extremely interesting and pathetic beauty. From her garb and the arrangement of her hair, it had evidently been painted about the end of our civil war. In it was to be observed the same haunting quality of intellectual charm visible in the man lying prone upon the floor, and though she was fair and he dark, there was sufficient likeness between the two to argue some sort of relationship between them. Below this picture were fastened a sword, a pair of epaulettes, and a medal such as was awarded for valor in the civil war.

"Mementoes which may help us in our task," mused the detective.

Passing on, he came unexpectedly upon a narrow curtain, so dark of hue and so akin in pattern to the draperies on the adjoining walls that it had up to this time escaped his attention. It was not that of a window, for such windows as were to be seen in this unique apartment were high upon the wall, indeed, almost under the ceiling. It must, therefore, drape the opening into still another communicating room. And such he found to be the case. Pushing this curtain aside, he entered a narrow closet containing a bed, a dresser, and a small table. The bed was the narrow cot of a bachelor, and the dresser that of a man of luxurious tastes and the utmost nicety of habit. Both the bed and dresser were in perfect order, save for a silver-backed comb, which had been taken from the latter, and which he presently found lying on the floor at the other end of the room. This and the presence of a pearl-handled parasol on a small stand near the door proclaimed that a woman had been there within a short space of time. The identity of this woman was soon established in his eyes by a small but unmistakable token connecting her with the one who had been the means of sending in the alarm to the police. The token of which I speak was a little black spangle, called by milliners and mantua-makers a sequin, which lay on the threshold separating this room from the study; and as Mr. Gryce, attracted by its sparkle, stooped to examine it, his eye caught sight of a similar one on the floor beyond, and of still another a few steps farther on. The last one lay close to the large centre-table before which he had just been standing.

The dainty trail formed by these bright sparkling drops seemed to affect him oddly. He knew, minute observer that he was, that in the manufacture of this garniture the spangles are strung on a thread which, if once broken, allows them to drop away one by one, till you can almost follow a woman so arrayed by the sequins that fall from her. Perhaps it was the delicate nature of the clew thus offered that pleased him, perhaps it was a recognition of the irony of fate in thus making a trap for unwary mortals out of their vanities. Whatever it was, the smile with which he turned his eye upon the table toward which he had thus been led was very eloquent. But before examining this article of furniture more closely, he attempted to find out where the thread had become loosened which had let the spangles fall. Had it caught on any projection in doorway or furniture? He saw none. All the chairs were cushioned and—But wait! there was the cross! That had a fretwork of gold at its base. Might not this filagree have caught in her dress as she was tearing down the cross from the wall and so have started the thread which had given him this exquisite clew?

Hastening to the spot where the cross had hung, he searched the floor at his feet, but found nothing to confirm his conjecture until he had reached the rug on which the prostrate man lay. There, amid the long hairs of the bearskin, he came upon one other spangle, and knew that the woman in the shiny clothes had stooped there before him.

Satisfied on this point, he returned to the table, and this time subjected it to a thorough and minute examination. That the result was not entirely unsatisfactory was evident from the smile with which he eyed his finger after having drawn it across a certain spot near the inkstand, and also from the care with which he lifted that inkstand and replaced it in precisely the same spot from which he had taken it up. Had he expected to find something concealed under it? Who can tell? A detective's face seldom yields up its secrets.

He was musing quite intently before this table when a quick step behind him made him turn. Styles, the officer, having now been over the house, had returned, and was standing before him in the attitude of one who has something to say.

"What is it?" asked Mr. Gryce, with a quick movement in his direction.

For answer the officer pointed to the staircase visible through the antechamber door.

"Go up!" was indicated by his gesture.

Mr. Gryce demurred, casting a glance around the room, which at that moment interested him so deeply. At this the man showed some excitement, and, breaking silence, said:

"Come! I have lighted on the guilty party. He is in a room upstairs."

"He?" Mr. Gryce was evidently surprised at the pronoun.

"Yes; there can be no doubt about it. When you see him—but what is that? Is he coming down? I'm sure there's nobody else in the house. Don't you hear footsteps, sir?"

Mr. Gryce nodded. Some one was certainly descending the stairs.

"Let us retreat," suggested Styles. "Not because the man is dangerous, but because it is very necessary you should see him before he sees you. He's a very strange-acting man, sir; and if he comes in here, will be sure to do something to incriminate himself. Where can we hide?"

Mr. Gryce remembered the little room he had just left, and drew the officer toward it. Once installed inside, he let the curtain drop till only a small loophole remained. The steps, which had been gradually growing louder, kept advancing; and presently they could hear the intruder's breathing, which was both quick and labored.

"Does he know that any one has entered the house? Did he see you when you came upon him upstairs?" whispered Mr. Gryce into the ear of the man beside him.

Styles shook his head, and pointed eagerly toward the opposite door. The man for whose appearance they waited had just lifted the portière and in another moment stood in full view just inside the threshold.

Mr. Gryce and his attendant colleague both stared. Was this the murderer? This pale, lean servitor, with a tray in his hand on which rested a single glass of water?

Mr. Gryce was so astonished that he looked at Styles for explanation. But that officer, hiding his own surprise, for he had not expected this peaceful figure, urged him in a whisper to have patience, and both, turning toward the man again, beheld him advance, stop, cast one look at the figure lying on the floor and then let slip the glass with a low cry that at once changed to something like a howl.

"Look at him! Look at him!" urged Styles, in a hurried whisper. "Watch what he will do now. You will see a murderer at work."

And sure enough, in another instant this strange being, losing all semblance to his former self, entered upon a series of pantomimic actions which to the two men who watched him seemed both to explain and illustrate the crime which had just been enacted there.

With every appearance of passion, he stood contemplating the empty air before him, and then, with one hand held stretched out behind him in a peculiarly cramped position, he plunged with the other toward a table from which he made a feint of snatching something which he no sooner closed his hand upon than he gave a quick side-thrust, still at the empty air, which seemed to quiver in return, so vigorous was his action and so evident his intent.

The reaction following this thrust; the slow unclosing of his hand from an imaginary dagger; the tottering of his body backward; then the moment when with wide open eyes he seemed to contemplate in horror the result of his own deed—these needed no explanation beyond what was given by his writhing features and trembling body. Gradually succumbing to the remorse or terror of his own crime, he sank lower and lower, until, though with that one arm still stretched out, he lay in an inert heap on the floor.

"It is what I saw him do upstairs," murmured Styles into the ear of the amazed detective. "He has evidently been driven insane by his own act."

Mr. Gryce made no answer. Here was a problem for the solution of which he found no precedent in all his past experience.

CHAPTER III

The Mute Servitor

Meanwhile the man who, to all appearance, had just re-enacted before them the tragedy which had so lately taken place in this room, rose to his feet, and, with a dazed air as unlike his former violent expression as possible, stooped for the glass he had let fall, and was carrying it out when Mr. Gryce called to him:

"Wait, man! You needn't take that glass away. We first want to hear how your master comes to be lying here dead."

It was a demand calculated to startle any man. But this one showed himself totally unmoved by it, and was passing on when Styles laid a detaining hand on his shoulder.

"Stop!" said he. "What do you mean by sliding off like this? Don't you hear the gentleman speaking to you?"

This time the appeal told. The glass fell again from the man's hand, mingling its clink (for it struck the floor this time and broke) with the cry he gave—which was not exactly a cry either, but an odd sound between a moan and a shriek. He had caught sight of the men who were seeking to detain him, and his haggard look and cringing form showed that he realized at last the terrors of his position. Next minute he sought to escape, but Styles, gripping him more firmly, dragged him back to where Mr. Gryce stood beside the bearskin rug on which lay the form of his dead master.

Instantly, at the sight of this recumbent figure, another change took place in the entrapped butler. Joy—that most hellish of passions in the presence of violence and death—illumined his wandering eye and distorted his mouth; and, seeking no disguise for the satisfaction he felt, he uttered a low but thrilling laugh, which rang in unholy echo through the room.

Mr. Gryce, moved in spite of himself by an abhorrence which the irresponsible condition of this man seemed only to emphasize, waited till the last faint sounds of this diabolical mirth had died away in the high recesses of the space above. Then, fixing the glittering eye of this strange creature with his own, which, as we know, so seldom dwelt upon that of his fellow-beings, he sternly said:

"There now! Speak! Who killed this man? You were in the house with him, and should know."

The butler's lips opened and a string of strange gutturals poured forth, while with his one disengaged hand (for the other was held to his side by Styles) he touched his ears and his lips, and violently shook his head.

There was but one interpretation to be given to this. The man was deaf and dumb.

The shock of this discovery was too much for Styles. His hand fell from the other's arms, and the man, finding himself free, withdrew to his former place in the room, where he proceeded to enact again and with increased vivacity first the killing of and then the mourning for his master, which but a few moments before had made so suggestive an impression upon them. This done, he stood waiting, but this time with that gleam of infernal joy in the depths of his quick, restless eyes which made his very presence in this room of death seem a sacrilege and horror.

Styles could not stand it. "Can't you speak?" he shouted. "Can't you hear?"

The man only smiled, an evil and gloating smile, which Mr. Gryce thought it his duty to cut short.

"Take him away!" he cried. "Examine him carefully for blood marks. I am going up to the room where you saw him first. He is too nearly linked to this crime not to carry some trace of it away with him."

But for once even this time-tried detective found himself at fault. No marks were found on the old servant, nor could they discover in the rooms above any signs by which this one remaining occupant of the house could be directly associated with the crime which had taken place within it. Thereupon Mr. Gryce grew very thoughtful and entered upon another examination of the two rooms which to his mind held all the clews that would ever be given to this strange crime.

The result was meagre, and he was just losing himself again in contemplation of the upturned face, whose fixed mouth and haunting expression told such a story of suffering and determination, when there came from the dim recesses above his head a cry, which, forming itself into two words, rang down with startling clearness in this most unexpected of appeals:

"Remember Evelyn!"

Remember Evelyn! Who was Evelyn? And to whom did this voice belong, in a house which had already been ransacked in vain for other occupants? It seemed to come from the roof, and, sure enough, when Mr. Gryce looked up he saw, swinging in a cage strung up nearly to the top of one of the windows I have mentioned, an English starling, which, in seeming recognition of the attention it had drawn upon itself, craned its neck as Mr. Gryce looked up, and shrieked again, with fiercer insistence than before:

"Remember Evelyn!"

It was the last uncanny touch in a series of uncanny experiences. With an odd sense of nightmare upon him, Mr. Gryce leaned forward on the study table in his effort to obtain a better view of this bird, when, without warning, the white light, which since his last contact with the electrical apparatus had spread itself through the room, changed again to green, and he realized that he had unintentionally pressed a button and thus brought into action another slide in the curious lamp over his head.

Annoyed, for these changing hues offered a problem he was as yet too absorbed in other matters to make any attempt to solve, he left the vicinity of the table, and was about to leave the room when he heard Styles's voice rise from the adjoining antechamber, where Styles was keeping guard over the old butler:

"Shall I let him go, Mr. Gryce? He seems very uneasy; not dangerous, you know, but anxious; as if he had forgotten something or recalled some unfulfilled duty."

"Yes, let him go," was the detective's quick reply. "Only watch and follow him. Every movement he makes is of interest. Unconsciously he may be giving us invaluable clews." And he approached the door to note for himself what the man might do.

"Remember Evelyn!" rang out the startling cry from above, as the detective passed between the curtains. Irresistibly he looked back and up. To whom was this appeal from a bird's throat so imperatively addressed? To him or to the man on the floor beneath, whose ears were forever closed? It might be a matter of little consequence, and it might be one involving the very secret of this tragedy. But whether important or not, he could pay no heed to it at this juncture, for the old butler, coming from the front hall whither he had hurried on being released by Styles, was at that moment approaching him, carrying in one hand his master's hat and in the other his master's umbrella.

Not knowing what this new movement might mean, Mr. Gryce paused where he was and waited for the man to advance. Seeing this, the mute, to whose face and bearing had returned the respectful immobility of the trained servant, handed over the articles he had brought, and then noiselessly, and with the air of one who had performed an expected service, retreated to his old place in the antechamber, where he sat down again and fell almost immediately into his former dazed condition.

"Humph! mind quite lost, memory uncertain, testimony valueless," were the dissatisfied reflections of the disappointed detective as he replaced Mr. Adams's hat and umbrella on the hall rack. "Has he been brought to this state by the tragedy which has just taken place here, or is his present insane condition its precursor and cause?" Mr. Gryce might have found some answer to this question in his own mind if, at that moment, the fitful clanging of the front door bell, which had hitherto testified to the impatience of the curious crowd outside, had not been broken into by an authoritative knock which at once put an end to all self-communing.

The coroner, or some equally important person, was at hand, and the detective's golden hour was over.

CHAPTER IV

A New Experience for Mr. Gryce

Mr. Gryce felt himself at a greater disadvantage in his attempt to solve the mystery of this affair than in any other which he had entered upon in years. First, the victim had been a solitary man, with no household save his man-of-all-work, the mute. Secondly, he had lived in a portion of the city where no neighbors were possible; and he had even lacked, as it now seemed, any very active friends. Though some hours had elapsed since his death had been noised abroad, no one had appeared at the door with inquiries or information. This seemed odd, considering that he had been for some months a marked figure in this quarter of the town. But, then, everything about this man was odd, nor would it have been in keeping with his surroundings and peculiar manner of living for him to have had the ordinary associations of men of his class.

This absence of the usual means of eliciting knowledge from the surrounding people, added to, rather than detracted from, the interest which Mr. Gryce was bound to feel in the case, and it was with a feeling of relief that a little before midnight he saw the army of reporters, medical men, officials, and such others as had followed in the coroner's wake, file out of the front door and leave him again, for a few hours at least, master of the situation.

For there were yet two points which he desired to settle before he took his own much-needed rest. The first occupied his immediate attention. Passing before a chair in the hall on which a small boy sat dozing, he roused him with the remark:

"Come, Jake, it's time to look lively. I want you to go with me to the exact place where that lady ran across you today."

The boy, half dead with sleep, looked around him for his hat.

"I'd like to see my mother first," he pleaded. "She must be done up about me. I never stayed away so long before."

"Your mother knows where you are. I sent a message to her hours ago. She gave a very good report of you, Jake; says you're an obedient lad and that you never have told her a falsehood."

"She's a good mother," the boy warmly declared. "I'd be as bad—as bad as my father was, if I did not treat her well." Here his hand fell on his cap, which he put on his head.

"I'm ready," said he.

Mr. Gryce at once led the way into the street.

The hour was late, and only certain portions of the city showed any real activity. Into one of these thoroughfares they presently came, and before the darkened window of one of the lesser shops paused, while Jake pointed out the two stuffed frogs engaged with miniature swords in mortal combat at which he had been looking when the lady came up and spoke to him.

Mr. Gryce eyed the boy rather than the frogs, though probably the former would have sworn that his attention had never left that miniature conflict.

"Was she a pretty lady?" he asked.

The boy scratched his head in some perplexity.

"She made me a good deal afraid of her," he said. "She had very splendid clothes; oh, gorgeous!" he cried, as if on this question there could be no doubt.

"And she was young, and carried a bunch of flowers, and seemed troubled? What! not young, and carried no flowers—and wasn't even anxious and trembling?"

The boy, who had been shaking his head, looked nonplussed.

"I think as she was what you might call troubled. But she wasn't crying, and when she spoke to me, she put more feeling into her grip than into her voice. She just dragged me to the drug-store, sir. If she hadn't given me money first, I should have wriggled away in spite of her. But I likes money, sir; I don't get too much of it."

Mr. Gryce by this time was moving on. "Not young," he repeated to himself. "Some old flame, then, of Mr. Adams; they're apt to be dangerous, very dangerous, more dangerous than the young ones."

In front of the drug-store he paused. "Show me where she stood while you went in."

The boy pointed out the identical spot. He seemed as eager as the detective.

"And was she standing there when you came out?"

"Oh, no, sir; she went away while I was inside."

"Did you see her go? Can you tell me whether she went up street or down?"

"I had one eye on her, sir; I was afraid she was coming into the shop after me, and my arm was too sore for me to want her to clinch hold on it again. So when she started to go, I took a step nearer, and saw her move toward the curbstone and hold up her hand. But it wasn't a car she was after, for none came by for several minutes."

The fold between Mr. Gryce's eyes perceptibly smoothed out.

"Then it was some cabman or hack-driver she hailed. Were there any empty coaches about that you saw?"

The boy had not noticed. He had reached the limit of his observations, and no amount of further questioning could elicit anything more from him. This Mr. Gryce soon saw, and giving him into the charge of one of his assistants who was on duty at this place, he proceeded back to the ill-omened house where the tragedy itself had occurred.

"Any one waiting for me?" he inquired of Styles, who came to the door.

"Yes, sir; a young man; name, Hines. Says he's an electrician."

"That's the man I want. Where is he?"

"In the parlor, sir."

"Good! I'll see him. But don't let any one else in. Anybody upstairs?"

"No, sir, all gone. Shall I go up or stay here?"

"You'd better go up. I'll look after the door."

Styles nodded, and went toward the stairs, up which he presently disappeared. Mr. Gryce proceeded to the parlor.

A dapper young man with an intelligent eye rose to meet him. "You sent for me," said he.

The detective nodded, asked a few questions, and seeming satisfied with the replies he received, led the way into Mr. Adams's study, from which the body had been removed to an upper room. As they entered, a mild light greeted them from a candle which, by Mr. Gryce's orders, had been placed on a small side table near the door. But once in, Mr. Gryce approached the larger table in the centre of the room, and placing his hand on one of the buttons before him, asked his companion to be kind enough to blow out the candle. This he did, leaving the room for a moment in total darkness. Then with a sudden burst of illumination, a marvellous glow of a deep violet color shot over the whole room, and the two men turned and faced each other both with inquiry in their looks, so unexpected was this theatrical effect to the one, and so inexplicable its cause and purpose to the other.

"That is but one slide," remarked Mr. Gryce. "Now I will press another button, and the color changes to—pink, as you see. This one produces green, this one white, and this a bilious yellow, which is not becoming to either of us, I am sure. Now will you examine the connection, and see if there is anything peculiar about it?"

Mr. Hines at once set to work. But beyond the fact that the whole contrivance was the work of an amateur hand, he found nothing strange about it, except the fact that it worked so well.

Mr. Gryce showed disappointment.

"He made it, then, himself?" he asked.

"Undoubtedly, or someone else equally unacquainted with the latest method of wiring."

"Will you look at these books over here and see if sufficient knowledge can be got from them to enable an amateur to rig up such an arrangement as this?"

Mr. Hines glanced at the shelf which Mr. Gryce had pointed out, and without taking out the books, answered briefly:

"A man with a deft hand and a scientific turn of mind might, by the aid of these, do all you see here and more. The aptitude is all."

"Then I'm afraid Mr. Adams had the aptitude," was the dry response. There was disappointment in the tone. Why, his next words served to show. "A man with a turn for mechanical contrivances often wastes much time and money on useless toys only fit for children to play with. Look at that bird cage now. Perched at a height totally beyond the reach of any one without a ladder, it must owe its very evident usefulness (for you see it holds a rather lively occupant) to some contrivance by which it can be raised and lowered at will. Where is that contrivance? Can you find it?"

The expert thought he could. And, sure enough, after some ineffectual searching, he came upon another button well hid amid the tapestry on the wall, which, when pressed, caused something to be disengaged which gradually lowered the cage within reach of Mr. Gryce's hand.

"We will not send this poor bird aloft again," said he, detaching the cage and holding it for a moment in his hand. "An English starling is none too common in this country. Hark! he is going to speak."

But the sharp-eyed bird, warned perhaps by the emphatic gesture of the detective that silence would be more in order at this moment than his usual appeal to "remember Evelyn," whisked about in his cage for an instant, and then subsided into a doze, which may have been real, and may have been assumed under the fascinating eye of the old gentleman who held him. Mr. Gryce placed the cage on the floor, and idly, or because the play pleased him, old and staid as he was, pressed another button on the table—a button he had hitherto neglected touching—and glanced around to see what color the light would now assume.

But the yellow glare remained. The investigation which the apparatus had gone through had probably disarranged the wires. With a shrug he was moving off, when he suddenly made a hurried gesture, directing the attention of the expert to a fact for which neither of them was prepared. The opening which led into the antechamber, and which was the sole means of communication with the rest of the house, was slowly closing. From a yard's breadth it became a foot; from a foot it became an inch; from an inch—

"Well, that is certainly the contrivance of a lazy man," laughed the expert. "Seated in his chair here, he can close his door at will. No shouting after a deaf servant, no awkward stumbling over rugs to shut it himself. I don't know but I approve of this contrivance, only—" here he caught a rather serious expression on Mr. Gryce's face—"the slide seems to be of a somewhat curious construction. It is not made of wood, as any sensible door ought to be, but of—"

"Steel," finished Mr. Gryce in an odd tone. "This is the strangest thing yet. It begins to look as if Mr. Adams was daft on electrical contrivances."

"And as if we were prisoners here," supplemented the other. "I do not see any means for drawing this slide back."

"Oh, there's another button for that, of course," Mr. Gryce carelessly remarked.

But they failed to find one.

"If you don't object," observed Mr. Gryce, after five minutes of useless search, "I will turn a more cheerful light upon the scene. Yellow does not seem to fit the occasion."

"Give us rose, for unless you have someone on the other side of this steel plate, we seem likely to remain here till morning."

"There is a man upstairs whom we may perhaps make hear, but what does this contrivance portend? It has a serious look to me, when you consider that every window in these two rooms has been built up almost under the roof."

"Yes; a very strange look. But before engaging in its consideration

I should like a breath of fresh air. I cannot do anything while in confinement. My brain won't work."

Meanwhile Mr. Gryce was engaged in examining the huge plate of steel which served as a barrier to their egress. He found that it had been made—certainly at great expense—to fit the curve of the walls through which it passed. This was a discovery of some consequence, causing Mr. Gryce to grow still more thoughtful and to eye the smooth steel plate under his hand with an air of marked distrust.

"Mr. Adams carried his taste for the mechanical to great extremes," he remarked to the slightly uneasy man beside him. "This slide is very carefully fitted, and, if I am not mistaken, it will stand some battering before we are released."

"I wish that his interest in electricity had led him to attach such a simple thing as a bell."

"True, we have come across no bell."

"It would have smacked too much of the ordinary to please him."

"Besides, his only servant was deaf."

"Try the effect of a blow, a quick blow with this silver-mounted alpenstock. Some one should hear and come to our assistance."

"I will try my whistle first; it will be better understood."

But though Mr. Gryce both whistled and struck many a resounding knock upon the barrier before them, it was an hour before he could draw the attention of Styles, and five hours before an opening could be effected in the wall large enough to admit of their escape, so firmly was this barrier of steel fixed across the sole outlet from this remarkable room.

CHAPTER V

Five Small Spangles

Such an experience could not fail to emphasize Mr. Gryce's interest in the case and heighten the determination he had formed to probe its secrets and explain all its extraordinary features. Arrived at Headquarters, where his presence was doubtless awaited with some anxiety by those who knew nothing of the cause of his long detention, his first act was to inquire if Bartow, the butler, had come to his senses during the night.

The answer was disappointing. Not only was there no change in his condition, but the expert in lunacy who had been called in to pass upon his case had expressed an opinion unfavorable to his immediate recovery.

Mr. Gryce looked sober, and, summoning the officer who had managed Bartow's arrest, he asked how the mute had acted when he found himself detained.

The answer was curt, but very much to the point.

"Surprised, sir. Shook his head and made some queer gestures, then went through his pantomime. It's quite a spectacle, sir. Poor fool, he keeps holding his hand back, so."

Mr. Gryce noted the gesture; it was the same which Bartow had made when he first realized that he had spectators. Its meaning was not wholly apparent. He had made it with his right hand (there was no evidence that the mute was left-handed), and he continued to make it as if with this movement he expected to call attention to some fact that would relieve him from custody.

"Does he mope? Is his expression one of fear or anger?"

"It varies, sir. One minute he looks like a man on the point of falling asleep; the next he starts up in fury, shaking his head and pounding the walls. It's not a comfortable sight, sir. He will have to be watched night and day."

"Let him be, and note every change in him. His testimony may not be valid, but there is suggestion in every movement he makes. Tomorrow I will visit him myself."

The officer went out, and Mr. Gryce sat for a few moments communing with himself, during which he took out a little package from his pocket, and emptying out on his desk the five little spangles it contained, regarded them intently. He had always been fond of looking at some small and seemingly insignificant object while thinking. It served to concentrate his thoughts, no doubt. At all events, some such result appeared to follow the contemplation of these five sequins, for after shaking his head doubtfully over them for a time, he made a sudden move, and sweeping them into the envelope from which he had taken them, he gave a glance at his watch and passed quickly into the outer office, where he paused before a line of waiting men. Beckoning to one who had followed his movements with an interest which had not escaped the eye of this old reader of human nature, he led the way back to his own room.

"You want a hand in this matter?" he said interrogatively, as the door closed behind them and they found themselves alone.

"Oh, sir—" began the young man in a glow which made his more than plain features interesting to contemplate, "I do not presume—"

"Enough!" interposed the other. "You have been here now for six months, and have had no opportunity as yet for showing any special adaptability. Now I propose to test your powers with something really difficult. Are you up to it, Sweetwater? Do you know the city well enough to attempt to find a needle in this very big haystack?"

"I should at least like to try," was the eager response. "If I succeed it will be a bigger feather in my cap than if I had always lived in New York. I have been spoiling for some such opportunity. See if I don't make the effort judiciously, if only out of gratitude."

"Well, we shall see," remarked the old detective. "If it's difficulty you long to encounter, you will be likely to have all you want of it. Indeed, it is the impossible I ask. A woman is to be found of whom we know nothing save that she wore when last seen a dress heavily bespangled with black, and that she carried in her visit to Mr. Adams, at the time of or before the murder, a parasol, of which I can procure you a glimpse before you start out. She came from, I don't know where, and she went—but that is what you are to find out. You are not the only man who is to be put on the job, which, as you see, is next door to a hopeless one, unless the woman comes forward and proclaims herself. Indeed, I should despair utterly of your success if it were not for one small fact which I will now proceed to give you as my special and confidential agent in this matter. When this woman was about to disappear from the one eye that was watching her, she approached the curbstone in front of Hudson's fruit store on 14th Street and lifted up her right hand, so. It is not much of a clew, but it is all I have at my disposal, except these five spangles dropped from her dress, and my conviction that she is not to be found among the questionable women of the town, but among those who seldom or never come under the eye of the police. Yet don't let this conviction hamper you. Convictions as a rule are bad things, and act as a hindrance rather than an inspiration."

Sweetwater, to whom the song of the sirens would have sounded less sweet, listened with delight and responded with a frank smile and a gay:

"I'll do my best, sir, but don't show me the parasol, only describe it. I wouldn't like the fellows to chaff me if I fail; I'd rather go quietly to work and raise no foolish expectations."

"Well, then, it is one of those dainty, nonsensical things made of gray chiffon, with pearl handle and bows of pink ribbon. I don't believe it was ever used before, and from the value women usually place on such fol-de-rols, could only have been left behind under the stress of extraordinary emotion or fear. The name of the owner was not on it."

"Nor that of the maker?"

Mr. Gryce had expected this question, and was glad not to be disappointed.

"No, that would have helped us too much."

"And the hour at which this lady was seen on the curbstone at Hudson's?"

"Half-past four; the moment at which the telephone message arrived."

"Very good, sir. It is the hardest task I have ever undertaken, but that's not against it. When shall I see you again?"

"When you have something to impart. Ah, wait a minute. I have my suspicion that this woman's first name is Evelyn. But, mind, it is only a suspicion."

"All right, sir," and with an air of some confidence, the young man disappeared.

Mr. Gryce did not look as if he shared young Sweetwater's cheerfulness. The mist surrounding this affair was as yet impenetrable to him. But then he was not twenty-three, with only triumphant memories behind him.

His next hope lay in the information likely to accrue from the published accounts of this crime, now spread broadcast over the country. A man of Mr. Adams's wealth and culture must necessarily have possessed many acquaintances, whom the surprising news of his sudden death would naturally bring to light, especially as no secret was made of his means and many valuable effects. But as if this affair, destined to be one of the last to engage the powers of this sagacious old man, refused on this very account to yield any immediate results to his investigation, the whole day passed by without the appearance of any claimant for Mr. Adams's fortune or the arrival on the scene of any friend capable of lifting the veil which shrouded the life of this strange being. To be sure, his banker and his lawyer came forward during the day, but they had little to reveal beyond the fact that his pecuniary affairs were in good shape and that, so far as they knew, he was without family or kin.

Even his landlord could add little to the general knowledge. He had first heard of Mr. Adams through a Philadelphia lawyer, since dead, who had assured him of his client's respectability and undoubted ability to pay his rent. When they came together and Mr. Adams was introduced to him, he had been struck, first, by the ascetic appearance of his prospective tenant, and, secondly, by his reserved manners and quiet intelligence. But admirable as he had found him, he had never succeeded in making his acquaintance. The rent had been uniformly paid with great exactitude on the very day it was due, but his own visits had never been encouraged or his advances met by anything but the cold politeness of a polished and totally indifferent man. Indeed, he had always looked upon his tenant as a bookworm, absorbed in study and such scientific experiments as could be carried on with no other assistance than that of his deaf and dumb servant.

Asked if he knew anything about this servant, he answered that his acquaintance with him was limited to the two occasions on which he had been ushered by him into his master's presence; that he knew nothing of his character and general disposition, and could not say whether his attitude toward his master had been one of allegiance or antagonism.

And so the way was blocked in this direction.

Taken into the room where Mr. Adams had died, he surveyed in amazement the huge steel plate which still blocked the doorway, and the high windows through which only a few straggling sunbeams could find their way.

Pointing to the windows, he remarked:

"These were filled in at Mr. Adams's request. Originally they extended down to the wainscoting."

He was shown where lath and plaster had been introduced and also how the plate had been prepared and arranged as a barrier. But he could give no explanation of it or divine the purpose for which it had been placed there at so great an expense.

The lamp was another curiosity, and its varying lights the cause of increased astonishment. Indeed he had known nothing of these arrangements, having been received in the parlor when he visited the house, where there was nothing to attract his attention or emphasize the well-known oddities of his tenant.

He was not shown the starling. That loquacious bird had been removed to police headquarters for the special delectation of Mr. Gryce.

Other inquiries failed also. No clew to the owner of the insignia found on the wall could be gained at the pension office or at any of the G. A. R. posts inside the city. Nor was the name of the artist who had painted the portrait which adorned so large a portion of the wall a recognized one in New York City. Otherwise a clew might have been obtained through him to Mr. Adams's antecedents. All the drawers and receptacles in Mr. Adams's study had been searched, but no will had been found nor any business documents. It was as if this strange man had sought to suppress his identity, or, rather, as if he had outgrown all interest in his kind or in anything beyond the walls within which he had immured himself.

Late in the afternoon reports began to come in from the various tradesmen with whom Mr. Adams had done business. They all had something to say as to the peculiarity of his habits and the freaks of his mute servant. They were both described as hermits, differing from the rest of their kind only in that they denied themselves no reasonable luxury and seemed to have adopted a shut-in life from a pure love of seclusion. The master was never seen at the stores. It was the servant who made the purchases, and this by means of gestures which were often strangely significant. Indeed, he seemed to have great power of expressing himself by looks and actions, and rarely caused a mistake or made one. He would not endure cheating, and always bought the best.

Of his sanity up to the day of his master's death there was no question; but more than one man with whom he had had dealings was ready to testify that there had been a change in his manner for the past few weeks—a sort of subdued excitement, quite unlike his former methodical bearing. He had shown an inclination to testiness, and was less easily pleased than formerly. To one clerk he had shown a nasty spirit under very slight provocation, and was only endured in the store on account of his master, who was too good a customer for them to offend. Mr. Kelly, a grocer, went so far as to say he acted like a man with a grievance who burned to vent his spite on someone, but held himself in forcible restraint.

Perhaps if no tragedy had taken place in the house on —— Street these various persons would not have been so ready to interpret thus unfavorably a nervousness excusable enough in one so cut off from all communication with his kind. But with the violent end of his master in view, and his own unexplained connection with it, who could help recalling that his glance had frequently shown malevolence?

But this was not evidence of the decided character required by the law, and Mr. Gryce was about to regard the day as a lost one, when Sweetwater made his reappearance at Headquarters. The expression of his face put new life into Mr. Gryce.

"What!" he cried, "you have not found her?"

Sweetwater smiled. "Don't ask me, sir, not yet. I've come to see if there's any reason why I should not be given the loan of that parasol for about an hour. I'll bring it back. I only want to make a certain test with it."

"What test, my boy? May I ask, what test?"

"Please to excuse me, sir; I have only a short time in which to act before respectable business houses shut up for the night, and the test I speak of has to be made in a respectable house."

"Then you shall not be hindered. Wait here, and I will bring you the parasol. There! bring it back soon, my boy. I have not the patience I used to have."

"An hour, sir; give me an hour, and then—"

The shutting of the door behind his flying figure cut short his sentence.

That was a long hour to Mr. Gryce, or would have been if it had not mercifully been cut short by the return of Sweetwater in an even more excited state of mind than he had been before. He held the parasol in his hand.

"My test failed," said he, "but the parasol has brought me luck, notwithstanding. I have found the lady, sir, and—"

He had to draw a long breath before proceeding.

"And she is what I said," began the detective; "a respectable person in a respectable house."

"Yes, sir; very respectable, more respectable than I expected to see. Quite a lady, sir. Not young, but—"

"Her name, boy. Is it—Evelyn?"

Sweetwater shook his head with a look as naive in its way as the old detective's question.

"I cannot say, sir. Indeed, I had not the courage to ask. She is here—"

"Here!" Mr. Gryce took one hurried step toward the door, then came gravely back. "I can restrain myself," he said. "If she is here, she will not go till I have seen her. Are you sure you have made no mistake; that she is the woman we are after; the woman who was in Mr. Adams's house and sent us the warning?"

"Will you hear my story, sir? It will take only a moment. Then you can judge for yourself."

"Your story? It must be a pretty one. How came you to light on this woman so soon? By using the clew I gave you?"

Again Sweetwater's expression took on a touch of naïveté.

"I'm sorry, sir; but I was egotistical enough to follow my own idea. It would have taken too much time to hunt up all the drivers of hacks in the city, and I could not even be sure she had made use of a public conveyance. No, sir; I bethought me of another way by which I might reach this woman. You had shown me those spangles. They were portions of a very rich trimming; a trimming which has only lately come into vogue, and which is so expensive that it is worn chiefly by women of means, and sold only in shops where elaborate garnitures are to be found. I have seen and noticed dresses thus trimmed, in certain windows and on certain ladies; and before you showed me the spangles you picked up in Mr. Adams's study could have told you just how I had seen them arranged. They are sewed on black net, in figures, sir; in scrolls or wreaths or whatever you choose to call them; and so conspicuous are these wreaths or figures, owing to the brilliance of the spangles composing them, that any break in their continuity is plainly apparent, especially if the net be worn over a color, as is frequently the case. Remembering this, and recalling the fact that these spangles doubtless fell from one of the front breadths, where their loss would attract not only the attention of others, but that of the wearer, I said to myself, 'What will she be likely to do when she finds her dress thus disfigured?' And the answer at once came: 'If she is the lady Mr. Gryce considers her, she will seek to restore these missing spangles, especially if they were lost on a scene of crime. But where can she get them to sew on? From an extra piece of net of the same style. But she will not be apt to have an extra piece of net. She will, therefore, find herself obliged to buy it, and since only a few spangles are lacking, she will buy the veriest strip.' Here, then, was my clew, or at least my ground for action. Going the rounds of the few leading stores on Broadway, 23d Street, and Sixth Avenue, I succeeded in getting certain clerks interested in my efforts, so that I speedily became assured that if a lady came into these stores for a very small portion of this bespangled net, they would note her person and, if possible, procure some clew to her address. Then I took up my stand at Arnold's emporium. Why Arnold's? I do not know. Perhaps my good genius meant me to be successful in this quest; but whether through luck or what not, I was successful, for before the afternoon was half over, I encountered a meaning glance from one of the men behind the counter, and advancing toward him, saw him rolling a small package which he handed over to a very pretty and rosy young girl, who at once walked away with it. 'For one of our leading customers,' he whispered, as I drew nearer. 'I don't think she is the person you want.' But I would take no chances. I followed the young girl who had carried away the parcel, and by this means came to a fine brownstone front in one of our most retired and aristocratic quarters. When I had seen her go in at the basement door, I rang the bell above, and then—well, I just bit my lips to keep down my growing excitement. For such an effort as this might well end in disappointment, and I knew if I were disappointed now—But no such trial awaited me. The maid who came to the door proved to be the same merry-eyed lass I had seen leave the store. Indeed, she had the identical parcel in her hand which was the connecting link between the imposing house at whose door I stood and the strange murder in —— Street. But I did not allow my interest in this parcel to become apparent, and by the time I addressed her I had so mastered myself as to arouse no suspicion of the importance of my errand. You, of course, foresee the question I put to the young girl. 'Has your mistress lost a parasol? One has been found—' I did not finish the sentence, for I perceived by her look that her mistress had met with such a loss, and as this was all I wanted to know just then, I cried out, 'I will bring it. If it is hers, all right,' and bounded down the steps.

"My intention was to inform you of what I had done and ask your advice. But my egotism got the better of me. I felt that I ought to make sure that I was not the victim of a coincidence. Such a respectable house! Such a respectable maidservant! Should she recognize the parasol as belonging to her mistress, then, indeed, I might boast of my success. So praying you for a loan of this article, I went back and rang the bell again. The same girl came to the door. I think fortune favored me today. 'Here is the parasol,' said I, but before the words were out of my mouth I saw that the girl had taken the alarm or that some grievous mistake had been made. 'That is not the one my mistress lost,' said she. 'She never carries anything but black.' And the door was about to close between us when I heard a voice from within call out peremptorily: 'Let me see that parasol. Hold it up, young man. There! at the foot of the stairs. Ah!'

"If ever an exclamation was eloquent that simple 'ah!' was. I could not see the speaker, but I knew she was leaning over the banisters from the landing above. I listened to hear her glide away. But she did not move. She was evidently collecting herself for the emergency of the moment. Presently she spoke again, and I was astonished at her tone: 'You have come from Police Headquarters,' was the remark with which she hailed me.

"I lowered the parasol. I did not think it necessary to say yes.

"'From a man there, called Gryce,' she went on, still in that strange tone I can hardly describe, sir.

"'Since you ask me,' I now replied, 'I acknowledge that it is through his instructions I am here. He was anxious to restore to you your lost property. Is not this parasol yours? Shall I not leave it with this young girl?'

"The answer was dry, almost rasping: 'Mr. Gryce has made a mistake. The parasol is not mine; yet he certainly deserves credit for the use he has made of it, in this search. I should like to tell him so. Is he at his office, and do you think I would be received?'

"'He would be delighted,' I returned, not imagining she was in earnest. But she was, sir. In less time than you would believe, I perceived a very stately, almost severe, lady descend the stairs. She was dressed for the street, and spoke to me with quite an air of command. 'Have you a cab?' she asked.

"'No,' said I.

"'Then get one.'

"Here was a dilemma. Should I leave her and thus give her an opportunity to escape, or should I trust to her integrity and the honesty of her look, which was no common one, sir, and obey her as every one about her was evidently accustomed to do?

"I concluded to trust to her integrity, and went for the cab. But it was a risk, sir, which I promise not to repeat in the future. She was awaiting me on the stoop when I got back, and at once entered the hack with a command to drive immediately to Police Headquarters. I saw her as I came in just now sitting in the outer office, waiting for you. Are you ready to say I have done well?"

Mr. Gryce, with an indescribable look of mingled envy and indulgence, pressed the hand held out to him, and passed out. His curiosity could be restrained no longer, and he went at once to where this mysterious woman was awaiting him. Did he think it odd that she knew him, that she sought him? If so, he did not betray this in his manner, which was one of great respect. But that manner suddenly changed as he came face to face with the lady in question. Not that it lost its respect, but that it betrayed an astonishment of a more pronounced character than was usually indulged in by this experienced detective. The lady before him was one well known to him; in fact, almost an associate of his in certain bygone matters; in other words, none other than that most reputable of ladies, Miss Amelia Butterworth of Gramercy Park.

CHAPTER VI

Suggestions from an Old Friend

The look with which this amiable spinster met his eye was one which a stranger would have found it hard to understand. He found it hard to understand himself, perhaps because he had never before seen this lady when she was laboring under an opinion of herself that was not one of perfect complacency.

"Miss Butterworth! What does this mean? Have you—"

"There!" The word came with some sharpness. "You have detected me at my old tricks, and I am correspondingly ashamed, and you triumphant. The gray parasol you have been good enough to send to my house is not mine, but I was in the room where you picked it up, as you have so cleverly concluded, and as it is useless for me to evade your perspicacity, I have come here to confess."

"Ah!" The detective was profoundly interested at once. He drew a chair up to Miss Butterworth's side and sat down. "You were there!" he repeated; "and when? I do not presume to ask for what purpose."

"But I shall have to explain my purpose not to find myself at too great a disadvantage," she replied with grim decision. "Not that I like to display my own weakness, but that I recognize the exigencies of the occasion, and fully appreciate your surprise at finding that I, a stranger to Mr. Adams, and without the excuse which led to my former interference in police matters, should have so far forgotten myself as to be in my present position before you. This was no affair of my immediate neighbor, nor did it seek me. I sought it, sir, and in this way. I wish I had gone to Jericho first; it might have meant longer travel and much more expense; but it would have involved me in less humiliation and possible publicity. Mr. Gryce, I never meant to be mixed up with another murder case. I have shown my aptitude for detective work and received, ere now, certain marks of your approval; but my head was not turned by them—at least I thought not—and I was tolerably sincere in my determination to keep to my own *metier* in future and not suffer myself to be allured by any inducements you might offer into the exercise of gifts which may have brought me praise in the past, but certainly have not brought me happiness. But the temptation came, not through you, or I might have resisted it, but through a combination of circumstances which found me weak, and, in a measure, unprepared. In other words, I was surprised into taking an interest in this affair. Oh, I am ashamed of it, so ashamed that I have made the greatest endeavor to hide my participation in the matter, and thinking I had succeeded in doing so, was congratulating myself upon my precautions, when I found that parasol thrust in my face and realized that you, if no one else, knew that Amelia Butterworth had been in Mr. Adams's room of death prior to yourself. Yet I thought I had left no traces behind me. Could you have seen—"

"Miss Butterworth, you dropped five small spangles from your robe. You wore a dress spangled with black sequins, did you not? Besides, you moved the inkstand, and—Well, I will never put faith in circumstantial evidence again. I saw these tokens of a woman's presence, heard what the boy had to say of the well-dressed lady who had sent him into the drug-store with a message to the police, and drew the conclusion—I may admit it to you—that it was this woman who had wielded the assassin's dagger, and not the deaf-and-dumb butler, who, until now, has borne the blame of it. Therefore I was anxious to find her, little realizing what would be the result of my efforts, or that I should have to proffer her my most humble apologies."

"Do not apologize to me. I had no business to be there, or, at least, to leave the five spangles you speak of, behind me on Mr. Adams's miserable floor. I was simply passing by the house; and had I been the woman I once was, that is, a woman who had never dipped into a mystery, I should have continued on my way, instead of turning aside. Sir, it's a curious sensation to find yourself, however innocent, regarded by a whole city full of people as the cause or motive of a terrible murder, especially when you have spent some time, as I have, in the study of crime and the pursuit of criminals. I own I don't enjoy the experience. But I have brought it on myself. If I had not been so curious—But it was not curiosity I felt. I will never own that I am subject to mere curiosity; it was the look on the young man's face. But I forget myself. I am rambling in all directions when I ought to be telling a consecutive tale. Not my usual habit, sir; this you know; but I am not quite myself at this moment. I declare I am more upset by this discovery of my indiscretion than I was by Mr. Trohm's declaration of affection in Lost Man's Lane! Give me time, Mr. Gryce; in a few minutes I will be more coherent."

"I am giving you time," he returned with one of his lowest bows. "The half-dozen questions I long to ask have not yet left my lips, and I sit here, as you must yourself acknowledge, a monument of patience."

"So you thought this deed perpetrated by an outsider," she suddenly broke in. "Most of the journals—I read them very carefully this morning—ascribed the crime to the man you have mentioned. And there seems to be good reason for doing so. The case is not a simple one, Mr. Gryce; it has complications—I recognized that at once, and that is why—but I won't waste another moment in apologies. You have a right to any little fact I may have picked up in my unfortunate visit, and there is one which

I failed to find included in any account of the murder. Mr. Adams had other visitors besides myself in those few fatal minutes preceding his death. A young man and woman were with him. I saw them come out of the house. It was at the moment I was passing—"

"Tell your story more simply, Miss Butterworth. What first drew your attention to the house?"

"There! That is the second time you have had to remind me to be more direct. You will not have to do so again, Mr. Gryce. To begin, then, I noticed the house, because I always notice it. I never pass it without giving a thought to its ancient history and indulging in more or less speculation as to its present inmates. When, therefore, I found myself in front of it yesterday afternoon on my way to the art exhibition, I naturally looked up, and—whether by an act of providence or not, I cannot say—it was precisely at that instant the inner door of the vestibule burst open, and a young man appeared in the hall, carrying a young woman in his arms. He seemed to be in a state of intense excitement, and she in a dead faint; but before they had attracted the attention of the crowd, he had placed her on her feet, and, taking her on his arm, dragged her down the stoop and into the crowd of passers-by, among whom they presently disappeared. I, as you may believe, stood rooted to the ground in my astonishment, and not only endeavored to see in what direction they went, but lingered long enough to take a peep into the time-honored interior of this old house, which had been left open to view by the young man's forgetting to close the front door behind him. As I did so, I heard a cry from within. It was muffled and remote, but unmistakably one of terror and anguish: and, led by an impulse I may live to regret, as it seems likely to plunge me into much unpleasantness, I rushed up the stoop and went in, shutting the door behind me, lest others should be induced to follow.

"So far, I had acted solely from instinct; but once in that semi-dark hall, I paused and asked what business I had there, and what excuse I should give for my intrusion if I encountered one or more of the occupants of the house. But a repetition of the cry, coming as I am ready to swear from the farthest room on the parlor floor, together with a sharp remembrance of the wandering eye and drawn countenance of the young man whom I had seen stagger hence a moment before, with an almost fainting woman in his arms, drew me on in spite of my feminine instincts; and before I knew it, I was in the circular study and before the prostrate form of a seemingly dying man. He was lying as you probably found him a little later, with the cross on his breast and a dagger in his heart; but his right hand was trembling, and when I stooped to lift his head, he gave a shudder and then settled into eternal stillness. I, a stranger from the street, had witnessed his last breath while the young man who had gone out—"

"Can you describe him? Did you encounter him close enough for recognition?"

"Yes, I think I would know him again. I can at least describe his appearance. He wore a checked suit, very natty, and was more than usually tall and fine-looking. But his chief peculiarity lay in his expression. I never saw on any face, no, not on the stage, at the climax of the most heart-rending tragedy, a greater accumulation of mortal passion struggling with the imperative necessity for restraint. The young girl whose blond head lay on his shoulder looked like a saint in the clutch of a demon. She had seen death, but he—But I prefer not to be the interpreter of that expressive countenance. It was lost to my view almost immediately, and probably calmed itself in the face of the throng he entered, or we would be hearing about him today. The girl seemed to be devoid of almost all feeling. I should not remember her."

"And was that all? Did you just look at that recumbent man and vanish? Didn't you encounter the butler? Haven't you some definite knowledge to impart in his regard which will settle his innocence or fix his guilt?"

"I know no more about him than you do, sir, except that he was not in the room by the time I reached it, and did not come into it during my presence there. Yet it was his cry that led me to the spot; or do you think it was that of the bird I afterward heard shouting and screaming in the cage over the dead man's head?"

"It might have been the bird," admitted Mr. Gryce. "Its call is very clear, and it seems strangely intelligent. What was it saying while you stood there?"

"Something about Eva. 'Lovely Eva, maddening Eva! I love Eva! Eva! Eva!'"

"Eva? Wasn't it 'Evelyn? Poor Evelyn?'"

"No, it was Eva. I thought he might mean the girl I had just seen carried out. It was an unpleasant experience, hearing this bird shriek out these cries in the face of the man lying dead at my feet."

"Miss Butterworth, you didn't simply stand over that man. You knelt down and looked in his face."

"I acknowledge it, and caught my dress in the filagree of the cross. Naturally I would not stand stock still with a man drawing his last breath under my eye."

"And what else did you do? You went to the table—"

"Yes, I went to the table."

"And moved the inkstand?"

"Yes, I moved the inkstand, but very carefully, sir, very carefully."

"Not so carefully but that I could see where it had been sitting before you took it up: the square made by its base in the dust of the table did not coincide with the place afterwards occupied by it."

"Ah, that comes from your having on your glasses and I not. I endeavored to set it down in the precise place from which I lifted it."

"Why did you take it up at all? What were you looking for?"

"For clews, Mr. Gryce. You must forgive me, but I was seeking for clews. I moved several things. I was hunting for the line of writing which ought to explain this murder."

"The line of writing?"

"Yes. I have not told you what the young girl said as she slipped with her companion into the crowd."

"No; you have spoken of no words. Have you any such clew as that? Miss Butterworth, you are fortunate, very fortunate."

Mr. Gryce's look and gesture were eloquent, but Miss Butterworth, with an access of dignity, quietly remarked:

"I was not to blame for being in the way when they passed, nor could I help hearing what she said."

"And what was it, madam? Did she mention a paper?"

"Yes, she cried in what I now remember to have been a tone of affright: 'You have left that line of writing behind!' I did not attach much importance to these words then, but when I came upon the dying man, so evidently the victim of murder, I recalled what his late visitor had said and looked about for this piece of writing."

"And did you find it, Miss Butterworth? I am ready, as you see, for any revelation you may now make."

"For one which would reflect dishonor on me? If I had found any paper explaining this tragedy, I should have felt bound to have called the attention of the police to it. I did notify them of the crime itself."

"Yes, madam; and we are obliged to you; but how about your silence in regard to the fact of two persons having left that house immediately upon, or just preceding, the death of its master?"

"I reserved that bit of information. I waited to see if the police would not get wind of these people without my help. I sincerely wished to keep my name out of this inquiry. Yet I feel a decided relief now that I have made my confession. I never could have rested properly after seeing so much, and—"

"Well?"

"Thinking my own thoughts in regard to what I saw, if I had found myself compelled to bridle my tongue while false scents were being followed and delicate clews overlooked or discarded without proper attention. I regard this murder as offering the most difficult problem that has ever come in my way, and, therefore—"

"Yes, madam."

"I cannot but wonder if an opportunity has been afforded me for retrieving myself in your eyes. I do not care for the opinion of any one else as to my ability or discretion; but I should like to make you forget my last despicable failure in Lost Man's Lane. It is a sore remembrance to me, Mr. Gryce, which nothing but a fresh success can make me forget."

"Madam, I understand you. You have formulated some theory. You consider the young man with the tell-tale face guilty of Mr. Adams's death. Well, it is very possible. I never thought the butler was rehearsing a crime he had himself committed."

"Do you know who the young man is I saw leaving that house so hurriedly?"

"Not the least in the world. You are the first to bring him to my attention."

"And the young girl with the blonde hair?"

"It is the first I have heard of her, too."

"I did not scatter the rose leaves that were found on that floor."

"No, it was she. She probably wore a bouquet in her belt."

"Nor was that frippery parasol mine, though I did lose a good, stout, serviceable one somewhere that day."

"It was hers; I have no doubt of it."

"Left by her in the little room where she was whiling away the time during which the gentlemen conversed together, possibly about that bit of writing she afterward alluded to."

"Certainly."

"Her mind was not expectant of evil, for she was smoothing her hair when the shock came—"

"Yes, madam, I follow you."

"And had to be carried out of the place after—"

"What?"

"She had placed that cross on Mr. Adams's breast. That was a woman's act, Mr. Gryce."

"I am glad to hear you say so. The placing of that cross on a layman's breast was a mystery to me, and is still, I must own. Great remorse or great fright only can account for it."

"You will find many mysteries in this case, Mr. Gryce."

"As great a number as I ever encountered."

"I have to add one."

"Another?"

"It concerns the old butler."

"I thought you did not see him."

"I did not see him in the room where Mr. Adams lay."

"Ah! Where, then?"

"Upstairs. My interest was not confined to the scene of the murder. Wishing to spread the alarm, and not being able to rouse any one below,

I crept upstairs, and so came upon this poor wretch going through the significant pantomime that has been so vividly described in the papers."

"Ah! Unpleasant for you, very. I imagine you did not stop to talk to him."

"No, I fled. I was extremely shaken up by this time and knew only one thing to do, and that was to escape. But I carried one as yet unsolved enigma with me. How came I to hear this man's cries in Mr. Adams's study, and yet find him on the second floor when I came to search the house? He had not time to mount the stairs while I was passing down the hall."

"It is a case of mistaken impression. Your ears played you false. The cries came from above, not from Mr. Adams's study."

"My ears are not accustomed to play me tricks. You must seek another explanation."

"I have ransacked the house; there are no back stairs."

"If there were, the study does not communicate with them."

"And you heard his voice in the study?"

"Plainly."

"Well, you have given me a poser, madam."

"And I will give you another. If he was the perpetrator of this crime, how comes it that he was not detected and denounced by the young people I saw going out? If, on the contrary, he was simply the witness of another man's blow—a blow which horrified him so much that it unseated his reason—how comes it that he was able to slide away from the door where he must have stood without attracting the attention and bringing down upon himself the vengeance of the guilty murderer?"

"He may be one of the noiseless kind, or, rather, may have been such before this shock unsettled his mind."

"True, but he would have been seen. Recall the position of the doorway. If Mr. Adams fell where he was struck, the assailant must have had that door directly before him. He could not have helped seeing any one standing in it."

"That is true; your observations are quite correct. But those young people were in a disordered state of mind. The condition in which they issued from the house proves this. They probably did not trouble themselves about this man. Escape was all they sought. And, you see, they did escape."

"But you will find them. A man who can locate a woman in this great city of ours with no other clew than five spangles, dropped from her gown, will certainly make this parasol tell the name of its owner."

"Ah, madam, the credit of this feat is not due to me. It was the initial stroke of a young man I propose to adopt into my home and heart; the same who brought you here tonight. Not much to look at, madam, but promising, very promising. But I doubt if even he can discover the young lady you mean, with no other aid than is given by this parasol. New York is a big place, ma'am, a big place. Do you know how Sweetwater came to find you? Through your virtues, ma'am; through your neat and methodical habits. Had you been of a careless turn of mind and not given to mending your dresses when you tore them, he might have worn his heart out in a vain search for the lady who had dropped the five spangles in Mr. Adams's study. Now luck, or, rather, your own commendable habit, was in his favor this time; but in the prospective search you mentioned, he will probably have no such assistance."

"Nor will he need it. I have unbounded faith in your genius, which, after all, is back of the skilfulness of this new pupil of yours. You will discover by some means the lady with the dove-colored plumes, and through her the young gentleman who accompanied her."

"We shall at least put our energies to work in that direction. Sweetwater may have an idea—"

"And I may have one."

"You?"

"Yes; I indulged in but little sleep last night. That dreadful room with its unsolved mystery was ever before me. Thoughts would come; possibilities would suggest themselves. I imagined myself probing its secrets to the bottom and—"

"Wait, madam; how many of its so-called secrets do you know? You said nothing about the lantern."

"It was burning with a red light when I entered."

"You did not touch the buttons arranged along the table top?"

"No; if there is one thing I do not touch, it is anything which suggests an electrical contrivance. I am intensely feminine, sir, in all my instincts, and mechanisms of any kind alarm me. To all such things I give a wide berth. I have not even a telephone in my house. Some allowance must be made for the natural timidity of woman."

Mr. Gryce suppressed a smile. "It is a pity," he remarked. "Had you brought another light upon the scene, you might have been blessed with an idea on a subject that is as puzzling as any connected with the whole affair."

"You have not heard what I have to say on a still more important matter," said she. "When we have exhausted the one topic, we may both feel like turning on the fresh lights you speak of. Mr. Gryce, on what does this mystery hinge? On the bit of writing which these young people were so alarmed at having left behind them."

"Ah! It is from that you would work! Well, it is a good point to start from. But we have found no such bit of writing."

"Have you searched for it? You did not know till now that any importance might be attached to a morsel of paper with some half-dozen words written on it."

"True, but a detective searches just the same. We ransacked that room as few rooms have been ransacked in years. Not for a known clew, but for an unknown one. It seemed necessary in the first place to learn who this man was. His papers were consequently examined. But they told nothing. If there had been a scrap of writing within view or in his desk—"

"It was not on his person? You had his pockets searched, his clothes—"

"A man who has died from violence is always searched, madam. I leave no stone unturned in a mysterious case like this."

Miss Butterworth's face assumed an indefinable expression of satisfaction, which did not escape Mr. Gryce's eye, though that member was fixed, according to his old habit, on the miniature of her father which she wore, in defiance of fashion, at her throat.

"I wonder," said she, in a musing tone, "if I imagined or really saw on Mr. Adams's face a most extraordinary expression; something more than the surprise or anguish following a mortal blow? A look of determination, arguing some superhuman resolve taken at the moment of death, or—can you read that face for me? Or did you fail to perceive aught of what I say? It would really be an aid to me at this moment to know."

"I noted that look. It was not a common one. But I cannot read it for you—"

"I wonder if the young man you call Sweetwater can. I certainly think it has a decided bearing on this mystery; such a fold to the lips, such a look of mingled grief and—what was that you said? Sweetwater has not been admitted to the room of death? Well, well, I shall have to make my own suggestion, then. I shall have to part with an idea that may be totally valueless, but which has impressed me so that it must out, if I am to have any peace tonight. Mr. Gryce, allow me to whisper in your ear. Some things lose force when spoken aloud."

And leaning forward, she breathed a short sentence into his ear which made him start and regard her with an amazement which rapidly grew into admiration.

"Madam!" he cried, rising up that he might the better honor her with one of his low bows, "your idea, whether valueless or not, is one which is worthy of the acute lady who proffers it. We will act on it, ma'am, act at once. Wait till I have given my orders. I will not keep you long."

And with another bow, he left the room.

CHAPTER VII

Amos's Son

Miss Butterworth had been brought up in a strict school of manners. When she sat, she sat still; when she moved, she moved quickly, firmly, but with no unnecessary disturbance. Fidgets were unknown to her. Yet when she found herself alone after this interview, it was with difficulty she could restrain herself from indulging in some of those outward manifestations of uneasiness which she had all her life reprobated in the more nervous members of her own sex. She was anxious, and she showed it, like the sensible woman she was, and was glad enough when Mr. Gryce finally returned and, accosting her with a smile, said almost gayly:

"Well, that is seen to! And all we have to do now is to await the result. Madam, have you any further ideas? If so, I should be glad to have the benefit of them."

Her self-possession was at once restored.

"You would?" she repeated, eying him somewhat doubtfully. "I should like to be assured of the value of the one I have already advanced, before I venture upon another. Let us enter into a conference instead; compare notes; tell, for instance, why neither of us look on Bartow as the guilty man."

"I thought we had exhausted that topic. Your suspicions were aroused by the young couple you saw leaving the house, while mine—well, madam, to you, at least, I may admit that there is something in the mute's gestures and general manner which conveys to my mind the impression that he is engaged in rehearsing something he has seen, rather than something he has done; and as yet I have seen no reason for doubting the truth of this impression."

"I was affected in the same way, and would have been, even if I had not already had my suspicions turned in another direction. Besides, it is more natural for a man to be driven insane by another's act than by his own."

"Yes, if he loved the victim."

"And did not Bartow?"

"He does not mourn Mr. Adams."

"But he is no longer master of his emotions."

"Very true; but if we take any of his actions as a clew to the situation, we must take all. We believe from his gestures that he is giving us a literal copy of acts he has seen performed. Then, why pass over the gleam of infernal joy that lights his face after the whole is over? It is as if he rejoiced over the deed, or at least found immeasurable satisfaction in it."

"Perhaps it is still a copy of what he saw; the murderer may have rejoiced. But no, there was no joy in the face of the young man I saw rushing away from this scene of violence. Quite the contrary. Mr. Gryce, we are in deep waters. I feel myself wellnigh submerged by them."

"Hold up your head, madam. Every flood has its ebb. If you allow yourself to go under, what will become of me?"

"You are disposed to humor, Mr. Gryce. It is a good sign. You are never humorous when perplexed. Somewhere you must see daylight."

"Let us proceed with our argument. Illumination frequently comes from the most unexpected quarter."

"Very well, then, let us put the old man's joy down as one of the mysteries to be explained later. Have you thought of him as a possible accomplice?"

"Certainly; but this supposition is open to the same objection as that which made him the motive power in this murder. One is not driven insane by an expected horror. It takes shock to unsettle the brain. He was not looking for the death of his master."

"True. We may consider that matter as settled. Bartow was an innocent witness of this crime, and, having nothing to fear, may be trusted to reproduce in his pantomimic action its exact features."

"Very good. Continue, madam. Nothing but profit is likely to follow an argument presented by Miss Butterworth."

The old detective's tone was serious, his manner perfect; but Miss Butterworth, ever on the look-out for sarcasm from his lips, bridled a little, though in no other way did she show her displeasure.

"Let us, then, recall his precise gestures, remembering that he must have surprised the assailant from the study doorway, and so have seen the assault from over his master's shoulder."

"In other words, directly in front of him. Now what was his first move?"

"His first move, as now seen, is to raise his right arm and stretch it behind him, while he leans forward for the imaginary dagger. What does that mean?"

"I should find it hard to say. But I did not see him do that. When I came upon him, he was thrusting with his left hand across his own body—a vicious thrust and with his left hand. That is a point, Mr. Gryce."

"Yes, especially as the doctors agree that Mr. Adams was killed by a left-handed blow."

"You don't say! Don't you see the difficulty, then?"

"The difficulty, madam?"

"Bartow was standing face to face with the assailant. In imitating him, especially in his unreasoning state of mind, he would lift the arm opposite to the one whose action he mimics, which, in this case, would be the assailant's right. Try, for the moment, to mimic my actions. See! I lift this hand, and instinctively (nay, I detected the movement, sir, quickly as you remembered yourself), you raise the one directly opposite to it. It is like seeing yourself in a mirror. You turn your head to the right, but your image turns to the left."

Mr. Gryce's laugh rang out in spite of himself. He was not often caught napping, but this woman exercised a species of fascination upon him at times, and it rather amused than offended him, when he was obliged to acknowledge himself defeated.

"Very good! You have proved your point quite satisfactorily; but what conclusions are to be drawn from it? That the man was not left-handed, or that he was not standing in the place you have assigned to him?"

"Shall we go against the doctors? They say that the blow was a left-handed one. Mr. Gryce, I would give anything for an hour spent with you in Mr. Adams's study, with Bartow free to move about at his will. I think we would learn more by watching him for a short space of time than in talking as we are doing for an hour."

It was said tentatively, almost timidly. Miss Butterworth had some sense of the temerity involved in this suggestion even if, according to her own declaration, she had no curiosity. "I don't want to be disagreeable," she smiled.

She was so far from being so that Mr. Gryce was taken unawares, and for once in his life became impulsive.

"I think it can be managed, madam; that is, after the funeral. There are too many officials now in the house, and—"

"Of course, of course," she acceded. "I should not think of obtruding myself at present. But the case is so interesting, and my connection with it so peculiar, that I sometimes forget myself. Do you think"—here she became quite nervous for one of her marked self-control—"that I have laid myself open to a summons from the coroner?"

Mr. Gryce grew thoughtful, eyed the good lady, or rather her folded hands, with an air of some compassion, and finally replied:

"The facts regarding this affair come in so slowly that I doubt if the inquest is held for several days. Meanwhile we may light on those two young people ourselves. If so, the coroner may *overlook* your share in bringing them to our notice."

There was a sly emphasis on the word, and a subtle humor in his look that showed the old detective at his worst. But Miss Butterworth did not resent it; she was too full of a fresh confession she had to make.

"Ah," said she, "if they had been the only persons I encountered there. But they were not. Another person entered the house before I left it, and I may be obliged to speak of him."

"Of him? Really, madam, you are a mine of intelligence."

"Yes, sir," was the meek reply; meek, when you consider from whose lips it came. "I ought to have spoken of him before, but I never like to mix matters, and this old gentleman—"

"Old gentleman!"

"Yes, sir, very old and very much of a gentleman, did not appear to have any connection with the crime beyond knowing the murdered man."

"Ah, but that's a big connection, ma'am. To find someone who knew Mr. Adams—really, madam, patience has its limits, and I must press you to speak."

"Oh, I will speak! The time has come for it. Besides, I'm quite ready to discuss this new theme; it is very interesting."

"Suppose we begin, then, by a detailed account of your adventures in this house of death," dryly suggested the detective. "Your full adventures, madam, with nothing left out."

"I appreciate the sarcasm, but nothing has been left out except what I am about to relate to you. It happened just as I was leaving the house."

"What did? I hate to ask you to be more explicit. But, in the interests of justice—"

"You are quite right. As I was going out, then, I encountered an elderly gentleman coming in. His hand had just touched the bell handle. You will acknowledge that it was a perplexing moment for me. His face, which was well preserved for his years, wore an air of expectation that was almost gay. He glanced in astonishment at mine, which, whatever its usual serenity, certainly must have borne marks of deep emotion. Neither of us spoke. At last he inquired politely if he might enter, and said something about having an appointment with someone in the study. At which I stepped briskly enough aside, I assure you, for this might mean—What did you say? Did I close the door? I assuredly did. Was I to let the whole of —— Street into the horrors of this house at a moment when a poor old man—No, I didn't go out myself. Why should I? Was I to leave a man on the verge of eighty—excuse me, not every man of eighty is so hale and vigorous as yourself—to enter such a scene alone? Besides, I had not warned him of the condition of the only other living occupant of the house."

"Discreet, very. Quite what was to be expected of you, Miss Butterworth. More than that. You followed him, no doubt, with careful supervision, down the hall."

"Most certainly! What would you have thought of me if I had not? He was in a strange house; there was no servant to guide him, he wanted to know the way to the study, and I politely showed him there."

"Kind of you, madam—very. It must have been an interesting moment to you."

"Very interesting! Too interesting! I own that I am not made entirely of steel, sir, and the shock he received at finding a dead man awaiting him, instead of a live one, was more or less communicated to me. Yet I stood my ground."

"Admirable! I could have done no better myself. And so this man who had an appointment with Mr. Adams was shocked, really shocked, at finding him lying there under a cross, dead?"

"Yes, there was no doubting that. Shocked, surprised, terrified, and something more. It is that something more which has proved my perplexity. I cannot make it out, not even in thinking it over. Was it the fascination which all horrible sights exert on the morbid, or was it a sudden realization of some danger he had escaped, or of some difficulty yet awaiting him? Hard to say, Mr. Gryce, hard to say; but you may take my word for it that there was more to him in this meeting than an unexpected stumbling upon a dead man where he expected to find a live one. Yet he made no sound after that first cry, and hardly any movement. He just stared at the figure on the floor; then at his face, which he seemed to devour, at first with curiosity, then with hate, then with terror, and lastly—how can I express myself?—with a sort of hellish humor that in another moment might have broken into something like a laugh, if the bird, which I had failed to observe up to this moment, had not waked in its high cage, and, thrusting its beak between the bars, shrilled out in the most alarming of tones: 'Remember Evelyn!' That startled the old man even more than the sight on the floor had done. He turned round, and I saw his fist rise as if against some menacing intruder, but it quickly fell again as his eyes encountered the picture which hung before him, and with a cringe painful to see in one of his years, he sidled back till he reached the doorway. Here he paused a minute to give another look at the man outstretched at his feet, and I heard him say:

"'It is Amos's son, not Amos! Is it fatality, or did he plan this meeting, thinking—'

"But here he caught sight of my figure in the antechamber beyond, and resuming in an instant his former debonair manner, he bowed very low and opened his lips as if about to ask a question. But he evidently thought better of it, for he strode by me and made his way to the front door without a word. Being an intruder myself, I did not like to stop him. But I am sorry now for the consideration I showed him; for just before he stepped out, his emotion—the special character of which, I own to you, I find impossible to understand—culminated in a burst of raucous laughter which added the final horror to this amazing adventure. Then he went out, and in the last glimpse I had of him before the door shut he wore the same look of easy self-satisfaction with which he had entered this place of death some fifteen minutes before."

"Remarkable! Some secret history there! That man must be found. He can throw light upon Mr. Adams's past. 'Amos's son,' he called him? Who is Amos? Mr. Adams's name was Felix. Felix, the son of Amos. Perhaps this connection of names may lead to something. It is not a common one, and if given to the papers, may result in our receiving a clew to a mystery which seems impenetrable. Your stay in Mr. Adams's house was quite productive, ma'am. Did you prolong it after the departure of this old man?"

"No, sir, I had had my fill of the mysterious, and left immediately after him. Ashamed of the spirit of investigation which had led me to enter the house, I made a street boy the medium of my communication to the police, and would have been glad if I could have so escaped all responsibility in the matter. But the irony of fate follows me as it does others. A clew was left of my presence, which involves me in this affair, whether I will or no. Was the hand of Providence in this? Perhaps. The future will tell. And now, Mr. Gryce, since my budget is quite empty and the hour late, I will take my leave. If you hear from that bit of paper—"

"If I hear from it in the way you suggest I will let you know. It will be the least I can do for a lady who has done so much for me."

"Now you flatter me—proof positive that I have stayed a minute longer than was judicious. Good evening, Mr. Gryce. What? I have not stayed too long? You have something else to ask."

"Yes, and this time it is concerning a matter personal to yourself. May I inquire if you wore the same bonnet yesterday that you do today?"

"No, sir. I know you have a good reason for this question, and so will not express my surprise. Yesterday I was in reception costume, and my bonnet was a jet one—"

"With long strings tied under the chin?"

"No, sir, short strings; long strings are no longer the fashion."

"But you wore something which fell from your neck?"

"Yes, a boa—a feather boa. How came you to know it, sir? Did I leave my image in one of the mirrors?"

"Hardly. If so, I should not have expected it to speak. You merely wrote the fact on the study table top. Or so I have dared to think. You or the young lady—did she wear ribbons or streamers, too?"

"That I cannot say. Her face was all I saw, and the skirt of a dove-colored silk dress."

"Then you must settle the question for me in this way. If on the tips of that boa of yours you find the faintest evidence of its having been dipped in blood, I shall know that the streaks found on the top of the table I speak of were evidences of your presence there. But if your boa is clean, or was not long enough to touch that dying man as you leaned over him, then we have proof that the young lady with the dove-colored plumes fingered that table also, instead of falling at once into the condition in which you saw her carried out."

"I fear that it is my boa which will tell the tale: another proof of the fallibility of man, or, rather, woman. In secret search for clews I left behind me traces of my own presence. I really feel mortified, sir, and you have quite the advantage of me."

And with this show of humility, which may not have been entirely sincere, this estimable lady took her departure.

Did Mr. Gryce suffer from any qualms of conscience at having elicited so much and imparted so little? I doubt it. Mr. Gryce's conscience was quite seared in certain places.

CHAPTER VIII

In the Round of the Staircase

The next morning Mr. Gryce received a small communication from Miss Butterworth at or near the very time she received one from him. Hers ran:

You were quite correct. So far as appears, I was the only person to lean over Mr. Adams's study table after his unfortunate death. I have had to clip the ends of my boa.

His was equally laconic:

My compliments, madam! Mr. Adams's jaws have been forced apart. A small piece of paper was found clinched between his teeth. This paper has been recovered, and will be read at the inquest. Perhaps a few favored persons may be granted the opportunity of reading it before then, notably yourself.

Of the two letters the latter naturally occasioned the greater excitement in the recipient. The complacency of Miss Butterworth was superb, and being the result of something that could not be communicated to those about her, occasioned in the household much speculation as to its cause.

At Police Headquarters more than one man was kept busy listening to the idle tales of a crowd of would-be informers. The results which had failed to follow the first day's publication of the crime came rapidly in during the second. There were innumerable persons of all ages and conditions who were ready to tell how they had seen this and that one issue from Mr. Adams's house on the afternoon of his death, but when asked to give a description of these persons, lost themselves in generalities as tedious as they were unprofitable. One garrulous old woman had observed a lady of genteel appearance open the door to an elderly gentleman in a great-coat; and a fashionably dressed young woman came in all breathless to relate how a young man with a very pale young lady on his arm ran against her as she was going by this house at the very hour Mr. Adams was said to have been murdered. She could not be sure of knowing the young man again, and could not say if the young lady was blonde or brunette, only that she was awfully pale and had a beautiful gray feather in her hat.

Others were ready with similar stories, which confirmed, without adding to, the facts already known, and night came on without much progress having been made toward the unravelling of this formidable mystery.

On the next day Mr. Adams's funeral took place. No relatives or intimate friends having come forward, his landlord attended to these rites and his banker acted the part of chief mourner. As his body was carried out of the house, a half-dozen detectives mingled with the crowd blocking the thoroughfare in front, but nothing came of their surveillance here or at the cemetery to which the remains were speedily carried. The problem which had been presented to the police had to be worked out from such material as had already come to hand; and, in forcible recognition of this fact, Mr. Gryce excused himself one evening at Headquarters and proceeded quite alone and on foot to the dark and apparently closed house in which the tragedy had occurred.

He entered with a key, and once inside, proceeded to light up the whole house. This done, he took a look at the study, saw that the cross had been replaced on the wall, the bird-cage rehung on its hook under the ceiling, and everything put in its wonted order, with the exception of the broken casings, which still yawned in a state of disrepair on either side of the doorway leading into the study. The steel plate had been shoved back into the place prepared for it by Mr. Adams, but the glimpses still to be seen of its blue surface through the hole made in the wall of the antechamber formed anything but an attractive feature in the scene, and Mr. Gryce, with something of the instinct and much of the deftness of a housewife, proceeded to pull up a couple of rugs from the parlor floor and string them over these openings. Then he consulted his watch, and finding that it was within an hour of nine o'clock, took up his stand behind the curtains of the parlor window. Soon, for the person expected was as prompt as himself, he saw a carriage stop and a lady alight, and he hastened to the front door to receive her. It was Miss Butterworth.

"Madam, your punctuality is equal to my own," said he. "Have you ordered your coachman to drive away?"

"Only as far as the corner," she returned, as she followed him down the hall. "There he will await the call of your whistle."

"Nothing could be better. Are you afraid to remain for a moment alone, while I watch from the window the arrival of the other persons we expect? At present there is no one in the house but ourselves."

"If I was subject to fear in a matter of this kind, I should not be here at all. Besides, the house is very cheerfully lighted. I see you have chosen a crimson light for illuminating the study."

"Because a crimson light was burning when Mr. Adams died."

"Remember Evelyn!" called out a voice.

"Oh, you have brought back the bird!" exclaimed Miss Butterworth. "That is not the cry with which it greeted me before. It was 'Eva! Lovely Eva!' Do you suppose Eva and Evelyn are the same?"

"Madam, we have so many riddles before us that we will let this one go for the present. I expect Mr. Adams's valet here in a moment."

"Sir, you relieve me of an immense weight. I was afraid that the privilege of being present at the test you propose to make was not to be accorded me."

"Miss Butterworth, you have earned a seat at this experiment. Bartow has been given a key, and will enter as of old in entire freedom to do as he wills. We have simply to watch his movements."

"In this room, sir? I do not think I shall like that. I had rather not meet this madman face to face."

"You will not be called upon to do so. We do not wish him to be startled by encountering any watchful eye. Irresponsible as he is, he must be allowed to move about without anything to distract his attention. Nothing must stand in the way of his following those impulses which may yield us a clew to his habits and the ways of this peculiar household. I propose to place you where the chances are least in favor of your being seen by him—in this parlor, madam, which we have every reason to believe was seldom opened during Mr. Adams's lifetime."

"You must put out the gas, then, or the unaccustomed light will attract his attention."

"I will not only put out the gas, but I will draw the portières close, making this little hole for your eye and this one for mine. A common expedient, madam; but serviceable, madam, serviceable."

The snort which Miss Butterworth gave as she thus found herself drawn up in darkness before a curtain, in company with this plausible old man, but feebly conveyed her sensations, which were naturally complex and a little puzzling to herself. Had she been the possessor of a lively curiosity (but we know from her own lips that she was not), she might have found some enjoyment in the situation. But being where she was solely from a sense of duty, she probably blushed behind her screen at the position in which she found herself, in the cause of truth and justice; or would have done so if the opening of the front door at that moment had not told her that the critical moment had arrived and that the deaf-and-dumb valet had just been introduced into the house.

The faintest "Hush!" from Mr. Gryce warned her that her surmise was correct, and, bending her every energy to listen, she watched for the expected appearance of this man in the antechamber of Mr. Adams's former study.

He came even sooner than she was prepared to see him, and laying down his hat on a table near the doorway, advanced with a busy air toward the portière he had doubtless been in the habit of lifting twenty times a day. But he barely touched it this time. Something seen, or unseen, prevented him from entering. Was it the memory of what he had last beheld there? Or had he noticed the rugs hanging in an unaccustomed way on either side of the damaged casings? Neither, apparently, for he simply turned away with a meek look, wholly mechanical, and taking up his hat again, left the antechamber and proceeded softly upstairs.

"I will follow him," whispered Mr. Gryce. "Don't be afraid, ma'am. This whistle will bring a man in from the street at once."

"I am not afraid. I would be ashamed—"

But it was useless for her to finish this disclaimer. Mr. Gryce was already in the hall. He returned speedily, and saying that the experiment was likely to be a failure, as the old man had gone to his own room and was preparing himself for bed, he led the way into the study, and with purpose, or without a purpose—who knows?—idly touched a button on the table top, thus throwing a new light on the scene. It was Miss Butterworth's first experience of this change of light, and she was observing the effect made by the violet glow now thrown over the picture and the other rich articles in the room when her admiration was cut short, and Mr. Gryce's half-uttered remark also, by the faint sound of the valet's descending steps.

Indeed, they had barely time to regain their old position behind the parlor portières when Bartow was seen hurrying in from the hall with his former busy air, which this time remained unchecked.

Crossing to his master's study, he paused for an infinitesimal length of time on the threshold, as if conscious of something being amiss, then went into the room beyond, and, without a glance in the direction of the rug, which had been carefully relaid on the spot where his master had fallen, began to make such arrangements for the night as he was in the habit of making at this hour. He brought a bottle of wine from the cupboard and set it on the table, and then a glass, which he first wiped scrupulously clean. Then he took out his master's dressing gown and slippers, and, placing them to hand, went into the bedroom.

By this time the two watchers had crept from their concealment near enough to note what he was doing in the bedroom. He was stooping over the comb which Mr. Gryce had left lying on the floor. This small object in such a place seemed to surprise him. He took it up, shook his head, and put it back on the dresser. Then he turned down his master's bed.

"Poor fool!" murmured Miss Butterworth as she and her companion crept back to their old place behind the parlor curtains, "he has forgotten everything but his old routine duties. We shall get nothing from this man."

But she stopped suddenly; they both stopped. Bartow was in the middle of the study, with his eyes fixed on his master's empty chair in an inquiring way that spoke volumes. Then he turned, and gazed earnestly at the rug where he had last seen that master lying outstretched and breathless; and awakening to a realization of what had happened, fell into his most violent self and proceeded to go through the series of actions which they were now bound to consider a reproduction of what he had previously seen take place there. Then he went softly out, and crept away upstairs.

Mr. Gryce and Miss Butterworth stepped at once into the light, and surveyed each other with a look of marked discouragement. Then the latter, with a sudden gleam of enthusiasm, cried quickly:

"Turn on another color, and let us see what will happen. I have an idea it will fetch the old man down again."

Mr. Gryce's brows went up.

"Do you think he can see through the floor?"

But he touched a button, and a rich blue took the place of the violet. Nothing happened.

Miss Butterworth looked disturbed.

"I have confidence in your theories," began Mr. Gryce, "but when they imply the possibility of this man seeing through blank walls and obeying signals which can have no signification to any one on the floor above—"

"Hark!" she cried, holding up one finger with a triumphant air. The old man's steps could be heard descending.

This time he approached with considerable feebleness, passed slowly into the study, advanced to the table, and reached out his hands as if to lift something which he expected to find there. Seeing nothing, he glanced in astonishment up at the book shelves and then back to the table, shook his head, and suddenly collapsing, sank in a doze on the nearest chair.

Miss Butterworth drew a long breath, eyed Mr. Gryce with some curiosity, and then triumphantly exclaimed:

"Can you read the meaning of all that? I think I can. Don't you see that he came expecting to find a pile of books on the table which it was probably his business to restore to their shelves?"

"But how can he know what light is burning here? You can see for yourself that there is no possible communication between this room and the one in which he has always been found by any one going above."

Miss Butterworth's manner showed a hesitation that was almost naive. She smiled, and there was apology in her smile, though none in her voice, as she remarked with odd breaks:

"When I went upstairs—you know I went upstairs when I was here before—I saw a little thing—a very little thing—which you doubtless observed yourself and which may explain, though I do not know how, why Bartow can perceive these lights from the floor above."

"I shall be very glad to hear about it, madam. I thought I had thoroughly searched those rooms—"

"And the halls?"

"And the halls; and that nothing in them could have escaped my eyes. But if you have a more patient vision than myself—"

"Or make it my business to look lower—"

"How?"

"To look lower; to look on the floor, say."

"On the floor?"

"The floor sometimes reveals much: shows where a person steps the oftenest, and, therefore, where he has the most business. You must have noticed how marred the woodwork is at the edge of the carpeting on that little landing above."

"In the round of the staircase?"

"Yes."

Mr. Gryce did not think it worth his while to answer. Perhaps he had not time; for leaving the valet where he was, and Miss Butterworth where she was (only she would not be left, but followed him), he made his way upstairs, and paused at the place she had mentioned, with a curious look at the floor.

"You see, it has been much trodden here," she said; at which gentle reminder of her presence he gave a start; possibly he had not heard her behind him, and after sixty years of hard service even a detective may be excused a slight nervousness. "Now, why should it be trodden here? There is no apparent reason why any one should shuffle to and fro in this corner. The stair is wide, especially here, and there is no window—"

Mr. Gryce, whose eye had been travelling over the wall, reached over her shoulder to one of the dozen pictures hanging at intervals from the bottom to the top of the staircase, and pulling it away from the wall, on which it hung decidedly askew, revealed a round opening through which poured a ray of blue light which could only proceed from the vault of the adjoining study.

"No window," he repeated. "No, but an opening into the study wall which answers the same purpose. Miss Butterworth, your eye is to be trusted every time. I only wonder you did not pull this picture aside yourself."

"It was not hanging crooked then. Besides I was in a hurry. I had just come from my encounter with this demented man. I had noticed the marks on the landing, and the worn edges of the carpet, on my way up-stairs. I was in no condition to observe them on my way down."

"I see."

Miss Butterworth ran her foot to and fro over the flooring they were examining.

"Bartow was evidently in the habit of coming here constantly," said she, "probably to learn whether his master had need of him. Ingenious in Mr. Adams to contrive signals for communication with this man! He certainly had great use for his deaf-and-dumb servant. So one mystery is solved!"

"And if I am not mistaken, we can by a glance through this loophole obtain the answer to another. You are wondering, I believe, how Bartow, if he followed the movements of the assailant from the doorway, came to thrust with his left hand, instead of with his right. Now if he saw the tragedy from this point, he saw it over the assailant's shoulder, instead of face to face. What follows? He would imitate literally the movements of the man he saw, turn in the same direction and strike with the same hand."

"Mr. Gryce, we are beginning to untangle the threads that looked so complicated. Ah, what is that? Why, it's that bird! His cage must be very nearly under this hole."

"A little to one side, madam, but near enough to give you a start. What was it he cried then?"

"Oh, those sympathetic words about Eva! 'Poor Eva!'"

"Well, give a glance to Bartow. You can see him very well from here."

Miss Butterworth put her eye again to the opening, and gave a grunt, a very decided grunt. With her a grunt was significant of surprise.

"He is shaking his fist; he is all alive with passion. He looks as if he would like to kill the bird."

"Perhaps that is why the creature was strung up so high. You may be sure Mr. Adams had some basis for his idiosyncrasies."

"I begin to think so. I don't know that I care to go back where that man is. He has a very murderous look."

"And a very feeble arm, Miss Butterworth. You are safe under my protection. My arm is not feeble."

A-Table. B-Small Stand. C-Door to Bedroom. D-Evelyn's Picture
E-Loophole on Stair Landing. F-Entrance to Study.[5]

CHAPTER IX

High and Low

At the foot of the stairs, Mr. Gryce excused himself, and calling in two or three men whom he had left outside, had the valet removed before taking Miss Butterworth back into the study. When all was quiet again, and they found an opportunity to speak, Mr. Gryce remarked:

"One very important thing has been settled by the experiment we have just made. Bartow is acquitted of participation in this crime."

"Then we can give our full attention to the young people. You have heard nothing from them, I suppose?"

"No."

"Nor from the old man who laughed?"

"No."

Miss Butterworth looked disappointed.

"I thought—it seemed very probable—that the scrap of writing you found would inform you who these were. If it was important enough for the dying man to try to swallow it, it certainly should give some clew to his assailant."

"Unfortunately, it does not do so. It was a veritable scrawl, madam, running something like this: 'I return your daughter to you. She is here. Neither she nor you will ever see me again. Remember Evelyn!' And signed, 'Amos's son.'"

"Amos's son! That is Mr. Adams himself."

"So we have every reason to believe."

"Strange! Unaccountable! And the paper inscribed with these words was found clinched between his teeth! Was the handwriting recognized?"

5   Since my readers may not understand how an opening above the stairway might communicate with Mr. Adams's study, I here submit a diagram of the same. The study walls were very high, forming a rounded extension at the back of the house.

"Yes, as his own, if we can judge from the specimens we have seen of his signature on the fly-leaves of his books."

"Well, mysteries deepen. And the retaining of this paper was so important to him that even in his death throe he thrust it in this strangest of all hiding-places, as being the only one that could be considered safe from search. And the girl! Her first words on coming to herself were: 'You have left that line of writing behind.' Mr. Gryce, those words, few and inexplicable as they are, contain the key to the whole situation. Will you repeat them again, if you please, sentence by sentence?"

"With pleasure, madam; I have said them often enough to myself. First, then: 'I return your daughter to you!'"

"So! Mr. Adams had someone's daughter in charge whom he returns. Whose daughter? Not that young man's daughter, certainly, for that would necessitate her being a small child. Besides, if these words had been meant for his assailant, why make so remarkable an effort to hide them from him?"

"Very true! I have said the same thing to myself."

"Yet, if not for him, for whom, then? For the old gentleman who came in later?"

"It is possible; since hearing of him I have allowed myself to regard this as among the possibilities, especially as the next words of this strange communication are: 'She is here.' Now the only woman who was there a few minutes previous to this old gentleman's visit was the light-haired girl whom you saw carried out."

"Very true; but why do you reason as if this paper had just been written? It might have been an old scrap, referring to past sorrows or secrets."

"These words were written that afternoon. The paper on which they were scrawled was torn from a sheet of letter paper lying on the desk, and the pen with which they were inscribed—you must have noticed where it lay, quite out of its natural place on the extreme edge of the table."

"Certainly, sir; but I had little idea of the significance we might come to attach to it. These words are connected, then, with the girl I saw. And she is not Evelyn or he would not have repeated in this note the bird's catch-word, 'Remember Evelyn!' I wonder if she is Evelyn?" proceeded Miss Butterworth, pointing to the one large picture which adorned the wall.

"We may call her so for the nonce. So melancholy a face may well suggest some painful family secret. But how explain the violent part played by the young man, who is not mentioned in these abrupt and hastily penned sentences! It is all a mystery, madam, a mystery which we are wasting time to attempt to solve."

"Yet I hate to give it up without an effort. Those words, now. There were some other words you have not repeated to me."

"They came before that injunction, 'Remember Evelyn!' They bespoke a resolve. 'Neither she nor you will ever see me again.'"

"Ah! but these few words are very significant, Mr. Gryce. Could he have dealt that blow himself? May he have been a suicide after all?"

"Madam, you have the right to inquire; but from Bartow's pantomime, you must have perceived it is not a self-inflicted blow he mimics, but a maddened thrust from an outraged hand. Let us keep to our first conclusions; only—to be fair to every possibility—the condition of Mr. Adams's affairs and the absence of all family papers and such documents as may usually be found in a wealthy man's desk prove that he had made some preparation for possible death. It may have come sooner than he expected and in another way, but it was a thought he had indulged in, and—madam, I have a confession to make also. I have not been quite fair to my most valued colleague. The study—that most remarkable of rooms—contains a secret which has not been imparted to you; a very peculiar one, madam, which was revealed to me in a rather startling manner. This room can be, or rather could be, cut off entirely from the rest of the house; made a death-trap of, or rather a tomb, in which this incomprehensible man may have intended to die. Look at this plate of steel. It is worked by a mechanism which forces it across this open doorway. I was behind that plate of steel the other night, and these holes had to be made to let me out."

"Ha! You detectives have your experiences! I should not have enjoyed spending that especial evening with you. But what an old-world tragedy we are unearthing here! I declare"—and the good lady actually rubbed her eyes—"I feel as if transported back to mediæval days. Who says we are living in New York within sound of the cable car and the singing of the telegraph wire?"

"Some men are perfectly capable of bringing the mediæval into Wall Street. I think Mr. Adams was one of those men. Romanticism tinged all his acts, even the death he died. Nor did it cease with his death. It followed him to the tomb. Witness the cross we found lying on his bosom."

"That was the act of another's hand, the result of another's superstition. That shows the presence of a priest or a woman at the moment he died."

"Yet," proceeded Mr. Gryce, with a somewhat wondering air, "he must have had a grain of hard sense in his make-up. All his contrivances worked. He was a mechanical genius, as well as a lover of mystery."

"An odd combination. Strange that we do not feel his spirit infecting the very air of this study. I could almost wish it did. We might then be led to grasp the key to this mystery."

"That," remarked Mr. Gryce, "can be done in only one way. You have already pointed it out. We must trace the young couple who were present at his death struggle. If they cannot be found the case is hopeless."

"And so," said she, "we come around to the point from which we started—proof positive that we are lost in the woods." And Miss Butterworth rose. She felt that for the time being she, at least, had come to the end of her resources.

Mr. Gryce did not seek to detain her. Indeed, he appeared to be anxious to leave the place himself. They, however, stopped long enough to cast one final look around them. As they did so Miss Butterworth's finger slowly rose.

"See!" said she, "you can hardly perceive from this side of the wall the opening made by the removal of that picture on the stair landing. Wouldn't you say that it was in the midst of those folds of dark-colored tapestry up there?"

"Yes, I had already located that spot as the one. With the picture hung up on the other side, it would be quite invisible."

"One needs to keep one's eyes moving in a case like this. That picture must have been drawn aside several times while we were in this room. Yet we failed to notice it."

"That was from not looking high enough. High and low, Mr. Gryce! What goes on at the level of the eye is apparent to every one."

The smile with which he acknowledged this parting shot and prepared to escort her to the door had less of irony than sadness in it. Was he beginning to realize that years tell even on the most sagacious, and that neither high places nor low would have escaped his attention a dozen years before?

CHAPTER X

Bride Roses

"A blonde, you say, sir?"

"Yes, Sweetwater; not of the usual type, but one of those frail, ethereal creatures whom we find it so hard to associate with crime. He, on the contrary, according to Miss Butterworth's description (and her descriptions may be relied upon), is one of those gentlemanly athletes whose towering heads and powerful figures attract universal attention. Seen together, you would be apt to know them. But what reason have we for thinking they will be found together?"

"How were they dressed?"

"Like people of fashion and respectability. He wore a brown-checked suit apparently fresh from the tailor; she, a dove-colored dress with white trimmings. The parasol shows the color of her hat and plumes. Both were young, and (still according to Miss Butterworth) of sensitive temperament and unused to crime; for she was in a fainting condition when carried from the house, and he, with every inducement to self-restraint, showed himself the victim of such powerful emotion that he would have been immediately surrounded and questioned if he had not set his burden down in the vestibule and at once plunged with the girl into the passing crowd. Do you think you can find them, Sweetwater?"

"Have you no clews to their identity beyond this parasol?"

"None, Sweetwater, if you except these few faded rose leaves picked up from the floor of Mr. Adams's study."

"Then you have given me a problem, Mr. Gryce," remarked the young detective dubiously, as he eyed the parasol held out to him and let the rose-leaves drop carelessly through his fingers. "Somehow I do not feel the same assurances of success that I did before. Perhaps I more fully realize the difficulties of any such quest, now that I see how much rests upon chance in these matters. If Miss Butterworth had not been a precise woman, I should have failed in my former attempt, as I am likely to fail in this one. But I will make another effort to locate the owner of this parasol, if only to learn my business by failure. And now, sir, where do you think I am going first? To a florist's, with these faded rose-leaves. Just because every other young fellow on the force would make a start from the parasol, I am going to try and effect one from these rose-leaves. I may be an egotist, but I cannot help that. I can do nothing with the parasol."

"And what do you hope to do with the rose-leaves? How can a florist help you in finding this young woman by means of them?"

"He may be able to say from what kind of a rose they fell, and once I know that, I may succeed in discovering the particular store from which the bouquet was sold to this more or less conspicuous couple."

"You may. I am not the man to throw cold water on any one's schemes. Every man has his own methods, and till they are proved valueless I say nothing."

Young Sweetwater, who was now all nerve, enthusiasm, and hope, bowed. He was satisfied to be allowed to work in his own way.

"I may be back in an hour, and you may not see me for a week," he remarked on leaving.

"Luck to your search!" was the short reply. This ended the interview. In a few minutes more Sweetwater was off.

The hour passed; he did not come back; the day, and still no Sweetwater. Another day went by, enlivened only by an interchange of notes between Mr. Gryce and Miss Butterworth. Hers was read by the old detective with a smile. Perhaps because it was so terse; perhaps because it was so characteristic.

Dear Mr. Gryce:

I do not presume to dictate or even to offer a suggestion to the New York police, but have you inquired of the postman in a certain district whether he can recall the postmark on any of the letters he delivered to Mr. Adams?

A. B.

His, on the contrary, was perused with a frown by his exacting colleague in Gramercy Park. The reason is obvious.

Dear Miss Butterworth:

Suggestions are always in order, and even dictation can be endured from you. The postman delivers too many letters on that block to concern himself with postmarks. Sorry to close another thoroughfare.

E. G.

Meanwhile, the anxiety of both was great; that of Mr. Gryce excessive. He was consequently much relieved when, on the third morning, he found Sweetwater awaiting him at the office, with a satisfied smile lighting up his plain features. He had reserved his story for his special patron, and as soon as they were closeted together he turned with beaming eyes toward the old detective, crying:

"News, sir; good news! I have found them; I have found them both, and by such a happy stroke! It was a blind trail, but when the florist said that those petals might have fallen from a bride rose—well, sir, I know that any woman can carry bride roses, but when I remembered that the clothes of her companion looked as though they had just come from the tailor's, and that she wore gray and white—why, it gave me an idea, and I began my search after this unknown pair at the Bureau of Vital Statistics."

"Brilliant!" ejaculated the old detective. "That is, if the thing worked."

"And it did, sir; it did. I may have been born under a lucky star, probably was, but once started on this line of search, I went straight to the end. Shall I tell you how? Hunting through the list of such persons as had been married within the city limits during the last two weeks, I came upon the name of one Eva Poindexter. Eva! that was a name well-known in the house on —— Street. I decided to follow up this Eva."

"A wise conclusion! And how did you set about it?"

"Why, I went directly to the clergyman who had performed the ceremony. He was a kind and affable dominie, sir, and I had no trouble in talking to him."

"And you described the bride?"

"No, I led the conversation so that he described her."

"Good; and what kind of a woman did he make her out to be? Delicate? Pale?"

"Sir, he had not read the service for so lovely a bride in years. Very slight, almost fragile, but beautiful, and with a delicate bloom which showed her to be in better health than one would judge from her dainty figure. It was a private wedding, sir, celebrated in a hotel parlor; but her father was with her—"

"Her father?" Mr. Gryce's theory received its first shock. Then the old man who had laughed on leaving Mr. Adams's house was not the father to whom those few lines in Mr. Adams's handwriting were addressed. Or this young woman was not the person referred to in those lines.

"Is there anything wrong about that?" inquired Sweetwater.

Mr. Gryce became impassive again.

"No; I had not expected his attendance at the wedding; that is all."

"Sorry, sir, but there is no doubt about his having been there. The bridegroom—"

"Yes, tell me about the bridegroom."

"Was the very man you described to me as leaving Mr. Adams's house with her. Tall, finely developed, with a grand air and gentlemanly manners. Even his clothes correspond with what you told me to expect: a checked suit, brown in color, and of the latest cut. Oh, he is the man!"

Mr. Gryce, with a suddenly developed interest in the lid of his ink-stand, recalled the lines which Mr. Adams had written immediately before his death, and found himself wholly at sea. How reconcile facts so diametrically opposed? What allusion could there be in these lines to the new-made bride of another man? They read, rather, as if she were his own bride, as witness:

I return your daughter to you. She is here. Neither she nor you will ever see me again. Remember Evelyn!

Amos's Son.

There must be something wrong. Sweetwater must have been led astray by a series of extraordinary coincidences. Dropping the lid of the inkstand in a way to make the young man smile, he looked up.

"I'm afraid it's been a fool chase, Sweetwater. The facts you relate in regard to this couple, the fact of their having been married at all, tally so little with what we have been led to expect from certain other evidences which have come in—"

"Pardon me, sir, but will you hear me out? At the Imperial, where they were married, I learned that the father and daughter had registered as coming from a small place in Pennsylvania; but I could learn nothing in regard to the bridegroom. He had not appeared on the scene till the time for the ceremony, and after the marriage was seen to take his bride away in one carriage while the old gentleman departed in another. The latter concerned me little; it was the young couple I had been detailed to find. Employing the usual means of search, I tracked them to the Waldorf, where I learned what makes it certain that I have been following the right couple. On the afternoon of the very day of Mr. Adams's death, this young husband and wife left the hotel on foot and did not come back. Their clothes, which had all been left behind, were taken away two days later by an elderly gentleman who said he was her father and whose appearance coincides with that of the person registering as such at the Imperial. All of which looks favorable to my theory, does it not, especially when you remember that the bridegroom's name—"

"You have not told it."

"Is Adams, Thomas Adams. Same family as the murdered man, you see. At least, he has the same name."

Mr. Gryce surveyed the young man with admiration, but was not yet disposed to yield him entire credence.

"Humph! I do not wonder you thought it worth your while to follow up the pair, if one of them is named Adams and the other Eva. But, Sweetwater, the longer you serve on the force the more you will learn that coincidences as strange and unexpected as these do occur at times, and must be taken into account in the elucidation of a difficult problem. Much as I may regret to throw cold water on your hopes, there are reasons for believing that the young man and woman whom we are seeking are not the ones you have busied yourself about for the last two days. Certain facts which have come to light would seem to show that if she had a husband at all, his name would not be Thomas Adams, but Felix, and as the facts I have to bring forward are most direct and unimpeachable, I fear you will have to start again, and on a new tack."

But Sweetwater remained unshaken, and eyed his superior with a vague smile playing about his lips.

"You have not asked me, sir, where I have spent all the time which has elapsed since I saw you last. The investigations I have mentioned did not absorb more than a day."

"Very true. Where have you been, Sweetwater?"

"To Montgomery, sir, to that small town in Pennsylvania from which Mr. Poindexter and his daughter registered."

"Ah, I see! And what did you learn there? Something directly to the point?"

"I learned this, that John Poindexter, father of Eva, had for a friend in early life one Amos Cadwalader."

"Amos!" repeated Mr. Gryce, with an odd look.

"Yes, and that this Amos had a son, Felix."

"Ah!"

"You see, sir, we must be on the right track; coincidences cannot extend through half a dozen names."

"You are right. It is I who have made a mistake in drawing my conclusions too readily. Let us hear about this Amos. You gathered something of his history, no doubt."

"All that was possible, sir. It is closely woven in with that of Poindexter, and presents one feature which may occasion you no surprise, but which, I own, came near nonplussing me. Though the father of Felix, his name was not Adams. I say was not, for he has been dead six months. It was Cadwalader. And Felix went by the name of Cadwalader, too, in the early days of which I have to tell, he and a sister whose name—"

"Well?"

"Was Evelyn."

"Sweetwater, you are an admirable fellow. So the mystery is ours."

"The history, not the mystery; that still holds. Shall I relate what I know of those two families?"

"At once: I am as anxious as if I were again twenty-three and had been in your shoes instead of my own for the last three days."

"Very well, sir. John Poindexter and Amos Cadwalader were, in their early life, bosom friends. They had come from Scotland together and settled in Montgomery in the thirties. Both married there, but John Poindexter was a prosperous man from the first, while Cadwalader had little ability to support a family, and was on the verge of bankruptcy when the war of the rebellion broke out and he enlisted as a soldier. Poindexter remained at home, caring for his own family and for the two children of Cadwalader, whom he took into his own house. I say his own family, but he had no family, save a wife, up to the spring of '80. Then a daughter was born to him, the Eva who has just married Thomas Adams. Cadwalader, who was fitted for army life, rose to be a captain; but he was unfortunately taken prisoner at one of the late battles and confined in Libby Prison, where he suffered the tortures of the damned till he was released, in 1865, by a forced exchange of prisoners. Broken, old, and crushed, he returned home, and no one living in the town at that time will ever forget the day he alighted from the cars and took his way up the main street. For not having been fortunate enough, or unfortunate enough, perhaps, to receive any communication from home, he advanced with a cheerful haste, not knowing that his only daughter then lay dead in his friend's house, and that it was for her funeral that the people were collecting in the green square at the end of the street. He was so pale, broken, and decrepit that few knew him. But there was one old neighbor who recognized him and was kind enough to lead him into a quiet place, and there tell him that he had arrived just too late to see his darling daughter alive. The shock, instead of prostrating the old soldier, seemed to nerve him afresh and put new vigor into his limbs. He proceeded, almost on a run, to Poindexter's house, and arrived just as the funeral cortège was issuing from the door. And now happened a strange thing. The young girl had been laid on an open bier, and was being carried by six sturdy lads to her last resting place. As the father's eye fell on her young body under its black pall, a cry of mortal anguish escaped him, and he sank on his knees right in the line of the procession.

"At the same minute another cry went up, this time from behind the bier, and John Poindexter could be seen reeling at the side of Felix Cadwalader, who alone of all present (though he was the youngest and the least) seemed to retain his self-possession at this painful moment. Meanwhile the bereaved father, throwing himself at the side of the bier, began tearing away at the pall in his desire to look upon the face of her he had left in such rosy health four years before. But he was stopped, not by Poindexter, who had vanished from the scene, but by Felix, the cold, severe-looking boy who stood like a guard behind his sister. Reaching out a hand so white it was in itself a shock, he laid it in a certain prohibitory way on the pall, as if saying no. And when his father would have continued the struggle, it was Felix who controlled him and gradually drew him into the place at his own side where a minute before the imposing figure of Poindexter had stood; after which the bearers took up their burden again and moved on.

"But the dramatic scene was not over. As they neared the churchyard another procession, similar in appearance to their own, issued from an adjoining street, and Evelyn's young lover, who had died almost simultaneously with herself, was brought in and laid at her side. But not in the same grave: this was noticed by all, though most eyes and hearts were fixed upon Cadwalader, who had escaped his loathsome prison and returned to the place of his affections for *this*.

"Whether he grasped then and there the full meaning of this double burial (young Kissam had shot himself upon hearing of Evelyn's death), or whether all explanations were deferred till he and Felix walked away together from the grave, has never transpired. From that minute till they both left town on the following day, no one had any word with him, save Poindexter, whom he went once to see, and young Kissam's mother, who came once to see him. Like a phantom he had risen upon the sight of the good people of Montgomery, and like a phantom he disappeared, never to be seen by any of them again, unless, as many doubt, the story is true which was told some twenty years ago by one of the little village lads. He says (it was six years after the tragic scene I have just related) that one evening as he was hurrying by the churchyard, in great anxiety to reach home before it was too dark, he came upon the figure of a man standing beside a grave, with a little child in his arms. This man was tall, long-bearded, and terrifying. His attitude, as the lad describes it, was one of defiance, if not of cursing. High in his right hand he held the child, almost as if he would hurl him at the village which lies under the hill on which the churchyard is perched; and though the moment passed quickly, the boy, now a man, never has forgotten the picture thus presented or admitted that it was anything but a real one. As the description he gave of this man answered to the appearance of Amos Cadwalader, and as the shoe of a little child was found next morning on the grave of Cadwalader's daughter, Evelyn, it has been thought by many that the boy really beheld this old soldier, who for some mysterious reason had chosen nightfall for this fleeting visit to his daughter's resting-place. But to others it was only a freak of the lad's imagination, which had been much influenced by the reading of romances. For, as these latter reasoned, had it really been Cadwalader, why did he not show himself at John Poindexter's house—that old friend who now had a little daughter and no wife and who could have made him so comfortable? Among these was Poindexter himself, though some thought he looked oddly while making this remark, as if he spoke more from custom than from the heart. Indeed, since the unfortunate death of Evelyn in his house, he had never shown the same interest in the Cadwaladers. But then he was a man much occupied with great affairs, while the Cadwaladers, except for their many griefs and misfortunes, were regarded as comparatively insignificant people, unless we except Felix, who from his earliest childhood had made himself feared even by grown people, though he never showed a harsh spirit or exceeded the bounds of decorum in speech or gesture. A year ago news came to Montgomery of Amos Cadwalader's death, but no particulars concerning his family or burial place. And that is all I have been able to glean concerning the Cadwaladers."

Mr. Gryce had again become thoughtful.

"Have you any reason to believe that Evelyn's death was not a natural one?"

"No, sir. I interviewed the old mother of the young man who shot himself out of grief at Evelyn's approaching death, and if any doubt had existed concerning a matter which had driven her son to a violent end, she could not have concealed it from me. But there seemed to have been none. Evelyn Cadwalader was always of delicate health, and when a quick consumption carried her off no one marvelled. Her lover, who adored her, simply could not live without her, so he shot himself. There was no mystery about the tragic occurrence except that it seemed to sever an old friendship that once was firm as a rock. I allude to that between the Poindexters and Cadwaladers."

"Yet in this tragedy which has just occurred in —— Street we see them brought together again. Thomas Adams marries Eva Poindexter. But who is Thomas Adams? You have not mentioned him in this history."

"Not unless he was the child who was held aloft over Evelyn's grave."

"Humph! That seems rather far-fetched. What did you learn about him in Montgomery? Is he known there?"

"As well as any stranger can be who spends his time in courting a young girl. He came to Montgomery a few months ago, from some foreign city—Paris, I think—and, being gifted with every personal charm calculated to please a cultivated young woman, speedily won the affections of Eva Poindexter, and also the esteem of her father. But their favorable opinion is not shared by every one in the town. There are those who have a good deal to say about his anxious and unsettled eye."

"Naturally; he could not marry all their daughters. But this history you have given me: it is meagre, Sweetwater, and while it hints at something deeply tragic, does not supply the key we want. A girl who died some thirty years ago! A father who disappeared! A brother who, from being a Cadwalader, has become an Adams! An Eva whose name, as well as that of the long-buried Evelyn, was to be heard in constant repetition in the place where the murdered Felix lay with those inscrutable lines in his own writing, clinched between his teeth! It is a snarl, a perfect snarl, of which we have as yet failed to pull the right thread. But we'll get hold of it yet. I'm not going to be baffled in my old age by difficulties I would have laughed at a dozen years ago."

"But this right thread? How shall we know it among the fifty I see entangled in this matter?"

"First, find the whereabouts of this young couple—but didn't you tell me you had done so; that you know where they are?"

"Yes. I learned from the postmaster in Montgomery that a letter addressed to Mrs. Thomas Adams had been sent from his post-office to Belleville, Long Island."

"Ah! I know that place."

"And wishing to be assured that the letter was not a pretense, I sent a telegram to the postmaster at Belleville. Here is his answer. It is unequivocal: 'Mr. Poindexter of Montgomery, Pa. Mr. Thomas Adams and Mrs. Adams of the same place have been at the Bedell House in this place five days.'"

"Very good; then we have them! Be ready to start for Belleville by one o'clock sharp. And mind, Sweetwater, keep your wits alert and your tongue still. Remember that as yet we are feeling our way blindfold, and must continue to do so till some kind hand tears away the bandage from our eyes. Go! I have a letter to write, for which you may send in a boy at the end of five minutes."

This letter was for Miss Butterworth, and created, a half-hour later, quite a stir in the fine old mansion in Gramercy Park. It ran thus:

Have you sufficient interest in the outcome of a certain matter to take a short journey into the country? I leave town at 1 P.M. for Belleville, Long Island. If you choose to do the same, you will find me at the Bedell House, in that town, early in the afternoon. If you enjoy novels, take one with you, and let me see you reading it on the hotel piazza at five o'clock. I may be reading too; if so, and my choice is a book, all is well, and you may devour your story in peace. But if I lay aside my book and take up a paper, devote but one eye to your story and turn the other on the people who are passing you. If after you have done so, you leave your book open, I shall understand that you fail to recognize these persons. But if you shut the volume, you may expect to see me also fold up my newspaper; for by so doing you will have signaled me that you have identified the young man and woman you saw leaving Mr. Adams's house on the fatal afternoon of your first entrance. E. G.

CHAPTER XI

Misery

It is to be hoped that the well-dressed lady of uncertain age who was to be seen late that afternoon in a remote corner of the hotel piazza at Belleville had not chosen a tale requiring great concentration of mind, for her eyes (rather fine ones in their way, showing both keenness and good nature) seemed to find more to interest them in the scene before her than in the pages she so industriously turned over.

The scene was one calculated to interest an idle mind, no doubt. First, there was the sea, a wide expanse of blue, dotted by numerous sails; then the beach, enlivened by groups of young people dressed like popinjays in every color; then the village street, and, lastly, a lawn over which there now and then strayed young couples with tennis rackets in their hands or golf sticks under their arms. Children, too—but children did not seem to interest this amiable spinster. (There could be no doubt about her being a spinster.) She scarcely glanced at them twice, while a young married pair, or even an old gentleman, if he were only tall and imperious-looking, invariably caused her eyes to wander from her book, which, by the way, she held too near for seeing, or such might have been the criticism of a wary observer.

This criticism, if criticism it would be called, could not have been made of the spruce, but rather feeble octogenarian at the other end of the piazza. He was evidently absorbed in the novel he held so conspicuously open, and which, from the smiles now and then disturbing the usual placidity of his benevolent features, we can take for granted was sufficiently amusing. Yet right in the midst of it, and certainly before he had finished his chapter, he closed his book and took out a newspaper, which he opened to its full width before sitting down to peruse its columns. At the same moment the lady at the other end of the piazza could be seen looking over her spectacles at two gentlemen who just at that moment issued from the great door opening between her and the elderly person just alluded to. Did she know them, or was it only her curiosity that was aroused? From the way she banged together her book and rose, it looked as if she had detected old acquaintances in the distinguished-looking pair who were now advancing slowly toward her. But if so, she could not have been overjoyed to see them, for after the first hint of their approach in her direction she turned, with an aspect of some embarrassment, and made her way out upon the lawn, where she stood with her back to these people, caressing a small dog in a way that betrayed her total lack of sympathy with these animals, which were evidently her terror when she was sufficiently herself to be swayed by her natural impulses.

The two gentlemen, on the contrary, with an air of total indifference to her proximity, continued their walk until they reached the end of the piazza, and then turned and proceeded mechanically to retrace their steps.

Their faces now being brought within view of the elderly person who was so absorbed in his newspaper, the latter shifted that sheet the merest trifle, possibly because the sun struck his eyes too directly, possibly because he wished to catch sight of two very remarkable men. If so, the opportunity was good, as they stopped within a few feet of his chair. One of them was elderly, as old as, if not older than, the man watching him; but he was of that famous Scotch stock whose members are tough and hale at eighty. This toughness he showed not only in his figure, which was both upright and graceful, but in the glance of his calm, cold eye, which fell upon everybody and everything unmoved, while that of his young, but equally stalwart companion seemed to shrink with the most acute sensitiveness from every person he met, save the very mild old reader of news near whom they now paused for a half-dozen words of conversation.

"I don't think it does me any good," was the young man's gloomy remark. "I am wretched when with her, and doubly wretched when I try to forget myself for a moment out of her sight. I think we had better go back. I had rather sit where she can see me than have her wonder—Oh, I will be careful; but you must remember how unnerving is the very silence I am obliged to keep about what is destroying us all. I am nearly as ill as she."

Here they drew off, and their apparently disinterested hearer turned the page of his paper. It was five minutes before they came back. This time it was the old gentleman who was speaking, and as he was more discreet than his companion or less under the influence of his feelings, his voice was lower and his words less easy to be distinguished.

"Escape? South coast—she will forget to watch you for—a clinging nature—impetuous, but foolishly affectionate—you know that—no danger—found out—time—a cheerful home—courage—happiness—all forgotten."

A gesture from the young man as he moved away showed that he did not share these hopes. Meanwhile Miss Butterworth—you surely have recognized Miss Butterworth—had her opportunities too. She was still stooping over the dog, which wriggled under her hand, yet did not offer to run away, fascinated perhaps by that hesitating touch which he may or may not have known had never inflicted itself upon a dog before. But her ears, and attention, were turned toward two girls chatting on a bench near her as freely as if they were quite alone on the lawn. They were gossiping about a fellow-inmate of the big hotel, and Miss Butterworth listened intently after hearing them mention the name Adams. These are some of the words she caught:

"But she is! I tell you she is sick enough to have a nurse and a doctor. I caught a glimpse of her as I was going by her room yesterday, and I never saw two such big eyes or such pale cheeks. Then, look at him! He must just adore her, for he won't speak to another woman, and just moves about in that small, hot room all day. I wonder if they are bride and groom? They are young enough, and if you have noticed her clothes—"

"Oh, don't talk about clothes. I saw her the first day she came, and was the victim of despair until she suddenly got sick and so couldn't wear those wonderful waists and jackets. I felt like a dowdy when I saw that pale blue—"

"Oh, well, blue becomes blondes. You would look like a fright in it. I didn't care about her clothes, but I did feel that it was all up with us if she chose to talk, or even to smile, upon the few men that are good enough to stay out a week in this place. Yet she isn't a beauty; she has not a good nose, nor a handsome eye, nor even an irreproachable complexion. It must be her mouth, which is lovely, or her walk—did you notice her walk? It was just as if she were floating; that is, before she fell down in that faint. I wonder why she fainted. Nobody was doing anything, not even her husband. But perhaps that was what troubled her. I noticed that for some cause he was looking very serious—and when she had tried to attract his attention two or three times and failed, she just fell from her chair to the floor. That roused him. He has hardly left her since."

"I don't think they look very happy, do you, for so rich and handsome a couple?"

"Perhaps he is dissipated. I have noticed that the old gentleman never leaves them."

"Well, well, he may be dissipated; handsome men are very apt to be.

But I wouldn't care if—"

Here the dog gave a yelp and bolted. Miss Butterworth had unconsciously pinched him, in her indignation, possibly, at the turn these rattle-pated young ladies' conversation was taking. This made a diversion, and the young girls moved off, leaving Miss Butterworth without occupation. But a young man who at that moment crossed her path gave her enough to think about.

"You recognize them? There is no mistake?" he whispered.

"None; the one this way is the young man I saw leave Mr. Adams's house, and the other is the old gentleman who came in afterward."

"Mr. Gryce advises you to return home. He is going to arrest the young man." And Sweetwater passed on.

Miss Butterworth strolled to a seat and sat down. She felt weak; she seemed to see that young wife, sick, overwhelmed, struggling with her great fear, sink under this crushing blow, with no woman near her capable of affording the least sympathy. The father did not impress her as being the man to hold up her fainting head or ease her bruised heart. He had an icy look under his polished exterior which repelled this keen-eyed spinster, and as she remembered the coldness of his ways, she felt herself seized by an irresistible impulse to be near this young creature when the blow fell, if only to ease the tension of her own heartstrings, which at that moment ached keenly over the part she had felt herself obliged to play in this matter.

But when she rose to look for Mr. Gryce, she found him gone; and upon searching the piazza for the other two gentlemen, she saw them just vanishing round the corner in the direction of a small smoking-room. As she could not follow them, she went upstairs, and, meeting a maid in the upper hall, asked for Mrs. Adams. She was told that Mrs. Adams was sick, but was shown the door of her room, which was at the end of a long hall. As all the halls terminated in a window under which a sofa was to be found, she felt that circumstances were in her favor, and took her seat upon the sofa before her in a state of great complacency. Instantly a sweet voice was heard through the open transom of the door behind which her thoughts were already concentrated.

"Where is Tom? Oh, where is Tom? Why does he leave me? I'm afraid of what he may be tempted to do or say down on those great piazzas alone."

"Mr. Poindexter is with him," answered a voice, measured, but kind. "Mr. Adams was getting very tired, and your father persuaded him to go down and have a smoke."

"I must get up; indeed I must get up. Oh! the camphor—the—"

There was a bustle; this poor young wife had evidently fainted again.

Miss Butterworth cast very miserable glances at the door.

Meanwhile in that small and retired smoking-room a terrible scene was in progress. The two gentlemen had lit their cigars and were sitting in certain forced attitudes that evinced their non-enjoyment of the weed each had taken out of complaisance to the other, when an old man, strangely serious, strangely at home, yet as strangely a guest of the house like themselves, came in, and shut the door behind him.

"Gentlemen," he at once announced, "I am Detective Gryce of the New York police, and I am here—but I see that one of you at least knows why I am here."

One? Both of them! This was evident in a moment. No denial, no subterfuge was possible. At the first word uttered in the strange, authoritative tone which old detectives acquire after years of such experiences, the young man sank down in sudden collapse, while his companion, without yielding so entirely to his emotions, showed that he was not insensible to the blow which, in one moment, had brought destruction to all their hopes.

When Mr. Gryce saw himself so completely understood, he no longer hesitated over his duty. Directing his full attention to Mr. Adams, he said, this time with some feeling, for the misery of this young man had impressed him:

"You are wanted in New York by Coroner D——, whose business it is to hold an inquest over the remains of Mr. Felix Adams, of whose astonishing death you are undoubtedly informed. As you and your wife were seen leaving that gentleman's house a few minutes before he expired, you are naturally regarded as valuable witnesses in determining whether his death was one of suicide or murder."

It was an accusation, or so nearly one, that Mr. Gryce was not at all surprised to behold the dark flush of shame displace the livid terror which but an instant before had made the man before him look like one of those lost spirits we sometimes imagine as flitting across the open mouth of hell. But he said nothing, seemingly had no power to do so, and his father-in-law was about to make some effort to turn aside this blow when a voice in the hall outside was heard inquiring for Mr. Adams, saying that his wife had fainted again and required his help.

The young husband started, cast a look full of despair at Mr. Poindexter, and thrusting his hand against the door as if to hold it shut, sank on his knees before Mr. Gryce, saying:

"She knows! She suspects! Her nature is so sensitive."

This he managed to utter in gasps as the detective bent compassionately over him. "Don't, don't disturb her! She is an angel, a saint from heaven. Let me bear the blame—he was my brother—let me go with you, but leave her in ignorance—"

Mr. Gryce, with a vivid sense of justice, laid his hand on the young man's arm.

"Say nothing," he enjoined. "My memory is good, and I would rather hear nothing from your lips. As for your wife, my warrant does in no way include her; and if you promise to come with me quietly, I will even let you bid her adieu, so that you do it in my presence."

The change which passed over the young man's face at these significant words was of a nature to surprise Mr. Gryce. Rising slowly, he took his stand by Mr. Poindexter, who, true to his inflexible nature, had scarcely moved in limb and feature since Mr. Gryce came in.

"What have you against me?" he demanded. And there was a surprising ring to his voice, as if courage had come with the necessity of the moment. "Of what am I accused? I want you to tell me. I had rather you would tell me in so many words. I cannot leave in peace until you do."

Mr. Poindexter made a movement at this, and cast a half-suspicious, half-warning glance at his son-in-law. But the young man took no notice of his interference. He kept his eye on the detective, who quietly took out his warrant.

At this instant the door shook.

"Lock it!" was the hoarse command of the accused man. "Don't let any one pass that door, even if it is to bring the tidings of my wife's death."

Mr. Gryce reached out his hand, and turned the key in the lock. Young Adams opened the paper which he had taken from the detective's hand, and while his blood-shot eyes vainly sought to master the few lines there written, Mr. Poindexter attracted the attention of Mr. Gryce, and, fixing him with his eye, formed his lips with three soundless words:

"For murder? Him?"

The detective's bow and a very long-drawn sigh from his son-in-law answered him simultaneously. With a curious lift of his upper lip, which showed his teeth somewhat unpleasantly for a moment, he drew back a step, and sank into his previous immobility.

"I am indebted to you," declared the young man. "Now I know where I stand. I am quite ready to go with you and stand trial, if such be deemed necessary by the officials in New York. You," he cried, turning with almost an air of command to the old gentleman beside him, "will watch over Eva. Not like a father, sir, but like a mother. You will be at her side when she wakes, and, if possible, leave her only when she sleeps. Do not let her suffer—not too much. No newspapers, no gossiping women. Watch! watch! as I would watch, and when I come back—for I will come back, will I not?" he appealed to Mr. Gryce, "my prayers will bless you and—" A sob stuck in his throat, and he turned for a minute aside; then he took the detective's arm quite calmly and remarked:

"I do not want to say good-by to my wife. I cannot bear it. I had rather go straight from here without another glance at her unconscious face. When I have told my story, for I shall tell it to the first man who asks me, I may find courage to write her. Meanwhile, get me away as quickly as you can. Time enough for the world to know my shame tomorrow."

Mr. Gryce tapped on the window overlooking the piazza. A young man stepped in.

"Here is a gentleman," he cried, "who finds himself forced to return in great haste to New York. See that he gets to the train in time, without fuss and without raising the least comment. I will follow with his portmanteau. Mr. Poindexter, you are now at liberty to attend your suffering daughter." And with a turn of the key, he unlocked the door, and one of the most painful scenes of his long life was over.

CHAPTER XII

Thomas Explains

Mr. Gryce was not above employing a little finesse. He had expressed his intention of following Mr. Adams, and he did follow him, but so immediately that he not only took the same train, but sat in the same car. He wished to note at his leisure the bearing of this young man, who interested him in quite a different way from what he had anticipated, a way that vaguely touched his own conscience and made him feel his years as he had no right to feel them when he had just brought to an end an intricate and difficult pursuit.

Seated at a distance, he watched with increasing interest the changes which passed over his prisoner's handsome countenance. He noted the calmness which now marked the features he had so lately seen writhing in deepest agony, and wondered from what source the strength came which enabled this young man to sit so stoically under the eyes of people from whose regard, an hour before, he had shrunk with such apparent suffering. Was it that courage comes with despair? Or was he too absorbed in his own misery to note the shadow it cast about him? His brooding brow and vacant eye spoke of a mind withdrawn from present surroundings. Into what depths of remorse, who could say? Certainly not this old detective, seasoned though he was by lifelong contact with criminals, some of them of the same social standing and cultured aspect as this young man.

At the station in Brooklyn he rejoined his prisoner, who scarcely looked up as he approached. In another hour they were at Police Headquarters and the serious questioning of Mr. Adams had begun.

He did not attempt to shirk it. Indeed, he seemed anxious to talk. He had a burden on his mind, and longed to throw it off. But the burden was not of the exact nature anticipated by the police. He did not acknowledge having killed his brother, but confessed to having been the incidental cause of that brother's death. The story he told was this:

"My name is Cadwalader, not Adams. My father, a Scotchman by birth, was a naturalized citizen of Pennsylvania, having settled in a place called Montgomery when a young married man. He had two children then, one of whom died in early life; the other was my brother Felix, whose violent death under the name of Adams you have called me here to explain. I am the fruit of a later marriage, entered into by my father some years after leaving Montgomery. When I was born he was living in Harrisburg, but, as he left there shortly after I had reached my third year, I have no remembrances connected with that city. Indeed, my recollections are all of very different scenes than this country affords. My mother having died while I was still an infant, I was sent very early in life to the Old World, from which my father had originally come. When I returned, which was not till this very year, I found my father dying, and my brother a grown man with money—a great deal of money—which I had been led to think he was ready to share with me. But after my father was laid away, Felix" (with what effort he uttered that name!) "Felix came to New York, and I was left to wander about without settled hopes or any definite promise of means upon which to base a future or start a career. While wandering, I came upon the town where my father had lived in early youth, and, hunting up his old friends, I met in the house of one who had come over from Scotland with my father a young lady" (how his voice shook, and with what a poignant accent he uttered that beloved name) "in whom I speedily became interested to the point of wishing to marry her. But I had no money, no business, no home to give her, and, as I was fain to acknowledge, no prospects. Still I could not give up the hope of making her my wife. So I wrote to my brother, Felix Cadwalader, or, rather, Felix Adams, as he preferred to be called in later years for family reasons entirely disconnected with the matter of his sudden demise, and, telling him I had become interested in a young girl of good family and some wealth, asked him to settle upon me a certain sum which would enable me to marry her with some feeling of self-respect. My only answer was a repetition of the vague promise he had thrown out before. But youth is hopeful, even to daring, and I decided to make her mine without further parley, in the hope that her beauty and endearing qualities would win from him, at first view, the definite concession he had so persistently denied me.

"This I did, and the fault with which I have most to reproach myself is that I entered into this alliance without taking her or her father into my confidence. They thought me well off, possibly rich, and while Mr. Poindexter is a man of means, I am sure, if he had known I had nothing but the clothes I wore and the merest trifle in the way of pocket money, he would have cried halt to the marriage, for he is a very ambitious man and considers his daughter well worth a millionaire's devotion—as she is.

"Felix (you must pardon me if I show no affection for my brother—he was a very strange man) was notified of my marriage, but did not choose to witness it, neither did he choose to prohibit it; so it was conducted quietly, with strangers for witnesses, in a hotel parlor. Then, with vague hopes, as well as certain vague fears, I prepared to take my young bride into the presence of my brother, who, hardened as he was by years of bachelorhood, could not be so entirely impervious to feminine charms as not to recognize my wife as a woman deserving of every consideration.

"But I had counted without my host. When, two days after the ceremony which had made us one, I took her to the house which has since become so unhappily notorious, I found that my brother had but shown me one facet, and that the least obdurate, of his many-sided nature.

"Brilliant as steel, he was as hard, and not only professed himself unmoved by my wife's many charms, but also as totally out of sympathy with such follies as love and marriage, which were, he said, the fruit of unoccupied minds and a pastime wholly unworthy of men boasting of such talents and attainments as ourselves. Then he turned his back upon us, and I, moved by an anger little short of frenzy, began an abuse for which he was so little prepared that he crouched like a man under blows, and, losing minute by minute his self-control, finally caught up a dagger lying close at hand, and crying, 'You want my money? Well, then, take it!' stabbed himself to the heart with one desperate blow.

"I fear I shall not be believed, but that is the story of this crime, gentlemen."

CHAPTER XIII

Despair

Was it? Tragedies as unpremeditated as this had doubtless occurred, and inconsistencies in character shown themselves in similar impetuosities, from the beginning of time up till now. Yet there was not a man present, with or without the memory of Bartow's pantomime, which, as you will recall, did not tally at all with this account of Mr. Adams's violent end, who did not show in a greater or less degree his distrust and evident disbelief in this tale, poured out with such volubility before them.

The young man, gifted as he was with the keenest susceptibilities, perceived this, and his head drooped.

"I shall add nothing to and take nothing from what I have said," was his dogged remark. "Make of it what you will."

The inspector who was conducting the inquiry glanced dubiously at Mr. Gryce as these words left Thomas Adams's lips; whereupon the detective said:

"We are sorry you have taken such a resolution. There are many things yet left to be explained, Mr. Adams; for instance, why, if your brother slew himself in this unforeseen manner, you left the house so precipitately, without giving an alarm or even proclaiming your relationship to him?"

"You need not answer, you know," the inspector's voice broke in. "No man is called upon to incriminate himself in this free and independent country."

A smile, the saddest ever seen, wandered for a minute over the prisoner's pallid lips. Then he lifted his head and replied with a certain air of desperation:

"Incrimination is not what I fear now. From the way you all look at me I perceive that I am lost, for I have no means of proving my story."

This acknowledgment, which might pass for the despairing cry of an innocent man, made his interrogator stare.

"You forget," suggested that gentleman, "that you had your wife with you. She can corroborate your words, and will prove herself, no doubt, an invaluable witness in your favor."

"My wife!" he repeated, choking so that his words could be barely understood. "Must she be dragged into this—so sick, so weak a woman? It would kill her, sir. She loves me—she—"

"Was she with you in Mr. Adams's study? Did she see him lift the dagger against his own breast?"

"No." And with this denial the young man seemed to take new courage. "She had fainted several moments previously, while the altercation between my brother and myself was at its height. She did not see the final act, and—gentlemen, I might as well speak the truth (I have nothing to gain by silence), she finds it as difficult as you do to believe that Mr. Adams struck himself. I—I have tried with all my arts to impress the truth upon her, but oh, what can I hope from the world when the wife of my bosom—an angel, too, who loves me—oh, sirs, she can never be a witness for me; she is too conscientious, too true to her own convictions. I should lose—she would die—"

Mr. Gryce tried to stop him; he would not be stopped.

"Spare me, sirs! Spare my wife! Write me down guilty, anything you please, rather than force that young creature to speak—"

Here the inspector cut short these appeals which were rending every heart present. "Have you read the newspapers for the last few days?" he asked.

"I? Yes, yes, sir. How could I help it? Blood is blood; the man was my brother; I had left him dying—I was naturally anxious, naturally saw my own danger, and I read them, of course."

"Then you know he was found with a large cross on his breast, a cross which was once on the wall. How came it to be torn down? Who put it on his bosom?"

"I, sir. I am not a Catholic but Felix was, and seeing him dying without absolution, without extreme unction, I thought of the holy cross, and tore down the only one I saw, and placed it in his arms."

"A pious act. Did he recognize it?"

"I cannot say. I had my fainting wife to look after. She occupied all my thoughts."

"I see, and you carried her out and were so absorbed in caring for her you did not observe Mr. Adams's valet—"

"He's innocent, sir. Whatever people may think, he had nothing to do with this crime—"

"You did not observe him, I say, standing in the doorway and watching you?"

Now the inspector knew that Bartow had not been standing there, but at the loophole above; but the opportunity for entrapping the witness was too good to lose.

Mr. Adams was caught in the trap, or so one might judge from the beads of perspiration which at that moment showed themselves on his pale forehead. But he struggled to maintain the stand he had taken, crying hotly:

"But that man is crazy, and deaf-and-dumb besides! or so the papers give out. Surely his testimony is valueless. You would not confront me with him?"

"We confront you with no one. We only asked you a question. You did not observe the valet, then?"

"No, sir."

"Or understand the mystery of the colored lights?"

"No, sir."

"Or of the plate of steel and the other contrivances with which your brother enlivened his solitude?"

"I do not follow you, sir." But there was a change in his tone.

"I see," said the inspector, "that the complications which have disturbed us and made necessary this long delay in the collection of testimony have not entered into the crime as described by you. Now this is possible; but there is still a circumstance requiring explanation; a little circumstance, which is, nevertheless, one of importance, since your wife mentioned it to you as soon as she became conscious. I allude to the half dozen or more words which were written by your brother immediately preceding his death. The paper on which they were written has been found, and that it was a factor in your quarrel is evident, since she regretted that it had been left behind you, and he—Do you know where we found this paper?"

The eyes which young Adams raised at this interrogatory had no intelligence in them. The sight of this morsel of paper seemed to have deprived him in an instant of all the faculties with which he had been carrying on this unequal struggle. He shook his head, tried to reach out his hand, but failed to grasp the scrap of paper which the inspector held out. Then he burst into a loud cry:

"Enough! I cannot hold out, with no other support than a wicked lie. I killed my brother for reasons good as any man ever had for killing another. But I shall not impart them. I would rather be tried for murder and hanged."

It was a complete breakdown, pitiful from its contrast with the man's herculean physique and fine, if contracted, features. If the end, it was a sad end, and Mr. Gryce, whose forehead had taken on a deep line between the eyebrows, slowly rose and took his stand by the young man, who looked ready to fall. The inspector, on the contrary, did not move. He had begun a tattoo with his fingers on the table, and seemed bound to beat it out, when another sudden cry broke from the young man's lips:

"What is that?" he demanded, with his eyes fixed on the door, and his whole frame shaking violently.

"Nothing," began the inspector, when the door suddenly opened and the figure of a woman white as a wraith and wonderful with a sort of holy passion darted from the grasp of a man who sought to detain her, and stood before them, palpitating with a protest which for a moment she seemed powerless to utter.

It was Adams's young, invalid wife, whom he had left three hours before at Belleville. She was so frail of form, so exquisite of feature, that she would have seemed some unearthly visitant but for the human anguish which pervaded her look and soon found vent in this touching cry:

"What is he saying? Oh, I know well what he is saying. He is saying that he killed his brother, that he held the dagger which rid the world of a monster of whose wickedness none knew. But you must not heed him. Indeed you must not heed him. He is innocent; I, his wife, have come twenty miles, from a bed of weakness and suffering, to tell you so. He—"

But here a hand was laid gently, but firmly on her mouth. She looked up, met her husband's eyes filled with almost frantic appeal, and giving him a look in return that sank into the heart of every man who beheld it, laid her own hand on his and drew it softly away.

"It is too late, Tom, I must speak. My father, my own weakness, or your own peremptory commands could not keep me at Belleville when I knew you had been brought here. And shall I stop now, in the presence of these men who have heard your words and may believe them? No, that would be a cowardice unworthy of our love and the true lives we hope to lead together. Sirs!" and each man there held his breath to catch the words which came in faint and fainter intonation from her lips, "I know my husband to be innocent, because the hand that held the dagger was mine. I killed Felix Cadwalader!"

* * * *

The horror of such a moment is never fully realized till afterward. Not a man there moved, not even her husband, yet on every cheek a slow pallor was forming, which testified to the effect of such words from lips made for smiles and showing in every curve the habit of gentle thought and the loftiest instincts. Not till someone cried out from the doorway, "Catch her! she is falling!" did any one stir or release the pent-up breath which awe and astonishment had hitherto held back on every lip. Then he in whose evident despair all could read the real cause of the great dread which had drawn him into a false confession, sprang forward, and with renewed life showing itself in every feature, caught her in his arms. As he staggered with her to a sofa and laid her softly down, he seemed another man in look and bearing; and Mr. Gryce, who had been watching the whole wonderful event with the strongest interest, understood at once the meaning of the change which had come over his prisoner at that point in his memorable arrest when he first realized that it was for himself they had come, and not for the really guilty person, the idolized object of his affections.

Meanwhile, he was facing them all, with one hand laid tenderly on that unconscious head.

"Do not think," he cried, "that because this young girl has steeped her hand in blood, she is a wicked woman. There is no purer heart on earth than hers, and none more worthy of the worship of a true man. See! she killed my brother, son of my father, beloved by my mother, yet I can kiss her hand, kiss her forehead, her eyes, her feet, not because I hate him, but because I worship her, the purest—the best—" He left her, and came and stood before those astonished men. "Sirs!" he cried, "I must ask you to listen to a strange, a terrible tale."

CHAPTER XIV

Memoranda

"It is like and unlike what I have just related to you," began young Adams. "In my previous confession I mixed truth and falsehood, and to explain myself fully and to help you to a right understanding of my wife's act, I shall have to start afresh and speak as if I had already told you nothing."

"Wait!" cried Mr. Gryce, in an authoritative manner. "We will listen to you presently;" and, leaning over the inspector, he whispered a few words, after which he took out a pencil and jotted down certain sentences, which he handed over to this gentleman.

As they had the appearance of a memorandum, and as the inspector glanced more than once at them while Mr. Adams (or Cadwalader, as he should now rightfully be called) was proceeding with his story, I will present them to you as written.

Points to be made clear by Mr. Adams in his account of this crime:

1. Why a woman who was calm enough to stop and arrange her hair during the beginning of an interview should be wrought up to such a pitch of frenzy and exasperation before it was over as to kill with her own hand a man against whom she had evidently no previous grudge. (Remember the comb found on the floor of Mr. Adams's bedroom.)

2. What was the meaning of the following words, written just previous to this interview by the man thus killed: "I return you your daughter. Neither you nor she shall ever see me again. Remember Evelyn!"

3. Why was the pronoun "I" used in this communication? What position did Mr. Felix Adams hold toward this young girl qualifying him to make use of such language after her marriage to his brother?

4. And having used it, why did he, upon being attacked by her, attempt to swallow the paper upon which he had written these words, actually dying with it clinched between his teeth?

5. If he was killed in anger and died as monsters do (her own word), why did his face show sorrow rather than hate, and a determination as far as possible removed from the rush of over-whelming emotions likely to follow the reception of a mortal blow from the hand of an unexpected antagonist?

6. Why, if he had strength to seize the above-mentioned paper and convey it to his lips, did he not use that strength in turning on a light calculated to bring him assistance, instead of leaving blazing the crimson glow which, according to the code of signals as now understood by us, means: "Nothing more required just now. Keep away."

7. What was the meaning of the huge steel plate found between the casings of the doorway, and why did it remain at rest within its socket at this, the culminating moment of his life?

8. An explanation of how old Poindexter came to appear on the scene so soon after the event. His words as overheard were: "It is Amos's son, not Amos!" Did he not know whom he was to meet in this house? Was the condition of the man lying before him with a cross on his bosom and a dagger in his heart less of a surprise to him than the personality of the victim?

9. Remember the conclusions we have drawn from Bartow's pantomime. Mr. Adams was killed by a left-handed thrust. Watch for an acknowledgment that the young woman is left-handed, and do not forget that an explanation is due why for so long a time she held her other arm stretched out behind her.

10. Why did the bird whose chief cry is "Remember Evelyn!" sometimes vary it with "Poor Eva! Lovely Eva! Who would strike Eva?" The story of this tragedy, to be true, must show that Mr. Adams knew his brother's bride both long and well.

11. If Bartow is, as we think, innocent of all connection with this crime save as witness, why does he show such joy at its result? This may not reasonably be expected to fall within the scope of Thomas Adams's confession, but it should not be ignored by us. This deaf-and-dumb servitor was driven mad by a fact which caused him joy. Why?

12. Notice the following schedule. It has been drawn up after repeated experiments with Bartow and the various slides of the strange lamp which cause so many different lights to shine out in Mr. Adams's study:

> White light—Water wanted.
> Green light—Overcoat and hat to be brought.
> Blue light—Put back books on shelves.
> Violet light—Arrange study for the night.
> Yellow light—Watch for next light.
> Red light—Nothing wanted; stay away.

The last was on at the final scene. Note if this fact can be explained by Mr. Adams's account of the same.

With these points in our mind, let us peruse the history of this crime and of the remote and possibly complicated causes which led to it.

BOOK II: REMEMBER EVELYN

CHAPTER I

The Secret of the Cadwaladers

Thomas Cadwalader suggested rather than told his story. We dare not imitate him in this, nor would it be just to your interest to relate these facts with all the baldness and lack of detail imposed upon this unhappy man by the hurry and anxiety of the occasion. Remarkable tragedies have their birth in remarkable facts, and as such facts are but the outcome of human passions, we must enter into those passions if we would understand either the facts or their appalling consequences. In this case, the first link of the chain which led to Felix Adams's violent death was forged before the birth of the woman who struck him. We must begin, then, with almost forgotten days, and tell the story, as her pleader did, from the standpoint of Felix and Thomas Cadwalader.

Thomas Cadwalader—now called Adams—never knew his mother; she died in his early infancy. Nor could he be said to have known his father, having been brought up in France by an old Scotch lawyer, who, being related to his mother, sometimes spoke of her, but never of his father, till Thomas had reached his fifteenth year. Then he put certain books into his hands, with this remarkable injunction:

"Here are romances, Thomas. Read them; but remember that none of them, no matter how thrilling in matter or effect, will ever equal the story of your father's bitterly wronged and suffering life."

"My father!" he cried; "tell me about him; I have never heard."

But his guardian, satisfied with an allusion which he knew must bear fruit in the extremely susceptible nature of this isolated boy, said no more that day, and Thomas turned to the books. But nothing after that could ever take his mind away from his father. He had scarcely thought of him for years, but now that that father had been placed before him in the light of a wronged man, he found himself continually hunting back in the deepest recesses of his memory for some long-forgotten recollection of that father's features calculated to restore his image to his eyes. Sometimes he succeeded in this, or thought he did; but this image, if image it was, was so speedily lost in a sensation of something strange and awe-compelling enveloping it, that he found himself more absorbed by the intangible impressions associated with this memory than by the memory itself. What were these impressions, and in what had they originated? In vain he tried to determine. They were as vague as they were persistent. A stretch of darkness—two bars of orange light, always shining, always the same—black lines against these bars, like the tops of distant gables—an inner thrill—a vague affright—a rush about him as of a swooping wind—all this came with his father's image, only to fade away with it, leaving him troubled, uneasy, and perplexed. Finding these impressions persistent, and receiving no explanation of them in his own mind, he finally asked his guardian what they meant. But that guardian was as ignorant as himself on this topic; and satisfied with having roused the boy's imagination, confined himself to hints, dropped now and then with a judiciousness which proved the existence of a deliberate purpose, of some duty which awaited him on the other side of the water, a duty which would explain his long exile from his only parent and for which he must fit himself by study and the acquirement of such accomplishments as render a young man a positive power in society, whether that society be of the Old World or the New. He showed his shrewdness in thus dealing with this pliable and deeply affectionate nature. From this time forth Thomas felt himself leading a life of mystery and interest.

To feel himself appointed for a work whose unknown character only heightened its importance gave point to every effort now made by this young man, and lent to his studies that vague touch of romance which made them a delight, and him an adept in many things he might otherwise have cared little about. At eighteen he was a graduate from the Sorbonne, and a musical virtuoso as well. He could fence, ride, and carry off the prize in games requiring physical prowess as well as mental fitness. He was, in fact, a prodigy in many ways, and was so considered by his fellow-students. He, however, was not perfect; he lacked social charm, and in so far failed of being the complete gentleman. This he was made to realize in the following way:

One morning his guardian came to him with a letter from his father, in which, together with some words of commendation for his present attainments, that father expressed a certain dissatisfaction with his general manner as being too abrupt and self-satisfied with those of his own sex, and much too timid and deprecatory with those of the other. Thomas felt the criticism and recognized its justice; but how had his father, proved by his letter to be no longer a myth, become acquainted with defects which Thomas instinctively felt could never have attracted the attention of his far from polished guardian?

His questions on this point elicited a response that confounded him. He was not the only son of his father; he had a brother living, and this brother, older than himself by some twenty years or more, had just been in Paris, where, in all probability, he had met him, talked with him, and perhaps pressed his hand.

It was a discovery calculated to deepen the impression already made upon Thomas's mind. Only a purpose of the greatest importance could account for so much mystery. What could it be? What was he destined to do or say or be? He was not told, but while awaiting enlightenment he was resolved not to be a disappointment to the two anxious souls who watched his career so eagerly and exacted from him such perfection. He consequently moderated his manner, and during the following year acquired by constant association with the gilded youth about him that indescribable charm of the perfect gentleman which he was led to believe would alone meet with the approval of those he now felt bound to please. At the end of the year he found himself a finished man of the world. How truly so, he began to realize when he noted the blush with which his presence was hailed by women and the respect shown him by men of his own stamp. In the midst of the satisfaction thus experienced his guardian paid him a final visit.

"You are now ready," said he, "for your father's summons. It will come in a few weeks. Be careful, then. Form no ties you cannot readily break; for, once recalled from France, you are not likely to return here. What your father's purpose concerning you may be I do not know, but it is no ordinary one. You will have money, a well-appointed home, family affection, all that you have hitherto craved in vain, and in return you will carry solace to a heart which has awaited your healing touch for twenty years. So much I am ordered to say; the rest you will hear from your father's own lips."

Aroused, encouraged, animated by the wildest hopes, the most extravagant anticipations, Thomas awaited his father's call with feverish impatience, and when it came, hastened to respond to it by an immediate voyage to America. This was some six months previous to the tragedy in —— Street. On his arrival at the wharf in New York he was met, not by his brother, as he had every reason to expect, but by a messenger in whose face evil tidings were apparent before he spoke. Thomas was soon made acquainted with them. His father, who he now learned was called Cadwalader (he himself had always been called Adams), was ill, possibly dying. He must therefore hasten, and, being provided with minute instructions as to his way, took the train at once for a small village in northern Pennsylvania.

All that followed was a dream to him. He was hurried through the night, with the motion of the ship still in his blood, to meet—what? He dared not think. He swam in a veritable nightmare. Then came a stop, a hurrying from the train, a halt on a platform reeking with rain (for the night was stormy), a call from someone to hurry, the sight of a panting horse steaming under a lamp whose blowing flame he often woke in after nights to see, a push from a persuasive hand, then a ride over a country road the darkness of which seemed impenetrable, and, finally, the startling vision of an open door, with a Meg Merrilies of a woman standing in it, holding a flaming candle in her hand. The candle went out while he looked at it, and left only a voice to guide him—a voice which, in tones shaken by chill or feeling, he could not tell which, cried eagerly:

"Is that you, laddie? Come awa in. Come awa in. Dinna heed the rain. The maister's been crying on you a' day. I'm glad you're no ower late."

He got down, followed the voice, and, stumbling up a step or two, entered a narrow door, which was with difficulty held open behind him, and which swung to with a loud noise the minute he crossed the threshold. This or the dreariness of the place in which he found himself disturbed him greatly. Bare floors, stained walls, meagre doorways, and a common pine staircase, lighted only by the miserable candle which the old woman had relit—were these the appointments of the palatial home he had been led to expect? These the surroundings, this the abode of him who had exacted such perfection on his part, and to satisfy whose standard he had devoted years of hourly, daily effort, in every department of art and science? A sickening revolt seized him, aggravated by the smiles of the old woman, who dipped and courtesied before him in senile delight. She may have divined his feelings, for, drawing him inside, she relieved him of his overcoat, crying all the while, with an extravagant welcome more repulsive than all the rest:

"O the fine laddie! Wad your puir mither could see you the noo! Bonnie and clever! No your faither's bairn ava! All mither, laddie, all mither!"

The room was no better than the hall.

"Where is my father?" he asked, authoritatively, striving to keep down his strong repugnance.

"Dinna ye hear him? He's crying on ye. Puir man, he's wearying to see ye."

Hear him? He could scarcely hear her. The driving rain, the swish of some great boughs against the house, the rattling of casements and doors, and the shrieking of wind in the chimney made all other sounds wellnigh inaudible. Yet as he listened he seemed to catch the accents of a far-off voice calling, now wistfully, now imperatively, "Thomas! Thomas!" And, thrilled with an emotion almost superstitious in its intensity, he moved hastily toward the staircase.

But the old woman was there before him. "Na! Na!" she cried. "Come in by and eat something first."

But Thomas shook his head. It seemed to him at that moment as if he never could eat or sleep again, the disillusion was so bitter, his disappointment so keen.

"You will na? Then haste ye—haste ye. But it's a peety you wadna ha'e eaten something. Ye'll need it, laddie; ye'll need it."

"Thomas! Thomas!" wailed the voice.

He tore himself away. He forced himself to go upstairs, following the cry, which at every moment grew louder. At the top he cast a final glance below. The old woman stood at the stair-foot, shading the candle from the draught with a hand that shook with something more than age. She was gazing after him in vague affright, and with the shadow of this fear darkening her weazen face, formed a picture from which he was glad to escape.

Plunging on, he found himself before a window whose small panes dripped and groaned under a rain that was fast becoming a torrent. Chilled by the sight, he turned toward the door faintly outlined beside it, and in the semi-darkness seized an old-fashioned latch rattling in the wind that permeated every passageway, and softly raised it.

Instantly the door fell back, and two eyes blazing with fever and that fire of the soul of which fever is the mere physical symbol greeted him from the midst of a huge bed drawn up against the opposite wall. Then two arms rose, and the moaning cry of "Thomas! Thomas!" changed to a shout, and he knew himself to be in the presence of his father.

Falling on his knees in speechless emotion, he grasped the wasted hands held out to him. Such a face, rugged though it was and far from fulfilling the promise held out to him in his dreams, could not but move any man. As he gazed into it and pressed the hands in which the life blood only seemed to linger for this last, this only embrace, all his filial instincts were aroused and he forgot the common surroundings, the depressing rain, his own fatigue and bitter disappointment, in his lifelong craving for love and family recognition.

But the old man on whose breast he fell showed other emotions than those by which he was himself actuated. It was not an embrace he craved, but an opportunity to satisfy an almost frenzied curiosity as to the appearance and attributes of the son who had grown to manhood under other eyes. Pushing him gently back, he bade him stand in the light of the lamp burning on a small pine table, and surveyed him, as it were, from the verge of his own fast failing life, with moans of mingled pain and weariness, amid which Thomas thought he heard the accents of a supreme satisfaction.

Meanwhile in Thomas himself, as he stood there, the sense of complete desolation filled his breast almost to bursting. To have come home for this! To find a father only to be weighed in the scales of that father's judgment! To be admired, instead of loved!

As he realized his position and listened to the shrieking of the wind and rain, he felt that the wail of the elements but echoed the cry of his own affections, thus strangled in their birth. Indeed the sensations of that moment made so deep an impression upon him that he was never afterward able to hear a furious gust of wind or rain without the picture rising up before him of this great hollow room, with the trembling figure of his father struggling in the grasp of death and holding it at bay, while he gauged with worldly wisdom the physical, mental, and moral advantages of the son so long banished and so lately restored to his arms.

A rush of impetuous words followed by the collapse of his father's form upon the pillow showed that the examination was over. Rushing forward, he grasped again that father's hands, but soon shrank back, stunned by what he heard and the prospect it opened before him. A few of his father's words will interpret the rest. They came in a flood, and among others Thomas caught these:

"The grace of God be thanked! Our efforts have not failed. Handsome, strong, noble in look and character, we could ask nothing more, hope for nothing more. My revenge will succeed! John Poindexter will find that he has a heart, and that that heart can be wrung. I do not need to live to see it. For me it exists now; it exists here!" And he struck his breast with hands that seemed to have reserved their last strength for this supreme gesture.

John Poindexter! Who was he? It was a new name to Thomas. Venturing to say so, he reeled under the look he received from his father's eyes.

"You do not know who John Poindexter is, and what he has done to me and mine? They have kept their promise well, too well, but God will accord me strength to tell you what has been left unsaid by them. He would not bring me up to this hour to let me perish before you have heard the story destined to make you the avenger of innocence upon that enemy of your race. Listen, Thomas. With the hand of death encircling my heart, I speak, and if the story find you cold—But it will not. Your name is Cadwalader, and it will not."

Constrained by passions such as he had never imagined even in dreams, Thomas fell upon his knees. He could not listen otherwise. His father, gasping for breath, fixed him with his hollow eyes, in which the last flickering flames of life flared up in fitful brightness.

"Thomas"—the pause was brief—"you are not my only child."

"I know it," fell from Thomas's white lips. "I have a brother; his name is Felix."

The father shook his head with a look suggestive of impatience.

"Not him! Not him!" he cried. "A sister! a sister, who died before you were born—beautiful, good, with a voice like an angel's and a heart— she should be standing by my side today, and she would have been if—if he—but none of that. I have no breath to waste. Facts, facts, just facts! Afterward may come emotions, hatred, denunciation, not now. This is my story, Thomas.

"John Poindexter and I were friends. From boyhood we shared each other's bed, food, and pleasures, and when he came to seek his fortune in America I accompanied him. He was an able man, but cold. I was of an affectionate nature, but without any business capacity. As proof of this, in fifteen years he was rich, esteemed, the master of a fine house, and the owner of half a dozen horses; while I was the same nobody I had been at first, or would have been had not Providence given me two beautiful children and blessed, or rather cursed, me with the friendship of this prosperous man. When Felix was fourteen and Evelyn three years older, their mother died. Soon after, the little money I had vanished in an unfortunate enterprise, and life began to promise ill, both for myself and for my growing children. John Poindexter, who was honest enough then, or let me hope so, and who had no children of his own, though he had been long married, offered to take one of mine to educate. But I did not consent to this till the war of the rebellion broke out; then I sent him both son and daughter, and went into the army. For four years I fought for the flag, suffering all that a man can suffer and live, and being at last released from Libby Prison, came home with a heart full of gratitude and with every affection keyed up by a long series of unspeakable experiences, to greet my son and clasp once more within my wasted arms the idolized form of my deeply loved daughter. What did I find? A funeral in the streets—hers—and Felix, your brother, walking like a guard between her speechless corpse and the man under whose protection I had placed her youth and innocence.

"Betrayed!" shrieked the now frenzied parent, rising on his pillow. "Her innocence! Her sweetness! And he, cold as the stone we laid upon her grave, had seen her perish with the anguish and shame of it, without a sign of grief or a word of contrition."

"O God!" burst from lips the old man was watching with frenzied cunning.

"Ay, God!" repeated the father, shaking his head as if in defiance before he fell back on his pillow. "He allowed it and I—But this does not tell the story. I must keep to facts as Felix did—Felix, who was but fifteen years old and yet found himself the only confidant and solace of this young girl betrayed by her protector. It was after her burial—"

"Cease!" cried a voice, smooth, fresh, and yet strangely commanding, from over Thomas's shoulder. "Let me tell the rest. No man can tell the rest as I can."

"Felix!" ejaculated Amos Cadwalader below his breath.

"Felix!" repeated Thomas, shaken to his very heart by this new presence. But when he sought to rise, to turn, he felt the pressure of a hand on his shoulder and heard that voice again, saying softly, but peremptorily:

"Wait! Wait till you hear what I have to say. Think not of me, think only of her. It is she you are called upon to avenge; your sister, Evelyn."

Thomas yielded to him as he had to his father. He sank down beneath that insistent hand, and his brother took up the tale.

"Evelyn had a voice like a bird. In those days before father's return, she used to fill old John Poindexter's house with melody. I, who, as a boy, was studious, rather than artistic, thought she sang too much for a girl whose father was rotting away in a Southern prison. But when about to rebuke her, I remembered Edward Kissam, and was silent. For it was his love which made her glad, and to him I wished every happiness, for he was good, and honest, and kind to me. She was eighteen then, and beautiful, or so I was bound to believe, since every man looked at her, even old John Poindexter, though he never looked at any other woman, not even his own wife. And she was good, too, and pure, I swear, for her blue eyes never faltered in looking into mine until one day when—my

God! how well I remember it!—they not only faltered, but shrank before me in such terror, that, boy though I was, I knew that something terrible, something unprecedented had happened, and thinking my one thought, I asked if she had received bad news from father. Her answer was a horrified moan, but it might have been a shriek. 'Our father! Pray God we may never see him or hear from him again. If you love him, if you love me, pray he may die in prison rather than return here to see me as I am now.'

"I thought she had gone mad, and perhaps she had for a moment; for at my look of startled distress a change took place in her. She remembered my youth, and laughing, or trying to laugh away her frenzy, uttered some hurried words I failed to understand, and then, sinking at my knee, laid her head against my side, crying that she was not well; that she had experienced for a long time secret pains and great inward distress, and that she sometimes feared she was not going to live long, for all her songs and merry ways and seeming health and spirits.

"'Not live, Evelyn?' It was an inconceivable thought to me, a boy. I looked at her, and seeing how pale, how incomprehensibly pale she was, my heart failed me, for nothing but mortal sickness could make such a change in any one in a week, in a day. Yet how could death reach her, loved as she was by Edward, by her father, and by me. Thinking to rouse her, I spoke the former's name. But it was the last word I should have uttered. Crouching as if I had given her a blow, she put her two hands out, shrieking faintly: 'Not that! Never that! Do not speak his name. Let me never hear of him or see him again. I am dead—do you not understand me?—dead to all the world from this day—except to you!' she suddenly sobbed, 'except to you!' And still I did not comprehend her. But when I understood, as I soon did, that no mention was to be made of her illness; that her door was to be shut and no one allowed to enter, not even Mrs. Poindexter or her guardian—least of all, her guardian—I began to catch the first intimation of that horror which was to end my youth and fill my whole after life with but one thought—revenge. But I said nothing, only watched and waited. Seeing that she was really ill, I constituted myself her nurse, and sat by her night and day till her symptoms became so alarming that the whole household was aroused and we could no longer keep the doctor from her. Then I sat at her door, and with one ear turned to catch her lightest moan, listened for the step she most dreaded, but which, though it sometimes approached, never passed the opening of the hall leading to her chamber. For one whole week I sat there, watching her life go slowly out like a flame, with nothing to feed it; then as the great shadow fell, and life seemed breaking up within me, I dashed from the place, and confronting him where I found him walking, pale and disturbed, in his own hall, told him that my father was coming; that I had

had a dream, and in that dream I had seen my father with his face turned toward this place. Was he prepared to meet him? Had he an answer ready when Amos Cadwalader should ask him what had become of his child?

"I had meant to shock the truth from this man, and I did so. As I mentioned my father's name, Poindexter blanched, and my fears became certainty. Dropping my youthful manner, for I was a boy no longer, I flung his crime in his face, and begged him to deny it if he could. He could not, but he did what neither he nor any other man could do in my presence now and live—he smiled. Then when he saw me crouching for a spring—for, young as I was, I knew but one impulse, and that was to fly at his throat—he put out his powerful hand, and pinning me to the ground, uttered a few short sentences in my ear.

"They were terrible ones. They made me see that nothing I might then do could obliterate the fact that she was lost if the world knew what I knew, or even so much as suspected it; that any betrayal on my part or act of contrition on his would only pile the earth on her inno-cent breast and sink her deeper and deeper into the grave she was then digging for herself; that all dreams were falsities; that Southern prisons seldom gave up their victims alive; and that if my father should escape the jaws of Libby and return, it was for me to be glad if he found a quiet grave instead of a dishonored daughter. Further, that if I crossed him, who was power itself, by any boyish exhibition of hate, I would find that any odium I might invoke would fall on her and not on him, making me an abhorrence, not only to the world at large, but to the very father in whose interest I might pretend to act.

"I was young and without worldly experience. I yielded to these ar-guments, but I cursed him where he stood. With his hand pressing heav-ily upon me, I cursed him to his face; then I went back to my sister.

"Had she, by some supernatural power, listened to our talk, or had she really been visited by some dream, that she looked so changed? There was a feverish light in her eye, and something like the shadow of a smile on her lips. Mrs. Poindexter was with her; Mrs. Poindexter, whose face was a mask we never tried to penetrate. But when she had left us alone again, then Evelyn spoke, and I saw what her dream had been.

"'Felix,' she cried as I approached her trembling with my own emo-tions and half afraid of hers, 'there is still one hope for me. It has come to me while you have been away. Edward—he loves me—did—perhaps he would forgive. If he would take me into his protection (I see you know it all, Felix) then I might grow happy again—well—strong—good. Do you think—oh, you are a child, what do you know?—but—but before I turn my face forever to the wall try if he will see me—try, try—with your boy's wit—your clever schemes, to get him here unknown to—to—the one I fear, I hate—and then, then, if he bids me live, I will live, and if he bids me die, I will die; and all will be ended.'

"I was an ignorant boy. I knew men no more than I knew women, and yielding to her importunities, I promised to see Edward and plan for an interview without her guardian's knowledge. I was, as Evelyn had said, keen in those days and full of resources, and I easily managed it. Edward, who had watched from the garden as I had from the door, was easily persuaded to climb her lattice in search of what he had every reason to believe would be his last earthly interview with his darling. As his eager form bounded into the room I tottered forth, carrying with me a vision of her face as she rose to meet—what? I dared not think or attempt to foresee. Falling on my knees I waited the issue. Alas! It was a speedy one. A stifled moan from her, the sound of a hoarse farewell from him, told me that his love had failed her, and that her doom was sealed. Creeping back to her side as quickly as my failing courage admitted, I found her face turned to the wall, from which it never again looked back; while presently, before the hour was passed, shouts ringing through the town proclaimed that young Kissam had shot himself. She heard, and died that night. In her last hour she had fancies. She thought she saw her father, and her prayers for mercy were heart-rending. Then she thought she saw him, that demon, her executioner, and cringed and moaned against the wall.

"But enough of this. Two days after, I walked between him and her silent figure outstretched for burial. I had promised that no eye but mine should look upon her, no other hand touch her, and I kept my word, even when the impossible happened and her father rose up in the street before us. Quietly, and in honor, she was carried to her grave, and then—then, in the solitude of the retreat I had found for him, I told our father all, and why I had denied him the only comfort which seemed left to him—a last look at his darling daughter's face."

CHAPTER II

The Oath

A sigh from the panting breast of Amos Cadwalader followed these words. Plainer than speech it told of a grief still fresh and an agony still unappeased, though thirty years had passed away since the unhappy hour of which Felix spoke.

Felix, echoing it, went quickly on:

"It was dusk when I told my story, and from dark to dawn we sat with eyes fixed on each other's face, without sleep and without rest. Then we sought John Poindexter.

"Had he shunned us we might have had mercy, but he met us openly, quietly, and with all the indifference of one who cannot measure feeling, because he is incapable of experiencing it himself. His first sentence evinced this. 'Spare yourselves, spare me all useless recriminations. The girl is dead; I cannot call her back again. Enjoy your life, your eating and your drinking, your getting and your spending; it is but for a few more years at best. Why harp on old 'griefs?' His last word was a triumph. 'When a man cares for nothing or nobody, it is useless to curse him.'

"Ah, that was it! That was the secret of his power. He cared for nothing and for no one, not even for himself. We felt the blow, and bent under it. But before leaving him and the town, we swore, your father and I, that we would yet make that cold heart feel; that some day, in some way, we would cause that impassive nature to suffer as he had made us suffer, however happy he might seem or however closely his prosperity might cling to him. That was thirty years ago, and that oath has not yet been fulfilled."

Felix paused. Thomas lifted his head, but the old man would not let him speak. "There are men who forget in a month, others who forget in a year. I have never forgotten, nor has Felix here. When you were born (I had married again, in the hope of renewed joy) I felt, I know not why, that Evelyn's avenger was come. And when, a year or so after this event, we heard that God had forgotten John Poindexter's sins, or, perhaps, remembered them, and that a child was given him also, after eighteen years of married life, I looked upon your bonny face and saw—or thought I saw—a possible means of bringing about the vengeance to which Felix and I had dedicated our lives.

"You grew; your ardent nature, generous temper, and facile mind promised an abundant manhood, and when your mother died, leaving me for a second time a widower, I no longer hesitated to devote you to the purpose for which you seemed born. Thomas, do you remember the beginning of that journey which finally led you far from me? How I bore you on my shoulder along a dusty road, till arrived within sight of his home, I raised you from among the tombs and, showing you those distant gables looming black against the twilight's gold, dedicated you to the destruction of whatever happiness might hereafter develop under his infant's smile? You do? I did not think you could forget; and now that the time has come for the promise of that hour to be fulfilled, I call on you again, Thomas. Avenge our griefs, avenge your sister. *Poindexter's girl has grown to womanhood.*"

At the suggestion conveyed in these words Thomas recoiled in horror. But the old man failed to read his emotion rightly. Clutching his arm, he proceeded passionately:

"Woo her! Win her! They do not know you. You will be Thomas Adams to them, not Thomas Cadwalader. Gather this budding flower into your bosom, and then—Oh, he must love his child! Through her we have our hand on his heart. Make her suffer—she's but a country girl, and you have lived in Paris—make her suffer, and if, in doing so, you cause him to blench, then believe I am looking upon you from the grave I go to, and be happy; for you will not have lived, nor will I have died, in vain."

He paused to catch his failing breath, but his indomitable will triumphed over death and held Thomas under a spell that confounded his instincts and made him the puppet of feelings which had accumulated their force to fill him, in one hour, with a hate which it had taken his father and brother a quarter of a century to bring to the point of active vengeance.

"I shall die; I am dying now," the old man panted on. "I shall never live to see your triumph; I shall never behold John Poindexter's eye glaze with those sufferings which rend the entrails and make a man question if there is a God in heaven. But I shall know it where I am. No mounded earth can keep my spirit down when John Poindexter feels his doom. I shall be conscious of his anguish and shall rejoice; and when in the depths of darkness to which I go he comes faltering along my way—

"Boy, boy, you have been reared for this. God made you handsome; man has made you strong; you have made yourself intelligent and accomplished. You have only to show yourself to this country girl to become the master of her will and affection, and these once yours, remember *me! Remember Evelyn!*"

Never had Thomas been witness to such passion. It swept him along in a burning stream against which he sought to contend and could not. Raising his hand in what he meant as a response to that appeal, he endeavored to speak, but failed. His father misinterpreted his silence, and bitterly cried:

"You are dumb! You do not like the task; are virtuous, perhaps—you who have lived for years alone and unhampered in Paris. Or you have instincts of honor, habits of generosity that blind you to wrongs that for a longer space than your lifetime have cried aloud to heaven for vengeance. Thomas, Thomas, if you should fail me now—"

"He will not fail you," broke in the voice of Felix, calm, suave, and insinuating. "I have watched him; I know him; he will not fail you."

Thomas shuddered; he had forgotten Felix, but as he heard these words he could no longer delay looking at the man who had offered to stand his surety for the performance of the unholy deed his father exacted from him. Turning, he saw a man who in any place and under any roof would attract attention, awake admiration and—yes, fear. He was not a large man, not so large as himself, but the will that expressed itself in frenzy on his father's lips showed quiet and inflexible in the gray eye resting upon his own with a power he could never hope to evade.

As he looked and comprehended, a steel band seemed to compress his heart; yet he was conscious at the same time that the personality before which he thus succumbed was as elegant as his own and as perfectly trained in all the ways of men and of life. Even the air of poverty which had shocked him in his father's person and surroundings was not visible here. Felix was both well and handsomely clad, and could hold his own as the elder brother in every respect most insisted upon by the Parisian gentleman. The long and, to Thomas, mysterious curtain of dark-green serge which stretched behind him from floor to ceiling threw out his pale features with a remarkable distinctness, and for an instant Thomas wondered if it had been hung there for the purpose of producing this effect. But the demand in his brother's face drew his attention, and, bowing his head, he stammered:

"I am at your command, Felix. I am at your command, father. I cannot say more. Only remember that I never saw Evelyn, that she died before I was born, and that I—"

But here Felix's voice broke in, kind, but measured:

"Perhaps there is some obstacle we have not reckoned upon. You may already love some woman and desire to marry her. If so, it need be no impediment—"

But here Thomas's indignation found voice.

"No," said he; "I am heart-whole save for a few lingering fancies which are fast becoming vanishing dreams."

He seemed to have lived years since entering this room.

"Your heart will not be disturbed now," commented Felix. "I have seen the girl. I went there on purpose a year ago. She's as pale as a snowdrop and as listless. You will not be obliged to recall to mind the gay smiles of Parisian ladies to be proof against her charms."

Thomas shrugged his shoulders.

"She must be made to know the full intoxication of hope," Felix proceeded in his clear and cutting voice. "To realize despair she must first experience every delight that comes with satisfied love. Have you the skill as well as heart to play to the end a rôle which will take patience as well as dissimulation, courage as well as subtlety, and that union of will and implacability which finds its food in tears and is strengthened, rather than lessened, by the suffering of its victim?"

"I have the skill," murmured Thomas, "but—"

"You lack the incentive," finished Felix. "Well, well, we must have patience with your doubts and hesitations. Our hate has been fostered by memories of her whom, as you say, you have never seen. Look, then, Thomas. Look at your sister as she was, as she is for us. Look at her, and think of her as despoiled, killed, forgotten by Poindexter. Have you ever gazed upon a more moving countenance, or one in which beauty contends with a keener prophecy of woe?"

Not knowing what to expect, anticipating almost to be met by her shade, Thomas followed the direction of his brother's lifted hand, and beheld, where but a minute before that dismal curtain had hung, a blaze of light, in the midst of which he saw a charming, but tragic, figure, such as no gallery in all Europe had ever shown him, possibly because no other limned face or form had ever appealed to his heart. It did not seem a picture, it seemed her very self, a gentle, loving self that breathed forth all the tenderness he had vainly sought for in his living relatives; and falling at her feet, he cried out:

"Do not look at me so reproachfully, sweet Evelyn. I was born to avenge you, and I will. John Poindexter shall never go down in peace to his tomb."

A sigh of utter contentment came from the direction of the bed.

"Swear it!" cried his father, holding out his arms before him in the form of a cross.

"Yes, swear it!" repeated Felix, laying his own hand on those crossed arms.

Thomas drew near, and laid his hand beside that of Felix.

"I swear," he began, raising his voice above the tempest, which poured gust after gust against the house. "I swear to win the affections of Eva Poindexter, and then, when her heart is all mine, to cast her back in anguish and contumely on the breast of John Poindexter."

"Good!" came from what seemed to him an immeasurable distance. Then the darkness, which since the taking of this oath had settled over his senses, fell, and he sank insensible at the feet of his dying father.

* * * *

Amos Cadwalader died that night; but not without one awful scene more. About midnight he roused from the sleep which had followed the exciting incidents I have just related, and glancing from Thomas to Felix, sitting on either side of the bed, fixed his eyes with a strange gleam upon the door.

"Ah!" he ejaculated, "a visitor! John Poindexter! He comes to ask my forgiveness before I set out on my dismal journey."

The sarcasm of his tone, the courtesy of his manner, caused the hair to stir on the heads of his two sons. That he saw his enemy as plainly as he saw them, neither could doubt.

"Does he dread my meeting with Evelyn? Does he wish to placate me before I am joined to that pathetic shade? He shall not be disappointed. I forgive you, John Poindexter! I forgive you my daughter's shame, my blighted life. I am dying; but I leave one behind who will not forgive you. I have a son, an avenger of the dead, who yet lives to—to—"

He fell back. With these words, which seemed to seal Thomas to his task, Amos Cadwalader died.

CHAPTER III

Eva

Felix had not inherited his father's incapacity for making money. In the twenty years that had passed since Thomas had been abroad he had built up a fortune, which he could not induce his father to share, but which that father was perfectly willing to see devoted to their mutual revenge. There was meaning, therefore, in the injunction Felix gave his brother on his departure for Montgomery:

"I have money; spend it; spend what you will, and when your task is completed, there will still be some left for your amusement."

Thomas bowed. "The laborer is worthy of his hire," was his thought. "And you?" he asked, looking about the scanty walls, which seemed to have lost their very excuse for being now that his father had died. "Will you remain here?"

Felix's answer was abrupt, but positive. "No; I go to New York to-morrow. I have rented a house there, which you may one day wish to share. The name under which I have leased it is Adams, Felix Adams. As such you will address me. Cadwalader is a name that must not leave your lips in Montgomery, nor must you forget that my person is known there, otherwise we might not have been dependent on you for the success of our revenge." And he smiled, fully conscious of being the handsomer man of the two. "And now how about those introductions we enjoined you to bring from Paris?"

* * * *

The history of the next few weeks can best be understood by reading certain letters sent by Thomas to Felix, by examining a diary drawn up by the same writer for his own relief and satisfaction. The letters will be found on the left, and the diary on the right, of the double columns hereby submitted. The former are a summary of facts; the latter is a summary of feelings. Both are necessary to a right comprehension of the situation.

FIRST LETTER.

Dear Felix:

I am here; I have seen her. She is, as you have said, a pale blonde. Tomorrow I present my credentials to John Poindexter. From what I have already experienced I anticipate a favorable reception.

Yours aff., Thomas.

FIRST ENTRY

I could not write Felix the true story of this day. Why? And why must I write it here? To turn my mind from dwelling on it? Perhaps. I do not seem to understand my own feelings, or why I begin to dread my task, while ardently pressing forward to accomplish it.

I have seen her. This much I wrote to Felix, but I did not say where our meeting took place or how. How could I? Would he understand how one of Poindexter's blood could be employed in a gracious act, or how I, filled with a purpose that has made my heart dark as hell ever since I embraced it, could find that heart swell and that purpose sink at my first glimpse of the face whose beauty I have sworn to devote to agony and tears? Surely, surely Felix would have been stronger, and yet—

I went from the cars to the cemetery. Before entering the town or seeing to my own comfort, I sought Evelyn's grave, there to renew my oath in the place where, nineteen years ago, my father held me up, a four-year-old child, in threat, toward John Poindexter's home. I had succeeded in finding the old and neglected stone which marked her resting-place, and was bending in the sunset light to examine it, when the rustle of a woman's skirts attracted my attention, and I perceived advancing toward me a young girl in a nimbus of rosy light which seemed to lift her from the ground and give to her delicate figure and strangely illumined head an ethereal aspect which her pure features and tender bearing did not belie. In her arms she carried a huge cluster of snow-white lilies, and when I observed that her eyes were directed not on me, but on the grave beside which I stood, I moved aside into the shadow of some bushes and watched her while she strewed these flowers—emblems of innocence—over the grave I had just left.

What did it mean, and who was this young girl who honored with such gracious memorials the grave of my long-buried sister? As she rose from her task I could no longer restrain either my emotion or the curiosity with which her act had inspired me. Advancing, I greeted her with all the respect her appearance called for, and noting that her face was even more beautiful when lifted in speech than when bent in gravity over her flowers, I asked her, in the indifferent tone of a stranger, who was buried in this spot, and why she, a mere girl, dropped flowers upon a grave the mosses of whose stone proved it to have been dug long before she was born.

Her answer caused me a shock, full as my life has lately been of startling experiences. "I strew flowers here," said she, "because the girl who lies buried under this stone had the same birthday as myself. I never saw her, it's true, but she died in my father's house when she was no older than I am today, and since I have become a woman and realize what loss there is in dying young, I have made it a custom to share with her my birthday flowers. She was a lily, they say, in appearance and character, and so I bring her lilies."

It was Eva Poindexter, the girl I—And she was strewing flowers on Evelyn's grave.

LETTER II

Dear Felix:

I have touched the hand of John Poindexter. In order to win a place in the good graces of the daughter I must please the father, or at least attract his favorable notice. I have reason to think I have done this.

Very truly, Thomas.

ENTRY II

I no longer feel myself a true man. John Poindexter is cold in appearance, hard in manner, and inflexible in opinion, but he does not inspire the abhorrence I anticipated nor awaken in me the one thought due to the memory of my sister. Is it because he is Eva's father? Has the loveliness of the daughter cast a halo about the parent? If so, Felix has a right to execrate me and my father to—

LETTER III

Dear Felix:

The introductions furnished me have made me received everywhere. There is considerable wealth here and many fine houses. Consequently I find myself in a congenial society, of which she is the star. Did I say that he was, as of old, the chief man of the town?

Yours truly, Thomas.

ENTRY III

She is beautiful. She has the daintiness of the lily and the flush of the rose. But it is not her beauty that moves me; it is the strange sweetness of her nature, which, nevertheless, has no weakness in it; on the contrary, it possesses peculiar strength, which becomes instantly apparent at the call of duty. Could Felix have imagined such a Poindexter? I cannot contemplate such loveliness and associate it with the execrable sin which calls down vengeance upon this house. I cannot even dwell upon my past life. All that is dark, threatening, secret, and revengeful slips from me under her eye, and I dream of what is pure, true, satisfying, and ennobling. And this by the influence of her smile, rather than of her words. Have I been given an angel to degrade? Or am I so blind as to behold a saint where others (Felix, let us say) would see only a pretty woman with unexpected attractions?

LETTER IV

Dear Felix:

Rides, dances, games, nonsense generally. My interest in this young girl is beginning to be publicly recognized. She alone seems ignorant of it. Sometimes I wonder if our scheme will fail through her impassibility and more than conventional innocence. I am sometimes afraid she will never love me. Yet I have exerted myself to please her. Indeed, I could not have exerted myself more. Today I went twenty-five miles on horseback to procure her a trifle she fancied.

Yours aff., Thomas

ENTRY IV

All will not go as easily as Felix imagines. Eva Poindexter may be a country girl, but she has her standards, too, and mere grace and attainment are not sufficient to win her. Have I the other qualities she demands? That remains to be seen. I have one she never dreams of. Will its shadow so overwhelm the rest that her naturally pure spirit will shrink from me just at the moment when I think her mine? I cannot tell, and the doubt creates a hell within me. Something deeper, stronger, more imperious than my revenge makes the winning of this girl's heart a necessity to me. I have forgotten my purpose in this desire. I have forgotten everything except that she is the one woman of my life, and that I can never rest till her heart is wholly mine. Good God! Have I become a slave where I hoped to be master? Have I, Thomas Cadwalader, given my soul into the keeping of this innocent girl? I do not even stop to inquire. To win her—that is all for which I now live.

LETTER V

Dear Felix:

She may not care for me, but she is interested in no one else. Of this I am assured by John Poindexter, who seems very desirous of aiding me in my attempt to win his daughter's heart. Hard won, close bound. If she ever comes to love me it will be with the force of a very strong nature. The pale blonde has a heart.

Yours aff., Thomas

ENTRY V

If it were passion only that I feel, I might have some hope of restraining it. But it is something more, something deeper, something which constrains me to look with her eyes, hear with her ears, and throb with her heart. My soul, rather than my senses, is enthralled. I want to win her, not for my own satisfaction, but to make her happy. I want to prove to her that goodness exists in this world—I, who came here to corrode and destroy; I, who am still pledged to do so. Ah, Felix, Felix, you should have chosen an older man for your purpose, or remembered that he who could be influenced as I was by family affections possesses a heart too soft for such infamy.

ENTRY VI

The name of Evelyn is never mentioned in this house. Sometimes I think that he has forgotten her, and find in this thought the one remaining spur to my revenge. Forgotten her! Strange, that his child, born long after his victim's death, should remember this poor girl, and he forget! Yet on the daughter the blow is planned to fall—if it does fall. Should I not pray that it never may? That she should loathe instead of love me? Distrust, instead of confide in my honor and affection? But who can pray against himself? Eva Poindexter must love me, even if I am driven to self-destruction by my own remorse, after she has confided her heart to my keeping.

LETTER VI

Dear Felix:

Will you send me a few exquisite articles from Tiffany's? I see that her father expects me to give her presents. I think she will accept them. If she does, we may both rest easy as to the state of her affections.

Very truly, Thomas

ENTRY VII

I cannot bring myself to pass a whole day away from her side. If Felix were here and could witness my assiduity, he would commend me in his cold and inflexible heart for the singleness with which I pursue my purpose. He would say to me, in the language of one of his letters: "You are not disappointing us." Us! As if our father still hovered near, sharing our purposes and hope. Alas! if he does, he must penetrate more deeply than Felix into the heart of this matter; must see that with every day's advantage—and I now think each day brings its advantage—I shrink further and further from the end they planned for me; the end which can alone justify my advance in her affections. I am a traitor to my oath, for I now know I shall never disappoint Eva's faith in me. I could not. Rather would I meet my father's accusing eyes on the verge of that strange world to which he has gone, or Felix's recriminations here, or my own contempt for the weakness which has made it possible for me to draw back from the brink of this wicked revenge to which I have devoted myself.

LETTER VII

Dear Felix:

This morning I passed under the window you have described to me as Evelyn's. I did it with a purpose. I wanted to test my own emotions and to see how much feeling it would arouse in me. Enough.

Eva accepted the brooch. It was the simplest thing you sent.

Aff., Thomas.

ENTRY VIII

I hate John Poindexter, yes, I hate him, but I can never hate his daughter. Only Felix could so confound the father with the child as to visit his anger upon this gentle embodiment of all that is gracious, all that is trustworthy, all that is fascinating in woman. But am I called upon to hate her? Am I not in a way required to love her? I will ask Felix. No, I cannot ask Felix. He would never comprehend her charm or its influence over me. He would have doubts and come at once to Montgomery. Good God! Am I proving such a traitor to my own flesh and blood that I cannot bear to think of Felix contemplating even in secret the unsuspicious form of his enemy's daughter?

LETTER VIII

Dear Felix:

A picnic on the mountains. It fell to me to escort Miss Poindexter down a dangerous slope. Though no words of affection passed between us (she is not yet ready for them), I feel that I have made a decided advance in her good graces.

Yours, Thomas.

ENTRY IX

I have touched her hand! I have felt her sweet form thrilling against mine as we descended the mountain ledges together! No man was near, no eye—there were moments in which we were as much alone in the wide paradise of these wooded slopes as if the world held no other breathing soul. Yet I no more dared to press her hand, or pour forth the mad worship of my heart into her innocent ears, than if the eyes of all Paris had been upon us. How I love her! How far off and faint seem the years of that dead crime my brother would invoke for the punishment of this sweet soul! Yes, and how remote that awful hour in which I knelt beneath the hand of my dying father and swore—Ah, that oath! That oath!

ENTRY X

The thing I dreaded, the thing I might have foreseen, has occurred. Felix has made his appearance in Montgomery. I received a communication to that effect from him today; a communication in which he commands me to meet him tonight, at Evelyn's grave, at the witching hour of twelve. I do not enjoy the summons. I have a dread of Felix, and begin to think he calculates upon stage devices to control me. But the day has passed for that. I will show him that I can be no more influenced in that place and at that hour than I could be in this hotel room, with the sight of her little glove—is there sin in such thefts?—lying on the table before us. Evelyn! She is a sacred memory. But the dead must not interfere with the living. Eva shall never be sacrificed to Evelyn's manes, not if John Poindexter lives out his life to his last hour in peace; not if Felix—well; I need to play the man; Felix is a formidable antagonist to meet, alone, in a spot of such rancorous memories, at an hour when spirits—if there be spirits—haunt the precincts of the tomb.

ENTRY XI

I should not have known Felix had I met him in the street. How much of a stranger he appeared, then, in the faint moonlight which poured upon that shaded spot! His very voice seemed altered, and in his manner I remarked a hesitation I had not supposed him capable of showing under any circumstances. Nor were his words such as I expected. The questions I dreaded most he did not ask. The recriminations I looked for he did not utter. He only told me coldly that my courtship must be shortened; that the end for which we were both prepared must be hastened, and gave me two weeks in which to bring matters to a climax. Then he turned to Evelyn's grave, and bending down, tried to read her name on the mossy stone. He was so long in doing this that I leaned down beside him and laid my hand on his shoulder. He was trembling, and his body was as cold as the stone he threw himself against. Was it the memory of her whom that stone covered which had aroused this emotion? If so, it was but natural. To all appearance he has never in all his life loved any one as he did this unhappy sister; and struck with a respect for the grief which has outlived many a man's lifetime, I was shrinking back when he caught my hand, and with a convulsive strain, contrasting strongly with his tone, which was strangely measured, he cried, "Do not forget the end! Do not forget John Poindexter! his sin, his indifference to my father's grief; the accumulated sufferings of years which made Amos Cadwalader a hermit amongst men. I have seen the girl; she has changed—women do change at her age—and some men, I do not say you, but some men might think her beautiful. But beauty, if she has it, must not blind your eyes, which are fixed upon another goal. Overlook it; overlook her—you have done so, have you not? Pale beauties cannot move one who has sat at the feet of the most dazzling of Parisian women. Keep your eyes on John Poindexter, the debt he owes us, and the suffering we have promised him. That she is sweet, gentle, different from all we thought her, only makes the chances of reaching his heart the greater. The worthier she may be of affections not indigenous to that hard soul, the surer will be our grip upon his nature and the heavier his downfall."

The old spell was upon me. I could neither answer nor assert myself. Letting go my hand, he rose, and with his back to the village—I noticed he had not turned his face to it since coming to this spot—he said: "I shall return to New York tomorrow. In two weeks you will telegraph your readiness to take up your abode with me. I have a home that will satisfy you; and it will soon be all your own."

Here he gripped his heart; and, dark as it was, I detected a strange convulsion cross his features as he turned into the moonlight. But it was gone before we could descend.

"You may hear from me again," he remarked somewhat faintly as he grasped my hand, and turned away in his own direction. I had not spoken a word during the whole interview.

LETTER IX

Dear Felix:

I do not hear from you. Are you well, or did your journey affect your health? I have no especial advance to report. John Poindexter seems greatly interested in my courtship. Sometimes he gives me very good advice. How does that strike you, Felix?

Aff., Thomas

ENTRY XII

I shall never understand Felix. He has not left the town, but is staying here in hiding, watching me, no doubt, to see if the signs of weakening he doubtless suspects in me have a significance deep enough to overthrow his planned revenge. I know this, because I have seen him more than once during the last week, when he thought himself completely invisible. I have caught sight of him in Mr. Poindexter's grounds when Eva and I stood talking together in the window. I even saw him once in church, in a dark corner, to be sure, but where he could keep his eye upon us, sitting together in Mr. Poindexter's pew. He seemed to me thin that day. The suspense he is under is wearing upon him. Is it my duty to cut it short by proclaiming my infidelity to my oath and my determination to marry the girl who has made me forget it?

LETTER X

Dear Felix:

Miss Poindexter has told me unreservedly that she cares for me. Are you satisfied with me now?

In haste, Thomas

ENTRY XIII

She loves me. Oh, ecstasy of life! Eva Poindexter loves me. I forced it from her lips today. With my arms around her and her head on my shoulder, I urged her to confession, and it came. Now let Felix do what he will! What is old John Poindexter to me? Her father. What are Amos Cadwalader's hatred and the mortal wrong that called so loudly for revenge? Dead issues, long buried sorrows, which God may remember, but which men are bound to forget. Life, life with her! That is the future toward which I look; that is the only vengeance I will take, the only vengeance Evelyn can demand if she is the angel we believe her. I will write to Felix tomorrow.

ENTRY XIV

I have not written Felix. I had not the courage.

ENTRY XV

I have had a dream. I thought I saw the meeting of my father with the white shade of Evelyn in the unimaginable recesses of that world to which both have gone. Strange horrors, stranger glories met as their separate paths crossed, and when the two forms had greeted and parted, a line of light followed the footsteps of the one and a trail of gloom those of the other. As their ways divided, I heard my father cry:

"There is no spot on your garments, Evelyn. Can it be that the wrongs of earth are forgotten here? That mortals remember what the angels forget, and that our revenge is late for one so blessed?"

I did not hear the answer, for I woke; but the echo of those words has rung in my ears all day. "Is our revenge late for one so blessed?"

ENTRY XVI

I have summoned up courage. Felix has been here again, and the truth has at last been spoken between us. I had been pressing Eva to name our wedding day, and we were all standing—that is, John Poindexter, my dear girl, and myself—in the glare of the drawing-room lights, when I heard a groan, too faint for other ears to catch, followed by a light fall from the window overlooking the garden. It was Felix. He had been watching us, had seen my love, heard me talk of marriage, and must now be in the grounds in open frenzy, or secret satisfaction, it was hard to tell which. Determined to know, determined to speak, I excused myself on some hurried plea, and searched the paths he knew as well as I. At last I came upon him. He was standing near an old dial, where he had more than once seen Eva and me together. He was very pale, deathly pale, it seemed to me, in the faint starlight shining upon that open place; but he greeted me as usual very quietly and with no surprise, almost, in fact, as if he knew I would recognize his presence and follow him.

"You are playing your rôle well," said he; "too well. What was that I heard about your marrying?"

The time had come. I was determined to meet it with a man's courage. But I found it hard. Felix is no easy man to cross, even in small things, and this thing is his life, nay, more—his past, present, and future existence.

I do not know who spoke first. There was some stammering, a few broken words; then I heard myself saying distinctly, and with a certain hard emphasis born of the restraint I put upon myself:

"I love her! I want to marry her. You must allow this. Then—"

I could not proceed. I felt the shock he had received almost as if it had been communicated to me by contact. Something that was not of the earth seemed to pass between us, and I remember raising my hand as if to shield my face. And then, whether it was the blowing aside of some branches which kept the moonlight from us, or because my eyesight was made clearer by my emotion, I caught one glimpse of his face and became conscious of a great suffering, which at first seemed the wrenching of my own heart, but in another moment impressed itself upon me as that of his, Felix's.

I stood appalled.

My weakness had uprooted the one hope of his life, or so I thought; and that he expressed this by silence made my heart yearn toward him for the first time since I recognized him as my brother. I tried to stammer some excuse. I was glad when the darkness fell again, for the sight of his bowed head and set features was insupportable to me. It seemed to make it easier for me to talk; for me to dilate upon the purity, the goodness which had robbed me of my heart in spite of myself. My heart! It seemed a strange word to pass between us two in reference to a Poindexter, but it was the only one capable of expressing the feeling I had for this young girl. At last, driven to frenzy by his continued silence, which had something strangely moving in it, I cried:

"You have never loved a woman, Felix. You do not know what the passion is when it seizes upon a man jaded with the hollow pleasures of an irresponsible life. You cannot judge; therefore you cannot excuse. You are made of iron—"

"Hush!" It was the first word he had spoken since I had opened my heart to him. "You do not know what you are saying, Thomas. Like all egotists, you think yourself alone in experience and suffering. Will you think so when I tell you that there was a time in my life when I did not sleep for weeks; when the earth, the air, yes, and the heavens were full of nothing but her name, her face, her voice? When to have held her in my arms, to have breathed into her ear one word of love, to have felt her cheek fall against mine in confidence, in passion, in hope, would have been to me the heaven which would have driven the devils from my soul forever? Thomas, will you believe I do not know the uttermost of all you are experiencing, when I here declare to you that there has been an hour in my life when, if I had felt she could have been brought to love me, I would have sacrificed Evelyn, my own soul, our father's hope, John Poindexter's punishment, and become the weak thing you are today, and gloried in it, I, Felix Cadwalader, the man of iron, who has never been known to falter? But, Thomas, I overcame that feeling. I crushed down that love, and I call upon you to do the same. You may marry her, but—"

What stopped him? His own heart or my own impetuosity? Both, perhaps, for at that moment I fell at his feet, and seizing his hand, kissed it as I might a woman's. He seemed to grow cold and stiff under this embrace, which showed both the delirium I was laboring under and the relief I had gotten from his words. When he withdrew his hand, I feel that my doom was about to be spoken, and I was not wrong. It came in these words:

"Thomas, I have yielded to your importunity and granted you the satisfaction which under the same circumstances I would have denied myself. But it has not made me less hard toward you; indeed, the steel with which you say my heart is bound seems tightening about it, as if the momentary weakness in which I have indulged called for revenge. Thomas, go on your way; make the girl your wife—I had rather you would, since she is—what she is—but after she has taken your name, after she believes herself secure in her honorable position and your love, then you are to remember our compact and your oath—back upon John Poindexter's care she is to be thrown, shortly, curtly, without explanation or excuse; and if it costs you your life, you are to stand firm in this attitude, using but one weapon in the struggle which may open between you and her father, and that is, your name of Cadwalader. You will not need any other. Thomas, do you swear to this? Or must I direct my own power against Eva Poindexter, and, by telling her your motive in courting her, make her hate you forever?"

"I will swear," I cried, overpowered by the alternative with which he threatened me. "Give me the bliss of calling her mine, and I will follow your wishes in all that concerns us thereafter."

"You will?" There was a sinister tone in this ejaculation that gave a shock to my momentary complacency. But we are so made that an anticipated evil affects us less than an immediate one; and remembering that weeks must yet elapse, during which he or John Poindexter or even myself might die, I said nothing, and he went icily on:

"I give you two months, alone and untrammelled. Then you are to bring your bride to my house, there to hear my final decision. There is to be no departure from this course. I shall expect you, Thomas; you and her. You can say that you are going to make her acquainted with your brother."

"I will be there," I murmured, feeling a greater oppression than when I took the oath at my father's death-bed. "I will be there."

There was no answer. While I was repeating those four words, Felix vanished.

LETTER XI

Dear Felix:

Have a fresh draft made. I need cigars, clothes, and—a wedding ring. But no, let me stop short there. We will be married without one, unless you force it upon us. Eva's color is blue.

Very truly, Thomas

ENTRY XVII

Today I wrote again to Felix. He is at home, must be, for I have neither seen nor felt his presence since that fateful night. What did I write? I don't remember. I seem to be living in a dream. Everything is confused about me but Eva's face, Eva's smile. They are blissfully clear. Sometimes I wish they were not. Were they confused amid these shadows, I might have stronger hope of keeping my word to Felix. Now, I shall never keep it. Eva once my wife, separation between us will become impossible. John Poindexter is ill.

LETTER XII

Dear Felix:

Congratulations: visits from my neighbors; all the éclat we could wish or a true lover hate. The ring you sent fits as if made for her. I am called in all directions by a thousand duties. I am on exhibition, and every one's curiosity must be satisfied.

In haste,
Thomas

ENTRY XVIII

The wedding is postponed. John Poindexter is very ill. Pray God, Felix hears nothing of this. He would come here; he would confront his enemy on his bed of sickness. He would denounce him, and Eva would be lost to me.

LETTER XIII

Dear Felix:

Eva is not pleased with the arrangements which have been made for our wedding. John Poindexter likes show; she does not. Which will carry the day?

Yours aff.,
Thomas

ENTRY XIX

Mr. Poindexter is better, but our plans will have to be altered. We now think we will be married quietly, possibly in New York.

LETTER XIV

Dear Felix:

A compromise has been effected. The wedding will be a quiet one, but not celebrated here. As you cannot wish to attend it, I will not mention the place or hour of my marriage, only say that on September 27th at 4 P. M. you may expect my wife and myself at your house.

Aff.,
Thomas

ENTRY XX

We have decided to be married in New York. Mr. Poindexter needs the change, and Eva and I are delighted at the prospect of a private wedding. Then we will be near Felix, but not to subject ourselves to his will. Oh, no!

ENTRY XXI

Married! She is mine. And now to confront Felix with my determination to hold on to my happiness. How I love her, and how I pity him! John Poindexter's wickedness is forgotten, Evelyn but a fading memory. The whole world seems to hold but three persons—Eva, Felix, and myself. How will it end? We meet at his home tomorrow.

CHAPTER IV

Felix

Meanwhile there was another secret struggle going on in the depth of a nature from which all sympathy was excluded both by the temperament of the person concerned and the circumstances surrounding him.

I can but hint at it. Some tragedies lie beyond the ken of man, and this one we can but gather from stray scraps of torn-up letters addressed to no one and betraying their authorship only through the writer's hand. They were found long after the mystery of Felix Cadwalader's death had been fully accounted for, tucked away under the flooring of Bartow's room. Where or how procured by him, who can tell?

* * * *

"Madness!

"I have seen Eva Poindexter again, and heaven and hell have contended for me ever since. Eva! Eva! the girl I thought of only as our prey. The girl I have given to my brother. She is too lovely for him: she is too lovely for any man unless it be one who has never before thrilled to any woman's voice, or seen a face that could move his passions or awaken his affection. Is it love I feel? Can I, Felix, who have had but one thought, known but one enthusiasm, retain in this breast of iron a spot however secret, however small, which any woman, least of all his daughter, could reach? Never! I am the prey of frenzy or the butt of devils. Yet only the inhabitants of a more celestial sphere brighten around me when I think of those half-raised eyes, those delicately parted lips, so devoid of guile, that innocent bearing, and the divine tenderness, mingled with strength, by which she commands admiration and awakens love. I must fly. I must never see her again. Thomas's purpose is steady. He must never see that mine rocks like an idol smitten by a thunderbolt.

"If Thomas had not been reared in Paris, he too—But I am the only weak one. Curses on my—

"Did I say I would fly? I cannot, not yet. One more glimpse of her face, if only to satisfy myself that I have reason for this madness. Perhaps I was but startled yesterday to find a celestial loveliness where I expected to encounter pallid inanity. If my emotion is due to my own weakness rather than to her superiority, I had better recognize my folly before it proves my destruction.

I will stay and—

Thomas will not, shall not—

dexter's daughter—

hate, hate for Thom—

"My self-esteem is restored. I have seen her again—him—they were together—there was true love in his eye—how could I expect him not to love her—and I was able to hide my anguish and impose his duty on him. She loves him—or he thinks so—and the work goes on. But I will not stay to watch its accomplishment. No, no.

"I told him my story tonight, under the guise of a past experience. Oh, the devils must laugh at us men! They have reason to. Sometimes I wonder if my father in the clearness of his new vision does not join them in their mirth.

"Home with my unhappy secret! Home, where nothing comes to distract me from my gnawing griefs and almost intolerable thoughts. I walk the floors. I cry aloud her name. I cry it even under the portrait of Evelyn. There are moments when I am tempted to write to Thomas—to forbid him—

"Eva! Eva! Eva! Every fibre in my miserable body utters the one word. But no man shall ever know. Thomas shall never know how the thought of her fills my days and nights, making my life a torment and the future—

"I wait for his letters (scanty they are and cold) as the doomed criminal awaits his executioner. Does she really love him? Or will that exquisite, that soulful nature call for a stronger mate, a more concentrated temperament, a—a—

"I thought I saw in one of my dark hours my father rising up from his grave to curse me. Oh! he might curse on if—

"What have I said about no man knowing? Bartow knows. In his dumbness, his deafness, he has surprised my secret, and shows that he has done so by his peering looks, his dissatisfied ways, and a jealousy at which I could shout aloud in mirth, if I were not more tempted to shriek aloud in torment. A dumb serving-man, picked up I have almost forgotten where, jealous of my weakness for John Poindexter's daughter! He was never jealous of my feeling for Evelyn. Yet till the day I dared fate by seeking out and looking for the second time upon the woman whose charms I had scorned, her name often resounded through these rooms, and my eyes dwelt upon but one spot, and that was where her picture hangs in the woeful beauty which has become my reproach.

"I have had a great surprise. The starling, which has been taught to murmur Evelyn's name, today shrieked out, 'Eva! Eva!' My first impulse was to wring its neck, my next to take it from its cage and hide it in my bosom. But I did neither. I am still a man.

"Bartow will wring that bird's neck if I do not. This morning I caught him with his hand on the cage and a murderous light in his eye, which I had no difficulty in understanding. Yet he cannot hear the word the wretched starling murmurs. He only knows it is a word, a name, and he is determined to suppress it. Shall I string the cage up out of this old fellow's reach? His deafness, his inability to communicate with others, the exactness with which he obeys my commands as given him by my colored slides, his attention to my every wish, consequent upon his almost animal love for my person, are necessary to me now, while the bird—Ah! there it goes again, 'Eva! Eva!'

"Is it hate or love I feel, abhorrence or passion? Love would seek to save, but I have no thought of saving her, since she has acknowledged her love for Thomas, and since he—Oh, it is not now for Evelyn's sake I plan revenge, but for my own! These nights and days of torture—the revelation I have had of my own nature—the consent I was forced to give to a marriage which means bliss to them and anguish beyond measure to me—all this calls for vengeance, and they will not escape, these two. I have laid my plans deep. I have provided for every contingency. It has taken time, thought, money. But the result is good. If they cross the threshold of my circular study, they must consent to my will or perish here, and I with them. Oh, they shall never live and be happy! Thomas need not think it. John Poindexter need not think it! I might have forgotten the oath made on my father's crossed arms, but I will never forget the immeasurable griefs of these past months or the humiliation they have brought me. My own weakness is to be avenged—my unheard-of, my intolerable weakness. Remember Evelyn? Remember Felix! Ah, again! Eva! Eva! Eva!"

CHAPTER V

Why the Iron Slide Remained Stationary

The rest must be told in Thomas's own words, as it forms the chief part of the confession he made before the detectives:

According to my promise, I took my young wife to Felix's house on the day and at the hour proposed. We went on foot, for it was not far from the hotel where we were then staying, and were received at the door by an old servant who I had been warned could neither speak nor hear. At sight of him and the dim, old-fashioned hall stretching out in aristocratic gloom before us, Eva turned pale and cast me an inquiring look. But I reassured her with a smile that most certainly contradicted my own secret dread of the interview before us, and taking her on my arm, followed the old man down the hall, past the open drawing-room door (where I certainly thought we should pause), into a room whose plain appearance made me frown, till Bartow, as I have since heard him called, threw aside the portière at one end and introduced us into my brother's study, which at that moment looked like fairyland, or would have, if Felix, who was its sole occupant, had not immediately drawn our attention to himself by the remarkable force of his personality, never so impressive as at that moment.

Eva, to whom I had said little of this brother, certainly nothing which would lead her to anticipate seeing either so handsome a man or one of such mental poise and imposing character, looked frightened and a trifle awe-struck. But she advanced quite bravely toward him, and at my introduction smiled with such an inviting grace that I secretly expected to see him more or less disarmed by it.

And perhaps he was, for his already pale features turned waxy in the yellow glare cast by the odd lantern over our heads, and the hand he had raised in mechanical greeting fell heavily, and he could barely stammer out some words of welcome. These would have seemed quite inadequate to the occasion if his eyes which were fixed on her face, had not betrayed the fact that he was not without feeling, though she little realized the nature of that feeling or how her very life (for happiness is life) was trembling in the balance under that indomitable will.

I who did know—or thought I did—cast him an imploring glance, and, saying that I had some explanations to make, asked if Mrs. Adams might not rest here while we had a few words apart.

He answered me with a strange look. Did he feel the revolt in my tone and understand then as well as afterward what the nature of my compliance had been? I shall never know. I only know that he stopped fumbling with some small object on the table before him, and, bowing with a sarcastic grace that made me for the first time in my intercourse with him feel myself his inferior, even in size, led the way to a small door I had failed to notice up to this moment.

"Your wife will find it more comfortable here," he observed, with slow pauses in his speech that showed great, but repressed, excitement. And he opened the door into what had the appearance of a small but elegant sleeping-apartment. "What we have to say cannot take long. Mrs. Adams will not find the wait tedious."

"No," she smiled, with a natural laugh, born, as I dare hope, of her perfect happiness. Yet she could not but have considered the proceeding strange, and my manner, as well as his, scarcely what might be expected from a bridegroom introducing his bride to his only relative.

"I will call you—" I began, but the vision of her dimpled face above the great cluster of roses she carried made me forget to complete my sentence, and the door closed, and I found myself face to face with Felix.

He was breathing easier, and his manner seemed more natural now that we were alone, yet he did not speak, but cast a strange, if not inquiring, glance about the room (the weirdest of apartments, as you all well know), and seeming satisfied with what he saw, why I could not tell, led the way up to the large table which from the first had appeared to exert a sort of uncanny magnetism upon him, saying:

"Come further away. I need air, breathing place in this close room, and so must you. Besides, why should she hear what we have to say? She will know the worst soon enough. She seems a gentle-hearted woman."

"An angel!" I began, but he stopped me with an imperious gesture.

"We will not discuss your wi—Mrs. Adams," he protested. "Where is John Poindexter?"

"At the hotel," I rejoined. "Or possibly he has returned home. I no longer take account of his existence. Felix, I shall never leave my wife. I had rather prove recreant to the oath I took before I realized the worth of the woman whose happiness I vowed to destroy. This is what I have come to tell you. Make it easy for me, Felix. You are a man who has loved and suffered. Let us bury the past; let us—"

Had I hoped I could move him? Perhaps some such child's notion had influenced me up to this moment. But as these words left my lips, nay, before I had stumbled through them, I perceived by the set look of his features, which were as if cast in bronze, that I might falter, but that he was firm as ever, firmer, it seemed to me, and less easy to be entreated.

Yet what of that? At the worst, what had I to fear? A struggle which might involve Eva in bitter unpleasantness and me in the loss of a fortune I had come to regard almost as my own. But these were petty considerations. Eva must know sooner or later my real name and the story of her father's guilt. Why not now? And if we must start life poor, it was yet life, while a separation from her—

Meanwhile Felix had spoken, and in language I was least prepared to hear.

"I anticipated this. From the moment you pleaded with me for the privilege of marrying her, I have looked forward to this outcome and provided against it. Weakness on the part of her bridegroom was to be expected; I have, therefore, steeled myself to meet the emergency; for your oath must be kept!"

Crushed by the tone in which these words were uttered, a tone that evinced power against which any ordinary struggle would end in failure, I cast my eyes about the room in imitation of what I had seen him do a few minutes before. There was nothing within sight calculated to awaken distrust, and yet a feeling of distrust (the first I had really felt) had come with the look he had thrown above and around the mosque-like interior of the room he called his study. Was it the calm confidence he showed, or the weirdness of finding myself amid Oriental splendors and under the influence of night effects in high day and within sound of the clanging street cars and all the accompanying bustle of every-day traffic? It is hard to say; but from this moment on I found myself affected by a vague affright, not on my own account, but on hers whose voice we could plainly hear humming a gay tune in the adjoining apartment. But I was resolved to suppress all betrayal of uneasiness. I even smiled, though I felt the eyes of Evelyn's pictured countenance upon me; Evelyn's, whose portrait I had never lost sight of from the moment of entering the room, though I had not given it a direct look and now stood with my back to it. Felix, who faced it, but who did not raise his eyes to it, waited a moment for my response, and finding that my words halted, said again:

"That oath must be kept!"

This time I found words with which to answer. "Impossible!" I burst out, flinging doubt, fear, hesitancy, everything I had hitherto trembled at to the winds. "It was in my nature to take it, worked upon as I was by family affection, the awfulness of our father's approaching death, and a thousand uncanny influences all carefully measured and prepared for this end. But it is not in my nature to keep it after four months of natural living in the companionship of a man thirty years removed from his guilt, and of his guileless and wholly innocent daughter. And you cannot drive me to it, Felix. No man can force another to abandon his own wife because of a wicked oath taken long before he knew her. If you think your money—"

"Money?" he cried, with a contempt that did justice to my disinterestedness as well as his own. "I had forgotten I had it. No, Thomas, I should never weigh money against the happiness of living with such a woman as your wife appears to be. But her life I might. Carry out your threat; forget to pay John Poindexter the debt we owe him, and the matter will assume a seriousness for which you are doubtless poorly prepared. A daughter dead in her honeymoon will be almost as great a grief to him as a dishonored one. And either dead or dishonored he must find her, when he comes here in search of the child he cannot long forget. Which shall it be? Speak!"

Was I dreaming? Was this Felix? Was this myself? And was it in my ears these words were poured?

With a spring I reached his side where he stood close against the table, and groaned rather than shrieked the words:

"You would not kill her! You do not meditate a crime of blood—here—on her—the innocent—the good—"

"No," he said; "it will be you who will do that. You who will not wish to see her languish—suffer—go mad—Thomas, I am not the raving being you take me for. I am merely a keeper of oaths. Nay, I am more. I have talents, skill. The house in which you find yourself is proof of this. This room—see, it has no outlet save those windows, scarcely if at all perceptible to you, above our heads, and that opening shielded now by a simple curtain, but which in an instant, without my moving from this place, I can so hermetically seal that no man, save he be armed with crowbar and pickaxe, could enter here, even if man could know of our imprisonment, in a house soon to be closed from top to bottom by my departing servant."

"May God protect us!" fell from my lips, as, stiff with horror, I let my eyes travel from his determined face, first to the windows high over my head and then to the opening of the door, which, though but a few steps from where I stood, was as far as possible from the room into which my darling had been induced to enter.

Felix, watching me, uttered his explanations as calmly as if the matter were one of every-day significance. "You are looking for the windows," he remarked. "They are behind those goblin faces you see outlined on the tapestries under the ceiling. As for the door, if you had looked to the left when you entered, you would have detected the edge of a huge steel plate hanging flush with the casing. This plate can be made to slide across that opening in an instant just by the touch of my hand on this button. This done, no power save such as I have mentioned can move it back again, not even my own. I have forces at my command for sending it forward, but none for returning it to its place. Do you doubt my mechanical skill or the perfection of the electrical apparatus I have caused to be placed here? You need not, Thomas; nor need you doubt the will that has only to exert itself for an instant to—Shall I press the button, brother?"

"No, no!" I shouted in a frenzy, caused rather by my knowledge of the nature of this man than any especial threat apparent in his voice or gesture. "Let me think; let me know more fully what your requirements are—what she must suffer if I consent—and what I."

He let his hand slip back, that smooth white hand which I had more than once surveyed in admiration. Then he smiled.

"I knew you would not be foolish," he said. "Life has its charms even for hermits like me; and for a *beau garçon* such as you are—"

"Hush!" I interposed, maddened into daring his full anger. "It is not my life I am buying, but hers, possibly yours; for it seems you have planned to perish with us. Is it not so?"

"Certainly," was his cold reply. "Am I an assassin? Would you expect me to live, knowing you to be perishing?"

I stared aghast. Such resolve, such sacrifice of self to an idea was beyond my comprehension.

"Why—what?" I stammered. "Why kill us, why kill yourself—"

The answer overwhelmed me.

"Remember Evelyn!" shrilled a voice, and I paused, struck dumb with a superstitious horror I had never believed myself capable of experiencing. For it was not Felix who spoke, neither was it any utterance of my own aroused conscience. Muffled, strange, and startling it came from above, from the hollow spaces of that high vault lit with the golden glow that henceforth can have but one meaning for me—death.

"What is it?" I asked. "Another of your mechanical contrivances?"

He smiled; I had rather he had frowned.

"Not exactly. A favorite bird, a starling. Alas! he but repeats what he has heard echoed through the solitude of these rooms. I thought I had smothered him up sufficiently to insure his silence during this interview. But he is a self-willed bird, and seems disposed to defy the wrappings I have bound around him; which fact warns me to be speedy and hasten our explanations. Thomas, this is what I require: John Poindexter—you do not know where he is at this hour, but I do—received a telegram but now, which, if he is a man at all, will bring him to this house in a half-hour or so from the present moment. It was sent in your name, and in it you informed him that matters had arisen which demanded his immediate attention; that you were on your way to your brother's (giving him this address), where, if you found entrance, you would await his presence in a room called the study; but that—and here you will see how his coming will not aid us if that steel plate is once started on its course—if the possible should occur and your brother should be absent from home, then he was to await a message from you at the Plaza. The appearance of the house would inform him whether he would find you and Eva within; or so I telegraphed him in your name.

"Thomas, if Bartow fulfils my instructions—and I have never know him to fail me—he will pass down these stairs and out of this house in just five minutes. As he is bound on a long-promised journey, and as he expects me to leave the house immediately after him, he has drawn every shade and fastened every lock. Consequently, on his exit, the house will become a tomb, to which, just two weeks from today, John Poindexter will be called again, and in words which will lead to a demolition which will disclose—what? Let us not forestall the future, our horrible future, by inquiring. But Thomas, shall Bartow go? Shall I not by signs he comprehends more readily than other men comprehend speech indicate to him on his downward passage to the street that I wish him to wait and open the door to the man whom we have promised to overwhelm in his hour of satisfaction and pride? You have only to write a line—see! I have made a copy of the words you must use, lest your self-command should be too severely taxed. These words left on this table for his inspection—for you must go and Eva remain—will tell him all he needs to know from you. The rest can come from my lips after he has read the signature, which in itself will confound him and prepare the way for what I have to add. Have you anything to say against this plan? Anything, I mean, beyond what you have hitherto urged? Anything that I will consider or which will prevent my finger from pressing the button on which it rests?"

I took up the paper. It was lying on the table, where it had evidently been inscribed simultaneously with or just before our entrance into the house, and slowly read the few lines I saw written upon it. You know them, but they will acquire a new significance from your present understanding of their purpose and intent:

> I return you back your daughter. Neither she nor you will ever see me again. Remember Evelyn!
> Amos's Son.

"You wish me to sign these words, to put them into my own handwriting, and so to make them mine? Mine!" I repeated.

"Yes, and to leave them here on this table for him to see when he enters. He might not believe any mere statement from me in regard to your intentions."

I was filled with horror. Love, life, human hopes, the world's friendships—all the possibilities of existence, swept in one concentrated flood of thought and feeling through my outraged consciousness, and I knew I could never put my name to such a blasphemy of all that was sacred to man's soul. Tossing the paper in his face, I cried:

"You have gone too far! Better her death, better mine, better the destruction of us all, than such dishonor to the purest thing heaven ever made. I refuse, Felix—I refuse. And may God have mercy on us all!"

The moment was ghastly. I saw his face change, his finger tremble where it hovered above the fatal button; saw—though only in imagination as yet—the steely edge of that deadly plate of steel advancing beyond the lintel, and was about to dare all in a sudden grapple with this man, when a sound from another direction caught my ear, and looking around in terror of the only intrusion we could fear, beheld Eva advancing from the room in which we had placed her.

That moment a blood-red glow took the place of the sickly yellow which had hitherto filled every recess of this weird apartment. But I scarcely noticed the change, save as it affected her pallor and gave to her cheeks the color that was lacking in the roses at her belt.

Fearless and sweet as in the hour when she first told me that she loved me, she approached and stood before us.

"What is this?" she cried. "I have heard words that sound more like the utterances of some horrid dream than the talk of men and brothers. What does it mean, Thomas? What does it mean, Mr. —"

"Cadwalader," announced Felix, dropping his eyes from her face, but changing not a whit his features or posture.

"Cadwalader?" The name was not to her what it was to her father. "Cadwalader? I have heard that name in my father's house; it was Evelyn's name, the Evelyn who—"

"Whom you see painted there over your head," finished Felix, "my sister, Thomas's sister—the girl whom your father—but I spare you, child though you be of a man who spared nothing. From your husband you may learn why a Cadwalader can never find his happiness with a Poindexter. Why thirty or more years after that young girl's death, you who were not then born are given at this hour the choice between death and dishonor. I allow you just five minutes in which to listen. After that you will let me know your joint decision. Only you must make your talk where you stand. A step taken by either of you to right or left, and Thomas knows what will follow."

Five minutes, with such a justification to make, and such a decision to arrive at! I felt my head swim, my tongue refuse its office, and stood dumb and helpless before her till the sight of her dear eyes raised in speechless trust to mine flooded me with a sense of triumph amid all the ghastly terrors of the moment, and I broke out in a tumult of speech, in excuses, explanations, all that comes to one in a more than mortal crisis.

She listened, catching my meaning rather from my looks than my words. Then as the minutes fled and my brother raised a warning hand, she turned toward him, and said:

"You are in earnest? We must separate in shame or perish in this prison-house with you?"

His answer was mere repetition, mechanical, but firm:

"You have said it. You have but one minute more, madam."

She shrank, and all her powers seemed leaving her, then a reaction came, and a flaming angel stood where but a moment before the most delicate of women weakly faltered; and giving me a look to see if I had the courage or the will to lift my hand against my own flesh and blood (alas for us both! I did not understand her) caught up an old Turkish dagger lying only too ready to her hand, and plunged it with one sideways thrust into his side, crying:

"We cannot part, we cannot die, we are too young, too happy!"

It was sudden; the birth of purpose in her so unexpected and so rapid that Felix, the ready, who was prepared for all contingencies, for the least movement or suggestion of escape, faltered and pressed, not the fatal button, but his heart.

One impulsive act on the part of a woman had overthrown all the fine-spun plans of the subtlest spirit that ever attempted to work its will in the face of God and man.

But I did not think of this then; I did not even bestow a thought upon the narrowness of our escape, or the price which the darling of my heart might be called upon to pay for this supreme act of self-defence. My mind, my heart, my interest were with Felix, in whom the nearness of death had called up all that was strongest and most commanding in his strong and commanding spirit.

Though struck to the heart, he had not fallen. It was as if the will which had sustained him through thirty years of mental torture held him erect still, that he might give her, Eva, one look, the like of which I had never seen on mortal face, and which will never leave my heart or hers until we die. Then as he saw her sink shudderingly down and the delicate woman reappear in her pallid and shrunken figure, he turned his eyes on me and I saw—good God!—a tear well up from those orbs of stone and fall slowly down his cheek, fast growing hollow under the stroke of death.

"Eva! Eva! I love Eva!" shrilled the voice which once before had startled me from the hollow vault above.

Felix heard, and a smile faint as the failing rush of blood through his veins moved his lips and brought a revelation to my soul. He, too, loved Eva!

When he saw I knew, the will which had kept him on his feet gave way, and he sank to the floor murmuring:

"Take her away! I forgive. Save! Save! She did not know I loved her."

Eva, aghast, staring with set eyes at her work, had not moved from her crouching posture. But when she saw that speaking head fall back, the fine limbs settle into the repose of death, a shock went through her which I thought would never leave her reason unimpaired.

"I've killed him!" she murmured. "I've killed him!" and looking wildly about, her eyes fell on the cross that hung behind us on the wall. It seemed to remind her that Felix was a Catholic. "Bring it!" she gasped. "Let him feel it on his breast. It may bring him peace—hope."

As I rushed to do her bidding, she fell in a heap on the floor.

"Save!" came again from the lips we thought closed forever in death. And realizing at the words both her danger and the necessity of her not opening her eyes again upon this scene, I laid the cross in his arms, and catching her up from the floor, ran with her out of the house. But no sooner had I caught sight of the busy street and the stream of humanity passing before us, than I awoke to an instant recognition of our peril. Setting my wife down, I commanded life back into her limbs by the force of my own energy, and then dragging her down the steps, mingled with the crowd, encouraging her, breathing for her, living in her till I got her into a carriage and we drove away.

For the silence we have maintained from that time to this you must not blame Mrs. Adams. When she came to herself—which was not for days—she manifested the greatest desire to proclaim her act and assume its responsibility. But I would not have it. I loved her too dearly to see her name bandied about in the papers; and when her father was taken into our confidence, he was equally peremptory in enjoining silence, and shared with me the watch I now felt bound to keep over her movements.

But alas! His was the peremptoriness of pride rather than love. John Poindexter has no more heart for his daughter than he had for his wife or that long-forgotten child from whose grave this tragedy has sprung. Had Felix triumphed he would never have wrung the heart of this man. As he once said, when a man cares for nothing and nobody, not even for himself, it is useless to curse him.

As for Felix himself, judge him not, when you realize, as you now must, that his last conscious act was to reach for and put in his mouth the paper which connected Eva with his death. At the moment of death his thought was to save, not to avenge. And this after her hand had struck him.

CHAPTER VI

Answered

A silence more or less surcharged with emotion followed this final appeal. Then, while the various auditors of this remarkable history whispered together and Thomas Adams turned in love and anxiety toward his wife, the inspector handed back to Mr. Gryce the memorandum he had received from him.

It presented the following appearance:

1. Why a woman who was calm enough to stop and arrange her hair during the beginning of an interview should be wrought up to such a pitch of frenzy and exasperation before it was over as to kill with her own hand a man she had evidently had no previous grudge against. (Remember the comb found on the floor of Mr. Adams's bedroom.)
   Answered

2. What was the meaning of the following words, written just previous to this interview by the man thus killed: "I return you your daughter. Neither you nor she will ever see me again. Remember Evelyn!"

Answered

3. Why was the pronoun "I" used in this communication? What position did Mr. Felix Adams hold toward this young girl qualifying him to make use of such language after her marriage to his brother?

Answered

4. And having used it, why did he, upon being attacked by her, attempt to swallow the paper upon which he had written these words, actually dying with it clinched between his teeth?

Answered

5. If he was killed in anger and died as monsters do (her own word), why did his face show sorrow rather than hate, and a determination as far as possible removed from the rush of over-whelming emotions likely to follow the reception of a mortal blow from the hand of an unexpected antagonist?

Answered

6. Why, if he had strength to seize the above-mentioned paper and convey it to his lips, did he not use that strength in turning on a light calculated to bring him assistance, instead of leaving blazing the crimson glow which, according to the code of signals as now understood by us, means: "Nothing more required just now. Keep away?"

Answered

7. What was the meaning of the huge steel plate found between the casings of the doorway, and why did it remain at rest within its socket at this, the culminating, moment of his life?

Answered

8. An explanation of how old Poindexter came to appear on the scene so soon after the event. His words as overheard were: "It is Amos' son, not Amos!" Did he not know whom he was to meet in this house? Was the condition of the man lying before him with a cross on his bosom and a dagger in his heart less of a surprise to him than the personality of the victim?

Not Answered

9. Remember the conclusions we have drawn from Bartow's pantomime. Mr. Adams was killed by a left-handed thrust. Watch for an acknowledgment that the young woman is left-handed, and do not

forget that an explanation is due why for so long a time she held her other arm stretched out behind her.

Answered

10. Why did the bird whose chief cry is "Remember Evelyn!" sometimes vary it with "Poor Eva! Lovely Eva! Who would strike Eva?" The story of this tragedy, to be true, must show that Mr. Adams knew his brother's bride both long and well.

Answered

11. If Bartow is, as we think, innocent of all connection with this crime save as witness, why does he show such joy at its result? This may not reasonably be expected to fall within the scope of Thomas Adams's confession, but it should not be ignored by us. This deaf-and-dumb servitor was driven mad by the fact which caused him joy. Why?[6]

Answered

12. Notice the following schedule. It has been drawn up after re-peated experiments with Bartow and the various slides of the strange lamp which cause so many different lights to shine out in Mr. Adams's study:

White light—Water wanted.
Green light—Overcoat and hat to be brought.
Blue light—Put back books on shelves.
Violet light—Arrange study for the night.
Yellow light—Watch for next light.
Red light—Nothing wanted; stay away.

Answered

The last was on at the final scene. Note if this fact can be explained by Mr. Adams's account of the same.

* * * *

Two paragraphs alone lacked complete explanation. The first, No.

---

6   It must be remembered that the scraps of writing in Felix's hand had not yet been found by the police. The allusions in them to Bartow show him to have been possessed by a jealousy which probably turned to delight when he saw his master smitten down by the object of that master's love and his own hatred. How he came to recognize in the bride of another man the owner of the name he so often saw hovering on the lips of his master, is a question to be answered by more astute students of the laws of perception than myself. Probably he spent much of his time at the loophole on the stairway, studying his master till he understood his every gesture and expression.

9, was important. The description of the stroke dealt by Mr. Adams's wife did not account for this peculiar feature in Bartow's pantomime. Consulting with the inspector, Mr. Gryce finally approached Mr. Adams and inquired if he had strength to enact before them the blow as he had seen it dealt by his wife.

The startled young man looked the question he dared not ask. In common with others, he knew that Bartow had made some characteristic gestures in endeavoring to describe this crime, but he did not know what they were, as this especial bit of information had been carefully held back by the police. He, therefore, did not respond hastily to the suggestion made him, but thought intently for a moment before he thrust out his left hand and caught up some article or other from the inspector's table and made a lunge with it across his body into an imaginary victim at his right. Then he consulted the faces about him with inexpressible anxiety. He found little encouragement in their aspect.

"You would make your wife out left-handed," suggested Mr. Gryce. "Now I have been watching her ever since she came into this place, and I have seen no evidence of this."

"She is not left-handed, but she thrust with her left hand, because her right was fast held in mine. I had seized her instinctively as she bounded forward for the weapon, and the convulsive clutch of our two hands was not loosed till the horror of her act made her faint, and she fell away from me to the floor crying: 'Tear down the cross and lay it on your brother's breast. I would at least see him die the death of a Christian.'"

Mr. Gryce glanced at the inspector with an air of great relief. The mystery of the constrained attitude of the right hand which made Bartow's pantomime so remarkable was now naturally explained, and taking up the blue pencil which the inspector had laid down, he wrote, with a smile, a very decided "answered" across paragraph No. 9.

CHAPTER VII

Last Words

A few minutes later Mr. Gryce was to be seen in the outer room, gazing curiously at the various persons there collected. He was seeking an answer to a question that was still disturbing his mind, and hoped to find it there. He was not disappointed. For in a quiet corner he encountered the amiable form of Miss Butterworth, calmly awaiting the result of an interference which she in all probability had been an active agent in bringing about.

He approached and smilingly accused her of this. But she disclaimed the fact with some heat.

"I was simply there," she explained. "When the crisis came, when this young creature learned that her husband had left suddenly for New York in the company of two men, then—why then, it became apparent to every one that a woman should be at her side who understood her case and the extremity in which she found herself. And I was that woman."

"You are always that woman," he gallantly replied, "if by the phrase you mean being in the right place at the right time. So you are already acquainted with Mrs. Adams's story?"

"Yes; the ravings of a moment told me she was the one who had handled the dagger that slew Mr. Adams. Afterward, she was able to explain the cause of what has seemed to us such a horrible crime. When I heard her story, Mr. Gryce, I no longer hesitated either as to her duty or mine. Do you think she will be called upon to answer for this blow? Will she be tried, convicted?"

"Madam, there are not twelve men in the city so devoid of intelligence as to apply the name of crime to an act which was so evidently one of self-defence. No true bill will be found against young Mrs. Adams. Rest easy."

The look of gloom disappeared from Miss Butterworth's eyes.

"Then I may return home in peace," she cried. "It has been a desperate five hours for me, and I feel well shaken up. Will you escort me to my carriage?"

Miss Butterworth did not look shaken up. Indeed, in Mr. Gryce's judgment, she had never appeared more serene or more comfortable. But she was certainly the best judge of her own condition; and after satisfying herself that the object of her care was reviving under the solicitous ministrations of her husband, she took the arm which Mr. Gryce held out to her and proceeded to her carriage.

As he assisted her in, he asked a few questions about Mr. Poindexter.

"Why is not Mrs. Adams's father here? Did he allow his daughter to leave him on such an errand as this without offering to accompany her?"

The answer was curtness itself:

"Mr. Poindexter is a man without heart. He came with us to New York, but refused to follow us to Police Headquarters. Sir, you will find that the united passions of three burning souls, and a revenge the most deeply cherished of any I ever knew or heard of, have been thrown away on a man who is positively unable to suffer. Do not mention old John Poindexter to me. And now, if you will be so good, tell the coachman to drive me to my home in Gramercy Park. I have put my finger in the police pie for the last time, Mr. Gryce—positively for the last time." And she sank back on the carriage cushions with an inexorable look, which, nevertheless, did not quite conceal a quiet complacency which argued that she was not altogether dissatisfied with herself or the result of her interference in matters usually considered at variance with a refined woman's natural instincts.

Mr. Gryce, in repressing a smile, bowed lower even than his wont, and, under the shadow of this bow, the carriage drove off. As he walked slowly back, he sighed. Was he wondering if a case of similar interest would ever bring them together again in consultation?